**MOUTH OPEN WIDE,
IVORY SPIKES SET
TO SEIZE HIS THROAT,
THE VAMPIRE LEAPED AT CHONDOS.**

Fingers like claws clamped, inhumanly strong, on his arm. Chondos swung his free arm around. The sleeve, loaded with glowing Hastur stones, slapped the pallid face.

The vampire screamed and flung him through the air. As he got to his feet, it rushed him, hissing like a cat.

Chondos had just time to drop a large rock from his sleeve into his hand. As the creature sprang for his throat, he heaved the stone high and brought it down with both hands. The skull caved in like a wasp's nest; the bony figure fell.

But still it was not dead. On hands and knees, the corpse crawled toward him....

Also by
PAUL EDWIN ZIMMER

The Dark Border Volume One:
The Lost Prince

THE DARK BORDER
VOL. 2
KING CHONDOS' RIDE
PAUL EDWIN ZIMMER

BERKLEY BOOKS, NEW YORK

THE DARK BORDER VOL. 2: KING CHONDOS' RIDE

A Berkley Book / published by arrangement with
the author

PRINTING HISTORY
PBJ Books edition / October 1982
Berkley edition / March 1983

For my Daughter:
FIONA LYNN ZIMMER,
*who is almost exactly
as old as this book*

Prologue: What Has Gone Before

Ten thousand years ago, Hastur drove the Dark Things from the world, and repeopled it with men brought from another universe. A thousand years later, human greed accidentally opened the barriers Hastur had set between the worlds, and once more the Eight Dark Lords walked, eating up whole nations as they passed.

The Children of Hastur were able to hurl the Eight back to their own place, but the lesser Dark Things remained, and raised a spell of darkness on the spine of the mountain chain that ran from north to south on the western shore of the main continent, hiding the mountains from the light of the Twin Suns.

Slowly, over the ages, the Shadow grew. A thousand years ago it rolled over the Empire of Takkaria, and the last of the proud Takkars fled from their mountain home to the tiny northern province that was all that remained of their land.

Over centuries, feuding between branches of the ancient royal house broke the kingdom into three tiny, warring principalities that shrank as the Shadow moved down from the mountains.

The weak fled, and the cowardly. Those that remained, defying not only ravening Night Walkers but the dark magic that blighted crops and killed the babe in the womb, became the Bordermen, fighting for every scrap of land.

The hardest struggle for the poorest land was fought in the westernmost principality of Manjipé—the land surrounding the ancient city of Manjipor, said to have been built by the first Takkars that Hastur brought into the world. Again and again the Shadow covered the city; again and again the Manjipéans drove it back.

Far to the east, the Princes of the rich city of Mahapor, the proud Mondavan line, controlled a tract that stretched far enough north, away from the Border, to give their people grazing for cattle and crops the Dark Things could not blight, making Mahavara the strongest of the Border Principalities.

Between Manjipé and Mahavara, bounded by rivers, lay the last remnant of the Kantara forest that had once covered all the land.

Four hundred years ago, Rojer of Aqilla, a bandit from Devonia or Alferrida, built a robbers' hold at the meeting of three rivers, north of the Kantara, and grew rich and powerful from the tolls he levied on the river trade. Around his castle grew the city of Tarencia.

When the Kantara branch of the old royal line was failing, a Lord of Tarencia married the last Princess of the house, and the upstart Aqillas ruled the Kantara as Princes of Tarencia. North of the Border country, the rich port cities along the Sea of Ardren had long forgotten the glories of the Takkarian Empire, and felt only scorn for the ragged Bordermen.

Little more than a century ago, a Seynyorean mercenary, Riccarho DiVega, of the great DiVega family, married a Princess of the Aqillas whom war and chance then made the heir. Taking the throne in time of war, he humbled the proud Mondavans and conquered Mahapor, and then began to forge the myriad squabbling principalities and city-states into a kingdom. His son Olansos continued the work, conquering the rich city-states of the seacoast and the fertile lands north of the Border countries. In his old age he married Tarani, Princess of the failing line of Manjipor.

With wealth taxed from the port cities, Olansos hired Seynyorean mercenaries in great numbers, and supplied the Bordermen with food, fuel, and weapons to stop the advance of the Shadow. Tarani's cousin Jagat led an army over the Border, and with fire and steel and the magical aid of the Children of Hastur, carved out of the Shadow his realm of Damenco, a land of poisonous Demon-blasted dust, where nothing could grow until the land had been scoured down to bedrock and new soil built laboriously.

Queen Tarani bore Olansos two sons—twins—but one of them, Jodos, vanished soon after birth, carried into the Shadow by a renegade wizard. Twenty years later, the dying King Olansos summoned his famous cousin, Istvan DiVega, the most reknowned swordsman and general in the world, and made him swear to support Chondos, the remaining twin. For the conquered lands were rebellious. The gold of the merchant cities flowed in a brisk traffic in treason, and old Prince Hansio of Mahapor, "the Old Fox," was only biding his time before he would rebel. Unfortunately, the tactless tongue of Prince Chondos was making him many enemies, and Jagat's son Pirthio was almost his only friend.

Istvan was pleased to learn that Martos, a pupil of an old comrade, a Kadarin Swordmaster, was leading a mercenary troop serving Lord Jagat. Indeed, Jagat's niece and adopted daughter Kumari was pregnant by Martos, who had begged her to come away with him. But Kumari was undecided, for over the centuries it had become a point of pride with Borderwomen not to flee the dangers of their land.

The death of King Olansos set many forces in motion. A violent assault on the Hastur-towers that guarded the Border sent Hasturs and men to battle the Dark Things with need-fire and sword; while the Dark Things used the commotion of the magical war to send

Jodos, the Lost Prince, unnoticed across the Border. The plotters in the port cities were also taking advantage of the confusion surrounding the coronation to complete their plans. Istvan DiVega single-handedly killed the twenty assassins sent to eliminate him, and Martos, protecting Lord Jagat, disposed of as many.

During the coronation, the Hastur who crowned Chondos King also made for him a mind-shielding spell to protect him from the Dark Things. But Prince Jodos secretly entered the palace that night, and was able to cast Chondos into a deep trance before the mind-shield could protect him; in the process, Jodos acquired enough of his brother's memories to impersonate him as King while a winged Demon carried Chondos into captivity in the Shadow.

In the drunken revelry of Coronation night, a group of young Borderers, including Jagat's son Pirthio, attempted a mock-attack on the merchants, and both Pirthio and the young Prince of Mahapor were killed by the Seynyorean mercenary on guard. The carefully insulting message of condolence sent by Jodos to the grieving Lord Jagat was enough to send the old Lord back to Damenco in rebellion.

While Borderers and port cities prepared for war and Istvan DiVega began to gather the mercenary forces into a powerful army, the Dark Things assaulted a distant part of the Border to keep the Children of Hastur from investigating the troubles in Tarencia. Meanwhile, Jodos began to infiltrate and take over the minds of all about him except for Istvan DiVega, who was protected by the spells on his Hastur-made sword.

Chondos, held captive in the ruined city of Rashnagar deep in the Shadow, refused to serve the Dark Things and planned his escape. Martos and Kumari quarreled when she refused to go away with him because their child was now Lord Jagat's only heir. Martos rode south to help besiege the city of Manjipor, to whose relief Jodos was sending an army under Istvan and Prince Phillipos, hoping to destroy all the Bordermen and expose the kingdom to invasion from the Shadow.

Istvan heard a rumor that Martos had been killed at Manjipor, and realised that this young man, heir to the skills of the Three Swords School (of which Istvan himself is the most famed Master), should have been like a son to him.

Istvan readied his army to march to the relief of Manjipor. A nobleman of the Kantara, Ballo of Kotulmer, claimed the ancient right of his clan, to lead the vanguard of the Kantara in war, and rather than risk offending his only allies among the bordermen, Istvan allowed him to march at the head of the van, although he had been warned that Kotulmer was proud and headstrong.

Arming himself with makeshift weapons, Chondos escaped from the ruins of Rashnagar, and fled through the barren, Demon-haunted mountains under the Shadow, taking refuge in the broken Hastur-towers. Meanwhile, Martos was riding with a small force to delay and harass Istvan's army. . . .

Chapter One

Streams met and mingled as Chondos followed falling water down the mountain, and each day seemed darker than the last. Beyond the Shadow, the cloud masses sweeping down from the Sea of Ardren in the north had rolled up against the Border, and the dwellers in the darkness had seized upon their vapours to weave into the web of spells which hid the mountains from the light of the Twin Suns.

Twice he had to hide, crouching among boulders, while emboldened night-things prowled: once a troll, and once a pack of giant ghouls twice as tall as a man. But neither struck his trail. He had to wade through foul black waist-high water, gripping his spear tightly, need-fire flaming on its blue stone point. But the things that hid in the waters beneath the Shadow did not sense him, and he waded out alive though filthy.

Several times he glimpsed behind him a tiny brown shape. He wanted to believe that there was more than one of the things, and it was only by chance that he kept seeing them. But when he remembered the shrill, piping voice that had called his name in the night, that hope faded. The creature was some spy of the Master, no doubt.

When the black bars of sunset banded the sky, something large and hairy and many-legged leaped from behind a rock. He killed it with his flame-pointed spear, glad he could not see it clearly, and ran like a rabbit toward the faint need-fire glow far down the canyon.

This was the third of the broken towers he had found in his flight from Rashnagar. A huge tree reared up in the ring of glowing stone, its leaves thick and beautiful, its trunk gnarled and old. Inside the walls, dead leaves and fallen branches lay thick in long rich grass. He gathered a pile to make a fire on a flat section of the wall, and stared at the colours that darted through the flames, trying to forget the greyness of earth and sky. Outside the tower's light, dim shapes circled in the dark. Peering through the glare above the wall, he made out the looming figure of a troll beyond a pair of wary, man-sized ghouls. He threw a blazing branch at them, and a few bright chunks of rock, and they scattered away from the light.

Squeals and roars woke him later in the night, and looking out, he saw the troll tearing at the carcass of one of the ghouls. The other

11

had fled. The morning came as dark as an overcast night. Hours passed before Chondos could believe it was really day.

The bones of the ghoul lay broken and scattered. The troll was gone. Something brown and ratlike scurried through the broken ribcage. Chondos threw a stone and watched the creature run. He filled his sleeves with broken chunks of glowing stone, and used his knife to whittle a point on one of the straighter branches. It was no sword, but it was the best he could hope for now.

What was left of his meagre stolen grain tasted foul, and he was still hungry after he devoured the tiny ration he dared allow himself. He wondered how long his food could last; there was no way to tell how far it was to the Border.

The leaden ash was pale under the black sky. Twisting lines of light writhed and vanished above the glowing wall. Gathering his spears, and wood for extra torches, he heaved himself up onto the flat section beside the ashes of his fire and sat staring across the leprous dust, looking for some hint of the light of the Border. But all he could see was the wide dark river flowing through a sparse forest of flabby, branching, leafless growths between stony bluffs.

A warm tingling pulsed through him from the stone beneath, sharpening his senses. He felt more alert, as though fed by the power that still burned in the shattered stone. Sliding reluctantly from the wall, he began to plod, with torch raised, across ashen powder toward the foul black river.

A clump of leafless plants bore the marks of teeth. He stared at them, thinking. The deer ate them, he knew, but that meant nothing—a man could not live on grass. In Rashnagar his captors had fed him something that he thought must be a kind of large mushroom. Could this be the same? He hesitated, rubbing his fingers through the thick, curly stubble on his cheeks, and gingerly touched the plant. After a moment, he broke off a piece and put it in his mouth.

Hard to chew, and almost tasteless, he thought, and yet—familiar. Yes, it was the same stuff they had fed him in the city. The plants seemed to grow all down the river. He broke off a larger piece and chewed on it. It might or might not keep him alive, but it should at least still the pains of hunger. If he could keep going until he reached the border . . .

He slid the stone-tipped spear from his shoulder. Torch in one hand, glowing spear in the other, he set off through the darkness of the Shadow's day.

"What does that fool think this is?" Aimon DiBraise snarled irritably on the third day's ride out from Ojaini. "A race?" Gone was the good-natured smile: the frown that furrowed the freckled forehead almost made him seem a different man.

"He probably does, in a way," Pression D'Olafos said, riding at DiBraise's side.

Behind the two mercenary captains the hooves of six hundred horses drummed on the hard parched earth. Armour clattered and leather squeaked. Sun-browned grass stretched wide and flat away to north and east beneath the fleecy sky. Before them, grey blotches of poisoned dust blighted the rougher land ahead. On their left, the glassy Shadow darkened the southern sky.

First one sun and then the other peeked between piled storm clouds, pricking painful points of light from the tiny mail-rings of distant horsemen—the vanguard of the army that marched to Manjipor.

D'Olafos rose in his stirrups, shading his eyes with a broad, bronzed hand. "DiSezrotti's stringing his men out in a long thin line," he said, puzzled. "Now why . . . ? Ah! Very good!" He settled back into his saddle. "That way, we can keep his tail in sight, no matter how fast that idiot, Kotulmer, drags them along."

"They should let him go!" DiBraise snapped. "If Kotulmer wants to ride into an ambush unsupported, let him! If his glory is so dear to him—"

"It's DiVega's order," D'Olafos said with a shrug. "He told them to keep him in sight! Oh, I agree with you! And I think DiVega will change the orders once he realises what Kotulmer's doing. But, you saw Kotulmer at the council! How he just stood up and demanded to lead the vanguard, and all the Kantarans backed him. DiVega doesn't want to offend the—"

"*Offend* them!" DiBraise snarled. "Bugger them, if they can't obey orders!"

"We have enough enemies in the Border country as it is," D'Olafos pointed out, reasonably. "Remember, the Old Fox will be just waiting to pounce, and we have only the Kantara to guard our backs, along with the two or three companies DiVega left to guard Ojaini. If all the Bordermen were to unite against us, then we—"

"Is Kotulmer fighting for us or against us?" DiBraise broke in. "And which way would be better?"

"Don't underestimate the Bordermen!" D'Olafos' tone was sombre. "There are virtues beside discipline, and strengths that depend on neither size nor skill. You've been here long enough to know that!"

Clouds shrouded the sunlight: the pinpricks of glare faded, and the distant mail was the colour of tears. D'Olafos' horse shook its head, its bit jingling.

"This will be no easy war," D'Olafos went on, after a moment. "Men who face death and horror worse than death every day of their lives—"

"Yes, yes, I know all that!" DiBraise scolded, his usually soft voice high-pitched with irritation. "Will the Bordermen blame *us* if Kotulmer rides into an ambush? Are we his nursemaids?"

"You know DiVega," said D'Olafos. "He never wastes men. Some would call that a weakness. I do not. But since he couldn't stop Kotulmer from taking the lead, he'll try to make sure there's someone to get him out of trouble if he gets into it."

"Even if he has to risk the whole army?"

"No." D'Olafos shook his head. "Once he finds out that Kotulmer is placing the rest of the vanguard in danger, he'll change the order and let the fool run as far ahead as he wants."

"We'll catch up with him when his horses wear out," said DiBraise. "He can't keep this pace long. We'll find them limping along ahead of us in a day or so." He chuckled.

D'Olafos nodded and grinned, but his eyes rose to the hilly, grey-dappled distances ahead, where, someplace beyond the long line of mail-clad men, the little troop that followed Kotulmer's proud banner had dwindled out of vision.

Far ahead, other eyes watched Kotulmer's banner.

Martos peered above dried brown grass-stalks, and down the scout's pointing finger. The Shadow's black wall held grey earth from grey sky. Tiny mounted figures marched against the dark curtain: makeshift armour hanging loosely around them made the men look hunched, like beetles in the saddle. Their armour differed subtly from that of Manjipor.

"That's Kotulmer's banner," said Suktio, beside him. "Ah! He must have claimed the old Omdavan privilege, then, and forced DiVega to allow it!" He smiled at the confusion on Martos' face. "The Omdavans of Kotulmer have led the vanguard of the Kantara for a thousand years."

The smile was friendly, but sharp to Martos' mind came the sudden memory of Kumari's angry voice and of Suktio glaring, fingers clenched tight on his sword-hilt. . . . No time to think of that now! He forced his mind away from her face and the hateful words that haunted him, and made himself look at the barren ash-grey wastes, where Demons had devoured the land and left only leaden dust.

Now, behind the grotesque, shabbily armoured Bordermen, he saw in the distance other men marching, mail-shirts rippling like water in the gloom—a long thin column that stretched back out of sight. Beyond, straining his eyes, he could sense a crawling, a faint hint of dust clouds blurring innumerable tiny dots too small to see: DiVega's vast Seynyorean army, which so greatly outnumbered his own. Then his eye caught on a deep fold of land that ran down next to the road, and sudden creative fervour leaped through him, driving all thought of Kumari from his head.

"That—that—ravine. He stuttered a moment before his tongue came under his control. "Can the bottom be seen from—from the road? Could men—can men hide there? And horses?" He pointed, and Suktio followed his arm.

"Why, yes," said the Borderer. "A good place for an ambush! In fact, there was an old battle fought here . . ."

"If we move men down it from . . ." His elation faded. He watched the enemy scouts, in drab Border armour, prowl to each side of the road. "But that's no good," he said, frowning. "Their scouts would find us before we could get into position."

"Perhaps not!" Suktio straightened. "Not if—listen! Lord Ballo of Kotulmer is said to be a rash and headstrong man. Now, if a small group of men were to show themselves ahead of his troop— say, back there, on that rise—then he might well rush to the attack."

Martos' heart soared. Pulling his dagger, he began to scratch plans in the dry earth.

Frowning at the Seer's report, Istvan DiVega stared into the distant dimness that hid the vanguard. Behind and around him horseshoes chimed on stone, thudded on earth, fell soundless on the ever-thickening patches of dust.

Sweat rolled down his face. His body longed for the cooling rains that his mind dreaded. This was the third dawn that Kotulmer had broken camp early and pushed his men on at a pace that put them far ahead of Cousin Enjanton's company. The Bordermen had no Seer: messengers sent after them had reported arrogant answers that implied the Seynyoreans were slugabeds and slackers, whose plain duty was to keep up.

Istvan snorted. He would just have to let the fool push ahead. Already, Cousin Enjanton's attempts to keep Kotulmer's men in sight had drawn both his company and DiSezrotti's dangerously far from the main part of the army. The gloom on sky and land seemed to settle into his heart, and he wished vainly for a tree or a bird. The land ahead rose in long brown waves, scarred with twisting patches of dust. North he could see broad stretches of brown grassland, but along the Border all was grey and ruined.

And there would be worse to come. On their left, the Shadow was falling away to the south. Over his shoulder, beyond swaying rows of helmets, Istvan could see the blue shimmer of Vajrakota Tower, dim against darkness in the east, at the corner of the great bite Lord Jagat had carved out of the Shadow. From here to Manjipor they must march through miles of poisoned dust, depending on the ponderous supply train to bring food for men and horses.

Yesterday they had had to cross their first wide stretch of dust, on their way to Vajrakota. And a little before there had been a broad plain of clattering stone where the dust had been scoured away around one of the little Border castles. They had passed several deserted castles, but here scouts reported a challenge, shouted in a woman's voice. He and Arjun DiFlacca had ridden with the scouts to the gates. An arrow shattered beside his horse's hooves. "That was no accident!" a woman had shouted from inside the wall.

Shocked, Istvan realised that to these Borderwomen, he was no longer human, but only another enemy, like a ghoul or a troll. He shuddered again at the memory. What could a man do if a woman attacked him? The Ban of Hastur awaited any man who broke Hastur's Law by killing women! But how well could the Borderwomen defend their little fort against the *real* Dark Things, if the Border broke while their men were still away fighting in this *stupid* war? He had asked Lord Rinmull to leave a few men camped near the castle, ready to ride to its rescue. But they must end this war quickly.

A sudden thought seized him, and he turned his head to look back over his shoulder at Vajrakota's blue flame in the east. Before Lord Jagat had driven the Dark Things from Damenco—*as Hastur drove them from the world in the dawn of time,* he thought; that was why Jagat was so revered among his people—surely, then, the Border here had been farther to the north?

Yet that same tower still stood at the Border, holding back the dark. He had never believed old stories that the Hasturs could move their towers. Sometimes, he knew, they abandoned them to the use of men, and there were castles all along the rim of Shadow built with such a tower at its core. Ekakin was one such. *Had* the tower moved? Had it grown legs and walked? Flown through the air? Or simply vanished, to reappear in its new place?

"Lord Istvan?" Arjun DiFlacca's voice broke rudely into his thoughts. "There is something you said earlier I do not understand."

There is a great deal you do not understand, Istvan thought, biting the sarcastic rejoinder back. He was beginning to regret the generous impulse which had made him ask the boy to ride with him. The young Borderman's naïve self-righteousness was beginning to get on his nerves. He remembered how, as they had ridden away from the castle full of women, he had turned to Arjun and snapped, "Where now is your courtesy of war?"

That castle could not move, if the Dark Things came . . .

"What is it?" Istvan asked with a sigh. After all, the boy had never been more than a hundred miles from the Border in his life: the wide world that Istvan knew was to him a wonder and a dream. And besides, his advice had already allowed Istvan to foresee and prevent two dangerous conflicts between touchy Border honour and Seynyorean pride.

"You said that one of the heroes gathered at Rath Tintallain had been a companion of Fendol. But I thought Fendol lived long ago. Ages ago!"

"Five thousand years ago," Istvan said. "Before the fall of Galdor. But Tuarim MacElathan comes of an undying race, although some say he has mortal blood. He is older than Kandol Hastur-Lord. But there are elves in Elthar—that is the Hastur's great city in Y'Gora, like Carcosa on this continent—who are older still, who came to the aid of the Children of Hastur when the Dark Things first returned to the world."

And they are not old, he thought, in mingled wonder and envy. Bitterness washed through him. *See what only sixty years have done to me,* he thought.

"I wish I could cross the ocean," said Arjun. "Or even *see* the ocean! But I would rather go to Carcosa than Y'Gora, and see a land that has never been ruined by the Dark Things."

Istvan smiled down at the boy. Arjun's trotting Border pony was almost lost among the tall, bony, Seynyorean war-horses that towered above it on every side.

"And a land where the young men speak of nothing but leaving dull Carcosa, where nothing can ever happen, and going to the Border, where life is dangerous and exciting," said Istvan with a smile. Arjun gaped up at him.

While the boy was still thinking about that, Prince Phillipos came riding, white plumes waving against the leaden sky, glorious on his white horse. "Grey silk!" the Prince said, indignantly. "So much for my Chamberlain's ideas on fashion! Bales and bales of it he bought! When I get home, he'll have to throw out the whole lot! *I'll* not wear it! Not after this!" The white plumes bobbed pallid and ghostly above his helmet. His armour was dull in the gloom; its polished steel demanded sunlight. Lost and sad and out of place in this cheerless waste, it screamed for sunbeams.

"You know, Lord DiVega," said the Prince cheerfully, "that land up ahead is a lot rougher than it looks. Are you sure you have the best formation for it? We might run into an ambush."

Istvan gaped at him. This decorative, empty-headed young man had never opened his mouth on military matters before.

"There was an ambush laid here during the Gonshi Wars, eight hundred years or so ago," the Prince said. "I don't remember the name of the battle but—"

"Arankila?" said Arjun DiFlacca.

"Why yes! That was it!" Phillipos grinned. "Thank you! Arankila! Yes, the Mondavans had made a temporary alliance with the

Aryarajans of the Kantara, because the Arthavans of Manjipor had gained control of the royal family and . . . Well, that's all very complicated.

"In any case, the two clans crossed the Yukota—the largest army to take the field since Rashnagar fell, I understand—but the Arthavans used one of the folds in the land ahead to hide a fair-sized body of men, and put their main army in clear view just beyond. The enemy marched right past them, and when—"

"That was a long time ago!" Arjun broke in scornfully. "You couldn't hide a covey of rabbits there now!"

"Well, I suppose not," Phillipos said, his smile unruffled, while Istvan scanned the vague grey wastes ahead, trying to pick out the shapes of men he knew were there. "There *was* a lot more cover then. It must have been beautiful, all fertile land, green and wooded. I suppose you must know more about the Gonshi Wars than I do. I've only read the account in the *Rajaji,* and Jaya Charun's *Gonshi Chronicles,* of course."

Mysterious names of long-dead kings and heroes lilted meaninglessly in Istvan's ears, fascinating as fragments of fading tapestry, as Arjun and the Prince talked of ancient struggles of the Arthavans and Mondavans for the regency, in days when the old imperial line had become mere puppets, hostages to the ambitions of the rival clans. Ghostly armies contended in their voices; long-dead courtiers plotted. Istvan listened, silent, to scraps of a history that was not his, but which meant as much to his companions as the Defense of Heyleu, or the old feud between the Vegas and DiVegas, did to him.

". . . why, Prince Rutna would have been taken or killed, here at Arankila," Arjun was saying, "had not Kailun, the Omdavan chief, seized the Prince's helm, with its royal crest, and fought in his place while my ancestor Chichak, Kailun's brother, dragged the Prince's horse from the battlefield and back across the Yukota. Some say Kailun fell fighting in the middle of the battle, but there is an old story that he was captured, and killed himself to keep the Arthavans from learning the truth, so there would be more time for his Prince to escape."

"Such a waste!" Prince Phillipos shook his head.

Arjun bristled. "*A waste!* He saved his Lord! Had Prince Rutna died the last of the Aryarajans, there would have been no strain of the ancient blood to pass down through the Aqillas to King Olansos, and the Kantara would have come under the rule of the Manjipor or Mahapor. Men killed themselves in the old days for far more trivial things than that!"

"The war itself was a waste," Phillipos said stubbornly. "While the Arthavans and Aryarajans and Mondavans were killing each other off, the Dark Things ate the land for which they fought."

"At least it was a clean war between honourable men," Arjun snapped, "and not this bloody Border butchery!" He shook his fist at the Shadow that hid the southern horizon. "If only they could be driven from the world, there would be no other kind of war!"

Istvan stirred and spoke. "I'm not so sure of that." The younger men turned, gaped at him. "I think sometimes you Border folk are fortunate to have true evil lurking at your door." He shook his head sadly. "I think sometimes that man is born with the need to fight against evil, and if there is no evil for him to fight against, he will make it himself."

"What *are* you talking about?" Prince Phillipos asked with a perplexed frown.

"Look you," said Istvan, "do you think Lord Jagat is evil?"

"*Jagat?*" they chorused, staring.

"Of course not!" said the Prince.

"Of course not." Istvan nodded. "Here you know what evil is. Yet, in lands far from the Shadow, where the Dark Things are only a rumour, I have seen men act like Dark Things themselves in war, and lose all humanity, imagining their foes to be evil. That is how criminals like Sandor of Anganvar come to be, men who let hatred blind them to all honour. If the Dark Things were gone, all war might turn to that kind of madness."

"Surely not!" exclaimed Phillipos. "However a few madmen may behave, most men, surely, will respect the Rules of War!"

"I hope you are right," said Istvan. "But remember the women at the castle, yesterday? They would have murdered us, even though they *knew* the Law of Hastur forbade us to harm them and would keep us from defending ourselves. And for what? A quarrel between two kinsmen, a foolish contest to see who can hold the throne."

Water-worn stones in a dry creekbed rolled and clattered under hoof. Arjun stared at him, shocked. "You speak as though—as though you did not believe—that this war is just, or that it matters?"

"Wars are rarely fought over things that matter," said Istvan bitterly. "Oh yes, this matters! Because the Dark Things are waiting, and because no one but Chondos can hold the realm together." *Not that he's done very well so far,* he thought. "And if Jagat wins, it will be the same story as before, when the Arthavans and Mondavans fought here!" His arm waved across the grey dust of the ancient battlefield. "That is why we must end this war quickly! But if the other provinces would accept Jagat, he would be a good king." *Better than Chondos.* "And as long as the realm is united, it does not matter who rules it."

As he stopped, he became aware of an uncanny silence. The grey powder was all around them now, muffling the horses' hoofbeats. "But most wars—and I've fought in many," he went on, "are stupid. One King decides he wants some patch of land—or the taxes from it anyway—that belongs to some other King, who then feels he has to defend it. Usually it doesn't matter that much to the people who live there which way their tax money goes after it leaves them, but after the armies have marched over the fields a few times, there's nothing left to pay taxes with anyway!'' He was surprised by the anger in his voice. ''Stupidity and greed—that's all you need for war!''

''What about King Olansos!'' Arjun demanded. ''If he had not conquered all the little city-states and principalities, there would have been no kingdom! And the Border would have been up around Inagar or the Hinarion by now!''

''Softly,'' Istvan said. ''I did not say war between men was never justified, nor that good could not come of it. But all too often, the reasons men give for war are trivial, mere excuses to justify their greed or their desire for glory and action.'' *And this war?* he wondered. *No one wanted it. Both sides were forced to it. Or were we?*

''If the need to unite the kingdom justifies Olansos' wars,'' said Phillipos, thoughtfully, ''what justifies the men who fought against him? Some of my father's vassals never forgave him for submitting to—now, what was it they called him? Yes!—*that bloody-handed robber and oppressor of Princely states!* Even today,'' he said with a laugh, ''there are men who would cheer if I rebelled against the Crown.''

''One of the Kadarin philosophers,'' Istvan said, ''wrote that war was only justified to defend your home against foreign conquest. Yet, without the conquests of Ore the Great, there would be no Kadar.''

As his voice stopped, he felt again the wide desolation. For nine days hoofbeats had hammered in his ears. Now, despite the creak and the jingle of leather and steel, and the pitiful voices of men all around, the army seemed to march in unnatural silence.

Demons had eaten this land to the bare bones, and turned those to grey dust. Here, where men long dead had fought over a kingdom, and where many a man beside Kailun of Kotulmer had died a hero's death before the shouting of battle faded, poisoned ash covered the field of Arankila, hardly stirring in the lonesome winds. It barely puffed above the fetlocks of the horses before settling again to the ground. Good thing, too: the stuff destroyed men's lungs, and Istvan remembered friends who had come back to Carcosa coughing blood.

''Look at those fellows there, slogging along!'' Phillipos gestured at the long column of footmen. ''Such long faces! It's all this gloom and quiet. They need cheering up. I'll soon see to that!'' The beautiful white horse whirled and cantered back toward the marching men.

Istvan was homesick for Carcosa: for children playing beside sparkling fountains; for sunlight glowing on leaves and windows of hidden houses peering through ordered ranks of trees all up the mountain slope, between little steep streets and stairways. But before him now lay rolling waves of leaden dust, which stole the sound of hooves. All the ancient Takkar heroism at Arankila had not stopped that. Now men were dying again at Manjipor, and more would die before this war ended. First Jagat's son, then Birthran's pupil, Martos, and Cousin Raquel's student, Nurin Kimerosa—how many others? So many young men, dead! Young men died—the young men always died, while he lived on!

A sudden whistling trill startled him. A bird? But birds had long ago flown away from the Border. Twisting on his swaying horse, he saw Prince Phillipos laugh above a silver flute. Marching men looked up. Again the Prince set the flute to his mouth and twittered another chirping call. Then his fingers danced in an old tune, one that had long ago made its way across the world to Carcosa.

Istvan felt his horse sway and dance between his thighs, and for a moment, he was young again, part of a crowd of young men on high-spirited horses thronging brightly lit streets in festival finery, while giggling girls watched, or rode pillion behind the bolder and luckier. Only a moment; then he was old again, riding the grey wasteland at the foot of the Shadow, leading a host of younger men to battle and death, while the night-things watched and waited behind the dark veil.

Nervous men waited in a giant ditch.

Martos tried to count companies of tiny toy figures moving on the endless grey: little knots of Bordermen jogging on earth-coloured ponies between the orderly blocks of tall Seynyorean horses. But even so huge an army was dwarfed by the ocean of dust and the looming mass of the Shadow.

A hundred and forty men left in his own company, and a few hundred Borderers and Massadessans, against how many thousand Seynyoreans? The Seynyoreans, he recalled, counted a company as three hundred men.

Behind him horses snorted and bits jingled. He heard Paidros' low voice talking to the men. His stomach was bitter: probably the cold chicken and hardtack he'd eaten that morning. At least they'd not yet brought him raw fish.

Faint shouting drew his eyes down the road. Under Kotulmer's banner he saw waving arms and unsheathed swords, and looked quickly down the road past them, far to his right. There were

Suktio's men in the agreed-on place, outlined against the sky. Shifting clouds opened overhead, and sunlight poured out. Swords flared; Suktio's mail-rings glittered like jewels; hanging strips and plates of lacquered horsehide glowed rich brown.

Milling horses were spurred to a run as Kotulmer's banner surged to meet the challenge. On the road behind, long legs of sombre, gaunt, Seynyorean horses shifted to a trot. The Twin Suns vanished in the swirling clouds. A scout in Border armour came racing past, followed by another. Neither even glanced at the fold where Martos hid.

Martos whirled and sprang down the slope to where Paidros held Thunderhead's bridle, then swung himself into the saddle. The company was mounted and formed up for the charge. The small group of Massadessans and Bordermen who would lend weight to their wedge clustered behind them.

Thunderhead shook himself eagerly and pawed at the dust. With a thump of his heels Martos urged the war-horse up the slope at a walk, but reined him in as soon as he could see over the rim. He freed the long blade from its sheath. *Dwarf-forged,* he thought, *in Y'Gora beyond the sea, and able to cut troll's flesh.*

A fleck of dark rock stared at him like Kumari's eyes. He shook his head angrily. There was no time for that! Down the slight slope from the rim, the Seynyorean line was passing from left to right. Thinly though they were spread, he guessed the line ahead numbered six hundred. They had quickened their horses' pace to a canter; in a moment he would face the long line's center. His sword stretched high, he rose in his stirrups.

Now! The sword snapped down.

"Charge!" Paidros yelled.

Thunderhead surged under Martos' thighs, lunging up and over the rise, scrambling in slippery dust. Ugly jumping horses bounded past. Martos heard whispering arrows splinter on his steel breastplate. He clenched his teeth, sheathed his sword, and reached for the bow by his boot.

Confused Seynyoreans swung their horses round, but had no time to re-form. Air swarmed with spike-headed arrows; their needle tips slipped through mail-rings, and riderless horses plunged in the Seynyorean line as the Kadarins shot left and right.

A last arrow whistled from Martos' bow. Men galloped over the ashen dust that ate the sound of hooves. The Jumpers raced before, like lean and ugly hounds. Martos' morion rocked on his head, a shaft glancing from its brim, as he bent to slide the bow back into its case. He ripped his shield from the saddle. His wrist scraped painfully against the leather back as he shrugged his sleeve through the enarmes. Sudden weight tugged at his shoulder.

He pulled free his sword, and a thicket of steel sprouted behind him. The Jumpers soared like birds above the Seynyorean line. Martos saw men reel back, staring at the huge horse-bodies in the air, the hooves so close to their helms. Airborne riders bent with curved bows, and arrows smashed down from the sky. Seynyoreans pitched from their saddles, blood pouring out of their mouths, feathers brushing their ears.

A wave of steel struck the staggered line: Martos at its crest, rising in the stirrups, shield clasped tight to his shoulder, his sword blurred to a silver fan. A corpse flopped from a saddle, smearing blood and brains on the poisoned ash. Martos' sword, a red fan now, crashed on a quickly raised shield. A thin slice of steel planed at his eyes. The brown back of his shield blotted it away, and his armbones shook with the shock. Twisting in the saddle, he lashed out, and felt mail-rings grate under his edge. Thunderhead shouldered a riderless horse aside, and grey dust stretched empty to the Shadow's foot.

Behind, men shrieked. Beaten armour knelled; horses neighed and snorted. A wedge of living men hurtled through the broken line. Ahead, the riders of the jumping horses were still trying to get their frantic, bucking mounts under control. Trumpets shrilled, signalling the turn, and then the whole force followed as Thunderhead swung wide.

Seynyoreans stared over their shoulders, and then, with a sudden pounding of heels, the entire line burst into full flight.

"Look at them run!" someone cried, and men laughed jubilantly. But Martos did not laugh. These were Seynyoreans.

Whooping men began to spur their horses after the fleeing men, but Paidros' voice snapped out: "Keep together! Trot! Slow trot! Form up!"

Martos twisted in the saddle, counting the bobbing faces behind him. A long scratch bled on Paidros' cheek, and to right and left were other wounded: Oton, Huaris, Diegos . . .

Against the grey clouds, the Ghost-Wolf of his father's house rattled on the shaft below Jagat's Sword-Wheel, and Martos felt generations of ancestors watching him through the blank cloth eyes. He struggled with his tongue.

"Wounded men fall back!" he croaked. Paidros echoed the command, louder, but did not fall back himself, Martos noticed—but then, the scratch was nothing.

Fresh men moved to the front, took their distances, and formed themselves for the second charge. Ahead, beyond the fleeing riders, Martos could see manoeuvring horsemen. He dared not hope the Seynyoreans would crash into their comrades and throw them into confusion, but it *could* happen.

He heard Valiros' voice behind him, and turning, saw him with the others on the neurotic, misshapen Jumpers, prancing toward the front. The Seynyoreans whirled their horses and formed into a line, weapons poised and ready. Admiration was like wine to Martos' mood: a worthy foe, and glory to be fought.

"Look, they stopped!" Valiros jeered. "Resting their horses, do you think, before they run again?"

What a stupid thing to say! Martos thought. The enemy ranks would be too deep to jump. And there were nearly twice as many Seynyoreans as his own little force. He spurred Thunderhead across the ashen dust. An arrow flickered past him, splintered on steel. Where was Suktio?

Loud of a sudden, hooves drummed on solid earth as they rode across an unblasted patch. Arrows hissed by him, crackling on helmets, splintering on armour, quivering in flesh. Seynyoreans shouted, and enemy hooves crashed into a trot. Martos heard Paidros shout his name. He turned. The little man was waving at something, off to the left. Earth-brown ponies ran over grey dust, carrying little dark men in drab leather armour, skirted breeches and wide sleeves flapping comically in the wind; and before them, a savage banner: the Lord of Kotulmer's head on a spear.

Raising his long sword high, Martos spurred Thunderhead, drove the great horse ahead through swarming arrows. Seynyoreans sheathed their bows and drew their swords. He saw the ends of the line in motion, drawing forward, ready to lash like twin whips on his flanks while the centre took the brunt of his charge.

A crescent! Suddenly his mind seethed with the familiar symbols of strategy as taught in the Three Swords School: inspiration flared like lightning in his brain. He fought his frozen tongue, reached with the flat of his sword to touch Paidros on the arm.

"Right!" he croaked. Paidros stared at him. "Right! The horns!" And he wheeled and charged toward the enemy left, where the advancing wings had thinned and their shields, turned away from him, were useless. Jumping horses scattered from his path. Valiros stared at him, pop-eyed.

"To the right, wheel!" came Paidros' crisp voice.

A trumpet echoed the command. Seynyorean horsemen gaped as Martos rose in his stirrups, heavy blade raised. Jumping horses soared past him, leaping over the line of cavalry in a rain of arrows.

A horseman in Martos' path tried to wheel and face him. His lifted sword crashed under Martos' falling blade. Thunderhead's shoulder sent the long-legged Seynyorean horse sprawling, its rider flying from the saddle. Another horseman was rushing; his falling sword crashed on Martos' lifted shield. The dwarf-blade circled about Martos' head: bone and steel broke under its edge.

He saw Paidros crashing through the press, needle-sword red in his hand. The belling of battle battered Martos' ears; swords sought his life, leaping in metal rainbows against the clouds. His shield was clanging like an anvil.

Now he heard, over the hammering and shrieking, the shouting voices of many men, raised in an ancient war-cry he had heard but once before: "The Barrier of Blood!"

He shivered in sudden memory. Jagat had told him this war-cry was never used in a battle against men. It was the rallying cry of those who fought against the Shadow.

"The Barrier of Blood! The Barrier of Blood!"

Far in the north the false King sat, like a spider in the web of his court. Dreams were his haunt and his hunting ground, and his prey the minds of men; but by day he sat on Chondos' throne, to act the part of King.

Jodos feared the hold this gave his brother's ghost upon his mind. Chondos' memory, not his, held all the rituals he had expected to know. Not only the rituals of court, but all the strange little rituals of courtesy and friendship, of greeting and parting and friendly talk.

The thought of the Master, and the torture that failure would bring, forced him to smile and laugh, despite his fear of this corrupting humanity, while he waited impatiently for news from the south of the war he had begun. Yet it pleased him, watching old Lord Zengio and his son, to see in their sidelong glances distrust and fear, and the beginnings of hate. Gazing into the depths of their minds, he could see growing the seed he had planted in their dreams. And all around the court, other minds showed similar stirrings. Spinning his web, he smiled, waiting for word of the war in the south.

The first reports came in whirling confusion. One Seer pitched from his horse in the middle of a word, clawing at his throat in some comrade's death-shock. Red-robed Healers dragged him away, while Istvan stared into the grey blur where men fought and died beyond the range of sight.

DiBraise and D'Olafos were already moving in. Istvan ordered six companies forward to their support, while the muscles of the lean mare rippled between his thighs as he raced toward the battle, dragging his Seers with him.

Martos rode through the screaming and the booming of battle. Sweat ran like rain, though his mouth was dry. Hand and sleeve were thick with blood that drooled down from his sword-guard.

The Seynyorean spirit was breaking. Too many lay in purple drying blood under the horses' hooves. Hammer blows from each end had crushed their line. Commands were drowned in death-screams and the clamour of steel; each living man was cut off from his fellows by his kinship to the stained corpses his horse danced to avoid.

Across rumpled ashen dust, Istvan saw swarming motes: DiBraise and D'Olafos joining their companies, riding to aid the vanguard. And beyond them a milling, a stirring of other dots too small to see.

Remembering, he fumbled in his saddlebag. His fingers closed on a tube. Pulling his horse to a stop, he drew the glass out and set it to his eye: a black horse plodded out of greyness, an armoured rider on its back. A small brown horse darted in. A man in reddish lacquered leather swung a vague grey sword. The sword was a sudden red. The grey figure fell from the black horse's back, and a red thread stained its side.

Sombre horses gathered and scattered again, under phantom men in watery mail; dull steel blended with the dust. Small solid Bordermen harassed the ghostly riders. A snow-white horse flamed in the glass. It's rider's cuirass gleamed, a dull, wet sheen, under a whipping scarlet cloak. A Kadarin!

Something like a great wave of water seemed to rise up, flooding the plain. Istvan started; the glass jerked. Then he saw he was looking over the mail-clad shoulders of men, their ranks tossing like waves with the stride of their horses. Dim light rippled on sunless armour as on a shadowed pool.

Martos and Paidros rode together. Swords thundered and clanged. Above his foemen's heads, Martos could see approaching horsemen: six hundred men in dull metal. The Ghost-Wolf glared down. Wounded men screamed; whole men shouted. Muffled hooves stirred leaden dust.

Martos raised high his dripping sword. Men rallied behind him, gathering into a tense line at the rim of the battle. Paidros shouted an order. Styllis' trumpet repeated it.

Arrows arched high in a sudden swarm above the tangle of mingled friend and foe, and dropped into the oncoming ranks. Before the thrum of bowstrings died, Martos' blade snapped down, spattering blood over poisoned dust. Paidros shouted; a trumpet cried. Kadarin and Bordermen spurred to a sudden charge that lifted the remnants of broken companies and swept them into the ranks of their rescuers. Martos saw Seynyoreans kill Seynyoreans in the confusion of that first blind shock.

Inside the Shadow, grey dusk covered grey dust: Chondos could not see far. Flat grey roofed the little valley, and the mountain behind him vanished.

Once he climbed up the earth banks—lower now, closer to the level of the river—and found himself peering across a broad, dim plain. Sparse blobs might have been bushes or rocks or fungi, but were few and far between. He thought he saw vague shapes moving, far across the barren plain, and quickly scrambled down.

Cautiously, he followed the stream, testing the earth with the glowing stone point of his spear. Ahead the grey seemed brighter. He hoped it was the sign of another tower. A skeletal figure rose from behind a rock.

"King Chondos!" a harsh voice croaked.

Chondos planted the butt of his torch in the dust and gripped his levelled spear with both hands.

"Do you not know me, Lord?" There was something familiar about the rasping voice. "Do not fear me, Prince; I have been wandering in this dust as long as you."

It came crouching into the open. Rags covered flesh that barely covered bone, yet the dried, leathery face *was* familiar.

"I served you in Rajinagara! Do you not remember? I have been alone for a long time. And I thirst—I thirst!"

"Drink then," said Chondos, gesturing to the broad black water on his left. He recognised the face now: one of his "servants"—the one who had vanished just before Chondos' own escape.

The wretched figure staggered across Chondos' path, watching him sidelong as it moved toward the stream. Chondos kept his spear ready, but the man seemed very weak, and unarmed. What had kept him alive through the dangers of the mountains?

Pressure surged in Chondos' head, and a sudden buzzing sounded in his ears. The Hastur-spell rose from the depths of his mind.

The bony figure twisted in a blur of speed. Chondos drove the flaming spearpoint toward the rib-ridged chest, but it was no longer there. It had writhed aside and fleshless hands locked on the spear shaft. Tough wood snapped. The flaming stone tip flew glittering, and Chondos was jerked from his feet.

Pale lips lifted from long white needles. Red eyes glared into his own.

Muscles ached in Martos' arms. His great sword rose and fell. Metal tore: a bundle of meat that had once been a man catapulted from a saddle, down under the hooves where other bundles lay, and parts of living men that screamed and spattered blood from waving stumps. Men shouted exultantly, drunk with life and war.

Steel boomed on his shield. Light-headed, he swayed, sword arm lurching rhythmically, returning stroke for stroke. Shields rose and fell. Aching knees pressed Thunderhead this way and that. The enemy's gaunt steed shied away, and a riderless horse galloped between them, blood pouring from a wound in its flank. The Seynyorean horse bucked frantically; Thunderhead shivered, but calmed quickly: Kadarin war-horses were bred to bear worse than this.

Hunger scalded Martos' stomach, and there was nothing to look forward to but hardtack and cold chicken—or raw fish! A roast of beef floated in his mind, brown and steaming. He could almost smell its juices.

The bucking Seynyorean steed carried its master away. Men shouted and screamed above the clattering of metal; riderless horses stampeded through the fray.

Beef. Mutton. Pork. He pictured meat roasted, stewed, broiled, pictured it red and dripping. Then he saw and smelled the blood dripping from his sword arm and his empty belly tried to heave itself up through his throat.

Above hammering bells he heard Paidros' voice shouting. He turned Thunderhead toward the sound. Paidros pointed; Martos stared stupidly past the little man's waving arm. Empty greyness swayed before his eyes a moment before he saw them. Still small in the distance, evenly spaced blocks of horses swarmed toward the battle. Six companies—nearly two thousand men.

"Any more bright ideas?" Paidros spat. "Or can we get out of here?"

Martos gazed frowning at the nearing swarms of swift-moving dots. Behind him Borderers' voices were still shouting.

"The Barrier of Blood," he muttered, and turned back to Paidros. "Do you suppose the Bordermen know what 'retreat' means?"

"If not," Paidros snarled, "we'd better give them a fast lesson!"

Chondos let go the broken spear shaft and staggered back. Out of his childhood he had heard Lord Jagat's voice: *Do not look in their eyes!* He forced his eyes away from the red stare. *Strike for the heart if at all,* Jagat had said, *or take the head off cleanly. Nothing else will kill a vampire—not with plain steel.* And he didn't even have plain steel.

Fingers like claws, inhumanly strong, clamped on his arm. Racking his shoulder joint with a sudden wrench, it plucked him from his feet as though he were a doll made of rags.

His sleeves were still filled with glowing stone. He swung his free arm around fast, and the loaded sleeve slapped the pallid face. He heard a scream, and flew through the air. His shoulder blade pushed the breath from his lungs as grey dust puffed around him. An open mouth gaped wide, ivory spikes set to seize his throat. The thick, sickening smell of blood and decay choked him.

He kicked up with both feet. It was like kicking a leather sack of dry stricks. The creature sailed weightless through air, and fell yards away. But it was on its feet before he was, hissing like a cat as it rushed him. He had just enough time to drop a large rock from his sleeve into his hand, and as the corpse sprang for his throat, he pressed the stone to its face.

The stone chip flared. Chondos felt no heat; though a pleasant tingle ran up his arm. The vampire screamed and staggered back, a brand of seared flesh across its eyes. Chondos heaved the stone chip high and brought it down with both hands. The skull caved in like a wasp's nest; the bony figure fell. But still it was not dead. Crawling on hands and knees, it tried to rise.

Chondos remembered the sharpened stake, carried like a sword in his belt, and reached for it. Bony fingers gripped his ankle, sinking into flesh. He struck down with the rock. A scream grated from empty lungs. As the fingers fell from the crushed flesh of his leg, he kicked it over onto its back and stabbed the stick down into its chest. Papery skin parted; bone splintered; dull brownish blood spurted. Chondos hammered the stake down with the rock, down into the ground. He limped to where his torch stood in the dust and, lifting it, whipped it into flame. He shivered. The new-made vampire had not been aware of its power. But an older one . . .

He set fire to the dry scraps of cloth. The parched flesh caught. Breathing hard, he turned away and began limping onward along the stream, toward the Border.

Istvan's heart twisted at the screaming of men and horses. The vanguard still milled in confusion, but the Bordermen and their Kadarin allies were gone. He saw Pression D'Olafos spurring his horse to meet him, with DiSezrotti and Cousin Enjanton close behind, and another man Istvan did not know. Blood was oozing from a rent in Enjanton's mail.

"Where's DiBraise?" Istvan asked, as D'Olafos saluted. He had to shout above the cries of the wounded.

"DiBraise is dead!" D'Olafos shouted back. "Omartos DiMadyar" —he jerked a thumb at the stranger who rode with him, a bulky black-bearded man—"has taken command of his company."

"What happened?" Istvan asked.

"That idiot, Kotulmer—" DiSezrotti's voice was a snarl.

"He's dead," Enjanton DiVega cut in. "His head was on a spear. I saw it." His voice was weak.

"More use there than it ever was on his shoulders!" D'Olafos snorted.

"Speak no ill of the dead!" said DiMadyar. He swayed in the saddle, though Istvan could see no wound.

"I said, *What happened?*" Istvan snapped, in the command voice he rarely had to use.

"Kotulmer went charging off suddenly," Enjanton said. "There was an enemy force ahead. All the Bordermen who were acting as flankers bolted past. We increased our pace, and then—I heard shouting behind me, and horsemen were charging—out of nowhere!"

"They appeared out of the ground. There must be ravines or something over there," said DiSezrotti. "But they had Jumpers, DiVega! Five or six of them! That's how they broke our line so quickly!"

"What?" Istvan stared. "Jumping horses, here?"

"They went over our line like rabbits jumping a row of cabbage. Then the rest hit, a wedge of them charging in close order, so that more than a hundred of them were riding down ten of us. Hastur forgive me, I started shooting at the horses."

"How badly were you outnumbered?" Istvan asked.

"We outnumbered them, actually. I'd say they were about half bordermen and half Kadarins. And there's only one Kadarin company in these parts I know of: Martos of Onantuga's. Kadarins call a hundred and fifty men a company, and that's what Martos had. It was him, all right. I saw him at the point of the wedge."

"*What?*" Istvan wondered at the strength of his reaction. "He's alive?"

"He certainly is."

So he would not have to carry that news to Birthran after all, Istvan thought. Not yet, anyway.

Chapter Two

Bordermen's voices chanted in the dusk.

> *Earth shall eat*
> *The Seed of Man,*
> *And Man shall drink Her milk . . .*

Firelight throbbed. Thick, oily smoke coated the dull red glow of the funeral pyres.

> *Earth must be fed,*
> *For all food comes*
> *From the breasts of Earth . . .*

Istvan tried to keep from smelling the burnt-meat odor that rode on the smoke as it rolled slowly south. He had feared he might have to carry the bodies to Manjipor, despite the heat, for the Bordermen will not burn bodies on the dust, mingling the life-giving ashes with the poisonous powder that the Demons leave. But the Kantarans had found this little island in the dust, less than a mile from the battlefield: a few pitiful acres of unblasted soil.

Much of the wood they had brought from the Kantara had gone to build these pyres. If the Dark Things attacked there would be that much less to face them with. But the ashes of the dead would be saved for the land. In the fields of the Border they would lie together: Seynyorean and Kadarin, a handful of Massadessans, all of Kotulmer's men, fifty of them, and the single Manjipéan whose comrades had missed him. For Jagat's men, following long habit from a lifetime of struggle against the Shadow, had carried away their dead and wounded, although the Kadarin wounded had been left behind—safe under Hastur's Law—to be an added burden on Istvan's army.

Earth must be fed, Istvan thought. He had heard Bordermen use that saying to explain their poverty, or even to excuse themselves when going to defecate, but most often he had heard it in connection with death, as comfort to widower and widow. A Borderwoman would mutter, "Earth must be fed," over one stillborn child after another; she would say the same when husbands and lovers were brought home dead from the constant war on the Border, and then look for someone else to give her children. When childbirth or age or the fangs of some marauding night-thing claimed her at last, her lovers and her children would say, "Earth must be fed," and fight on.

31

At least a Borderman need never wonder *why* he died.

Istvan felt a faint spray of moisture across his face, but it was soon gone. He heard a shout. Someone pointed north. Then he saw, tiny in the dark, a row of reddish sparks. *Jagat's men*, he thought. *Earth must be fed.*

His joints ached in a cold wind that whipped flames from the pyres and rolled greasy smoke south, to the Shadow. The Dark Things would weave the smoke into the spell that hid the mountains. The pyres would burn all night, and in the morning the Kantarans would collect the sacred ashes to hallow their fields. Men born beneath Hastur's Citadel would nourish the gardens of the Border.

D'Olafos' company had been decimated, with thirty men dead. Other companies had fared worse: close to half of DiSezrotti's company had been killed or wounded, and nearly a third of Enjanton DiVega's men, including Enjanton himself. Istvan remembered helping his bleeding cousin down from his horse.

". . . they had us at open shields," the wounded DiSezrotti had said. "How I lived through it, I'll never know. . . . I managed, somehow, to twist in the saddle and get my shield up over my head, and seven or eight of them hit it one after another as they rode by. The last one knocked me off my horse, or maybe the horse bucked me off."

That idiot, Ballo of Kotulmer! Dead now, his head on a spear. No use blaming him. It was always the Commander's fault, whatever happened, and he'd been warned. He should have kept Kotulmer on a tighter rein. He could have ridden after him when the Borderers first began to draw ahead, and taken Rinmull of Ojaini along to back him.

If! Useless "ifs"! Grey dust was poisoning his men's wounds. The Healers were working hard. How many more of his men would die, to bless with burnt bones the Bordermen's fields?

> But Man is a part of the Earth!
> All must go back to the Earth!
> Man is the flesh of the Earth.

Bordermen chanted in the death-fire's glow. Stars and moons were hidden by thick clouds. On nights like this the Dark Things walked—and wounded men would be choice prey.

South and east the towers glowed—Ketusima, Vajrakota, Agnasta— against the black wall looming above the leprous land. Istvan watched grimly for any ripple of need-fire, but the towers were pale stalks of dim light against a blank southern sky. Without them, on such a night, it would have been hard to tell that the Shadow was there at all.

Jodos wore the face and body of Lord Zengio's son as he stalked down dream corridors in the castle of the old man's sleep. In shifting crystal dreams of the work that was his pride, Zengio the Constable heard his son's voice say, *It is mine now, Old Man!* Rough hands seized him, tore the mantle of his office from his shoulders; his son's face glared into his own. Zengio struck that face as hard as he could, but the young man only laughed and pushed him away.

Outside a crystal window, Zengio saw Istvan DiVega riding back from war, covered with a glory that he did not need. *You are old, Old Man!* His son's mask mocked. *But he is older still. You could have commanded that army, had you not allowed command to be stolen from you—worthless Old Fool!*

In a rage Lord Zengio searched for a battlefield, and found one in a courtyard that widened to a broad plain, where old King Olansos' army was drawn up. The Constable rode to his place by the King, but was rudely pushed aside.

I am the Constable! his son Mario announced, standing there, wrapped in the stolen mantle of the Constable's office. Zengio felt for his sword, but already the army was in motion, and the ungrateful son was leading his men to battle and glory.

Zengio turned to appeal to King Olansos, but young King Chondos was there instead. *He has robbed you of your Post!* The King laughed.

Angrily, Zengio ran. Drawing his sword and holding it high, he addressed his troops. *Obey me,* he said. *Am I not the Constable?*

You are dead, they said. *Your son has inherited your mantle.*

But I am not dead! Zengio shouted.

You will be, the false son cried, drawing a sharp dagger.

Zengio felt its point pierce his breast, and fell, whirling, whirling into flickers of red. A grey plain stretched lightless around him. Dog-headed shapes like ghouls bubbled out of the ground, which seemed to be shifting ooze. Ahead of him a dark tower rose against the sunless sky.

Inside, the tower seemed empty at first. Nothing moved. Human bones littered the floor. The winding stair climbed empty into darkness under the roof. Yet he felt brooding all around him a presence and a will. Two red flares glowed near the roof. The air moved, came to life.

Zengio fled. When he looked back, he saw, rising mountain-high behind him, a pillar of dark mist, and at its top, stone-black against the sky, the long-jawed head like a dragon's glaring down with eyes of hate-filled flame.

His heart was bursting, and the world was cold. He ran into the comfort of his own mind, but at the door of the fortress the usurper stood: his son's face mocked him with long knife raised. From under the stolen mantle came Olansos' crown, dripping with blood. Cruel laughter split his son's mask as he set the dripping crown on his head.

Stunned by his son's treason, Lord Zengio fled to his youth, far from his white hair and the pains in his chest, to the arms of a wife grown once more young and beautiful. In her bed he found solace, until the sharp-toothed child crawled biting from her womb. Zengio screamed as sharp teeth mutilated him, then screamed again as the child turned and devoured its mother.

He woke screaming, and lay sweating and trembling in the darkness with the horror of the dream he could not remember. Jodos, smiling to himself, put on Lord Zengio's face, and went to haunt the dreams of the new Constable, Mario.

Sadly Istvan mounted his tired mare. The rites were ended; he had honoured the dead. Death-fires would burn all night, but living men must sleep and the Commander keep his mind clear for another day of war.

Like windborne mist, fine cold spray flew into his face. He flinched, then looked up at the cloud-mottled night sky. The dry season was gone, and soon those clouds would drop the winter rains: once they started, they seldom stopped. He had been lucky to have these three rainless days. When the rain began, there would be only a few days before the sea of dust around Manjipor became an impassable morass. The dust never turned to true mud, but the dust grains slipped and slid with water between them, until neither man nor horse could find footing. The horses' hooves would swell and crack with wet, and then the dust would poison the wounds.

Only a little delay, and Manjipor would be beyond help; Maldeo would have to hold it on his own. If Jagat's men could slow this army down, the rain and the dust would do the rest.

And Istvan still did not know how large a force he had to fight! D'Olafos and DiSezrotti had estimated five hundred or six hundred men in the force that had attacked them. DiCalvados, who had seen the enemy force cross his line of march after the battle, and had pursued until Istvan called him back, guessed a thousand men. But that was just this one group; Jagat might have several parties of the same size waiting along the route at various strategic points.

None of the Kantarans he had sent out as scouts had reported any sign of an enemy—though Jagat's scouts, clearly, had found this army quickly enough! But then, it was their own country, after all. And many of the Kantaran scouts, he suspected, would never return.

The hoofbeats of the horses around him in the dark suddenly faded as they rode off the solid earth onto the dust. If he listened he could hear faint squeakings under the horses' weight, but that was all. After the battle, D'Olafos had said, the Kadarins had rounded up all the riderless horses and driven them away. That was probably where DiCalvados had gotten his guess. But that meant that only five hundred men had shattered four Seynyorean companies! It must have been Martos, Istvan thought, who had devised that last daring charge: the tactics bore the stamp of the Three Swords School.

"They rode into our ranks all mixed with our friends, just driving them along," D'Olafos had said. "The fighting caught our left wing first, Seynyoreans and Kadarins all mixed together, cutting away like mad." Seynyoreans had killed Seynyoreans in that first wild flurry. "I thought a third force had hit our rear," DiSezrotti had mumbled apologetically.

Omartos DiMadyar rode at Istvan's side, his grotesquely splinted leg dangling awkwardly. Like many another man, he had broken a knee when Kadarins charging on the left and Bordermen from the right had hurled together the tight-packed horsemen battling boot-to-boot in the centre.

Only Kadarin cavalry could have rallied or charged so decisively. Istvan remembered Ovimor Field: the orderly blocks of Kadarin cavalry charging in bright steel waves, and his own youthful wonder at the riders in the air as the jumping horses soared.

"What kind of men are we fighting?" D'Olafos had asked.

"Well-trained Kadarin cavalry," Istvan had answered. D'Olafos was too young to remember Ovimor Field, though an older brother had been killed there.

But there was only that one small company of Kadarins, Istvan thought. *Fewer now. They, too, lost men in this battle. And there were only five or six of the jumping horses.* The Bordermen, he recalled, usually fought in a looser order, acting more as individuals than as a body.

Again the wind slapped his face with a fine spray of rain, interrupting his thoughts. It was still hot between bursts of wind, though not the usual stifling heat. His body delighted in the bracing relief of the wet wind, even while his mind shuddered, picturing the campaign he might have to fight.

He heard, above the faint squeaking of the dust, Omartos DiMadyar's harsh breathing. He'd told the man not to come, but DiMadyar had insisted; he had seen DiBraise plucking at the arrow in his throat, choking on his own blood. Most of the unwounded survivors of the battle were here.

The camp ahead was dark. Most of the wood that would have made torches was charring their dead comrades left behind. Hoof-beats were muffled by the shrouding dust. He wondered if the guards would hear them at all.

"Halt!" a guard shouted. "Give the password!"

"Heyleu Pine-stakes!"

"Heyleu *what?*" Paidros whispered to Martos.

"Hush!" Martos hissed back.

"Heyleu Pine-stakes it is!" The voice reached them clearly at the end of the line, where they rode mixed with Seynyoreans and Bordermen. "Pass, General DiVega!"

Martos filed the password in his mind, but it did not look as if they would need it. The group of horsemen to which they had attached themselves filed past the pickets without further challenge: Martos and Paidros, in dark cloaks atop tall stolen Seynyorean horses, were, with the three Bordermen who accompanied them, only five more. *And no wonder,* Martos thought, *with Istvan DiVega himself leading, What luck!*

"Heyleu?" questioned Paidros, as the horsemen dispersed inside the camp. The sheer size of the encampment was daunting, but it would be their protection. In so large an army, a strange face would not be noticed, certainly not on such a dark night. And a few of the Seynyoreans wore Kadarin-style armour.

"Heyleu is the great Seynyorean port, and Heyleu Pine-stakes are ships' masts seen in the harbour," Martos whispered to Paidros. "It's from a famous poem. Heyleu is supposed to be very beautiful in the spring."

"Pine-stakes!" Paidros shook his head. "What a watchword! Why—"

"Hush!"

Martos smelled horses. His listening ears picked out snorts and muffled stamps nearby. He followed the sounds. Horses were tethered in a long line slung between two sagging stakes. They champed noisily on wide sheets of cloth, spread to keep the metallic dust from the hay and to catch the dung for the Bordermen to gather.

Sleeping men huddled in blankets under the clouded sky: a single tent was most likely the Commander's.

There were empty places in the line, and the single sleepy guard barely glanced up as Martos and Paidros tied the stolen Seynyorean horses and filled nosebags for them from a half-empty sack of grain. But the guard came alert as a strange Borderman approached, leading his rough-coated pony.

"Your pardon, Lord," the stranger said, "but I seem to have missed my way in the dark. I am one of Lord Ajeysio's men, and he has sent me to fetch feed for our horses from the baggage wagons. But this army is—so big . . ." He spread his hands helplessly, and Martos smiled to himself. The man was doing well.

"You have missed your way indeed," said the guard. "You're way forward of where you want to be! You want to go back that way and—wait a moment! You there!" He gestured at Paidros, who stood beside the open sack of grain, a nosebag in his hand. Martos cursed silently. "How much is left in that bag?"

Martos' fingers crept to his hilt. If the guard realised the voice was a stranger's . . .

"It's more than half empty!" Paidros called back. Martos' hand tensed, ready to draw.

"I thought as much," said the guard. "We'll be needing more feed ourselves," he said, turning back to the Borderman. "I'll send a man to get it now, and he can show you the way."

Martos wondered if, laughably, he or Paidros would be assigned to guide the Borderman to the wagons, but the guard turned and walked down the row of sleeping men. Finally he stopped, and kicked accurately into a pile of blankets. A man erupted, cursing, sword drawn.

"Put that away, you dung-dauber! I told you we needed more grain! Get down to the wagons now, and bring up another bag! And you can show this Fish"—he coughed—"this *Border gentleman* the way. He's lost himself in the big city."

Grumbling, the sleepy man put up his sword and, rubbing his eyes, staggered toward the picket line. Martos faded into darkness, while Paidros worked his way around the horse, fixing his nosebag, stroking him, until he was out of the guard's sight and could slip away to join Martos.

As the Seynyorean went off, with Jagat's vassal beside him, he was unaware of the four men who followed through the dim cloudlight.

Jodos followed Lord Mario down dim dream corridors: the face that he wore was Lord Zengio's face.

I brought you into the world, he cackled in the old man's voice. *And I can take you out of it!*

Through nightmare chambers of his own mind Lord Mario fled, but the aged death with his father's face met him at every turn.

Thief, the shrill voice cried. *You have stolen my mantle!*

Mario ran, sobbing. Why did his father hate him so? He ran under the arch where an iron dragon watched over the courtyard, but his father's face waited at the door to his refuge.

Father! No, Father! he shrieked, falling back. Gargoyles grinned as a sharp knife sliced. He felt blood pouring from where his ear had been. He left his ear on the floor and ran.

Thief! His father's voice cackled behind him. *I brought you into the world. I'll take you out, too.*

Mario ran around a corner. A hand seized his shoulder and lifted him from the ground. Pain cracked across his back. He kicked and struggled, but he was child-sized again in a giant father's grip. The Constable's staff beat upon his back.

Ungrateful scum! Thief and liar, his father's voice raged. *You have stolen my mantle. You and the King.* He was hurled to the ground, saw his father's giant foot swing. Ribs drove breath from his lungs and the pain lifted him. *Wretch!* the voice cried. *Thief!*

He rolled to his feet and ran. Carvings stared with mocking stone eyes. Why did the old man hate him so?

His mother would save him. He ran to her room, and threw himself sobbing in her lap. A cackling voice sounded. Mother screamed. Mario fumbled for his dagger. His mother's blood poured down her dress. With a shout, Mario drove the knife into his father's throat.

Istvan DiVega's eyes opened in the darkness of his tent, and he sat up, shouts ringing in his ears, his sword already rasping from the scabbard by his bed. Faint need-fire on its blade lit the walls of the tent. But through the tent flap came a different light: a dull red glow. His bare feet hit the floor, and he crossed the tent in a long swordsman's stride, soft dust shifting underfoot. The Border was aflame; the Dark Things were moving! He heard his name shouted as he ripped the tent flap open, the cool grip of his sword warming in his hand.

"What is it? The Border—" But on the horizon his eyes found only the usual starless blankness behind the dim light of distant towers.

"No, Lord," the voice said. "It is not the Border. The baggage wagons are on fire."

It seemed at first no one would notice them in the confusion, but as Martos finished pulling tight the saddle girth on the nervous, stamping horse he had picked, a voice shouted: "Hey! What do you think you're doing?"

Two men ran toward him, across the long rows of abandoned bedding. One was the guard who had been so helpful earlier. Paidros was already in the saddle. Martos swung himself up, whooping at the horses, flapping his cloak to frighten them. Picket stakes fell and the cut line parted as three hundred horses, already spooked by noise and smoke, reared and pulled and stampeded free.

Running men cursed, waving drawn swords. The horse guard ran in front of the stampede, waving his arms, trying to turn the horses. The leading horses veered away, but the herd was too big, too tightly packed. The horse guard went down, and Martos heard him screaming under the hooves. He shuddered. He'd not meant that to happen. Shouting men came running at their heels, but that only made the horses run faster.

Wind fanned wild flames and rolled the thick smoke south. *More smoke for the Shadow,* Istvan thought bitterly. Men ran through oily clouds, carrying smouldering bags of grain. Bags burst, and precious feed mingled with the poisoned ash.

The hay was gone. There was no saving it. The food for the men was burning too. Flame flickered through smoke like lightning in dark clouds and, fading, haunted blinded eyes with its pale blue ghost. Men ran from the furnace of fire to the angry wind, saving grain, bread, and meat.

A sudden spot of cold on his forehead jerked Istvan's head up. Large drops of water spattered on his face. Through shouting he heard a dull rattle as raindrops pummelled leprous poison dust, and in a moment his face was wet.

Rain poured down, spitting in the flames, drenching the rescued sacks of smoking grain. Hot steam mingled with the smoke. Exhausted men with blackened faces tried to cough smoke from their lungs, while icy rain poured down around them. Others ran sodden and dripping into steaming flames, and staggered out again with their clothes nearly dried, under half-burnt bags with sparks still crawling in the threads. Wagons collapsed, their smouldering wheels folding under them, tipping their glowing loads onto the dust. Rain hissed on thick beds of orange coals.

Tents had been in the wagons and were burned, except for the officers' tents, and these must be used to try to keep dry what little grain was not already soaked. Most of the cooked wet grain would sour, and a horse could die from eating too much of it.

It was nearly dawn before the fire showed signs of dying. A thick pillar of mist hung above sputtering black ashes. All that could be saved had been saved. Istvan ordered men to get what sleep they could, huddled under sodden blankets, two by two for warmth, while the cold rain fell all around.

Two or three times Chondos woke in the night, hearing down the stream a distant doleful wailing and howling, as of human and animal voices blending together, that seemed to fade in the distance, without stopping. But when he looked over the wall of the broken tower, the land was empty.

At dawn, mingled with the usual chorus of screams and roars, he heard it again; but as far downstream as he could see, nothing moved along the shores of the river—nor was there any sign of life on the fungi-dotted grey plain above the banks at the valley's edge. He shivered, and wondered how secure his refuge was. Against trolls and ghouls it served well enough, but the Dark Things had broken it before.

A verse from "Pertap's Ride" sang in his mind . . .

> Demons have shattered Hastur's Tower,
> Against their power it might not stand.

They have cast it down in molten stone,
And laid their Shadow on the land.

When he was sure the grey-black sky would grow no lighter, he climbed reluctantly over the dimly glowing wall and followed the sluggish water toward the Border. He noticed the fungi grew more sparsely as encroaching Demon-dust thickened in the valley. The food he had brought from Rashnagar was gone.

The haze was growing thicker, and the air seemed to crawl before his eyes. He stopped, muscles tensing, listening intently. Again he heard the sobbing, faint and far across the poisoned wastes. It could have been wind in a forest: the Kantara sounded like that in the great winter storms. But even the ghosts of trees were gone from the poisoned plains ahead.

It grew steadily louder, nearer. The human sound grew clearer. Chondos felt a shiver leaping up and down his spine. There *were* human voices in that eerie keening chorus, the voices of women as well as men. But mingled with them were other sounds, deep mournful howling like a lonely dog, and shrill piglike squealing. Slowly the sound faded. It was as if, he thought, the creatures travelled in a great circle, moaning as they went.

He moved cautiously, spear ready in his hand. After a time the sound rose again. He scrambled up the bank and looked out across the plain, trying to see the things that made the sound. Haze baffled his eyes: the plain of grey dust was empty.

As he turned back to the stream, he glimpsed a small brown head peering over a rock. It whisked out of sight as soon as it saw him looking. For a mad moment he wondered what would happen if he called it back. He was so used to the creature following him that he had lost his fear. He was almost lonely enough to try to make a pet of it—*almost* lonely enough.

The wailing faded in the distance. The turgid river gurgled on his left, but otherwise the wastes were silent—except for the pattering of tiny paws behind him.

Raindrops battered at the hood of Istvan's cloak. His ears fought to make out words:

". . . Martos of Onantuga, I'm sure of it!" Kardom D'Aglar shouted above the rain. "I saw him with Jagat several times, after Ukarakia, and the little man with him. They stampeded the horses right over the horse guard."

"I'll kill him for that," screamed the other man, a trooper in D'Aglar's company, his voice shrill with shock. "Poor Nico never had a chance! They drove the horses right over him! You know a horse won't step on a man if he can help it! I heard him scream. Why? Why did the—" Clattering rain drowned phrases of hatred;

then the shriek in the taut voice rose: "But I'll get them, I'll kill the—"

"That's enough!" Istvan roared, forced to shout above the mutter of water, although a soft voice would have cut more deeply. "We're at war! Men die in a war. Men kill each other. But it is foolish to hate. It is war that kills. Soldiers, on each side, only do their duty."

"That wasn't war!" the soldier howled, but his own Commander spoke harshly. Istvan closed his eyes and let the clamour of the rain shut away the angry voices. Could he have stopped this war? Could he stop it now?

"Commander!" It was Firencio's voice. Istvan opened his eyes. Beyond grey strings of rain a vague figure saluted. "All companies ready to move out."

"Good." Istvan shouted. "Carry on." His horse moved, and wind peppered his face with a swarm of icy raindrops.

"Move *out!*" voices commanded, up and down the line. "For— *ward!*" Sleepless men on weary beasts staggered over poison dust through pelting icy rain. Istvan's mare lurched and swayed as her hooves slipped on uncertain footing. Already water crept between the tiny flecks of poison. Istvan patted her neck and crooned pet names to calm her, as raindrops trickled down his nose.

He pitied his soldiers, stumbling through the downpour, and wished he could have let them sleep a little longer. But horses would hunger before they reached Manjipor. Some would go lame, water soaking their hooves until they cracked. Many would die, then, as poisoned dust, and spores from the Shadow got into the cracks. But if he turned aside to the grasslands in the north, he might as well turn back. The rain and the dust would seal Manjipor away, and the city would fall before the rains ended. Even if he went north, the poor land would provide scant grazing for six hundred hungry mounts.

That morning men had eaten meat seared black on the outside, cooked in the burning baggage wagon. But food for the men would last to Manjipor, with even a little to spare. It was feed for the horses that was low.

Kardom D'Aglar's company trudged through the rain with Prince Phillipos' men. Their horses were far away, with Martos.

Martos had done this. Birthran's best pupil. Birthran had wanted Istvan to meet the boy, but not like this. What twist of fate had set them—swordsmen of the same school, natural allies—on opposite sides in this war? Now, because of Martos, his men were drowsing on the backs of hungry horses, while an enemy force of unknown size hovered around them, ready to strike.

Istvan thought of the trampled horse guard and his comrade. He heard the hate-filled voice: *I'll kill him for that!* Istvan had not gone to look at the body, but he knew what he would have seen. He could not blame the man for his hate. Ordinary war was hard enough on the nerves . . .

He remembered the curious relief he had felt upon learning that Martos was not dead. For a time he had mourned the boy as though it had been one of his own kin who'd died. Now one of his men was dead because Martos was alive. Trampled. A nasty way to die. *No worse than old age, though. A lot quicker.* Joints ached in the rain.

He thought of Birthran, as he had last seen him, bragging of Martos' exploits, boisterous with pride. Something in his memory made him pause. He stared unseeing into colourless meshes of falling water, but behind his eyes candlelight glowed on the rich red-and-gold hangings on Birthran's walls, and instead of the purring chatter of the rain, he heard the old swordsman's voice: "He will be a hero like those in old songs," Birthran had said. "Such an earnest young man. A student of the philosophers Atrion and Eldir. He breathes honour."

That did not fit. It was a cutting action with a needle-sword, a thrust with an axe. How could the young man Birthran had described bear to sneak into an enemy camp at night, to kill a man with a stampede instead of a sword, to make war not on his human foes but on their innocent horses? Unless . . .

He smiled, and straightened in the saddle. Unless Martos had too few men to mount an effective attack on a host this size. Martos must have thrown every man he had into the attack on the vanguard—typically Kadarin, now that he thought about it. Less than two companies, DiSezrotti had said. In the back of his mind, the immense, shadowy host he had imagined hovering just out of sight vanished like a pricked bubble.

"They're not turning back!" said Valiros.

Martos rubbed sleep from his eyes, started to stutter above the storm's babble, then, shutting his mouth, turned his face to the black-and-silver sky and let cloud-chilled water wake him.

Valiros' face was barely visible. Martos knew the face of the Borderman beside him, but could not remember his name. The man's armour was a drum on which the rain hammered: water ran slick over lacquered leather, pouring around the Borderer's legs like a transparent skirt. Beyond, Martos could see horses huddled in clumps, heads together, tails to the wind. A few wandered, sweeping wet grass with their manes as they grazed. The wind's whine made him shiver as he remembered the trampled guard's screams.

Not turning back? was DiVega mad?

"I am awake now," he said, mustering his dignity and wrapping his cloak more tightly around him. "Give me your report."

The Borderman bowed from the waist. "The Seynyoreans have broken camp and are marching toward Manjipor. A small group of Red-robes, with wounded men in carts, have left the army and are moving north—toward Inagar, I believe."

Not turning back! Martos stared south. Beyond endless veils of colourless rain, the Border was like black rock glimpsed at the back of a waterfall. He saw Thunderhead standing, braced into the wind, mane and tail blowing, creamy coat dampened to old ivory. *Not turning back!* He pictured Thunderhead thin and starved, and remembered the trampled sentry's screams; the jubilation with which he had watched sparks swirl up from flaring hay.

He had fed the great war-horses when he was still too young to reach their shoulders by standing on his toes. His forefathers had raised horses and ridden them to battle as far back as history told. Now horses must starve because of him. Horses were innocent tools in war: they cared nothing for the stupid strife of men, nothing whether Chondos or Jagat ruled Tarencia. All cavalrymen agreed that killing the men on the other side was one thing, but to kill a horse was a coward's deed, stupid and unnecessary, like killing children or unarmed men. He remembered his grandfather saying that this new style of war with bows was wrong, because arrows were sure to hit the horses.

Men blind themselves to the evil they do, Atrion had written, *by looking to some goal beyond the deed. But the Self-judged Man sees through such folly.*

So much for the Self-judged Man!

A virtuous deed is it's own reward. But a wicked deed cheapens life for all men. Horses that died because of him would still be dead when this trivial war was over—dead and useless when next the Dark Things crossed the Border. What would it matter then who wore Olansos' crown?

The Self-judged Man cannot be drawn into evil, for he knows his acts affect the body of mankind.

The sudden soft *tap-tap* on the dust startled Chondos before the first raindrops hit his face. The river beside him was suddenly tinkling, dimpled with ripple rings. Raindrops thudded on the dust. Clammy droplets spattered on his forehead, bouncing from his cheek-bones with surprising force.

He glimpsed brown fur darting between two rocks. His tiny watcher was scrambling for cover. Could it be a kind of squirrel, he wondered, that had survived the destruction of the ancient forests, sneaking like the ghost deer through remote hollows of the hills?

Then what had called his name?

He stayed close to the bank, as he moved on, and that offered some protection from the harsh rain. The rhythmic clatter grew pleasant to his ears. Ahead now the grey Demon-dust thinned. The river flowed between banks of thick red clay.

He held the broken stone-tipped spear before him like a sword, its jagged glassy tip where he could see it if it flamed. This way he would know if under the mud, at least, Demons were waiting. He rejoiced, after walking on dust for so long, in the slippery squishiness under his feet. Strange, to be so happy just to walk on mud! Its clotted-blood colour was beautiful after the endless dull grey.

He struggled over a rise, red clay smearing under his feet, and found himself staring through the gossamer flicker of water at the squat brown walls of a castle ruin out of old songs. It reared out of the middle of the river, covering the little island on which it was built, though centuries of currents had laid silt against its walls. The long tongue of a broken bridge jutted almost to the shore on Chondos' side of the river. At its end water foamed around massive fallen blocks. Ground and river dipped here: tributaries made a maze of side canyons, walled with red clay.

Out of his childhood, legends came rushing: memories of storied battles and desperate sieges, and of the last tragic defence against the dark. For he knew that stubby brown-walled tower. All through his boyhood he had sat dreaming before its woven likeness.

> The men that sleep in Kudrapor
> Must sleep with weapons in their hands:
> For Kudrapor the Border guards,
> Where Demons watch the Mortal lands.

Kudrapor! Through long ages it had guarded the crossing of the Yukota and the road to Rashnagar. Through ages of warfare it had held back invading armies, and at last had stood guard as the Shadow crept north. Here Pertap had made his famous ride, with all the terrors of the Shadow at his heels. And here, a generation later, he had died with all his men, rather than abandon the strategic fortress. Somewhere in the ruins below mouldered their gnawed and scattered bones.

Chondos stepped toward the famous fortress, glory tingling down his back—and stopped, his feet sliding in mud, as he glimpsed through veiling rain the stunted, distorted figures loitering near crumbled pillars where the broken bridge had once touched shore.

He crouched in mud that smeared his robe's hem. The things were mere blobs at this distance, pipestem arms and legs thin lines jutting from their rotund bodies. But if he could see them, they could see him. He was larger.

He studied the dim land carefully and crept back behind a drift of mud. He needed to think before he tried to sneak past the goblin guards below, and he was hungry. He was always hungry now. He suspected that the fungus, though it kept life in his body, provided little real nourishment.

As he ate, he heard a faint scrabbling sound, and something small and furtive peeped over the top of a nearby boulder. He was no longer afraid of the thing. He would have worried if it had vanished. Loneliness was beginning to tell. Even the most despised sycophant at court would have found a warm welcome now.

He wondered if the rat-thing was as hungry as he was. He broke off a piece of the flabby branch he was eating and tossed it at the rock. The tiny head vanished. He smiled and then lobbed another piece high in the air, so it sailed completely over the boulder.

Rain sprinkled about him while he sat chewing the tasteless stuff, trying to think. He must get past the goblins, somehow, and follow the Yukota. His ears caught faint crunching sounds from behind the boulder. A moment later the tiny head appeared.

He watched it out of the corner of his eye. The brown thing whisked around the rock and darted to the first piece he had thrown. It bolted it down, watching Chondos warily, as though expecting him to pounce. He could see it clearly now, for the first time. The rain had plastered its fur to its body. It was certainly no ordinary rat. Its head was the wrong shape. It was not a rat's head, nor a squirrel's head. It seemed almost like a tiny human head.

The creature finished the fungus and glared at him warily. He tossed another piece, and it jumped away, poised to run, its naked pink tail twitching. Chondos did not move. After a moment, the little beast slunk toward the piece, and began to nibble cautiously. Its eyes never left him.

Perhaps, Chondos thought, if he continued to feed it, the creature would lose its fear of him. He caught his thoughts suddenly. He was wasting time! The light was passing. He must find a way past the goblins at Kudrapor and reach the next tower before night—or spend the night in the haunted darkness.

He crawled, crouching behind rocks, soft mud squishing around his knees and lapping at his wrists. The sharp stone tip of his broken spear shimmered with a faint blue flame. It grew brighter as he drew near the old fort and the goblins clustered there. He hugged it close, twisting his shoulders around it, lest the light betray him, until smeared mud hid the flame.

The brown walls loomed under the black conical roof. Blurred by the rain, it seemed as soft as the woven image he had dreamed before as a boy. But the sky was no longer blue: Kudrapor had fallen.

> About the middle of the night,
> When Mortal Men were sleeping sound,
> The army of the Demon Lords
> Rose up from underneath the ground.

Bright the power of Hastur's Tower
Went blazing up as need-fire high;
But Demons shattered Hastur's Tower,
And drew the Dark across the sky.

Raindrops pitted the mud, splashing into his eyes. Runny red clay smeared his arms to the elbows; his robe was clammy. He crept to a low wall of fallen mud, where the rains of a thousand years had piled clay washed down from the bank above. Above it he saw Kudrapor rearing out of muddy water. The glassy haze of rain hid the damage of age and war; almost he could imagine that the massive walls still sheltered men of the Imperial Guard, watching the crossings of the Yukota—except for the goblins at the water's edge.

The goblins wore rusty coats of ancient Takkarian mail. Round helmets covered pointed heads; beneath their iron rims, huge slant-ing eyes glared evilly. A few carried curved swords out of the earliest days of Takkarian history. Chondos eyed the green-stained brass hilts at their belts hungrily. *Oh, for a sword!*

Some of the goblins were hairless, pallid like slugs; others were covered with dirty whitish fur. He could hear their harsh voices: they snarled when they spoke, their voices so bestial that he paid no attention to words, until he realised, with sudden shock, that they were speaking in the tongue of Hastur—the common language of men.

"How much longer?" he heard one say.

Several other voices were raised then, but Chondos could under-stand no words. Spears were shaken by skeletal hands. Then, through the snarls, he heard again the distinct wailing. The goblins were suddenly silent. Mingled with the sorrowful sobbing, a deep baying chilled the heart. The sounds grew louder and louder.

"They're coming again!" a goblin squealed, fear in its voice.

"What if they can't turn them this time?" another asked.

"Then we'll be a nice meal for them," snarled the first.

"We run for the fort," said another, but his comrades only grunted and cowered on the ground while the rain pattered down around them, and the mingled sobbing, squealing, and baying grew and grew.

Chondos started and looked up as something moved on the cause-way of the castle. He saw a goblin figure scutting across the long bridge. It, too, wore ancient, rusted-mail armour. Its legs were shorter and thicker than those of the white goblins and, like its face and hands, were covered with short black fur. It balanced, swaying on the broken end of the bridge, then leaped across the water to one of the fallen stones. Cruel red eyes burned under its helmet's rim as it hopped from rock to rock, long arms spread like wings.

The eerie wailing swelled, and slowly faded again. The fear-hunched goblins began to stir. The black figure bounded to the bank as the white goblins turned menacingly toward it, snarling and hissing.

Chondos guessed the newcomer was from another tribe, but he could make out no words until the black goblin raised its voice angrily: "Watch your tongue or I'll have it to eat! Or would you rather be fed to *them?* They're short of food."

"Everyone's low on food," snarled the biggest of the white goblins. "Skinned, you'll taste just like anybody else. What are you doing on our side of the river?"

Chondos began to move, looking uncomfortably at the large bare space between him and the next rock. All eyes were turned away, toward the black goblin. But as he poised to run, a shrill voice rose behind him—the same squeaking voice that had warned him of the troll.

"Here!" it shrieked. "King Chondos is here, behind the mudbank! Come and take him! But remember, the reward is mine!"

Uselessly, Chondos dodged back behind the mudbank. Over his shoulder he saw the tiny brown thing that had followed him for so long well out of reach on top of a boulder. Anger sickened him—a stupid, baseless anger that grew from an even stupider sense of betrayal. He had thrown it food. But it was not on his side, had never been on his side.

Goblin feet slapped the mud. This was no time for foolishness! He dipped the stone tip of the broken spear into a puddle, and the jagged chip of flame glittered, free of mud.

The first goblin to scuttle around the end of the mudslide skidded to a halt, flat feet slipping in blood-red mud as the bright light burned its eyes. Its chest was covered by rusty mail, but its eyes were at the height of a man's heart. Chondos lunged, gripping the spear like a sword. The thing shrieked once, raising a rusty curved sword, before the flaming glass chip vanished in a slanting crescent the size of a man's mouth.

The old carved blade fell spinning from the goblin's hand, and Chondos let go the spear shaft. A dozen other goblins came swarming over the mudslide, but by then Chondos DiVega, King of Tarencia, had a sword in his hand.

Heavy steel whipped out at the end of his arm, and a goblin head splashed mud in the eyes of the rest. He spun at another that cut at his head from the top of the mudbank: the curved blades clashed, and Chondos thrust over the other sword as it glanced aside. But the curve of the blade made him miss the throat; the point caught in a

ring of mail, throwing the goblin back off the bank unhurt. Chondos
stepped away from a flailing cut, his sword slicing through a wrist
no thicker than a candle. He swept aside a spear that darted at his
legs, and stepping past the point, stretched to shear the skinny neck.

In the back of Chondos' mind, Istvan DiVega danced in the castle
garden, sunlight flaring on his sword. Chondos' rusty blade whipped
in a brown blur to meet a spearpoint lunging at his throat. He felt the
edge catch in tough wood, and in heart-gripping panic wrenched
savagely. Wood cracked, and the spearhead fell to the ground as he
twisted away from another weapon, sweat mingling with icy rain on
his forehead. His enemies were armoured. He was not.

"Take him alive!" a goblin shouted; and from the rock behind
him, the rat-thing's thin voice shrilled like an echo: "Take him
alive! The Master promised death to whoever harmed him! Remember! Death if he is harmed! The Master promised! Remember! The
reward is mine!"

Alive? Chondos' teeth gritted in a grim grin. They would not find
that easy!

The wounded goblin, screaming and clutching its bleeding wrist,
was staggering away. One of the others tripped it, and slashed the
tendons of its legs. A horn buzzed, hoarse and tuneless. Chondos
saw the black goblin blowing it, standing well back from the fight,
horn raised to the sky.

The goblins hung back, spreading out cautiously, trying to get
behind Chondos without coming into reach of his sword. Sickle eyes
glowed in the half-light. Mixed rain and sweat blurred his sight.
With a shout he heaved up his sword and shifted his weight as
though to charge. As the goblins scuttled back squealing, he whipped
the driest part of his dangling sleeve across his eyes, and the stones
pouched there hit his cheek.

His left hand writhed into the pocket, and a stone slid into
Chondos' palm. Shouting, he drove his sword point toward the sky
and ran at the goblins edging past on his left. They scattered from
his path, but behind him he heard the expected slap of flat feet
rushing for his back. Treacherous mud churned underfoot as he
whirled and hurled the stone. It struck the great eyes of the nearest
goblin, and flared with blue-white flame.

Howling, hands over its eyes, the creature crumpled to the ground
as Chondos dodged under a poised spear butt, his arm guiding the
falling weight of his sword through a skinny, white-furred elbow.
He jumped back, whirling the old blade down, as a goblin dived at
his leg. He felt the steel quiver as it bounded from an iron helmet.
The bronze hilt stung his hand, and the goblin fell stunned in the
mud.

Hordes of pale goblins shrieked and milled about him, waving their weapons out of reach of his sword. And beyond them, he saw black-furred goblins swarm down the jutting tongue from Kudrapor.

> *Through all the years our tales can trace,*
> *No hostile foot could gain this floor.*
> *I'll face the death that's more than death*
> *To keep the Dark from Kudrapor!*

"Kudrapor!" he shouted, heaving his blade high. They reeled back screaming, and he whirled away and ran, up the canyon, into the maze of channels he had glimpsed there.

Whooping, horrid laughter followed. They were after him at once, but his legs were longer: he drew steadily ahead. For a moment it seemed the trick had worked, and he would lose his pursuers in the maze of gullies. Rain would wash out his tracks and his scent, and he would find another way down the river to the next fallen tower— perhaps the very one to which Pertap had ridden.

Holes gaped in the earth, and scores of pallid figures, white fur stained with mud, rose to block his way. A city of the goblins spread before him. Filling his left hand with flaming pebbles, he turned at bay, rushing to meet his pursuers. The old brown sword purred through the air, rust hidden in blood.

Back the way he had come he went, hurling flaming fragments of a broken tower like hot coals in their faces; slicing left and right, his sword a wind of death in his hand. Those swiftest on his track died before they knew their prey had turned. Some hesitated, remembering the Master's command, trying to take him alive. Others tried to kill him. But now hope of escape fled. Sword and mind became one in the purity of a single purpose. He would force them to kill him, and until he died, he would kill.

His sword-hilt was hot in his hand, his swaying arm spattered with foul blood. He danced down the canyon, and corpses fell as he passed. Mail-rings grated under his edge; dark blood spurted. Suddenly the goblins were running. He chased them toward the canyon's mouth. Kudrapor loomed beyond the fleeing mob. Hope returned. Free of the banks that packed them together, they would scatter and he would run on.

A tight wedge of black-furred globins with small round shields forced their way through the fleeing mob. They spread into a line across the canyon. His left hand ripped the carving knife from his belt. The rusty sword lashing in great circling strokes, he hurled himself upon them, trying to break through by sheer savagery.

His blade thudded on wood and leather. They closed around him, raised shields walling in his sword. A spear shaft thrust between his feet, tripping him, and he slipped in rain-washed clay. His blade flailed on upraised shields as he fought for balance. Something hit the back of his knee, and he was down, his left hand and the knife it held plunged deep in mud. His sword lashed out under the shields, and a goblin screamed as the curved blade slashed through spindly legs.

He felt a blow at the back of his head; pain flashed blue-white before his eyes. Shields drove his sword down into the mud. Blurred figures leaped on him, hands gripping his arms and legs. He dropped his useless sword and rolled, ripping his knife out of the mud, up into flesh. Hot blood spurted on his hand. He writhed and stabbed. Then another sharp pain crashed in his head, and he could not find his arms and legs in the sudden dark.

Chapter Three

Istvan DiVega drowsed on his horse's swaying back. The sodden weight of his cloak hunched his shoulders, but it was a good thick cloak. Except for the water's constant mutter he would not have known it was raining at all, as long as the wind blew the rain away from his face. He drifted between sleep and waking, sure that most of the others did the same. He pitied the sentries tonight. His body longed for the march to end, for time to stretch out and sleep, but there were still miles to cover. Miles of poisoned dust . . .

His ankles ached in the stirrups, and sometimes it felt as though icy water were trickling painfully through holes drilled in his joints. The rain was finer now, a shimmer against grey earth and sky. The Seynyoreans staggered on. They had gone without sleep before; they expected to go without sleep again. The Kalascorians were footsore and weary, and even the Bordermen were sluggish.

Waking, Istvan saw through the rain that one of the nearby companies had dismounted and were walking their horses. He shook himself, trying to remember if it was time for him to get down and lead the mare, and then remembered that it was Ciavedes' company that he'd been using to pace himself.

Turning in the saddle, he got a face full of cold, rain-laden wind. Blinking the icy water from his eyes, he saw that Ciavedes' men were still mounted. He yawned, shifted in the saddle, and stretched: his knee clicked with a passing stab of pain. He flexed the wrist of his sword hand under the cloak, trying to drive away the dull ache that gnawed his knuckles and the base of his thumb. He drifted off to sleep again, but was rudely awakened by Firencio's voice, almost drowned in the rattle of rain.

". . . forward scout on the right," Firencio was saying. "His horse was gone, and it was only luck they stumbled over the body."

"What?" Istvan yelled. "Speak up, lad! I can't hear a thing in all this racket."

The forward man of the string of scouts that paralleled the army on the north had been found dead. "His sword was out," Firencio said, "and there may even have been blood on it, but the rain would have washed it away, of course. But all his wounds were in front.''

Barely had Firencio finished when two more reports came in, one on the heels of the other. A small party of men had been glimpsed through the rain ahead of the army, crossing its path and headed south. And another scout had been killed, this time within full sight of two companies. Fifteen or twenty men had materialised out of the blur of rain to the north, pursuing and intercepting the scout, cutting him off from the army. One man had fought the scout while the others sat their horses and watched.

Men had ridden to the rescue, but the scout was dead before they could reach him, and his slayers already vanishing in the grey haze of rain. Twenty men from DiCalvados' company had followed. They had not returned.

"Idiots!'' Istvan snapped, and then was silent, thinking furiously, while rain chattered on his hood. It would do no good to waste wrath on men who might well be dead already.

The men crossing the road ahead—were they part of a larger force? Was the enemy set ahead of them to block their advance? Or was this a trick, to make him think so, to delay him on the dust while precious supplies ran out? Too much caution could destroy him now.

Martos—he remembered what Birthran had told him. If Martos had the men to stand against this army in a pitched battle . . .

There were so few Bordermen left that Jagat's whole army couldn't outnumber his by more than a few thousand or so. And there were at least two thousand Seynyoreans in Manjipor, plus however many of Jagat's own people had chosen to stand with Maldeo, and Ironfist's men, too. Jagat could not put an army in the field to match his without stripping the force that was besieging Manjipor, or giving up the siege altogether.

"What news from Manjipor?'' he demanded sharply. Cold wet drops spattered on his nose as he straightened.

"Um—nothing new—that I've heard—'' Firencio looked confused.

"Get me one of the Seers, fast. Now!''

Firencio saluted and rode off, and Istvan settled himself in his saddle, waiting. Before Firencio could return with the Seer, two more reports arrived. The lead scout on the left was missing, and a riderless Border pony that looked to be his had blundered in among the ranks of Alon Robardin's men. While Istvan pondered this, Rupiros D'Ascoli rode up, bearing his own message. His men, and those of the next company in line—also led by a D'Ascoli—had seen a small band of horsemen pursuing another scout. Within sight of the two companies, they had circled to cut the scout off and intercepted him: one man had engaged him while others watched.

This time, it seemed, the scout had overcome his attacker, for a second horseman had left the group and fought. D'Ascoli had sent men to the scout's rescue, but the party made off before they arrived, leaving the scout's dead body behind. D'Ascoli had called back pursuit, aware of the danger.

Istvan sent for Lord Rinmull of Ojaini and Arjun DiFlacca as Firencio came with the Seer. The Seer, too, had news. Moments before, a man had come riding out of the south, with the Shadow looming behind him in the rain like black glass seen through lace. Galloping to within a few yards of the outriders of Chalcondiel's company, he had stood in his stirrups and thrown something down before turning his pony and pounding away. The thing he had thrown rolled between the hooves of the horses: it was the head of a missing scout.

"What word from Manjipor?" asked Istvan.

"They beat off another assault on the walls yesterday, but today Jagat's men seem to be waiting out the rain."

"Ask D'Oleve if he can get an estimate of how many men are still out there. Better get an estimate of how many there were yesterday morning, too. I want to hear about *any* change in numbers—anything that would indicate how many of them will have left the siege to come here."

"Very good, my Lord, but it may take time." The Seer closed his eyes and went into a trance.

Istvan straightened and turned to D'Ascoli. "They fought him one at a time, you said?"

"Yes." D'Ascoli nodded thoughtfully. "Of course, if he'd killed the second one there would have been a third, and so on, until he killed all twenty. Not as fair as it looks, but at least they didn't smother him in numbers."

Istvan grunted. "Firencio, I want all the scouts called in. Now. And—" He stopped, listening. "What in Hastur's name is that?"

Out of the moving mists of rain came a high, musical humming.

"If we weren't so far from the ocean," said Firencio, "I'd say it was a—" D'Ascoli's laugh interrupted him.

"That's what it is!" he said. "You're quite right, it's a conch shell. The Bordermen use them as war-horns sometimes. The Old Takkarians imported them from the sea, and some houses still have them, as precious heirlooms. They have all kinds of strange legends about them."

A few moments later, an exhausted, bleeding man rode into the lines of DiGasclon's company, which brought up the rear on the right. He was the last survivor of the twenty men from DiCalvados' company, who had ridden after the killers of the scout; all the others lay dead, out of sight in the rain to the north.

Cold rain poured over Chondos' face and rolled like icy sweat over his skin to drip on the mud beneath. His head throbbed. Harsh croaking voices meant nothing to him, nor the ache in his shoulders, nor the chafing on his wrists.

Sudden wild screaming startled him, and his eyes snapped open. Raindrops leaped out of vague greyness. A pain-filled voice babbled and pleaded. Other voices jeered. Chondos, blinking, rolled his head over in the mud.

The goblins he had wounded were being cut apart, while others laughed and jeered in a mob around them, mocking their cries and struggles. He saw one clawing at his torturer, but the other goblin caught its hand and sneered.

"Thought you'd live to eat the rest of us, didn't you?" The long knife slashed away. The butcher stuffed a handful of bleeding meat into its mouth and chewed, then stretched out something like a thin white string, and began scraping it with the edge of the knife. The screaming became more frenzied. The goblin with the knife laughed through the mouthful of meat, spitting blood all over.

Sickened, Chondos closed his eyes. Then, above the screaming, he heard a sudden snarl behind him and then a deep, harsh voice said, "No you don't!" More snarling, the sound of blows, and a sudden squealing. "He's not to eat! Keep your hands off!"

Chondos tensed his arms, trying to roll up and fight. Harsh bristles rasped his wrists. His hands were tied behind his back. His shoulder joints ached.

"Keep off, yourself! He's ours! He's on our side of the river!" This voice was shriller, grating.

"And who caught him? You maggots would be running yet, and he'd be long gone, if we'd stayed on our side."

Above him, Chondos saw struggling figures black and white against the greyness, blurred by the rain that poured into his eyes. The white one went staggering back. A crouching black shape, armour grey around its body, stood over him, sword raised.

"So keep away from him!" growled the deep, grim voice. "There's plenty of meat, and there'll be more if you try to touch him again! He's for the Master, and the reward—"

"Mine!" a squealing voice shrilled, a voice that Chondos knew well. "The reward is mine! None of you could have caught him except for me! He is mine!"

"Come and take him then," the black goblin snarled under his breath; even Chondos could barely hear him over the screams.

The rain began to slacken, and in a moment only a fine drizzle came down, almost a mist.

"Flesh!" the shrill voice cried. "The Master promised you would give me flesh!"

Above him Chondos saw the great slanted eyes of white and black goblins exchanging half-lidded looks. Sharp teeth were bared in a smile, and slits flared in the noseless space between the black goblin's eyes and mouth.

"Get him some meat," said the black goblin, with a jerk of his head toward the screaming creatures behind them. Again Chondos saw a look pass between the two, and then the white figure moved away, out of the range of his vision.

A startling red tongue darted between the black lips, and the nostril slits flared. Then the huge eyes dropped to Chondos, too quickly for him to close his own. The vast mouth widened; thin lips drew away from spikes of teeth.

"Awake, are you?" it whispered. It laughed, a horrible, gurgling chuckle. "All ready for carving. You're a lot of more meat than any of those!" It gestured toward the screaming creatures behind him. "*Much* more meat."

Chondos felt as though a stone had fallen onto his chest, but he mastered his face and gazed calmly and unblinkingly into the goblin's great red eyes. The Master wanted him; this creature would not dare to touch him. The lips writhed, as though to utter more threats, but then the red eyes shifted away. The white goblin came back, its stained hands heaped with quivering, bleeding flesh. Blood clotted in white fur.

"Here's your meat and your prisoner both!" the black goblin shouted. "Come and get them!" Out of the corner of his eyes, Chondos again saw the goblins exchange glances. He rolled his head to look where the goblins looked, away from the feeding mob and their shrieking food. He saw a ball of brown fur drop from the top of a rock and race toward them.

The creature paused warily, watching the goblins, out of their reach. "Throw the meat here!" the shrill voice commanded.

With a grimace, the white goblin lobbed the mound of meat toward the creature. A red, dripping mass came apart in the air and scattered across the ground. Even the smaller pieces fell short, and scraps of meat littered several feet.

"Now back away!" the shrill voice commanded. Silently, slowly, they began to fall back. But again Chondos saw that malicious glance pass between black face and white face. Between the black lips, the red tongue leaped and licked the needle fangs.

Chondos remembered the troll. Before it had betrayed him, the thing had saved his life. What did that matter now? It was an enemy; it had saved him only for the reward.

The goblins were moving away from him. He tried to move his feet—tied, of course. With a convulsive movement that sent jolts of pain through his skull, he squirmed into a sitting position. He felt weak and sick; flashes of pain blurred his vision. His hair was plastered with mud—blood too, maybe.

He had thought he could make them kill him. He wriggled his knees up toward his chest and looked at the ropes wrapped around and around his ankles. They were plaited of long strips of hide, still bristling with fur. The lumps of several knots discouraged him.

Even had his legs been free, there seemed little point in dashing with bound hands into the Shadow, weaponless. Suddenly he realised that his sleeves had been torn away: the few remaining fragments of stone were gone. He could feel the weight of silver rings still on his fingers, but with his hands tied behind him they would be no help.

Warily, the rat-thing watched the goblins shuffle slowly away. Satisfied that they were far enough back, it sniffed the nearest piece of meat and began chewing greedily.

Behind Chondos, the cries of the butchered goblins sank to a pitiful mewing. Cold rain chilled his skin and ran like tears down his face. Strained shoulders ached, and the bristles on the cord grated the soft skin of his wrists. His eyes searched over the mud for an abandoned knife or sword, although he knew that even if he found one, there was no way to reach it or use it unseen.

Out of the corner of his eye he saw the black and white goblins move apart, slowly circling the scattered meat. The rat-thing fed, unheeding, moving from one piece of meat to another, gorging itself and drawing closer to the slowly moving goblins. They were going to catch it. Why should he care?

The white goblin tensed to spring. Chondos shouted. The tiny head came up, mouth dripping. It sprang away as the white shape leaped. Evading the clutching hands, it doubled back and raced for the safety of the high rocks.

The black goblin ran to block its way. The rat-thing turned and tried to dash around, but it was sluggish from heavy feasting. The long-fingered black hand swooped down and closed on the tail and one hind leg. Then the creature was dangling from the black-furred hand, and the goblin laughed, stretching its long arm up, as the rat-thing wriggled and squealed.

"Here's your reward," the goblin mocked, pitching its voice as shrilly as it could. Opening its mouth, it lowered the struggling creature towards the long, yellow teeth.

The rat-thing writhed, and sank its fangs into the goblin's upper lip. Roaring in pain, the goblin jerked it away, and the tiny teeth tore through flesh. Dark blood ran. The rat-thing curled and bit the hand that held it.

Snarling, the black goblin lashed the creature like a whip against the rock it had tried to reach. The small body crunched on stone; a shrill cry stopped short. Chondos closed his eyes. . . . When he opened them, the goblin was staring at the limp body in its hand. Snarling, it began to rip away furred skin with its teeth.

The white goblin walked toward it. The black goblin glared, and insolently tore a strip of red muscle from the rat-thing's back.

"I suppose *this* is yours, too? I caught it on this side of the river." Blood-smeared lips sneered. "Take it then! But the man is ours." It hurled the tiny bleeding body into the white goblin's face.

Wiping blood from its eyes, the white one staggered back, tugging at the sword-hilt jutting from its belt, but a rusty knife lashed out at the end of a long black arm. The brown blade vanished in the white-furred body.

The black goblin laughed, and raised its muzzle to the sky. "More meat!" it shouted. "Fresh meat!"

Chondos heard the rush of goblin feet. The white one tried to run, but fell, bleeding. Running goblins, black and white, blotted it from sight. Chondos closed his eyes. The screaming began—went on and on. Chondos pushed his eyelids hard together and wished he could close his ears. Then, beside him, the deep voice spoke.

"Cut the leg ropes. Make him walk."

They would cut his legs free, and he would run, run, run away from the screaming and the smell of blood, even with his hands tied.

Something harsh and rasping slipped over his face. He opened his eyes. Black goblins stood around him, armoured and grim. One had pulled a noose over his head. Unthinkingly, he jerked away. Goblins laughed, a harsh gargling sound like the coughs of a drowning cat, and the rope tightened around his neck.

One leaned down, a long knife in his hand. Chondos kicked out with his bound feet, but a goblin heel in the ribs sent him sprawling. As he tried to roll over, two goblins landed on his legs and held them down. The creatures weighed no more than children, but were stronger than he had thought. He heaved and bucked, but could not shake them off. A foot drove into his belly, and he lay gasping.

Before he had his breath back, they hauled him to his feet. He stood bent over, breathing harshly, laughing to himself. If he ran *toward* the goblin with the rope, he could knock it down with his shoulder. . . .

Pain cracked across his back. Starting, he saw a whip writhing in the air. It slashed down on his back again.

"Get moving!" the deep voice snarled. "Let's get out of here!"

The noose tightened around his neck, pulling him forward. The whip burned across his back, curling down his fingers. He staggered forward, unwilling, down the road that led back into the mountains, back to Rashnagar.

Wind-driven drops lashed Martos' face. He rode toward the line of carts where his own men and Istvan's men lay together, united by their spilled blood. The carts of the Healers rolled slowly toward the north, pulled by patient cattle. Rows of red-robed men walked beside them. Above the whining creak and rumble of the wheels came the moans of men in pain. Rough canvas had been spread above the wagons, to shelter the wounded.

The men behind him had laughed and jested merrily as they rode from camp, but their mouths closed solemnly when they saw the sombre, brightly robed procession emerge, blood-coloured, out of the vagueness of grey dust and rain. In a few moments they would know for certain which of their missing comrades still lived, and which had crackled in the pyres they'd glimpsed the night before. Some among the Kadarins were thinking of the quiet tombs of their forefathers, where those who fell would never lie; others were remembering swordblades and arrows that had come uncomfortably close to them in the battle. All knew that, without luck and skill combined, they might be lying in those carts—or else the greasy smoke of their burnt flesh would be rolling before the wind, and the ashes of their bones be collected to hallow the Bordermen's gardens.

Scarlet cowls lifted as they rode up, and one tall, red-robed figure turned and strode from his place to meet them. The others marched on, unperturbed, while water hurtled upon red hoods.

A sudden shift of wind whipped Martos' face with icy rain. He blinked. The Red-robe reached them and halted. A hand threw back the scarlet hood; and a calm dark face appeared. Serene brown eyes gazed at them from beneath a mass of black hair, which the slanting rain soaked in an instant and plastered flat over the scalp. Martos felt his own scalp cowering under his hood at the sight, but the Healer seemed unconcerned, and the dark eyes never wavered. It seemed to Martos that nothing could disturb the perfect calm of that face.

"Welcome, my son," the Red-robe said. "What is it that you wish?"

Martos had to fight with his tongue a moment to make it answer. "I've come to see"—he stammered for a second, and went on— "my wounded men." The calm dark eyes were still looking at him in silence. "My men," he said again, stammering slightly. The rain-soaked head nodded. Water beat down on it.

"Come then." The Healer turned away, and as Martos scrambled down from his horse to follow, the carts stopped. Paidros and Valiros came up behind him.

"We may not keep from our journey for long." The Healer reached up and pulled the cowl forward to cover his wet hair. "Look in these carts first. They hold the most gravely wounded, who must go on soon. Much wrong this weather can do them: if we are to save them we must not delay. In such a rain, a sudden chill may put into the grave a man who would heal quickly were no strain put on him. Make whatever speed you can! It means their lives."

In the dimness of the wagon lay men without limbs, with stumps of arms or legs tied and bandaged. Groaning drowned out the rattle of rain on canvas.

"We can do more for pain when we reach Inagar," the Healer said. "It is our plan to spend the night at Rungpor north of here, and go on in the morning. Is that man not one of yours?"

"Emilio," Paidros said. "At least we know he's alive."

"Only barely, I fear," the Healer said. Martos could say nothing: he was looking at Emilio's wounds, remembering the jolly boy who had come all the way from Northern Sardis, up by the Seynyorean border, to find a place in the company.

There were fewer of his own men than he had hoped. Grimmer and grimmer he grew as the numbers of the missing swelled: Tibalo, Linardo, and Garsio were here; Inigos, Espris, Luvicos, and Luego . . . He remembered Paidros calling the roll before they left the camp, and the long silences as name after name went unanswered.

There were three Massadessans in the cart too, and Martos sent Valiros running to fetch the Massadessan leader, Buldeo, to identify them. There were also Seynyoreans in plenty, but no Bordermen. He had tried to order them to leave the wounded behind, as he had done, to burden the other army, but from long habit of Border warfare they had carried off both dead and wounded, just as though they had been fighting Dark Things instead of honourable men.

Most of the wounded in the carts were Seynyoreans, a fact that Martos felt *should* bring considerable pride. The Seynyoreans had held a reputation as the premier soldiers of the world for thousands of years, and these were hardy veterans of many years of warfare. To have defeated them even with equal numbers would have been accounted a notable deed; to have met them when outnumbered and broken them as he had was a marvel. Yet he found a curious emptiness where the pride should be, as he looked into carts full of wounded men.

The first carts, with the most seriously wounded, were moving again. The men in the other carts were livelier, less thoroughly drugged, less seriously wounded.

"Commander!" cried Quintis, as he saw Martos' face at the end of the cart. "I didn't think—why, I never expected—I'm very pleased to see you, sir. Did we win?" One of the Seynyoreans in the cart laughed.

"Yes!" Martos answered. The Seynyorean continued to chuckle. Martos pointedly did not look at him, and continued, "Just count up the number of Kadarins here and subtract them from the number of Seynyoreans. I'm proud of you men! You engaged a Seynyorean force twice your own number, and took only minor losses!"

The chuckling had stopped.

Martos went on, forcing his voice to remain level. He had an uncomfortable feeling that he was blushing, but hoped the light was dim enough that no one would notice. "I'm proud, and you can be proud. You have followed the best traditions of the Kadarin—warrior." He'd almost said "army," but had stopped himself just in time. Platitudes! Did what he was saying sound as idiotic to other people as it did to him? He decided he'd better shut up before he said something really silly.

"You'd not have done so well if—" came an angry and scornful voice from the wagon, but there was a hiss and a sound almost of scuffling, and then another voice spoke.

"Yes, Kadarin, it *was* well done." Martos saw the speaker, in the far corner of the cart—an older man—and for a startled second he thought it might be Istvan DiVega himself. But no, the face was fuller, and this man was younger. "But you cannot empty the ocean with a wine cup. You do not have the force to turn our army aside. You can delay us, but we will get there."

"Then you can meet us with equal numbers," said Paidros, his voice lightly mocking. "If you don't lose too many more on the way."

"Well spoken," said the Seynyorean calmly. "But there is only one company of you Kadarins. The rest—"

"*Hai mai!*" came an angry voice, and beside Quintis a heavyset Massadessan, swathed in bandages, heaved himself painfully to a sitting position. "Were there no Bordermen or Massadessans in the charge that broke your line, DiSilva? It was I myself who—"

A Healer thrust Martos rudely aside, and at the same moment he felt Paidros pull him away. For only a second he resisted, and then realised that they were right. He heard the Healer speaking calmly and authoritatively.

Men who had the day before been trying their best to kill each other must now bear their common misfortune on what tradition and Hastur's Law declared neutral ground. The Seynyorean veterans were used to this, and none knew better than they the truth of the old maxim:

The man you try to slay today
May save your life tomorrow.

Tradition among the roving mercenary bands—and, to a lesser extent, among the class of warriors throughout the world—stressed the camaraderie that could grow between men, even men from opposing sides, who suffer and wait for healing, united by the blood they have lost.

It was an ideal—and any ideal believed in by enough men becomes a truth—but Martos knew how easily that ideal could shatter. The hardest part of a Healer's task might well be to keep peace among his charges, to keep the pain of wounds and grief for slain comrades from bursting into hatred and violence.

The Seynyorean veterans were used to spending the onerous time of healing in cheerful companionship with their former enemies, and his own men—he hoped—were at least used to the idea of doing so. But the Massadessans, whose experience was confined to the pursuit of rare thieves and occasional plundering bands of Dark Things, were not steeped in these traditions of the warrior class. Or was he wronging them? Jagat had spoken of old wars in which the Massadessans had taken land from the Borderers—no small feat.

Diego lay in the next cart, arrow wounds in his arm and shoulder bandaged, his leg splinted. Another Massadessan . . . And then that was all, and a courteous Healer—a younger man, less controlled than the first—was escorting them back to their horses, while Martos' brain still hunted for the men who were not there, the missing men, the dead men: Carlos and Matios, Ijinio, Balsaro, Octios . . . Gomis, and Tomis too . . . Eliso, Hosio . . . Andrios . . .

Thunderhead stirred under him as he came down in the saddle. He patted the horse absently, his mind whirling. Just before the battle, in the grey-walled ravine, Andrios had been telling the old joke about the nearsighted duenna and the twin sisters. And now Andrios was dead, his body burned to ashes, the remnants of his bones collected to fertilise some Borderman's fields. No more jokes about Tomis and Gomis, either . . .

After a moment he realised that the Healer was talking to him, assuring him that the men would get the best care.

"Yes, of course," Valiros was saying. "In fact, I believe Martos has ordered that the rest of the wounded be sent to Inagar also. Isn't that so, Martos?"

Martos' tongue was numb again. He struggled for a moment, then stuttered out an affirmative grunt and jerked his head up and down. He licked his lips, angry at this stupid handicap that crippled his tongue whenever it was most needed.

"Yes!" he blurted. His voice was harsh and ugly in his own ears. "We're sending them!" He felt another stutter start, and clamped his jaws until it went away. "To Inagar!" he finished, and pulled Thunderhead around. Water splashed across his face as though someone had emptied a goblet of rain into the opening of his hood. He pounded his heels on the horse's side and was off through the blur of rain that washed his eyes like tears.

The shock of the cloud-cold water was good. It cleared his head and brought him back to the present. He slowed Thunderhead's pace, and after a moment Valiros and Paidros caught up with him. They did not speak, but their simple presence was comforting. They rode three abreast, and after a moment he bowed his head and let the rain clatter on the cloth of his hood as it fell forward over his face. His soaked beard dripped down the front of the cloak. He lifted his head, and shook the hood from his face, letting the rain bathe it. Paidros was looking at him impatiently, and as he saw Martos' face, he spoke.

"Shouldn't we be turning south sometime soon? We must be nearly abreast with the tail of their army now. Or have you changed your—" He saw the look in Martos' eyes and shut up.

"Where is that scout?" Martos asked. "He said he could take us to Suktio."

Paidros grunted. His horse dropped away to the rear.

Martos straightened and looked around. How dark it was! But it could not be night already, surely? The blur of falling water was all about them, but above it the sky was a writhing mass of mottled black. The Shadow was no longer visible through the curtain of rain: it was as though the clouds held an army of men bailing with buckets.

Then the Borderman rode up, the little Border pony trotting along beside Thunderhead. Martos had to look down at him. Mounted, the man's head only came to his elbow. He struggled to remember his name. The man had regularly been on guard at Jagat's castle; he ought to know his name.

"Shiraj," he said after a moment, plucking a name from his mind.

"Mulraj, Lord," said the Borderman quietly. Embarrassment warmed Martos' face briefly, and for a moment his tongue stalled again.

"Mulraj." He wavered between words of apology, then plunged on. "You said that Lord Suktio—that he would divide his men up to—to—" Cold water peppered his face. What was he trying to say? He couldn't seem to think. "To pick off scouts and stragglers, and to—to cause as much confusion as possible. Do you think—" A sudden gust of wind whipped the hood from his head, and icy wet hammers pounded his scalp, driving whatever he'd been saying clean out of his mind. He reached up and pulled the hood back over his drenched hair, and said simply, "Take us to Suktio."

"Yes, Lord," said Mulraj. "We must turn off to the south now, then. Tell your men to keep together, for it is easy to lose one another in this rain. Follow!"

Grass-grown mud squished under their horses' feet, and broad puddles splashed water on their stirrups. The roar of falling rain deafened them, and the silver-grey curtain cut away the world. How Mulraj could find his way through this, Martos could not understand.

Then of a sudden the squelching, quaking soil was gone from under their hooves, and instead the horses were sliding and neighing as slippery dust shifted under water that foamed around their knees.

"Go slowly now!" Mulraj said, his shout barely audible above the hammering of water. "This is low ground, and the water has flooded the dust. Very slippery, Lords! But soon the land rises, and the going will be easier."

Martos felt Thunderhead lurching uneasily under him as they moved. Water thrown up by the horse's passage soaked the hem of his cloak and splashed down into one boot.

The ground *did* rise, and the treacherous dust, though still uncertain under them, was no longer the terrifying ooze it had been. At the tops of the ridges there were stretches of bare slick rock. Martos heard Mulraj's voice.

"Curse this war!" the little Borderman was saying. "We have hoped for such a rain as this. See, Lord, how it has washed away even the dust? It takes a heavy rain to do that, and were these normal times we would ride to the towers and beg the Hasturs to come and finish the job. All this area could be cleansed, and though it would stay barren for many years, with the dust gone . . ." He shook his head irritably, and his voice was lost again in the rumble of the rain.

Ahead of them, the Shadow glowered through watery veils. Martos rode through sad grey rains, but still, behind his eyes, red and stark, blood was flowing from severed veins. He could almost smell it, as in the dark of the wagons where it had filled his nose.

Men who fear death should not go to war. Had Atrion written that? Or one of the others? He could not remember.

His men had not followed him from Kadar for their health! They could have stayed safely at home, whole and sound in the peace and safety they had all found so stifling. In their first employment they had ridden over the soldiers of the League of Ardren without losing a man, and with only the most minor, trifling wounds. Fighting the Dark Things at Ukarakia had been terrifying enough, but it had been a simple, uncomplicated matter. Not like this . . .

Could he force his men to pay the price for *his* honour? As their Commander, did he not owe them—what? Safety? There was no safety in a war. He had promised no safety to those who followed him: he had promised war. Battle and adventure. They were not trapped here, like the Bordermen. They had come seeking war, and they had found it. Why should a few severed limbs . . .

A high, shrill musical whine cut through the mutter of the rain. Startled, his thoughts scattered, Martos reined in his horse and looked around. Could that be a Demon's cry? Had the Border broken and brought the war to an end?

"Lord Suktio is near!" said Mulraj. "Listen! That is the Conch-horn of Chandra, the heirloom of the Hara Clan, which the great hero Chandra bore in the great wars of the past. It has been kept in honour in Varakota for age upon age, and Lord Suktio got it from his mother, who was the last of that line."

Martos had never heard a conch-horn—or, indeed, heard of one before, for there were no conches in the little inland Sea of Kadar, nor even in the greater landlocked Sea of Arden. But now that he knew it was a horn of some kind, and that Suktio was blowing it, the problem of finding Suktio seemed simple enough. He called up his trumpeters, Romulos and Styllis, and bade them sound their horns. And as the note of the conch-shell died away, a golden blare of Kadarin trumpets answered it, rising and falling like a cock crowing in the dawn.

It was not long before Suktio himself came through the grey threads of rain, with sixteen men at his back. Martos rode to greet them. The Borderman bowed in the saddle, and then cracked a groundnut between his fingers.

"Well done, Lord!" The Borderer popped the two kernels into his mouth, and tucked the husks neatly into a small bag that hung at his saddlebow. Eventually everything in that bag, Martos supposed, would go into the fields. "The Seynyoreans will be expecting us to attack any minute now." He produced another handful of nuts and politely offered some to Martos. Martos took one, and rolled it between his thumb and forefinger while Suktio talked. "When I heard those bugles of yours, it took me a moment to realise it must be you; it gave me quite a start. It should have stopped them, and if we give them another fanfare, they'll be sitting there for hours waiting for us to attack! Probably send their scouts back out, too."

"Go ahead," said Martos, and gestured to Romulos and Styllis. The two raised their long trumpets. Martos looked with interest at the domed conch-shell in Suktio's hand. It did not look as though it could produce any such sound. He had expected some sort of strange animal horn.

Then the trumpets belled out above the rain, and the shrill drone of the great conch of Varakota rose above them and blended with them. From various points beyond the silvery lattice of rain, cow's-horns echoed them.

Suktio lowered the conch from his lips. The trumpeters rested the bells of their bugles on their thighs. Into the void where their tones had been, rushed the rapid patter of splattering water.

"That should make them worry a little," Suktio said with a satisfied smile. "After that, they'll think there's a big force out here and expect an attack at any moment." He chuckled.

Raindrops rattled on the dusty plain. Martos listened: through the chatter of water he heard the splashing of a galloping rider. A Borderman came riding hard out of the haze of rain. Suktio cantered out to meet him. The Borderman reined in his horse and gestured frantically.

Martos remembered the nut in his fingers and, pressing his thumb down, cracked it. Suktio and the newcomer were jabbering excitedly, words lost in the sonorous rhythm of rain. The newcomer kept gesturing back in the direction from which he had come.

Martos stuffed the kernels into his mouth and chewed. In Kadar, groundnuts were eaten only for their pleasant flavour, and no one thought of them as food. But they were a major staple of the Borderman's diet. One of the more tasty ones, even if they did get monotonous after a while. He started to throw away the shell, and stopped, remembering Suktio's bag. The shell should not be thrown away on the dust. It should be saved for the horses, or the fields. Rain was pouring all around, washing the poisoned soil free of all organic impurity: the blood of his men and DiVega's both . . .

Suktio and the other came clattering back. The rain hammered on their helmets. "They haven't stopped," Suktio said. "They're still marching. I do not understand it."

"What have you been doing?" Martos asked. "Mulraj said something about old Takkarian ways of war."

"Indeed, Martos, he spoke truth," Suktio said. "Thus fought Kaljit the Bandit Prince, in days that are now legend. And Chandra who bore this conch-horn before me—and many other heroes in the ancient days.

"They can see no farther in this rain than we, and we know the country as they do not. To keep track of so large an army is a simple task, but scattered groups of men cannot be found so easily. All my men are broken into little groups, riding just out of sight. When we see one of their scouts, we cut him off so that he cannot flee to the main body. Then one of us will fight him, while the others watch, within sight of the army. Twenty men rode to save one scout, and they followed out into the rain, where our comrades waited. They are dead now."

"But there are more that are alive," interrupted the man who had just ridden in. "And it seems as though nothing we can do will slow them in their march."

Suktio nodded, chagrin on his face. "Boktio was watching them. He tells me there was a momentary confusion when we sounded the trumpets, but then they went right on with their march. They've drawn in all their scouts, which means they're marching blind." Suktio paused, thinking, and said, "They are drifting south, a little, off the main route. If we—if they get turned far enough, they will find themselves marching deeper into the dust, and miss Manjipor altogether." Again he paused, rain drumming on his helmet, then shook his head. "I thought they'd stop to defend themselves, or at least send out more scouts."

"They gambled we wouldn't dare attack," said Martos, "and won." *DiVega's doing*, he thought. "We should offer them the same gamble again, but this time make them lose."

"They are in very tight formation, Lord," said the scout. "If we try to attack any single company, the others will have us surrounded at once. And we are too few."

"If we rode in and loosed arrows at them," said Martos thoughtfully, with a glance at Paidros, "they would have to stop and fight back. We could withdraw without coming to blows, and they would have to wait, to see if we were going to attack again."

"That would slow them. *Hai*, I like that!" said Suktio. "We should be able to keep them here all day—might even draw some after us. Well thought of!"

Martos was surprised to find that he was beginning to like Suktio. It was strange. He remembered the quarrel with Kumari, Suktio glaring, his knuckles white on his sword-hilt.

"I'll gather the men, then, and we'll attack." Suktio raised the great conch to his lips, and its high call rang above the clamouring rain. Again it cried, a short blast; then once more, a long wailing cry. Paidros spoke to Romulos and Styllis, and their trumpets sounded. Men snapped to attention.

Martos saw Kumari's eyes, ghostlike against the grey screen of rain. Was Suktio one of her former lovers? Best not to know, he thought; and then remembered an old proverb: *All kinship comes through a woman's womb*.

"If they respond with any real force," the scout was saying, "we can be crushed by numbers in a moment!"

"That is true, of course." Suktio shrugged. "Earth is the Bride of the Warrior."

Chapter Four

"Yes, I heard the trumpets! I may be old, but I'm not deaf yet!"
Istvan sat on his grey mare's back, and water poured down all
around. His knee cracked as he shifted in the saddle, and suddenly
he smiled at the indignation in his tone. After all, many men his
age—and younger—*were* deaf. "Just keep moving!" he said.

"But if we're attacked—" Firencio shut up as Istvan looked at
him.

Rupiro's D'Ascoli began talking instead. "Come now, DiVega,
you can't just ignore the menace of a force of unknown size massing
on our right flank this way. Those horns must mean something!"

"Of course," said Istvan. "The trumpets mean that Martos of
Onantuga is out there with somewhere under a hundred and fifty
men—since that's what he had to start with—and there were dead
and wounded Kadarins here after the battle. The conch-horn means
that his Border and Massadessan allies are with him. About how
many would you say, DiSezrotti?"

"Four, five hundred maybe, if he has no more than he had at the
battle. But he might have gotten reinforcements. Or he might have
had some as a reserve."

"He might have, but he didn't," said Istvan, shaking his head.
"Attacking a large force with a smaller is either idiotic, brilliantly
subtle, or rash but necessary. I've never heard that Martos was an
idiot. He *might* have a long and involved plan that depends on
making us underestimate his numbers—in which case, indeed, we
may be attacked at any moment. If we weren't down to the last of
the grain, I'd halt and turn to set a front, just to be on the safe
side—or better still, go after him! But if we don't get off the dust,
we'll arrive at Manjipor on foot; we may still find ourselves walking! So I'm gambling that he attacked with no more than six hundred
men because that's all he has. He *does* have reinforcements on the
way, I'm sure, but they can't have gotten here yet, unless they can
fly. My guess is that he's trying to make us stop, to delay us until
his reinforcements arrive, or else to draw us back into the dust. He's
buying time for Jagat."

"Well, I hope you're right," Ciavedes growled. "But I wish
you'd let us send out scouts to see! If they do have any real force out
there, they could split us in half!"

67

Istvan sighed, and listened to the clatter of water on the dust. "I'm not going to order any man to certain death," he said. "Fighting fifteen men, even if it's only one at a time—and they might not stick to that—is not something I—"

"*You've* done it!" Arjun DiFlacca cut in. Istvan blinked at the boy.

"Well, yes, I suppose I have, but—" He was interrupted by loud laughter from Servara and Rupiros D'Ascoli.

"Tell me, DiVega, is that modesty, or is your memory just getting bad?" Servara chuckled. "I had to count them, you know!"

Istvan shook his head. "All right!" he snapped. "But that's beside the point. Those were riffraff! These are trained and seasoned Border warriors! And just because I've had to do that sort of thing once or twice doesn't mean that I could do it again. Or that I do it out of choice! Most particularly, it doesn't mean I expect everybody to be able to do it. If everybody could, then we wouldn't need to worry about the size of the force out there. Even if it were—let me see, six times fifteen—even if it were ninety thousand men, we would be a match for them! So why bother with scouts?" They laughed again.

Istvan had sent the remaining scouts forward to DiBolyar's company and to Robardin's. They now led the army, with the shattered remnants of the former vanguard grouped between them.

The rain poured down as they rode. At their left, the long line of Kalascorean footmen plodded sturdily through the rain, heavy cloaks dripping, the heads of their pikes and halberds covered with loose waterproof scabbards, the thongs dangling. A shake, and all those deadly points would be free.

Off to the right, DiCalvados' men walked their horses. The tired beasts trudged head-down, rain running from their manes, shivering, snorting with annoyance and hunger. There would be less than a handful of grain for each of them tonight. How much less than a handful, Istvan wasn't sure. There was a little bread and dried fruit that could be used to stretch it out, but among six thousand horses it would not go far. How could they fight a battle on hunger-weakened mounts? Even when they reached the area of occasional grass beyond the dust, there would not be enough grazing there to do much good. By the time they got to Manjipor . . .

Something was nagging at the back of Istvan's brain. He scowled and tried to tease it out, but it remained shapeless in a corner. There was something he had failed to take into account. What was it?

The men around had begun talking again, but it was mostly idle chatter. He ignored it, concentrating on the elusive thought, until D'Ascoli's voice broke in:

". . . don't you think so, Istvan?"

"Umm. Good question! What is it that I'm supposed to think?"
D'Ascoli laughed. "You weren't listening."

"Listening to what?"

"I was just saying that they wouldn't be bothering about the scouts if—"

A sudden shout cut him off. A Seer rode into their midst, crying, "An attack!" DiGasclon's company is under attack! Listen."

Through the dumbness that followed his words, they heard above the clatter of rain the distant shouts of men. DiGasclon straightened in the saddle. "Vega! DiVega!" he shouted. "Come on!" And then he was off, his horse galloping back toward the rear.

"They are attacking Vega's company now," the Seer said.

"What!" said Istvan. "What kind of an attack is it?"

"Arrows," the Seer said. "They are riding—" He closed his eyes more tightly. "Yes, they are riding along the line, about a hundred yards out, firing into the ranks and riding on."

"We've *got* them!" said Istvan. The rest stared. "DiCalvados! Ciavedes! Get your men and follow me. Back to your companies, the rest of you; tell your men to shoot at them as they come! But *don't* let them draw you out to pursue them! That's what they want. Don't leave the line without my order!" He turned to the Seer. "Pass the word back. Tell them to string their bows."

Istvan wheeled his horse and galloped toward the gap that separated the two nearest companies, DiCalvados and Ciavedes riding at his heels. In a short time both companies were in motion. DiCalvados' company rode straight at a right angle to the line of march for two hundred yards, and then whirled to face the rear. Ciavedes' company wheeled out like a door opening. Istvan rode between them.

Barely was the manoeuvre completed when they saw horsemen rushing toward them from the shadowy rain. Istvan's sword slid from its scabbard, need-fire glittering on its blade. His sword was poised to signal the charge, his lungs were filled with air. But the enemy horsemen were already angling away from the main body, and as those in the front rank saw the two companies awaiting them, they yelled over their shoulders, and loud above the rain and shouting rose the clear dove-note of the great conch-horn.

Like a startled flock of birds, Borderman and Kadarin wheeled in an instant and darted away to the north. Even as Istvan's blade snapped down to signal the charge, he knew it was too late.

Long before the conch-shell sounded, Martos and his men had been prepared to turn. The danger was obvious. Already Seynyorean arrows arched through the rain to fall among them.

They rode in a long thin line, and when the conch called there was no hesitation: each man turned his horse and fled. They scattered as they rode, but that was all to the good. Behind them, Seynyoreans and Kantarans milled in confusion. The rain was thickening. Soon, Martos knew, it would change to that crushing downpour through which he had ridden here.

Then that waterfall roared from the clouds. Raindrops clamoured on Martos' helm. Beyond his horse's ears, he saw only vague greyness shot with silver strings. The men around him vanished, and after a moment it was as though he were alone. He slid his bow into its case and pulled out the flap that would shield it from the water. One of the men near him had had an arrow through his arm, and Martos supposed there must be others wounded. But they had not come off badly: the enemy had had little time to react. The attack had been timed well. It had not done a great deal of damage—the light was too dim for good shooting—but the Royal Army had stopped, milling in confusion while men scrambled for bows. It would take them time to re-form and move on.

He himself had not aimed to kill until the end, when they had begun shooting back. But with six thousand men, there was little space for his arrows to find the ground, so he had undoubtedly hit some of them.

It was necessary, he told himself, angrily.

Let the man who is no danger to you go his way, Atrion answered. *No man's life is worth more than another's. If Death is not already present at a gathering, it is folly to invite him. Death is a capricious guest: his appetite may be larger than his host expects.*

But that had been a warning against forcing a duel, or drawing steel on an unarmed man. Surely, this was different? But a part of his mind persisted in imagining himself dodging arrows, scrabbling for the bow in his boot, helpless to reply, while arrows came out of nowhere.

The conch-horn sang the gathering-call above the clatter of the rain. He turned his horse toward the sound. The light grew steadily dimmer. Beyond the Shadow, the Twin Suns were settling toward the sea. All around him raindrops flicked across his sight, blurring the world with glassy haze. It would be dark in a few short hours.

Suddenly the conch was silent. Above the rain he heard the babbling of voices and the clatter of steel. He pulled the dwarf-sword free, and spurred his horse. Rain splashed his face as though he rode through a river. Through the glassy streaks he glimpsed a struggling dark mass, heard men shouting, and the clamour of battle. He checked his horse and stared in confusion at a battle of Bordermen.

Men from the Kantara must have followed them. Apparently the Bordermen could tell friend from foe in that rain-laced tangle; Martos could not. The skinny little men in lacquered leather armour all looked the same on their earth-coloured horses, except for a few he knew well. Bimsio he recognised, the best blade on the Border, emptying men's saddles with well-placed cuts. And he saw Suktio raging through the press, his red sword mingling blood with the rain, spattering crimson droplets as it rose and fell.

Martos' men came riding up, and gathered behind him, as confused as he by the homemade Border armour. Bordermen came rushing out of the rain and hurled themselves into the fight, their swords whirling about their heads, lashing down on leather shields with a deep-toned *boom!* Strange war-cries lilted above the clangour of battle. The watching Kadarins were stunned by the fury of the fight.

Bordermen fought Bordermen. Memories of more than a thousand years of fratricidal feuds rose up to claim their due, strengthened by all the tenacity and courage developed in the survivors of centuries of hopeless struggle. Martos felt a terrifying chill. Such warriors! They hurled themselves upon their foemen's swords. More than once he saw a dying man forcing himself up a sword, toward the hilt of the blade that pierced him, striking for the man behind it. Maimed men heaved themselves up out of pools of their own blood, trying to strike one last blow. One-handed men attempted to snatch the swords from their severed arms. Men fell in pairs, with blades driven through one another's bodies. They were not as skilled or disciplined as the Seynyoreans. They lacked the horsemanship of his own Kadarins, and the size and weight of northerners in general, but they were unmatched in their total disregard of pain and death.

Martos had seen Bordermen face the Dark Things, he had seen them against foreigners, and fighting their own kin in Manjipor, but never until now had he seen the ancient enmities between the principalities stirred to life. Suddenly he understood why the Old Takkarian Empire had shattered to such tiny fragments, how the Dark Ones had taken so much of the ancient land.

Suddenly the fight was over. Bordermen glared suspiciously at each other, but the swords ceased their dance. Rain clattered from the silver sky. He saw Suktio, standing in his stirrups, raise the ancient conch-shell with a bloodstained hand. It shrilled above the gurgle of the rain, crowing in victory above the tangled dead. Martos rode up slowly, followed by his men. Bordermen were lying on the wet grey dust, wasting their blood on poisoned ash. Rainwater splashed on their armour, running in a thick film over the lacquer.

Suktio lowered the horn, and Martos saw blood oozing from rents in his mail. It had been a costly victory. There were more dead than wounded, and among those who had reached Suktio before the battle ended, more wounded than whole.

The enemy, riding in a body, had followed the neigh of the

conch-horn through the rain, and reached Suktio before more than a handful of his own men had gathered around him, so that at first they had outnumbered the Manjipéans. And all the Manjipéan Healers were still in the camp to the north.

Water poured down all around them, washing blood and sweat from the bodies of the dead. Martos tried to look up at the sky, and got a face full of cold water. But the sky was still grey with black mottlings, so there must be some light above the clouds. He felt suddenly weary. Tense muscles ached in neck and shoulder; the day seemed very long. How long now, until dark? The blank clouds gave no clue. The horses were worn out. . . .

The horses. The hungry horses in the Seynyorean camp. He'd slowed their march; night would come and they would still be on the dust. Could they have any hay left? Not much: those had been the first wagons Paidros had set afire. The horses would be hungry. He should steal them, take them away to the north where they could graze.

If he only had enough men and horses to make a decent frontal assault, instead of this contemptible business of ambush, striking and running! But even with the force Jagat was sending, he would be outnumbered more than six to one.

For a moment, it seemed the rain was lessening. Then the mutter of water turned to a roar.

"Never mind all that!" snapped Istvan. "Get them moving again, fast! Delay was the whole point of that—exercise. If we get back to our full pace we should still be past the worst by sundown. If not, we'll just have to march on in the dark! Now if you want any sleep—for yourselves, for your men, for your horses—get your men *marching!*"

Sleep! Need of it weighted his limbs more than his sodden cloak. His eyelids crawled with weariness. He shook himself, then turned his head up and let the rain wash the sweat from his face. The bracing icy water helped. He would have fallen asleep hours ago had it not been for the continual cold slap of the rain. He lowered his head and let the tiny pellets of water batter his cloak like pecking birds.

The few remaining Healers, red robes vivid against the grey, were hunting out the wounded, pulling out arrows while the Bordermen attended to the dead. There were fewer dead than wounded, and not even many of those. Two men at least had gone down with Kadarin spike-headed arrows through their mail, and one man had gotten one of the Border arrows through his throat. But mostly the broad-headed arrows had caught in mail-rings, leaving a mere pin-prick or nothing at all. And most of the arrows had simply missed. Shooting through such rain was not easy, even from a standing position, riding at full speed.

He hated bows. *Istvan the Archer*. The name mocked him, the filthy name he could never be rid of. Martos, too, must be sick of this kind of fighting. He chuckled, remembering Birthran's description, and wondered what Fendol would have done in such a situation— or Tuarim . . .

"Lord! Lord-Commander DiVega!" Istvan looked up and saw Rinmull of Ojaini riding toward him, his shaggy brown pony solid against the vagueness of rain and dust.

"Lord Rinmull." Istvan saluted. "What is it?"

The Borderman pulled the little horse to a stop and made a rapid, awkward bow from the saddle. "I have discovered, Lord, that several of my men pursued the enemy after the attack. And your men allowed them—" He stopped, controlling the anger that had crept into his voice. "And your men, Lord DiVega, were under orders not to leave their place in line, so that my men were unsupported."

Istvan sat stunned, shock and anger warring in him. His first impulse was to scream at the man that the orders were supposed to apply to his men, too; that the men who had ridden out had done so against orders, and whatever happened was their own fault, not his. But this was no time to dodge responsibility. *Whatever happens is the Commander's fault*, he thought. And he had been proud and relieved that none of the companies had left their place in line.

"I do not think that anyone knew," he said. "I did not know until—" He stopped as a sound came out of the dim rain haze: the high, clear hum of the conch-shell.

There are your men, he thought, but kept the words inside his mind where they belonged. But from Rinmull's face, he knew he thought the same. More dead men, red blood running in the rain, empty eyes staring at the weeping sky.

"How many?" he asked softly, and had to repeat it, louder, to be heard above the drumming of rain. Rinmull looked up at him, eyes wide, mouth twisted.

"I don't know. Perhaps fifty. They—I don't know!"

Firencio came rushing up, urging a horse already drooping with weariness. Behind, DiCalvados, Ciavedes, and others were coming.

"You heard the horn!" said Firencio. "They're coming again!"

"If they are, we'll be ready for them this time," Istvan said. "But I don't think that's what it was. I almost wish it was." He gestured to Lord Rinmull. "We've lost some of our Border allies."

"I lost some of my men, too!" snapped Firencio. "Most of the companies were lucky, but three of my men—"

"*Fifty!*" Istvan said, his voice cutting across the younger man's with a tone he seldom used. "They left the line and followed." He saw Firencio's mouth shut. "I'm afraid that conch-horn may be sounding in celebration."

"Could your men not have supported them?" Rinmull burst out, passionately. "Oh, I know, Lord Istvan, it was stupid of them to leave their place, and it was against orders, but when you saw—"

"I truly do not think anyone saw," said Istvan.

"I saw a number of Bordermen," said Firencio.

"But of course, all Bordermen look alike!" snapped Rinmull. "Perhaps you foreigners should leave us to fight our own battles. We can at least tell each other apart!"

"In this rain," Istvan said quickly, "I do not know that I could recognise my own brother at ten feet, let alone a hundred yards! And the armour *is* much the same." Rinmull sighed, and his head drooped until rain leaped from the back of his helmet.

"You have the right of it, Lord," he said. "It was not your fault. But men who were my vassals and kinsmen are dead. And also, Pirthio was a good friend of mine."

Far off in the rain, the conch-horn crowed, rising and falling in an exultant tune. Rinmull turned in the saddle and stared out. Istvan, too, gazed into the crystal blur, trying to find the tiny shapes of distant men.

"We've got to get some scouts out, DiVega!" It was Ciavedes' voice. "I know your objections, but we've got to find out what's going on out there! If we'd had a scout out before, we would have had some warning of that attack."

"No," said Rinmull. "This is an old tradition, Lord Ciavedes. A scout would simply have died first."

"Maybe," said Ciavedes. "But that's a risk we all take. Perhaps we should send out a small party of scouts, enough to defend themselves if attacked."

"And there's another matter, DiVega," DiCalvados cut in. "The scouts you sent to the front tell me that it looks like we've missed our road and are moving too far south. If we miss Manjipor, we may find ourselves wandering in the dust until our horses run out. We need someone to look for the guideposts by the old road."

"If we're too far south, it shouldn't be any trouble to just swing north a little," Istvan said.

Rinmull and Firencio both spoke at once. Istvan raised a hand, and they quieted.

"It is not that easy, Lord Istvan," said Rinmull. "If we have gotten off the old road, and missed the guideposts, the danger of becoming lost in the dust, in winter, is very real. In summer it is simple enough, but the rain makes it difficult to find the true way."

"And the scouts themselves are worried, Cousin," said Firencio.

"I talked to one of them just now. He said it was better for one man to die than for the whole army to go astray. He was quite willing to go."

"Send me, Lord DiVega!" It was Arjun DiFlacca's voice. Istvan turned, and saw him riding behind on his little pony. His eyes were very bright and eager. "I can find the guidepost! Earth is the Bride of the Warrior; but my horse is fast, and I can fight!"

Istvan gritted his teeth. Somehow the boy's eagerness made him sound even younger than he really was, as though he were ten instead of seventeen.

"I can go, if need be," said Rinmull with a shrug. "Perhaps I'll learn what became of my men."

The rain seemed to be slacking off. Istvan stood in his stirrups, and halting the mare a moment, looked out across the plain. He could see through the rain now, a little, anyway. He was able to make out the army behind him and the vast grey wasteland beyond. Against the greyness he saw tiny hints of shape and colour. Men and horses? He strained his eyes to see. The distant shapes were blotted from sight by a curtain of grey rain that swept down out of the north. Even as he watched, the storm moved toward them, roaring like a waterfall.

"Keep moving!" he shouted, dropping back into the saddle. He urged the mare on. Then falling water rumbled his hood, and men and animals were staggering forward blindly under a weight of water. Istvan saw Ciavedes' mouth opening and shutting as he shouted against the rain, but whatever he was saying was drowned in the stutter of the storm. The mare balked and lurched. Istvan patted his mount, then climbed down from the saddle and began to lead her.

Booming water flattened his hood against his skull and soaked it through. The mare put her head down and stumbled shivering along. Istvan played nervously with the reins in his hands. Jagat's men were resting through this. They would be finding shelters and keeping themselves dry. And he would come staggering in tomorrow evening with an army of tired men on tired horses. Hungry horses. Sick horses . . .

He raised his head to peer through the rain streams, and spray from shattered droplets on the edge of his hood leaped to fill his eyes. He could see no more than a few yards away. All around him, the Royal Army blundered through the storm. Time became a constant battering. A cold wind whooped out of the north and cut through Istvan's wet cloak to hunt out the cracks of his joints and stiffen them. It whipped the torrent sideways and pelted the army with rain like thrown stones.

Man and beast plodded on in a deadness of misery. At last, the cataract began to ebb. The roar of the crashing water sank and scattered to a clattering tattoo. It could not have been long, Istvan thought, but it seemed as though he had always been leading his horse through the crushing downpour. Now, through the flooded air, other men emerged. He could see the army around him again. But only a few miles off, the world still ended in a cloud-pale curtain.

"Does it rain like that often?" Ciavedes' voice carried easily above the rain.

"Often, Lord?" said Rinmull of Ojaini. "Not very often, no." He turned and rode toward Istvan. "Do you wish me to go out? This might be the best time for it, and that wind, coming with the rain, has undoubtedly caused us all to drift toward the south."

"Scattered us all over, too," said Ciavedes. "Look at them! No two companies together! We've got to close up! If the enemy were to attack—"

"No fear of that," said Rinmull. "They are in no better case then we. But do you wish me to ride out, Lord-Commander?"

Istvan considered. Rinmull was probably right. There was less likelihood of an attack now, and if they did miss Manjipor itself . . .

On the other hand, they could not afford to lose Rinmull. Ojaini had become the most important city in the Kantara, and its Lord the most important man in the province, next to the King himself. Only Rinmull could control the unruly Border nobles. Yet it had to be done.

"You say this business of killing scouts is old Border custom, Lord Rinmull?"

"The custom is older than the Border," said Rinmull grimly. "Long before the Dark Things came out of the north, the ancient heroes of the Takkarian Empire fought so when faced with a host greater than their own. Indeed, even before the Barriers of Hastur were broken, in the golden Age of Peace when the Dark Things were still banished from the world, Prince Ranjit fought alone against the armies of his usurping uncle. Or so they tell the tale." Rinmull paused and gazed out into the mournful wilderness of rain.

"There are many tales of Prince Ranjit, and once there were more," he said, thoughtfully. "In the old books preserved in Ojaini I have found many old ballads and fragments of tales that have been forgotten, and references to still more. But when the usurper's army hunted Ranjit in the mountains of his home province, and all but a handful of his men had deserted him, the tale says that he sought out the scouts of the army and challenged them to single combat, then slew them one by one. And that great army went astray in the mountains and was forced to turn back from hunger and cold. And Ranjit's fame grew so great that men flocked to his banner, and so in time he regained the throne that was rightfully his.

"And when the Army of Adlerheim invaded the empire, it is told that the great hero Virata remembered the tale of Prince Ranjit, and although he had far fewer men than the invaders, he was able to slow their advance until a greater army could be raised. And Kaljit the Bandit Prince, too, long defied the army of the Emperor, until he was betrayed." For a moment Rinmull was silent, while the clouds wept above the bones of the land; and then, instead of speaking, he sang softly:

> *And none can say where Kaljit's grave*
> *Is hid among the mountains high.*

The wind moaned, setting icy spikes in Istvan's joints. He closed his eyes and hunted through his memory for times he had ridden to Manjipor in the past. He remembered the little markers set up by the road, tiny flat pillars set in cairns of stones. He would know them if he saw them.

"Well, DiVega?" said Ciavedes. "Are you going to *do* anything? Or do we just blunder around in the dust?"

"I am willing to go, Lord," said Rinmull.

"I am not willing to have you go," Istvan said. "You are the leader of the Kantarans, and you are needed here. Send me instead the scout Kurrun. And you are quite right, Ciavedes, in saying that the army is a mess. Look at your own company, for example! Do they not need to be put in order?"

Ciavedes stiffened, then laughed. "I've burned my own dinner while trying to season yours, eh? All right, DiVega, it's back to my own pot!" He turned his horse, and rode toward his own men.

Istvan halted the mare and scrambled back on. "Firencio!" he said. "I want this army straightened out! I want every company pulled in tight, so that we're marching in a solid formation, without all these gaps between the companies. DiCalvados and DiGasclon should act as flanking wings on the north, and Chalcondie and Servara on the south. I want just enough room between each block for a single horseman to get through . . ." He issued orders in a steady stream.

When the scout Kurrun arrived a few moments later, he found Commander DiVega alone. "How exactly would you get us back on the road to Manjipor?" DiVega asked him. "If you rode out scouting, what would you look for?"

"The road itself, Lord," the man said. "It is clearly marked along here. That is how I knew that we must have drifted away from it."

"How do you know we are south instead of north?"

"That is only a guess, Lord. The wind has been blowing from the north, and it seems likely to me that that has caused us to veer to the south. Also, we have been attacked from the north. If I do not find the road north of us, I shall search for it to the south."

"How can you keep yourself from being lost in the rain?"

"An army as large as this makes much noise, Lord," Kurrun said, puzzled. "The wind is steady enough to be some guide. And when the rain drops, you can see the Shadow to the south of us. And I know this country well, Lord. I have guarded many convoys from Ojaini."

"Suppose you could not find the army, and missed it in the rain. What would you do?"

"I would go west to the little stream, the one we camp by tonight, and follow its banks until I came to the camp."

Istvan nodded to himself. "Very well, Kurrun. Thank you. Now report to Captain DiBolyar, and take the lead for his men."

"But Lord-Commander," the man protested, "do you not wish me to—?"

"You heard the order, Kurrun." Istvan's voice was gentle, but implacably firm. The man blinked, made an awkward bow from the saddle, and was gone.

Istvan turned his horse north. He stopped at DiCalvados' company, just long enough to send Firencio a message: "You are in command until I return."

A simple enough message, he thought, and laughed. He turned the mare to the north. The wind whistled, and whipped his face with water. He kicked the mare's ribs gently and rode out into the rain.

Every time Chondos tripped, the noose cut off his wind, and then the whip would whistle down on his shoulders. Sometimes they kicked him. Rage built up inside him, but all he could do was clench his bound hands furiously and unclench them again, straining angrily at the ropes. The muscles in his shoulders were rigid bars, aching as they wrenched futilely at the ropes that held him. The rough rope chewed the skin of his wrists.

Blood pounded furiously in his battered head, and his feet hurt. The goblins were setting a fast pace. If he lagged, the noose tightened around his neck, and then the whip cracked on his shoulders. He felt rain on the tender flesh there; knew that the cloth had been cut by repeated whip strokes. Cool rain trickled down his back, mingling with warm blood.

Rashnagar and the Master. Better if he had been killed in the fight. Better if the troll had gotten him. Better if he had cut his own throat that first night. *Death is the Bride of the Warrior*, the Bordermen said. It was a common thing for the Bordermen to kill themselves to avoid capture by the Dark Things. He remembered the screaming goblins, and knew why.

They began to clamber up a narrow ravine. The ground was rising under his feet, and the rope ahead of him grew taut. *A man can always die*, the Bordermen said. He felt the rope tighten around his neck, and smiled.

He planted his feet on the slope, and leaned back, against the pressure of the taut rope. At once he felt his neck caving in, his throat closing. He pushed with his feet, ignoring the pain. His lungs were numb and aching.

A beastly voice snarled a harsh command. Sound came and went in waves as blood bubbled in his ears. His heart was trying to batter its way out of his chest. Another pain ripped across his back, but he was beyond that. He could feel numbness swirling down his forehead into his eyes. He felt his legs folding up, and saw the ground coming toward him as though through fog. . . .

Something burned at his neck, something fumbled. There was a sense of something cold, and suddenly his lungs betrayed him and sucked in deep ragged gasps of burning cold air. But he was falling. It didn't matter. He was almost asleep.

Something fumbled with his arms. His shoulders were wrenched with sudden violence, as both his arms were twisted. He was floating, or flying, except he could feel his toes bumping and bumping. Then the ground came up and hit him, smashing the newly precious air out of his lungs.

He lay and breathed in great shuddering gasps, feeling the beauty of the air chilling his trembling lungs. There was nothing more precious than air. Goblins were jabbering and quarreling above him. Water dripped on his aching back. He tried to roll over. The first time he fell back, his cheek splashing mud over his face as it slapped the ground. The second time he managed to roll up onto his shoulder. One elbow was trapped beneath him, twisting the arm and throwing new pain into his already sore shoulder joints. With a jerk, he rolled onto his back.

Black goblins clustered around. Water fell into his eyes, making him blink. Angry goblins snarled and hissed. Strange black shapes loomed nearby. Blinking rain from his eyelashes, he saw huge boulders. The rope around his neck was gone.

He kicked his feet and wriggled toward the nearest of the boulders. Its sides bulged out. He wriggled in close to its base, out of the rain. He felt utterly exhausted. His limbs were too heavy to move. He closed his eyes and fell asleep.

The rain closed around Istvan like a wall. It beat on his hood and splashed into his eyes. The weight of his wet cloak dragged on his shoulders. After he had ridden for a few moments it was as though there were no one else in the world: nothing but grey dust and the colourless curtain of water that hissed and clattered around him.

Yet when he listened, he was able to hear behind him a murmur of blended sounds: voices, the jingle of metal, the creak of leather, the blowing and snorting of horses, the splash of water. The scout had been right. So great an army made much noise. He listened a moment, then urged the tired mare on. Through the glassy blur of the rain, the dust seemed featureless, endless, a monotonous flat plain that went on forever with no landmark, no change.

He counted his horse's strides mechanically, trying to keep track of the distance. Rain in his face kept him moving roughly north. He tried to hold his head turned one way or the other, to keep the rain from flooding his eyes. When the wind blew, his eyelashes blurred with spray and his joints ached with chill. The blank land unrolled in the rain.

Out of the murk ahead came a faint cough. For a moment Istvan thought he had lost his way and circled back, but the wind blew water into his face, and he realised that Martos' men must be out here somewhere. He heard a faint murmur of voices and the rattling snort of a horse. Cautiously, trying to make as little noise as possible, he eased the heavy shield from his saddle and shrugged it onto his arm, wondering if they would really attack him one at a time.

If they were Bordermen they would. Not only because it was their own tradition, but because fear—the only reason, after all, for packing to kill a single man—had long been burned out of any man who chose to stay on the Border. A man who was not willing to face death constantly, fighting against impossible odds, went and found another place to live. Anybody with any sense went and found another place to live.

He smiled suddenly, remembering an old joke. *Bordermen are so stupid they always run the wrong way. . .*

Something caught his eye, a solid blotch against the vague gloom. He urged the mare toward it. Other dim shapes emerged nearby. And then he was looking down on the pillar-topped cairns that marked the road. He nodded to himself, thoughtfully. It would not take long to get back on course. Under the mare's feet, under the pooling water, dust drifted over the remnants of the ancient road.

He heard the snuffle of a horse, loud above the purr of the rain. Hazy figures of mounted men appeared out of the dappled veil of water. The dense shower drummed on homemade leather armour. The rough coats of little Border ponies were slicked down and soaked. They spread out in a circle. The steel of their swords was flecked with droplets. One man wore one of the rare old mail-shirts.

"That's a Seynyorean!" a Borderman cried.

They stared at Istvan uncertainly through the cobweb lines of water.

"Take him!" snapped the mail-clad man. "Sujio!"

"Defend yourself, scout!" shouted one, and clapped his heels to his horse.

Istvan's Hastur-blade came flaming from its scabbard. The Borderman checked his pony a moment, staring at the need-fire, then spurred the horse again, waving his sword above his head. Istvan let the rein drop from his shield hand and nudged the tired mare with his knees. She moved only a step or so.

The Borderman stood in his stirrups to cut. His horse was taller than most Border ponies, and his blade came lashing up at Istvan's head. Istvan's shield rose to meet it, blocking his vision. But even as the shield rang with the blow, his sword arm was whipping above his helm; and as the shield dropped, the flaming blade sliced out toward his foe's right temple. It ripped across the Borderer's leather shield, leaving a fine incision straight across. At the end of the stroke, Istvan's arm paused and reversed, driving the point past the edge of the shield. It was an expert's move, and a dangerous one. His arm from the elbow down was exposed, and if the other caught the point in his shield . . .

Istvan felt the point pierce as the shield came down and the other blade lifted for a blow. Cold prickles swept from elbow to wrist, but the sword fell from the Borderer's limp hand, and the shield dropped to show Istvan's point buried in an eye, driven deep into the brain. Then he jerked the sword free, and the horse dashed past while the corpse tumbled from its back.

There was a hiss above the sputter of the rain as every Borderman breathed at once. Istvan's shield dipped as he gathered the reins to lie along the shield-grip in his left hand.

Shouting, a Borderman rushed from behind him. Istvan pulled the weary mare around, and wind squirted rain into his eyes. A blurred figure galloped out of the rain, and Istvan heard an edge hissing in the air. He hunched himself down behind his shield, drawing up the knee on that side, pulling his sword hand in tight to give himself as much protection as possible. His shield thundered against his helm, and his crouched neck ached with the strain. He uncurled his body, his burning ears trying to separate the soft sound of hoofbeats on dust from the eternal chatter of rain.

He heard the squelching hooves turn behind him, and then they were coming on his right side, where he had only his sword to guard. No time to turn the tired horse, barely time enough to turn his face from the rain and blink the blinding water from his eyes. He saw a sword lashing for his face, and met it with his own.

Steel belled on steel. The Borderman pulled up his horse, holding to his advantage of position. Istvan heaved the glowing blade above his head and slashed. The Borderer's sword moved in the counter-stroke as his shield came up. But as his eyes vanished behind the shield, Istvan leaned his body back in the saddle, turning his wrist so that the sword flipped in the air and missed the Borderman complete-ly, to come down flat across the horse's withers.

Then he was whipping it up frantically, trying to meet the sword that was lashing toward his chest. There was a rasp of steel as the blades met, and the Borderman's point bounced harmlessly from the metal of Istvan's shield as he pulled it hurriedly before him.

Then the Borderman was clinging tightly to his bucking, kicking horse. Istvan settled himself firmly in the saddle. Someone laughed, and several voices joined. Istvan braced himself for another attack. None came. The Borderman got his horse under control, and turned it back toward Istvan. Istvan rode to meet him. His sword flamed through the rain as though the suns shone on it. The last of the laughter died.

The Borderman brought his shield up, and poised his sword above his head. Istvan prodded the tired mare foward, and anger rippled in the muscles of his arm as he squeezed the sword-hilt. He raised the shield to the tip of his nose. Now he would not have to use his sword for guarding while the other was free to guard and strike at the same time! Now it would be the Borderman's turn to—

He wondered why he was so angry. The man was only trying to stay alive, and Istvan was the enemy he had to kill. Anger still knotted his arm. And anger was stupid, it could kill you, it cut into the oneness between mind and sword.

Water clattered on armour as the two horses came closer. Istvan willed the rage in his arm and shouder to relax, but there was no more time. With a sudden burst of speed the Border pony darted in, and the leather-armoured figure loomed up through the mesh of water, spattering raindrops from a blurred grey sword.

Istvan hurled up his shield and cut under it as it boomed on his arm. He felt his blade sink into leather and jerked it back sharply. His own shield dropped out of his vision, and over it he saw the deep cut in the edge of the Borderer's buckler. That was the danger of a Hastur-blade: so sharp, and so hard of edge, it could slice through almost any armour, but could easily be trapped in a shield.

The Borderman's sword whistled toward him again, a wheel of silver above its owner's head, angling up for Istvan's eyes. His shield-edge lifted the blade, letting it keen harmlessly over his helm, and his own sword followed it down. His shoulder crackled as he leaned with the stroke, trying to use the advantage of his horse's height to pass over his enemy's shield. The Borderman swayed frantically back in the saddle, and the glowing point snicked across his nose, leaving a bright thread of blood at the very tip, as though he had been scratched by a thorn.

There! Istvan exulted, remembering himself leaning out of a blow, and another part of his mind mourned the savage joy.

The Borderman heaved himself erect, and with the movement, arm and blade snapped in an arc aimed at Istvan's head, the shield drifting to the side. Istvan saw the shoulder moving out with the blow.

As Istvan's shield went up, his sword lashed along its inner edge, toward the unseen foe. Metal pealed on the steel of his shield. He felt his edge slice through leather and flesh. His shield came down, and he saw a cloud of blood. His blade, aimed in that instant before his shield blinded him, had sunk deep into the shoulder where it joined the neck, slashing through the leather to open the artery. Red drops fountained, to mingle with the rain. The blade jerked free. The corpse toppled.

Low short words sounded all around. Istvan tightened his grip on his sword and waited, his shoulders aching in the rain.

Chapter Five

A kick in the ribs jarred Chondos awake. He clenched his bound hands and futilely tried to jerk them apart. Bristles grated against his wrists.

"Up, slave!" a harsh voice sneered.

A whistle in the air laid a stripe of pain across his legs. He rolled up enraged, tugging at his bonds. Goblin laughter filled his ears. The whip lashed down on his shoulders. He got his feet under him and staggered up. Laughter sounded all around him. He stepped toward his tormenters.

Ropes around his ankles tightened and tripped him. He crashed awkwardly onto his face and lay struggling in the mud, listening to their ugly laughter in the rain. The whip flicked his back lightly.

He wriggled awkwardly onto his side, his shoulders aching from the strain, and sat up, then managed to get his knees under him. Rain chilled his head. He glared at his tormenters. None would come up to his shoulder, and few would reach his elbow. But they were armed, and he was not; his hands were bound, theirs were free. And the noose was gone. They had taken his hope of death from him.

A hunk of raw meat hit the ground in front of him. He stared. Did they expect that he would grovel for it with his teeth? He remembered the butchered goblins, and his stomach squirmed. He kept his face calm and looked away. Goblins jeered.

At least there was plenty of water. It dripped from the Shadow's greasy roof. He threw back his head and opened his mouth. The rain had an odd, bitter taste, but that was to be expected.

"Get up!" the goblin voice snarled again.

Once more the lash whistled through the air. Chondos' shoulder muscles ached with impotent rage. If only his hands had been tied in front of him, he would have made a grab for the whip. What matter if they killed him? Was he not better dead, if he could not escape? Would not death be better than the betrayal they wished from him?

Pain flicked across his shoulders. Chondos lurched to his feet. Bound hands wrestled at the ropes around them. His shoulders strained and ached, but the ropes held.

"Walk, slave!"

The whip curled around his hobbled legs. His helpless hands

clenched and unclenched. If he could only get them around that black-furred throat!

The goblin's mouth gaped with inhuman mirth. It raised the whip again, but another voice snarled a command Chondos did not catch. The arm with the whip stopped in mid-motion. Eyes like coals glared at him, and then the whip hand dropped.

They came crowding up around him, pushing, pinching, jostling. He lurched and staggered, one step and then another. With his hands bound behind him he could keep his balance only by moving his feet. After a moment, he realised that this was how they planned to keep him moving.

He braced his feet and tried to stand. He nearly fell, but long black arms caught him and pushed him rudely, and he went staggering on. Jabbering goblins crowded all around him, and his nose was full of their beastly stench. They kept pushing. Again and again he recovered his balance, and then another long arm sent him staggering once more.

Why had they stopped using the whip, he wondered. Was it because this worked better? Or, more likely, because the Master wanted him unharmed, and they were afraid they might do him too much damage?

He was sweating. His shoulders and bound arms hurt. It was sprinkling, but the tiny drops of rain were lost in sweat. He felt dizzy.

They pushed him on, now from one direction, now from another. His head spun. They swarmed like rats around him: giant rats that walked like men, wore armour, and carried spears and swords. And whips . . .

It seemed hours that he stumbled on. Then, suddenly, it ended. When he staggered off balance, there were no hands to catch him. He saw the ground coming up to meet him and wrenched his shoulder muscles trying to bring his hands around to break his fall. He managed to twist, and hit the ground with one shoulder. Impact emptied his lungs. Then he was lying full-length on the earth, gasping for breath, while goblin voices jabbered in the gathering dark.

The air rasped in and out of his lungs. For a while he paid no attention to the quarreling voices. They were less important than the rain that dripped on his face. He opened his dry mouth, and let the tiny trickles from the sky dribble slowly in. After a time his breath came easier. The intensity of the voices demanded his attention, and he listened.

"Our torches will go out," one was squealing. "We'll have nothing. They'll eat us!"

"I'll eat you myself if you keep squeaking," said a harsh, snarling voice that Chondos had heard before. "Have you forgotten that I can summon a Blood Drinker? None will dare approach us then!"

The other goblin muttered something unintelligible.

"No," the deep voice snarled, "this Blood Drinker knows the Master Words, all the names of the Great Ones. He will command them to turn aside, and they will cower away."

There came a babble of voices in which words were lost, and the rain thickened on his face. In the middle of it all, a goblin walked over and kicked him.

"Walk!" came the harsh voice. "Walk or be dragged."

His hands clenched and unclenched behind his back, but there was nothing he could do. Except, perhaps, tire his captors by forcing them to lift him. He gritted his teeth together and staggered to his feet.

Weariness seemed to flow through every bone. Would they ever let him sleep, he wondered, or did they plan to keep him awake and walking until he dropped? Did goblins tire as humans did, or would they just go on and on, never weakening? What would they do if he could not keep up? The masses of screaming raw flesh that they had eaten writhed in his mind; but even as he shuddered, he remembered that the Master wanted him alive. Better if they killed him. Perhaps they would force him to walk until he died. That would be the best thing.

Horror sickened him. Weariness made the thought of such a death very real. Some sentinel of firmness deep in his mind began to struggle with another part that only wanted life, and freedom from pain and fear; that wanted to go peacefully to the Master, to beg the goblins not to hurt him.

What had the men of Kudrapor faced before they died? The thought steadied him. The sentinel in his mind thrust the gibbering, terrifying thing deep, and slammed the lid. "Pertap's Ride" sang inside his brain:

> The bells rang out in Kudrapor,
> And men rose up with faces stern.
> They looked far out into the night
> But saw no tower's need-fire burn.
>
> Where is the light of Hastur's Tower?
> Why are there no stars in the sky?

The beat of the ballad steadied his feet as he staggered on. He moved aching shoulders. Goblins crowded around him, but did not touch him now.

> With fire and steel and silver blade
> The warriors battled through the night:
> Then far away, beyond the foe,
> Men thought they saw a glint of light.

Istvan peered between raindrops, awaiting the next attack. Resting his shield on his saddle, he crouched on the grey mare's back, eyes moving quickly about him. Knees and shoulders ached with chill.

How long before he tired? How long before his aching joints slowed him at a crucial moment? He shuddered. He did not want to die. *I should*, he thought. Soon the pains of age in his bones would chain him crippled to his bed. Then the slow waiting. Better to die here, to let life go in the midst of action.

A horseman rode from the circle that surrounded him. Istvan gritted his teeth and lifted his fiery sword. When you have fought for years to survive, and have come out of every battle with a thankful "I'm alive!" on your lips, it is not easy to let go.

Pain does not hurt, he told himself sternly. *Fear of pain hurts!* So it must be with death, surely? And there was an army of men depending on him.

The Borderman rode slowly through the rain. Istvan saw between the curved flaps of the leather helmet a young man's beardless face: a boy, even younger than King Chondos.

His joints hurt, and he *did* fear the pain—doubly. It could kill him now, or if it did not, it could keep him prisoner in his bed for age to kill.

The boy stopped his horse and bowed in the saddle, then drew his sword with a flourish. "You have seen scant courtesy so far, Seynyorean!" the boy said above the rain. "I would not have you die thinking ill of us. I am Shiraj, a vassal of Lord Jagat, and I come of the blood of the Maldawuts, the Clan of Pertap! Who is it that I have the honour of facing?"

Nice boy, Istvan thought. *Pity to kill him.* "Istvan DiVega," he said.

"DiVega! DiVega!" ran like a whispering echo around the ring of men. The boy's face was suddenly set and pale. But he was a Borderman. With clenched lips he raised his blade in a sketchy salute, and urged his little pony forward. Istvan loved him then. He would rather die than kill this boy.

Then Shiraj's sword was lashing toward his face, Istvan's shield rising to meet it, and he could feel his sword arm coiling back behind his head to strike. He did not want to die. Must he kill this young man, this courageous and worthy—child? Why could he not let go, and die? Die now, and get it over with!

He swept his sword high on the return cut, letting the boy's shield lift it easily away. He did not want to kill this boy, just to save his own worthless life for the few pitiful years left him. But would Shiraj give him any choice?

He could look down over the wood-and-leather shield: the little Border pony accentuated the boy's youth. He was fighting a child!

He could so easily use his height to cut down over the shield.

Then Shiraj was standing in his stirrups, and his blade drove up in a thrust. Istvan let the point slide harmlessly from the steel of his shield, checking his almost automatic cut at the wrist so innocently offered. He could get killed playing games like this!

The boy's arm drew back for another cut. Istvan raised his sword above his head, and let his shield drop. The boy's shield flinched up, but his arm crooked to deliver the countercut at the opening offered.

Istvan's sword hissed around in a half cut, and paused as Shiraj's arm lashed out. The waiting point sheathed itself in flesh just below the elbow and grated on bone. A shriek choked to a gurgle in the boy's throat. The sword fell from his hand. Istvan jerked back his own point before the boy's movement severed the muscles completely.

A chorus of gasps drowned the murmur of the rain. Istvan let his swordpoint drop, and rested the weight of his shield against his thigh. Shiraj swayed in the saddle, and Istvan saw the boy's teeth worrying his lip. Shiraj let the wood-and-leather target slide from his arm to the ground, and clapped the freed hand over the bleeding wound.

"My thanks for the honour, Lord Istvan!" His voice was shrill above the murmuring rain. Then he clapped his heels to his horse and was riding away, while blood ran down his arm and spattered on the saddle.

"No, Bimsio!" a sharp voice said. Istvan turned toward it. A Borderman was riding slowly toward him. A big man, by Border standards. On his face, Istvan could see a rapturous, exultant look, the look of a man who sees a dream coming true. Istvan had seen that look before. It meant death.

"Bismio!" the sharp voice cried again. This time Istvan saw the speaker, a lean scarred man, hawk-faced, all bone and whipcord beneath one of the old mail-shirts that came down from the legendary days of Takkarian power. Slung by a cord over his shoulder was an ancient conch-shell. He came cantering out, and the big man turned toward him, a dreamy smile on his rapt face.

"Istvan DiVega, Suktio!" he said. "Istvan the Archer!"

"I forbid it, Bimsio!" the scarred man said. "I have lost three men already. I cannot afford to lose more—and especially not you!"

"But with a shield—" Bimsio began, but Suktio cut him off.

"Even with a shield, Bimsio, his skill passes yours. Were Martos with us, he might be a match for him."

"He is their commander! Without him—"

"Without him they will still go on. They are veterans, professionals, and every company has an experienced commander. They can afford to lose him better than we can afford to lose another man."

He rode toward Istvan, his open hand raised, and stopped a few paces away.

"If I order my men to attack you all at once, Istvan DiVega," he said, "it is likely that even you would die. But so would many of my men. Go your way, Istvan DiVega. We will go ours."

Istvan looked at him closely, surprised and suspicious. It seemed to him unusually sensible for a Borderman. *Bordermen always run the wrong way . . .*

But the Borderer's sword was still in his scabbard. Istvan sheathed his own, watchfully, but the other made no move. The rain shifted its volume again, pouring down more heavily, and the wind cut through Istvan's soaked clothes. He shivered.

His hand was on his sword-hilt and his shield on his arm. If they thought to take him off guard it would be they who were surprised. He became aware of the sodden weight of his cloak hanging between his shoulder blades. At least the wind would be behind him.

They watched him expectantly. They had all sheathed their weapons now. Bowing from the saddle, Istvan turned his horse away.

The sky was still a greasy film of grey. Martos saw light above the clouds; behind the western Shadow the Twin Suns hung over the horizon. They could not be much longer, though. The cold wind rose hooting out of the north, and he wrapped his cloak more tightly around him. Where was Suktio? He had told him to hurry and get back!

The thick grey rain came battering down, drumming in his ears like a shaken rattle. Through it now he heard splashing sounds, and out of the rain came men and horses. He recognised Suktio riding in the lead, and rode to meet him, with Paidros and Valiros behind.

"What took you so—" He started to say *long*, but then he saw the horses with the bodies of men strapped across their backs. He was suddenly dumb. He heard Paidros' voice from behind.

"What happened? Did you ride into an ambush?"

"No." Suktio shook his head sadly. Suddenly he let out a bark of bitter laughter. "Or maybe we did. We saw a scout leave the main body and went after him."

"I see!" Paidros scowled at the corpses. "One less of them and two less of us."

"Three less of us," said Suktio. "Shiraj has a hole in his arm. But we couldn't kill the scout. It was Istvan DiVega."

All three Kadarins echoed the name.

"I could have killed him!" Bimsio came riding up from behind Suktio. "I may not be as good with a sword alone, but with shields I can take him! Suktio stopped me."

"You should have all gone after him at once!" Paidros snapped.

"And how many men would I have had left then?" snarled Suktio. "We didn't have time. Look! The sky's darkening now! Do you still want to attack, Martos? If so, we'll have to attack in the dark! They haven't stopped, and their vanguard must be reaching the edge of the dust. They were still drifting south, but DiVega will stop that, I imagine. He was at the road when we caught up with him. Well, Martos?"

Martos struggled with his frozen tongue. He glanced up at the sky again, blinking as water splashed into his face. At first he thought the drenched twilight had not changed, but then he saw that the drizzling roof of cloud was in fact darkening even as he watched.

On the other side of the wall of Shadow, hidden now by the rain, the sky would be glowing with sunset. No longer could the rays of the Twin Suns pass over Dark Things' stronghold to turn the sky blue above the clouds. Up there now stars would wink to life, and a host of wandering moons would bleach the top of the clouds with brilliant light; but here below was only deepening gloom and drizzling rain. And Istvan DiVega's vast army still marched toward Manjipor.

"We ride," he said, his stutter gone. "If we hit their rear hard, we can push them south and confuse them, and maybe keep them from finding their way back to the road, and if they turn on us we may be able to draw them back into the dust."

Paidros frowned and shook his head. A few moments later his little force was on the move, riding through the rain toward the rear of the huge army.

Istvan's mustache dripped with rain, and his tired mare plodded wearily through pooling water, dust sliding under her hooves. The drizzling twilight was dimming all around him. The stars would be coming out above the clouds soon, as the Twin Suns vanished. But by then he should have reached the army.

Alive! But why should he be happy over that, he wondered. It was not as though he would live forever. Death was behind him, creeping closer and closer. Whenever he tried to force himself to turn and meet the enemy, habit made him flinch away.

Death! Why should he fear it so? Everyone went through it, sooner or later, hundreds of times if what they said was true—*if* it was true. He'd read enough of the philosophers to know the usual theory—the only one the Hasturs did not snicker at, or so it was claimed—that there was in truth only one soul, or being, and that the whole universe, substance and spirit alike, was compounded from the same stuff. But some maintained that individuals were splintered fragments of the whole; others that all grew from a kind of common center.

One of the Kadarin philosophers claimed that the single soul raced back and forth in time, so that a man might die and be reborn as his father. Or his mother. Or a pheasant he had killed for his dinner. The man you killed might have been yourself a thousand lifetimes back. Another sage maintained that the dead were absorbed back into the Primal Being, and that memories of former births were merely accidentally acquired by the new growths. The Hasturs were of little help, commenting that the truth was more than a mortal mind could grasp, but that all theories were partly true.

Istvan sighed, and peered through the crystal wires of rain. Ahead of him, beyond the shrouding storm, he could hear the mingled sounds of the army: creaking, chattering, jingling, splashing. The wind still blew on his back, but the sounds were a little to the right. He turned the mare toward them.

All those theories, but he still did not know what to expect when he died. What happened between death and rebirth, assuming there was a rebirth? Was it like sleep? Like a visit to some marvellous spiritual realm? *When people grow old, their bodies wear out, and they have to go find new ones.* He had told that to a child once. He wished that he could look at it that simply.

He had come very close to finding out, back there by the road. If they had forgotten the ancient tradition, and rushed him all at once, they might well have killed him. Some men would have laughed at the Bordermen for throwing that advantage away. But Istvan would not. He knew the life the Bordermen must live, and he knew the purpose such traditions served, however much "practical" men might laugh at them. They burned away fear and hardened the will.

Above the jumbled pulse of water pounding down around him, he could hear clearly the various mingled noises of the army ahead. Then the rainbeat quickened, swelling to a din that drowned out the sounds of the marching men. It lasted only a short time and then began to slacken.

He listened through the lessening mutter of the rain and heard faint splashing and the creaking of gear, but his eyes were still baffled by the chattering water and could guess no direction. Somewhere in this rain, two armies moved. One was in front of him, but where was the other? He thought furiously, and urged on his exhausted mare.

The light was fading now. Dusk crept over the dust and darkened the rain-filled air. The clouds were black above the teeming drops; the cold wind gnawed at his joints. The murmur of the rain grew loud and soft by turns.

He listened uneasily. He could hear his own men ahead, but

where were the Bordermen he had fought? And the rest of Martos'
army? It was their lack of fear that made the Bordermen what they
were—but why had their leader acted so cautiously? That was
unusual. There was something odd, something that didn't quite fit,
about a Borderman who worried about losses. Had there been some
other reason? Time, perhaps? Time to do what?

In the lessening rain he heard faint splashing sounds: the feet of
many horses churning shallow pools. His heels hit his horse's ribs.
Through the thinning veil of rain, he saw before him the vast black
mosaic of his army. Twisting in the saddle he saw behind, half-
hidden by the gloaming and the storm, misty figures in a moving
swarm, like the ghosts of toy men on toy horses.

Swarming goblins jabbered and snarled as Chondos staggered
through the gloom of the Shadow.

> *What is that light that gleams afar,*
> *Flaming white and gold and red?*
> *Hastur has built him his new tower,*
> *And counts us now among the dead.*

The old ballad steadied his feet. Sweat and rain rolled down his
face, and spattered his sleepy eyes with spray.

> *If a man might ride to Hastur's Tower,*
> *To tell them that we still fight on,*
> *Might not the men of Kudrapor*
> *Yet live to see another dawn?*

The road ran between steep, undercut cliffs. Jumbled foothills
rose up before them, a maze of caverns dividing massive mounds of
stone. The roof of the Shadow was scored with stripes of black and
grey. Nightfall. Goblins clustered under an overhang. Tiny flashes
sought Chondos' eyes. Flickers of light outlined black shapes. Light
flared: a moment later the goblins emerged with torches that sputtered in the rain.

Puffs of smoke and steam obscured the light. The goblins dodged
back into the recess, waiting for the rain to lessen. Bands of grey
faded above, and blackness claimed the sky. Torches wavered,
washing red light over dark rock. Piggish goblin eyes glowed; sharp
fangs glistened.

"Hurry," the deep-voiced leader snarled from Chondos' elbow.
Goblins, Chondos recalled, were among the few servants of the
Dark Lords who could or would handle fire.

"We must go to the caverns," a shrill voice shrieked. "But with
this much water the torches won't even get us that far!"

"Call up your Blood Drinker," called another voice. "You've
been boasting of your power; now use it!"

Other voices joined in, but now they seemed to lose all human semblance, and Chondos, swaying on his feet, could no longer recognise words in the chorus of beastial sounds. Exhaustion crept over him in waves, despite the rain that pounded on his head, spattering on the already soaked hair slicked against his scalp.

Chondos closed his eyes, and slumped. He felt his knees hit ground. His shoulders were aching and his arms were numb; he could no longer feel the cords around his wrists. Pain and exhaustion drove all thought from his mind as he swayed on his knees. The red light blurred, and the bestial voices faded. A foot slammed into his ribs. He felt himself falling, and then cruel hands seized him and jerked him roughly to his feet.

The rain was lighter. He must have slept. He heard the leader's voice in an eerie, cracked singsong, chanting strange words. Turning, he saw one armoured, black-furred shape standing apart from the others. In its hand a moving torch created patterns of flame.

"Vidraj! Arise Vidraj!" it chanted. The torch rose high on the end of a long black arm, whipped down again, then shot sharply to the side. *"Corpse Immortal! Lord of the Night! Vidraj! Vidraj! Come from the shelter that enfolds you! Arise! Vidraj! Amivahi! Amarkaya!"*

Chondos shook his head, confused. Something very strange about the pitch and tone of the creature's voice grated along his spine and made him shudder, as though the sounds were somehow piercing his brain.

"Vidraj! By the Eight Lords from the Dark World, Arise! Vidraj! Arise!"

Sleep, and the pain in his shoulders and neck, seemed remote.

"By the Covenant! Kravya Amarta! Arise! Vidraj! Arise! Come to my calling! Come through the air! Vidraj! Arise! Vidraj!" The voice went on.

Suddenly a shriek behind him brought Chondos' head around. The chant was cut off as a white shape darted into torchlight. Something long and brown whirled at the end of its arm. A black goblin fell. More white shapes came scuttling from the darkness. Chondos realised that these were the other goblins that had fled from him by the river.

Many of the black goblins had already fallen, cut down from behind. Shrieking, the survivors turned on the intruders. Rusty blades were bathed in blood. The screams of the dying drowned out the rain. The reek of burning fur reached Chondos' nose: the black goblins were using their torches as weapons, thrusting them into their opponents' eyes. And above the war-cries and death-screams, Chondos heard the leader's voice again, rising in a triumphant, rasping chant:

"Vidraj! Blood now is poured for you! Cringing we wait for you! Vidraj! Arise Vidraj! Amivahan! Lord of the Night! Vidraj!" The voice rose to a triumphant shriek, and the leader turned to face a bounding white shape, whipping the burning torch into its eyes, while his other hand ripped his sword from his scabbard. The white goblin reeled back, and the leader's brown blade hissed as he hacked through its ankle.

Chondos staggered back against the cliff and leaned on the stone to keep from falling. All around him goblins struggled, screaming and jabbering, stabbing, biting, gouging. He closed and reopened his sleep-soused eyes and wondered what would happen if he tried to run. He gathered himself, feeling his muscles leaden and flaccid.

Something crashed against his mind. He reeled against the rock, feeling the mind-shield spell leap into memory. The goblins were suddenly silent. Shouting and fighting stopped; even the wounded stopped screaming. A man strode into the light of the torches. Not tall, but lean and elegant and unafraid. He wore Border dress, but his face was pale. Bloodless. The goblins cringed at his feet.

Chondos blinked his sticky eyes, realising that the clothes were older than any of the patched heirlooms his Borderers wore; more like clothing from some ancient tapestry. Chondos' knees gave way and he slid down the stone. His mind was blank; he did not even care that his bound arms wrenched their sockets.

"Down, Kravyad!" The power of the voice made him tremble, and the goblins fell to earth and clawed the dust. "Who has dared to summon me! Should I care if you eat each other? Fools!" His eyes threw back the light like burning rubies. Then Chondos felt those eyes come to rest upon him, and suddenly the figure blurred and it was standing over him. Red eyes looked into his own.

"What is this?" the voice said softly. "A gift for me?"

"No!" That was the leader's voice. He came running up and threw himself down in the grey dust before the pale one's feet. "No, Vidraj, he is for the Master. That is why I summoned you."

Wounded goblins whimpered.

"So *you* summoned me? Beware, Kravyad, such knowledge is dangerous! And beware how you thwart me! If the Master wishes . . ." He stopped, looking at Chondos closely. "Ah," he said, more softly, "this is the one for whom they hunted? This, then, is the new King of the Takkars? And it is for the Master alone." Pale lips writhed back from needle fangs, and a hiss sounded. "I am thirsty, I am dry as a stone, and the Master forbids me this!" A pale tongue darted over the white fangs, over the ivory lips.

"There is blood spilled here, great one!" The goblin leader leaped up, seized a black goblin that lay nearby, dying, its bowels spread around, blood pouring out. It whimpered, then screamed as he dragged it roughly over. The vampire looked down coldly.

"Foul blood," he said. "But it is wet." He knelt, and pushed his face down to the wound, the long white tongue lapping out.

Chondos shuddered, and closed his eyes. Wounded goblins began to scream again. Suddenly he heard the goblin leader snarl, and then another voice: "Great one! Lord!"

"What is it, Kravyad?" said Vidraj.

Chondos opened his eyes. The vampire was kneeling only a few feet away. His face was smeared with blood from the torn goblin body that lay in front of him. One of the white goblins grovelled nearby, clawing at the dust. The leader of the black goblins stood over him, scowling.

"The prisoner was *ours*, Lord. He was on our side of the river. They stole him from us! We should get the reward!"

Needle teeth flashed between blood-smeared lips. "Why should *I* care?" sneered Vidraj.

"Drive these worms away!" snarled the black goblin. "Then we can take this to the Master and get the reward. Chase them back to their holes!"

"No," said Vidraj. He licked black blood from his lips with a grimace, and Chondos saw that tongue and lips were coloured now, a faint bluish-purple flush. "What do I care for you rat-folk and your petty quarrels? You're barely good enough for food." In a sudden blur of movement he was on his feet, towering above the stunted creatures. "So you summoned *me* to take your prisoner to the Master?"

"To guard us, and take us past the great ones who hunt!"

"So that *you* can get the reward!" The purple lips writhed, and Chondos shivered as the vampire laughed. "And now you wish me to drive away these others?" Another laugh, and the red eyes glowed with malicious humour. "Are there then so many of you? You were killing each other when I arrived; and I see much dead meat on the ground, much blood wasted."

Suddenly the scarlet eyes were turned on Chondos. He shrank back. This was no mere walking corpse with teeth, like the one he had killed the day before. This was a Master Vampire, filled with power and skilled in its use—and old, old . . .

"I shall take this to the Master. Those who wish to claim the reward may come." The red eyes glowed, and Chondos felt them beat upon the barriers of his mind.

The symbols of the spell that shielded Chondos' mind filled his eyes and ears, blinding him to the glowing eyes, drowning the restless mutter of the rain. The wave of power fell from his brain, and he was back, crouching at the foot of the stone, with cold water spattering over him, a mass of goblins huddled nearby, and the glowing eyes of the vampire red in the darkness.

"So," said Vidraj. "You think your puny memorised spell will protect you from *me!* Fool!" He laughed, and the red eyes glowed.

Chondos' leg twitched. He looked down and saw the muscles in both legs begin to jerk in uncontrollable spasms. They began to move. His heels dug into the mud, and his legs began to straighten. He tried to kick out, but his legs were numb. He could only watch them move, sink into the mud, press his back against the rock. Something flowed about him like water, lifting his body as the legs pushed him up. His back and bound hands scraped along the rough stone. One foot drew back and dug in, then the other.

He tried to struggle, to throw himself off balance and fall forward, but something like a solid slab of air caught him and pushed his head back against the stone. Then he was standing, leaning against the boulder. One foot jerked in an awkward step—then the other, and he was tottering forward.

"You see, fool?" Vidraj whispered. "You cannot fight me." Chondos felt his body totter ahead, step after step.

The red eyes moved away, and suddenly Chondos' aching legs belonged to him again. He stood swaying while the vampire's voice hissed softly through the thudding rain:

"If need be, I can march you all the way to Rajinagara. But there is no need. You will remember that it is useless to resist my power." The voice changed, became powerful, commanding. "You *will* walk. Or *they* shall drive you! Bring him, Kravyad!"

The vampire turned away. Goblins came crowding through the pounding rain: black-furred and white-furred, and smooth-skinned pallid goblins, their white skin wet and thick. Bloody meat was in their mouths. Torches smoked and sputtered in their hands: he saw the dim flames reflected glittering in the huge sickle eyes. But all he saw was blurred by exhaustion. He felt sick and dizzy, and his head ached. As they crowded in around him, he staggered on behind the vampire, wondering if they would ever let him sleep.

Pounding his heels on his horse's sides, Istvan DiVega urged her through drumming rain, hearing the splashing of an army at his heels. Men of Nomenos DiGasclon's company stared slack-jawed as he galloped into their lines. He slid down from his exhausted mare, and leaned his head against the saddle, feeling the need for sleep in the hollows of his aching bones.

"Commander DiVega!" A young officer, one of the lieutenants in charge of a third of the company, reined up beside him. "Where have you been? The Captain said—"

"No time for that," Istvan interrupted. "There's an army right behind. Where's your Captain? Get him, and get your Seer here, fast! Tell your men to be ready!" He closed his eyes for a moment, feeling the hard leather of the saddle wet against his forehead, sleep crawling behind his eyes.

There were sharp voices and commands behind him, and the rasping clatter of steel. Suddenly he realised that the danger of falling asleep was very real. He jerked hs head up from the saddle, blinking as thin rain sprinkled his face. The sky above was dark: the suns had set. Then he saw that the men had stopped and were pulling out their bows, slipping shields on their arms, buckling helmets under their chins . . .

Nomenos DiGasclon came riding up, and behind him Boros DiVega.

"DiGasclon! Get your men moving again. Have them ride as they arm! Where's your Seer?"

"He's coming now," DiGasclon said, and turning his horse, he began barking orders to the men.

"Find the Seer closest to Firencio DiVega. Tell him that every company that is not attacked directly . . . No, wait—" Istvan rubbed his brows furiously, trying to think through the fog of weariness. "Tell him that the front part of the army must keep moving. The whole point of this attack is delay. Now, we're about three miles south of where we ought to be; if we angle north we'll hit the road. He's to take all the forward companies, march on to make camp, and—"

"Here they come, sir!" It was a young man's voice—the lieutenant's. Istvan's head snapped up, and his eyes hunted through the twilight and the rain and focussed at last on a mottling of moving shadow. They were still a few miles out, there was still time—a little time. . . .

"Keep moving! Don't stop or turn until they're close. Wait for my order," he shouted. "Cousin Boros! Get your company ready to support us." Boros saluted and rode off. Istvan turned back to the Seer. "Message to Prince Phillipos, Kardom D'Aglar, Esrith Gunnar, and Asbiorn Kung. The footmen should stop and form up ranks. Then I want the DiFlaccas . . ."

He went on giving orders, his voice calm, as he watched the blurred pattern in the twilight turn into tiny shapes of men and horses growing slowly out of the distance.

Chapter Six

Martos watched tiny black flecks like flocking birds grow out of the rainy twilight into a vast herd of horses with men on their backs.

"We must strike quickly and get away!" said Paidros. He pointed. "There, at the rear, where the companies branch out."

The Seynyorean army looked like a huge fallen tree, leaves hidden by a mist of rain. At the rear they could see the companies spread out like roots, with little clumps of Bordermen between them like clods of earth.

"That exposed wing—" Martos pointed to a company that jutted north toward them. "Circle ahead, and come in from the northwest." If they could move in fast enough, he thought, they would crash right through that stippling of horsemen and ride on south and east, drawing any pursuit deeper into the dust.

"Right," said Paidros. "I see it." He rose in his stirrups. "At the canter!" his calm voice rolled. "To the right—wheel!"

Martos' saddle jolted under him: Thunderhead's muscles bunched and stretched.

Raindrops clanged on his morion's brim. He ran his dry tongue futilely over dry lips, then leaned his head back to drink from the sky. His heart pounded in his chest as though to batter through his breastplate.

Suddenly he remembered Kumari's ear pressed to his ribs, her laugh: "*A dance!*" And her heart pounding in the white valley between crushed breasts under him. Would he ever feel her heart beating against his again? Would his heart still beat tomorrow? It beat now, louder than hooves on muffling dust, louder even than the clatter of water on steel.

"To the left—wheel!" Paidros sang from beside him. "Steady at the canter! Bows—out!"

The Seynyoreans marched on as though the grey waste was empty about them. *Surely*, Martos thought, *they must see us now?*

"Bows up!" Paidros shouted. "Nock!"

Enemy animals suddenly milled, as the horsemen shifted out of marching order into line.

"Pick your target!" Paidros called. "Aim!"

Balanced on the swaying saddle, Martos stretched the string, sighting over the arrowhead at a moving mounted figure. The air ahead filled with tiny black bristles that were not rain.

"Loose!" Paidros yelled, and the thrumming of strings was followed by the hiss of arrows.

"Charge!"

Then they were galloping over grey dust, while enemy arrows whistled down around them.

The Conch-horn of Chandra bayed behind them, and Jagat's men howled Border war-cries.

All around him Martos heard the strumming of bows as he drew and nocked and loosed and drew and nocked and loosed and shapes ahead grew nearer and larger, bulking through the rain.

"Bows down!" Paidros screamed. "Swords out!"

The bow went into the case by his boot. He felt the weight of the shield on his arm and the sword sweeping free in the air.

Out of the gloom of rain, Martos saw rushing eyes glaring over shield-rims, and raised wet swords.

His horse crashed into the other line: the dwarf-blade poised above his head swung hawk-swift at the nearest pair of eyes. A shield rose to hide them, pealing like a bell beneath his steel. A wet sword lifted and lashed at his head as his own shield roared on his arm; his blade hissed along his shield-edge. He felt metal parting and soft flesh beneath. Thunderhead hurtled on, through the hammering clamour of battle.

Istvan listened to the belling of metal, tense on his tired mare's back. Shame swept through him. He should be there, in the middle of the battle, leading his men.

But that was Nomenos DiGasclon's work, and he was doing it well. Istvan saw him, looming in his saddle, grey sword whirling. His voice was a trumpet.

Prince Phillipos cantered up, shining in the twilight on his fine white horse. Rain ran ruinously over his polished armour.

"Everything as you ordered," said Phillipos, first saluting, then gesturing at the long pike-line.

A solid wall of shields bristled with pikes; men with halberds and longer spears stood behind, and mixed among them were Carrodians with their short heavy axes, and the men of Kardom D'Aglar's company with drawn swords.

The covers were gone from the sharp points of pikes; raindrops shattered on the edges of halberds.

"Advance!" Istvan said. His bright blade waved. The bristling wall stalked toward the swirling horsemen. Istvan knew that Boros DiVega's company was poised now on the enemy flank, and Rinmull of Ojaini's men were moving in. He had kept three companies in reserve.

Ahead, the rest of the army marched on. Kadarins came crashing through DiGasclon's line; a clamour of battered metal rang. Rinmull shouted the Ojaini war-cry, and Bordermen like bees were all around them: Kadarin and Kantaran fought.

Whirling his deadly sword in a circle, Martos hurtled through the enemy line. Suddenly, little leather-covered men came swarming in from the left, milling madly on earth-coloured ponies.

Two of them rode at him. His great sword flew up weightless in his hand, swept the head from one, then spun to shear through the shoulder of the other. Blood pumped onto poisoned dust.

He saw Rodericos surrounded by Bordermen, his shield leaping up to block a cut from the left. Another stabbed from the right, under the sword arm drawn back from the counter. Martos saw bright blood burst from the artery.

Raging in grief, he spurred through the press, his sword soaring in his hand. Raindrops clattered on his helm; sword-strokes thundered on his shield. Water spattered from his wheeling blade as he hurled a Borderman flying from the saddle, shattering his wood-and-leather helm.

Then Martos saw beyond them a thicket of spears, sprouting from a dyke of shields. Steel pealed on his shield; another sword stabbed from his right.

Martos' heavier blade beat the thrust away, then spun at the swordsman's wrist. A hand dropped, blood pulsing, but Martos' long blade swept on in a deadly circle, up behind his back and over his helmet, and, swooping like a swallow in his hand, dipped past the shield-edge of the man on his left. He felt steel quiver as his edge slashed wood and splintered frail bones in the temple.

Then his eyes flew back to the moving hedge of spears. Even at full tilt a charge would break on such a wall. His men had been slowed and scattered in the fighting; they would shatter on that phalanx, futile as a child's toy against a grown man's breastplate.

And the tongue in his mouth was dead.

Istvan's wet cloak seemed made of lead under the weight of crushing rain. His sword's flame gleamed on Phillipos' breastplate, and glittered on the deadly points of pikes.

Feet splashing above grey dust, the phalanx advanced, pikes stretched out, halberds drawn back to strike. Double-bitted Carrodian axes and fine Seynyorean swords were raised in the rust-bringing rain.

Water ran down over Prince Phillipos' armor. The plumes on his helm were a tangle of dripping fibers and spines. Istvan saw determined calm in his face: the Prince was a warrior; Istvan had no more doubt.

Booming mixed with shouting made Istvan twist in his saddle. A horse had backed into the line of shields and, startled, was kicking the offending metal while its shaken rider clung to its back. Ahead, milling horsemen were slashing at each other. The hammering of metal drowned the clamour of water.

The phalanx pushed into the press, grinding friend and foe together. The hooves of startled horses pounded bronze. Istvan nudged his tired mare forward, watching the battle through a veil of falling water. Raindrops stung his eyes with savage force.

Martos struggled with his leaden tongue, and pulled up his restive horse, staring about wildly. He could not find Paidros in the tumult around him, but he saw Valiros not far away, trading sword-strokes with a Seynyorean veteran.

Martos reared Thunderhead around. He had outrun most of his men, cleaving through the fighting with a skill few could match. A Borderman, rushing him, battered on his shield. Fending away a cut at his temple, Martos sent steel swooping over the rim of the smaller man's buckler. Wood and leather crunched under his edge.

With a savage cut at a second man who tried to close on his right, he clapped spur to horse. Thunderhead bounded through dusk, and startled Bordermen watched them pass.

Leather bucklers rattled under hammering blows; steel shields boomed like gongs. Men shouted and screamed as they killed and died. Riderless Border ponies plunged. Pealing armour parted beneath the sword's edge, and steel-clad Kadarins tumbled to the ground.

Martos sensed behind him a half-seen horseman rushing at his back, sword raised and ready. A tug at Thunderhead's bridle brought the vague figure near: the sword swung down at his back. Twisting in his saddle, Martos whirled a lashing cut across the falling blade's flat. Steel chimed as he dashed it down. The man's dangling sword arm hampered his shield-edge as Martos' point flipped up through the open mouth.

Martos felt the dead jaws clamp on his blade: blood flooded out between them. Then he felt the sword-hilt wrench in his hand as the body toppled. Teeth grated on the steel as he pulled it free.

Thiondos and Odessis fought at Valiros' side, shields roaring under sword-strokes, making Valiros' stolen Seynyorean steed prance skittishly. Empty saddles told of others. Martos' heart contracted. Where was Paidros?

Martos burst through the line of mail-clad men, his sharp sword flying on the wind. Thunderhead's shoulder hurled one bony steed staggering into another, long legs scrabbling on slippery ash: both went down in an ungainly sprawl.

Seynyoreans scattered. Martos' sword sliced steel and bone. Fighting to Valiros' side he tried to speak. But only a gurgle would come from his throat, drowned in the drumming of the rain.

He heard the war-cries of Jagat's men, turning to meet an attack on their flank, and the hammering crash of weapons on armour. Martos waved his sword frantically, pointing out the way. Dim in rainy darkness he saw surging figures fight.

Valiros knew Martos well, and recognised the plea in his eyes.

"You want me to give the order?" he asked, watching Martos' face closely. "You want the company to turn—that way?" He stood in his stirrups, frowning to the left, where the Kantaran Bordermen swarmed. "To wheel left?" Martos nodded dumbly. Valiros frowned, and stared into the fight.

"You're mad!" he said, shaking his head. Then, raising his voice above the clatter of battle: "Rally! To the left—wheel!"

From somewhere in the darkness Paidros echoed the command.

Istvan DiVega saw the big white horse turn and dash back into the melee, but that meant nothing to him then. He longed to hurl himself into the battle, to offer his life to protect his men, but his part now was to watch. Pattering raindrops pecked at his hood.

A Kadarin came storming through the Kantaran men, red steel spinning in his hand. Prince Phillipos clapped spurs to his horse. Istvan saw him plunge into the Kadarin's path, his fine blade belling on the Kadarin's shield.

A glancing sword-cut scraped sodden feathers from the Prince's helm. Istvan watched the tension in Phillipos' wrist, and relaxed: the Prince was a fair match for his foe.

A Kadarin war-horse checked, rearing at the barricade of shields. The man on its back stared too long: a pike darted out; his shield knocked it away, but a swinging halberd caught him by his shoulder and dragged him from the saddle, down, out of Istvan's sight.

Martos' little army was trapped now, Istvan thought in sour triumph. Boros DiVega was closing on their flank. He could hear Border war-cries on the far side of the fight. *How shall I tell Birthran?* It would be a bloody victory. Most of Martos' company would feed the Border fields.

Istvan heard a command shouted above the clatter of steel and sensed ominous changes in the pattern of battle. Wildly lashing sword arms switched their slant, as though sudden winds were ruffling a thicket of steel. Metal-clad Kadarins were clustering together. Ordinary horsemen would have milled in confusion, their mounts still skittish from the charge, but the Kadarin war-horses were the best in the world, utterly calm in the madness of battle. It was horse-breeding that made the Kadarin cavalry great.

Prince Phillipos' whistling blade lashed in a circle, his steel shield tolling. The Kadarin's helmet shattered and rang, and limp as a scarecrow he flew from the saddle, dead or unconscious—the Healers would learn which later.

As Istvan watched, the battle's shape changed. Like a river current shifting at the turn of the tide, swarming figures eddied in the dark. A sudden gap of silence opened in the middle of the fight, as Kadarin warriors vanished from the centre, to plunge into the flurry of the Kantaran attack.

Little Border ponies scattered in shoals as tight-packed massive Kadarin horses crashed between them, sharp death swinging in their riders' hands. Leather bucklers rattled under hammering swords; steel shields boomed like gongs.

In a moment the Kadarins had burst free, with only empty dust before them. But beyond, Istvan could hear Border war-cries across the dark, where Jagat's men still fought.

Amid the clangour of metal, Martos and Valiros rode through battle, grating steel battering their ears. Valiros shouted as loud as he could, but the Bordermen paid no heed.

All of Suktio's men fought here against Seynyoreans crowding in from the rear, crushing the Bordermen into enemy ranks. Martos saw Suktio and spurred to his side. Valiros followed him, close as a shadow.

"Move out!" Valiros shouted. "Turn your men left! Get them out of here!"

Suktio's sword clattered off a helmet; his leather buckler rattled as he guarded the return. Martos spurred Thunderhead. The big horse's shoulder sent a bony steed staggering, its rider clinging helplessly to its back.

"Turn your men!" shouted Valiros. "Get them moving north!"

"We're busy here!" Suktio snapped with a shake of his head. A Seynyorean sword-stroke rattled his buckler. Another hissed at Martos' face, and belled on his lifted shield.

Seynyoreans swirled in from every side. Swords lashing all around him, Martos struggled with his leaden tongue, desperately hunting for words, his blade a sharp pendulum at the end of his arm.

"Suktio—" Words burst into Martos' mind. He struggled to stutter them. "Suktio! *You're not fighting for the land!*" A swordpoint darted at his eyes. His rising shield blinded him. He heard a shrill tinkle like shattering glass, felt his shield lurch as the stabbing sword broke.

"What?" shouted Suktio. "What's that you say?"

Thunderhead reared up, hammering with iron-shod hooves. Martos fought his frozen tongue, tried to find words as a sword-edge came sighing. He sucked in breath and swung up his shield, licking his lips as the weapon crashed on his arm.

"Will the death of all your men buy back a foot of land?" he shrieked. His sword skittered off a helmet. Words, words, trying to move arms and tongue at the same time: "If not, get them *away* from here!"

A sword flicked across the top of his lifting shield. It stopped at the end of the stroke, and suddenly its point was lancing at his eye. Chin slamming into his breastplate, he bent toward his horse's mane, his blade spinning on the pivot of elbow and wrist toward the hand he could not see.

His morion rocked on his head; ears trembled with the grating of metal on metal as the sharp point slid on steel above his ear. Then it fell away, sword and bleeding arm together. Thunderhead shuddered as a red flood dyed his coat. The falling forearm bounced from Martos' knee and dropped to the poisoned ash.

Suktio's pony reared and whirled. "Away, now, away!" Martos heard the Borderman shout. "Need lies elsewhere! Follow me! Away!"

The whining hum of the Conch-horn of Chandra rose above the clamour of metal. Little Border ponies whirled and scattered from the battle.

Freed from the need for words, Martos lashed his sword back and forth in a dance of slaughter: saddle after saddle was emptied by whistling strokes. Ranging up and down the line, hewing left and right, he built such a barricade of riderless horses that the Bordermen were gone before any Seynyorean knew of their retreat.

Then he whirled Thunderhead and followed the Bordermen into the rain-dark night, Valiros riding amazed behind him. Pride swelled up warm inside him. Despite the odds, he had delayed the Royal Army, made it stop to fight.

Yet even that was a little thing. More importantly, he had conquered his tongue in the middle of a battle: he had needed to speak, and he had spoken.

Istvan watched the enemy host vanish in the darkness and the rain. His back ached, and weariness weighted his eyes. He listened to the groans of wounded men. Splashing water clattered on his helm. Weary, aging muscles ached. Sleep! He needed it, needed it badly. So did his men. Sleep, hot food, and shelter from the rain. Dry clothes, warm beds, a solid roof above their heads, that was what they needed. That was what they couldn't get.

By now the rest of the army would be starting to set up camp. A cold camp, lashed by pitiless rain and beaten by the vicious, bitter wind; but a place to sleep. But these tired men, weary from the battle, must march on through the rain with no chance of rest, must carry their dead and wounded. The three companies that had been left out of the fighting could act as a guard for the others. Not that Martos would attack again tonight. Both sides had been severely mauled in this battle: Martos' troops must be as weary as his own men.

Those Healers who had not left after the last battle were busy in the dark shambles where the wounded lay bleeding and groaning while the savage rain poured down.

Disspirited, Istvan slumped in the saddle, listening to water beating on his hood. Tonight he must march men worn out by slaughter across weary miles to their waiting camp. But then in the morning they must march again: to leave them resting would invite an attack.

They were barely a day's march from Manjipor, but at Manjipor they must fight still another battle; this time not against Martos' little troop, but against the assembled army of Lord Jagat. By morning, Martos' reinforcements would have arrived. He would no doubt attack on the road to the city, and then fall back to—

Ojakota!

It flashed into Istvan's brain sudden as lightning: the fact his weary mind had hunted for hours. He had forgotten Ojakota: that could mean disaster—or salvation. He shouted for the Seer.

Were there supplies on Ojakota? Or had Ironfist's men stripped the castle in leaving?

Martos saw Paidros ride out of the darkness with blood running down his face, but the little man chuckled at Martos' worried look.

"Scratch!" he said with a shake of his head. Then his face grew sober. "There are others with worse. Patraclos is dead. And Darios, Evarin, and Pirasos, either dead or close to it. Out of the fighting anyway! And what have we gained by it?"

"Time!" Martos said. "We stopped them! We've done what Jagat sent us to do. Do you think they will go on tonight? If they follow us, we can draw them on, back into the dust!" Pride strengthened his voice and banished the stutter; he spoke clearly above the rustle of rain. "They cannot go on. They must camp where they are. Morning will find them still on the dust! Tomorrow we'll turn them with larger numbers."

"You think so?" said Paidros. "Fool! Look behind you! Look back at the place where we fought them! Five, perhaps six companies are there! The rest went on marching. They'll be setting up camp and spreading out their blankets. They'll be at Ojakota an hour after noon, and nuzzling Jagat's pickets before nightfall!"

Startled, Martos turned in his saddle and stared through the rain-laced night. There was little he could see, now that the storm clouds no longer glowed. The wind battered his face with cold drops, and water clattered and rattled on his helm. But that mottled patch of shade—the enemy host—was smaller than it ought to have been. Smaller than it had been when he and his men had attacked.

He peered west, through the veil of falling water, trying to find the rest of Istvan's army, but the darkness had hidden them long ago. The hollow applause of the rain drummed on his helmet. He sat slumped in the saddle and heard Paidros bellow for Romulos and Styllis. His tongue was again a lump of useless meat. He had felt so proud of this battle! But he had only thrown away men's lives for nothing! Failure curdled sour inside him. He heard the growl of Paidros' voice, issuing orders above the rain.

"Follow the Seynyoreans," the little man said. "Settle yourselves in close to their camp. And when you think they're about to go to sleep—play them every trumpet-call you ever learned! Wake them up! Make them think they are under attack! Don't let them go back to sleep."

Martos stirred, but his tongue was numb. He could only make inarticulate sounds that were drowned in the rush of the rain.

"There he is!" said Paidros. "Wait here a moment!" He spurred his horse off, into the weeping night, and vanished among the mob of earth-coloured Border ponies. When he came back, Suktio rode beside him, and other Bordermen behind.

"Watch out for their scouts," Martos heard Paidros say. "They'll be hunting for you! But keep them awake! Play them a reveille in the middle of the night! Then sound the charge, just as they start to go back to sleep."

Sleep! Martos slumped, weary, defeated, in his saddle. He remembered Rodericos falling from his horse, and the memory mocked him with his failure, mocked his vanity and stupidity. The rain beat down, pattering on his helmet. The sound was growing softer: the rain was lessening again.

Blunders like this would bring no fame.

And where was Kumari tonight? Asleep in her bed, far, far away. Did she think of him? Or had she taken another lover already, with Martos' child barely stirring in her womb?

He realised Paidros was speaking to him. He looked up, blinking, and wondered if it was rain in his eyes.

"Come along, Martos," said Paidros. "Back to the horses! We'll get some sleep. Sleep will be our most potent weapon now."

Chondos staggered sleepless over poisoned ash. Water slicked his hair flat against his scalp, a clammy cap that made him shiver. Sleep! Would they ever let him sleep?

The world was a blur that swayed before his eyes. Sleep was a mystery, unknown and wonderful, rare and unobtainable. He staggered on. The wet dust was slippery underneath his feet. All around him goblins jabbered and laughed, driving him through the cold rain.

Sometimes they hurried him on too fast, and the hobbles on his ankles tightened and tripped him. Then all the goblins tittered and jeered, kicking his ribs hard, while the dust made him cough and gasp for air. Then the whip would whistle down on his shoulders, *crack* on the tender weals it had already left there . . .

Pain filled his senses. Pain and hate.

. . . And then would come the bell of the vampire's voice, warning them in tones rich with menace. Suddenly the goblins would cower and quail, and soon they would be marching on as before, Chondos' back sticky with blood from the whip.

His wounds were washed by the beat of the rain, as he staggered on through the night of Shadow. Icy water hammered on his head. His feet stumbled on in darkness. He tottered, eyelids drooping, while the black sky wept, dripping on his skull.

Istvan shivered in the icy wind and wrapped his rain-soaked cloak more tightly about him. The rain was lighter, but the wind had risen. Ironfist's deep voice spilled, incongruously, out of the lips of a slender Seer:

"Well, we locked up Ojakota when we left it, but I didn't expect that to do any good. Anyone can get into an empty fort. But there are plenty of supplies there—we couldn't carry much. There wasn't time. I wanted to defend it, but Lord Maldeo insisted. And it's true enough that we were needed here. Some of Jagat's assaults came closer than he knew to carrying the walls. But if I had held the fort, you would have a base: now Jagat's men can use it against you."

"Perhaps," said Istvan. "But were there supplies for horses?"

"Of course!" said Ironfist. "It's a major way station on the road. Plenty of hay and grain—bread and dried fruits, too. You can feed your horses—if you can get inside. It's a strong place. If you have to besiege it, you'll be in trouble. You know what Bordermen are like."

"Yes," said Istvan, thinking furiously. "But I doubt that Jagat could spare many men. What do you think?"

"Forty men could hold it," Ironfist said, through the Seer's mouth. Istvan struggled to suppress a yawn, feeling his eyelids dragging. "It's a strong fort, right enough. If I were going to try to take it, I'd concentrate my forces on the western wall. It's older than the others, and in poor repair. But probably you're better off just surrounding it, and cutting your way through into the city."

Istvan saw DiGasclon waiting to speak.

"One moment, Ironfist," he said. DiGasclon saluted.

"The men are ready to march, Commander." Istvan nodded and turned back to the Seer.

"I must go now, Ironfist. I'll see you tomorrow. Or perhaps the day after."

"Good luck, DiVega! We'll be ready!" The Seer shook himself, and came out of trance, blinking earth-brown eyes in confusion. Istvan walked toward his tired mare.

Through most of the march, Istvan nodded in the saddle. At one point he stirred, listening intently, hearing a change in the sound of the downpour. Was it only that the rain was softer? Then he heard his mare's hooves squelching in soft mud.

Other hooves were hammering on hard stone: some men were riding on the old road itself. The camp must be close now. Sleep would be sweet . . .

Angrily, he shook himself awake. At the rear the Healers were tending the wounded. He could be no more tired than they! And the weary mare between his knees—she would be hungry, and the grain nearly gone! Why should he sleep while others laboured?

He swayed in the saddle, fighting sleep, while the thin rain blurred the world before his eyes. The monotonous beat of water, thrumming musically on his wet hood, went on and on.

When he woke they were riding into camp.

The Duke of Ipazema lay sleepless. Only one more day of waiting! Then he would strike! All was ready. With their leader gone, Prince Phillipos' forces would crumple quickly, assailed at once from both north and south. *If* Prince Hansio kept to his bargain! Men said that Bordermen always kept their word, but with that old fox—who could say? Well, no matter! He had men enough! Probably. Still, it was better to wait for Hansio's signal.

The capture of Thantakkar! That was a strong fort. Was Hansio boasting? Well, he'd wait and see—but not too long.

The Duke kept his Seer beside him all day, so Hansio could reach him if he wanted. Tomorrow his army would be poised and ready, and the day after, it would strike down like a thunderbolt out of the north. He'd wait for word of an attack on Thantakkar, yes—but not

too long. Only one more day of waiting, and then he would rule all
the north!

Prince of Kalascor! He savoured the title: an intoxicating taste of
the wine of power. It warmed him as he lay sleepless in his golden
bed.

Jodos cast early sleep across the court and castle, and free from
prying eyes, sent his summons into the night. Then he rose and crept
down to the gates. The rain here had stopped. Small swift moons
shot, painfully bright, across gaps between clouds; guards slept
unheeding at their posts, sprawled on the cold wet stones.

Jodos reached into the night. The Spider was coming now, he
could feel it moving through the chill dank mists that rose from the
river and swirled through the filthy alleys by the docks.

He waited at the gate, tasting the night with his mind. Sleepers
stirred, but he drove them back to haunted dreams whose forms he
had shaped long before. Briefly he toyed with their fears and hatreds, but he had other work now. Later he would hunt them through
the chambers of their minds.

He waited, feeling the Dead Man walking through the fog-filled
city, coming to fulfill his commands.

Firencio DiVega was angry.

"Supposing I'd just ridden off and left the army? I *should* have—
and gone after you! Think what this does to discipline!"

"Indeed." Istvan smiled. "Younger officers shouting at their
superiors—disgraceful! The effect on discipline has been bad, I must
admit." He chuckled at the chagrin on Firencio's face, behind
lashing strands of rain. "You were all insisting someone had to go
out. I thought it should be someone who had a chance to return."

"That, Cousin, was said with less than your usual modesty!"
Firencio exclaimed. "You thought no other could bring the information back? You are not only overly proud, but wrong. Someone else
did bring the information back—*after* you did, as it happened, so
that when we met him on the way here, he had but found the road,
and was on his way back to tell us."

"Who?" asked Istvan.

"Arjun DiFlacca," Firencio answered.

"That young fool!"

"Why is he a fool, and not you? He came back alive. And he did
not leave the whole army leaderless!"

"The army wasn't leaderless. You were in command. I'm not
important. Any man here could lead this army as well as I, and some
of them, better. Which is why, instead of standing around worrying

about what I *should* have done, I should talk about what we *will* do tomorrow, so that if any of you''—he waved his hand to include all the commanders gathered around him—''have a better idea about the approach to Manjipor, I'll be able to hear it while I'm still awake enough to think. And *that* doesn't give us much time!'' The chattering sound of falling water filled the silence as he paused. Even scowling Firencio was quiet.

''Martos will have reinforcements tomorrow,'' Istvan continued, ''and will no doubt try to turn us aside once more. He'll probably try to stop us and hold us at Ojakota, though he'll almost certainly attack us before we reach the place. He's a Kadarin: he'll think in terms of cavalry. Though he can't match our numbers, he'll try to hit us and slow us down.

''But he knows he'll be driven back to Ojakota! That's a strong fort. If we try to go around it, he'll hit us from the rear when we come up against Jagat's main force. If we lay siege, that'll slow us down and give Jagat's men the initiative. Jagat has, according to D'Oleve, more men than we; although the numbers inside the city make us roughly even. But he can leave enough men at the city to drive back a sortie and still have enough to do us a great deal of damage. Especially if we have to go in on foot, with our horses hungry. But that's the important point. There is grain in Ojakota.'' He let that sink in, then turned to Rupiros D'Ascoli, whose company was guarding what remained of the baggage. ''How much grain do we have here?''

''None,'' said D'Ascoli, shaking his head. ''We fed them the last of it an hour ago. There was about a mouthful for each horse here, but as carefully as we rationed it, we couldn't stretch it to leave enough for the companies you had, or for the Bordermen; so those horses will have to get by on the dried fruit and bread. We've rationed out enough to keep them alive, but what we're going to do tomorrow I don't know.''

''How much *is* there?'' said Istvan—then as D'Ascoli frowned, considering—''Wait: what I *should* ask is how many horses could we give a *full* meal to?''

''Humph! Not many! I'd say we could feed . . . oh, maybe fifty horses, or a hundred Border ponies, since they eat about half what ours do. That's not going to go far among six thousand!''

''Then there's not that much use rationing it, is there?'' said Istvan. ''But that's actually very good; better than I expected!'' They stared at him. ''I want all the companies that wear Kadarin-style armour to pick out their fastest horses—fifty of them. I want all of those to march together in a single unit tomorrow. I want the horses fed all they need, and their riders well-rested. Tomorrow they're to march—let's see—probably on the south side, toward the centre. I want them somewhere where they won't come under direct attack, but where they can get out instantly.''

"What are you going to do?" asked Ciavedes. "Send them around in a flanking action? It's hardly enough."

"No." Istvan shook his head. "The moment we have Martos' forces engaged, I'm going to send them off for Ojakota, riding as fast as they are able."

Istvan yawned and shook his head. He could feel slow sleep creeping across his forehead, pressing down his eyebrows and the lids beneath. The quarreling voices of his commanders seemed to come from behind a wall of mist.

The Dead Man walked through the city. Jodos tasted the pain of the Spider-ridden corpse as it drew near the fiery ghost of the broken spell that had covered the castle before Chondos had been taken.

The smell of death tainted the mist that crept from the river to gird the castle wall. Black shapes blotched the fog that filled the gate, but no guard stirred from slumber on the cold stone to challenge them.

The Dead Man walked from the mist, and behind him, sharp-angled, squared black silhouettes, Hotar and the others came, in blocky homemade armour taken from men killed and eaten on the Border.

The smell of death wrinkled the noses of the helpless sleepers. No longer would the corpse of the guard Tonios pass as a living man, but there were bodies in plenty sprawled about the castle.

The Pure-in-Blood cowered as Jodos met them at the gate. He said no word, but gestured contemptuously for them to follow. They trembled at his power as he led them through the long corridors of the silent castle where bespelled men slept.

Dimly, Martos heard through sleep the sound of tramping feet. Horses snorted. His fingers sought his sword-hilt.

"Martos! Wake up!" It was Valiros' voice. "They've come!"

"Who? What?"

"The men Jagat sent. They marched all night. Ymros has a message for you, from Lord Jagat."

Martos rolled up, resheathing his half-drawn sword. The warmth of his blankets tried to pull him back down: sleep crawled in his brain.

Dim, fragmented memories ran through his mind, of a dream in which he had searched madly for Kumari in a room full of women, all of whom had looked like her from the back. But each of them had turned to him a stranger's face.

Above, the clouds were streaked with light. Black patches rippled through translucent grey masses. The rain was a fine mist, easy to ignore. But the man stepping between blanket-bundled sleeping bodies dripped both rain and sweat. Martos sat up and began to rise; but the Borderer dropped to his knees and then, to Martos' surprise, bent his body forward, face to the ground, in the seldom-seen, ancient Takkarian court bow.

"Lord Martos?" It was Ymros' deep, quiet voice. The Borderman bobbed up again to sit Border-fashion, feet under him, hands resting on his thighs. "Lord Jagat said that I must make clear to you that you are still in command. Lord Hamir is here, and Lord Bajio of Kaligaviot." Martos tried to find faces to fit those names, but his head felt numb and he wanted to sleep. The battering rain thickened, then suddenly stopped. "My Lord has told them both that you are in command. Lord Hamir will give no trouble, but our Lord says that Lord Bajio takes himself far too seriously and is always looking for a way to make himself important." Ymros chuckled. "Lord Bajio was furious that a 'foreigner' should be given command, but my Lord told him he was like the Takkarian noble in the old story, who died of thirst because he was too proud to accept water from the hands of a low-born man, even though it was Hastur's boon.

"But if Lord Bajio attempts to take command, *I* know, and all of my Lord's vassals who came with me know, that you are in command. And Lord Hamir knows, although he, too, feels slighted, and may not try to stop Lord Bajio—though he will do nothing to rouse my Lord's anger. But Bajio is a fool, and there is no knowing what he will do."

"Have you—" Martos had to struggle to keep from a stutter. He fought to wake fully. This could be serious. He chose his words with care. "Have you spoken to Lord Suktio about this?"

"No, Lord. He is not here. But I will tell him when he returns. All of my Lord's men will stand with you on this, and will follow your orders without question."

Out of the heavens a spatter of rain, rapid and furious, danced in a flurry. So inured was Martos to the rain that he did not even trouble to pull his blanket up to cover his head, but only moved it a bit to keep the water from wetting the inside of his bedding. Ymros seemed not to note the raindrops that shattered on his helmet.

"It would seem a light enough matter, then," said Martos. "If I call on Hamir of Inagar directly, he must obey."

"Indeed, Lord." Ymros nodded. "A good plan. That should serve." He yawned, and Martos remembered that this man had marched all day on foot and had had far less sleep than he.

"Get to bed, man!" he said. "Find a place to spread your

blankets. You'll be more useful after you've slept.'' As though to set an example, Martos snuggled into his own blanket and, covering his wet scalp, let himself drift back to the warmth of dreams.

Trumpets blared in darkness. Istvan jerked awake. His sword flamed as he rolled to his feet. The rain had stopped, and the cold wind had torn a jagged rent in the roof of clouds: bright moons glowed pearl and crystal against the naked sky. All around him wakened men snatched up weapons and, rubbing their eyes, stared into moonlight. The eerie wail of the conch-horn rose above the wind.

Istvan's bones ached. Cold mud crawled between his toes. His sword-guard was cold between forefinger and thumb. Men's voices drowned the music, voices hoarse from sleeplessness and fear.

"Here they come!'' someone shouted. Men ran wildly, gathering at one end of the camp, staring into darkness.

Istvan took two quick steps in that direction, and stopped, listening. The direction was wrong. The merry call of the trumpets burst through the high shrill song of the conch: he turned his head toward the sound, then back to the gathered men.

Conch and trumpet sang together, then both stopped. Cold wind whispered in Istvan's ear. Dim moonlight whitened dingy ash: cloud-shadows drifted on the pallid plain, but there was no sound of hooves. Tiny black patches seemed to move against the pale ash. Was that a horse? Were there two? A shape came running on great flapping squares: Istvan blinked and recognised Border garments.

"Commander DiVega!'' It was Rinmull of Ojaini's voice. "I truly think there is no one out there, except the men with the horns.''

"I'm quite sure of it,'' said Istvan, sheathing his sword. He filled his lungs. "Listen, men!'' he shouted. "Back to your beds! There's no attack! It's just a trick to rob you of sleep.''

Chondos' feet hurt as he stumbled through pale dust: walking, walking, endlessly, all night, walking, in darkness and cold rain. Welts on his back burned. The dull pain was cruel, so cruel . . .

He staggered on through ebon night. Plummeting water from slavering clouds beat on his head. Goblins snarled and jabbered all around him, ready to torment him. Cold water wet their dirty fur.

In a storeroom in the castle, Hotar's men had changed their clothes. Now in gaudy royal livery, they followed Jodos' lead. There were empty soldiers' quarters in a little-used wing, where few officials of the court would go. A new troop stationed there would strike no one as strange.

Searching through the dreams of the court, Jodos found a victim for the Spider. Sleeping in a nearby room, a young clerk dreamed in peace: a minor figure at the edge of the court, alone and friendless—noticed seldom, yet his business might take him to the King.

Homesick meadows filled with flowers stirred by gentle winds of dream, where people danced in a childhood glow. Rustic music played about him; all the world was gay and sweet . . .

Jodos poisoned the dream.

Poison crawled over his landscape. Flowers died, and grass was withered. Something crawled, invisible, toward him. The dreamer leaped to his feet. In the waking world, Jodos made the dreamer's muscles obey. Fleeing shapeless fear, the dreamer lurched from bed and blindly walked. Across a ruined landscape fled the clerk, over his shoulder seeming to see Fear following.

Dead! It must be dead! A human body staggered behind him.

The sleeper lurched from his chamber, into the corridor where Jodos waited with the Dead Man. Though he ran in dream, his living body stumbled slowly down the hall. Now he smelled the corpse as it overtook him, coming nearer, nearer . . .

Jodos let the sleeping man fall at the door of the soldiers' quarters. The sleeper lay twitching as the Dead Man knelt.

Jodos smiled. After the change, Hotar and his men would drag the old body inside and dispose of it. Later, if there was need, its gnawed bones could always be thrown into the river. But more than likely, no one would look inside the room until after the Shadow had covered the city.

In his dream, the young clerk still fled the corpse that pursued him.

The Dead Man knelt at the victim's side. The Spider ran down the arm, jumped onto the sleeper's neck. Tonio's body toppled, to lie beside the sleeper. Cruelly, Jodos let the man wake, to stare into the dead guard's face. He caught the scream in the young man's throat.

The Spider bit.

Thrice in the night Istvan woke, hearing conch and bugle, and each time rolled over, back to sleep. Now the conch-horn woke him once again—but mingled with hooves and the shouting of men. His Hastur-blade flared from the scabbard as he came to his feet and darted between the bundled bodies of sleeping men.

Through fine rain Istvan saw swirling swordblades. Gaunt Seynyorean horses ran, with Bordermen on their backs. Bugles sounded, far off in the night.

A tall horse bore down on him. He jumped at its nose and it shied. He sprang in next to its shoulder: a scything blade swept harmlessly past him as he hurled his back against the horse, feeling mighty muscles clench along his spine as his point drove up through leather and flesh. Bleeding dead weight toppled, brushing his shoulder.

Somewhere in the dark beyond the camp, the conch-horn wailed, and stopped. Bugles answered from the distance. The conch called twice more, plaintively. Riderless horses ran loose, with cursing men chasing them—but there was no more shouting or clanging of steel. Wiping blood from his sword, Istvan DiVega went back to his blankets.

Chapter Seven

The furred black roof of the Shadow was grey-streaked with dawn when Vidraj allowed Chondos' captors to halt. Pallid poisoned dust swayed before Chondos' eyes. Vague light filtered through the darkened air.

His head throbbed from the spear-butt crack; his back was an aching net of welts.

Goblins gathered around Vidraj.

"I shall return, Kravyad," he sneered down at them, "nor will you need to summon me again. I shall find you when the light is gone."

The tall form blurred and shifted. A bat wheeled in the gloom. Chondos blinked and slumped. Was he awake, still, or dreaming? His eyes closed.

Rough goblin hands seized him, and dragged him into darkness.

"They really *do* eat raw fish!" Valiros said with a shudder.

Martos sat up, shivering, and wrapped his blanket more tightly around him. He blinked doubtfully at the lump in Valiros' hand.

Fine, gentle rain pattered down on their camp, washing the blood from the coats and hooves of the horses. Martos' head felt stuffed with wool. He almost drifted back to sleep.

"I like it!" said Paidros, striding out of the rain. "That sauce of theirs hides the flavour so that you wouldn't know it was fish at all."

"If I didn't *know* it was fish—at all!" Valiros said, and bit. Hardtack crackled.

Martos chuckled in relief. Only the same hardtack, unleavened— Bordermen never used yeast—dry, and hard as wood to chew.

Cold chicken and hardtack. How long had it been since they'd had anything else to eat? Now the Borderers really were eating the fish that they caught in the little streams that fed the Marunka, eating it raw. Each of them carried a cooking mirror strapped to his saddle— but the mirrors were of no use now.

"Here come our musicians! Paidros exclaimed. "I must go see how the Seynyoreans enjoyed our concert!" He wiped his hands, and with a smug smile strode into the rain.

Martos rubbed his sleep-smeared eyes and saw Suktio riding on a pony, leading a tall Seynyorean horse on a lead-rope. Romulos and Styllis followed. They all looked subdued and sad.

Valiros handed him some hardtack and Martos began to chew. He shivered. It was cold—not *really* cold, but colder than he was used to now. All through the summer he had longed for rain and cold weather. When he had arrived, at the very end of last year's rains, the unblasted parts of the plain had been covered with thick green grass. But summer had baked it brown, and he had baked too.

"What's wrong?" Valiros asked as Paidros came back. His smile was gone.

"That—" Paidros shook his head. "Our friend Suktio tried to repeat our horse-catching trick, and lost four men. That horse he's leading is the one he rode out of the Seynyorean camp. It's the only one!"

Martos saw Suktio talking to Ymros. Suddenly the hardtack exploded in his mouth as he bit down hard, remembering Ymros' words of the night before. He chewed.

"Valiros!" he called when his mouth was empty at last. "You too, Paidros, this is important! Ymros"—he had to stop and struggle with his tongue—"he said that—that Lord Bajio—might—" Martos foundered, and took another bite of hardtack to cover his confusion. It grated on his gums.

"Lord Jagat has said I am—am in command. But Bajio—and Hamir, too—are angry that—a foreigner should be—be set over them. Jagat sent Ymros to—he thinks Bajio may try—and Hamir may—back him—Bajio may try to take command away from me."

"*That* donkey?" Paidros snorted. "What does he think *he* can do against Istvan the Archer?"

"How will you stop him?" Valiros asked.

"I—I don't know yet. Ymros said—" Martos fought his tongue. Why should the command mean so much to him? *The Self-judged Man cares nothing for titles of Power, or the esteem of men . . .*

"You said Hamir would support him?" Valiros asked. "What about Jagat's own men?"

"Ymros said—that's what he's talking to Suktio about now. Jagat's men will all—back me. And I don't think Hamir will—want to anger Lord Jagat—"

Valiros laughed. "No one in his right mind would anger Lord Jagat!" he said.

"If it comes to—if he's forced to it, he'll—back me—reluctantly— but Jagat told him—I was in command. He won't—"

"Push him, then!" snapped Paidros. "Put him in a position where he has to confirm you, or defy Jagat directly. But whatever you do, do it quickly. There's a war to be fought!"

*   *   *

Mud squelched under Istvan's boots as he led his tired mare through the rain. The entire army walked, sparing their hungry horses. Plaintive whinnies and squeals were all around. Only seventy-five of the horses were full-fed and content: the elite force that would ride for Ojakota at the first sign of an attack. Istvan marched beside the little force. Seveny-five men, to take one of the strongest forts in Manjipé!

Istvan could hear Arjun DiFlacca's voice off to his left, raised to tell some spirited tale of Border warfare. He had one of the fastest horses among the Bordermen, and so he was one of the little party, and Istvan had made him second-in-command, aide to Boros DelContar.

". . . miles of woodland would have been lost that day," Arjun was saying, "except for Prince Hansio. He led his men into the Shadow, with the Border aflame, and the night-things hunting, and crossed the Atvanadi at the old bridge of Gajguna—that's a good ten miles or more inside the Shadow—and rode back over the Border of the Kantara side, attacking the Dark Things' rear before they knew his men were not part of their own force."

Istvan listened. He had never been able to reconcile the reckless hero of Border lore with the cunning plotter whose intrigues had troubled the kingdom before most of these men had been born. Yet it was the same man.

"No one ever said the Old Fox lacked nerve," said one Seynyorean. "It's a wonder the Hasturs did not fry him by mistake, when he crossed the Border from the wrong side."

"He has a Hastur—blade!" said Arjun. "Did you not know? The Guardians of the Towers recognised it and brought magic to his aid—like Pertap. I have heard that the flames from his sword shot out like thunderbolts to strike Demons that were far away, and sparks of need-fire whirled like stars around him. So men say. But I did not see that myself."

Istvan smiled.

"What I've never understood," said DelContar slowly, "is why so great a warrior should—well, why is he the Fox? Why does he plot with merchants? If he wishes to rebel, why does he—why are we not marching against *him*, instead of against Jagat?"

"Didn't he rise against Olansos in his youth?" someone asked.

"Yes, and Olansos smashed his army in a fortnight, they say," answered another. *Poets' lies*, Istvan thought.

"So they say," said Arjun, "and ever since, he has laid plans for Olansos' death. But Lord Rinmull believes that by now the habit of caution has grown so strong that he will never move, but will always watch and wait for a better chance."

A habit of caution, Istvan thought. Was that not the root of his own foolish fear of death? Before age had bleached his hair, in the days when death seemed far away, older men had warned him against rashness, again and again.

Had Hansio, too, been trapped in that game? Fellow-feeling swept over him. Did the Old Fox feel shame, as he did, to hear lying poets' songs? Caution? Folly! Better not to fear . . .

The Bordermen sometimes seemed to throw their lives away as casually as other men might throw away dung or old clothing. But death was all about them here, in poisoned ash where no grass grew and no bird sang. A Borderman who reached old age—the rare ones, like Hansio or Jagat—could look at coming death with equanimity. They had never expected to live so long. As a child a Borderman would face a simple choice: to run away and leave the land, or to stay and die in its defence. Men who had fled the Border could be found all through the port cities—and women, but the women had an even harder choice.

And Hansio, who had spent years plotting against his human foes, never committing himself, always scheming for some advantage to make the outcome certain, would yet hurl himself into battle against the Dark Things with no advantage, risking his life and those of all his men upon a mad hazard.

If he had been fighting Hansio's army instead of Jagat's, Istvan wondered, would Hansio have sent men one at a time to fight the scouts? The reckless Border hero would; the cunning schemer would not. Which would Hansio prove to be in the field?

Istvan was suddenly reminded of the fight in the rain, and his stupid rage at the man who had closed on his sword-side to keep him from using his shield. He had been enraged at the man for clinging to that advantage, yet the man had only been trying to overcome the obvious advantage of Istvan's skill. How could there be even combat, with equal risk, when he had spent forty years teaching himself to be a better swordsman than other men? How dared he scorn another for taking advantage, when he had such an advantage as that?

It was an unattainable ideal, he supposed—a totally fair fight, where each man had an equal chance, with no difference in speed or strength or skill, or even in courage. The victor would win because he was right.

A moral advantage? Was that not what swordsmanship was, or should be? Once the movements had been drilled into the muscles and nerves and mind, did not the action of the blade become the pure outflow of the heart, the flowering of the inner, basic nature?

He shook his head, frowning. What was this nonsense? Ridiculous! Poetic, even, like something spouted on a street corner in Carcosa by one of the ragged wanderers who flooded into the "City of Poets'' every year, to be a nuisance until winter and lack of funds drove them home.

This was no time for nonsense! Before the Shadow hid the suns, his tired men must fight and hungry horses must be fed.

The rain had stopped. Martos pulled on the cinch-strap, cursed, and pounded Thunderhead's ribs. He planted his foot and pulled until he was sure the cinch was tight.

All the camp was astir. The men of Martos' company dried their bowstaves carefully, then pulled dry bowstrings from their packs and strung their bows anew. Bordermen were rigging makeshift saddles for the stolen horses.

Ymros came slipping through the crowd. "Arm quickly, Lord!" he hissed. "Lord Bajio is already giving orders as though he were in command. Lord Hamir only smiles, but his men obey.''

"My thanks, Ymros.'' Odd words chased themselves through Martos' head. "Get back to your men, now,'' was all he sai ', finally. Should he say something else, he wondered. While he thought, Ymros left. Martos' brain went round and round. Had that been the right thing to say?

He hurried the gear onto the horse quickly, then forced himself to stop and, despite teeth-gritting impatience, to check and make sure everything was in order. There was a battle to fight, after all, and that was more important than this nonsense with Lord Bajio.

Then the armour, pressing cloth tight against skin, the familiar comfortable stiffness straightening his spine and pressing in his stomach while his fingers fumbled with the buckles. He felt cold through the cloth, like back home, rather than the stifled feeling he had always gotten arming in the furnace of the southern summer. He swung himself up on the big horse's back, the familiar weight of the morion rocking his head.

Almost at once he saw Lord Bajio, riding on one of the small Border ponies like a general marshalling his troops. He steered Thunderhead out of the Kadarin lines and rode toward the Border Lord.

As he drew near, Bajio looked up. Martos saw a frown quickly replaced by a sneer.

"Are you coming, Kadarin?" The Borderman called in a mocking tone. "I was beginning to wonder if you were tired of fighting and had decided to go home to your own country!"

Martos had not expected quite so studied an affront, but although he felt the surge of anger inside him, he kept his face impassive and made no reply—knowing that his tongue would be useless anyway. Instead, he walked Thunderhead around the smaller horse until the two were nose to nose, and then gently patted Thunderhead's neck and let him walk forward.

The Border pony seemed almost paralysed at the sight of the gigantic animal before it: Thunderhead ambled forward and leaned his head down to touch the other's nose with an explosive sniff. The small horse shied, and backed away a few dancing steps. Someone laughed among the ranks, and Martos saw a flush spread across the Borderman's dark face. A lazy smile came to Martos' lips, and he felt his tongue freed from the chains of emotion.

"My thanks, Lord Bajio!" he said loudly, looking down at the Borderman on his little horse. Even had their horses been the same size, he would have towered over Bajio; and with Thunderhead beneath him, he might have been bending down to speak to a child. "I see all your men are in order." He moved his eyes calmly to look across the Kaligaviot men. Then quickly, he turned to look at the men from Inagar. "Lord Hamir, too, has his men prepared. I thank you, Lord Hamir! Ymros, are your men ready to ride?"

"Yes Lord!" came Ymros' voice. "We await your orders!"

"Very good!" said Martos. He had deliberately kept his voice very loud, so that it carried all across the field. Now, in the same tone, he said, turning back to Lord Bajio, "Your men will ride with Lord Hamir's on the left, and Lord Hamir will be in charge as my lieutenant." And now it had come. This was the crisis point. He felt some emotion struggling inside him, straining to seize his tongue, but he drew a deep breath and concentrated on one of the meditation symbols Birthran had taught him.

Lord Bajio's face grew dark and pale by turns. It paled to an odd yellowish colour, then reddened. "Foreigner!" he hissed, his voice choked with anger. "I am not some lesser vassal of Jagat's for you to order about! I am the Lord of Kaligaviot, and this is *my* army!"

The Borderer had played so perfectly into Martos' hands that the emotion that had gripped his tongue vanished. "Lord Hamir!" he called, his voice still at the same loud pitch. "Come here please!"

He saw Hamir hesitate, and then come riding out. Unlike Bajio, Hamir had taken one of the long-legged Seynyorean horses, and the rawboned beast was so tall on its thin legs that Hamir, on its back, could have looked Martos straight in the eye. He did not; he was plainly uncomfortable so far from the ground, and he rode unsurely, with eyes constantly glancing at the ground below him.

"Lord Hamir, I am placing Lord Bajio and his men under your command," said Martos. Hamir shot an angry glance at him, then looked away and nodded sullenly.

"Hamir!" Lord Bajio hissed. "Are the Takkarians to take orders from northern mercenaries forever?" Hamir looked uncertain and unhappy.

Martos filled his lungs again, and spoke. "Lord Hamir, who did Lord Jagat tell you was in command?"

"You," said Hamir with a glance of sharp hatred, his voice choked to a whisper.

"We are about to go into battle, Lord Hamir," Martos said softly. And then, raising his voice slightly, though not as loudly as before, he said, "Would you speak up, Lord Hamir?" Hamir looked at him sharply, then bit his lip. He glanced quickly at Lord Bajio, and then away again.

"You are in command, Lord Martos!" said Hamir, his voice loud enough to carry through the camp. "We await your orders!"

"*You* may await his orders," said Bajio, raising his own voice. "You and your vassals. But I am no vassal of yours—or Jagat's either! Kaligaviot is no part of Damenco! What right has he to set this—foreigner above me!"

"If you do not recognise Lord Jagat's claim as Prince of Manjipor," said Martos calmly, "are you sure you are in the right army?"

All around he heard a sinister hissing, like wind in reeds. As one, all of Lord Jagat's men had drawn their swords.

Lord Bajio's face turned an unhealthy yellowish tinge, like stained ivory. He stared at Martos. "Someday, I will kill you, Kadarin. After this war is over." His voice was very low. "But for now"— he raised his voice, and brought his arm up in satirical mockery of a Kadarin salute—"what are your orders, Commander?"

"You have heard them," said Martos, and turned Thunderhead away. "Ymros! Buldeo! Paidros! Valiros!" He hesitated, uncertain whether to call Suktio or not, knowing the man had been up all night. As he tried to determine which of Jagat's vassals he should call to replace him, he saw that Suktio rode at Ymros' side, his eyes somewhat bleared but alert. He cursed Paidros' "cleverness": the Seynyoreans might have been robbed of sleep, but Suktio certainly had been. But there were other things to think about now, as the various leaders rode up.

"We'll have to look at their dispositions before we draw up a final battle plan," said Martos, "but if their order of march is as it was yesterday, what I want to do is threaten their rear, and possibly attack with a small portion of our forces, while the main body moves ahead to block their road. I was hoping to draw them out, but it's plain that DiVega plans to march straight on, whatever happens. We do not have the strength to stop them. We will be forced to retreat. But if we retreat in good order, and fall back on Ojakota, we may be able to hold them there.

"They cannot devote the time to taking Ojakota while Jagat's men close in on them. If they try to pass Ojakota and go on to the city, we need only bide our time and strike when they are engaged with

Jagat. A sortie from the city will not help them, for Jagat will be expecting that.

"Hamir, you and Lord Bajio will be on the left; Ymros, Suktio, and Buldeo on the right. I will be in the centre with the company. Valiros, you and the Jumpers will ride directly to my rear, so that we can bring you out when needed. Let us go."

Horses neighed. Hooves kneaded mud as the different groups sorted themselves out. Martos raised an arm, shouted. The command was passed from group to group, and then all that long line of horsemen were in motion, nine hundred horses, riding south to where six thousand Seynyoreans marched steadily toward the city.

"Lord Istvan, there are horsemen moving down from the north. It looks to be at least a thousand men."

Istvan frowned, and looked over at the little force he had designated to take Ojakota. So soon . . . He had hoped Jagat's force would not be moving in for hours yet. He turned back to the scout.

"How far are we from Ojakota now?"

"No more than a day's march, at this speed, Lord." The Kantaran knitted his brows. "Perhaps as little as half a day."

Istvan smiled. That was better than he had hoped! They had not lost as much time as he had feared.

"I know how outnumbered we are!" Martos snapped, his temper worn thin by Paidros' constant nagging. "If we could draw them back into the dust—but DiVega just keeps marching. But by hitting the rear—or seeming to—we will get some of them stopped! Maybe half. Then if we run ahead of the ones that are still marching—"

"They'll march right over us," said Paidros.

"We have a horseflesh advantage," Martos said. "We can fight them, stop them, retreat to Ojakota."

"Why not just go to Ojakota now?" asked Paidros. "Clip them in passing, perhaps use arrows on them as we go by, make them *think* we're attacking. That will slow them down, keep them busy. But we have less than a thousand men. We can't fight six thousand in the open!"

"I have fought worse than that in the open," Lord Hamir burst in. "If you give up all idea of living through a battle, you may win even a hopeless fight. It will not matter if we are all killed, if DiVega's army is weakened enough. They cannot afford delay. The city will fall soon, if DiVega cannot drive Jagat from the walls."

Martos pondered. Paidros was right, he knew. Once behind those massive walls, they could hold off DiVega's army forever. And with Jagat's army so near . . .

Yet the thought of being trapped behind walls annoyed him:

cavalry was the proper form of war. To it he had been raised, and his fathers before him. Grandfather had fought at Ovimor Field, when King Manuel was a boy, to smash the power of Chelebinor, and regain the eastern provinces.

His brain roared in the fever of insight. "We'll retreat to Ojakota in good time!"—he snapped. "But we'll shake them up first! We hit their rear, and the rear stops, while the rest go on. But that means they have a new rear. Then we move on, and hit that too." He looked at Paidros exultantly.

The little man frowned, and after a moment nodded reluctantly. "Might work. Our horses are better fed; we can outrun them if we need to. If we hang on their rear for a while, and get them good and nervous—"

"We'll sprinkle them with arrows," Martos said, nodding jubilantly. "Try to tempt them into a charge. We'll rush them and—pass them. You take a small group and go by their left. The rest of us swing right. While they're still confused, we'll go on—"

"But," Lord Buldeo, the Massadessan, broke in, "we will be trapped between the two. We'll be crushed between them like grain in a mill!"

"Commander DiVega?" It was Arjun DiFlacca's voice.

"Yes, DiFlacca?"

"Why are you letting your—"

"An attack!" shouted the Seer, straightening in his saddle. "Arrows are falling among the DiFlacca companies and Kantarans!"

"Tell them to shoot back!" snapped Istvan.

"Sir! They're out of bowshot!"

"*What*?"

"They—I do not understand. DiVarro says—he showed me through his own eyes, Lord! The attack force is at least five or six hundred yards away! Well beyond bowshot! Some men are shooting back, but their arrows are falling short. But the enemy arrows are—a man just went down next to—to DiVarro! The shaft went through the mail! The Bordermen are mounting."

Istvan's memory heard King Olansos' voice: *Hamir of Inagar hired a troop of N'lantian bowmen . . .*

"N'lantians, of course!" he exclaimed. "One of Jagat's allies has a troop of N'lantians!" *The Farshooters, they call themselves.*

"Of course!" said the Seer. Istvan saw his eyes flicker in and out of trance. "Sir! Some of the Bordermen have mounted and are turning to charge! There they go! Ivailos DiFlacca wants to know if he should hold his position or support the Bordermen? And Endrios DiFlacca wants to know the same thing!"

Istvan closed his eyes, thinking furiously. "Yes!" He snapped his eyes open again. "I want all three DiFlacca companies, and I want—let me think—I want Servara and DiGasclon to support them! And all Lord Rinmull's men! Everyone else is to keep marching! Transmit the orders!" The Seer was already in trance. Istvan rubbed his eyes. Half a day or more, to Ojakota. It was still too far. He'd planned to be closer; he'd not expected an attack so soon—

"Commander DiVega?" Arjun DiFlacca again. Istvan shook his head. "Not now, boy!" He would wait until they were closer, until an hour or so's hard riding—

"It *is* important, Lord!"

Istvan fought down anger. "What is it?"

"Why are you letting your horses go hungry like this, when—"

"Because there isn't any *food*, you—" He bit off the end of his shout and turned away. *Important, he said! The idiot!*

"There is meat, Lord! Dried meat, smoked and salted! More than you need for your men!"

"*What?*" Istvan stared at him. "What are you talking about? You can't feed horses meat!"

"The Manjipéans do, Lord! They have to feed their horses all kinds of things when they are fighting on the dust. When the horses are this hungry, they will eat anything they can chew—wood, meat, anything you give them! Especially anything with salt. You cannot give them much, or feed them too long, but it will build their strength and calm them down."

Istvan stared at him.

Martos watched the Farshooters. Their arms were gnarled, swollen trees as they stood and shot. Across the stony plain, the vast army's roots writhed and broke away from the trunk. Bordermen came riding like dolls on horseback, dolls in leather armour lifting tiny bows or waving dull grey steel. Arrows dropped into mud, yards ahead of Martos' men.

Paidros rode over to the Farshooters. "Mount up!"

Massive-shouldered figures scrambled onto horses. Spent arrows slithered through the mud, slowly drawing nearer to the horses' hooves. Martos slid his bow from its case. All around him men nocked arrows.

Paidros' voice echoed up and down the line as he issued orders. The jumping horses pranced nervously.

"Charge!" Paidros yelled. Valiros and the Jumpers soared ahead. Martos felt Thunderhead's muscles gather, as his knees pressed ribs. Shod hooves were thundering, pounding in unison. Arrows came flying and splintered on armour. Martos' bowstring hummed. A mist of arrows hit the enemy.

Paidros shouted an order, and Ymros answered it. Bordermen on the left pulled up their horses. Paidros' voice barked again, Paidros and Valiros, with twenty horsemen, wheeled their horses to the left, crossing the front of Ymros' men.

Martos glanced over his shoulder, down the long, staggered line. Each horse's nose was next to another's haunches. He sheathed his bow, drew his sword, and standing in the stirrups, filled his lungs with air. "To the right—wheel!" His last word was a scream, but it was obeyed. Suddenly they were riding away from the centre of the milling cloud of Bordermen.

Bordermen at the end of the line stared at them over their swords and clapped their shields across their chests, trying to stretch them around to protect their right sides.

The little Border ponies were bucking, panicked by the huge horses bearing down on them. The Bordermen fought their horses, but now they were scattering out of the way. In the centre, men tried to turn their horses, but those behind crashed into them.

Beyond the scattering Bordermen, steel-clad Seynyoreans appeared. Sudden sunlight poured through broken clouds, and Seynyorean mail glittered as though each ring were wet with tiny jewels. Martos laid the flat of his sword on his shoulder and dressed his shield to guard. He saw a Seynyorean rise in his stirrups to shout—doubtless the commander. Martos' line ploughed into the Seynyoreans before the man had time to shout. Martos' shield crashed and shuddered on his arm.

A horse reared as Martos' shield-rim struck its nose. A startled Seynyorean tried to guard with his sword, but the heavy dwarf-blade drove it from his hand. From behind him came the cry of Suktio's conch and rasping notes of metal on metal. He cut left and right; felt his blade grate through mail rings; heard it thunder on a shield. Then he was through the Seynyorean line. Twisting in the saddle, he watched ten of his men emerge. Some had red swords and some had bleeding wounds. Sparkling swords whirled and flickered behind them, as Ymros and his men followed through the broken Seynyorean ranks.

Men from the Kantara charged in pursuit and crashed into the melee; but to the Seynyoreans, in the confusion, all Bordermen looked alike. Ymros and his men burst out through the ranks—and behind them, their enemies fought each other, unknowing. Hungry horses flagged and fell behind as Martos led his men west, toward the rest of Istvan's army.

Istvan looked quickly up at the Twin Suns in the grinning gap between clouds, then blinked blue sparks from his eyes and looked out across the treacherous desert of bared stone.

". . . several of Lord Rinmull's men were killed—some of DiGasclon's too. Lord Rinmull is very angry."

"He has cause to be," said Istvan. *Whatever happens is the commander's fault*, he thought, feeling old. He stared across bared bedrock where water glittered. The narrow road was a low wall.

The Bordermen had wrapped their horses' hooves and lower legs with leather, and veteran Shadowland fighters were doing the same. Even so, many horses would be lame before they reached Ojakota.

"Commander!" The Seer's voice broke into Istvan's thoughts. "Boros DiVega reports a large body of men approaching his rear."

Martos saw the Jumpers bounding up like rabbits. One was bucking and gyrating madly, as its rider clung white-faced to the saddle. Valiros was close behind. He reached out and caught the wildly leaping beast's rein. Martos saw that its tail was dappled with blood. An arrow stuck through the tail, its sharp point pricking the beast as it thrashed. Valiros' own high-strung mount exploded in a frenzy of bucking. Paidros spurred his great calm horse closer and grabbed the rein just as Valiros was forced to let go.

Men ran to help the rider down and tried to calm the frenzied creature enough to get the arrow out. The jumping horse thrashed and kicked, and bit one of the big war-horses on the shoulder. Paidros let others struggle after a moment, and slid from the back of his stolid mount, shaking his head.

"Crazy animals!" he snorted. "I'd rather ride a ferret! More even-tempered!" That, Martos suspected, explained why Paidros had left his enviably secure position in the army; men of his size were needed for the Jumpers. "At least there was only one," said Paidros. "We'd never have managed two of them."

"No other injuries? No—no losses?"

"They didn't see us until we were almost on them," said Paidros. "The Jumpers went over the line, and the rest of us rode past shooting. They thought there were more of us, I think."

Shading his eyes against sunlight, Martos looked at the milling cloud of horsemen miles behind. "They've dismounted again!" he exclaimed. "I thought they'd be after us, with whatever speed they could get out of their horses!"

"Smarter not to," said Paidros. "They know we're outnumbered. Why should they ruin their horses? But are you still planning to attack this next batch?" He waved a hand at the glittering river of armoured horsemen flowing away from them.

Martos felt like a ghost. They were in full sight of the Seynyoreans, but the soldiers marched on as though they had not an enemy in the world.

"Rub down the horses and rest them," said Martos. "Then we'll move in." His teeth worrying his lip, he watched the moving pattern of glittering dots. "Tariohan Ro!" he shouted.

The N'lantian named came striding, nearly naked. His mountainous shoulders were mismatched with the slim, graceful body beneath. Even the broad chest under the crossed baldrics seemed too small for arms thicker than Martos' thighs, with muscles bulging like bags of rocks. Grotesque homemade armour flapping around them, Hamir and Bajio came riding up behind the bear-shouldered bowman.

"Take your men down to the edge of bowshot," Martos said, "and shoot into the Seynyorean ranks." Tariohan Ro cast a quick glance at his employer. Lord Hamir nodded; the N'lantian, saluting, slipped from his shoulder the massive bow no normal man could bend, and strung it with a ripple of muscles that could twist iron bars.

"When are we going to attack?" Lord Bajio demanded, as the N'lantian strode back to his men. "Or are we going to sit here and watch them march away?"

"Against—against so many, the speed of our horses is all we have," said Martos, fighting the rage that wrestled with his tongue. "They will hold up better if we rest them between charges."

"*Our* horses are rested!" Bajio snapped. "How long do we have to wait for these oversized pets of yours? What if the Seynyoreans charge Hamir's mercenaries, whom you have just ordered into action? Will you support them?" Lord Hamir opened his mouth to speak, frowned, and shut it again.

"We are still closer to the N'lantians than the Seynyoreans are," said Martos. "But since you say your horses are rested, and since it worries you, you may walk your horses down and stand guard beside them." *That will keep you busy,* he thought.

After they had gone, Paidros spoke. "You should have sent Bajio to garrison Ojakota," he said. "He's going to make trouble before this battle is over. You know it, I know it, and worst of all, *he* knows it. We need more men in Ojakota anyway. If DiVega gets there before we do—"

Valiros laughed, and shook his head. "They way you talk, Paidros, you must think DiVega will sprout wings, fly to Ojakota, and capture it single-handedly! And after he kills the men we left there, he'll hold it against us himself until his army comes up! What's got under your helmet? Did somebody knock you over the head, or is it just the heat?"

"Well," said Paidros, smiling wryly, "I'll admit none of the stories about Istvan the Archer indicate that he can sprout wings, but nothing else you've said is beyond him if half the stories are true."

"Well then, we'll just have to send Martos in after him!" Valiros said, chuckling.

* * *

"Arrows falling among Boros DiVega's company!" the Seer exclaimed. "Two men down!"

"Are they in bowshot?" Istvan asked.

"No! It must be the N'lantians again. Arrows have started landing among Vega's and D'Aglar's companies now, sir."

Istvan frowned. He hated bows, but at least with ordinary bowmen you could shoot back. It had only been within the last thirty years or so that the N'lantians had begun to emerge from their mountain-girdled land to hurl a new force into the wars of men.

"Tell Cousin Boros to keep his men moving. Tell prince Phillipos to halt his phalanx and form up with shields facing north. Tell Vega to send his horses around behind the phalanx, and have his men and D'Aglar's halt and form into a shield-wall, kneeling in front of the phalanx."

His mare dropped her nose to the bare rock and licked it, then scraped with her forefoot, as though she hoped to find grass beneath. Istvan pulled a scrap of broken, seared salt meat from his pouch. Her rough tongue scraped it from his palm.

The thrum of bowstrings died, and the Farshooters scrambled onto the saddles of horses that looked absurdly small under their massive shoulders.

The riders of the jumping horses had their bows out, but the heavy cavalrymen drew their swords. Martos shrugged his shoulders to the side, so his shield was foremost, and laid the flat of his sword against his shoulder with his elbow cocked beside his head.

They started at a walk. The walk turned to a trot, the trot to a canter. Four hundred yards . . . three hundred yards . . .

"Charge!" Paidros yelled.

Martos' knees squeezed his horse's ribs. Hooves splashed at his left and clacked on his right. Ahead, bronze shields gleamed, and above them thirsty pikes glittered like daggers, mixed with the curved axe-heads of halberds. At the foot of the metal fence men crouched behind small round shields. The Jumpers bounded, about to spring over the brazen plates, the riders ready to shoot down.

Shouting, the kneeling men sprang to their feet. Martos felt himself lifted, his saddle rising under him as Thunderhead reared and checked. All the war-horses plunged and halted; jumping horses flew in all directions.

Men on foot came rushing. Martos fought Thunderhead down and heaved his sword around in a scything cut. Shock jarred his arm: a half-seen figure reeled away bleeding. Far on the right he glimpsed shining horsemen galloping past, and wondered if they were his own men fleeing or Seynyoreans circling from his rear.

A Jumper hurtled over his head: a white face stared down. A line of Border ponies rushed the hedge of spears, their riders crouched in the saddle like frogs, feet free of the stirrups. A jumping horse screamed as it came down on the points of pikes. Its rider flew from the saddle and vanished behind bronze plates. The dying horse kicked and struggled: pikes broke, or twisted from the hands that held them, and the beast crashed down on the phalanx, smashing a hole in its wall. Thunderhead raced for the gap.

Crouching Bordermen leaped from their saddles as ponies balked at the dagger-points of pikes. Some fell across spear shafts, pressing the points to the ground. Others, leaping farther, hooked leather bucklers over the tops of huge bronze slabs and pulled them down. Swords flashed.

Thunderhead drove between tall standing shields, and leaped the Jumper's still-kicking body. Martos' buckler thundered on his arm. A thrust flexed tough dwarf-steel against a shield: a cut belled on a helm.

"Back!" Paidros' voice shouted above the ringing and screaming of battle. "Turn back! They're closing on our rear!"

A halberd's axe-edge flew at Martos' face, and he lifted it with his shield. Steel scraped across the metal face, bruising his shield arm against his helm. A pike-point skidded over his breastplate; lashing out, he felt metal part under his edge.

The meaning of Paidros' words seeped into Martos' mind. Pikes and halberds poked at him. He whirled Thunderhead and rode out of the breach, over fallen bodies. Bordermen shouted war-cries; spear-splinters flew above honey-coloured bronze.

Istvan sprang to the grey mare's back and raced to the men who waited on full-fed horses.

"Mount up!" he shouted. "Watch the footing on this rock! Make the best time you can without killing the horses! When you reach Ojakota, act like you're being chased! Wave to the men on the walls! Shout for them to open the gates! We'll hold here as long as we can! *Go!*"

Ignoring salutes and shouted assurances, he spurred his horse toward Chalcondiel's company. Behind him, seventy-five horses pounded the slick black rock.

"Follow them!" he ordered. "Walk and trot by turns until you reach the fields. Find a place where the horses can graze. Unbit them, unsaddle them, let them roll. Then mount up and act as though you were pursuing an enemy. Make the men in Ojakota think you're after their friends!"

*   *   *

Martos spurred Thunderhead. Air squealed under his gliding sword; red rain spattered from the steel. Voices shouted above the metallic jangle: orders, war-cries, death-screams. Paidros' voice was among them, but Martos could not see him.

Seynyorean horsemen came crashing through the shifting mosaic of battle. Tall, bony steeds crashed together, swords whistled, ringing on metal shields, drumming on leather. A dying Borderman reeled from his horse. A Seynyorean on foot battered Martos' shield: his sword flew with his hand. A wild rapture thrilled up his arm, spinning the heavy blade.

In the delirium of battle, a scarlet flower nodded above a jewel-studded stem. Martos blinked, then saw it was a headless corpse, still upright in the saddle, blood gushing in a fountain from the jagged neck. It swayed and slid from sight. Martos leaned forward, emptying his aching stomach over Thunderhead's shoulder and foreleg.

Istvan watched the shrinking horsemen race for Ojakota: long-legged Seynyorean horses quickly outpaced the Border ponies. All around him leather-wrapped hooves clapped stone, as six companies spread out into a two-mile line, cutting Martos' men off from Ojakota.

Suddenly he saw a tall horse slip on the slick stone, its rider falling, skidding over wet dark rock. Bony steeds behind swerved barely in time to avoid a pile of stumbling horses. The fallen horse rolled up and ran, riderless. Border ponies swerved—all but three. One followed the risen horse. Two other men, riding abreast, bent from their saddles, their hands nearly brushing the stone. As they galloped past the man on the ground, each caught an elbow and straightened in the saddle. The Seynyorean hung between two horses. Thus, Istvan realised, the bordermen carried away their dead and wounded. A Healer had once told him that injured men often died from this rough handling. In a moment the Seynyorean was clinging behind his rescuer as they raced toward the riderless horse. The party had barely broken stride.

Martos fought nausea amid screaming men and hammering metal. But the headless man was gone. Spitting vileness from his mouth, he wrestled his shield in front of a red-and-silver blur: it shuddered on his arm, and red drops spattered past the rim.

Martos saw Paidros at last, rallying men against a Seynyorean charge. Kadarins rose up in their stirrups, sword—arms lashing like wind-whipped boughs. The stolid horses under them stood like rocks in a stream, while lighter steeds, colliding, reeled back. His sword whining like a wild red wind, Martos spurred Thunderhead and battered through the echoing clamour to Paidros' side.

Domed shields boomed as the sharp swords flew. On the ground, wounded men screamed, trying to roll away from bloody hooves. Wet blades scattered crimson rain; steel shields were furrowed with dints. Martos' soaring blade danced and swooped above his head, dragging his aching arm. Death knocked on his shield. He heard Paidros' voice behind him, but he dared not turn.

"If any of us are going to get out of here alive," Paidros shouted, "we've got to go now! There's only one chance!"

Martos hunted for his tongue. His arms ached as sword and shield swayed and crashed. *Paidros should be in command*, he thought. *I'm no good at this!* All around was a clangour like tormented bells.

"Give—the—order!" Martos managed to shriek. Breaking mail-rings rasped under his edge. A bleeding Seynyorean reeled back.

"Form—up!" Paidros shouted above clanging metal. 'Dress-ranks!'' Martos blinked. This was no parade-ground!

Yet horses moved. Some danced back, others must surge into spaces cleared by sharp-edged swinging steel. Martos saw startled looks on the faces of Seynyoreans as confused as he

"To the right oblique—wheel!" Paidros cried. Thunderhead turned, and over his shield-edge Martos glimpsed sudden panic in Seynyorean eyes that looked up to meet his past an unprotected arm.

"At a trot, for—*ward!*" Paidros called.

Massive Kadarin mounts shouldered the leaner horses aside. Steel drummed madly on Kadarin shields; Seynyorean saddles emptied. As the horses picked up their pace, the mail-clad men fell back and scattered; and as their foes rushed past, they cut at their shieldless right sides.

Jodos' body sat quite still on Chondos' throne. Yet the old castle stood not only by the river, on solid earth and stone, but in the minds of men. And through that castle Jodos walked. . . .

Old Lord Zengio wished he had never resigned, never let his ungrateful son take his post as Constable. Now he was trapped here, in the court, while in the war Istvan the Archer stole glory that he did not need.

But worst of all, his son had turned against him! His beloved son, whom he had groomed so carefully to follow him, was deliberately doing everything wrong! Just for spite, just to bring his father shame, he was ruining everything. He would not listen! And all of Zengio's old enemies were gathering, with treason spreading through the court, as his son dragged them both down to ruin and shame!

Why did the boy hate him so? He should never have given the ungrateful whelp his post. He should have strangled him as a baby.

"Never count the numbers of the foe!" Bajio of Kaligaviot snapped. Martos stared across bared stone, sudden weariness weighting his heart. Two miles of armour sparkled between Ojakota and his little force, and the horses were nearly blown.

"It was not to march past an enemy without fighting that I left Manjipor!" Bajio went on. "If we die in the assault, is that not why we are here? He who feeds our Mother the Earth feeds all mankind!"

He had only six hundred men left. When the Seynyoreans had flanked him, the Massadessans had bolted, and even a few of the company had fled with them.

"A man may always die," Lord Hamir said, unexpectedly. "We will all feed the Earth in time, Bajio. But if our deaths will not turn this army aside, then our Lord will have need of us, and it will be our duty to live."

"Maldeo cannot hold out without hope of relief!" snarled Bajio. "If we break this host—even though we die—the city will fall! I say attack! We will never have them this scattered, so apt to the purpose, again! And battles have been won against far greater odds than this!"

It was for the Bordermen's sake, most of all, that Martos wanted to find some way past that glittering line, get to Ojakota, and rest. The Bordermen were burdened with wounded and dead—yet still Bajio was ready to fight.

"If we hold Ojakota against them," Paidros was explaining patiently, yet again, "they will be forced to retreat."

Jodos crept through the corridors of his courtiers' minds, ferreting out the hidden rooms and deep cellars of their secret fears. . . .

Lord Zengio's cousin, Rojero, fingered his dagger's hilt, brooding on his wrongs. He had served the old King well—as long and hard as any—but others were always preferred before him. Once he had blamed the King for this, but now he knew better; now he knew it was Zengio and Shachio and their fawning friends.

He knew they hated him. Zengio had always hated him. But they would suffer, when the time came! And Lord Arricos' daughter, too—he'd show her! Too good for him, was she? All a part of their plot to rob him of his status in the court. But she'd suffer for it! When the time came, she'd grovel and beg him for mercy!

Brooding on their wrongs, men wronged each other daily, as Jodos twisted their minds, infecting them with sneers and sullen, furtive glances. Men trapped in visions of suspicion and fear saw in the sidelong looks of others proof that the horrors in their minds were real.

Less and less now, he feared discovery, as men sank deeper in their own concerns. They had not time to watch him: they watched each other, frightened, while secret hate burrowed beneath the surface of their minds, fear growing while unthinking hands stroked the hilts of their daggers.

"Remember," Istvan said, "killing them isn't important. Break them into little groups and scatter them."

"*I* think killing them is important," growled D'Olafos. "They've killed enough of us!"

Istvan had no answer to that. He stared across bare stone at Martos' little group of horsemen. Heavy clouds hid the Twin Suns, and gloom lay over cheerless stone.

Twice now he'd ordered his line to mount and move as the horsemen had tried to ride around them. Now they looked to be resting their horses. If they rested them enough, he would not be able to keep up with them; but if they rested them long enough, it would not matter and he would happily let them ride past. But he must be sure that the men who raced for Ojakota had a long start.

Frowning, he saw them mount and mill, forming into three long lines, with the heavy Kadarin cavalry at the front. He shook his head. He'd hoped to be able to avoid more fighting. Had his riders a long enough start? Just a little longer and he would have been able to retreat before them, but it looked to be too late now. He searched his brain for some way to stop this battle—or better, to stop this war.

The three lines advanced, like waves rolling across a stone sea. Arrows began to fall, although the enemy was still far out of bowshot. The Farshooters again! But the arrows seemed mostly to skitter harmlessly away on the rock. N'lantians normally fought on foot; they were probably finding it difficult to aim from horseback.

He mounted his mare and rode across his line, to where Rupiros D'Ascoli's company waited, advanced from the rest, and turned inward. When the battle started, D'Ascoli's men would move down the face of the line to catch the Kadarins from the flank, and on the left wing Robardin's company was poised to do the same.

He watched the enemy waves roll in, at a trot now. They seemed to be angling away, to strike the line farther to the left than he had expected.

"Mount up!" he called. Men scrambled into their saddles. His sword hung free at the end of a loose, relaxed arm.

In a moment they would charge. He swung up his blade and signalled the advance. Cloth-wrapped hooves padded on stone. He kept an easy lope. He heard distant shouting and the sound of a trumpet, swung up his sword again.

Kadarins and Bordermen wheeled and galloped. Suddenly the three lines were three columns, rushing toward the end of the line at a speed his starving horses could not match.

But one tiny group of Bordermen ran straight in, charging the waiting swords.

Martos laughed and twisted in the saddle, lifting his bow. The trick had worked! He cast a quick glance over his shoulder at the column behind.

Earth-coloured ponies dashed over the stone toward the waiting line of foes. He wheeled Thunderhead out of line, staring. Had Paidros' voice failed to carry? Bajio of Kasthapor rode at the head of the Kaligaviot men. A single sun peered through torn clouds, glittering on mail and raised swords.

Martos groped for words: "To the left—wheel!" Though he forced his tongue to grapple the command, his voice was not loud: barely fifty of his own men heard and swung out of line to follow him. But already Hamir and the Inagar men were moving.

Istvan stared at the Bordermen and at the retreating columns drawing rapidly away. His sword had swept down and already he was riding with D'Ascoli's men upon their flank.

They saw their danger; part of their rear turned and came rushing to meet D'Ascoli's men, even as the rest rushed on against the line. Istvan's heart leaped at their courage—then it ached. Less than a dozen men were charging his three hundred.

Sunlight flashed on a Borderman's sword as he rose in his stirrups, cutting at Istvan's face. Istvan's shield rose, and in the same motion his Hastur-blade looped out above the leather buckler. He remembered his own words: *Killing them isn't important* . . .

He pulled back his arm and felt his point slide through softness. Past the rim of his falling shield he saw the Borderman clap his buckler to his face and drop it again. Istvan's heart twisted to see the cloven eyeball and the hanging flap of bloody skin that hid the other. Howling, the blinded man lashed out wildly, Istvan drove the sword from his hand, turned the other horse by urging his mare's shoulder against it, then swatted the flat of his blade on the pony's flank. It galloped away from the battle, the blind man clinging to its back.

Ahead Martos glimpsed surprised men scrambling to arm, but he paid them no heed and kept his chin pressed to his left shoulder, watching the Kaligaviot men and the two companies that had closed on them—one from somewhere down the line and the one that had advanced to meet them. Behind the block of men that had moved out of line he could see empty stone through a broad gap where only a scattered handful of men hung back.

"Oblique to the left—charge!" he yelled, and swung away from the hastily arming men toward the rear of battle already joined. With his fifty men he plunged into the gap, while Hamir's men, behind, with no orders and no need of any, swung farther, to crash into the rear of the Seynyoreans who fought Bajio's men.

Istvan's shield hummed on his arm. He could see the weakness in his foeman's guard. It would be easy to kill. But who could show mercy if he could not?

The enemy edge was a silver line. He thrust at the wrist below, knowing that if he missed, his sword arm would hinder his own shield. He felt steel spring as his point caught in bone. The sword, flying from its holder's hand, bounced clanging from his helmet and fell to the stone.

Swords drummed on shields and rang on armour. Seynyoreans and Bordermen milled. But there seemed to be more Bordermen than he had thought.

"Where did *they* come from?" D'Ascoli exclaimed. "How did they— *Look out!*"

Istvan twisted and his lifted blade chimed against a Borderman's sword. But there had been no Bordermen on that side! The other sword wheeled like a hawk and swooped again, but the Hastur-blade brushed it aside. Istvan whirled his shoulders as the glancing sword fell atop the enemy shield. Sudden blood poured from leather armour.

Swords flailed on thundering shields. Gaunt Seynyorean horses ran by with empty saddles. Istvan's winging sword carried his hand above an enemy shield. In this madness it was harder not to kill. A Borderer swept up the man Istvan had slain, slinging the body across his saddle as his pony whirled away like a swallow.

Martos' sword sheared mail-rings. Riderless horses scattered. Before him bare stone stretched to Ojakota. Riding out, he whirled his men as though to charge back through the line. As he expected, the Seynyoreans turned to face him. He pointed his sword at the sky and waited.

Bordermen burst through the gap he had made, scattering mail-clad riders. Seeing open stone before them, they urged their horses to a gallop; some still slashed at Seynyoreans trapped in their ranks. And from somewhere on the far side of the Seynyorean line, Martos heard the high, shrill whine of the Conch-horn of Chandra, and knew that the rest of his men were fighting. With his fifty horsemen he went racing along the back of the enemy line, leaving the Bordermen to escape by themselves and cursing Lord Bajio's stupidity, which had splintered and scattered his army.

He rode toward the racket of battle and the shriek of Suktio's conch, and saw a frenzy of angry darting steel. He launched his fifty men with a shout. The shout brought men whirling to face him, and then he was among them, his great sword lashing left and right. Seynyoreans scattered from his path, panicked as death came from both sides.

A cheer rose. Suktio stared at him through red-shot eyes. Paidros shouted somewhere nearby. Waving his blade over his head, Martos reined around to the right, his men whirling with him, back into the disorder of broken Seynyorean ranks.

Startled men and horses scattered. Behind him the conch-horn crowed triumphantly as the rest of Jagat's men flooded through the gap, smiting to the stone any who tried to fight.

Istvan drew a deep breath and let it out again. *I'm alive*, he thought. *It's over, and I'm alive!*

Leather-covered hooves pattered all around. Martos' Kadarins were cantering away, dark-armoured Bordermen eddying around them. Horsemen were scattered all across the naked rock. The field was his! Louder than the hooves were the moans of wounded men.

"Shouldn't we follow them, sir?" asked young DiRonar at his elbow. "You said—"

"No boy," said Istvan, looking out across the stone. Kadarin armour shimmered in sunlight until clouds shrouded the single sun and armour faded to dreary grey. Horses' hooves flickered up and down. "Let them go."

Thunderhead was limping, favouring his right foreleg. Martos dismounted and checked the hoof under its leather wrapping but could find nothing wrong.

"All the horses will be lame if we stay on this rock much longer!" Paidros snarled. "Dis—*mount!*" He swung down from his saddle.

Ahead the fields emerged from the haze, and Bordermen were gathered at their edge. They were laying out bodies on the stone, along with broken arrows, bundles of reeds, saddles—anything that would burn.

Hamir of Inagar rose as they came up. At his feet a body moved and moaned. Hamir knelt down again. Martos handed Thunderhead's rein to Paidros and walked to where Hamir cradled the wounded man.

In the bloody mask of pain, Bajio's eyes opened.

"You! Foreigner!" Bajio's voice was a ragged whisper. Blood-crusted armour had been shredded on his body. "Hamir said—it was you—saved my men . . ." His chest heaved: breath rasped rapid in his throat. Lashes fell over his eyes.

"We should find a Healer," Martos said, fighting his tongue.

Bajio's eyes flew open.

"Healer!" he wheezed. "Dead men have no need for Healers!" Blood bubbled at his lips, and the wheeze turned to a cough.

"No," he said when the coughing had stopped, "the Red-robes should save their potions. The Bride of the Warrior waits for me; her flesh is warm with longing. Her breasts swell with milk for her children: milk that is grass and corn and apple trees. Earth must . . ." Coughing took his voice; he lay back, shaking, on Hamir's knee.

"Foreigner!" he gasped a moment later. "You broke their line for—my men and me! Good work! But you are still one of the . . ." His voice sank to a low mumble. Martos bent down to hear.

". . . from outside, you wipe your feet on us, but we still stand! Not give up a foot of . . . Earth must drink the seed of man, and men shall drink . . ." The eyelids snapped open, glared into Martos' eyes.

"*The Barrier of Blood!*" Bajio gasped. "We need no mercenaries to hold—to hold . . ."

A rattle rasped his throat: the black eyes froze.

Istvan saw smoke hanging in a thick pall at the edge of the fields. Figures scrambled away as the Seynyoreans approached.

Hours had passed: the dark wall of Shadow hid the suns. Hard stone underfoot slammed through boot soles and leather-wrapped hooves. Sad funereal smoke lay over a dying fire. There had not been enough to burn. Istvan averted his eyes from the half-burned corpses and sent for Lord Rinmull. He would deal with this.

Here at the edge were many fields still in preparation: squares laid out, filling slowly with dung and garbage. He saw fish heads, melon rinds, chicken legs, feathers. He shuddered. *Earth must be fed.*

He thought of Seynyor, where the dead would stay buried. Other fields here were partly prepared, with sand and clay worked into the rotting garbage. In some the soil was thoroughly mixed, just ground, waiting for the plow.

Farther on were fields of close-cropped clover, already grazed. He ordered the horses turned loose, to get what little they could. It was better than nothing. And if his men had not reached Ojakota, it would be the best they could get.

Martos had fallen far back, leading Thunderhead. Someone shouted his name, and he hurried forward to see several men surrounding a prisoner—a Seynyorean!

"I told you we should get on!" Paidros' voice was shrill. "There are Seynyoreans ahead of us, heading for Ojakota!" He turned to one of the others and snapped, "Fetch a fresh horse. Hurry!"

Moments later, mounted on a gaunt Seynyorean steed, Martos

rode with Paidros at the head of the men, racing toward Ojakota as it loomed up out of the haze.

"There they are!" Paidros pointed. In the failing light, a pattern of dark figures moved between them and the blocky shape of the fortress.

"Only one company!" Paidros said. "We have barely that ourselves now. But they'll be trapped against the walls, and if we can drive them a mile or so farther, Jagat's men will help."

Alternately galloping and cantering, they gained on the distant horsemen, while the stark wall of the fort grew closer and clearer.

"The gates are open!" Paidros shouted. "They'll get in! Gallop! Charge!"

Hooves pounding together, they closed in on the Seynyoreans. The enemy, aware of them, milled a moment, then moved off the road and formed a line—but not between Martos' men and the fort.

"Ride past them!" Paidros shouted. "Form into columns, and get between them and the gate!" They swerved away, falling into a column as they galloped past: Martos expected some flanking move from the enemy, but the Seynyoreans only watched. Cold prickles climbed Martos' back.

The gateway's vast mouth opened before them, and he glimpsed men moving on the stone beyond the archway. The gate swung shut. They pulled up their horses beneath the frowning stone wall.

"Who's in command up there?" Paidros shouted.

"I, Arjun DiFlacca!" A voice laughed down, and a young man in Border armour leaned out above the gate.

"Do you not—" Paidros' voice stopped. He stared. "*DiFlacca?*"

"DiFlacca!" crowed the boy proudly. A man in steel plate like their own appeared on the wall beside him. "And with me in this fortress are DiCedaspis, DiArnacs, and even, I believe, a few DiVegas! And behind you, if I am not mistaken, is a Chalcondiel!"

Startled, Martos looked over his shoulder. Behind them, the Seynyorean ranks had swung out onto the road.

"I *told*—" Paidros shook his head, his face twisting in rage. "All right! Now what?"

"Ride on!" said Martos. "To Manjipor. And Jagat."

"Nothing else to do!" Paidros snarled. "Let's move!"

Chapter Eight

Chondos woke in darkness and stench, pain tearing at his shoulders. Something shook him. Voices snarled. Eyes floated in the dark like sickly moons. Rich orange light rippled along a slime-slick black wall.

"Up!" a shrill voice cried, and something pounded his ribs. He tried to struggle up, but his arms were numb. Voices shrieked over him; blows thudded on his flesh; hands wrenched at him and pulled him to his feet.

Red light flared in his eyes. He blinked. Black goblins waved torches. Fish-belly goblins crouched nearby, snarling, and a goblin with dirty white fur stood before him, showing its long yellow fangs.

His limbs were numb. He reeled on his feet, trying to find his arms so he could wrench at the ropes that held him, but it was as though his arms were gone, leaving only aching shoulders where they had been.

He blinked and looked away from the torches. The goblins, too, were looking away, but they were creatures of the darkness, dwellers in the deep mines under the Shadow. Yet legend held that their ancestors had once been men.

"Get him and go!" a black goblin snarled. "One of the Great Ones is hunting down the way!"

Small brown-furred goblins squealed and ran from the chamber.

"But where shall we go?" squeaked the white-furred one. "There is a troll hunting in the main cavern! He will care nothing for the Master's orders! Trolls are too stupid to be afraid! And this one is hungry. No one has been able to get through for a week!"

"We'll go around. We can take the ancient way, the Guakupa."

"You will never get a human alive through that!" scoffed another. "Only the upper tunnels are big enough, and those are nests of ghouls now. Where is your Blood Drinker? I thought he was to protect us!"

"Summon your Blood Drinker!" voices shouted. "Quickly!"

"He did not like being summoned," snarled the deep-voiced goblin. "He said he would return. We will wait."

"Wait, with a Great One hunting above?" shrilled the white-furred leader. "Something will eat the prisoner, and then the Master will blame us! All because you're afraid to summon your Blood Drinker, so that he is not here when we need him!''

"I am here, Kravyad.''

The voice shook the cave. The goblins cowered; Chondos felt his knees buckling, and struggled to stay on his feet.

A tiny shape fluttered from the dark. Vidraj fountained into the torchlight, shooting up from the floor to loom above them all.

"I am here, and—I thirst.'' Ivory spikes flashed back the torchlight. "Even had I time to hunt, there is nothing on this side of the mountains but you foul-blooded things. Nothing but—that!''

Suddenly he was beside Chondos, red eyes flaming dangerously close. Chondos stumbled back against the wall, the spell of his shield rising in his beleaguered mind.

"Only one vessel of clean blood this side of Rashnagar, and we are forbidden to cross the Border! And this must be dragged before the Master and Emicos, untouched, even though the smallest sip would make him beg to obey. What is this foolishness? What difference will it make? I spent years dried to skin and bone once, dust dry, a mere bundle of sticks and leather! Long ago. Must I dry up again to please them? No! Must I live only on foul blood like yours? No! I thirst! I am parched and hungry! Who is Emicos, or even the Master, that they should forbid me this?'' A white tongue like a pale worm licked the pallid lips. A long, graceful hand seized Chondos' shoulder, a grip like a vise, and the white fangs gleamed.

"Do not touch him.'' A voice like trumpets, golden, beautiful. Vidraj hissed like a cat.

A tall man appeared from nowhere.

"Emicos!'' Vidraj spat. He pushed Chondos away and whirled to face the other. "Will you dare to challenge *my* power?''

"I dare,'' said Emicos.

"Fool! I was old with power before your mortal mother and father were born! Before the ancestors of the King you served had built their little robber's hold between the Oda and Pavana, I had knelt in worship before Uoght, and had brought to his service thousands of descendants of the Takkars, draining the bounteous river of their blood!''

"And what were you before that?'' asked Emicos. "A common warrior, not skilled enough to keep from being bitten—nor brave enough to die with your companions when you saw what fate awaited you! Old Pertap died first, did he not? To show you younger warriors the way it should be done. He took—''

"*Silence!*'' roared Vidraj. "You were not there; you know nothing but the lies men sang a hundred years later!''

"You were a simple warrior,'' said Emicos, "but I was an Adept of Carcosa and Elthar, trained in the service of powers whose names you can no longer say. But *I* can.''

"Liar!" said Vidraj. "You would not dare."

"No?" Emicos laughed. "Even so, there are other names I might call. *You* have only your native power. Shall I call upon the Secret Name of Uoght? Or shall I call upon the Lord of the Eight, who seethes and burns in the centre of the Void? Shall I call upon the ghoul-guards of Uoght's Tower, and bid them bind you in your coffin and seal you there for a thousand years, thirsting? Or shall I have them cast you into the Dark World, and let the lesser Dyoles gnaw the scattered atoms of your body through a million years of torment? Doubt not, Vidraj, these things I can do.''

"I, too, have learned the Names and the Chants," said Vidraj. "Do you think, in the brief eyeblink of your mortal span, that you have learned more than I? You can no longer wield the Light Magic; and even if you called upon the Names of all the Eight, they could not pass the Blue-robes' barriers. If you can summon the Dyoles or the Zubweth, do so, and let *them* lead us over the Border: then there will be food enough for all. You have no power over me!''

Emicos made no answer in words, but instead whistled, a strange tune that seemed at times to vanish from human hearing to become a pointed shrill ache in the ear. Vidraj stared, and suddenly a sound twisted from Emicos' throat, a sound that seemed to throb in air and rock alike, making the bone crawl in Chondos' flesh.

The torchlight rippled, and something grey and ghoullike hung there. Chondos blinked, and looked quickly away. He had seen that doglike face before, and the soul-traps of its eyes; and the landscape behind it, glimpsed as though through a door, of bubbling ooze about a dread black tower.

"Would you go up before Uoght, Vidraj, and argue the matter with him? His Messenger shall take you, if I command.''

Suddenly the air seemed crowded with ghoul-faces, and Vidraj threw his arms over his eyes. Emicos laughed and spoke a single word. The rippling shapes vanished.

"Bring the mortal to Rashnagar, Vidraj. Bring him untouched, untasted, untainted. Will you obey?''

"I obey," said Vidraj slowly, his voice shaken.

"I am sure you will," said Emicos. "If not, you will suffer.''

"Arjun DiFlacca has to get a great deal of the credit," the young lieutenant was saying. "Things looked bad. One of the N'lantians was up on the wall with his bow, and another one ran to the stairs over there''—he gestured—"and got about halfway up. They had us between them, and I was sure they were going to pick us off one by one.

"The Bordermen had come in ahead of us—that was funny! It was like a race, and at the beginning we were all ahead, but at the end—" He shook his head. "Those little ponies are tough! But DiFlacca rode straight for the stairs when the arrows started falling. I was sure he was dead. I thought all of us were. I saw him cut one arrow out of the air with his sword. I think the point grazed him; he has quite a scratch along one thigh. But he made it into sword range and chopped the bow. His sword wouldn't go all the way through, but he cut just as the man started to bend it, and it shattered. Then he dived down the stairs and yelled for us to shoot at the fellow on the wall." He laughed. "We hadn't had time to think yet, really. But we pulled our bows out and made the N'lantian keep his head down, and DiFlacca went up the stairs again, ran around the wall, and cut the fellow's bowstring. We'd taken the rest of the garrison, of course, as soon as we'd come in. They hadn't even drawn their weapons: we just knocked them down and disarmed them. The N'lantian threw off the men who jumped him. DeCedaspi has a dislocated shoulder and one of the Bordermen a broken wrist—it was like jumping a bear."

"And they gave up after DiFlacca cut their bows?" Istvan asked.

"Well, he had to fight the one on the stairs. I was too busy shooting at the other one to see just what happened, but he managed to wound him—cut the tendon in one leg—and the man's sword got caught in his shield—cut through almost to the arm. The other one surrendered after that. He wasn't really dangerous once he lost his bow—no shield, no armour, and outnumbered like that—and, of course, it isn't really his quarrel."

"Right," Istvan nodded. *Is it ours?* He glanced around the courtyard. Men were rationing out hay and grain for another detachment of horses. The horses had to be fed very carefully, to make sure they did not swell up.

Once the smell of grain reached them, the weary, plodding horses suddenly perked up and tried to break away from their masters, meaning to break into the supplies and eat until they burst, eat until it killed them.

Witchlight and torchlight augmented the glow of a dozen tiny moons that shone through a long rift in the clouds. But the rift was narrowing, and many moons were speeding past and vanishing. Soon the gap would close, and Istvan did not like the look of those clouds. Much more rain and the whole army, men and horses alike, would be too sick to fight. Already a couple of men had been kicked by restive horses—as if their few remaining Healers did not have enough to do.

Rinmull of Ojaini walked up and bowed. "Plenty of fuel, sir. I have already ordered enough carried back to finish burning the remnants of the enemy dead. What of our own men? Do you still wish to start a new field at the edge of the rock?''

Istvan grimaced. ''No. Set up pyres—somewhere near the fort. When the siege is over we'll arrange with Maldeo for a place for their ashes.'' He shook his head. ''We've got a lot of them. If we give them a field apiece, we'll add a lot more land. Maybe we can fill the rock completely.'' He thought suddenly of the trail of the army, of the dung of men and horses that the Kantarans—after carefully collecting every horse-flop all across the dust—had left on the rock; of the blood-smears where the battles had been fought, blood now drying to powder. Already they had done much to bring the barren stretch of stone back to life.

''With your permission, Lord,'' said Rinmull, ''I would prefer to take the ashes of my own men back to the trees.''

Istvan nodded. ''Of course.''

The rift was thinning: the sky was almost covered now. New moons shot into sight; others vanished behind the filmy white roof. A few witch-stones burned around the walls, and someone had found one light-globe as large as a man's head, mounted on a tripod: this, glowing with diamond-fire, lit the area beside the stable door, and cast the black shadows of horses and men with hayforks across the stone floor. One company after another, until some six thousand horses were fed.

And Jagat's army waiting for him . . .

Jagat looked tired, Martos thought, tired and old. The pale moonlight gleamed on his snow-white hair. His eyes were sad, and his face more lined than Martos remembered.

''I—'' Martos felt his throat close and his tongue die again. What could he say? He had failed. ''I did all I—'' He forced a big lungful of air. ''Their army was too big to stop.'' Why was he making excuses? ''I am sorry, my—my lord.''

Jagat looked at him sadly, and then the frail ghost of a smile moved the sad lips.

''Do not blame yourself, boy,'' he said softly. ''I know you did the best you could, with the few men you had. And it has taken them longer. I have had extra time to assault the walls, and had I been able to carry them—'' He shrugged. ''Did you lose many men?''

''More than I should,'' said Martos. ''I truly do not know how many yet. I do not know for certain how many were wounded and how many—'' He shook his head. ''But through my—my stupidity, they had taken Ojakota. They will be . . .'' His voice trailed away miserably.

Jagat stared at the ground. ''So much death!'' He shook his head, and then the tragic eyes, glittering with moonlight, stared into Martos' own. "I have just returned from Suknia. I left the siege and—I should have sent for Kumari, but there was no time. But my boy is with the land now."

Martos stared at him, not understanding.

"There is a little field. There will be a tree—it will be very beautiful and green, someday. I had always thought it would be my own place, but it's my boy's now. Down toward the river, not too far from the gate. The clover is planted . . ."

Martos blinked at him, and then into his mind came the vision of the little coffer he had seen only once: Pirthio's ashes.

"All food comes from the breasts of the Warrior's Bride," said Jagat softly; then, "So, they have Ojakota. There are six thousand, I am told."

"Six thousand Seynyoreans," said Martos, "but there are a number of men from the Kantara, and—Kalascor, someone said. Maybe two thousand more, all told, eight thousand, perhaps. I'm not sure." He closed his eyes. "I don't seem to be very sure of anything, do I? I don't know how many men I lost. Not even from my own company! Nearly a third of them—missing, killed, wounded—I don't know!" He shuddered and realised that his voice was pitched wrong somehow, that a note of hysteria was making it shrill and womanish.

"Against Seynyoreans one may expect to lose men," said Jagat. "They are professionals, after all. I have seen them fight often enough." He paused and shook his head. "Seen them fighting for the land, fighting beside us to hold back the Shadow. What are we doing, Martos? What am I doing? Much of the land about us is hallowed with the ashes of Seynyorean dead.

"My boy died. He's with the land now. He could have died—he could have died before; he could have died during any raid by the Dark Things. Earth must be fed. I tell that to the men, and I will have to tell it to their widows! I meant to tell it to you, to tell you not to grieve too wildly; to tell you not to . . . And yet, what is this war about? My boy is with the land, he has gone to the bed of the Warrior's Bride, and here I sit, besieging the ancient city of my fathers, feeding the Earth, sending more men to her, sending to her bed the men who have come from Hastur's Mountain to share our trials, in a war that I strove to prevent in the first place."

Jagat's old eyes vanished behind his hands, and the white head bowed in the moonlight. Martos turned away, unable to look on the old man's anguish.

"But Chondos cannot rule," Jagat said after a moment. "I would have given my life to shield his throne, once! I worshipped his father. The kingdom suffers for the folly of the King, always. We must have another King. And yet . . .'' He shook his head.

Martos tried to think of some words of comfort, some antidote for the old man's despair; but all that came into his mind was a stale old Kadarin joke about a widow, in which a Borderman would see nothing funny at all.

He turned as he heard someone approach from behind. He could just make out Lord Hamir's face: a mass of clouds were drifting in from the north to fill in the twisting river of open sky through which the moon swam.

Other shapes appeared behind Hamir—fantastic shadows in Border dress: their legs truncated triangles, their arms wings, their heads distorted hillocks in leather helmets. Suktio he recognised by the rippling glint of the ancient mail-shirt that was his pride.

Hamir dropped to his knees in the Border fashion, and then bobbed quickly from the waist, one hand touching the ground in deference.

"Lord Prince, I must report the death of the Lord of Kaligaviot," he said, his tone formal. "He died valiantly in battle against the Seynyoreans." Martos heard Jagat's breath hiss from his throat. "He is part of the land."

"Has his heir been told yet?" Jagat asked.

"The Kaligaviot men have been sent word," came Ymros' quiet voice from behind Hamir. "But their new Lord is only a boy."

"Yes, I remember," said Jagat. "I suppose I'll have to appoint someone to take charge during his minority, and to command his vassals. Let's see—the boy's mother was married to someone else, wasn't she?"

"Yes," said Hamir. "Bajio made her husband Chamberlain when the boy was born, but I think he's dead now."

"Killed during the big raid a year or so back, as I recall," said Suktio. "The time the vampire managed to take his whole family—"

"And the man in Orissia was killed by his dogs?" said Jagat. "Yes, that one. Well, we can make the mother guardian, then. Who would you say would be best as war-leader? Hamir, you knew him better than I."

"Ramros of Pukota was a man on whom Bajio leaned heavily," said Hamir, slowly. "Either he or Mahdev, I'd say, Mahdev of—"

"With the Seynyorean army eight miles away," broke in Ymros, "we're likely to have one or the other of them removed shortly. They seemed to be cooperating pretty well the last I saw. But Ramros is wounded, and Mahdev should probably be the one to take command if we send them out to hold the Seynyoreans. But I think they deserve a rest, and some fresher troop might be sent to hold the road from Ojakota."

Jagat chuckled. "Back to business. Quite right! Do you think we'll be seeing any of them tonight, or will they wait until morning?"

"Morning," said Hamir. "They've been marching all day, and leading their horses, mostly."

"And they'll need to feed their horses," Suktio said, then yawned. "Martos burned their grain supply. If they hadn't managed to get into Ojakota, their horses would be in pretty bad shape by now. Nearly three days without food."

"They still won't be at their best," said Ymros. "If I were Lord Istvan, I would sit at Ojakota for two or three days before trying to attack; let the horses rest up and get them properly fed. What do you think, Lord Martos?"

Martos' mind seemed singularly empty. "I think," he said, slowly, "that DiVega will be most concerned with relieving the city by the most efficient method. How much danger is the city in? If the city can't hold out long, we may find him hitting our outposts tonight, just as a distraction. If the city is in no danger—well, his men are exhausted and his horses need food. They'll have sore feet from marching on stone, and they've gone through quite a bit of fighting over the last few days. And he'll want to use Ojakota to its best advantage."

"Well, he can't very well pick it up and carry it," said Hamir. "And he won't be able to fit his army inside. The fort was never meant to hold a garrison of more than three or four hundred. Most of his army will have to stay outside. We might try to cut them away from the fort. We can't capture it, but if we threw a force around it, so he couldn't get the grain out to his horses—"

"That would take most of the force from the city," objected Ymros.

"In terms of numbers, it's very close," said Jagat. "We couldn't maintain a siege of Ojakota and the city both. And if we tried to drive his army away, we'd have to leave at least"— he frowned, and grimaced—"at least half our force to prevent a sortie from the city."

"What about our supplies?" asked Martos.

The Bordermen looked at each other in dismay.

"He has us blocked off from Inagar, certainly," said Hamir after a moment.

"And that's where most of our food is coming from," said Jagat.

"Once he has his horses fed, he can block off any road just by keeping his patrols out," Ymros pointed out.

"How well can *we* bear a siege?" asked Martos.

"Better than we could have three days ago," Jagat said. "A big load of wagons arrived from Inagar and Massadessa day before yesterday. Still . . ."

"We've starved before, and fought," said Suktio.

"If he were to launch an attack and arrange a sortie at the same time," Jagat said thoughtfully, "we'd be outnumbered."

"We must keep him from choosing his own time of attack," said Martos. "We must fight him at our convenience, not his—see to it that he's too busy to set up a sortie."

Jagat stared thoughtfully into the night.

"Easier said than done," said Ymros. "If we move any large force away from the city to strike at him, he can order a sortie, through the Seers in the city—and with the amount of cavalry he has, even aid the sortie by sending a few companies circling around the attacking force."

"Give me fresh men," said Martos, "and I'll attack tonight. Even if he were to order a sortie, it would take them time to get out of bed."

Jagat looked at him and suddenly laughed. "Martos, you look as though you'd step on your eyelids if you tried to walk to your tent! If you can fight in your sleep, why assume the enemy cannot?"

Hamir and Ymros chuckled, and Ymros said, "Remember the fellow who got out of a sound sleep, killed a—what? A troll, wasn't it, Suktio? Killed a troll, or a ghoul, went back to sleep, and didn't remember a thing about it when he woke up. What was his name, Suktio? I've forgotten now. Suktio?"

"What?" murmured Suktio drowsily. "I'll be right with you!"

Martos tried to stop the laugh that hurtled into his throat, but he was too late; it had already seized his jaw and forced its way out of his open mouth. Then they were all laughing helplessly—all except Suktio, who was looking around, astonished, rubbing the sleep-drawn crescents of his eyes.

Suddenly Lord Jagat rose, tall in the darkness.

"Sleep is good after hard fighting," he said. "I have rested most of the day, since I returned to camp, and have made my men rest since noon, that they might be fresh if the Seynyoreans came. Sleep, all of you! It is an order! I myself shall ride to the Seynyorean camp. We shall see if they can drive the sons of the Takkars away from this city, where Hastur placed our fathers at the dawn of time! You have done your part: it is the turn of others now. Your duty is to rest. Sleep well!"

He strode off into thickening darkness.

The tall dark man Vidraj had called Emicos was gone. Goblins cowered about them; Vidraj stood, frowning and furious. Chondos felt a faint prickling in the space where arms ought to be, and a moment later an agony of returning circulation shot through them:

his mind was blurred with a blaze of pain. Angry red eyes glowed on him.

"You and your little mind-spell!" Vidraj snarled after a moment. "And the Master wants you untouched! They will suffer for it someday. But for now—"

Suddenly, a blur in the night, he whirled and snatched, and one of the white goblins was screaming in his grasp, kicking and squealing while Vidraj laughed. Fangs sank in. For a moment more the thing kicked frantically and waved its bony arms—then quieted. The shrieks became moans. The vampire cast the corpse away with a fastidious shudder of disgust, and spat a little dark blood from his mouth. The body crashed to the ground and bounced, with a splintering sound.

"Such filth I am forced to drink!" He stared at Chondos' throat, and then looked down at the sprawled and shattered corpse. "Well, now there is another of your filthy kind immortal—unless, of course, you are hungry, and wish to eat this flesh before it wakes."

He laughed as they scrambled round and began carving off slices with their knives. Chondos turned his eyes away.

"Enough!" he heard Vidraj snarl after a moment. "No time for you to stuff yourselves any fuller. And there are others living in this cave who will be glad enough to pick the bones. I am leaving now, with the prisoner. If you wish to come, come!"

He gave Chondos a push that sent him staggering along the corridor: he almost fell, but the bony hand pinched his arm in a painful grip.

"Walk!" said Vidraj.

Chondos walked, arms and shoulders and neck aching. If he refused to walk, the vampire would only seize his legs again. His mind tried to find some means of escape, at least of death, but futilely.

The Master wanted him untouched. *Why?*

There was a frantic scurrying behind him, and then black and white goblins jostled all around. Torches threw distorted shadows on the walls.

The corridor ended in a vast arch that opened into black emptiness. The air was still. Were they outside, Chondos wondered, or was this the cavern the goblins had mentioned, the cavern of the troll?

The goblins squealed and shrank from the opening, but Vidraj laughed harshly and ordered them on. Their torches lit up little spaces of floor around them; Chondos thought there was a hint of a great wall in the darkness but could not be sure. After a time he heard a faint, hollow dripping. The flapping of the goblins' feet sounded strange, too. It must be the cavern.

He was not long in doubt. Something rumbled in the distance, a roar magnified by echoes, echoes that went on and on, rumbling like thunder. Squealing goblins covered their ears with their hands; some fell to the ground and lay trembling. Dropped torches sputtered. Vidraj laughed.

The echoes did not die: the creature roared again, and once more the walls replied. Vidraj's eerie laughter, almost drowned in echoing thunder, rang all around the room.

Something moved beyond the light of the torches. Tiny reddish eyes glared at them. Another thundering bellow mingled with the echoes of the last, and a vast shadow appeared around the eyes, moving slowly toward them with a scrabbling shuffle.

It grew slowly out of darkness: grotesque, manlike, gigantic. Little piggish eyes gleamed in the torchlight. Roars echoed constantly from the hidden roof and walls. Vidraj smiled.

In the dim light, its green, scaled skin showed plainly. Great hands opened and closed, into fists as large as a man's head. Vidraj stepped to meet it.

Towering above him, it reached out with a huge hand. In a white blur of motion, the vampire evaded the grasping paw. There was a sudden sound of impact, and the creature bellowed more loudly than ever. Vidraj laughed impudently up into the giant's face.

A massive fist smashed into the vampire's shoulder. Chondos heard the sound of bone breaking, even through the echoing thunder. Sudden mist boiled where Vidraj had stood. It flowed around the troll.

The creature stared at the empty stone, and stood rocking back and forth, staring stupidly. A column of mist hung behind its shoulder. The little piggish eyes fixed on Chondos and the goblins, and with a roar it charged.

Suddenly it fell sprawling on its face, and Chondos saw Vidraj standing over it. Clumsily the monster clambered to its feet, hiding the vampire behind its massive form. Stony tusks glinted in its mouth like stalagtites as it moaned. It shuffled forward.

A sudden billow of mist, and Vidraj stood before it. The troll halted, staring.

"Go back!" said Vidraj. He raised his hand, and the troll shrank back, but then it glared past the vampire at Chondos and the others. An arm like a huge beam lifted to point at them; from its mouth came a deep, rumbled word:

"Food!"

"Not for you!" said Vidraj, his voice echoing trumpetlike through the vastness of the vault. "Go back, G'thon, or worse things will happen."

"Food," the troll rumbled. "I kill!"

A fist as large as a man's head went crashing through mist, and the huge form fell forward with the blow. Vidraj materialised, and

this time Chondos saw the vampire's arm swing around in a slap.
The giant's head rocked with the blow: the echoes repeated the sharp
sound endlessly. Another blur, and Vidraj was standing beside
Chondos.

"Go back!" he repeated. The troll rocked back and forth, glaring.
It hesitated a moment, looking over its shoulder, and then leaped
forward, roaring.

Something like a beam of blackness darted from Vidraj's hand.
The troll went crashing backward, kicking.

"Stupid beast!" shouted Vidraj. "Go back or I will destroy you!
G'thon! Go!"

Thunder echoed from the creature's mouth as it heaved itself to its
feet and lunged with amazing speed.

Vidraj sang out a word. Chondos felt vibrations aching and crawling in his bones. His empty stomach twisted. Again something shot
from Vidraj's hand, and the troll stopped as though it had crashed
into an invisible wall.

A high-pitched, shrill keening sounded through the cavern. The
troll glared fearfully around. Suddenly it turned and fled. Goblins
squealed near Chondos' feet.

At the edge of the torchlight the troll stopped. Sudden blackness
washed over it. A last bellow thundered around them, and then the
troll crumbled, like a mud fugure falling into dust. Blackness stood
at the edge of torchlight and whined.

Vidraj bent down and lifted one of the torches from the ground,
holding it well away from his body, handling it gingerly by the
extreme end. Darkness swirled into the torchlight. The shrill scream
rose, an aching needle in the ears.

Vidraj wrote in the air with the torch, and spoke a word. Chondos
felt his bones shudder and crawl. The blackness stopped. The pattern
of fire seemed to hang in the air. High-pitched Demon whistling rose
and fell, and slowly the blackness ebbed back from the light. But the
whining went on, insistently, piercing the ears.

Vidraj laughed. "Very well!" he said, and stooping, seized one
of the nearby goblins by the ankle and jerked it into the air; as though
it had no weight, he swung it at the end of his arm, and hurled it
toward the sharp edge of darkness that rimmed the torchlight.

The spinning white shape hurtled through the air and was suddenly shrouded in transparent blackness. Flesh dissolved from bone.
Bones fell to the floor and puffed into grey dust.

The whining rose shrilly, then died away. The torchlight was
clear.

Istvan had given orders to wake him at any sign of the enemy,
then gone to snatch what sleep he could.

It was only a few hours before he was wakened with the news that a large force was advancing from the city. He rubbed his eyes angrily and shook sleep from his brain to go sit by the Seer and wait . . .

More than a thousand Bordermen, mostly on foot, were advancing from the city. One of the scouts thought he had seen Jagat himself leading them, but could not be sure in the dark.

Istvan had ordered the companies that had not yet seen action— Troel DiBretan, Cassandor DiBathori, Erwan DiBolyar, Fernan DiRonar, Aurel Ciavedes, and Valanos Chalcondiel—to take up positions closer to the city, at strategic points from which they could move in quickly. He roused them—they had also been ordered to bed early—and set them to moving cautiously.

Word came of a brush with a mass of Bordermen: DiBathori, off on the left, had found himself fronted by the end of the enemy's right wing. He had been able to use an orchard to mask his movements, and had crashed into them before the rest of the line knew what was happening.

Istvan sent Erwan DiBolyar forward at high speed, and held the others back. DiBolyar reported that his men had found the enemy in confusion, and cut them to pieces. At almost the same time DiBathori reported that he had crashed through the enemy line and was now somewhere on their rear.

Istvan considered. He hated sitting comfortably in Ojakota while others died, giving orders blindly, based on reports that might be faulty. But there was no choice: he was simply too weary to ride out and give orders in person. These men were all competent commanders; he had to trust that their judgment would correct any mistakes he made.

He ordered DiBretan and Ciavedes to converge on the centre, and told DiBathori to hover in the rear until he recognised their attack, and then to strike the rear in the same place.

New estimates of the foes' numbers came in. Istvan scowled. It seemed likely there were at least three or four thousand. He waited grimly for reports.

Word came of battle in the centre: the three companies had found themselves outnumbered and had had to withdraw. Ciavedes had actually managed to smash through the line and join DiBathori at the army's rear, but DiBretan had been forced to fall back toward Ojakota. Several men were sure they had seen Lord Jagat.

There had been no word from DiBolyar for a time. His Seer was either dead or unconscious. Istvan swore, and sent Chalcondiel and DiRonar to support DiBretan.

Word came that DiBolyar's men had blundered into DiBathori's in the dark, and they had come close to fighting each other. Now four companies were poised on the enemy's rear. Then came word of grim fighting: DiBretan's force nearly overwhelmed, but for the timely arrival of Chalcondiel and DiRonar. Fernan DiRonar was sure he had recognised Lord Jagat, dashing about on a small Border pony, encouraging his men.

Istvan gave orders to wake more of the companies, but shortly after came tidings that the Bordermen were falling back, just as Istvan was preparing to order the four companies at the rear to aid the others.

And by the next report it was plain no such order had been needed. Hearing the clash of weapons, the four companies had advanced toward the sound; but missing their way a little in the dark, they had blundered upon Lord Jagat's left wing, already severely mauled by DiBathori's passing, and driven it before them in great confusion, into Jagat's main body.

Rain began to patter on the walls and roof of Ojakota, and Istvan shook his head and strode to one of the narrow openings. He could smell the rain, and when he put his hand to the slit, water splashed from his fingers: more of the heavy, drenching downpour of the winter rains. Istvan sighed. Most of his men were already suffering from the effects of the days of rain they had marched through.

The Bordermen's right wing came swooping in on Chalcondiel's flank, but he was aware of them in time to turn his men and charge. After great slaughter, Jagat's wing was sheared away completely from his main body, and Chalcondiel, too, was poised on Jagat's rear.

The four companies already there had fallen back after crushing Jagat's left, in order to avoid entanglement in the greater numbers of his main body. Jagat and his men seemed to be following them—but whether this was a pursuit or a retreat could not be said.

Jagat's separated right wing blundered in between two of the DiFlacca companies that had happened to camp in their path, and these, newly awakened by Istvan's earlier order, set upon them and harried them off to the south, still farther from Jagat's forces.

Istvan called Leonic Servara's company to reinforce DiBretan and DiRonar, and set them marching in pursuit of Jagat's men.

Wind whistled about the walls, and Istvan, shivering, pitied poor Jagat, out in such weather. But if Jagat could be taken or slain, that would bring this stupid war to an end—or, at least, bring the end far nearer. He shook his head sadly.

He recalled the DiFlaccas from their pursuit of the right wing, and set them to moving in on the main body.

Raindrops hammered on the castle wall. There were men fighting and dying out in that rain—wounded men lying helpless in the field.

"Are the Red-robes out?" Istvan snapped.

"Yes, Lord," the Seer replied calmly. Istvan closed his eyes, picturing the darkness and the rain hammering down.

Through the black of the vast cavern, through tunnels beyond, Chondos stumbled. Bones littered stone floors. The goblins' torches dredged from the darkness old skulls whose hollow eyes had long been hidden from light. Some were round and human; some pointed and misshapen. Here were spread the bones of men and ghouls, goblins and other creatures he could not identify.

Goblins kicked the bones aside as they marched through them. Horrid forms emerged out of the dark. Ghouls glared at them with blazing eyes like polished flat stones and writhed loose lips back from long fangs; nostrils wriggled at the tips of long muzzles. Vidraj spoke a word, and they fled. Twice more, filmy blots of blackness poured screaming into their path, and Vidraj dissolved them.

After a time, they turned into a side tunnel that swarmed with smaller, brown-furred goblins, who snarled at the intruders until they saw the vampire. Then they bowed and fled to the sides of the tunnel to let the procession pass. At times, Chondos had to walk crouching, while black, filthy, slimy rock scraped his head. Vidraj changed into mist that flowed before them.

Hours passed. Istvan, weary, yawned as he listened to the Seer. On the table where he sat he had arranged various objects—a dagger, two goblets, a handful of odd coins, and a small glass bottle—which he moved around to remind himself of the distant armies he commanded, and to keep their rough positions in his mind.

Incredible though it seemed, Jagat's men were in full retreat. He had ordered the five companies that menaced Jagat's path to Manjipor to move to block his advance, meaning then to bring Servara, DiBretan, the DiFlaccas, and DiRonar upon his rear, and then move up more force.

But Jagat, after a brief hesitation, had turned aside and marched to avoid the Seynyoreans, even though, by all reports, his number was the greater.

Istvan was sorely puzzled: Jagat's losses had been great, but no worse than his own. There had been no panic among Jagat's men—and these were Bordermen accustomed to fighting by night against all the terrors of the Shadow.

Bordermen are so stupid they always run the wrong way . . .

Well, they were running the right way now—or walking, anyway. Had Jagat been attempting to implement some plan that had depended on an unopposed approach? Or had the rain upset some vital calculation?

Istvan had roused Prince Phillipos and the footmen and set them marching, planning to use them as a major shock against Jagat, to support the cavalry already harassing the foe. But while they marched, Jagat's men were marching too. There seemed little hope of catching him before he had reached the rest of his army, encamped around the city walls.

He went again to the embrasure and peered out into the rain-laced blackness. There was nothing to see: no sign that a battle was being fought anywhere within a hundred miles. He ordered the five companies to make camp where they were, and watch Jagat's men warily. The other companies, moving in, he told to join them: but he ordered Prince Phillipos to march on past the position of the five, and to make his camp in front of the Seynyorean line.

The darkness was absolute. From this embrasure he could see no light from Manjipor, nor even from the distant towers along the Border. Strange to think that men were fighting out there in that calm. Stranger still to realise that *only* men fought there.

Why were the Dark Things so quiet? What were they waiting for? On a normal night, such a rain would have brought out dozens of lesser night-things: a rainy night near Manjipor was commonly as filled with haunts as a well-stocked pond with fish. Yet the Seer with him swore the night was clear.

Jagat's men were marching back to their own lines; Healers hunted for the wounded in the darkness and rain. Istvan felt sleep trickle through his body as the water trickled through the gutters. He left orders to be informed of any action by the enemy, and went back to bed.

The tunnels began to climb, to twist upward. Once something huge blocked the corridor ahead: Vidraj drove it on, but it moved very slowly, and at last Vidraj turned them out of that tunnel and led them through a maze of side corridors. Slimy things crawled over the floor; and once Chondos found himself wading in a pool of maggots.

It was a vast underground world through which he stumbled, thronged with the creatures of the night. The gaunt, bone-white shapes of vampires emerged from the gloom, spoke to Vidraj—staring hungrily at Chondos—and left. Goblins scurried from their path, ghouls snarled, then fled as Vidraj turned upon them.

Chondos staggered on, while the floor bent slowly upward under his feet. Would they ever, he wondered, come out into the open, or did they plan to make the whole journey under the earth?

He breathed foulness and horror: the air of the pits was clogged with an odour of ancient carrion and offal, and the still worse odours of the creatures that lived there. In the darkness they hunted each other. And Chondos realised that without Vidraj neither he nor the goblins could have followed these tunnels and lived. For the creatures that haunted these depths were starving, and eating each other in the darkness.

The corridors resounded to shrieks and howls. A ghoul moved from their path at Vidraj's command, dragging a half-eaten goblin corpse. Later, another ghoul ran frantically, blood pouring from a great wound in its leg. A pack of goblins with mole-grey fur ran at its heels, waving knives and swords, cutting it apart as it ran; and seizing the pieces, the goblins chewed them and fought over them on the run. All were gaunt, half-starved. These were the hordes that normally crept over the Border each night to raid the pens and folds of the Bordermen. But so many of them, and so hungry!

Martos woke to find Paidros beside him in the dim light of dawn. On the roof of the tent he heard the monotonous chatter of rain.

"Up," Paidros said. "Jagat wants you."

Martos crawled dully from his blankets, blinking groggily. His head and every muscle ached; his bones were heavy as lead. The taste of his teeth sickened him.

He staggered out into cold wind and icy water. Vague shapes around him must be men, horses, tents, and somewhere the wall of the city, but raindrops flooded his eyes and hid the darkness. He could barely see the inside of his hood.

But Paidros seemed to know, somehow, where he was going; so Martos allowed himself to be drawn through a mist of rain, and at last heard Jagat's voice speaking over the sputtering hiss of water.

" . . . saw Seynyoreans marching through the rain." The faceless voice was weary with despair. "Then I knew we had lost all hope of beating them back from the city. I saw the doom of the Borderlands, and the Dark Things creeping from the mountains of the Shadow. Who would remain to defend the land? Trolls and goblins would feast on our corpses—feast on the bodies of the men of both sides! Even if we killed all the Seynyoreans—"

"Do you mean, then, just to give up the city?" Hamir's voice was indignant. "Give up the fields of our ancestors' ashes? No! Let us show we can die as our fathers died, and leave our bones for the Warrior's Bride."

"You fool!" snarled Jagat. "This war is not for the land!"

Wiping the blur of water from his eyes, Martos saw their dim shapes through the weeping dark. Jagat stood with his arm stabbing through rain and darkness, pointing to the south.

"*There* is your enemy! *There* is your war! Yes, Istvan DiVega rides the road to Manjipor with an army at his back, but an army of men! Men who have helped us to drive the Shadow back again!''

''Foreigners!'' Hamir snarled. ''Mercenaries, and—''

''The ashes of their kinsmen fill our fields and heal our land,'' Jagat snapped, cutting him off. ''Any fool can die for the land! Now is the time to live for her! If there are only a few hundred of us left when next the Border flames, who then will die for the land? All will die, women, children and *all*, and the land will not be saved! Demons will devour your sacred fields. Trolls and goblins will haunt the halls of Manjipor, and ghouls will gnaw our unburnt bones!'' He looked up and saw Martos standing in the rain. ''Martos, you have fought in the outside world. Do you think you can talk some sense into these idiots?''

Martos blinked in surprise. For a moment his sleepy brain scurried frantically, his skull numb with the need for sleep.

''DiVega's forces were ready and drove me back,'' Jagat went on. ''In the morning they will move in and have us trapped against the gate. I feel that we should retreat. We can continue the war as well from Inagar.''

Inagar! Martos yawned and tried to think. He looked at the map in his head and remembered his years of training in strategy and tactics.

''Why, yes!'' he said, surprised. ''From Inagar we can control the Ojaini road. In truth, from Inagar we can hold the siege just as well, or better. DiVega's brought no new supplies—only extra mouths to feed.'' Sleepiness and misery dropped away as his mind soared above the Ojaini road. ''From Inagar we can use a small part of our men to keep supply trains from passing, and use the other to harass DiVega's men whenever they leave the city!'' He spun to face the watching Bordermen, his voice rich with excitement. ''We're not abandoning the siege at all! We're just''—he laughed suddenly— ''we're just moving our camp!''

Jagat laughed, but the others stared, muttering. Jagat stepped forward, his voice low and calm. ''There has been enough argument,'' he said. ''Waste no more time. Let us be like Kaljit the Bandit Prince—'as elusive as mist in the morning.' Let us vanish before morning comes! Quickly now!''

Chondos' shoulders and the back of his head scraped the rough roof of the tunnel. Goblins laughed when the rasping stone forced gasps of pain from his throat. Lower his head was forced, and lower; deeper his knees bent, and deeper, until at last they buckled under him and he fell, on the stone. The whip whistled on his back and bound arms, but he could feel nothing.

"Fools!" came Vidraj's golden voice. "He must crawl from here! Cut loose his arms!"

There was babbling and laughter. Sudden agony spouted from his shoulders. He fought the scream that came to his throat, knowing dimly that nothing would please his captors more. After a moment he realised that the pain was part of him: he had arms again, and they ached.

His eyes opened. Red light flashed and faded. He could see his arms stretched out beside his legs, pointing back toward his feet, limp and useless on the floor. He could feel bones aching, and blood prickling. The whip lanced across his shoulders.

"Leave him be!" said the vampire. "Rest yourselves. We shall go far before we stop again."

Chondos could not see the tall vampire. There was no room for him in this cramped tunnel. He tried to move a finger. He felt pain, but could see no movement.

The tunnel ahead was filled with mist.

Chapter Nine

Dawn light filtered through a drizzle of rain. Istvan swung himself into his saddle.

All around him, thousands of men were doing the same. Through grey strings of water came the racket of an army, mounting, marching, arming. Feet and hooves were pounding up and down on the sacred soil of the fields. Behind him, men were entering the fort. Not all the horses had been fed, and those last in line would hold Ojakota, while those with full-fed horses pushed ahead.

Horse and foot marched over rebuilt land. Dim in the drizzle, the city's dark shape was like a block of mist. All across the fertile land around it, Istvan's army swarmed. First bands of light horsemen— Seynyoreans mixed with Bordermen on horses that had had plenty of food and rest—rode zigzag across the plain, to probe for the weak points in the enemy array. Then came a long skirmish line of Kalascorian pikemen, with riders spaced here and there between them. After them, in orderly ranks, the two companies of Carrodian axemen flanked D'Aglar's dismounted company. Behind them the moveable wall of heavy bronze shields strode ponderously forward, bristling with halberds and pikes. At each end a cloud of horsemen hovered, ready to sweep out on order.

Pinkish light filtered through the web of rain and slowly brightened to gold. Istvan moved his horse at a steady trot through masses of marching men, riding toward the front.

The rain thinned. Boughs of trees dripped as he rode past little orchards. *Apples,* he thought, and his mouth wanted one. He had given orders against spoiling—not, he supposed, that it would do much good. It wouldn't have stopped him when he was young. There would be apples missing, and soldiers with stomachaches. He just hoped any idiot who had taken apples here wouldn't eat them in his presence, and force him to make an example . . .

The Twin Suns glowed vaguely through the mist of rain; then a thicker veil of cloud wrapped them away in a silver cloak. Gazing ahead through thinning rain, he could see thousands of men moving toward the city. He could even glimpse the vast areas of barren rock and dust that surrounded this tiny fertile space. But where was the enemy? The rain closed down again, dimming the distance, and

Istvan cursed himself for looking at scenery instead of searching for the enemy army.

Cocks were crowing somewhere beyond the rain. Ahead, the ancient city began to grow solid, stone by stone shaping itself out of surrounding greyness. The rain muted all colour to soft pastels. His eyes searched the spaces between the raindrops. Earth-brown, plant-green, the land ahead seemed empty through the wash of falling water. Unease pricked him. Where were they waiting? What were they planning? When would Lord Jagat's men come charging through the rain?

The great mount on which the city stood loomed. Stone walls frowned through the watery blur. Scouts reported glimpsing small bodies of men that rode away to vanish in the rain, but there was no sign of any forces gathering against them.

Were Jagat's men on the other side of the city? Or had they marched around, readying to take him in the rear? The empty fields mocked him.

It was a relief when a scout brought word of horsemen coming from the city. Istvan shook himself and felt some of the tension drain away from his stomach at the prospect of action. He ordered men forward. The whole army poised, to swirl like a great vortex around the advancing column.

A Seer dashed up. "Lord DiVega. D'Oleve is advancing with a column of men from the city. There is no enemy! These are troops from the city riding toward us."

Istvan checked his army and sent a small force riding warily up to the column. Half an hour later, his cousin Attilon DiVega rode up with two of the scouts and a young Borderman introduced as Jaimul, kinsman and vassal of Maldeo, Vicar of Manjipor.

"They've just packed up and left, as far as we can tell," Attilon said. "The guards on the wall heard a certain amount of bustle during the night, and assumed that they were getting themselves ready for you, but when we looked out this morning, there was no sign of them." He waved at the vast space of trampled mud around them. Here and there through the rain, small objects resolved themselves into the jetsam of an army: ruined boots, a scrap of torn blanket, a broken cooking pot. "This was part of their camp. But they just"— he shrugged—"gave up the siege and left! It doesn't make sense! Lord Maldeo had planned a sortie this morning, and then when we looked out—nothing! One of our scouts reported horsemen riding off to the north, but—"

"It seems strange," said Jaimul, "that Lord Jagat would simply give up the war."

"I doubt if we can hope for that," said Istvan. "If he were giving up, I'm sure he would have stayed to make peace."

"Then—why?"

Istvan laughed. "He may have realised we're less of a nuisance inside the city than out of it!" he said with a rueful smile. "Our supplies were burnt, remember, so we're going to have to depend on yours, with what's in Ojakota, until we can get a convoy here from Ojaini. And that may be difficult. The Ykota will be flooding, with all this rain."

"Yes," said Jaimul. "It usually is, this time of year. They'll ferry the stuff across, all right, but that *is* a long stretch of road."

Istvan nodded. "Makes a lot more sense than staying here, doesn't it? By avoiding battle, he keeps his army intact so he can resume the siege any time he wants, without losing a lot of men trying to beat us back from the city. Pretty smart . . ." *for a Borderman*, he thought, and wondered if Martos had suggested this.

Cautiously, the army moved toward the city. Still rife were rumours about the hidden host of the enemy that lurked around them, led by a Lord Jagat grown to legendary proportions.

The rain thinned. Men could see the vast reaches of dust and rock that stretched away around the little island of green. Once the great forest had covered all this land, and birds had sung in the trees. Istvan remembered old paintings that showed Manjipor surrounded by rippling fields and bright woodlands, set against the sunlit, white-capped mountains to the south.

Foreign soldiers marched on the bones of the dead, where once the army of the Takkarian Empire had guarded their most ancient city: the cradle, legend said, of all their race.

The road slanted upward. Istvan's horses began climbing the mound that was made of the rubble of ten thousand years. The maze of the gate opened its dark mouth. In the shadows beyond lurked memories of ancient glories, even though this was one of the newest parts of the city. Stone walls threw back the echo of horseshoes. The streets were like tunnels. The stones of the pavement were worn down, troughed by the passing of countless generations of feet.

Istvan had been in all the Old Takkarian cities that were still free of the Shadow—and, with Raquel, hunting for the Lost Prince, long ago, had even entered a few that were not. He knew the peculiarities of the Old Takkarian styles of architecture. But Manjipor was different even from these, and Istvan had always had the feeling that here he touched the stuff not only of another age, but another world as well. For legend said this was the city that the first Takkarians had built, when Hastur plucked them from their own world and set them here.

The corners of the houses were rounded by centuries of rain and wind; the stone was bleached and colourless, worn smooth by time. Under his feet, he knew, were the remains of still older houses. The tops of buried towers lifted out of the ground, their lower stories long lost in the slow accumulations of the debris of ages.

The clanging of the horseshoes of his cavalry rang louder and louder behind him, drowning the soft mutter of rain.

Cloaked, muscular Carrodian axemen stood guard at the door. One, hulking huger than the rest, vast inhuman shoulders bulging out his cloak, laughed and saluted as Istvan rode by: Ironfist Arac. Beyond, the streets were nearly empty. Even with the three or four thousand Seynyoreans added, Manjipor was still more than half empty. There were not enough people in the whole province to fill it.

Barred doors and blank walls and shuttered windows dripped with rain. Small groups of Bordermen moved here and there in the streets. Istvan saw only one woman—though he knew that most of the province's women lived in the city. But as they rode into the inner town, and up the broad, hollow street that ran to the old palace called the Rajmaul, he began to feel eyes on him. Once, glancing quickly up, he saw a face peering through the pierced holes in a strangely carved stone screen, peering with beautiful almond eyes that were feverishly bright as they studied the marching soldiers.

He flushed suddenly, thinking of the stupid jokes about Border-women that they told in the coastal towns. Behind the screens and shuttered windows, the women of Manjipor hungrily watched the men of his army. Women with empty wombs, and empty cradles, and an empty city all around them, on an island in the sea of dust.

Chondos crawled.

The goblins had put out their torches, so he crawled in darkness through the close stone tunnel. His back scraped against rough stone, tearing the welts and cuts left by the whip. If he hesitated or slowed, something sharp would prick his flesh to drive him on. His hands pushed dry bones aside as he crawled. His nose was filled with the smell of death.

The vampire was gone. Whether he waited for them somewhere in the darkness ahead or had gone back to his ancient grave, Chondos did not know; but he had learned to recognise the aura of the vampire's power, the particular pressure against the spell that guarded his mind, and now it was gone.

His ears grew used to the dry slithering and knocking of the bones that he disturbed: at first an awful shudder had wrenched his insides whenever he touched one, but now he had pushed past so many that he was immune to the horror.

Some, he was sure, were human bones, and others the bones of evil little creatures like those that drove him on. But now he was less concerned with whose bones they had been than he was with discovering who or what had littered this tunnel with them, and whether it still lived somewhere ahead.

Sometimes he crawled with his eyes closed, and sometimes he opened them, and much of the time he did not think about it, for it made no difference. He breathed the stench of corruption in great gasps that tore his throat. Sweat slimed his skin.

Then, opening his eyes after crawling with them shut for a while, he found that there *was* a difference. He blinked rapidly, and paused in his crawling until the prick of a spear urged him on. He could see pale streaks on the floor of the burrow, and whitish blobs his hands told him were skulls. A dim light floated in the blackness before him: the end of the tunnel.

He began to crawl more quickly. The tomblike air rasped his lungs.

"Lord King," Shachio's tired voice said, "there is great news."

Jodos could sense much of the old man's mind, and beyond it dimly feel the confusion of the other Seer, the Seer at Manjipor.

"Manjipor has been relieved," Shachio was saying. Jodos had picked the thought from Shachio's mind as he entered, and had had to control and disguise the demonic glee that had leaped into his face. "Lord Istvan wishes to report that Lord Jagat's forces have left the city. If your majesty will permit mind-touch—"

"No!" said Jodos hastily. "That will not be necessary. Say what he tells you."

Shachio blinked in surprise, as did the Seer in Manjipor.

"Very well." The tired eyes closed, and Jodos could feel a brief stir in the other Seer, who was worried that Lord Shachio might be too old to bear the strain involved in transmitting Istvan's message.

"Lord Istvan says that yesterday, after very little fighting, Lord Jagat's army retreated from Manjipor. He suspects that they will either fall back to Inagar or scatter to various Border castles near the Ojaini road. Thus, they continue to be a danger, and Lord Istvan's position is delicate, since they can still cut him off from Ojaini. He hopes, nevertheless, that Lord Jagat's retreat indicates a willingness to avoid further bloodshed, and hopes that he will soon be able to bring Lord Jagat to discuss peace terms—"

"With no further bloodshed!" Jodos shouted. "Will Lord Istvan coddle my enemies, then? Tell him that it is his duty to bring our enemies to their knees! It is his duty to capture Lord Jagat, to reduce the fortresses that menace his supply; to break his power to resist and—" He caught himself, remembering that most of the sensible ways to subdue your enemies were forbidden by the Blue-robes' Laws of War.

"Lord Istvan begs to remind Your Majesty that Lord Jagat was once counted the most loyal of your vassals, and—"

"Was *once* the most loyal! He is not loyal now! He has raised an army against me, and against the power of the Crown! How can the kingdom be secure until that army is humbled, broken, so it cannot strike against us again? Tell Lord Istvan to set to work! Manjipor is in his hands. Now he must take control of the province and break down whatever pockets of resistance remain. If Lord Jagat declines battle, you must seek out his armies and force battle upon them. Such is my command."

Istvan shook his head as the Seer repeated the words. Did the King forget that if the Bordermen were broken, the kingdom would be nearly helpless before the Dark Things? But there was no point in arguing. And, certainly, this war should be finished quickly.

"Very well," he said. "I shall send out men to take control of those castles that guard the Ojaini road, and when I have secured my supply lines, will move on Inagar. But I beg Your Majesty to remember that mercy is the mark of a great King."

Mercy! Jodos could barely keep from laughing. Mercy!

"You are in good spirits, Sire," said Lord Shachio.

"Yes," said Jodos, smiling. "Yes, the news is very good. Victory. Yes indeed!" Victory, indeed. Soon the Border would lie defenceless, its castles empty, their defenders slain or wounded, and then the slaves of the Lords Beyond the World would feed. Soon . . .

Soon—for every passing day made the risk greater. Praise Uoght, who kept the Blue-robes busy in the north!

The Duke of Ipazema rode at the head of his army, impatience seething inside him. Where was Hansio? His army was ready: he must use it soon, before his enemies noticed its movement.

The Duke's Seer straightened in his saddle, and turned to his master. "A message from Thantakkar, my Lord! An army has been sighted across the Oda, moving in from the south! They ask aid from the troops of the province. Soldiers are running to shut the gate."

Thantakkar! At last! The Duke straightened in the saddle and began giving orders. The time had come!

His Seer interrupted him. "A message from Prince Hansio, Lord. He says, 'Thantakkar is mine.'"

"What?" The Duke snorted in surprise. "So soon? The man's mad! There hasn't been time!"

Hansio was not mad, as Ipazema learned over the next few days. Months earlier, Hansio's men, disguised as merchants or travellers, had begun filtering into the fortress city, armour and weapons carefully hidden. The night before, they had assembled at various carefully selected inns and donned their distinctive Border armour; in the morning, they had marched to the gates while the troops outside held the attention of all the defenders.

Before most of the city folk had been awake long enough to realise there'd been an attack, Hansio's men had seized control of the city—even the ancient citadel that had given the town its name, and which was said to have never fallen in battle.

Kalascor was in a panic. Hansio's army was reported moving along both banks of the Oda, toward its junction with the Pavana. The garrisons of the northern province emptied as troops moved rapidly south to aid the threatened garrison at Iskoda, which alone stood between the hosting of Mahapor and the royal city of Tarencia.

The Duke of Ipazema laughed aloud when the summons came to assemble his army and march to the defence of Kalascor.

Two days later, Istvan stood with Phillipos at the gates of Manjipor. Rain muttered on all the roofs of the city, curtained the open archway with a dripping cascade.

"Three days now, with only a bit of light drizzle now and then," said Istvan, "and then, the minute you're ready to march, this!"

Phillipos' thousand Kalascorians were lined up to march, and Istvan had added several Seynyorean companies to escort them back as far as Ojaini. Some would turn back there and return as part of a convoy of supplies; others were to accompany the Prince, to help deal with the revolt.

Prince Phillipos stared disconsolately into the rain, muttering under his breath, and then looked down at the helmet he held in the crook of his arm. It had been scoured and scrubbed to remove all trace of its journey until it glistened. Bright new plumes nodded jauntily at its crest.

Far back in the line of men, someone sneezed. Istvan frowned.

"I'm still not sure it's wise to head back so soon," he said, thinking of the long march these men had just made. "It wouldn't hurt to take a few days to rest your troops. Ipazema and Hansio—"

"Will be fighting each other over the spoils?" interrupted Phillipos. "Maybe, but Ipazema won't come off well enough to make it worth watching. It's *my* inheritance, and *my* land, and I'm not going to let those two divide it up, or throw dice for it, or fight over it, or whatever! I have to go back. I'm the Prince. My people depend on me!"

"You may get there with a thoroughly exhausted army and find that your ministers—and your Lady Wife—have already trounced both of them," said Istvan.

"Or I may get home to find the two of them in my bedchamber, dividing up the sheets and quarreling over which of them gets my mirror," said Phillipos amiably. "I know: What do I expect to accomplish with a thousand men?"

"Three thousand," said Istvan.

"Well, I can make Ipazema very nervous, if nothing else. I've had my eye on that little sneak for a long time. If I hadn't been out of the province, he'd never have dared to revolt. As for Hansio, well, no one can say what Hansio will do. I expect he'll be besieging the capital by the time I get there. That's probably why his forces have backed off from the Oda."

"That doesn't make sense," said Istvan, shaking his head. "After he took Iskoda he had a clear road to the capital, but he didn't take it. And now nobody knows where he is—or most of his army."

"We'll know soon enough," said the Prince. He looked impatient.

Istvan let out his breath in an exasperated gasp. "At least leave your men here to rest, and let me give you four companies of Seynyoreans instead," he said. "I can send the men who were here in Manjipor. They're a lot fresher and have been able to keep themselves dry. Half the men you have there will be down with the ague by the time you get them home again, and too sick to fight! It's a wonder you've got as many able to march as you have! And you can use the cavalry!"

The Prince smiled and shook his head. "No, although I thank you truly. But you have not heard the stories that go through my men's barracks, or seen the way they look at the Shadow. They are not Bordermen, Captain DiVega, or Seynyoreans either. They are terrified here. If I left them, they would think I had abandoned them. They're brave enough against human enemies, but if the Border were to light up, I think half of them would go mad from fear. They hate the Blasted Lands, and the city itself bothers them. Just the age of it." He shrugged. "Probably they'd wind up fighting with the Bordermen, too, and you have enough trouble with Kantarans and Manjipéans snarling at each other. Kalascor was a province of the Old Empire once—a rebellious one—and these fellows were raised on stories of the great rebellion, and of a couple thousand years of raiding back and forth across the Oda. They're mostly simple men, and haven't caught on yet that the Takkarians aren't 'the enemy' anymore. . . . No, if I left them here, there'd be trouble."

The Prince's white horse was brought, shimmering in the dimness of the gate. Its horseshoes clanged on the stone, mingled with the hollow thrumming echo of the rain and the coughing of the men.

Phillipos mounted, then looked down and saluted. "Good fortune attend you, DiVega."

"A good road home, Prince Phillipos!"

Phillipos smiled wryly. "A *wet* road, most likely," he snorted, frowning down at the new plumes nodding on his helmet. He gestured to his trumpeter, pulled the hood over his head, and, carefully tenting his cloak to cover the cradled helmet, urged his horse at a walk into the waterfall curtain of the gate.

Echoing trumpets blared in aching ears, and the long line of Kalascorians marched out into the rain. Behind them, long files of Seynyorean horsemen clanged through the tunnel.

A bare forty miles to the northeast, that same rain battered the canvas roof of Martos' tent.

Far ahead, Jagat's army marched on, over soaked yellow grass, toward Inagar. Some might even have reached it already. But Martos was moving slowly, resting his men, waiting for stragglers, and nursing the great herd of ailing, weary horses.

Only the night before, Valiros had come in with his few men, mounted on the ugly, high-strung Jumpers, telling of his close brush with the Seynyorean rearguard when he had approached Manjipor, thinking to find Jagat's army there. And many other little groups of men, and one large one: the whole right wing of Jagat's army that had been broken off during Jagat's attempt on the Seynyorean camp.

But a full third of Martos' own company was gone. Barely a hundred remained with him of the young men who had set out with such high hearts from the great Kadarin city of Erthi, to seek battle and glory in the wars of the south. Some, he knew, waited among the wounded at Inagar, but others were ashes in fields of the dead.

Earth is the Bride of the Warrior . . .

Martos was pleased by the mournful mutter of the rain on the tent. The rain was outside, and he was warm and dry. There was little else to be cheerful about. Yet he and Paidros and Valiros laughed and pulled out their memories of every old joke that had ever been told in Kadar, and threw a mask of gaiety over the sorrow that all three shared. A few high-ranking Bordermen joined them, mystified by many of the jokes.

Outside, the horses were stripping away the sparse, rain-soaked yellow grass, making way for the new growth that would soon creep like a green blush over the broad plain as the rainy season wrought its yearly miracle. His men huddled in their tents, except for those who must watch the herd and stand guard against the coming of an enemy.

A Borderman came riding up from the south and, after a few words with the sentry, rushed dripping through the rain to the tent where Martos and the others were drowning their sorrows in stale jokes. He asked for pardon as he pushed through the tent flap and bowed, dripping water on the floor.

Paidros had been right in the middle of the story about the duenna of the prim girl from Thernhelm, but he paused, frowning, his expression so comical that Martos and several of his men laughed—mystifying the Borderers even more.

"Your pardon, Lords!" gasped the man who had come in out of the rain. He dropped to his knees in the doorway and bowed again. Water oozed from his wide-skirted trousers, and as his head bent forward, a trickle poured from one of the flaps of his leather helmet. "I am Akrit, a vassal of the Lady Rukmini of Shirkote. My mistress has sent me to tell you that an army of Seynyoreans are marching on the castle. They surrounded it as I rode away, Lords!"

They all sat up at this. Paidros, forgetting all about the duenna and her overly prim charge, rapped out, "How many men?"

"At least two hundred, Lord," said Akrit, "and perhaps more."

"DiVega isn't wasting any time," said Martos.

"He can't afford to!" exclaimed Paidros. "If he doesn't secure the road, he and his men won't eat, and he knows it!"

"But Shirkote isn't on the road," objected Valiros.

"No, but it's close enough to make a good raiding base, and it commands the road from Inagar," Paidros said. "He knows he'll have trouble if we hold it. He's probably grabbing up every fort within reach, and this is the closest to the city." He turned back to Akrit. "How many men does your mistress have?"

"Twenty-five, Lord," said the Borderman, "but she sent all but five to Inagar with Lord Jagat. Now there are only four men in the castle itself, as well as my lady and her serving-maids, and our children."

"The Seynyoreans count three hundred men as a company," Paidros mused. "We have more than that here—if you will ride with us, Lords?" He bowed to the Bordermen. The Bordermen bowed back.

In less than an hour, they were riding in the rain, peering through blurred veils of steel-pale water.

"The castle is near, Lord," Akrit said above the racket of the storm. "Listen! You can hear the enemy."

Martos listened, while clammy drops of rain washed his face, soaked his beard, and beat against the hood that covered his helmet. He could see nothing through the heavy rain, but he heard muffled sounds of men and horses in the distance. At least, Martos reflected, the Seynyoreans could not see them, either.

Suddenly the hammering of raindrops lessened, and through the thinning downpour, mile after mile of naked tableland opened out before them. Then he heard shouting: the sentries had seen them. Seynyorean trumpets bayed in brazen warning.

Martos charged, shouting, his sharp sword drawn, spurring on his war-horse. Like a wave his men followed. No time for formations or strategy, only to charge, in column, as they were. There was mounting and arming in the Seynyorean camp. Men on foot ran forward, waving their weapons.

Martos' sword was a scythe in his hand, sweeping low by his horse's side. It hummed in the air, reaping a man's head from his shoulders. Then he was past the dismounted men, hurtling toward the still confused soldiers who had scrambled onto their horses' backs and were trying to form a line. Before they could sort themselves out, Martos was in among them. He crashed into a standing horse and sent it sprawling; his sword smashed down on an armoured shoulder. The armour held, but the man went flying over his mount's tail.

Startled horses panicked. Martos saw one gallop away, dragging its rider by the foot. Another horse went bucking and rearing from Martos' path, its rider clinging to the saddle, unable to draw his sword. Out of the corner of his eye, Martos saw Valiros' ugly steed hanging in the air, soaring above the enemy; Akrit's sword was a wheel of blood.

All around him, men's voices were tangled in an echoing snarl. Confused soldiers and horses scattered from his path. A sword cut at him, but from so far away that it only hit a flying corner of his cloak, and the thick wool wrapped it for a second, then dropped away.

The Seynyoreans were fleeing! Already most of the horsemen were gone. Men on foot were scrambling after their vanishing comrades and panicked mounts, clumping together, staring slack-jawed over their shoulders, knowing that they would have to stand sooner or later.

Somewhere out there the commander would be trying to rally his men, get them into formation. And if he succeeded, Martos' troop was still disordered.

Martos reined in his horse and stabbed at the sky with his sword, trying to shape his tongue around the word, "Halt!" He stammered it out, but who could hear him above the shouting? Men went galloping past. A trumpet rang out behind him. Romulos or Styllis had seen the gesture and understood it.

Some of the Bordermen went on, intent on pursuit, or perhaps simply unfamiliar with the trumpet-calls. But his own men were pulling up their horses, and most of the Bordermen, seeing them, seemed to be doing the same.

Another bugle sounded behind, but it was neither Romulos nor Styllis. Martos whirled his horse around. Through the thin silver wash of rain he saw a steel-clad column advancing at a trot, deploying as it came, spreading out rapidly to right and left.

"Another company!" snarled Paidros, as though cursing.

Martos had been debating in his mind the virtues of various formations, but now the choice had been taken from him.

"Line!" he shouted. "Form on me!" He spurred his horse back through his own ranks, cantering past dropped weapons and abandoned cloaks and a head that grinned up from the ground with death-stiff lips. As he came abreast, the men of his crack troop turned their horses with parade-ground precision, until a hundred men were riding stirrup to stirrup, while their Border allies milled behind them.

The rain was thinning again as they rode, and he could see clearly the Seynyoreans ahead, shifting as they formed into line.

They were in three ranks, his men in one. He glanced over his shoulder and saw the milling cloud of Bordermen turning to follow him. All down the line on either side, dark grey swords pointed at the clouds. But the Seynyoreans were still forming.

"Charge!" he shouted, and snapped his sword down to point at the still-gathering foe. Romulos' trumpet sang, and Styllis' echoed the command.

Flying mud spattered from the horses' hooves: each hoofbeat jolted in the bones; speed-chilled winds rasped men's faces.

Seynyoreans shouted and spurred their own horses. The lines clapped together. Milky highlights rippled on charcoal-grey swords; shields were lifted to meet them, and the thunder of steel on iron numbed the ears. Horses fell, hurling their riders into mud; grey swords were stained crimson.

Martos' shield shuddered under a blow that bruised his arm beneath it. His sword rose and fell, hammering until his arm ached, as he drove his steed into the ranks before him. Men were yelling all around him, and the chiming of steel was an ache in his eardrums, but above it all he heard the crowing of Border war-cries.

And then suddenly it seemed that all the rearing, plunging horses that still had riders on their backs were running in the same direction, and the crowded mass was splitting apart. He blinked, stared about wildly, and saw little groups of Seynyoreans wheeling their mounts, trying to get free of the melee. Riderless Seynyorean horses bolted past. Bordermen came swarming from left and right, swords dripping. A dark grey horse was scrambling up from the mud. A Seynyorean vaulted onto his back and looked frantically around him. Martos saw terror on his face. A Borderman spurred in, and the Seynyorean whirled his horse and galloped away toward his comrades, who were streaming from the field.

Martos' steed reared and swerved away from another horse that lay writhing in the mud, moaning piteously with a shattered foreleg.

Its rider lay underneath, silent and inert: dead, Martos hoped, as the screaming horse rolled and pitched.

The impact had thrown the close-packed Seynyorean horses down in piles. The Bordermen, swarming in moments after the shock, had ridden around onto the flank and rear of a host already half-dismounted and fragmented by the shock of Martos' charge.

Demoralised, uncertain how large a force they were facing, those Seynyoreans still mounted had given back: the retreat quickly turned to a rout as the Bordermen, well-mounted and fresh, dashed in among them.

Bordermen, Kadarins, and Seynyoreans raced in a running battle for miles, until Martos called his own men back and rode to the gates of Shirkote.

Chondos did not know how long he crawled and staggered through the endless maze of bone-littered tunnels, with goblins jeering as they drove him on and the terrible presence of Vidraj looming over his life. After a time of nightmare delirium, he began to doubt that he had ever known any life beyond the tunnels, where dark things hunted and ate each other. Sunlight, and simple human joys, and freedom from pain, seemed dreamlike; he remembered his father's palace as one might remember some old tale. But at last they drove him up a slanting tunnel and turned into a slope of rough earth. Cold air struck his face, and he scrambled out of a hole into darkness under the shrouded night sky.

Dark shapes reared up about him: he recognised the roofless houses and crumbling towers. He had come back to ancient Rashnagar, where his forebears once had reigned as Kings; where now the Master waited for him.

The cold wind that raged through the dead city bit through his tattered clothing. His head whirled from weariness, and he sank to his knees. When had he last eaten? And what? He could not remember. . . .

"Get up!"

Chondos raised his head and met the baleful rubies of Vidraj's eyes.

"Get up!" the icy voice commanded again. "Get up, slave!"

He felt that terrible pressure again, and once more muttered the spell that shielded his mind. The effort made his head ache more than ever. The vampire hissed. A hand that felt like biting wire lifted him as though he were weightless, and set him on his feet.

Chondos stood, reeling. The bony hand seemed to crush his flesh.

"Walk, slave!" said the terrible voice. A push sent Chondos staggering forward. He was aware of eyes watching from the ruined buildings. Vidraj strode beside him, and goblins, white and black, came cringing behind.

Pale stone buildings like broken skulls lined the street. Furtive, misshapen silhouettes darted away from their torches. Once something came flapping from the sky, but Vidraj shouted a word and it veered away with a hoarse snarl.

A vast building appeared ahead, a grim, crumbling pile with empty, leering windows. A broken spike of tower stood at one corner, and farther away was another, unbroken, tower. The stone walls were still solid, although wind and rain had been working at them for a thousand years. A pale mist crept along the street toward them. It vanished as they approached, as mist does.

Emicos stepped into the torchlight. "You have done well, Vidraj," he said. His eyes glinted red, and they looked past Chondos and the vampire, lighting on the goblins who slunk behind them: "And with you, too, we are well pleased. Come, now, for your reward."

Was there mockery in that soft, intensely weary voice? Chondos could not be sure.

They followed Emicos down the cold street and into the darkness of a gaping archway. Goblins stood guard here: goblins of still another breed. These had noses, Chondos saw—noses as long as fingers—and tusks like a boar. Their skin in the torchlight was reddish-brown—lighter than that of many Bordermen. Some wore crude leather armour and some old mail; they bore halberds and spears in their hands. Their huge eyes glowed greenly at the newcomers; and dirty whitish hair straggled from under their helmets.

Stairways of mottled marble, and then a vast, echoing hall. Lights and shadows moved in it. Parts of the roof had fallen in: timbers and tiles lay scattered on the stone. At the far end, a ring of torches surrounded a stone throne. On it a black shape squatted.

Ahead of Chondos' captors, a body of men marched toward the throne. They wore ancient armour, and long lances were in their hands. Chondos was surprised to see that they marched in good order. They halted before the throne and crashed their spears upon the stone floor.

"We are the Chosen," their leader shouted. "We obey your summons, Lord! Command us!"

The black-robed figure shifted. As it moved, Chondos thought he saw a long, pallid, sticklike leg emerge from under the robe's hem, and a foot that put him in mind of a bird's claws, but then black cloth covered it so quickly that Chondos could not be sure just what he *had* seen.

"You have brought the rest of your tribe as well?" the deep voice hissed. "And your harvest?"

"As you ordered, Lord. All our women and children are here, and those few of our slaves that remain. They have been confined in the place your servant showed us.''

''You have done well,'' the Master replied in a hideous whisper. ''There are many to be fed. Join now my guard.'' A black sleeve gestured, and the armoured men moved to the side indicated. Many men were gathered here, Chondos saw, as well as armoured goblins of various breeds.

As the armoured men moved off, Emicos led Chondos and Vidraj forward. Suddenly Vidraj leaped in a blur of motion, and seized one of the men. There was a single loud shriek, and then Vidraj had bent the man back over his knee and his fangs were in his throat.

Armoured men shrieked and scattered. One, braver than the rest, turned and raised his spear. Without lifting his face from his victim's neck, Vidraj waved his hand at the spearman. The man shrieked, dropped the weapon, and fell to the ground, clutching his head with his hands.

''Vidraj!'' the Master's voice hissed. ''Is this seemly, before the throne of Emperors?''

Vidraj looked up, threw the man to the ground, and laughed. His victim lay quiet for a moment, and then crawled over to Vidraj's feet and sat staring up at his face.

''You may sit on the throne, Teratos, but do not try my patience too far! I have starved to bring this mortal to you; slaked my thirst with foul blood, and kept this prisoner untouched, by your order, for no reason I could see, when only a little nip, a sip, a scant cup of blood or less, would have bound him to obey—''

''And put your mark on him for all to see!'' said the Master. ''Fool! If all else fails, I may take that way to bind him; but for our plans, it would be best to send him forth with no detectable taint upon his body.''

''Do you not think that I desire his blood as much as you?'' said Emicos. ''I too could bind him to my will. Yet if we can send him, human and untouched, into the Bright Lands when the time comes, there is much he can do for us. If you bite him, he will begin to lose his immunity to the Powers of the Nameless. And that immunity we need.''

''Well enough,'' said Vidraj. ''I will not grudge you your prisoner, and you need not begrudge me this drink.'' He gestured at the man who knelt by his feet: the spearman looked up adoringly and reached out a hand to caress the vampire's knee.

''I would have given you blood,'' said the Master. ''You did not need to seize one of my guards.''

Vidraj stooped, picked up the man by the scruff of his neck, and tossed him sprawling before the throne.

''Have I harmed him? Back to your post!'' he commanded, and

the guardsman crawled to where he had dropped his spear, then rose and took his place among the others. But his eyes were still fixed in a dreamy stare upon Vidraj. "Even had I drained him as my reward for bringing back your prisoner, I would have taken nothing from you! He would serve you all the better!"

The Master tittered. "Have you lost all respect for the Emperors' throne?"

Vidraj straightened. "Had I still the respect for the ancient Kings that I had in life, I would rip your rotten body from the throne and tear your skinny bones apart. You have none of the ancient blood, you half-human—"

"Come forward, King Chondos!" The Master's voice broke through the vampire's tirade. "You wish one of the Old Blood, Vidraj? Here is the heir to the ancient Kings, the descendant of the Emperors! Come forward!"

Chondos blinked, and staggered a step toward the throne. His mind was blurred. Pain and exhaustion made it hard to think. The ancient throne? What good was it now? He had dreamed of it as a child, but it had been no such dream as this. He heard a chattering from the goblins behind him.

"Ah, yes," said Vidraj. "Our quarrel had nearly made me forget! These would claim the reward you promised for capturing the human. They summoned me from my sleep to help guard their prisoner!"

"They shall have their reward," said the Master. The face-cloth turned to the guards. "You, there, Leader of the Chosen. Guide these filth to where you penned your women and children. Let them eat their fill, and then, when they return, they may take three women with them, no more, to their tribes."

"As you command, Lord," said the Leader with a grave bow.

"And now, King Chondos," said the Master. "Do you wish to mount the throne of your ancestors? You have learned by now that you cannot escape. Are you willing now to do as you are told?" Whatever was under the black robe heaved and rippled as the Master laughed again. "Ah, we should summon old Sanga, and Isuri! It has been long indeed since either of them saw an Emperor by right of true descent sit upon *this* throne!"

Chondos stared at him, dully. The throne of his ancestors—the throne of the Emperor in Rashnagar! But all he wanted was food and water, and a chance to sleep.

"Come, King Chondos!" came the Master's voice. The black shape rose from the throne, and gestured at the vacant seat. "Will you not sit upon your ancestors' throne? Sit, and rule over all the Old Empire! I shall call up Isuri, who saw the last Emperor sit here, and he shall make the mark of sovereignty upon your brow, and our legions shall go forth to pacify your kingdom."

KING CHONDOS' RIDE 175

The throne, thought Chondos. Something at the back of his mind whispered that all he had to do was show them that he would do what they wanted, sit on the throne, and then he would get food and rest and water. All he needed to do was give in to them, and do what they wanted.

Sit on the throne. They were only mocking him, of course, but the throne was his by right. It had belonged to his ancestors, to the ancient Kings.

The ancient Kings . . . He straightened. His brain cleared.

"Yes, I will take the throne," he said. "I *will* sit on the throne. I will sit there after you, and these things that serve you, are dead, when the Twin Suns shine on this realm once more, and every foul creature has been hunted from this city! Then I will take the throne!"

The black cloth whipped toward him. "Will you indeed?" hissed the Master. "I think not! Guards! Bind him!"

Martos rode from Shirkote at dawn, having spent the night out of the rain, warmed and comforted by the chatelain. He rode out from Shirkote, north and east, toward Inagar.

Inagar—and Kumari. Her face was floating in his mind. He rehearsed the words he would say to her. Her eyes were in front of him when a scout rode up to report that a body of men was moving along the road in the distance.

Martos shook himself out of reverie and looked at the scout with no friendly eye.

"Men? What kind of men?"

"Seynyoreans, Lord, or so I would guess from their horses and gear. They are riding east along the road toward Nilakota. I could not see much at that distance, of course, but—"

But who else would be riding the Ojaini road from Manjipor, Martos thought, and rage roared up in him. He was on his way back to Inagar, he had fought yesterday, his men were tired, the horses were tired . . .

"How many?" he asked.

"I would say about a company, Lord. About three hundred men."

Martos frowned. Why not let the Seynyoreans go on? It was time for someone else to do the fighting. He was only about a day's march from Inagar. If he rode on, leaving the Seynyoreans to their own devices, he could be there by nightfall. By the morning, certainly. He could see Kumari tomorrow—if she would see him. If . . .

Rage twisted inside him and turned to bleak despair. How could he make plans until he had talked to Kumari? Why did this stupid war have to interfere? What did he care what the Seynyoreans did?

And all the time, the cold strategist in his mind was examining the situation, reminding him that if the Seynyoreans gained control of the road and opened it to their supply trains, then the war would be lost and all his men would have died in vain. An ominous rumble of thunder muttered from a distant bank of clouds.

How could he face Kumari if he let Jagat down? Jagat, and all the men who had gone to Inagar on *his* advice.

He had routed *two* Seynyorean companies yesterday—mostly by luck, and he had had more men yesterday. Nearly a hundred of the Bordermen had stayed at Shirkote. But there were still enough with him . . .

With a curse, he gave it up and, calling Paidros, picked out a fresh horse from the herd and prepared to ride off with the scout to look at the men on the road and decide on his plan of attack.

Chondos dangled: ropes chafed his wrists; his shoulders were being pulled apart. The golden-red glow of the brazier between his feet was very bright. And hot. Consciousness ebbed and flowed in red waves of pain. Once he came out of delirium to hear himself screaming.

That did nothing but make his throat raw and his enemies happy, so he forced himself to stop, closing his lips and setting his teeth in them. The blood from his lips dripped on the coals and steamed up, with his sweat, to scald his naked thighs. He nearly strangled before his throat would stop jerking. He could hear his breath rasp in and out in hoarse gasps.

About him the dimness of the ancient audience hall swam with memories of old glories like ghostly battle flags. Sometimes, in his delirium, he seemed to see throngs of fantastically robed courtiers, even to hear the stately cadence of the ancient Takkarian court music.

His arches ached from standing on tiptoe, keeping his feet away from the brazier, until he had to let go and hang loose in the ropes, suspended above the glowing coals while his nerves screamed that he was going to fall. The chains around his ankles caught his feet mere inches from the red-hot metal. They would not quite let him touch, but they were close enough that after a while he would force his toes down again and slowly move his feet away from the searing heat.

Through a haze of pain, he watched long-dead court officials in rich silken robes of purple, red, and gold, and richly clad embassies from all the countries of the world, prostrate themselves before the King of Kings, the Emperor of Takkaria. Then the pain in his shoulders would bring back the empty ruined hall, and he would look down and see the orange glow between his feet.

Every so often, someone in the darkness behind him would move one of the pins or needles or whatever it was sticking in his back, and at unexpected moments a whip would whistle out of the darkness to slash across his shoulders, his arms, or his belly. Or someone would throw a wisp of cloth or a scrap of wood into the glowing coals beneath him, and flames would leap to singe his legs. Sometimes water would splash across his face, and he could lick a little from his lips, while steam hissed up and burned. be did not know how long it had been since he had eaten.

He drifted back and forth between dream and waking. Was that moonlight peering through the roof? Or the pallid daylight of the Shadow? Here, where men long-dead had ridden through sunlit streets, or refreshed themselves in green gardens in the height of civilized elegance, starving ghouls and goblins hunted each other through windy streets between crumbling buildings under the dingy, sunless sky, screaming as they ate each other.

Lights and music and ancient ceremony filled the shadowy corners of his brain. But he could still hear screaming. He pressed his lips together and bit them, but the screams did not stop. After a while, he realised it was not his own voice. He forced his pain-dulled eyes open, and then wished he had not. They were cutting a girl up and eating her. He pressed his eyes shut and tried to wrench at his chains. He could not shut his ears, but after a while the pain did that for him.

Cold water splashing in his face. Licking wet lips. Scalding pain between his thighs.

There was something in his mind. Raw red flesh, torn from the wildly flailing bones. Blood, red and rich.

There was something in his mind. He tried to remember the symbols that Miron Hastur had given him, but they were lost somewhere in the abyss of pain.

Gongs, and deep braying horns. Richly robed courtiers bowed before the throne. The pride, the ancient power. The fear, the nightmare hordes thronging the city. Flaming towers shattered, men, women, and children fleeing, and the fangs in his throat.

There was something in his mind. He scrabbled for the symbols that could drive it out, but only broken and colourless fragments remained.

Was he going mad? The mournful call of a flute was echoing through the vast and empty hall. Inside his head he could hear the deep, roaring horns, the drums and gongs that accompanied it in the slow, pompous cadences of its ancient tune. But the flute sounded in his ears.

A bone-white face was before him. He blinked. Was it Vidraj? Emicos? He blinked again. The figure before him was clad in a long and flowing robe of brilliant silk, gold-coloured, such a robe as he had seen only in the pictures of old days, a robe of the kind worn by officials of the Imperial court, in the days when the Twin Suns glowed on Rashnagar. The flute played on.

Then he saw the flautist. Rich ring-mail and a purple cloak. And, nearby, another shape, a black-robed shape he had seen before.

"Take him down," said the hissing voice. "He will obey now."

The flute stopped, and the player turned; a rugged, white-mustached, red-eyed face stared. He remembered when the Dark Things had first come to Rajinagara.

The fangs in his throat, and the beginning of obedience.

Chapter Ten

While Chondos hung suffering in the old dark hall, Martos led his weary men southeast, into the dust.

Martos, riding with his hood thrown back, straightened in his saddle. Though there was no rain, a crack of thunder crashed and rumbled in the sky. Lightning glowed white through the far black clouds that glowered like a hill on the northern horizon.

No! Not more rain! he thought.

He could see blue sky through gaps in the clouds, and the light of the Twin Suns spread in broad golden bands through the gloom, although he and his men rode under a screen of cloud that dulled their armour.

Deeper and deeper into the dust they rode, south on a long curve that would bring them beside the road, down on the rear of the Seynyorean force. Ahead of him, his own scouts were busily hunting the enemy scouts. Their success would determine how much warning his foes would have: the outcome of the battle depended on a dozen grim little duels somewhere in the poisoned wastes. The two forces would be closely matched in numbers. Martos knew he could not depend on such a fluke of luck as the rain had twice handed him the day before.

He could easily have lost half his men, or more, in that second charge. By extreme good fortune none of his own men had been seriously injured when their horses went down—fortune and his very lack of numbers. His men, charging in a single line, had not piled up as the enemy had.

The plan he and Paidros had worked out a few hours before, crouching in the dust, watching the distant river of armour that was the enemy, had seemed good enough. As he rode, flaws in it kept occurring to him.

Barely visible to their left, and well out of sight of the road, a small body of Bordermen rode. A scout posted between them had no other duty than to carry news of the attack. Another little troop rode behind his line: they would circle to the right when the conflict began, to seek out the enemy flank.

The long-legged Seynyorean steed between his thighs trotted steadily over the poisoned dust, and the miles fell behind, vanished with the weight shifting from one pair of feet to the other. Its neck arched proudly. It was a far different beast from the powerful Kadarin horses he was used to. At first Martos had distrusted its small hooves and long, fine-boned legs; but as he rode it, his horseman's instincts, taking the measure of the beast beneath, told him that he had chosen well: that here was a horse born without fear, trained to battle, accustomed to noise and blood. He would soon see if he was right.

Sparkles of light in a patch of sun. He strained his eyes, watching them grow larger, nearer . . .

Then he saw the enemy, marching down the road, Seynyorean soldiers leading their horses. Beyond them reared the Shadow, blank and black. Grey dust muffled the sound of hooves as long-striding cavalry horses closed on the slow-moving column. Soon they would be within bowshot. But it would be better not to use the bow, if they could get close enough for a solid charge with the sword—if they could get close enough without being seen.

His scouts came riding out of the dust, waving, and joined themselves to the ranks behind. The line ahead stopped. Men were mounting their horses. Had the Kadarins been sighted? Even if they had not, surely some of the men must look up and see them any minute; surely someone must look over his shoulder, accidentally, and see the long line moving in.

Martos moved a hand toward the bow by his boot. A quick flight of arrows would knock out most of the men who could see them, and most of the column would still be uncertain of the direction of attack. The sunlight faded as a rift between clouds closed. The Seynyoreans were settled in their saddles, and the column rode on, shod hooves pounding the old stone road.

Martos left his bow in its case and drew his sword. Light rippled, white as curdled milk, down the shadowed blade. Muscles in wrist and forearm clamped tightly against the long weight. Left and right along his line, steel slipped silently from leather sheaths, pointing at the sky. He gathered his horse for the charge.

Crackling thunder boomed on high. Then he heard the trumpets— the bugles of the foe. Outriders, turning at the sound of the thunder, saw Martos' men bearing down upon them.

Romulos and Styllis sounded their horns. Horses stretched their long legs. Swords waved in the air. Swift hooves blurred in a jolting gallop.

Someone must have given contradictory orders in the Seynyorean column: the men milled in confusion, some whirling their horses to face the foe, while others spurred ahead, attempting to deploy and re-form. A shouted order rang out. The men who had turned to face the Borderers wheeled again, dashing away to join their comrades. But already Martos and his men were almost upon them.

The nearest horseman got bigger and bigger, and Martos could see the huge muscles of the horse throbbing; the face of its rider swiveled in the saddle to look back over his ready shield, no fear in it at all, like the face of a lion.

Martos' heart was jolting and his mouth was dry. He was breathing too fast. He forced himself to take a deep breath and hold it, concentrating, as Birthran had taught him, on the crystalline spiral. He was gaining on the man, but he would have him on his right side. His shoulder and elbow, at best, would be exposed.

Suddenly the Seynyorean pulled up his horse and cut at Martos' elbow as he hurtled into range. Martos whipped his arm down sharply, the pivoting weight of his sword dashing the other's blade back across the shield. The Seynyorean spurred his horse, and suddenly Martos was guarding furiously, unable to strike. The lighter blade flailed at him, and the Seynyorean's shield hovered in the way. Martos knew his arm would tire faster.

On a sudden inspiration, Martos jerked his horse to a stop, just as the two blades met. As the other hurtled past, Martos swept his heavy sword around in a low humming cut that glided above the horse's back, under the shield. The shield dipped, but not fast enough. Splinters flew from the cantle of the saddle. The Seynyorean bowed over his horse's neck, knocked forward by the blow, even though the saddle had probably taken most of its force. But now he was ahead of Martos again. And Martos' men were catching up: he had outridden them in the excitement of the chase.

He urged his horse forward, and rode now as part of the line. The milling Seynyoreans were still spreading out, trying to deploy.

The wild shouts of Bordermen rang out to the right. Leather-armoured men drove into the flank of the still unformed line.

Seynyorean horsemen were riding toward Martos' line, spreading out as they came: men from the front of the column, circling to left and right. Others were still facing away. Martos' line crashed into them. Horses scattered from Martos' path. He saw his previous opponent reel in his saddle, trying to prop himself up with his shield, but his horse would not turn and galloped rapidly away.

Other horses were panicking too, but some, better controlled, were turning. One, only half-turned, went down as Martos' steed crashed into it; the rider flew from its back and vanished in the storm of stamping hooves. Martos' steed plunged and danced back a few steps. A maddening ironwork clamour filled his ears.

On his left Martos saw another horse turn and bound toward him. A falling sword jarred his lifted shield, but his own sword was already twirling over his head. He felt his blade quiver against metal, and as his shield came down, saw his enemy reel in the saddle with a deep dent in his helm.

Something bright moved at the edge of his vision. His head snapped around as a sword swooped at his unprotected arm. He got his own blade down barely in time. Steel scraped his edge and nicked the iron guard above his finger, with a *ting!* that was drowned in the swelling battle-sound, the clamour of hammering and shouts of pain.

At least the other's shield was turned away. He could see the brown leather backing on the far side of the mailed body of the man whose arm was rising for a second cut. Martos' point darted at the armpit, but the other blade dropped atop it, drove it down, leaped at Martos' face. Steel rasped. Martos' horse danced under him. His sword swept up the other blade and carried it above his shoulder, then hissed back for the kill.

His helmet rang on his head like a bell, and he felt himself falling: his shield bruising his shoulder, his sword skittering harmlessly across metal. He clung to the saddle with his knees, tried to keep the reins from slipping through his fingers. His head felt swollen; his ears were aching with the hammering racket of battle. But air was rushing into his lungs; he must still be alive. Alive, and under attack by two men.

The sword on his right was driving straight down on his helmet. Somehow he got his suddenly heavy steel aloft and hurled a hurried look over his shoulder as the blade rang and trembled in his hand.

Sharp-edged steel swooped toward his eyes. He hurled his shield into its path, and cut to the right in the same movement. His shield shuddered, pealing on his arm, and he felt his sword crash against another. He snapped his face to the right. The blade on that side was flying toward his neck, and as he drove it aside, thought blossomed in his brain, and he turned and whirled the blade up in a cut above his shield, his elbow scraping his helmet.

He felt a shield-rim lift the blade, and then he whirled head and shoulders sharply, violently, blade-tipped arm lashing out to smash aside the steel that plunged at his arm. He leaned far to the right, hearing a sword sigh in the air behind him, and jerked his arm up, twisting to flip the pommel high. His point drove through mail-rings at the throat. Blood burst out, flooding grey steel.

Then he was turning, jerking the point free, and he saw his foe's shield flinch as the red tip of the long blade spun above his head on the way to a striking position. He cut as it began to drop, but the Seynyorean was too experienced to fall for that old trick, and his shield rose and rang as Martos' sword rebounded: the sharp edge lifted up behind.

Crackling thunder rumbled in the sky, drowning the metal racket of battle. Lightning seared men's eyes and left them filled with sparks. Martos' mount reared and danced. Dim shapes moved around him.

Then came the rush and clamour of rain, battering steel helmets with tinkling water. Horses were bucking and rearing in the tumult. Some, riderless, galloped away. There was a sudden outcry. Beyond the Seynyoreans, he saw small scurrying shapes in a dark mass and heard the mingled war-cries of Bordermen.

The Seynyorean ranks wavered and reeled in confusion. Horses were panicking, scattering. Martos controlled his own mount with difficulty, and wished he had Thunderhead or Warflame beneath him. Nothing disturbed the big Kadarin chargers, and they would be as calm in the thunder as in sunlight.

He heard leather bucklers rattle and steel shields groan as horsemen all around him scattered and fled. Where were his own men? Thunder rumbled in the sky again, and the clouds paled with lightning, but not so near or so dazzling. Raindrops splashed from the rim of his morion, and threw cold drops in his eyes.

Men in mail and men in breastplates were all mixed together in a swirling mass, hewing with darkened swords. A miniature horseman in dark, grotesque armour rammed through the shoal of frantic horses ahead, his bloody sword blurred to a looping, twisting ribbon, his shield drumming as he warded off the attacks of the taller horsemen around him.

Martos urged his stead forward. Horses were stampeding around him—many with riders on their backs. Sharp swords flailed at him, clashed on his shield-rim, glittered in lightning, as he rode on. He cut about him in the rain, his horse rearing as the shattering thunder crackled and roared, echoed by the hammering and crashing of metal.

There were Bordermen everywhere now, their little ponies seeming smaller than ever. He looked around for more Seynyoreans to fight, but the few he could see looked busy. He caught a flashing glimpse of Paidros as his sword hurled a mail-clad man from the saddle in a scarlet cloud; saw a Seynyorean burst out of a group of Bordermen, his sword whirling like a red windmill, spurring his horse unmercifully away.

Dimly, Martos realised that they had cut the Seynyorean force in two, and that the remaining pockets of men on the wings were disentangling themselves from the melee and fleeing.

A trumpet signalled the rallying-call—only one trumpet. Thunder drowned it out.

They had won. No doubt more Seynyoreans would be marching out of Manjipor to assail the castles that guarded the road, but he would let others attack them. He was tired. Perhaps two days' march due north now lay Inagar.

Inagar—and Kumari.

*   *   *

The thunder echoed through the streets of Manjipor, and rain muttered endlessly on the ancient stone. Lightning cast a pallid glare through the window where Istvan stood, and picked out a line of carved stone dancers on the facing wall, their rounded breasts smooth and nippleless from thousands of years of wind and water; their faces, mouthless and noseless, with only a hint of eyes.

"I never saw a troop of cavalry re-form so fast," Turul DiVega was saying, behind him. "They were all strung out and mixed in with DiArnac's men—what were left of DiArnac's men—and then they rallied and were in line and charging us while we were still forming. I don't think the men at the back of the column had time to realise that we were in a battle, really."

"What about the Bordermen?" asked Istvan, turning back from the window. The voice of the rain chattered behind him, fondling the carved women on the walls.

"I don't know where they came from; we couldn't see much in the rain. There were some with Martos, wiping up DiArnac's company, but I think there must have been more. They were everywhere, and hit both flanks at once, right after the Kadarins bowled into us. Thousands of them, it seemed like."

There was a warm fire in the grate, and the rain was outside. So why did Istvan's joints ache? He walked to the fire, shaking his head. It was warm, this room, but it was a trap. If Jagat's men controlled the road . . .

Boyaro DiArnac cleared his throat. There were bandages around his head, and one arm was in a sling.

"I'm afraid you're wrong there, Turul. There were a lot of Bordermen with Martos—two or three hundred, I'd say—and they all took off and followed the Kadarins. I didn't see any other force. I could be wrong, I suppose."

"Well, you weren't in a position to see very much!" Turul snapped. Istvan frowned at both of them impartially. This wasn't helping. He opened his mouth to speak, and shut it again as a voice sounded from the door.

"Commander DiVega!" Istvan recognised Garan D'Oleve, the Seer. "Rupiro Esnola's company just reported an attack, sir. The Kadarins again."

Jaws dropped. Istvan listened through the crackle of the fire and the rustle of the rain; opened his mouth to ask for more information, then shut it as thunder roared overhead.

"Well," he said after the thunder quieted. "He certainly does know how to use the rain, doesn't he? Let's hear it all, D'Oleve."

"He took them in the rear, by surprise, sir. They had no time to form up. Esnola started his men moving as fast as he could, but they were already on the tail of his column, and as the front went back to form a line, a force of Bordermen got in on the left flank. His center was in confusion and breaking, and then another pack of Bordermen came down the road and hit them from the rear—from the east, that is. That broke the line in two, and then the storm came up, and so many horses panicked that it started a rout."

"I'd like to fight him in the dry season sometime," said Istvan thoughtfully; then he shook his head. "Can't wait for it, though. What about the men with Phillipos? Any attack on them?"

"No, sir. Esnola's Seer said that he thought there was only about a company in the force that attacked him, that it was about equal numbers, but the Kadarins had the advantage of surprise."

"Well, the boy knows his business," Istvan grunted. He closed his eyes and listened to the rain drumming its fingers on the roofs of Manjipor, while his mind wrestled with the tiny force that was tying up his army. "We'll have to strip Ojaini to put a full-sized escort on the convoy. If we put a full . . ." He paused, thinking, his brows knotting. Martos was not attacking the men with Phillipos' force—or at least, had not done so yet—but appeared to prefer attacking single companies. He only had three or four hundred men.

But a convoy would be important enough to attack. And Martos had not hesitated to attack nine thousand men, before. . . . And the convoy would be under the same disadvantage as Istvan's army had been. . . . If he got to the wagons and burned them . . .

He shook his head. "I'll have to go after him myself," he said, and thought, suddenly uncomfortable, of Birthran's face.

It was two days later that Martos' tired troop limped into Inagar. Styllis was dead, cut down by a Seynyorean blade in the first clash of the charge. Emios, too, had been carried from the battlefield strapped to his saddle, and it was not likely that Donuon would live. And nearly a dozen other men were injured. The losses of the Bordermen had been worse, but then, they always were.

The brim of Martos' helmet, behind his left ear, was folded back, and in the centre of the fold was a deep cut.

The last time he had come this way, the road had been dry and dusty, and the fields and grasslands brown and seared. Now the road was mud, fetlock-deep, and in the distance faint hints of green had begun to dye the plain.

In the last dim beams of the falling suns, the ancient royal city glared like some forgotten ruin from a distance; yet it swarmed with life, and for the first time in perhaps centuries the old city, always too large for the tiny population, seemed full. Nearly every warrior in the province was there—more than two-thirds of all the people of Manjipé.

The great herd of tired, underfed horses had been left behind to graze in the care of a few men. They were now close enough to the city that Hamir's scouts and outriders would protect them against any movement from Manjipor.

Martos walked with his men through the great southern gate—the Imperial Gate, men called it—leading the tall Seynyorean horse he had picked that morning as a fresh mount. They had been able to make it to the city so quickly by changing horses often. From the stone pillars of the gate, weathered carved elephants stared down, warriors on their backs waving lances and swords; around them and beneath them, thousands of tiny figures danced, bought and sold, made war and love in eternal stone. Here and there, names had been scribbled in various scripts. The great bronze gates were of a later period, and the design hammered into them was different—a pattern of endlessly repeated flowers.

The little dark people swarmed about him as he entered: warriors in leather; here and there, little groups of women before whom the armoured men gave space with an almost superstitious reverence. Gaunt women in robes that had once been brightly coloured, a generation or so ago: women in new cheap dresses from the northern cities, bought as unbelievable luxuries with money that might have gone into the land; dark women, their eyes earth-brown. He searched among them, looking for Kumari's face.

There were women carved in the stone inside the walls, carved beads circling large breasts or drooping in a graceful curve between them, without hiding the weather-worn stubs of stone nipples.

No, she would not be in the crowd at the gate; she would be at Hamir's palace, the old summer palace of the Emperors: the old palace in exile of the dynasty's declining years.

Would she be waiting there? Would she be thinking of him? Would she be glad to see the company marching in? Or would she be busy with a new lover? He blinked his eyes furiously. That was no way to think!

The crowd was thinning now, letting them pass. Men were shouting questions, asking about the war, asking what the Seynyoreans were doing. Some of his men were answering them. Dark, hungry women watched the new soldiers through wide, earth-brown eyes.

The crowd thinned; he ordered his men to mount, and trotted down the long street to the palace. The city went by in a blinding blur. Then he was dismounting again before the great sprawling structure, and restraining himself from bounding up the steps like a child. Would she be waiting? Would she smile to see him? Would she greet him at all?

A horror settled on his heart. Suppose she would not speak to him? At the very thought, despair drowned his heart like chill water. She could not be so cruel! He could not bear that. He would go mad, he would pull out his dagger and stab himself there on the steps, or he would ride south into the Shadow and face the Dark Things.

"Look sharp!" Paidros muttered to the men behind him. "There's Lord Jagat!"

Martos looked up and saw her.

A thick group of men waited atop the stairs, and Jagat and Hamir were in the middle of them. Kumari was standing at Jagat's elbow, looking over his shoulder. He could only see her face and dark eyes, and a hint of bright cloth.

He wanted to shout, and run up the stairs. For once, it was a good thing his tongue would not move. He forced himself to take the steps one at a time, and twice slowed to a deliberate climbing pace as he realised his feet were skipping up the stairs.

He watched her face, seeking some sign she had seen him. His heart twisted. Was she looking at him? Or staring through him? Hamir moved, and Martos could see only her eyes and cap of night-black hair.

Not until one of his men, clattering up the steps behind him, bumped into him, did he realise that he had stopped dead on the stairs, staring at those eyes, his heart beating like a mad drum in his chest.

O Blessed Mother Earth! he thought. *Make her love me!*

Hamir moved, and Martos could see her face, the full red lips, white teeth suddenly flashing as she smiled. He fought the eagerness in his feet, and made himself climb slowly.

Jagat stepped to meet him, and caught hold of both his hands. "Welcome," said Jagat. "Word came that you have fought a battle at our backs while we sat here, and have saved the forts along the road from the Seynyoreans. Well done, Martos!"

He had to move his eyes then, and look into Jagat's proud, hawk-keen warrior's gaze, even though he wished to look at her. And he must make some answer, some formal speech, but his tongue was dead and his mind empty. Jagat had praised him, and what could he say? Could he say anything without stammering like an idiot? This was her uncle, almost her father, and his child was in Kumari's womb and—

His mind cleared. He remembered what Jagat had said—had it been only ten days ago?—when he had left to harass the Seynyoreans. Jagat wanted them to marry.

Words came to his mind. "I—I am glad to have been—pleased to have been of service, Lord. The road—control of the road should give us the victory, and—and—"

Jagat's hands tightened in a reassuring grip. "And I should be getting other troops down there!" Jagat rumbled, his voice stronger and more firm than Martos had heard it since Pirthio's death. Suddenly he had the feeling that those wise dark eyes had seen right through into his brain, seen all the fears and confusion whirling in his mind.

"You are tired, Martos," Jagat said calmly. "You and your men have marched far today. You need rest.

"Kumari! Show Martos to his lodging. The Rajtakun Chamber will do; it will be convenient to the Council Chamber. Lord Hamir, will you see to the lodging of Martos' men?"

"Yes, Lord," Hamir replied with poor grace.

And now Jagat was moving aside, his firm grasp drawing Martos past him, and Kumari was there.

Her wide brown eyes met his, and he had to fight the urge to take her in his arms. There were people all around them. He heard Suktio's voice, and a hand seized his and pressed it, and there was Suktio, white teeth flashing as he said something congratulatory, and Martos stammered some sort of reply without knowing what either of them had said, and Suktio was gone, and Kumari's eyes were there, and her hair black and fragrant, her slim body wrapped in blue and purple silk, and he wanted to kiss her and caress her and feel her pulse under his lips, and there were people all around them.

Full red lips opened in sudden laughter, white teeth flashed in her nut-gold face, and then her arms were around his neck and her mouth was on his.

His hand stroked the soft curves of her, the softness he had long missed. And then she let him go and stepped back, and he was aware of men staring at them as she drew him through the archway where painted figures in old court robes bowed and postured on white porcelain tiles.

He was dumb as she led him through long, dim-lit corridors: faded hangings and weary furniture that had been preserved from lost days of wealth. Forgotten Kings stared from age-bleached portraits.

She did not speak until they had followed a winding stairway up, and the crowd was left behind. He heard muffled footsteps, and looking back saw Mirrha and two other women, but they hung back, as though to stay out of earshot.

"I missed you," Kumari said.

He caught his breath, turned toward her, looked down at her. He glimpsed, from the corner of his eye, Mirrha's arm stretching out in front of the other women, saw them stop on the staircase, out of earshot. His throat felt swollen.

"I—I—I—" He fought against his stutter. "I—missed you." He swallowed, and wiped his lips with his tongue. "How is—is—are you well?"

She smiled up at him, and patted the front of her gown.

"We're both fine," she said. "I enjoy eating rice, Martos. I always wondered what it tasted like. It smelled so good when I was a girl, and attending the childing women. I almost took a grain once, but then Padmini—the older woman who was in charge of us—came into the kitchen, and I didn't dare. I felt *so* wicked!"

He realised that her face had begun to fill out and lose the hint of gauntness that all the Border women had unless they were pregnant, and he knew the slim body beneath the silk would be filling out too.

Suddenly he remembered her, teasing him: *But I always count the ribs of my lovers! How can I fell if you have any at all, under all that!*

Her smile faded, and her face became troubled. "But don't think I've changed my mind, Martos. I'm not going anywhere. I was ready to—I would have gone away with you once, but—I can't. I won't. You asked me to go with you, and I can't. So now it's time for me to ask you to stay with me instead."

He stared at her. There was a sudden stillness in his mind. He heard the voices of Mirrha and the other ladies-in-waiting, like doves cooing in the distance. He remembered the wall of Shadow, blank and black, and all the horrors he had ever heard of the Borderwomen's lives.

She would stay, would face those horrors, whatever he did. She would bear the baby—if it lived—here, with the Shadow and its makers barely fifty miles to the south. There was nothing he could do about that.

The choice was simple. To go, or to stay.

Go, and leave her to bear his child alone, to forget about it, to pretend it was some other man's child and nothing to do with him. Never to know whether it lived or died, to try to forget.

Or stay: stay to take up land along the Border—for Jagat would be generous, he knew. Father to the heir: heir to Damenco, at least; maybe, if all went well, heir to the kingdom. But an end to the life he had planned for himself. An end to the dreams of following in Birthran's footsteps, of founding his own school, after he'd had his fill of wandering and won a fame in war that would make his name a trumpet-call on the lips of poets for generations to come, and spend a calm old age watching boys grow up to be heroes.

He thought sadly of the ancient hall in Erthi where Birthran had taught for so many years, and the old man's face rose into his mind. He wondered if he would ever see Birthran again.

To stay, or to go: to live here with Kumari—or without her, anywhere else.

He had tried living without her for three weeks. He remembered, suddenly, the tense moments before the attack on the Seynyorean vanguard, and the stone that had shaped itself into her face, seeming to stare at him with her eyes.

A simple choice: to go, or to stay. The choice was no choice. It was already made.

"I'll—I'll—s—" He shook his head, angry at the stutter that always took away his words at the wrong time. "I—I've been without you for three weeks. That's enough. I thought I'd go mad! I couldn't—I thought you'd never forgive—" Then he caught her to him and crushed her tight against him.

She gasped when he let her go, and brought a hand to her bosom with a grimace. "Please, before you do that again," she said breathlessly, "will you please take off that—that—" Her little fist rapped against his breastplate, and it clanged like a muffled bell. "That basting pan? Ouch! Be careful of my breasts, dear, our baby's going to need them!"

"I'm sorry!" he said.

She laughed, grabbed his hand, and pulled him forward. "But I'm forgetting my orders from Uncle!" she said. "He told me to show you to your chamber!"

An ancient corridor opened out before them, and they went through like children, hand in hand, nearly running, and laughing. Martos could hear the faint cooing of her women, far behind.

"This chamber was panelled in silver once," she said, opening a door. "It was taken out centuries ago, of course, and sold to provide for the land. But they still call it the Silver Room. Wait here a moment." She moved away, stepped through another doorway a few strides down the hall, and came back with a lighted candle. "Your room, Lord," she said with mock gravity, and led the way inside. He stepped hesitantly after her, as she continued, "It is conveniently close to Lord Jagat's chamber, and his council, and" she winked—"convenient to other rooms as well."

The candlelight showed the rough unpainted boards where the silver panels had been. The wood between was even rougher, and he saw that it had been scraped: speckles of silver leaf told why. She closed the door behind them, and he heard the bolt click.

. "Now, will you please take that thing off?" she said. "I want to kiss you without getting bruises. You might as well take off everything else, while you're at it." There was a rustle of silk, and the robe began to slide from her shoulders.

He wet his lips and fumbled at the buckles that held breastplate and backplate together. Blood surged through his skin. A sound like cooing doves came dimly through the door.

"What—what about your—your women?" he asked.

She laughed. "They'll go and wait in my room. Next door. Convenient, isn't it?" The silk rustled to the floor, and Martos lost the power of speech again. But what they had to say to each other now was said, not in words, but in the tender language of flesh against flesh.

For three days Istvan and his men hunted Kadarins across the barren wastes around Manjipor. Single companies rode as decoys, their Seers ready to send word at the first sign of an attack. Seven companies were spread out over a vast area, all ready to rush to a single point when the word was given. Once the quarry revealed themselves, the chase would be short.

Istvan himself, with two thousand foot—D'Aglar's horseless company, the six hundred Carrodians, and a thousand of Maldeo's men from Manjipor—marched by the road, toward the slowly crawling convoy from Ojaini. Most of the time, he trudged among the men, while soldiers vied for the honour of leading his horse. But he tired more quickly than the younger men, and although he wanted to save the horse's strength as much as he could, sooner or later he was forced to mount and ride at the head of the column, with Ironfist Arac, whom he had made his second-in-command, striding easily alongside, cracking jokes.

Storms came and went. One day it rained steadily and heavily. On the fourth day it rained hardly at all, and between the rare, sparse drizzles, it was dank and hot. Their clothes clung stickily, drowning and suffocating their skin. The clouds that drifted across the Twin Suns did nothing to lessen the heat.

They halted shortly before noon, as the heat surged to a peak. Pale-skinned Seynyoreans, ruddy Carrodians, earth-brown Bordermen all sat or sprawled on the stone of the road, trying to avoid the dust that stretched away on either side; their weapons near to hand, they ate and talked and rubbed their aching feet, ready to spring up at any sign of the foe.

Istvan sat with Ironfist. They passed a slab of cheese and a leather bottle of wine back and forth as they talked.

"Three days now," said Istvan, "and no word or sign of Martos."

"Probably safe in Inagar with the rest of Jagat's men," said Ironfist. "Well," he said thoughtfully, "I can't say I'm really pleased to be hunting him down like this. He's a good lad, Martos." He took a long pull at the wineskin and passed it back to Istvan. "Pity he wound up on the other side. I always liked him."

"At Ojaini they told me you'd killed him," Istvan said.

"I thought I had," Ironfist said, hacking off a hunk of cheese with his dagger. "Wasn't happy about it. I was glad to learn I hadn't, though I suppose it would have saved everybody a lot of trouble if I had." He filled his mouth with cheese, and chewed thoughtfully.

"Must have been quite a fight," said Istvan.

Ironfist looked embarrassed. "Oh it was just—my strength, you know, these stupid overgrown muscles I inherited. Drove his sword down. I could have done it to you just as easily." He shook his head.

"I'd have had more sense than to try to block an axe with a sword," said Istvan with a slow smile. "Even when someone else is swinging them, those things are hard to stop."

Ironfist snorted, and shook his head again. Istvan felt sympathy. As a boy, he knew, Ironfist had been outlawed from his company because he had, by accident, killed a comrade during a wrestling match. The Carrodian's strength had been a curse to him all his life.

For Ironfist, like Istvan himself, was a man on whom the blood-guilt lay heavy: the curse of the hero, perhaps. For no more than Istvan himself could Ironfist escape the sense that all the men he fought were cripples, or children. Perhaps, in a way, it was worse for him, for he had been born with his terrible, smashing strength, while Istvan could always find comfort in the thought that any man who was willing to work long enough and hard enough could achieve his own level of skill.

Yet where, Istvan wondered, had that will and determination to work come from? Had he not been born with it, just as Ironfist had been born with massive, half-N'lantian muscles? Was a lazy man less to be pitied than a cripple? Should a man be praised for the virtues he had been born with? Were courage, willingness to learn, or determination more praiseworthy than the colour of a man's eyes? Were not all faults and virtues qualities that a man was born with, just as a man might be born with strength or intellect or quickness of hand, whether they were inherited from parents, or, as sages said, they were qualities of the soul, built up over ages of death and rebirth? What man could choose his past or control the forces that ruled over birth and death?

The sound of his name called Istvan from his thoughts. Looking up, he saw a Seer running over slippery stone.

"Lord, one of DiFlacca's scouts has brought word of a large body of men moving down from the north—from Inagar, Lord."

"How many?" Istvan asked. "And how far? Will they be at him soon?"

"At least two or three thousand, Lord—both mounted and afoot, though the scout could only make a rough guess at numbers. But they do not act as though they were aware of DiFlacca's company at all. They will pass across his front, some four or five miles ahead of him, and they seem to be moving a little toward the east. DiFlacca does not believe their scouts have discovered him."

"Moving to the east?" Istvan lunged to his feet. "Find out where the convoy is!" He turned toward his horse, and shouted at the young man who held it, "Hardyarl! Get the map out of my saddle-bag! Not that one—the left side! That's it! Then run and find Lord Rajan!"

"You think they're after the convoy?" Ironfist asked.

"Of course. I've been wondering how it got this far—ah!" He took the map from the young man's hand, thanking him carefully by name, and began to unroll it, while Svain Hardyarl went running over slick damp rock to fetch Lord Rajan.

Istvan wanted to pace back and forth in his impatience, but he schooled himself to squat and spread the map out on the stone of the road. They'd be tired soon enough, he thought.

"Have you gotten word from the convoy on their position yet?" he asked, searching his brain for the Seer's name.

"The Seers with the convoy are not yet sure, Lord. They are trying to find out."

There was nothing to be said to that, and Istvan turned his attention to the map, trying to work out just where he was and where DiFlacca's men were. When Lord Rajan arrived, he would be able to work out their position more exactly.

Rajan came a moment later, picking his way hastily among the reclining men. He was one of Maldeo's vassals from Manjipor, and knew the country as none of the Kantarans who had scouted for the army on the trek from Ojaini could.

The Seer—D'Arcor, this one's name was, Istvan remembered finally—closed his eyes, and through the eyes of one of the Seers riding with the convoy was able to describe a landmark—a small pile of stones and the dead shell of a tree—that allowed Lord Rajan to place them exactly on the map.

Istvan frowned. "That's—what? Fifteen, twenty miles?" He pursed his lips and shook his head as he calculated the distance. His breath hissed in exasperation. "It'll take us all day to get there, and the enemy will be at them in three or four hours. Five at the most!"

"It's not as bad as it looks," Ironfist's deep voice said. He leaned over Istvan's shoulder. "Men on foot can move at a better clip than you saddlebound people think! And the convoy is moving toward us at the same time. Make them pick up the pace to meet us. And what about DiFlacca?" He pointed. "He can ride in right on their tail! Just stay a few miles back until right before they reach the convoy."

It made sense. And there were two other mounted companies that should be able to catch up with DiFlacca.

Old Palos DiFlacca had ridden out with his Seer and his scout, and in a few moments D'Arcor, eyes closed again, was describing to

Istvan and his aides the swarms of tiny dots that were moving across the grey dust, and trying to count them.

Four thousand, perhaps more. Less than half of them mounted. The men on foot were hard to see without getting closer.

Two companies were moving to join DiFlacca; the others Istvan ordered to the road. Together with the companies that guarded the convoy, they would have clear superiority of numbers—if they could reach the convoy in time.

And that was Ironfist's job. Istvan told him to set the pace, and for the next several hours he marched with the men—his feet aching from stamping on the stone of the road. He marched until his heart was pounding and sweat was dripping from his sodden clothes, and his breath rasped in his lungs. Suddenly he felt strong hands close on him.

Before he could struggle, he found himself lifted in the air and deposited gently in the saddle of his horse. Blinking eyes that burned with sweat, he saw Ironfist holding him steady.

"I am—" But the words rasped so painfully in his throat that he did not go on to explain that he was perfectly all right. It took a while for his head to clear. The jolting of the horse made riding almost as bad as walking had been. Loud boots drumming on stone made a constant thunder beneath the pounding in his ears.

Under the glaring suns, over drying stone, Bordermen and mountaineers marched, their stout boots crashing on the road. While the Twin Suns slowly drifted west above them, soldiers quick-marched toward the east where evening waited, their legs jarred by constant pounding on the hard stone.

Istvan jounced beside them on his horse's back. When the throbbing in his ears died down, and the air he breathed no longer burned his throat, he felt ashamed—both because he could not keep the pace and because he had been so foolish as to think he could. His feet hurt. It had been stupid, at his age, to try to match Ironfist's pace. He must have his head clear for the war!

D'Arcor soon told him what little news there was to hear. DiFlacca was following the enemy force, staying well behind them, keeping out of sight but gradually gaining, creeping ever nearer to the enemy rear. Soon all would be ready, drawing into line, spurring to a gallop for a sudden charge.

The convoy from Ojaini was hurrying its pace, but the slow trundling wagons could only go so fast. The cavalry that guarded them were girding for the battle, riding in a screening column on the convoy's right. Scouts grimly watched the land to the north for signs of the foe.

Istvan's troops pressed on, stout boots shuffling over ancient stone. Istvan worried as he watched the suns slipping slowly westward. Could he win this race and reach the threatened convoy before Lord Jagat's men?

Sudden shouts rose from the Bordermen. The crash of boots softened and was suddenly stilled. Istvan pulled up his horse, trying to hear what the men were shouting.

"Look! There!" Lord Rajan pointed at the sky. There was awe in his voice. "I've never seen one this close to the Border—not outside the Kantara."

Istvan stared into the curdled blue and white sky, until it writhed with worms of light. Then he saw a tiny black speck that soared and circled, and suddenly he knew what the shouting was.

"A bird!" someone was saying.

"Look! There's another!"

"*Two* more!"

Istvan stirred with impatience and cleared his throat. He heard Esrith Gunnar's deep voice growling. But Ironfist was standing and staring, too, his eyes shaded by his broad palm.

"From the way that flies, I'd call that a vulture—carrion bird of some kind, anyway! Wouldn't you say so, Istvan?"

Istvan grunted, and then it struck him that it was one thing for the Borderers to stand staring at the bird, but Ironfist came from a country where birds were common.

"Vulture or crow, what difference does it make?" Esrith Gunnar's voice demanded. "I should think you'd see vultures all the time in this desert!"

Istvan straightened. "No," he said, startled. "No, you don't. There isn't enough for them to eat. Nothing lives here, so nothing dies here. Not this deep in the dust. What little carrion there is, the Dark Things get. Birds generally stay away from the Border anyway." He paused, thinking.

"It's an omen!" someone was saying. "The birds are coming back! Soon the land will be fertile and free!"

"A vulture!" Lord Rajan said.

"Have you ever seen one before?" asked Ironfist quietly.

"Oh yes," said Rajan, "but never before south of—" He stopped suddenly, and looked at them sharply. "Inagar!"

Istvan straightened in his saddle. "Of course!" he exclaimed. "They're following Jagat's army. They know that when armoured men gather, there's food for them."

"The birds always know," said Ironfist with a nod. "Look there! Quite a swarm of them! There's the enemy, I'll wager!" He turned away and began shouting orders. D'Arcor the Seer came rushing to Istvan's horse.

"Word from the convoy, Lord. The enemy is in sight."

Istvan grunted, and stared along the road, trying to make out the shape of the convoy. Was that a flash of metal ahead? He could not be sure.

"Where's DiFlacca?" he asked. The Seer closed his eyes a moment.

"He is closing in on the enemy rear, sir. They are well in sight now. He can see the convoy! Sir, he says . . ." He paused. "Captain DiFlacca says, unless you forbid, he will go straight in."

"Tell him to get moving," said Istvan.

There was no time for fine calculations now. Men were shouting orders, and in a moment the army was marching again.

Istvan strained his eyes against the greyness. Dim dots formed in the dull grey waste. Watching them, he realised they were still miles away. Sunlight glittered from tiny points.

Ironfist's deep voice roared an order. All the Carrodians broke into a jog. Heavy mail clashed and jingled from the jolting. Istvan urged his horse to match their pace. Slowly, so slowly, the distant dappling grew. And now he could see a second patch of dots, and in the air above it floated a dark shifting blur of birds. Another order, and the run dropped to a walk.

Ironfist shouted his name. "Take the cavalry and go on!" he said. "Go at your own pace! We'll catch up!" He was right, Istvan realised: a horse would not do well at this speed. But the men would catch up, for they could endure this grueling shift of paces as no horse could.

He spurred from the road, and waved to the horsemen drawing up alongside. As their leaders drew even, he set off at a canter. The marching men fell behind. Not for long, he knew.

The motes on the road had almost assumed the shapes of men and wagons now, and the other patch of milling dots was growing beneath its misty marbling of birds.

He ordered the pace to drop to a walk, and reined his horse in, watching the slowly growing masses of men ahead. He was certain that the battle would be joined before he got there. Jagat's army was moving in fast. He would build his pace slowly to a charge, and catch them in the flank. Where was DiFlacca? But of course, even were he in sight, it would be impossible to recognise him. He would only appear to be a part of the enemy.

Istvan heard a horse coming up behind him at a run. He turned, expecting one of the company captains, and saw instead the Seer, Garan D'Oleve, urging his horse beside the column.

"Commander DiVega!" D'Oleve called. "A message from Ojaini!"

"From Ojaini?" Istvan gaped at him. "Let it wait! What word from DiFlacca?"

"Commander! Ojaini is under siege!"

"*What?*" Istvan whirled his horse around. "Besieged? By whom?"

"Warriors from Mahavara, Lord. They think that—wait!" He closed his eyes a second, then said, "Yes, Prince Hansio *is* there. One of the Seers recognised him from the battlements, riding beneath his personal banner. He has at least ten thousand men."

A dozen questions rushed to Istvan's lips, but he choked them off and turned his eyes back to the battle ahead. If Ojaini was under siege, this might be the last convoy for quite a while.

Chapter Eleven

The harsh stone pile of Roger of Aqilla's old robber castle brooded on the rock of Tarencia, above the trading town, aloof from bustling and rumours. The soldiers that guarded its empty corridors had ceased to wonder at the silent, morose court officials they saw so seldom, for their minds were occupied with the petty slights they fancied from their superiors, and the revenge they would have someday—someday soon.

The servants, nervous and unobtrusive as their masters became more and more difficult, had their own wrongs to brood over— threads of hatred that drew them closer and closer to some half-dreamed day of butchery and reckoning.

Only old Lord Shachio—the only Seer who remained inside the walls—seemed to notice the change that had crept over the court; but whenever he began to wonder, a sudden twinge in his old joints would jerk his mind rudely away from the mystery and back to his own age and illness.

And Jodos, sitting like a spider in the midst of his web, would smile. He had done well: no thought stirred the surface of any mind in the castle that he had not touched. His own mind was a tangled web that filled the castle, and all other minds were inside it. Yet so cunningly wrought was that web that neither Lord Shachio nor any other Seer had yet noticed it.

He laughed as he watched the old man hobble through dreamlike corridors to find him and tell him the news. But he sobered as he penetrated the fringes of Shachio's mind: Hansio of Mahapor had crossed the Atvanadi and lain siege to Ojaini!

That could have been better than he had dared to hope, had it come a little later; had it come after DiVega had taken Inagar and broken the army of Lord Jagat. But now the combined armies of the two Border nations greatly outnumbered the Seynyorean force. If DiVega lost . . .

He was aware of Prince Phillipos marching at the head of his men, a little south of the city. Should he send Phillipos back to DiVega's aid? Or should he let him reach Kalascor, and then send him down through Mahavara with fire and sword to break the province while Hansio's army was absent?

There was much to be said for that: the hatred of the Kalascorians was old and bitter and easily roused; it might well drive them to deeds unthinkable to the Seynyoreans because of the Blue-robes' accursed rules. Yes, that would be best. Were it not for the Blue-robes' laws, these humans would have already done much of his work for him.

If DiVega lost, his men would still give a good account of themselves in dying, and the Border army would be weakened. And then, no doubt, Hansio and Jagat would hurl their power north, and leave the Border undefended behind them. Jodos smiled.

Yes, they would come after him, and he—he would call upon the Master at the proper time; and before they could turn, their homeland would be blotted out behind them. So, let DiVega persist. Phillipos would open the road through Mahavara.

He must hurry, though. They would be eating each other there, up in the hills, under the Shadow. He must not wait too much longer. But Phillipos would not be here for hours—would likely enough camp, then enter the city in the morning.

For now, however, there was time. He would go to bed and let his slave fawn upon him, and find ways to torment her. He need no longer do the disgusting thing she required of him, for, though she was not yet aware of it herself, the creature he had planted in her was growing, small and juicy. He licked his lips. But that was for later. Now he must be content with minor tortures. He would look into her mind to find some trivial thing she feared and then subject her to it.

He laughed cruelly. Such silly things she was afraid of, compared to what he would do to her later, when this city and all its lives were his!

Istvan DiVega spurred to a gallop, his Hastur-blade stretched out point-first before him, flaming with need-fire in the twilight. Soft dust swallowed the sounds of hooves. The battle was plain before him.

The companies defending the convoy had deployed to the north of the road in a steel-robed crescent. Bordermen swarmed down like a storm-driven wave, and carrion birds fluttered in circles above them.

Then, of a sudden, old Palos DiFlacca with nine hundred shouting men crashed into the rear of the Border army and hurled them, headlong and unprepared, into the waiting cup of Seynyoreans.

Border ponies crashed together and fell in piles; footmen jammed into crowding mobs; and now the crescent leaped forward. Tall Seynyorean steeds drove into the press: swords came spinning down among the tangled mass, shearing leather armour.

In the blink of an eye, Istvan saw that vast Border host hurled into utter confusion, and then he, with over a thousand horses at his back, was dashing in upon their right. Men looked up in surprise, taken at open shields, their chests and sword arms bared to his attack.

He pricked his horse to a run. His arm was straight as a spear shaft, and the keen blade in his hand darted to search out the muscles of arm and shoulder. He wished to wound, rather than kill. With these men dead, who would defend the Border holds when the Dark Things struck from the mountains?

Wounded men, swordless, scattered, with no choice but flight: any other army, taken so both in flank and rear, would have been in full flight by now. But the Bordermen were stubborn. Little knots of men gathered like rocks in a stream.

What they thought they were fighting for, Istvan could not tell; not the convoy, that was safe enough. *Bordermen are so stupid they always run the wrong way.*

Except for that, the battle was over. Istvan met Palos DiFlacca in the packed mass at the centre, laying about him with a bloody sword. Shortly the two of them, with men hastily gathered for the purpose, were riding into the ranks of the enemy left, scattering the Bordermen before them.

A conch-horn sounded above the battering of steel and leather, and the Border force began to fall back. Istvan wiped his brow and gave orders, allowing the Borderers to disengage themselves and retreat in good order. He pulled his horse free from the slaughter and rode toward the camp.

Ironfist had come running up with the foot, and a long line of axemen began combing little pockets of Bordermen out of the Seynyorean ranks. Heavy axes splintered shields of leather and bone. Bordermen staggered back with broken arms. Istvan, watching, felt his heart shudder. Nearly all the men of Manjipé—for no man lived on the Border who was not a warrior—had rallied to Jagat's cause, all but the few who followed Maldeo.

If many more of Jagat's men were killed, there would be little more than a handful of men, women, and children left to face the Dark Things when next the Border flamed. And that would likely mean that the new Border would be north of Inagar—perhaps far north, perhaps upon the sea itself; for who would dare to stand against the Dark Things once the Border folk were gone? The farmers and merchants of the north would fly in terror. Only the Hasturs themselves, and the mercenaries, would remain. And they would not be enough.

He watched, grimly, and then saw that Ironfist, too, was aware of the danger, and had given orders accordingly. Any eye accustomed to the grim efficiency of the Carrodian Mountaineers in battle could see that they were holding back, striking only when they must, and then striking to wound rather than kill.

They did not leap to follow the men reeling before them with shattered shields, but advanced cautiously, step by step, heavy axes raised menacingly above their heads. He saw a man rushing to attack that line crash senseless to the ground beneath a blow from the flat side of an axe. A comrade, diving to lift the unconscious man, passed under the stroke of that axe in safety, and drew back, burdened by the limp body, his sword gleaming defiantly in his hand as he backed away from the axemen's stately advance.

Most of the Borderers were now burdened by the dead and wounded they would never leave. They backed away, weapons in their hands, down the clear line of retreat Istvan had ordered made for them.

Beyond the ranks of the Seynyorean companies, Istvan saw the grey dust swarm with scattered men. But they were gathering, rallying, and Istvan sucked cold air through his teeth, wondering if he should have ordered pursuit after all. If they charged again . . .

Bordermen always run the wrong way.

How could he bring peace to this realm without destroying the very people essential to its preservation? Especially now, with Hansio of Mahapor sitting on his supply lines?

Jagat's army, with almost every man of fighting age in the principality behind him, was a little smaller than his own. How many men would Hansio have? More, probably: Mahavara was the larger and richer province, and much of its land was still unblasted, far enough from the Shadow that women and mares and cattle could give birth safely.

On the broad plains that stretched north to the Oda, the Mahavarans raised vast herds of cattle and horses. Oddly, they never ate beef, but lived on milk and cheese; and cow dung fed their fires.

At least ten thousand men, the Seer had said.

Would Hansio strike straight for the capital? Or would he, perhaps, clear away the Seynyoreans from his flank first? Men called him the Fox—and this despite a thousand more complimentary names that poets had made for him. He had stirred up treason and dissention through the kingdom before most of those he dealt with had been born.

Ojaini had been nearly stripped of defenders . . .

"DiVega!" a voice shouted from nearby, and turning, Istvan saw Rupiros D'Ascoli spurring his horse toward him.

"DiVega, are you asleep? Or drunk, or mad?" He pulled his horse up sharply, so sharply that it reared. "Can't you see they're rallying for another charge down there?" He waved a furious hand at the boiling mass of Bordermen. "Wake up, man! We've got to disperse them some way! Either throw another charge into their ranks, or else let off a flight of arrows! You told us 'no pursuit,' but that just gives them time to re-form! A little more and they'll be on us again! Don't just sit there!''

Istvan looked out at the milling men and horses. He could dimly hear voices from among their ranks, but men were shouting and talking among his own. A core was forming, of horsemen facing his line, and footmen behind them.

"If we let off a few volleys of arrows they'll scatter,'' D'Ascoli said. "They're burdened with their dead and wounded, and they know they can't get at the convoy now! Any other army would already be gone! And they don't have much in the way of arrows themselves.''

Istvan frowned at the gathering host. "I suppose you're right,'' he said. "A few volleys of arrows . . . No!'' He sat up in his saddle suddenly, his brain clearing. "No! Arrows will be certain to goad them into a charge!'' He paused, frowning at the two armies that stood fronting each other. "Have your men draw their bows and set arrows to the string, but don't shoot unless a charge is actually launched. And if they do charge, order the men—'' He paused, and his teeth clamped together as though to hold the order back in his throat. "Tell them to shoot at the horses.''

"At the *horses?*'' D'Ascoli stared at him. "Hastur's flames! Half of them are our own horses!''

"Better we lost some horses,'' Istvan said, "than lose all Tarencia the next time the Dark Ones move.''

He watched the armies below as D'Ascoli rode off with the orders. It looked to him as though there was some disagreement among the Borderers. Some hotheads were no doubt calling for another charge, and others arguing against it.

But to assume that Bordermen would retreat because arrows were landing among them—no, that was foolish. Perhaps the *threat* of arrows, arrows clearly visible on the string, would break their nerve enough. And it might still work just the other way.

"It is always folly to regard the enemy as lacking courage,'' Birthran had told him once. Fear was a chancy weapon at best: it could make an enemy fight all the harder, and spur him to actions he might not have taken otherwise.

They were quarreling over there, and a flight of arrows would have been just the thing to tip the scale toward another attack. The trick would be to tip it the other way. He thought about that for a few moments, then spurred to the convoy.

"Get those wagons moving!''

Soon the convoy and then the entire army was on the march, and still the Bordermen hesitated. Blocks of Seynyorean companies began to shift positions like migrating birds in spring, so that there was a continuous barrier between the Bordermen and the slow-moving wagons.

"We're just going to withdraw from the field?" Sandor D'Arnac exclaimed. "They're going to think we're afraid of them!"

Istvan laughed. "Excellent! That way they can feel they've won a victory of sorts, and go home and brag about it without feeling they have to fight another battle!" The younger man stared at him, but he heard Ironfist and old Palos DiFlacca chuckle behind them.

It was several hours before the Bordermen actually moved off to the north, after hanging on the army's right flank, parallel to the road, while Istvan and the older veterans calmed some of the younger commanders.

Again and again he would hear the same argument—that they should turn and drive the Borderers off, with either a charge or a shower of arrows. After a while, Istvan found that his answer had become a recitation to which he need not listen.

He sent scouts off to the east, to watch the west bank of the Yukota and learn what they could of Prince Hansio's movements.

Ten thousand men, the Seer had said, or more; between Maldeo's forces in Manjipor, and the men he had called out of Ojaini to guard the caravan, his own army had grown to near that number. But if he left Manjipor to relieve Ojaini, then Jagat would doubtless move, either to seize Manjipor or to attack Istvan's rear while he marched against Hansio.

Hansio was the more dangerous of the two, perhaps, but from Inagar Jagat would be a constant menace during the march to the Yukota. And after defeating Hansio—if he could defeat him—he would have to reconquer the principality again. And if they combined against him, they would outnumber his force by nearly two to one.

Well, he'd fought against worse odds than that. But not against Bordermen. And not against Hansio.

How had even the Fox been able to get his army to Ojaini so quickly, without giving warning of his coming? How could he have crossed the Atvandi unopposed, with so large a force?

By the time the Bordermen finally gave up and turned back to Inagar, his Seers had given him the answer to that question. Ajeysio of Kantakin had opened the gates of his impregnable fortress to Hansio, giving him control of the best crossing on the river.

For months Ajeysio had been wooing a girl across the Atvanadi—a girl distantly related to the old Prince and close kin to his Seneschal.

Istvan remembered the passion of the young man at Rinmull's council. Had he already decided, even then, to betray his castle into the Fox's hands? Or had it been DiFlacca's outburst that had decided him? No matter, now. What mattered was what Hansio would do.

Sometimes it seemed to Chondos that he walked in the living city of Rashnagar, in its days of glory, its streets swarming with the cultivated, happy people of its court, dressed in gorgeous robes of many-coloured silk, engaged in polite amusements and following rituals that reached far back into the earliest history. He drank fine teas and strange wines out of exquisite cups of delicate, paper-thin porcelain, or walked through gardens where brilliant-coloured carp swam in pools under green thickets of bamboo and rainbow-flowered bushes, or watched dancers whose steps were old as time, whose bodies were flames of passion beneath their butterfly robes.

Then, suddenly, he would be wandering the streets of a crumbling, ruined city where roofless houses leered at leaden, sunless skies, and bestial, misshapen creatures roamed. He could not tell which was real. Twice, as in a dream, he saw the city fall.

Twilight, and gay paper lanterns like glowing moons in the butterfly gardens: the real moons burning far above them—except in the west, where glowing towers flamed against ominous blackness.

A sudden glare of dull red light, the light of molten towers bursting, and dark shadowy forms, like ponderous shapes of mist, grew larger and larger. Fleshless black wings shadowed the stars. The people of the city wailed in terror. Other wails answered them, but they were not sounds from any human throat.

Men and women in fluttering robes ran panic-stricken through the streets. Black and sourceless shadows fell upon the crowds; where they passed, only grey dust remained. Flame-clad figures battled with the shadows. Need-fire lit the city. Stunted, misshapen hordes charged out of the dark, and at their head came a black-robed figure that laughed in malice. Pallid human figures grew out of mist.

Twice he saw the vision, and each time it was different—but each time it ended with a bone-white face and the sudden sinking of sharp teeth in his throat.

He remembered running, with sword in hand and great confusion, cutting down small, hairy figures that swarmed around him until the tall pallid shape at their head seized his sword arm in a grip of iron.

And that time he woke from the nightmare and found himself talking with old Sanga, the white-faced warrior who wrapped his helmet with cloth in the ancient style, and played chess with him in gardens that sometimes turned into an empty courtyard.

Again, seated with old Isuri, scholar and courtier, he remembered the chaos in the apartments of the Imperial family; remembered fleeing with King and court out of the city, down thickly-wooded slopes.

Shouting among the soldiers that guarded them. Stunted figures scuttling between night-shrouded trees, and the royal elephant screaming, and then only huge bones standing there, the flesh eaten away and the great bones falling, crashing into dust. The shrill screams of women and the hoarser cries of men, and the hideous cackling of uncanny shapes that ran in among them. Men scattered and ran between dark, gnarled tree-boles. Masses of needles and leaves and thin branches whipped his face as he ran, and then the frost-white face came out of darkness.

He awakened, and walked with Isuri through green gardens where gentle women in butterfly robes smiled and bowed as they passed.

It was confusing. He ate and drank, but could not tell whether what he ate was raw meat still filled with blood, or delicately roasted venison, drowned in sauce. He could not tell fine wine from foul water—or blood, which he once found himself sipping from a jewelled goblet that he hurled away in horror while Isuri and Sanga and a dark-robed shape laughed.

He knew that robed shape. He shook his head to clear it. He was Chondos, heir to the throne of Rashnagar, and what was this misshapen thing that covered itself beneath that black cloth to laugh at him? He balled his hands into fists. For a moment, he remembered what was under the black robe, the maggot-soft flesh he had glimpsed when Rashnagar fell and a dying soldier ripped the covering away.

Then he shook his head, dazed. How could he remember that? He had not even been born then! What was happening to him? What was all around him? He closed his eyes, and he felt the pain in his ankles and all up the inside of his legs, the tenderness of healing burns, and remembered a glowing brazier between chained ankles.

He opened his eyes on the dusty, ruined hall. But only a moment before it had been rich and splendid and thronged with the bright-robed nobles of his court.

His court? Curious confusion swept over him. He had been born to rule, yes, he had not escaped that. But surely there was a different throne, another castle? Another court? He remembered bowing before the throne, and intoning sonorous words of ancient ritual.

A thousand years ago.

He shook his head. That was all wrong.

"His mind is still strong, Emicos!" a hissing voice was saying, somewhere, echoing among stones. "Perhaps we should do more."

"It would be unwise to mutilate him, as I told you," another voice said. "He will do your will, given the right guidance."

"But he will be alone!" the first voice said, harshly. "We cannot send Isuri with him for the action we plan! If his mind should break free—"

"It would not matter," said the second voice. "The Chosen will not let him escape. Gates will still open for him. But he will not think to rebel once his memories have been taken from him.''

The voices echoed hollowly from the ancient walls of the empty hall, which was strange, because he was back in the light and music of ancient times, and the bright woven tapestries that covered the walls should have muffled the echoes.

He blinked. The rich colours of the room, bright tapestries, robed courtiers, padded furnishings, all became transparent, insubstantial, and cold stone walls appeared in pallid grey beams of light that crept through the gaping roof.

''Why will you not let me bite him?'' a soft voice said. It was old Isuri's voice—or was it his own voice?

''If you bite him, he will not deceive a Healer or a Seer,'' said Emicos. ''The compulsion will be too marked, too easily seen. I learned long ago to read the signs, and every Seer and Healer is taught to look for them.''

The insubstantial furnishings, tapestries, and people finally faded away. A cold wind blew in through the ruined roof and made Chondos shiver. He struggled to clear the numbness from his brain. The weathered stone, the pallid daylight, came and went as the dead city died and came to life around him.

Old Isuri stood close beside him, facing the black-robed shape and another white-faced man—Emicos. Chondos pondered the name, trying to remember how he knew it. Emicos. Emicos had stood against Vidraj. And there was something more . . .

Out of the corner of his eye, the empty magnificence of the hall began to creep back. All was grey stone when he looked at it directly, but as his eyes moved, flashes of colour crawled at the edge of his vision, as though the room behind him were filled with bright-coloured things that vanished when he looked at them.

''How long do you think you can starve us this way!'' said Isuri. ''It has been weeks since you allowed any to leave the mountains to feed! How much longer will you keep us here? Soon the last of the Chosen and the Pure-in-Blood will be gone! Already we have eaten the last of the Real Men! Over the Border is food in plenty, yet you will make us eat each other rather than let us hunt in the outer lands. I have had to kill a dozen ghouls who sought my flesh! And what good will *this* be, without the Pure-in-Blood to follow him? Soon all your human slaves will be gone!''

''There will be enough for the purpose, and then there will be new ones,'' the Master said. ''They are easily replaced. This plan was made when Emicos first brought the Lost Prince to us, nearly twenty years ago. We must let them grow lax and forget their fear of us. While we wait, they grow careless, or so Emicos says.''

''Emicos!'' Isuri snarled, and Chondos felt rage burning in his brain. "Why listen to one who was mortal only ten years ago, his blood as sweet and fresh as this one's." And Chondos tasted the salty sweetness of that blood in his mouth.

"Do not let my age deceive you," said Emicos. "You tasted my blood ten years ago, yes, you and Sanga and Vidraj and others. I nursed you from my veins while I passed from one form of life to another. But I was never your victim. Do not judge me by the walking dead that you rule. My mind was never numbed by death. I can still eat meat, or other food, if I wish to, and I have powers that you have not."

"And he is more useful than you, Isuri," the Master's voice rasped.

Chondos blinked, shaking his head as shadows of the past again clouded his vision. Transparent women in rich silk robes smiled at him; they flocked, chattering gaily, over the bright, ghostly carpets under which their bones lay.

One face out of the many looked at him, and suddenly he remembered her, fearfully. She, too, had fled from dread shapes under the trees, and then for long centuries afterward had crossed the Border in quest of food. But she had grown proud, too proud, and defied the Master. While she slept, ghouls had been guided to her resting place, and long ago her gnawed bones had been scattered across the mountain's slope.

This was madness! How could he remember such a thing? He shook his head, trying to clear it. What were they doing to him?

He heard Emicos and the Master laugh. His fists clenched in impotent rage. Transparent women, carpets, hangings, vanished. Dim light was fading from the ruined hall.

Pale mist fountained from a crack in the floor. Chondos stared as it flowed and drew together into a pillar, its surface pebbled, as though with tiny rings of frost. Frost hardened into metal.

Darkness came like a velvet blindfold, blotting all from his sight. A scratching sound, and a spark flared painfully and died again. Another scratch and a crackle, and then a tiny flame grew and sprinkled orange sparkles across the steel of Sanga's mail.

"Well, Sanga?" the Master hissed. "What do you want here? There is none here with blood for you! Or is it loneliness that draws you up from your grave tonight? Soon I will summon you, and then you will hunt on the other side, but for now, you might as well lie still."

"I am angry!" Sanga said. "You called me up to play with this man's mind for you, but now that the spell is broken, you tell me to lie down and gather dust until you decide to chase us over the Border again! Why this delay? When will we break the Barriers once more, and slake our thirst? While those fools out there are warring, we should attack!''

''Fool!'' said the Master. ''Have we never tried that before? You should remember other times, when we struck while our foes still fought. They will unite against us. War by itself will not win for us! But when they have weakened each other, when their attention is turned from us and King Chondos leads the Pure-in-Blood across the Border, then you may follow his army and feast in the castles he opens for us. Save up your thirst for then! There will be plenty of blood for all!

''Chondos!'' the Master hissed. ''Come now! Ascend your throne!''

Gongs boomed inside Chondos' head. Bright colours glowed before his eyes. Rich carpets covered the floor. On every side, kneeling courtiers in flowing robes knelt, and bent their heads to the floor in ritual salute to the King of Kings. Golden glory glowed around the throne, and he found himself stumbling toward it. The ancient court music, gongs and flutes, rippling strings and deep, braying horns, all rolling in ponderous, stately cadences, roared in his head.

At the foot of the steps of the empty throne he hesitated. Something was wrong, or different at least. Conch-horns brayed in chorus, saluting the heir of the ancient Kings. A black-robed figure materialised from mist on the steps of the throne.

''Who comes to claim the ancient seat of the Takkarian Kings?''

That confusing sense of familiarity that was somehow *wrong* became stronger than ever. There was something he must remember.

Deep horns moaned. His mind groped for words, and sought vainly for something he could not remember. In some other life, he had stood before a throne like this, and another figure had asked . . .

He could not remember.

''Chondos,'' he heard his own voice saying, as though from far away. ''Chondos, the heir of the Arthavan Kings.'' His voice sounded shrill and weak in his own ears, yet it echoed from the stone walls as the music did not.

''Come forward,'' whispered that harsh, inhuman voice, clear above the ghostly music. He set his foot on the stairs. But something was wrong. Something . . .

Gongs and horns, and tiny bells, and instruments he could not identify, deep and strange, and then Sanga's flute joined, strangely different from the others, echoing from stone. He could not feel the rich carpet he saw underfoot.

A dazzling blaze of torchlight and bright candles glowed on the rich fabrics of carpet, robes, and hangings. Pride swayed in him, princely, with the stately, ponderous beat of the old music. He set his feet on the second step. The world swayed about him.

But something was wrong. Something like cold tongs laid hold of his brain. Should not the figure by the throne have been robed in blue, rather than black?

Horns brayed in salute. Flutes trilled wildly above them, old Sanga's flute clear above the rest, echoing from the walls. He could feel the breathing of the black-robed shape.

"Something is wrong," he said, and staggered another step to the throne.

The hall was a mind about him, full of bright memories and ancient bowing courtiers whose bones had been scattered long ago, but behind the bright lights and rich-robed people lay slayings and bloody feasting and sardonic, mocking malice.

There was something he must remember. Had the robe been black or blue? The Blue-robe. Something was hidden in the blue robe! The black robe was chasing him now, up and down crazy winding stairways through skeletal buildings in a ruined city. But, no. He was on the steps, swaying on the stairs, and his throne was before him.

Deep gongs boomed. Horns roared. To a chiming of bells, he stepped onto the dais, turned his back upon the mighty throne of his forebears, and looked out over the brightly clad crowd below. Thousands of upturned faces looked at him expectantly. Horns bayed in salute.

"Sit, Chondos, Emperor of Takkaria, King of Kings, Ruler of Rajinagara!"

He sat down. The throne was cold and hard. The faces below vanished, every one turned to the floor as the people of the court prostrated themselves, and all he could see was thousands of richly robed backs. The music swelled, roaring in triumph, and the faces rose from the floor. Thousands of faces, subjects of the King of Kings. But they were all so white, so white . . .

The black-robed shape laughed. For a moment, an army of skeletons stared at him with eyes that were caves of bone. Then they vanished, and the courtiers were there again, in all the splendour of their robes, but there was something mocking and unclean in their eyes.

There was something he had to remember. Something a blue-robed man had given him.

The splendour vanished and flames of candle and torch were gone. Goblins were staring with huge round eyes, and ghouls were kneeling in a rubble of stone. The red eyes of vampires were hungry flames. Then they, too, vanished in a blare of horns, and in the velvet darkness that closed about him he reveled in the taste of the courtiers' blood. And the screams and the terror of the people of the city as his dread host poured into the streets, leaving behind them the burst and molten towers that Uoght had broken, and the long years of waiting and hatred were fulfilled at last.

The horde poured into the city. Bright-robed people squealed and fled. And he, the Child of Uoght, the scorned half-human child, was above them now, the descendants of the children who once had mocked when they thought him only a cripple, in the days when he had still *looked* human; now the time had come for revenge! Revenge, and wet red flesh, and the delightful terror and pain of writhing skinless things that had been men and women . . .

And Chondos screamed on his throne at the unbearable pain as he felt himself cut apart.

The Master laughed. "Remember that, King Chondos!" the cracked, inhuman voice said. Chondos blinked, saw the ruined hall about him, felt his broken fingernails still clawing the arms of the throne in agony—yet his body was sound and whole. "Even though I need you, I can bring you that pain! Only obedience can spare you."

Terror seized Chondos, and he ran and ran through tangled corridors in the Master's mind. But wherever he ran, the black shape was before him, and inhuman laughter met his every turn.

Again he found himself on the throne in the ancient hall. Isuri's finger smeared something wet on his forehead.

"There is no escape," said the Master. Old court music played on.

"Of course not, Martos," Kumari was saying. "If you had left, and I had decided to marry him, Suktio would have been a perfect father to the baby. He admires you greatly."

Martos' tongue was as useless as usual. Instead of speaking, he ran one finger down the soft skin of her side, bumping over ribs.

Someone pounded on the door. Martos tried to curse as he sat up, but his tongue would not do that either.

"Lord Martos!" a man's voice shouted through the locked door. "Lord Jagat wishes you to come to the Council Chamber! At once, Lord! It is very important! Hurry!"

"I—I'm coming," Martos stuttered, then shouted. He had to shout it twice before the knocking stopped and they heard quick feet hastening away from the door.

Angrily, he looked about for his clothes. A bare arm went around his chest; he felt soft breasts against his back. He turned his head. Their mouths met, and then she gave him a little push, and rolled away to pick her gown up from the floor.

"I'll be waiting," she said. "Come back if—if Uncle lets you. But—but if you don't come—if you have to go—" Her eyes met his. "If you don't come back—if Earth takes you—don't be afraid for the baby. He'll be cared for. Or she will." She smiled. "And remember that I love you!"

She pulled her gown over her head, hiding the start of tears.

Twenty miles south and east, Istvan's horses cropped wet brown grass in the light of a half-dozen moons.

"We've no choice," Istvan said. "A five-mile march in the morning and we'll be in good position to stop any attempt either to chase the convoy or to join with Hansio. We'll just have to sit there, until—"

"You can't bottle up nine thousand men with seven thousand!" a voice objected.

"Better than seven thousand against twenty thousand!" Istvan answered. "But it shouldn't come to that. Once Maldeo and his men move up—"

"Just abandon Manjipor? Lord Maldeo won't like that!"

"I don't suppose he will," said Istvan, "but let *him* argue it with me, if you please! By the third or fourth day, he should be southwest of the city, and we can close in from opposite sides."

"*If* Hansio marches north to Tarencia," Rupiros D'Ascoli cut in, "instead of just riding in on our tail!"

"That's a risk, I know," said Istvan. "But from here, we at least have a chance to keep his army away from Jagat's. If we can slow him down and harass his line of march until Lord Maldeo arrives, we can match his numbers—"

"His, *or* Jagat's," said D'Ascoli. "Not both! If they catch us between them, why—"

"If you have a better plan, let's hear it!"

"We can fall back on Manjipor. If Hansio does cross the river," said D'Ascoli, "he'll have to make the same march we did. Garrison Ojakota, and—"

"Not enough supplies," said Istvan. "If we'd gotten another convoy through, we might be able to hold out. But we'd be trapped there even so. This way, at least, we have room to manoeuvre, and a chance to keep Jagat and Hansio from joining forces."

"We should have attacked again!" Bimsio shouted. "We would have, but you sat there, you held us back! They didn't have the courage to follow us up! We could have broken through to the convoy if we'd charged!"

Martos glared. He'd been torn from Kumari's bed to listen to *this*?

"Idiot!" Suktio shrieked. "Couldn't you see they'd have killed us all!"

"Better that!" Bimsio yelled, and his voice warred with Hamir's and Suktio's, drowning out each other, drowning out even Jagat as he roared at them.

Hamir's wizard Arvesu rose, waving his arms, his shout for silence lost in their voices. The maddening torrent of sound went on, blending shouted words of taunting mercy and shame and Takkarian pride, while Jagat's angry face turned sunset-red.

Martos felt the hair on his spine lift. Voices died, and every eye turned to the wizard Arvesu. Into the aching emptiness in their ears came the wizard's soft, calm voice: "Quiet. I have a message from Prince Hansio."

Jagat's fist rested on the table it had pounded; wind hissed from his lungs.

"Thus says Hansio, Prince of Mahavara," Arvesu's soft voice continued—then, suddenly it changed, growing harsh and powerful, filling the room: "My army is ready to cross the Yukota at dawn, to march to Manjipor, and drive the Outlanders from the most ancient home of our race. When we have washed our swords in Seynyorean blood, we will join you in marching north on the stronghold of the upstart Aqillas and DiVegas, to cleanse our honour of the Outland yoke and avenge the deaths of our sons, the end of two lines of the Imperial House. In sympathy and friendship I extend my hand to Lord Jagat. We must take council to preserve what little remains of the old blood and to avenge our deaths—for it is we, surely, who have died! The murderer of our sons shall find no peace! Earth is thirsty! She will have blood!"

"Mad!" Jagat muttered to himself with a shiver. "Stark mad!" Then, straightening, "Tell Prince Hansio that our cavalry will march to meet him in the morning, under the command of my trusted aide, Martos of Onantuga. Phrase it just that way—*my trusted aide!* And tell him also that I will join him with the rest of my army within three days."

"D'Oleve!" Istvan called. The Seer walked between muttering voices in the dark. Istvan heard one, Aurel Ciavedes' deep bass, echoing his own thought: "Why do the Hasturs let this go on?"

"What news from the north, D'Oleve?" He had meant to ask quietly, but hearing Ciavedes made him speak more loudly, and the muttering quieted. The Seer's eyes closed.

"Bad," D'Oleve answered after a moment. "Uoght walks, and with him things summoned from the Dark World. Dyoles, I think. They walk like living mountains even in daylight, and the Hasturs fall back before them. They have broken several towers at the northern point of the Shadow, stretching it out to cover part of Kathor. By night they gather their hordes to sweep across the land.

The warriors of Kathor are dying where they stand. Beside them our kinsmen battle; with them our kinsmen die.

"South, in Handor and Orovia, the Dark Things are being pushed back. The giant King of Handor has gathered all his folk: the Hasturs fight beside them."

Istvan's hand covered his eyes. There was no hope, then, that the Hasturs could act as judges or mediators to settle this war. Not while the great Dyoles walked the world.

Chapter Twelve

The Twin Suns rose in the fleece-flecked sky, and glowed on the tawny plain. Istvan's sleepy men were breaking camp. Istvan, yawning, strode through mud. All around him was the clatter of armour and of pots.

Soon, mud squelching under their hooves, horses trotted toward the city. Istvan drowsed in the saddle, while on his right bright suns rose higher and higher, glowing cream-coloured through his closed eyelids. With a rapid spattering gallop, a scout dashed up. Istvan's eyes snapped open.

"Lord, there are men ahead—an army—see? There!"

Istvan looked out across the plain, shaping his eyes with his hand. North and east the land was brown, and flat as any floor. There he saw a mass of tiny dark dots: among them, mirror flecks of armour flared with light, not the jewelled pinprick sparkle of mail, but the polished glare of smooth steel plate. Kadarin plate. Martos and his men!

In a low voice he rapped out orders, never taking his eyes off the distant stippled pattern that grew nearer and nearer. Suddenly the crawling specks were still, frozen, like orderly rows of trees tiny with distance.

"They've seen us!" he snapped. "Move!"

Already the advance companies were hurrying out. Galloping horses streamed left and right, proud manes tossing as hooves churned mud. He held the main body back to a canter, and watched five companies dashing away from them, trampling wet earth to mud behind, toward the tiny blobs that were man and horse together.

Slowly, the little blobs grew. So many of them! Martos had not had so many before! He stood in his stirrups to estimate their numbers, and then, sinking back into the creaking saddle, ordered another four companies forward at the gallop.

He gnawed his lip, hating to stay here and send others into danger. But that was his duty now, much as it grated. He was stuck with the command: that was what happened when you became too famous, when the stinking poets got hold of your name and smeared it with glory; Seynyoreans expected to be led by famous men.

He saw rabbits bolting for their holes ahead of the speeding horses. Someone should try and catch some after the army passed, to help round out their rations—a dozen snares or so . . .

Suddenly he wondered what it was like to be a rabbit, to have everybody hunting you, both beast and man. It was like a soldier's life, he thought: you never knew whether your mate would come back or whether she had been eaten by a hawk or a fox. Not just a soldier's life, he thought with a sudden pang. An old man's life, all your friends and loved ones dying off around you, never knowing if you were seeing someone for the last time. With so much death in the world, why should men add to it by war?

He ordered a halt to breathe the horses, and watched the two thousand draw away, riding into danger and death. The dots in the distance milled. He heard a voice behind him, and turned to see D'Oleve.

"D'Ascoli and his men are close enough to see them clearly, sir. He reports that half their saddles are empty. There are around two thousand horses, but only a thousand men."

Istvan frowned, puzzled, and turned to watch the tiny, shifting dots.

"A full two thousand of them!" Martos said.

"And coming fast," said Paidros. "Their horses will be tiring fairly soon."

Each man stood between two horses, holding the reins, watching the enemy draw nearer and nearer. The minutes seemed long as the tiny dots swelled up to become horses with mail-clad men glittering on their backs. They were within a mile when Martos turned to Paidros and nodded.

"That's close enough."

"Fresh horses!" Paidros called out. "Re—mount!"

Leather rustled loud like tree limbs rubbing in the wind. The stolid Kadarin chargers stood still as stone, but most of the little Border ponies and even some of the proud Seynyorean steeds danced and jostled as men swarmed into their saddles. Martos reached down and patted Thunderhead reassuringly.

A sudden racket broke out down the line, and Martos saw that the Jumpers had become excited and were bucking and kicking irritably. He reached out to pat riderless Warflame, and then straightened, watching coldly the sea of riders that rolled toward them.

They were coming in at a canter now, two long lines that stretched across the plain, the sunlight leaping from countless tiny rings of armour. Glory thrilled through him as he watched, and he filled his lungs with air.

They were almost within bowshot when he called out, "To the right—wheel! At the canter—march!" A trumpet echoed the command.

The Kadarins swung about as one, the Bordermen more raggedly. Suddenly the entire force was cantering away, southwest across the line of Seynyorean riders and away from them.

Cheering rose among the watchers as they saw the tiny dots of the enemy wheel and flee before the mass of their own men. But Istvan snorted.

"They're going south," he said. "They're not running back to Inagar! They're after the convoy!" He turned to D'Oleve. "Have DiCedespi and his men met the wagons yet?"

D'Oleve closed his eyes briefly. "No, sir," he answered.

Istvan swore angrily, and frowned after the vanishing lines of men. "D'Ascoli will never catch them. They'll get well ahead and change horses." He paused, frowning, then added: "If he did catch them it would be after the horses tired out, and—tell D'Ascoli and the others to leave off the pursuit and hold their ground!"

He thought furiously. The enemy was out of sight now, and gaining distance every minute. But if they saw no pursuit behind them they might maintain a less grueling pace.

"I'll want you with me, D'Oleve," he said, "so I'll take your company—Sandor DiArnac's, right?" A nod. "I'm leaving D'Ascoli—Rupiros D'Ascoli—in command, with Ironfist as his lieutenant in charge of the foot. DiArnac's company and three more—Palos DiFlacca, Ciavedes—and let's see—Almos DiCassio." He frowned more deeply, weighing each company in his mind. D'Oleve stared at him and waited.

"Tell Emilio Vega—Milan Robardin," he said slowly, "Attilon DiVega, and Nomenos DiGasclon to dismount their men. They're to join D'Aglar and the foot, under Ironfist. We'll take good care of their horses."

After the pursuit had dropped away behind them, Martos and his men rode steadily until they were out of sight, and then, slowing their pace, turned east in a great circle that would carry them well to the south of the Seynyoreans. Long before there was any danger of the horses tiring, they halted and unsaddled them to graze.

Martos was jubilant. "That's at least half of their army back there!" he told Paidros. "We'll be able to lead Hansio straight on them, and crush them between the hammer and the anvil!"

"Well," said Paidros slowly, "I hope you're right. We've many a mile yet to go, and such plans do not always fall out so neatly when the time comes for the doing. And with DiVega metal between the hammer and anvil, we might find that it only toughens with the pounding!"

They rode on, and farther on, grey reaches of dust stretching away beyond their right knees, though they themselves still rode over tan grass. Later they would have to swing into the dust to reach the old road, but they would delay that to the last, so the horses could feed themselves, sparing the supplies for the long campaign ahead.

Far to the north, Phillipos had entered Tarencia at dawn, and as his men readied themselves for the crossing of the Oda, he sought the palace to speak with the King. With deliberate malice, Jodos kept him waiting; the man was an intrusion into the fine-spun web of court.

Jodos could sense Phillipos' growing unease as he fretted in an antechamber and tried to talk to man after man.

"But what do you mean by *they*, Lord Zengio?" he asked.

"Traitors!" Zengio snarled. "Traitors everywhere! Everything, the whole kingdom, is breaking apart, like flesh falling off bones. It's no good anymore. It's all rotten! There is no one to trust. Not even my own son! You should never let your seed escape you, young man! You never know when it's going to turn on you!"

Phillipos laughed weakly. "Come now, Lord Zengio! You cannot mean that!" He laughed again—too loudly this time.

"You haven't learned yet," muttered Zengio. "No woman has stolen your seed from you yet, to turn it into an enemy, a mockery. Never touch a woman—the people you trust are the ones who will hurt you!" His voice died away into incoherent mumblings, while Phillipos stared at him. The man was old, and bitter, but—

Jodos twitched a thread in Zengio's mind, and the old man wandered off.

"March south?" said the Captain of the Guard, a little later. "With Kalascor revolting?" He glared at Phillipos suspiciously. "Are you trying to sway me from my duty? Are you one of the commander's spies?"

Phillipos stared at him. After a moment the man's eyes dropped.

"Pardon! Pardon me, Lord Prince! I know *you* are beyond such stuff! But there are many who wish to topple me from my post, and put in some favorite of . . ." He paused and was silent.

Prince Phillipos had heard this sort of complaint before. He nodded sympathetically with a grunt, hoping he could head off the long, obscene, whining, self-pitying speech that always followed.

"But I don't understand why the question of marching south should be considered to conflict with—what do you mean by your duty?"

The soldier looked at him sharply, covert suspicion in his eyes. "Our duty is to guard the King, of course. To hold our ground and protect the city. If we march south, it will be open for Ipazema. If we go north, Hansio will move in. And you know well, Lord, that the city itself is filled with traitors!'' His voice grew shrill, hysteri-cal. "You'll get all the glory and the plunder, but we sitting here will do the work, holding down the kingdom's heart while you and the Seynyoreans scrabble around wading in traitors' guts! But we'll all be tricked and cheated out of our—but if we left our posts, so we get a share in the blood, then the city would fall and the King be caught and the whole stupid game be gone! But the commander will stop at nothing to get at me, the dirty blood-sucker. He'll see that I get nothing! He wants me to crawl and lick his vomit, but one day he'll go too far, I tell you, he'll go too far, and then he'll learn, that dung-head, he'll know who I am, that . . .''

Phillipos stared aghast. Was he awake? The soldier's voice went on and on in a stream of incoherent obscenities and threats, his eyes wide and wild, his face a nightmare mask.

Jodos smiled cruelly.

Old Shachio entered, talking with the son of Zengio. The guard's bitter black babble died away.

"There is no question,'' Lord Shachio said, "the army exists. It is gathering to march. But which side is it on? That is the question.''

"Orissia was always sick with treason,'' said the younger man. "Even under the Takkarians. Should we expect them to send us flowers now? Hate grows wild in the wheatfields over the bones of the men Olansos conquered.''

"Bitter fruit may grow from sowing such seed,'' said the Seer.

"Only on those you leave alive!'' the young man snorted.

"Enough of that, my Lord!''

"Wheat farmers!'' sneered the other, his face a hungry ferret's. "We'll reap wheat farmers, we'll scythe them down in heaps!''

Phillipos' nameless unease deepened, as though some hungry, evil beast had padded, unseen, into the chamber. His ears were buzzing and his heart beat much too fast.

Shachio turned on him the guileless eyes of a child. "Ah, there you are, Prince Phillipos! The King will see you now.''

And Phillipos rose, and felt as though he were diving into a dark, shark-haunted abyss.

Stark black storm clouds loomed like mountains floating high. Martos of Onantuga saw them flying in the blue, soaring above the plain. Swift winds hurried them high above the horizon. Suddenly thick rain battered like a waterfall across the land in front of them—a waterfall that walked.

Lightning dazzled eyes. Thunder drummed into an aching groan that stunned their ears, and then the speeding mountain was above them, and water crashed like sword-blows on their helmets. Their horses huddled together as the men pulled out heavy cloaks and threw them hastily over their armour, dreading rust as much as chill. A roof of clouds shrank the sky.

Then the swift-flying squall had passed them, and the hammering rain was suddenly gone without ever lessening its force. Lightning cracked the immensity of the sky. Looking over his shoulder, Martos saw the floating range of cloud-peaks careening madly away beneath the vast blue dome of the world, rushing to a collision with the Shadow in the west, while the hollow roar of thunder seemed to echo from endless horizons.

They halted then, trying to dry horses and armour, and watched piled-up mountains of mist hurry away, sweeping vast flats of land with rain and shade. They rubbed down the horses carefully and scrubbed their helmets as dry as they could. Now the Twin Suns burned down bright and hot on the barren land about them. The horses snatched hasty bites of the soaked grass. New green sprouts were beginning to force their way between the old brown stalks.

Mud steamed behind them as they mounted and rode on. The brief delay had rested the horses; they would soon make up the little time they had lost. But the mud, steaming now like hot soup, made slow going.

"We won't make any speed in this," said Paidros. "Heaven and Earth! There was a lot of water in that cloud! The mud wasn't this bad before!"

"Remember how dry it was?" asked Martos. "Like rock covered with grass, almost! And look Paidros, new grass is sprouting!"

"Green grass," said Paidros. "Certainly is a change! This is winter? More like spring!"

"At least we don't have to worry about one of the horses catching his hoof in a crack," Martos said.

"No," Paidros answered, "but one could break a leg slipping in this—" He stopped, straightening. "There's one of the scouts. Look, Martos! He's waving with his sword."

They turned their big steeds toward the little pony bounding on mud-caked legs. It's rider whipped his sword up in a kind of sketchy salute and then sheathed it. He shouted breathlessly, and had to repeat himself before they understood him.

"Seynyoreans, Lord!" he was saying. "A large body, moving down on us from the north!"

Jodos watched Phillipos' mind. The light was dim. Jodos liked it that way. It was bright enough for *him*. Far brighter, indeed, than he needed. But Phillipos, coming from the brightly lit Council Chamber, found himself in darkness, as though he had walked into night. He blundered into a low stool or table in the dimness and stood blinking while Jodos smiled to himself.

"Welcome, Prince Phillipos," he said, his tone casual, bantering. "From the battles in the south to the war in the north leaves little time for rest! You must be weary."

"Yes," said Phillipos, feeling exhaustion seeping through him, seeking tired muscles and stiffening joints. His eyelids fought to close, and at the hinges of his jaw he felt a yawn struggling. He longed to lie back, to fall into warm numbness and let his limbs drift prickling—vanish! But there was work to do.

"Yes, I am weary, but"—the conquering yawn forced his jaws apart—"your pardon, Highness! But with Hansio at Ojaini, this is a time"—again he yawned—"a time for decisive action. But I see the chief men in Your Majesty's service whining, backstabbing, plotting, living in a madman's dream . . ." He paused, groping for uneasy words.

Jodos looked through Phillipos' transparent brain, and said with a smile: "There is something wrong in the court, you think?"

He watched the vague unease in Phillipos' mind harden, crystallize.

"Something is very wrong!" Phillipos said. "There is a madness in your court!" Sudden suspicion flared at the back of his brain. "Have *you* not noticed it? The indecision, the distrust, the vengefulness—" Phillipos' mind was thrashing like a rabbit in a trap, trying to escape the sudden suspicion that had come to it.

Jodos laughed aloud.

Phillipos looked up, startled.

The King's eyes were shining in their own light.

Phillipos' eyes were caught and held. Suddenly the darkness around him seemed to swim with vague and menacing figures. Bones seemed to rattle in the room around him.

"How should I have noticed?" said the voice behind the glowing eyes. "Do you think you are awake?"

A huge spider, glowing like red-hot gold, reared up over the edge of a chest and huddled there, glaring.

"How rude, to sleep in the King's own court, while the King awaits!"

There were wolves in the room, and their great green eyes glowed in the dimness. And now worse things loomed and lurked in the corners of a vast dark space; for the little room was gone, and he was wandering through endless corridors and caverns where ghouls and goblins gnawed bloody bones.

Jodos wrapped the Prince's mind tighter and tighter in phantasms. Now, again, he spoke: "You are asleep now. Tell me, are you awake or asleep?"

"I am asleep," the Prince answered in a dull, dead voice.

"All you have seen is dream. You only dreamed that you spoke to the officers of the court. You will remember no more of what they said or what you thought of them than anyone remembers of a dream. If you remember anything, you will know that it was only a dream."

"It was only a dream."

"Does Lord Zengio hate his son?"

"I dreamed he did, but it was only a dream."

Jodos smiled a cruel smile. "When you wake, you will remember only tattered fragments of a dream. But you will march to war to destroy your enemies; you will have no mercy upon them. When you march into Mahavara you will drive your armies far south to the Border itself; you will burn fields and throw down castle walls. You will . . ."

He paused, suddenly uncertain. If Phillipos kept his army in the south for too long, that too could spoil all.

"But that must be a single rapid stroke, and then you must fare north again. You must do as much damage as you can; but your chief concern will be to harry Hansio's northern marches, to destroy his fields and crops, and to draw his army north after you."

He studied the pinioned mind he held so securely. What more should he command? He poured across Phillipos' captive eyes virulent visions of babies heaped writhing in fires, of men and women dying in slow torments, of an army marching on the screams of its victims.

The captive mind was writhing on the spike of vision. Coldly Jodos watched it flopping, then eased away the painful images. How had the Blue-robes done this, and why? The laws were inlaid on an inner core of softness, so tender it flinched from the delicious feast of suffering he offered. That part of his own mind which was now Chondos' mind was corrupt with the same weakness.

Could he command more? Days, if he had them, would break down the structure of thought and feeling that kept Phillipos tied to absurd humanity, and free the cruelty and death-scream hunger he knew must be there. But there was no time. A command to destroy the helpless would only strengthen this victim to struggle against him. And the soldiers would suspect something wrong, and obey only in a moment of passionate blood-lust.

And the Blue-robes might notice.

In his mind a heresy whispered that perhaps this tenderness of humanity was not a weakness after all, but a strength. That the links of humanity and sympathy bound the Sun People together and protected them against one another.

"Up!" he commanded in disgust. "Follow!"

Stumbling like a headless man, Phillipos followed him out of the room and dropped at his command into the seat in the antechamber where he had waited before. Those who were in the room left, but for a single liveried servant.

Inside his own skull, Phillipos wandered in a labyrinth, while dark shapes shambled all around him. A half-eaten figure ran past, screaming on bloody bones. Armies of Bordermen went riding through his cities. He saw houses burning, and women and children screaming and writhing in the flames. This was Hansio's doing, he knew. Hansio must pay—must pay . . . But no, not that other thought, no more destruction, his own soldiers murdering helpless Border folk.

He was moaning and struggling. A hand seized his shoulder. A giant ghoul had seized his shoulder and was tearing off his arm to eat it. He struck at it weakly, and it turned into a little old man in the King's livery, who looked at him in shock. He was sitting in a chair in the anteroom, blinking his eyes.

"You were dreaming, Lord," the servant was saying. "Bad dreams they must have been. You were lying and moaning in your sleep."

Phillipos rubbed his eyes. He *had* been asleep! Tattered fragments of dream came back to him, and he shuddered.

"The King will see you now, Lord."

"What?"

"The King is ready to receive you now." Jodos said again through the servant's lips, which moved in a subtle smile as Jodos, through the servant's eyes, watched Phillipos stagger drunkenly from the chair.

Phillipos rubbed numb eyelids furiously. He must have been more tired than he thought. How could he have drowsed off like that? It had been a hard march—Hansio's fault! Hatred flared up inside him.

Jodos smirked.

Hansio's fault, like so much else.! Phillipos thought, *When I catch up with him* . . . He saw himself riding as in his dreams through the land of Mahavara, with its burning fields and castles all around him and the bodies of the people . . . He caught himself with a shudder, and fought to subdue the wild hatred.

At the door to the chamber he stopped in shock, his mind taking in familiar images and shapes. *But I dreamed this!* Surely, that was the stool he had tripped over . . .

But this room was not dark; heavy drapes had been pulled from barred windows that glowed in glass panes of blue and red, with some figures out of old legend set in them; Fendol and the Black Dragon, he guessed. The King was busy at a desk in the corner, but he rose as Phillipos entered, and strode across the room to greet him with a laugh.

"Did you sleep well? Old Gido told me, when I sent for you, that you were sleeping like an old man with a young mistress, and I told him to let you sleep, but then he said you were moaning and muttering. Fighting your battles over in your dreams, I suppose? That was quite a march you made to get back here.''

Phillipos smiled at the warmth of the greeting. It was good. Better, indeed, than he had learned to expect from his wife's malicious little brother.

"Yes, it was a hard march, and worse on my men than on me,'' he said. "There are about fifty that I'll have to leave here; their shoes wore out—they can't walk.''

"Ah!'' the King said, "you would like me to give you fifty men to replace them, perhaps? That can be arranged, I should think. What else do you want from me?'' The unpleasant smile that Phillipos remembered had come back at that last sentence, and there was a nasty tone to the words. Yes, that was Chondos' way, thought Phillipos. If only the stupid brat would learn!

"In truth, more than fifty,'' Phillipos said. "With a few hundred more men, I'd have a better chance of getting Ipazema out of the way before Hansio moves north.''

"Well,'' said the King slowly, "that makes sense. But you must understand that we're busily preparing for a siege here. Between Hansio in the south and Ipazema in the north, we were already feeling like a grape between the teeth, and now this morning comes news of an army gathering in Orissia!''

Orissia? A voice spoke in Phillipos' memory: *Orissia was always sick with treason, even under the Takkarians.*

But he had dreamed that, had he not?

The army exists. It was Lord Shachio's voice. *There is no question the army exists.*

Orissia was always sick with treason . . . We'll reap wheat-farmers.

But he'd *dreamed* that.

Jodos saw the stir inside the skull, the writhing shift of the baffled brain, the soul trapped between two mirrors, and spoke quickly: "Yet, Kinsman, despite all this, it would no doubt be wise to send men with you, to strengthen you for the march into Kalascor. I must take thought as to how many men I will need to hold the city, to see how many I can spare. If Hansio comes north while you are embroiled in Kalascor, 'twould be sad if the city were too empty to give him a proper welcome!''

Phillipos laughed, and Jodos quickly reached to soothe the remaining tension from his mind as he spoke rapidly and smoothly of tactics.

"What are they doing *this* far east?'' Istvan wondered aloud. "I thought they'd be miles to the west by now, and hours ahead!''

Brooding, he looked out across the sombre tableland that stretched south to the slumbering Shadow. An hour before, all the world had been pressed to a thin strip of battering rain, roofed by jumbled, tossing clouds, floored by umber mud under their feet.

Now the Twin Suns from an immense blue sky glowed down over their shield shoulders, casting long dark shades off to the right, pointing to the cluster of tiny dots that were enemy horses and men.

Mirror-bright dots milled among duller dots that wheeled away to the south, where the sky was black beyond the dim grey dust.

"There they go!" said DiCassio. "Heading off south. Are we to try to catch them, sir?" He, with Ciavedes and DiFlacca, had joined Istvan at the first warning from the scouts that there were men ahead. Istvan ignored him.

"DiFlacca!" Istvan said. "Take your men out after them. Make the best speed you can in the mud, and try to close the gap a little. Be ready to retreat back to us if they turn on you. Halt before your horses get too tired."

"Going to walk them down?" said DiFlacca. "Right." He dashed off to his company. Istvan turned to the others.

"The rest of us must proceed at a slow and steady walk," he said. "The trick is to spare our horses and tire his. Next halt, change horses."

DiFlacca's men were moving out, splashing through the mud. Istvan watched them as they drew away, hoping none would go down in this soup as they galloped cautiously for a few yards before settling down to a steadier pace.

His mind was still gnawing at the puzzle of Martos' men riding east instead of west.

Mud splashed up Martos' legs, and some of it ran down into the tops of his boots. "We'll lead them right into Hansio's army," he said. "Are they still back there?"

Standing in the stirrups and craning his neck, he looked over the bobbing sea of his own men, trying to catch some glimpse of the enemy, but the sheen of the men's helmets behind him baffled his eyes with their glare.

Wheeling Warflame out of line, Martos shaded his eyes with his hand. Miles behind, mail sparkled. Above, farther back across the greening brown plain, he saw a second shimmer, like tiny moving stars.

All that day they raced and chased upon the plain, changing horses often, trampling old brown grass and new green shoots alike into the mud.

Slowly the Seynyoreans gained. Martos' horses were tiring more quickly as Istvan's slower-moving main force kept a reserve of rested men and mounts, but with a small force always at Martos' heels.

Ahead, the Border reared up like a black cliff, and at its foot the broad strip of grey crawled with twisting lines of light, as though lightning flickered on the ground. Stagnant water pooled above the surface of the dust, and the wind sent glaring snakes of sunlight rippling.

Istvan saw the tiny shapes ahead swing out into dust. Men and horses slipped on slick poisoned powder under fetlock-deep water. With every step, dust-grains shifted underfoot. Since the beginning of the rains, Istvan had dreaded this. He pushed his men on quickly while the enemy toiled ahead, and soon his army, too, was at the edge of the water-covered dust.

His men dismounted, and lurched and staggered in the foul, shallow water. Ahead he could see the Kadarins doing the same. Rapid and choppy splashing brought his head around, to see D'Oleve mounted, urging his horse to a precarious trot, hooves tossing up sheets of spray.

"A report from Vrijan," said the Seer as he reined up his horse cautiously. "One of the scouts you sent to watch the Yukota just rode in. He says an army of several thousand men is crossing the river."

"Prince Hansio," Istvan said grimly.

"Who else?" D'Oleve answered.

Istvan stared at the distant men toiling toward the old stone road, knowing at last why they were so far east. And once they reached the road, they would be gone long before he could get his men across the soaked dust.

He looked at D'Oleve again, wondering how he had managed his horse in this. Suddenly he remembered that D'Oleve was Seer for Sandor DiArnac's company. DiArnac had served at Ekakin, in the midst of the dust, for three years now. His men would have perforce more experience of the dust than anyone except the Bordermen. And if all of them could manage a trot . . .

"Martos! Look!" Valiros pointed. "Look at that!"

Martos followed the pointing finger. Off to the left, horses trotted across the water-shrouded flats, waves lashing from their feet, mailed men bouncing on their backs. As he watched, a horse went down, its rider leaping free, hurling up a fountain of water where he fell. A second slipped, its rider clearing the saddle just in time.

"They're making for the road!" Paidros exclaimed.

"They'll never make it!" Rojero said.

"Some will!" answered Paidros. "That's a full company—three hundred men."

Another horse went down. The wet plain was studded with wide-spaced horsemen. Riderless horses floundered through the dust; lone men scrambled on foot to follow their mounted comrades.

The Twin Suns were sinking in the west before Martos' men scrabbled up a slope of glass-slippery ash onto the solid stone road. But by then the way east was already blocked.

"Dis—*mount!*" Istvan shouted. "Bows—out!" He felt the spring of the bow in his hand as he hooked the string. Even though he never practiced, he could not seem to lose his skill with the hated weapon. At Rath Tintalain, after two years in which he had not touched a bow, his marksmanship had been praised by a legendary elvish archer. "Arrows—nocked!"

He lifted the bow, tested the string. It thrummed as clear as a deep-toned harp. He pulled a black-fletched arrow, and slitted his eyes against the glare of the falling suns.

A mile down the long stone road, Bordermen and Kadarins were struggling to drag their horses from the dust. Nearer, two Kadarins in mirror-bright steel were riding toward the line.

"Look! There!" said DiArnac, beside him. "That's Martos of Onantuga! The tall one!"

"Are you sure?" said Istvan, studying the figures, the tall man and the short one, as they slid from their horses and walked into the range of his bow.

"Yes," said DiArnac. "That's him all right!"

Istvan nodded. Birthran's face was suddenly in his mind, and Birthran's voice, bragging about his student, the boy who was almost a son to him.

Istvan nocked the black-feathered arrow and raised his bow to send death hissing toward Birthran's pride.

". . . barely two dozen, out of the whole company," Paidros was saying. "And the rest of them are still wading in. What can they do from out there?"

Martos looked from the double row of mailed men that blocked the road to the mass of men and horses still toiling in the water-logged desert, then glanced quickly over his shoulder at his own men. Sunlight dazzled his eyes. Turning back, he blinked, owl-blind.

"It won't take very many to—"

An inch below his throat something cracked and shattered on his steel breastplate. He staggered back a step, then stooped. Something whizzed past his head as he plucked a black-feathered splinter from the ground.

"What can they do from out there?" he mimicked. "They can fill our Border allies with arrows, little man! Or our horses! Spike our thighs to the saddle! Put holes in our boots!" Another arrow whispered past.

"We'd better get out of range then!" said Paidros. "Our Healer will have enough work as it is!"

Martos laughed, then straightened, pointing.

"That lean man—there!"

"That dried-up old fellow?" said Paidros. "What about him?"

"Is that not—Istvan DiVega?"

"Istvan the Archer!"

Istvan lowered his bow, watching the Kadarins move away with a sense of relief. Beyond them, leather-clad men dragged horses up onto the road.

Death and stark wounds waited: spike-tipped arrows and sharp-edged swords, with no earth to drink the blood, but only poisonous Demon-dung, where nothing would grow.

Birthran's best pupil, whom he had nearly killed, and the men who must defend this land when the Dark Things came, and the best blood of Seynyor, all fighting on this strip of stone—and for what?

"Why should we give back before them?" Suktio snapped. "They have not a man more than we! If we hold them until Prince Hansio comes—"

"It's two or three day's march from the river," snarled Paidros. "Hansio's army won't be here for another day at least. And this is no place to fight!"

Martos pulled off his helmet and ran his fingers through his sweat-drenched hair. "This dust doesn't go all the way to Manjipor!" he exclaimed. "There are patches of earth, too, I know. Where is the nearest?"

"There is good solid rock behind the Seynyoreans!" said Bimsio maliciously.

"Five miles to the west," Ymros' quiet voice said. "There is grass and clean water, too. Vajrakota is nearby, and Demons avoid it for fear of the Hasturs."

"Is there room to manoeuvre?" asked Paidros. Ymros nodded.

"Heaven and Earth!" Martos swore. "Let's go! Let us pick our own battleground, in Hastur's name, where we can at least have room to form a line!"

*   *   *

"The scouts say," D'Oleve reported, "that Hansio's vanguard is advancing at great speed and cannot be much more than a day's march east."

"How large is this vanguard?" Istvan asked.

"At least two thousand men, or so the scouts would guess," said the Seer. "They ride in a double column, on each side of the road. Conch-horns blow before them, as though for a procession, and a herald rides at the head of each column to proclaim the coming of the Prince of Mahavara."

"They're not moving toward Inagar?"

"They look to be marching straight to Manjipor."

Istvan listened while the Seer went on. An immense herd of horses followed the vanguard, providing fresh mounts: by old Mahavaran custom, most of the army walked, saving the horses for battle.

A soldier's shout turned Istvan west, to watch Bordermen and Kadarins moving in the twilight. Hansio on one side, Martos on the other. And he must get his men off the dust before he fought anyone. You could not fight bunched on the road like ants on a stick.

"Has DiCedaspi met the convoy yet?"

"Yes," D'Oleve answered. "And Lord Rinmull, too."

"Rinmull! What—" But he knew even before the Seer replied: Rinmull was marching to relieve Ojaini, of course, to attack Hansio's army of ten thousand with his fourteen hundred men—or was it twelve hundred?

Bordermen always run the wrong way.

Well, he could fight him now. Istvan gave orders for Rinmull and the convoy to turn and march toward the beacon of Vajrakota. Lord Maldeo had marched from Manjipor as Istvan had bidden and, moving northeast toward Inagar, was now camped within a day's march, at the edge of the dust. Istvan sent him orders through the Seer, to meet them at Vajrakota.

That was simple enough, but it left him worrying about the six thousand men sitting outside Inagar. Without them, he lacked the weight to turn the Mahavaran host. But dared he leave Lord Jagat free to join his force with Prince Hansio's?

He mulled that question in his mind while he prepared to free his army from the dust. Those companies still wading at the edge of the shallow swamp he ordered back to solid ground. That left some who were closer to the road, and long before the last of those could scramble to the stone, a message came from Ironfist Arac at Inagar: most of the Seynyoreans the Healers had taken to Inagar after the fighting at Arankila were healed now; Lord Jagat had ordered them out of the city, and sent with them a warning that if Istvan did not move the army from outside Inagar, his men would march on their bodies.

Martos' army choked the road in the dark. As they came to the end of the dust, horses grew wild from the smell of fresh grass. Even Thunderhead jerked frantically at his rein, and jostled other horses on the narrow path. Horses milled onto the grass, trying to stop and graze, blocking the way until orders were passed that each man reaching the solid ground should turn his horse's head south, to where Vajrakota Tower rose burning in the night. White mist swirled up from the pool that drowned the dust; soon men rode in fog-walled bubbles.

The road was like a bridge across a shallow sea. Martos studied it; he had meant to leave men here to hold it, to keep the Seynyoreans trapped on that strip of stone, or floundering in the dust.

He moved one sluggish arm, and tried to imagine fighting with it. His eyelids were numb, and tiny chills crawled through the marrow of his bones. His arms hung like logs. And all his men were as weary as he from the day's hard riding. Tomorrow there would be fighting enough, he thought. The enemy had no advantage of numbers now; sleep meant more than position or strategy. He ordered his men south, where creamy fog glowed around the gleaming tower.

Hours later, Istvan rode cautiously, peering through the mist, onto grass, surprised to find no guard set to bar his way. Six men rode cloaked at his back, behind them the long line of DiArnac's company; the rest of his men moved along the north edge of the dust. He had expected to bring them around on the rear of whatever force Martos had set to meet him here.

Blank mist floated just before them, closing off vision, except where the light of Vajrakota paled the fog. Grass sparkled with dew in the tower's light; Istvan could see a trampled space. He sent a man back swiftly to bid the company to move. He would turn north along the edge of the dust and ride until he met the rest of his force, and then camp. While they waited, a horse snorted somewhere nearby, and mud gurgled under a stamping hoof.

"Look, sir!" one of the men exclaimed. Turning in the saddle, Istvan saw a tall, long-legged horse gazing at them from out of the mist.

"One of Kardom D'Aglar's horses, I'll wager," the soldier said. "We should catch him and take him along. Those horse thieves! Attacking us with our own horses!"

Hooves clopped on the road behind, and the company began to appear through the mist. The watching horse whickered, and pounded across the road to join them.

,   *   *   *

And high in the cold hills, Chondos hunted through the rubble of his mind, searching for something he had lost—something hidden in a blue robe.

He sat on his throne: King of Kings, Emperor of Takkaria . . .

Phantoms of a former age swirled around him in the haunted city, and were vanquished by the starving, bestial servants of the Dark Lords, hunting each other in the crumbling ruins.

Something in his brain still fought, and sought whatever treasure had been hidden from him, wrapped in its blue cloth. But wrapped in black cloth, the Master mocked. Chondos fought the fear that washed over him every time he faced the twisted figure in black. The squat shape stirred under the robe, and laughed.

"Fear me, foolish little King!" the deep muffled voice hissed. "All fear me! In all your mortal lifetime you could never grow strong enough to eat me! You must live much longer to gain such power! Only fear will keep you alive—fear and obedience."

Rising from the throne, Chondos could feel stone flags cold and hard beneath his feet, even though his eyes showed him a bright-colored thick carpet. His head swirled with memories of ancient Rajinagara as it had been before its fall, but all mixed and jumbled with visions of a stark stone castle above a swarming city between two rivers.

The black-robed figure laughed. Fists clenched as rage swept fear away. Pain came from the Master, plucked out his eyes, stripped off his skin, and tore at his flesh. He doubled up, gasping. The pain vanished. Chondos cringed.

Had he ever known anything but fear? Was there a world beyond Rajinagara, a bright sunlit world?

Yes, a voice whispered in his mind. There was a sunlit world, and it was his! He must take it back.

The Master would give him an army to take it back. To take it back for the Old Ones, the Great Ones, who must return to reclaim the world they had gnawed in darkness before the Flaming One had come, burning, burning, from some deeper plane of the layered universes, to drive them in pain back into the oozing darkness.

He put his hand before his eyes, and squeezed his temples with thumb and forefinger. There was something wrong. How had such a vision come into his mind? He shook his head savagely, and let his hand slide down over his face, brushing the coarse hair that sprouted from lip and cheek. No razors here, of course.

Razors—that was something from that half-remembered sunlit world, the lost, hidden world that . . .

That the Master could give back to him.

The sunlit lands spread before him, lands subject to the ancient throne; he saw himself on horseback, lifted sword waving, with his Pure-in-Blood army following him against the fortresses where rings of invisible fire singed the Dark Ones that came too near; fortresses that would open their gates when their King called on them, open for their King and the pure blood of ancient Takkaria.

Again the land would be ruled by the King of Kings, once more the ancient throne hold sway. . . .

The ancient throne. He turned, and saw it once more, surrounded by guards of the Chosen and the Pure-in-Blood. Old court music gonged in his mind, and again he saw ambassadors from the far courts of the world prostrate themselves before him as he sank down on the throne, King of Kings, Emperor of Takkaria.

But inside his mind, something hunted for a lost blue robe.

Chapter Thirteen

Trumpets sang cockcrow.

Martos had never felt a Border dawn so cold: white plumes spiralled from the mouths of coughing men; thick marbled mists like curdled milk still hung above the dust; and gauze veils hid the northern flats.

Warflame was weary. Martos whistled up Thunderhead and began to rub him down. Many horses grazed on the dew-wet grass: some dragged the pegs to which they had been tethered. The ground was too wet to hold them. Men chased horses in the mist around the camp.

Groundnuts and cheese were the only food—at least it wasn't raw fish. Martos munched groundnuts while he saddled Thunderhead. As he tightened the cinch-strap, a shout brought his head up to see tiny mounted figures turn and vanish in opal-coloured mist.

Seynyorean scouts! he thought, and hurried to finish, then arm up, shivering as he strapped on cold armour.

"Look!" gasped Valiros, pointing.

Beyond ghostly fog-veils fading in the north, sun-jewels glittered on distant mail-rings. Doll-like figures bustled around tiny horses, mounting, arming.

"Bad!" said Paidros. "They're too close! We'll never get our own men mounted in time. A small raiding party, now, could cause enough confusion that we'd wind up fighting on foot!"

Glancing quickly around, Martos saw that most of his soldiers were still chasing horses or saddling them. He gazed north over grassy flats to the most-blurred glitter of the enemy array. They were not all armed or mounted, yet!

Decision came. Looking around him, he saw perhaps a dozen horses saddled and ready for battle.

"Paidros, you are in command!" he said. "I want you to get this army mounted and ready to fight! Retreat if you have to. Make sure there's room to manoeuvre!" He scooped up shield and quiver and fitted them to the saddle, then swung himself up onto Thunderhead's back.

"What are you doing?" Paidros asked.

"I—I'm going to give them something else to think about." Martos straightened in the saddle, and filled his lungs. "Men!" he shouted. "Any of you that are ready to ride *now*—to me! The rest of you, mount and arm! Obey Paidros and Valiros!"

Horses came darting from every quarter. There were more than he had thought, mostly Bordermen. Only four of his company: Quintis and Luego, healed of the wounds they had taken at Arankila, and Rojero and Donhanno. Ymros came riding, tall and calm, and Suktio hastily tightened his saddle-girth and sprang to his horse's back. When they were all gathered, he counted twenty men.

"Follow—" He stopped, and fought his stutter. "Does everyone have a bow?" Two of the Bordermen dashed quickly off, and came pounding back with long bows in their hands.

He led them north at a rapid canter over grass. They heard voices shout orders in the enemy ranks, saw hands point at them. Horsemen broke from the main body and sped to meet them.

Lifting his bow, Martos fitted an arrow to the string. He licked his lips and tried to force his tongue to stutter the command.

"Nock arrows!" Quintis shouted beside him.

Enemy horsemen grew, mail-rings shimmering in sunlight. Martos looked down his arrow-shaft, mastering his tongue, listening to the battering of hooves.

"Loose!" he screamed, and let the string slip from his fingers. Strumming bowstrings launched a cloud of arrows. "Left—wheel!" he shrieked. "Gallop!"

He glimpsed Seynyoreans reeling in their saddles as he turned, but then he and his men had left them behind, and were dashing toward the enemy right, where dismounted men were still saddling their horses. His fingers found another arrow.

"Nock—arrows!" he shouted, his voice shrill. "Loose!" His fingers found another arrow before the thrum of the string had died. "Nock!" Men and horses scattered. "Loose!" He saw a wounded horse bucking wildly and kicking. He saw a wounded man crawling on hands and knees. "Nock!" His voice quavered. "To the right—wheel!"

Men ran around them, waving swords, but they galloped through too quickly for any effective defence. But now mounted men came rushing after them. Twisting in the saddle, he sent shafts winging at them.

He saw an arrow glance from Rojero's helm, and another shatter on Quintis' backplate. One of the Bordermen shouted in pain as a spiked arrow pierced the leather over his shoulder.

One of Martos' arrows found a Seynyorean's throat. Another missed its mark and caught a horse in the whithers: Martos saw it leap and buck wildly, feathers waving in front of its shoulder, and his stomach writhed in protest. He'd not meant that.

"Form up," he muttered, then drew a deep breath, forced calm into his mind, and shouted, "Form into line! Down bows!"

The pursuit was drawing closer and closer. He drew his sword and flourished it, hoping to save himself further words, and ripped his shield from its place on the saddle.

The Bordermen were too close together. He had to fight his tongue and hunt for words.

"Spread out!" he shouted. "A horse's length!"

But there was no more time. They had ridden well away from the Seynyorean lines, but the thirty or forty men who pursued them were almost on their heels.

"Left, to the rear—wheel!" His voice sounded shrill and woman-ish in his own ears.

The five Kadarins turned as one. Behind, he heard shouting and stamping as the Bordermen reined their horses awkwardly around. A Seynyorean loomed in front of him, raising his bow in a futile attempt to stop Martos' falling sword. The bow shattered: Martos felt the fine steel in his hand flex against armour. The Seynyorean reeled back, but then the horses had run past, and beyond, other Seynyoreans were throwing down their bows and drawing swords.

All around burst the sounds of battle: clanging and crashing and cries of pain. He heard swords crash on shields and bell on armour; riderless horses raced past. His hand went flying on the wing of his sword. Mail-rings clinked beneath his edge. Bone cracked, blood flew. Bordermen reared their horses to cut at their high-mounted foes. Red swords and shouting were all around.

Rojero cried out, and reeled in the saddle, his face hidden in a veil of blood. Martos' heart lurched, and his pounding heels drove Thunderhead toward the bloody-sworded Seynyorean.

Dwarf-forged steel quivered like a harpstring against a rising shield. Flashing metal whirred; his own shield rose and took the shock of the stroke, shaking with thunder on his arm. Fine steel wheeled in the pivot of his hand, gliding in air. Shock quivered down the steel, through his palm, to his arm: the chiming scrape of tearing metal mingled with the crackle of splintering bone.

Men in mail ran, pursued by men in leather. Suktio raised the great conch-horn to his lips, and blew a long, shrill blast.

Istvan's eyes turned north across the plain, following the dashing troop of horsemen who had stung his ranks into confusion. The wounded horse screamed again, and his mare reared and bucked. He reined her down sternly.

Scarlet robes vivid against new green grass, two Healers worked, pulling out arrows and cleansing the wounds: D'Oleve and another

Seer helped them. Istvan had thought to fight by the convoy, with Healers in plenty.

"They're moving again, DiVega!" Aurel Ciavedes called.

Istvan turned his head south, where Kadarin plate flared in the long line of Bordermen moving against the blank black bank of gloom. They trotted west. Istvan frowned and slid down from his mare, patting her, and murmuring soothingly. Nearby, another horse let loose with his heels. Istvan felt the mare trembling under his hands.

Martos and his men behind the army, and that long line in front—brilliant, in a way. He did not dare move his whole line on either. But why did the army in the south not attack? What were they waiting for?

Men came riding toward the Healers. Blood oozed from rents in the netted rings of mail.

Martos blinked in surprise, seeing Rojero still clinging to his saddle, dabbing at his face with his sleeve. Spurring to the injured man's side, Martos saw the morion's brim folded and crumpled in, with a deep slit in the steel. Blood poured from a red line across the forehead.

"Rojero!" Martos croaked, his voice harsh and husky. "How bad—?" His tongue stuck.

"A scratch, I think, but—" The man's voice quavered. "I can't see. Blood keeps filling up my eyes!"

Martos glanced quickly back at the glittering enemy line. Beyond, another line moved. Paidros had mounted the men.

Already more Seynyoreans were moving, hunting his sadly shrunken little force. Four dead Bordermen were strapped across their saddles, and at least a dozen more were wounded. Quintis bled from a long gash in his arm; Luego's helm was dented, and one sleeve soaked with blood.

Yet the Seynyoreans, he knew, had lost more.

"I have to go after him myself," said Istvan.

"Who?" Ciavedes asked.

"Martos. Birthran's best student." Istvan sighed.

"They said in Manjipor that he'd killed Nurin Kimerosa," Ciavedes mused. "Well, if you can't take him, no one can."

Istvan smiled derisively. The reputation, the preposterous, over-blown reputation! He sobered. Martos might well have a better chance than any man he had ever faced. He remembered an old saying: *When heroes meet, no victory*. Was it a quotation from Eldir? He could never remember.

"Heaven and Earth!" Ciavedes swore. "Look! They're heading for the horses! If they stampede them . . ."

Istvan straightened. So that was what they were waiting for! "D'Oleve!" he shouted. The Seer looked up from the wounded man he was tending, then scrambled to his feet.

Martos raced for the great herd of loose horses. Kadarin chargers kept pace, hooves battering wet ground in blurred rhythm, but short-legged Border ponies dropped behind.

Further back, half-a-hundred hunters had swerved to follow, but he was still well ahead. Soon he would plunge into the heart of the herd, panicking them through the Seynyorean lines. But even if the pursuers caught up with him first, he was still close enough to carry the battle in among the horses, stampeding them just as well.

A fluff of cloud hid both suns. Silver flares of armour died to grey.

"*Look!*" Quintis shouted. From behind the nervous herd, mail-clad men rode: a hundred—two hundred—a full company!

Licking his lips, Martos muttered the order he must give, then filled his lungs: "To the left rear—wheel!" Five Kadarins turned as one; Bordermen scrambled to follow. Pursuing Seynyoreans milled, halted, then turned to the chase again, but in the time they had lost, Martos' men had drawn far ahead, looping away in a wide curve that would take them past the end of the Seynyorean line, on their road to join the rest of Jagat's men.

Amidst iron-grey mail, a sword flashed like a star. Twenty-one horsemen flew from the Seynyorean ranks: in the lead, one man's sword flashed as though in sunlight.

Twenty men rode at Istvan's back. His sword flamed with need-fire. Long-legged horses churned tender grass into mud. Hoofbeats seemed to chant in his ears. *When heroes meet—no victory!*

Istvan saw Bordermen on led horses, their armour dyed with blood; others draped across their saddles, hands swaying near the ground at the ends of stiffened, dangling arms. Grey Kadarin breast-plates loomed.

Off to the left, where the sky turned black, he saw the enemy army flowing like a river. His saddle jolted under him; his horse's back throbbed to the lunge of legs. Martos' men swelled larger and nearer, dead hands waved between the horses' hooves.

A shout turned his eyes over his left shoulder. Nearly a hundred horsemen dashed from the enemy line at a gallop, pounding toward him. They would swamp his men in a rain of swords.

He hauled his horse around in a wide circle, shouting to his men, and plunged into full flight. Jeering rose behind and brought angry heat to his ears. But foolish shame would not make him throw lives needlessly away. Rattling hoofbeats hammered, as enemy animals galloped behind.

Under the eye of Hastur and the Dark One, the two armies met at the edge of the Shadow. Half the sky was black, half streaked with bars of blue sky between wool-white clouds. Sunbeams walked golden through the gloom. Horses pranced and fretted, while their riders readied shield and bow, and loosened swords in scabbards.

From Vajrakota Tower, an Immortal watched. He could remember the fall of Rajinagara, and, before that, the Takkarian Empire in its days of glory. One level of his mind noted each man, each horse, and knew at a glance each creature's name and history, and mourned their wounds and weariness. But on another level, man and horse and grass were all the same: each a temporary flux in the endless field of sparkling particles.

Tiny flames danced. Through the rain of fire-flakes pelting from the suns, moving patterns came, swirling pieces of light. Earth and water were bound in long spiral chains: air flowed and changed, forging fire in the water of the veins. But all this was on the sunlit side of the Border. It was the other side that must be watched, where dim figures moved over the poisoned wastes, almost hidden by the mist of dark magic.

Totally exhausted, his powers worn down to the thinnest edge, Narmasil Hastur had flickered south from the battle against the Dyoles that Uoght had summoned from the Dark World. Kandol Hastur-Lord had ordered him to rest, but there was no rest, now, for any of the kindred, save the half-rest of duty in some unassaulted tower.

Through the minds of his kinsmen in the north, he watched the fighting. Uoght towered in a mighty column, shading himself with dark magic. Beside and before, in vast black spheres that were truly holes into the Dark World, the great Dyoles crawled. They could not exist unshielded in this world, but must wrap themselves in the other universe. Where they passed, the earth was gone, and deep grooves cut into solid bedrock. The flame-wrapped Children of Hastur fell back before them, though the surface of the globes hummed with need-fire.

The Shadow bulged past broken towers, and Demons gathered in the gloom, waiting for the dark. The mortal armies gathered on the plain of Vajrakota did not seem very important. Narmasil Hastur seethed with impatience to return to aid his kinsmen in the north.

Istvan could only see three Kadarins: the rest were masked by a shifting line of Bordermen. He studied the Kadarins carefully. Even at this distance, he could make out the wiry, spectral lines of the jumping horses. He smiled then.

This was how the Kadarins had fought when he was a boy, and the Jumpers were new and rare. The masking line of archers would part, and heavy cavalry would rush from the centre, to try to break through his line and then turn and ride back in a second place.

But I have a surprise for Martos, he thought. DiCassio's company was trained to fight in an even older way.

Southward he could see grey wastelands under the black sky of the Shadow, and vague hints in the mirk of mountains like crouching beasts. Nearer, running out of the Shadow, were the remnants of ruined walls, remains of some building long crumbled.

He ordered the advance. Through his spine he felt the drumming of the slow-trotting army that was now his sword. Across the green the Border ponies stopped milling, and cantered to meet him. Watching, he felt their tension and foresaw the instant of their charge. His hand dipped to pull his bow from its case.

The enemy cheered, and horses leaped forward at a gallop. His fingertips brushed soft feathers in his quiver.

Martos' ears drowned in voices as he cheered with the rest: his legs gripped the saddle. Thunderhead surged under him.

Over Valiros' shoulder, he saw Seynyoreans trotting to meet them. He breathed deeply, filling his mind with crystal calm, readying himself to rush into battle. Pounding hoofbeats jolted through his spine. Arrows rustled in the air: Borderers strummed their bows in answer. He threw his sword arm skyward, the iron guard pressing muscle between thumb and forefinger.

Paidros shouted the command.

String and arrow rasped from Istvan's fingers. His free hand dropped to the plumes in his quiver and plucked out another shaft. The bow strained in his hand. He saw a man's distant face tiny beside the point, and loosed. But the charging line was closing fast. Bows were of no use now. Trumpets echoed his shouted order as he drove the bow back into its case and shrugged his shield to his shoulder. His sword climbed the sky.

The running line of horses split, and Bordermen wheeled to left and right, their bows still hurling cascades of arrows. Through the parting line, titan horses appeared under grey steel figures with bristling swords.

Istvan almost laughed as he gave the signal. The trumpet behind him bayed. At each end of his line, men lashed out at a gallop, smashing into the bowmen. And in the centre, a grove of lances fell and jutted at the charging Kadarins, and the horses beneath sprang to a gallop. Jumping horses soared over them.

As Valiros' steed gathered itself and leaped, Martos saw above his shield-edge the clump of steel-tipped spines ahead. But *no one* used lances anymore! Not since his grandfather's time.

He hurled his shield up to fend off the spike that drove toward him. Thunder belled. He was riding air through darkness, clapped between giant palms. He ached.

Grey clouds floated between his bent knees and waving boots. His ears ached and his head was numb. Hooves crashed by: something bright dived at his legs. His shield was too heavy to move, but he curled his knees and the long shiny thing missed and went by with a sigh like a flute.

He rolled up, stunned, his head full of throbbing bells. Furred walls lurched above him; men fought on horseback with pearl-grey swords. His hand was empty. He blinked and saw his long sword lying on the grass. His shield weighed down his arm, too heavy to lift.

A horse's dark breast muscles rushed toward him, throbbing, as hooves pounded. Past it, he saw a sword drawn back. It scythed toward him. His shield-weighted arm hurled up, rang like a bell as he was thrown back, and the horse ran past.

Martos rolled, and crawled toward his sword, his head still buzzing. Hooves were all around him; horses kicked and stamped. Between a horse's hooves he saw a helmet lying on bloodstained grass. He blinked. Dead eyes stared from under the steel. The face was familiar.

His hands closed on his hilt. Hooves stamped near him, too near. He rolled away, trying to find the strength to climb to his feet. Eight hooves stamped round and round. Crashing bells drew his eyes up to the riders. They circled, swords thrashing back and forth. Rolling away from the hooves, he bumped into a Seynyorean corpse.

There was another world down here, glimpsed between the moving pillars of horses' legs. Wounded men were writhing and screaming; hooves danced away from them, backing and prancing.

A man pitched from the sky in a bloody rainbow, crashing into grass being trampled into mud. A Healer came dodging between hooves to kneel in the spreading red pool, then shook his head and ran off to kneel by another.

Hooves came crashing near again, and Martos, rolling away, used his shield to push himself up to his knees. Clanging filled his head. Every muscle ached: he could hardly breathe. Sweat had soaked through the thin leather palm of his glove, and he had to hold tightly to the slippery hilt of the unwieldy sword. Through the ringing in his ears, men were shouting, moaning, screaming. He shook his head: the world rocked.

A horse kicked and he dragged himself away from the heels. The bells in his head began to turn to the hammering clangour of war. In the constantly moving forest of horses' legs, wounded men moaned and screamed. He glimpsed some men crawling between the hooves; others lay still, in pools of purpling blood.

He heaved himself awkwardly to his feet. His sword dragged on the ground as he staggered up on numb, bloodless legs; his shoulders cramped as he tried to pull up the heavy blade.

Istvan's glowing sword tore through the leather of a shield and sank into the arm beneath. The Borderman's blade hesitated in the air, then fell, chiming harmlessly off Seynyorean mail. Istvan wrenched his sword free as his horse carried him past.

All around him, men killed each other with spiralling sword-strokes. Arrows swished in from the edge of the battle, where archers still dodged their enemies, but here most of the Bordermen had thrown down their bows to defend themselves with buckler and sword.

Borderman, Kadarin, Seynyorean, all were mixed together in a shouting, milling mass. Istvan's trained eyes looked through confusion to divine the mystery of the course of battle.

A Kadarin came dashing through the crush, his sword thrashing about him, coated with blood. Istvan's mind turned to steel in his hand as the great horse bounded toward him and the red sword came down on his quickly lifted shield. Poised steel in his hand hovered, swooped, struck: blood burst from the collapsing sack of the body.

The riderless horse ran past. Istvan's mind returned to the mystic vision of war, searching through the clamour and the flurry for the pattern of the whole.

The Bordermen fought with frantic desperation, but there was small cohesion among them. They had broken into the little groups that defended various undermanned castles.

The Kadarin wave had broken on the rock of spears. Although their commander was holding them together as well as he might, they were too few by themselves to turn the course of battle except by some stroke of genius.

But even in the tumult of the melée, the Seynyorean discipline held. He had a single army of a thousand men: against it fought many tiny armies. Gradually his formation was herding them in upon each other, crushing them together, driving the little groups on their flanks against the centre.

*   *   *

Martos heard hooves pounding, saw steel swoop. He wrenched up his leaden shield and poised his heavy sword.

Leaning out from the horse's side, an enemy face twisted; at the end of a diving mail-clad arm, white light rippled on waxy-grey blurred steel, ruby-flecked.

The weight of Martos' sword vanished as it glided on the wind. The hilt quivered against his palm as mail-rings shattered. Bone snapped. The Seynyorean blade bounced from his shield and fell at his feet. The horseman reeled in the saddle, crimson foaming from the severed links at the elbow of his flopping arm. His horse carried him away. Martos blinked, and tottered a few steps on chill feet.

Still all about him wild blades were battering, clattering on armour and on shields. Horses danced and circled under cursing men, while the dead and the maimed lay beneath. There were riderless horses running through the press. If he could catch one . . .

"Martos!" someone shouted.

The sound of his name brought him about. Three men on foot, in grass-stained Kadarin armour, were coming toward him—one running, the other two more slowly. He recognised the running man as Erivar. Something worked at the back of his mind, and he found himself trying to remember whose face he had seen looking out of the helmet under the hooves.

The sound of the shout had brought mounted men's eyes upon them, and another horse was suddenly rushing them, red sword swinging low. Erivar stumbled out of the way, lifting his shield. The wet sword barely scraped the steel face, but the horse-driven blow was enough to send him staggering.

Icy wrath cleared Martos' brain, and he bounded into the path of the flailing sword. His own blade was already whirring above his head, twirling high for the mailed shoulder.

The Seynyorean pulled his blade up and guarded, and the fine dwarf-forged blade came down on the lighter Seynyorean weapon. There was a glassy sound of shattering steel, and the Seynyorean was suddenly staring at the foot-long stub in his hand. Before he could recover or move, Martos' point drove up into his side. A mail-link burst around it, but then others caught and held it: less than an inch of the broad point pierced. The man jerked his flesh off the point, turned his horse, and dashed away.

Erivar ran to Martos' side as another horseman hurtled toward them; but then a mounted Kadarin loomed up, and the Seynyorean was forced to turn and defend himself. Quickly, in that precious breathing-space, Martos and Erivar ran to the other two. Romulos was supporting the other man, and both were bleeding. Horses bounded past them, and swords lashed out in passing, but for the most part the mounted Kadarins were giving the Seynyoreans little time to ride down dismounted comrades.

The staggering man was Rojero. The cut above his eyes was bleeding again, despite the crusted cloth still tied under his helm. He had several new wounds, and had hurt his ankle when he fell from his horse.

Now Quintis came dodging between blood-splashed hooves, and shoulder to shoulder they dressed their shields to guard each other. Horsemen looked down upon them; swords rose above them on every side. Ringed with danger, they marched together, weapons ready, through death and chaos.

Istvan sheathed his flashing sword and watched his army work. The echoing peal of hammered steel tortured his aching ears.

Earth must be fed, he thought. The violence of men enriched the ground with blood, fattening hungry grass. Under the sad grey clouds no sword flashed, now that his own was hidden; pearl-grey and sombre, swords splotched with rust-red blood battered on dull armour. The smell of blood was thick.

He glanced at the Shadow, beyond the flaming tower. He should ride to the tower and talk to the Hasturs. He should stop this clanging madness that was slaughtering good men!

He wheeled his horse away as a Borderman charged, and dodged around a knot of battling horsemen. Wounded men shouted from the ground; dead men lay in purple pools of blood.

Like an eagle in the eye of the storm, holding himself from wild winds with gentle twitches of wingtips, Istvan rode through battle, avoiding combat by skillful horsemanship, allowing the palm of his sword hand to cool as he studied the battle and encouraged his men. His side was winning. But what good was that?

Horses were frantic with the smell of blood. His mare wrenched the reins painfully into the flesh of his palm. He glanced up at the dreary skies, surprised that it was not raining. The sky should be weeping for the dead and maimed men, for the widows of the Border.

Suddenly a Kadarin came bouncing through the press, the ugly whiplash Jumper soaring out of nowhere. Arrows showered from the rider's bow. Something pounded Istvan's thigh, just above the knee. Mail-rings jangled. A sudden prick was followed by blushing warmth. He knew what that meant, even before he looked down. The Kadarin bounded away and vanished.

The feathers pointed across his lap at the cantle of the saddle. A long red splinter stuck out from the links on the other side of the leg, and as he watched, the sharp tip was hidden by blood that gathered on the end in a bead like a tiny cherry.

The arrowhead must have glanced off the wire of a ring and skittered aslant. How deeply it had pierced, or whether it had only cut the skin, he could not tell without removing his hauberk, and there was no time for that now.

And the few available Healers had far more serious injuries to deal with.

Striking to left and right, Martos and his men clove through the melee. Horses dashed about them. They kept their shields high. Swords lashed down from above, but there was as much to fear from the hooves of horses as from the steel of men. The horses, caught standing, would rear and back away as the slow-moving men trudged toward the furred walls of their sides. And now, among the horsemen, Kadarins saw their unhorsed comrades, and rallied to their aid. Horses were mountains around them, dancing, snorting hills from whose backs long tongues of sharp steel pitched down upon them: their shields thundered.

Martos stretched on his toes, cutting at a horseman whose steed twisted aside to draw his master out of reach. The heavy blade pulled Martos forward, off balance, and the steel from above came hurtling down again. Martos stepped to balance himself; his shield arm curled above his head and gonged under the stroke. His own point had dropped almost to the ground, so he could not cut. Instead he thrust upward, breaking mail-links under the man's arm and bringing blood; but the blade was too broad to go far. He heard the man curse through the crashing all around, and grinned savagely as he jerked the blade back behind him where it belonged.

Again the Seynyorean sword fell from the sky, but this time Martos was ready. He twisted forward, hurling his shield against the falling edge while his arm, pivoting from the shoulder, whipped out with all the concentrated power of his body, whirling down the blade to chisel through the mail-rings between shoulder and neck.

Bright arterial blood fountained, and the body toppled from the saddle. Before it had cleared the stirrups, Martos had leaped to the horse's head and seized the reins.

"Rojero!" he shouted. "Here! Mount! An empty saddle! Up!"

Rojero came staggering up, half leaning on Quintis, trying to protest that Martos should mount the horse himself. Martos, his tongue straining, barked inarticulately, then had to hold the horse's head down as the animal tried to rear. The smell of blood was making these Seynyorean beasts nervous as deer. Even the Kadarin chargers were less calm than usual.

Hoofbeats rushed toward them. Martos shouted for Rojero to hurry. There was a sudden flurry of ringing metal. Rojero scrambled

into the saddle; and as he gathered up the reins, Martos stepped
hastily away, balancing himself between shield and sword.

"Martos!" a voice shouted from above him. "You're alive! I saw
Thunderhead running loose and thought you were gone for sure!
Paidros was going crazy there, looking for— Watch out! Behind
you!"

Martos whirled. A Seynyorean came charging in, his sword reaping low. Martos crouched, dropping his point into the path of the
gliding scythe, hurling his shield-edge to meet it. The hilt wrenched
at his hand as the long blade rocked. Steel clattered; his wrist jerked:
he staggered backward. The enemy was past him. Hooves rattled
quickly, and the mounted Kadarin who had spoken to him—he had
still not seen his face nor recognised his voice—shot past, and then
the two horsemen were hammering each other, from the swaying,
dancing platforms of their horses' backs.

Who was that fighting for him?

Whose was the head he had seen on the ground?

Why was he fighting here, anyway?

The glory of war had fled from the crashing of the swords. His
enemies were men he might have been drinking with. Birthran's old
friend Istvan DiVega commanded them; Ironfist Arac and his son
were on their side.

Long strips of red-stained steel wheeled and stooped between the
circling horses, like grey-dappled rainbows. Long-haired tails whipped
violently.

Quintis and the others had run up and gathered about Martos.
Rojero, towering above them on his tall horse, moved toward the
fight, but now other Seynyoreans came rushing in, their swords hot
with blood.

The hugeness of horses blotted out his vision. His shield roared on
his arm; his sword twirled on the pivot of his shoulder, beating out
the bells of battle. Around him on the ground writhed weapon-
pierced bodies and severed limbs, and somewhere, unblinking eyes
under the brim of the helmet he had seen.

Mail parted under his sword-edge. A horse reared away, toppling
a body from its back, and he leaped to catch the reins, dodging
pawing forefeet, staggering back as a hoof bruised his arm through
the resonant steel of his shield. Then Quintis had the reins, and
Martos was shouting for him to mount, hurry, hurry.

Between massive moving shapes of horses, something white loomed
and reared. He swallowed a cool breath of hope. Nearer horses
blocked his view again. White horses were common enough, but
still . . .

Another sword was whirling at him. He guarded and struck, but the horseman went charging past and met Rojero. Steel shields gonged as they fought.

He dared another quick look. A lane cleared between horses, and he saw it again, the white shape rearing, mane and tail flowing. Heavy hooves pawed the air, and the stallion settled back on his haunches in the way that only the great Kadarin war-horses could.

"Thunderhead!" he shouted, and tried to whistle. His mouth was dry, and for a moment he struggled to raise enough spit as he ran toward the lane of horses.

A Seynyorean saw him and swept toward him, sword drawn back. Valiros came bouncing over the melee on Windracer, his hand flickering between string and quiver, arrows streaming from his bow.

The sword flew from the Seynyorean's hand and buried itself in the ground. The empty hand clutched vainly at the feathers rising from his hauberk. The horse went rushing past, the wounded man clinging to the saddle, face buried in the mane.

Martos whistled.

The white horse's forelegs struck the ground, and then he was coming, mane and tail flowing, running between circling horses and spiraling swords. Joy surged in Martos, seeing the foam-white horse, proud head tossing, quick hooves darting in a rapid stride. With a neigh like a trumpet-call, Thunderhead rushed to Martos and stood to be mounted, his head bobbing, tossing the creamy mane. Martos heaved himself up over the saddle, and as his other foot found the stirrup, he straightened, feeling himself fill with power.

Istvan's crystal gaze searched through the melee. Blood oozed down the red shaft projecting from his leg, gathered on the spike at the tip, and dripped down to the hungry earth.

Earth shall eat the seed of men and men shall drink her milk.

He started to break off the shaft and pull it out, but that might cause him to lose too much blood; the dart plugged the wound, and later he could get a Healer to tend it properly. He could bear the pain. He'd borne worse before.

Icy swords danced above shoaling horses, drumming on shields and armour. The rhythmic battering hammered at his ears and seemed to surge loud and soft, like the sea. But that, he knew, was the surging of the blood in his ears: the effect of his wound on his heart.

Horses, racing and rearing and milling. Some, riderless, dashed away. But those with men on their backs were turning and turning, dashing past each other while red swords rose and fell. They were all around him, churning and milling wildly, but he left the Hastur-blade in its sheath. This army was his sword, and he could not afford to be caught in the isolation of an individual fight now. When swords menaced him, he moved his horse away.

"Close your men together!" he shouted to DiArnac. "Close in on that space there!"

Then the saddle jounced under him and the arrow tore at his wound as he galloped to another point.

"Send fifty men to help DiArnac, on the left!" he ordered. "Hurry!" Then he was off again.

A blood-crusted sword swung at him, but he hurled his shield up and spurred his horse away, dodging around a mass of others to elude pursuit.

Slowly he was draining the weight away from his centre and building up the power on his wings. The Bordermen were being driven back, crushed in upon the Kadarins. Soon they would be fouling each other.

The hundred Kadarins in the centre—less than that, by now, he was sure—could be dealt with easily, despite their fine armour and heavy horses. Or they could run away, which he might well permit.

The blood on the arrow dried to brick-red, but every time he had to move the horse fast, the jouncing dyed it crimson again. The leg burned angrily with the feverish rush of blood, and the pain became harder to ignore as he rode.

Pain does not hurt, he reminded himself. *Only fear hurts.*

He smiled at himself. *I must be terrified!* he thought wryly.

All around him the boom of swords on shields and the blood-lust shouting of men in battle throbbed in his ears. Men died. Men killed. Wounded men dragged themselves along the ground or staggered up to fight on foot. Others lay among the dead, distinguished from them only by their still-bleeding wounds or gasping breath.

Between the crowding, blood-smeared horses, Istvan glimpsed a flash of red, where one of the Healers scrambled through the battle, dodging weapons and hooves to tend to the wounded. *Real courage,* he thought.

In the centre of the battle, where the Kadarins were mingled inextricably with his own men, Istvan sought for Almos DiCassio.

"The Captain?" a man said at last. "He's dead, sir! Over there!" His eyes were wide with shock. He was young.

"Who's in command, then?"

The young man licked his lips, dazed. "I—there's Lieutenant DiBahador, sir. He can tell you."

DiCassio's body was lying near the feet of DiBahador's horse. DiBahador himself was trading blows with a small Kadarin on a large horse. Istvan shouted and whipped out his sword: the Kadarin retreated.

"Ramanos was next in line, Commander, but I haven't seen him since the battle started, sir. For all I know, *I* may be in command!'' He shook his head and looked down, then started. ''Commander! You're wounded!''

So I am! Istvan thought. ''Just a scratch,'' was all he said aloud. ''I want fifty of your men, twenty-five to each wing, and I want you to pull your men back about a hundred yards.''

''Back?'' DiBahador blinked at him stupidly, and looked around at the heaving mountains of horses, confusion and madness. ''How? They're all mixed in together. I don't know where the trumpeter went, or if he's still alive!'' There was a faint touch of hysteria in the man's voice. Istvan looked at him sharply.

''Rally the men nearest you,'' Istvan said, speaking slowly and distinctly, making his voice as forthright and reassuring as he could manage, and holding the man's eyes with his own. ''Ride in groups at men in combat. I'll come with you, if you like.'' Shock, he supposed. The man certainly should know all this. He wouldn't have reached this rank otherwise. ''Come on!''

He urged his horse toward a little knot of men, where three Seynyoreans were battling four Kadarins.

''Rally! Rally!'' Istvan shouted, waving his sword. ''Form on me!''

Surrounded by death in the middle of the battle where the sharp swords slashed bones bare, Martos' long blade lifted like a wing on the wind.

He breathed life flowing into his lungs, drowning fear in the calm of control. His mind, at rest, watched his sword arm do the thinking, fingers twirling the hilt to bring the long steel tongue swinging round, down on jingling mail-rings or the gongs of lifted shields.

Thunderhead danced under him, hoofbeats jouncing the saddle. The warm horse between his legs was comforting, lifting him up above the jellied blood on the ground, the moaning maimed men and tumbled dead limbs.

Some of his comrades still fought there, and it was for them that he emptied saddles, his curled arm hurling sunless grey steel in rapid lashing loops and flowing swirls, until he was dizzy from the whirling of his horse and his arm was drenched to the elbow with sticky, clotting blood.

Now Erivar was mounted, and then Romulos, both in saddles he had emptied for them, but by then they had found other men fighting dismounted down among the hooves. A horse loomed up. Martos' sword flew skyward, but then, looking over his shield, he recognised the smooth grey mirror of Kadarin plate.

''Martos!'' Paidros' voice called. ''Oton said you were alive!''

He pulled his horse up, rearing. "I've been hunting all over! Heaven and Earth! When I saw Thunderhead bolting—"

"Spear knocked me out of my saddle," said Martos. "How'd you stay on?"

"Ducked under it," said Paidros, "and got into sword range. Man with a sword can always beat a lancer if he can get close enough; that's what Granpa always told me. But listen! We've got to rally and get out of here!"

"How—how bad is it?" said Martos.

"Bad. They're crushing the flanks in. The Bordermen don't have the weight for this kind of work. If we don't—"

Just then a Seynyorean hurtled down upon them, his sword battering on Martos' shield. After a few sweating moments, Martos felt his own edge grind through mail between neck and shoulder.

"Catch the horse!" he shouted, and looked around for Paidros, who was fighting a little ways off.

There were more Seynyoreans, and they seemed to be massing together. His own men were scattered, except for the little group with him, the men he had rescued from the ground. Above, horses and men's steel lashed wildly back and forth, like trees in a gale.

A sword flashed among the Seynyoreans. He blinked. In the sunless gloom most metal was dull and oily grey. Then he saw that the blade was flashing with its own light, glowing with need-fire: an elf-sword or Hastur-blade. *Istvan DiVega!* Sword aloft, Martos slammed his heels into Thunderhead's sides and drove toward that glittering flame of steel.

A tall Seynyorean steed dashed into his path. A glassy streak dappled with red shrilled toward him. His shield shuddered and boomed. Muscles clenched about his elbow as they hurled the dwarf-forged sword down.

It crashed back from the gong of the shield, and he saw the enemy blade ripple like water as it whirled in again. His shield came before his eyes and thundered with the blow; his sword took wing again, above the shield, aimed blindly at the flashing eyes he had glimpsed during the brief second of sight. He felt the edge twist upward as it glanced along metal, and knew the other shield had caught it. As the veiling leather dropped from before his eyes, he saw the other blade circling round again. His ears filled with the grating iron laughter of battle.

The bruise on his shield arm smarted with impact: metal thundered on his arm. His hurtling sword slammed into mail, and he felt a swaying limb knocked aside. Then his eyes were free again, and he saw the bloody rent in the mail sleeve—but the hand still gripped the sword, drawing it back behind the shoulder to strike again.

His sore muscles launched his own cut first this time: the long steel weight, lifted by the air, soaring for the retreating shoulder. Air chirped under his edge. A twist of the body and the shoulder was hidden; the enemy blade launched into flight. Martos turned his wrist. His sword swooped and scooped up the other blade, driving it aside, and with a jerk of his shoulders stabbed at the exposed eyes in the naked face.

The Seynyorean ducked his head and lurched forward in the saddle, trying to dive under the point. Plunging steel drove into his shoulder, shattering a mail-ring. Martos felt the point scrape bone, and heaved it back to cut again. Threads of crimson streamed behind his sword.

The Seynyorean wheeled his horse away, and the falling blade, instead of severing the arm, scored across with its point, tearing away mail-rings, ripping through cloth and skin.

A shout of command and a trumpet-call, and all the Seynyoreans were racing away. Martos blinked after them. His sword rose to hover above his shoulder, his heels poised to urge Thunderhead in pursuit.

Paidros shouted, "Rally! Quick now, quickly, before they re-form!"

Romulos pulled his trumpet around and raised it to his lips. The thunder of the battle dimmed, and above it rose the vibrant golden hum of the rallying-call. Horses came rushing, and men on foot. Martos tried a quick, rough count, and felt a stone between his lungs. There must be more! He could not have lost so many!

There were less than eighty-five men left of the hundred who had ridden with him from Inagar. The face under the helmet, rolling under the hooves of the horses, had been Thiondos' face.

Valiros bounded out of the melee on Windracer. His needle-sword was drawn, a sure sign he was nearly out of arrows. He pulled up the nervous Jumper—frantic now from the battle—and forced a grin to his drawn face.

"Somebody loan me some arrows. Mine are all—well, the enemy has them, so to speak." He tried to laugh, but the grating sound that came out was close to a sob.

"What about the rest of the Jumpers?" asked Paidros.

"Down. Gone. Dead or crippled." Valiros swore. "I think Greydoe broke a foreleg, I'm not sure, I don't know—" He bit off his words as a hysterical whine crept into his voice. The ugly horse began to prance again, ears flat against its tossing head.

"Everybody into line! Quickly! They'll charge again in a min-ute!" Paidros said. "Look! They're turning!"

Martos looked. A hundred yards away, the Seynyoreans—a whole company, more than three times their own number now—had formed into three lines and were wheeling their horses. They would trample his little command into the ground.

He looked around at the tossing thicket of swords on either side, and saw the rumps of Border ponies gradually backing toward them. Beyond, he saw gaunt horses towering, mesh-clad men on their backs, and the swords swaying frantically above them. On both sides, Bordermen were being forced back, herded into a single narrow corridor.

Paidros was still giving orders, readying the men to meet the charge. But that was no good! Martos struggled with his tongue.

"No!" he croaked.

Paidros looked at him.

"Take half the men!" Martos said, fighting his tongue. "Go down that side. Get the Bordermen. Cut them out. Herd them, fight them if you have to, but pull them out of here, retreat, move! Now!"

Paidros opened his mouth as though to say something, reddened, and shut it again. There was a sudden squeal as Windracer put his head down and hopped, nearly unseating Valiros, and then suddenly lashed out his lean head and nipped a nearby horse. The men on foot scrambled out of the way. Horses bucked and kicked, and for a moment the line was total chaos.

Martos rode to one of the dismounted men, reached down, and pulled the man up behind him. He gestured for others to do the same. Then, with a nod to Romulos, he turned his horse away.

The wild scream of a trumpet sounded the retreat.

Istvan, riding with his fifty men at the edge of the battle, heard above the belling steel the crystal trumpet-cry, and stood in his stirrups, peering through the tangle of tossing swords, ignoring the tearing in his leg.

If the Bordermen would only run away! Any other soldiers would have by now.

The Kadarins were moving, he saw: solid clumps of armour, riding through the scramble of the melee. Retreating, yes, but retreating through the turmoil, gathering their Border allies as they rode.

They drove down on little knots of fighting men, where blades black with dried blood pitched back and forth, pounding clanging shields. Seynyoreans wheeled away, and the Bordermen who started to pursue were cut off by Kadarin horsemen, their ponies herded away with the men on their backs riding willy-nilly.

Istvan smiled, then sobered instantly. He must organize a pursuit, and make sure they did not regroup for another charge. The thought spurred his horse's flanks, and set him galloping over pools of drying blood.

* * *

Martos on his fiery steed was sweeping through the carnage, herding away the Bordermen on their shaggy ponies. When they tried to fight on, Thunderhead blocked their charge with his shoulder, and shrugged the pony off to the side. The man who had ridden behind him transferred to a riderless horse.

But the Seynyoreans were gathering, closing on the flank, so Martos dropped back to the rear of his men. His warriors pounded by him. He called to Valiros. The jumping horse sprang from the ranks and nipped at Thunderhead. Valiros wrestled with the reins: the creature backed and danced. From the quiver by his stirrup, Martos jerked a handful of arrows. His bloody hands were slippery and the slim shafts hard to hold.

"Take them!" he yelled.

"Windracer! Whoa!"

They both could hear chiming steel. Men clad in mail rushed toward them on lanky, long-legged steeds. Their swords were dark and dripping as they fought with his rearguard.

Thunderhead whirled under him. Windracer sprang away. Martos hugged his shield against his chest and raised his long sword high. Hard-pressed, his men battled against the grim raiders at their rear. They had to use their swords to guard; their shields were useless weights as riders closed on their right sides and battered on their blades.

Martos crashed in among the foe. His sword soared out and struck. A riderless horse bolted past, its flanks all splotched with blood.

Arrows hissed down, piercing mail-rings: spike-tipped arrows from the sky. Martos' sword screeched through steel. Seynyoreans pulled up their horses as they saw their comrades fall.

A gap appeared between Martos' rear and the swarming Seynyoreans. Martos stormed into it, blade dripping. Two or three of his men turned and rallied behind him—but it was not enough, he saw.

Before him was an ocean of mail, an endless prairie of waving blades, and already it surged toward him. The corner of his eye saw Windracer high in the air, the men grabbing at the feathers of shafts that sprouted from their chests and shoulders. He slipped his arm free of the straps of the shield, and let the steel disc dangle from the strap across his shoulder.

Horses lunged toward him from either side. Long strips of red-dappled steel reached for him. His left hand closed on the hilt. He saw the man on his right twisting suddenly in the saddle, feathers jutting above his shield. The man on the left cut at him.

He heaved himself up in the stirrups, both hands sweeping the air with steel. Edges clashed as he rammed the enemy blade up and back, and then his two hands spun, snapping his sword down across the rising shield. Startled eyes vanished in a surge of blood.

Martos' knees whirled Thunderhead, and his heels urged him to overtake the riderless horses, running between them so that his flanks were protected for a precious few seconds, while his left hand tore at the buckle of the strap that held his shield. He yanked the leather hard, pulling it out until the shield was riding high between his shoulders, banging the dented brim of his morion. He fastened the buckle again, but by that time the riderless horses had bolted, and another with a rider was charging.

Valiros went bounding past. The others who had stayed with him had turned when they saw him turn. Valiros was shooting coolly, but his arrows would run out again.

A sword fell toward Martos. He turned away from it, digging his chin down against the metal collar of his breastplate, feeling it part the hairs of his beard, to scratch his sweating chin. The shield rocked and rang on his back.

As he felt the jolt, Martos lunged up, twisting with his thighs, feeling as never before the clamping vise of his breastplate. He swept the blade around in a thrust for the Seynyorean's face, his point following the retreating sword. The edge of the shield slammed into the flat, lifting the point so it only scraped across the bowl of the helm. But it was child's play to scoop up the returning blade with his own, heaving both swords high. His left hand let go of the hilt, and his right whirled the blade in a great curving swoop that went around the edge of the lifted shield, to clang on steel behind.

The Seynyorean reeled in his saddle. Probably only stunned, Martos guessed, but that was enough. The important thing was to get away.

The Conch-horn of Chandra shrilled loudly ahead.

Then they were racing away, Paidros' men rushing across to join them, and the Seynyoreans galloping behind. Miles vanished under their hooves.

Chapter Fourteen

Racing the Twin Suns down the western sky, Martos' men sheared off to the north, toward Inagar, seeing before them in the distance the tiny swarm of Lord Rinmull's men.

Istvan was glad enough to see them go, and turned his men back, to camp by the battlefield behind them. The wound in his leg was a savage, ripping pain; rust-red blood crusted the rings of his hauberk. Pain blurred the ride back, but he set his teeth and rode. *Pain does not hurt,* he reminded himself, sternly. *Only fear.*

White mists swirled up above the stagnant pools that covered the dust; the Twin Suns were falling toward the black smudge that marred the west.

Istvan pulled up his horse, and signalled a halt, listening intently. He called for silence. Bits jingled, horses stamped. He frowned, wondering if he had heard anything at all. Then, out of the mists in the east, it came again: a shrill, distant whine. He shot a quick glance to the south and the night-black wall, but the surface of the Shadow was still blank; the towers burned blue and dim. Not a Demon, then.

Again it came, like the distant cry of some strange bird, or the warble of a flute. He stiffened in the saddle, knowing that it must be the conch-horns of the vanguard of the army of Prince Hansio of Mahapor.

The smell of blood grew ever thicker. A lonely moon peered through clouds as they drew rein beside a field littered with groaning men with severed limbs and the wood-stiff bodies of the slain.

A red-robed Healer ran up to them and stopped by Istvan's horse. "Commander DiVega, are there tents? We must have some sort of protection from this mist—blankets, at least!"

"I'll see that you have all the blankets you need," said Istvan, "but we have no baggage, alas! Lord Rinmull's army is on its way here, and perhaps he will be better supplied. You should have D'Oleve or one of the other Seers contact his army—"

"I have done that, Lord," said the Healer. "Lord Rinmull and his men should be here in little more than an hour. There are several of our brothers with him, but he has no tents in his baggage."

"Well, we'll all lie in the open tonight, then, but I'll see what can be done. The horse blankets can be set up on bows and broken spear shafts perhaps.''

''Yes, that should be . . . Lord! You are wounded! Let me see!''

''A scratch,'' said Istvan, with an airy wave of his hand. ''I can attend to it myself, and there are others who need you more.''

He had already snapped off the feathered end, and now, calling old DiFlacca to help him, he jerked the arrow out through the wound. *Pain does not hurt,* he told himself, as pain like a burning monster roared up from the deep caverns of his being. He walled it away. It was only another sensation: pain and pleasure were alike; fear or longing made them different.

A bright spout of blood followed the shaft, covering with crimson the brown crust on the wire rings. He flipped up the skirt of his hauberk, and DiFlacca cut the stiff, caked cloth away. It was as he had thought. The arrow had pierced through a mere pinch of skin, missing most of the muscle beneath, though the skin was slashed badly. DiFlacca sponged the wound with wine and bandaged it. It would be stiff for a few days, and the blood he had lost would weaken him, but he'd been hurt worse.

He set men to fetch and carry for the Healers, and wrapped his cloak tightly around him as the cold mists came drifting in across spangled grass and trampled mud. He must have gotten groggy and dozed for a while. The shouted challenge of a sentry brought him up, groping for his sword. But it was only a large party of Healers, and behind them Rinmull's men marching out of the night.

He had to talk to Rinmull. He started to push himself up, then reeled, the grassy field spinning around him. *Ridiculous,* he thought. *The silly wound wasn't that bad!* He lay back. In a moment he would get up and look for Rinmull.

When he did manage to push himself up again, he saw that all the Bordermen had spread out blankets and gone to sleep. He shook his head angrily, groping for the quiver on the saddle behind him. His unslung bow would do for a cane. He snorted. *Best possible use for it!*

He blinked as light flashed. He stiffened. Had there been a flicker of light across the Shadow, there, between the towers? A grunt escaped him. His leg punished him as he stood up. He grabbed the bow and stood leaning on it until the sting lessened, then slid his sword flaming from its sheath.

Was the need-fire brighter on his blade? He could not tell. Far from the Shadow, the kindling of its blade would serve as a warning; but here, with so much dark magic so near, the blade burned all the time.

The Healers were still busy on the field of the dead: torchlight glowed on red robes. Off to one side, he saw Rinmull's men struggling to raise pyres, hunting for things that would burn: broken spears, arrow shafts . . . Others were carrying the wounded to a makeshift shelter of blankets. But most of the wounded were being treated where they lay.

A pair of moons shot between two clouds and vanished, leaving behind a single star in a patch of sapphire sky, which shrank as the clouds shifted. Istvan limped across the field, eyes searching the mist. Was that movement, there? Someone wailed like a child in the night. But that was to be expected on a battlefield. He drew a deep breath; forced himself to relax. Probably nothing.

Something huge and dark and torchless moved at the edge of the field. Istvan hobbled toward it, the hilt of his burning sword clammy against his palm, the wound gnawing his leg.

Larger it loomed, still indistinct, and behind it were other blurred shapes. A man screamed somewhere in the mist, and Istvan increased his pace, despite the pain in his leg, even though he was almost certain that the man had screamed because of some wound taken in the fight.

The shapes drew closer. Istvan's stomach lurched and his hair prickled. A low muttering and snarling came out of the mist. An inarticulate shout came from one of the Healers.

A troll reared up, twice as tall as a man. It seized one of the corpses and lifted it to its face. Beyond it, other dark creatures emerged from the mist—goblins, ghouls, shapes that seemed to be human figures.

Istvan threw the bow down and ran, forgetting the agony that lanced his leg with every step. Healers were running, waving their torches. A wounded man set up a harsh, ragged screaming. Between men and Night Walkers, mist suddenly swirled into a pillar. Sparks like red eyes glowed at its top. Istvan's leg folded under him, and he sprawled on the ground.

The pillar of mist fell in upon itself, darkened. A human shape stood there. Red eyes glowed in a long pale face. Istvan raised his sword against the menace of those eyes, but the vampire was not concerned with him. It strode toward the crowding night-things.

The troll roared thunderously, and hurled aside a half-eaten corpse. Snarls and low moans sounded from the skulking shapes behind it. The troll lumbered forward, bellowing with rage, towering over the other. The tiny figure raised a hand and spoke a single word. The roaring changed in timbre, and the troll drew back as though burned.

The elegant slim shape glanced quickly back over its shoulder. Again Istvan saw the long face, the hooked nose. A shiver went through him: it was a typically Seynyorean face.

The troll shambled into the mob of smaller forms. Low wails and moans sounded from the throng. Shoulders slumping, ravenous eyes turned down, the misshapen, gangling horde turned and shambled away into the mist, with the vampire walking purposefully behind, driving them with some invisible lash.

Istvan's fingers ached on the hot hilt in his fist, so tight was his grasp on his sword. He climbed painfully to his feet. Healers with torches and Bordermen with drawn weapons stood ranked behind him, staring into the mists where the nightmare procession had vanished.

And in the high hills, a few hours later, the dream world where Chondos lived, trapped, was shattered by the Master's anger.

Fragments of broken dream skittered away in the cold wind, the sudden, icy wind that roared through cracks in the castle wall. Butterfly girls smiled and faded. A gay-coloured bird croaked its single word, flapped its wings, and vanished in the starless night. Flowers and ancient pines fell into dark abysses filled with Demonic wings. Fine porcelain and carved jade were snatched away by the icy wind of the Master's voice.

"Punish them!" the voice was snarling. "Scatter them among a million mouths. Let tiny bites of their living flesh feed the hunger of our host. The fools! Now above all, with two armies ready to tear each other to shreds for us, now above all we must be still, and wait for the word. Soon the armies will leave their dead and go north, and all the land will lie empty and open for us."

Alone in his mind, Chondos reeled. He felt something thin and brittle break inside him. His mind was his own, but his memory was clouded yet. There in his mind, somewhere in his mind, was the tattered blue robe.

He stood by the steps, and the Blue-robe was there, and a voice rose, saying, *"Who comes to be crowned with the crown of the Kings of Tarencia?"*

He shivered as the wind blew cold. Old bones and new bones littered the flagstone floor. Fresh blood soaked into dust in the cracks. His memory fought through a fog: he slumped hopeless.

"Did the Blue-robes see?" the Master was asking.

"They struck at me as I flew between the towers, but with only a single bolt. There is little power in the towers now."

"That is why we must wait until we can strike swiftly and secretly!" the Master answered. "There must be no resistance—praise Uoght! There will be no resistance—none! *If* we wait for the signal! That is why we have planned so carefully. If the army there, with their flaming swords, could hold out against us long enough for the Blue-robes to fill their towers again, they could cut us off and drive us back." The hunched, muffled figure squirmed around and shook its black sleeve. "Feed them to the dwellers down below!"

Indistinct figures moved in the dark. Chondos blinked. The illusion that had filled his eye-sockets had been lit with torches and constellations of candles. Now the hall was dark: dim patches of vague half-light from the starless sky leaked through the broken roof to dapple the darkness with grey. Only the bones near his feet were clear. He must find a way to fight, but the will seemed drained from him. It was hopeless, there was no escape.

Even in the dark, he could sense the hooded thing turning to face him, shivered to realise that the unseen eye beneath that cloth saw him through cloth and darkness. A skittering spidery touch brushed lightly across the surface of his mind, and panic froze his thoughts in a stillness of absolute horror.

An echoing bass chuckle broke from the muffled figure before him, and the hoarse voice whispered in the dark: "Soon enough, little King. Soon enough your brother will call us, and you will leave at last, to lead your army against your disobedient servants. But I must see now to the punishment of *my* servants."

The black figure turned away, and was gone.

Faint and far in the morning mists, Istvan heard the Conch-horns of Mahapor shrill at dawn. A rich smell of roasting meat made him hungry. He sat up stiffly, and gagged as he saw that the smell came from the smoking pyres where Rinmull's men were burning the dead. His wounded thigh tugged and burned as he tried to get up. His joints creaking, he forced himself onto numb feet.

The mists glowed milky in the east, but slate-grey where they hid the Shadow in the south. Sullen smoke rolled from the funeral pyres. In his memory, red-eyed mist melted into human shape. A troll hurled away a body from which bones protruded. A gargoyle procession lurched into the night.

They were waiting, they were holding their hungry hordes in check, watching while *he* destroyed the Bordermen! They were starving their goblin armies to make the human world forget them! Had they somehow arranged this war? He did not see how that could have been managed—but everyone had expected war when the old King died.

He must end it, before the power of the Borderers was so greatly weakened that they could no longer hold the land. He must make peace, convince Jagat and Hansio that only the night-things could profit from this war.

The blood was returning to his feet. The sting in his thigh was a nuisance. Most of the training dances required a great deal of footwork. Perhaps he should devise a new one: a "Limping Dance."

With the thought, his fingers folded around the hilt, and the flame of his blade flashed free.

A thin rain began to drip from the silver skies, chilling Martos' men as they retreated slowly northward.

Valiros was almost in tears. "He's foundering!" he said. "Look at this! It's this damned rain. Softens the hooves and . . ." His voice faded, and his head shook. He put down Windracer's crumbling hoof, and stroked the horse's flank. Martos stood mute, his throat choked.

"If we could get him to one of the castles, into a dry stable," Paidros said sympathetically, "maybe we could fix a boot for him, and—"

"No." Valiros shook his head. "It's gone too far already—or certainly would, before we could get anywhere. And most of the castles near here have naked rock all around them. It would just . . ." He bit his lip, and shook his head.

"Want me to do it?" asked Paidros gently, but Valiros only shook his head again and wiped the rain from his face.

Martos, his throat too full to speak, was glad Paidros was so sympathetic. He was a bit surprised, too. Paidros' earlier comments about the Jumpers had been caustic. Martos kept trying to imagine how he would feel if it had been Warflame or Thunderhead. At least he still had both his horses. Most of the second horses had been left behind during the retreat, but Warflame had come running after them.

Wind dashed rain in his eyes. Valiros was stroking Windracer's neck, crooning to him softly. In his hand, the dim light rippled over steel.

Martos turned away, unable to watch, and strode back to his own horses, angry with himself. Here he was, all upset over a horse, when some of the Bordermen were dying slowly and in terrible pain because he had not been able to keep them from following their immemorial custom. Their single Red-robe had remained behind, at the battlefield. The wounded that had been carried away were receiving only their comrades' unskilled ministrations.

Rain thickened, then eased and stopped. Far above the northern horizon, a clenching of thunder clouds, interlaced with strings of light, muttered above the wind. They would be eating horsemeat for a while, and the Borderers would make new armour.

An hour or so later, as Martos and his men dragged their weary way toward Inagar through bursts of rain, a scout brought word of a large body of men, both foot and horse, marching down from Inagar.

*   *   *

Against the black sky ahead, Istvan could see the glowing tower looming larger and larger as he neared the Border of the Shadow. His wound itched and burned. The sky wept. And all around him, Bordermen carried the bodies of the dead.

Rinmull and Arjun DiFlacca were with them, and D'Oleve rode at his side. It had been nearly an hour ago that Lord Rinmull had come to him with the news that there was not enough wood to burn the men killed in this battle.

"It is a thing which has happened before, Lord," Rinmull had said, seeing Istvan's face. He pointed to Vajrakota. "We shall lay them out on the bottom floor of the tower. There they shall be safe from the night-things. Men have done this in the past, under similar need. Some have returned to find the bodies of their kin, uncorrupted, ready for the pyre. Some have found, instead, urns holding their ashes, ready to be poured upon the fields. Those fields are held doubly blessed."

There was an old song about that, which Rinmull sang as they rode toward the Border, slowly and sadly. Strange, Istvan thought, how his people had come to accept the Border funeral customs: though at home they preferred to bury the dead, that was impossible on the Border. They left the rites to the Borderers, trusting the dead to them as they trusted their wounded to the Red-robes. But then, if a Borderman did not understand death, who did?

Istvan and D'Oleve, on their gaunt, scarecrow horses, towered above the solemn procession of tiny, earth-coloured ponies. Some of his own men were among the bodies carried there—Almos DiCassio and various distant cousins, DiVegas and DiArnacs and so on. But that was not why he had come, nor why he had brought D'Oleve.

Behind, pale clouds crawled across the crowded sky; ahead, the shining column of burning stone shimmered blue through a mist of rain.

A great door swung open as they approached the Hastur-tower. Beyond was a haze of light. The Bordermen dismounted, and slinging the dead between them, carried them inside. Istvan's heart was still and aching as he watched men he remembered laughing, vanish, stiff and waxen, into that supernal light.

D'Oleve's eyes were rapt and blind. Istvan opened his mouth to speak, but D'Oleve's voice cut him off. "His mind is all about us. He sees. He knows," D'Oleve answered his unspoken question. "But the heart of his mind is in the north. If you could see, DiVega, the death and destruction in Kathor, you too would think little of the battle here. There, Uoght walks by day; the Dyoles crawl before him with the Dark World wrapped about them as a cloak. Where they pass, only bare rock remains, scraped and pitted. The Hasturs' need-fire cannot pierce their shells. It is a bad time, DiVega, for mortal men to fight among themselves.''

"How may I bring peace, then?" Istvan asked, not sure, indeed, whether he spoke to D'Oleve or directly to the Hastur. "Ask him that!"

Raindrops pattered around them.

"If you surrender, will the war not end? But mortals never see things so simply. Call for a truce, then, and a peace council. Call on your foes to join you in defence of the land, and bid them bring their grievance before the Hasturs when the Border is quiet again. Or talk your grievance over in council, with weapons laid aside, that stored-up anger may not burst forth with more bloodshed.''

Suddenly, D'Oleve swayed and blinked, and looked around wildly as though uncertain where he was. "He—he is gone!" he said, his voice changed and weak. "The call came while he spoke. Another Hastur, wounded, and weary from the struggle in the north, has taken the watch in this tower. But Narmasil Hastur stands now on the plains of Kathor, spraying need-fire upon the shells of the Dyoles. Shall I speak to—"

"No," said Istvan. "I think—I *think* I know what I must do."

As a cold wind whooped around him, splashing chill rain in his face, Martos shivered and remembered how he had cursed the heat of the parched golden summer. Raindrops battered at the metal of his helm.

Behind him, exhausted men stumbled through dreary rain. Not even Suktio had argued when Martos had ordered them to turn aside, out of the path of the Seynyorean army that was marching down from Inagar: there was little fight left in any of them now.

Gloomily he had wondered if he should try to keep this force from joining DiVega—but his scouts had told of six thousand men or more, fresh and marching jauntily. So there was no shame in marching to the east, getting out of their way, giving them a clear road, and hoping they would not pursue.

Through the streaked lens of rain, he saw, tiny in the distance, an antlered stag, with two hornless deer grazing at his side, throw up his lordly branching crown and gaze at them. Then all three animals wheeled and bounded away. Men and horses were too weary to pursue, so they would eat horseflesh tonight, not venison.

He thought of Valiros then, and clenched his jaw. Now all the Jumpers were gone, except the handful of mares they had left in Massadessa. No use going after those, even if they had time! And that would not bring the smile back to Valiros' eyes.

Dark and solid in the ghostly rain, a brown-armoured scout came splashing out of the south on his little pony.

"Prince Hansio's army marches on the road, Lord! Listen and you can hear the conches that blow before them!"

Martos listened: above the irregular rustling of rain, he heard a faint keening. It had been in his ears for some time, but half-hidden by rain and hoofbeats; he had assumed it to be wind.

"It is a great host, Lord! They ride fine horses, and their armour is rich and many-coloured."

They turned south. The wind was at their back now, and it was warmed. The cry of the horns grew louder. *Hansio!* Martos thought. So the goal of their march was at hand. But how different a meeting from Jagat's plan. Instead of riding in with a thousand men and two thousand horses, proud warriors ready for battle, he would lead in a stumbling, disspirited band of wounded men on overworked horses.

Thousands of conch-horns shrilled over miles of rain. The Conch-horn of Chandra sang in answer.

As they rode on through the ever-changing rhythm of rain, Martos gloomily anticipated his meeting with Jagat: Kumari's face, disappointed, in his mind; Jagat's face, frowning. Another face intruded: Thiondos, staring from the helmet that rolled under the hooves.

"Who is that?" Paidros pointed.

Five blurred shapes came riding through grey rain. Martos straightened. Border ponies, but the men on their back were not any of his scouts. Border armour, certainly, but different. Slowly his mind was beginning to adjust to the strangeness of Border armour. This was different from the style worn by Jagat's men, the leather dyed with bright-coloured lacquers.

"Mahavarans!" said Ymros.

Their armour is rich and many-coloured, the scout had said.

They rode up, lacquered leather glossy-wet and dripping, and bowed from their saddles.

"You are the army of Lord Jagat?" one inquired politely. The laces that bound together the leather and metal bands of his breastplate and shoulderpiece were dyed and tied in curious rows of knots, which gave a strangely braided look, striped with gold and red.

"Yes," said Martos. "I am Martos of Onantuga." *My trusted aide,* Jagat had said. His ears burned.

"Come! We will lead you to our Lord and Prince, Hansio of Mahavara."

And then more riding through the clammy drops of rain, his weary horses plodding behind the Mahavarans. Another scout came spurring from the north to tell of yet another army there—eight thousand men on foot—but the Mahavarans laughed.

"It is the rest of your own army," said one. "Had you ridden closer, you would have seen the sword-wheel of Lord Jagat."

*   *   *

Conch-horns shrilled in Istvan's ears as he rode back to camp. Beyond the bustling Red-robes, the rows of bedding where the wounded lay, and the peacefully grazing horses, he saw his men ranked across the road at the bank that rose from the dust. Beyond them, across the sheet of shallow water that hid the ghostly ash, the stone dyke of the road ran to the east, and in the distance, it was thronged with marching men.

The rustle of the rain slowly faded. Far in the north he saw slanting bars of transparent gold pierce the grey. He watched Hansio's army flow nearer and nearer. His own men seemed to be throwing up barricades across the road—though what they could be using to build it, he could not imagine, since Rinmull had burned most of the supply wagons and the broken spears and arrows. Dead men's swords? Empty Kadarin armour?

He must try to make peace. But if he failed—and making peace with Hansio seemed an ambitious and unlikely undertaking, when he thought about it—if it failed, he must be ready.

Beyond the still blankness of water he saw the long chain of men slow on the road. Horses left the packed bridge and foundered about in the water for a time. He smiled as he watched them struggling back.

The road was blocked. But most of Hansio's army was still on the other side of this stretch of dust, anyway. They could just swing north and go around it.

His mind busied itself with that thought, and then he called himself up sharply. Strategy could wait. At the moment, his task was to make peace, if he could. He summoned Rinmull's herald, and D'Oleve.

The armour of the enemy gleamed dully under the cloudy sky.

Martos could see Hansio's vanguard across the dust on his right, an endless chain of men that covered the road and seemed to vanish in the west. Conch-horns wailed proudly across the waste.

Jagat's men came striding out of the north. A flood of soldiers covered the grass. Slowly, the armies were converging. Perhaps they would meet before they reached Hansio.

Horses grazed in great herds on the grass before them. A dozen bodies of men, some mounted, some afoot, marched out from between the horses and passed on into the west. Not all of the horses were Border ponies, Martos saw. Many were of a larger breed, clean-limbed and smooth-coated, with long, flowing manes. None were as heavyset as his own war-horses, but they had war-horse lines. Kalascorian horses, he guessed, and remembered that from ancient times the province of Ipazema had been famous for its horses.

Their guide halted, and said to Martos, "Your men will camp here, Lord. I shall send for Healers to tend to your wounded. If you will accompany me, I will take you before our Prince."

Martos left Paidros in charge, and took Suktio and Ymros with him. He shifted his saddle to Warflame.

"We're surrounded here," Paidros whispered to him, frowning, as Martos prepared to leave. "Or will be, by the time the camp is set up. I don't like it. It looks to me as though Prince Hansio doesn't trust his allies much." He gestured. Warriors in shiny wet lacquer were still marching past them; and off in the direction from which they had come, men were at work setting up camp.

"I don't like it either," Martos murmured, "but I don't see much we can do about it." He glanced off to the north. Lord Jagat's men were still marching. Apparently Hansio did not plan to let them camp close together, but wished to scatter his allies among his own men.

He worried about it as he trotted after the Mahavaran, his mind counting the forest of weapons that had sprouted in the barren waste, wondering if this was mistrust or simple policy: a way to reduce Lord Jagat to just one more commander among Hansio's host.

He saw Jagat's army halt; a little later, he saw horsemen coming from that host—one a figure he thought he recognised. He pulled up his horse, his fingers loathing the slimy wet leather of the reins, and told the guide to wait. Was that a fleeting look of distress in the man's eyes? He could not be sure.

Jagat came, riding a little Border pony, dwarfed and plain among the taller, brighter Kalascorian horses of his Mahavaran escort. He looked sad and weary. Hamir, beside him, looked even smaller.

Martos cantered quickly up, and Suktio and Ymros rushed to greet their Lord. Was that displeasure on the faces of the Mahavarans? They did not look happy, he decided. But Jagat did. He smiled as Martos rode in, the Mahavarans making room for him—awed, perhaps, by Warflame's size and colour.

Jagat accepted Suktio's and Ymros' homage calmly, then turned to Martos. "So you did get here!" he said. "I was worried."

"I've failed again!" Martos blurted, his face hot. "DiVega chased me—caught me. Half the horses are gone—some of them running over by Vaj—Vajertuga or whatever it's called, and the others foundered, or killed, or dead with colic. I lost more than two hundred of your men; I had to leave the field, retreat." Shame claimed his tongue. He could feel the stammer building, and could not go on. Jagat was silent. Martos braced himself for withering scorn, but the old man simply sighed, and shook his head sadly.

"I've lost a battle or two myself, in my time, and had to answer to old King Olansos for it,'' said Jagat. ''And DiVega has beaten better men than either of us. We'll talk about it later.''

The merest shifting of his eyes pointed out the escort around them. Martos realised that Jagat, too, was uncomfortable with Hansio's welcome.

They rode on, and halted before a pavilion startling in its magnificence. Here and there, faint discolourations in the cloth hinted at its age, but it showed a richness Martos had not expected to see anywhere in the Border country.

Two guards stood beside an empty stool. A warrior in rich lacquered armour bowed and bade them sit: the Prince would return in a moment. He clapped his hands, and wine was poured.

Scarcely had they dismounted and taken the wine when there was a stir in the ranks behind them. A conch-horn sang, clear and high, and a horse came dashing up, splashing mud—a horse nearly as large and white as Thunderhead. A figure in magnificent armour of russet iron vaulted from the saddle and strode to the tent. He pulled an antlered helmet from his head, and the hair beneath was snow-white. He seated himself upon the guarded stool, and turned on them piercing yellow eyes from a face as dark as old, polished wood. All about, men bowed deeply. Hansio of Mahapor was seated on his throne.

Martos stared. *The Fox?* He looked more like an eagle now, his amber eyes keen and bright above the thin beak of his nose. His drooping white mustache hid his mouth.

Someone was calling out their names, presenting them to the Prince of Mahapor, naming them as servants of Jagat, Prince of Manjipé!

Hansio was off the stool at once to greet them. He grasped all their hands. His grip was firm: to Martos it seemed that he held a stone in his palm. A flash of those yellow eyes took the weariness out of his heart, and he understood, then, why men would follow Hansio even into the Shadow itself, and why he had remained a power and a menace in the kingdom through all the years of Olansos' reign.

But then, when Hansio was once more seated on the stool that served as a portable throne, while the acknowledged Prince of Manjipé still stood as a supplicant before him, something in Martos recoiled, stung by the callous, cynical display of charm and power. His vision opened out in a giddying glimpse of a golden mask, of a single untempered virtue: kingliness unmixed with kindness, fouled by the dross of a terrible self-regard.

His mind ran hunting for quotations from the Kadarin philosophers, and they swarmed up like schools of fish after clouds of flies: Eldir—*It is the task of a King or a Lord to lift men to his height;*

Atrion—*Talent is a gift to use for all men, that the world may be renewed. But the Merchant will use it to steal from the world* . . . And others, until it seemed a multitude of voices cried within him.

Seeing Lord Jagat still standing, humble, waiting, Martos forced his tongue to move, forced strength to his voice, turned his eyes to the officer who had greeted them.

"You there!" His voice was harsh and rough as he fought his stammer. "A seat for the Prince of Manjipé!"

Keen eyes moved in Hansio's brown face, and regarded him from under thunder-laded brows. White teeth flashed under silver hair. For a second, then, the eagle turned into the fox. Martos stared.

"Indeed!" The excitement of Hansio's presence had faded enough that Martos could note, coldly, the strong beauty of the ringing voice, the carefully chosen words. "A seat for our royal cousin, Prince Jagat!"

The official's eyes spat at Martos, and then he hurried away. After a moment of scrambling and bustling, a soldier came rushing up with a second stool. Suktio took it from the man's hands as he came up, and Jagat seated himself with all dignity. Suktio gave Martos an approving nod.

Hansio's eyes had not yet left Martos, and now the rich golden voice spoke again: "They tell me that freshly wounded men rode in with—Martos of Onantuga." He took great care in pronouncing the foreign word, and the accent still came out wrong. Martos had to fight back a smile. "You have been fighting, then. Tell me of it."

There was no denying the command in that voice, even were there reason. Martos swallowed. The stammer fought to destroy his tongue, and shame returned to him—but pride rose to fight it. He had already been forgiven by Lord Jagat; he owed no apology to Hansio of Mahapor.

"A force led by Istvan DiVega himself intercepted me on my way to join this army," he said. "We fought. I was forced to retreat."

The golden eyes had not left him. He shut his mouth, feeling his tongue ready to go bad on him again. Had he said enough? How much of a report would he have to give?

"How many men does DiVega have?" The voice was a flat whipcrack now, and Martos almost jumped. For a second his mind whirled with the shame of having to admit that DiVega had defeated him without having a man more than he. Then his head cleared, and good sense came to his rescue.

"He'll have close to eight thousand by now," he said. "Men were gathering to him from all over the countryside."

"As my men marched here," said Jagat, "my scouts told me of a force coming in from Manjipor of at least three thousand, probably more. That is in addition to the six thousand men he had left outside

Inagar, who marched away to join him as we left the city. I would guess that his total force is somewhere between twelve thousand and fourteen thousand men, mostly Seynyoreans.''

Behind the veiling mustache white teeth flashed. The fox looked out through the eagle's mask.

"We have him, then!" That was almost whispered, but then the voice changed, rang out boldly: "DiVega has sent an emissary, to beg for peace, no doubt. He is being escorted back through my vanguard, along the road, now. I invite you, Cousin Jagat, to be with me when he receives his answer." The tone had been that of one bestowing a gracious gift, but suddenly it changed and became harsh with excitement. "We will crush them!" The tall figure started up from the stool, and a knotted fist clenched in the air as though DiVega and his host were within. "When my main army comes up, we will have them! And I shall avenge the death of both our sons!" His eyes sought Lord Jagat's, held them.

"I will kill Istvan DiVega with this hand, with this sword." A Hastur-blade flashed from its sheath. "Just as he killed my son—and your son! I shall kill him with no more mercy than I would show any night-thing.''

"DiVega?" asked Jagat. "What has he to do with—"

"It was he who killed our sons!" Hansio shouted, and rage had carried away the music of his voice. It became a shrill scream. "His sword let out both their lives, when they played a harmless prank! Killed them, to protect the filthy merchants and money-lenders who defile our land while they pay his fee!"

"I had not heard anything of the kind," said Jagat, his face puzzled, his voice low and troubled.

"My men told me, who dared to return to Tarencia without my son!" Hansio was nearly screaming now. "Three strokes of the sword, and the ancient line was gone! Three strokes of the sword: three men dead, and only two women to bear the blood of the oldest royal line in the world! But he saved the merchants' money!

"But now it is my turn! He, too, bears a Hastur-blade, they tell me; but it shall not save him. I have slain northern swordsmen before! I have fought all along the Border. He'll not escape me!"

Jagat frowned. His eyes met Martos', and suddenly Martos remembered Jagat's words in Inagar—*He's mad!*

The tall figure was striding back and forth now, his drawn sword burning in his hand. Martos felt himself shrinking back, crouching, before the terrible energy of the man.

Hansio stopped in his pacing, and stood, glaring. With an impatient hiss of breath he sheathed his sword and stepped slowly back to the stool and sat once more.

"We shall cleanse the land forever of the stink of the DiVegas," he said after a moment. His voice was calmer now. "There will be no more of them to rule from Tarencia! We shall turn north after we have avenged the blood of our sons, and throw off the accursed foreign yoke."

Jagat was silent. Glancing up, Martos saw a long line of slow-moving wagons, tiny in the distance. Men laboured at the wheels, moving them through the mud. Around them, Hansio's vast army, like swarming ants, advanced out of the wastelands to the east.

Even though the rain had stopped, Istvan's joints ached so fiercely that the pain of his wound faded to nothing in his mind. Still, he kept busy: gritting his teeth, surveying the land on which he hoped he would not have to fight another battle.

With Arjun DiFlacca and one of the Seers, he rode to the Shadow's edge to take a closer look at the tumbled walls of the ruins there. Once it must have been a city of some size. The piled-up stones ran across the Border in ordered lines only legend could name. What had once been towering walls were now only breast-high, or waist-high: there were places where Istvan could step over them; others where the upper parts had fallen, making footing uncertain. On this side of the Border, grass hid all but the larger stones, sickly and yellowish toward the edge of the Shadow. On the other side, pallid blades of grass straggled among the stones, and then vanished, so that the stones stood on naked earth or grey dust under the sunless sky.

Istvan hobbled among the ruins, supporting himself on his un-strung bow. Gazing south into the murk, he started, thinking he saw tiny figures moving far off in the dimness. But the gloom was too thick: he could not be sure. Twice he thought he heard a far-off wailing, as of many voices, but it might have been the wind.

He stood behind a waist-high section of wall and gazed east. The rubble in front of the wall would slow down enemy cavalry, and even footmen would be hindered.

A plan was taking shape in his mind. If he was lucky—if they were all lucky, all, on both sides—this would be wasted effort. He let his eyes lift, to look across the grass to the ghostly stretch of dust beyond. Somewhere out there, D'Oleve and Rinmull's herald would meet Lord Hansio, sometime in the next few hours.

He asked the Seer, and learned that D'Oleve was still on the road. He puffed his lips away from his teeth. Carefully planting his feet, he raised his bowstave in both hands and cut the air above the wall with it several times. He nodded to himself: no question, Ironfist Arac could hold this!

He frowned then, and shook his head. The numbers were still too high. Eighteen or nineteen thousand men he would have to deal with, if Jagat's army joined with Hansio. Maybe a full twenty thousand.

"My Lord!" It was the Seer's voice. Istvan turned. "Rupiros D'Ascoli has reached camp with six thousand men. Also, there is word from Lord Maldeo that there is a large force moving in from the north and west, from Orissia, which he would guess at as about three thousand men."

Orissians! But whose side were they on?

Damenco must already be in twilight, Martos thought, watching the Twin Suns fading slowly behind the distant Shadow in the west.

He was suddenly intensely homesick for Suknia, remembering the bedroom where he had visited Kumari so often; where their child, no doubt, had been conceived. Would he ever see it again? He shook his head, angry at himself. What nonsense was this? Of course he would, when this stupid war was over.

"We cannot, of course, advance across the dust itself," Hansio was saying. "My vanguard, already on the road, will move to occupy them while our main strength goes around to the north."

Campfires were being lit: the Mahavaran host had brought what must seem to them an incredible treasure of wood out of the Kantara.

A horseman galloped up and, throwing himself from his horse, dashed to where Hansio stood with Lord Jagat and dropped to his knees.

"The embassy comes, my Prince!" He bowed his head to the ground, and then scurried away.

Hansio straightened, and his teeth glittered white. "Well! Shall we hear them, Cousin?" Without waiting for an answer, he turned and gestured, and men came running with the two low stools that served as thrones for Jagat and himself.

With Hamir, Ymros, and Suktio, Martos stood behind Jagat while some of Hansio's generals stood behind the other throne. Torches were brought, as the light was slowly leeched from the sky. A faint pink and white shimmer showed above the black band that bound the horizon in the west; beyond the dust, Vajrakota was a tiny stalk of light.

Horsemen came: tall above the Kalascorian steeds a gaunt Seynyorean war-horse swayed, and at its side the only Border pony. Two men dismounted and advanced toward the throne; the others rode away.

One was tall, hawklike, his long face pale under dark, faintly reddish hair. He wore Seynyorean court dress—which was to say, the Kadarin style of ten years before, Martos thought with a smile.

White lace cuffs and the narrow ruff were faintly yellowed and less than perfectly starched, but that was only to be expected.

His companion, clad in Border robes so well cared for that they looked almost new, stepped forward. His dark face was stretched across what should have been a fat man's skull, a round face whose broad cheekbones drew out the thin cheeks.

"I am the herald of Rinmull of Ojaini, and this"—he gestured to the other—"is a representative of Istvan DiVega, Commander of Mercenaries serving the court of Chondos, King of Tarencia.

"Our masters have bidden us to say this to Hansio, Prince of Mahapor, and Jagat, Lord of Damenco: Last night Dark Things crossed the Border, for the first time in many weeks, scenting the blood of the battle, seeking the flesh of the dead. But they were driven away, neither by mortal men nor by the power of the Hasturs, but by one of their own masters, a vampire that came out of the Shadow and compelled them to leave the battlefield."

A stir went through all that heard. Jagat sat upright, and his face became thoughtful. But Hansio sat still as stone.

"Think about this, Lords of the Border! Since the King died, no raiding party of Night Walkers has entered the land. Your livestock and your houses have been undisturbed. Is this not strange? Far in the north, we know the Children of Hastur battle with the greatest of the terrors out of the Dark World. Yet here it is quiet; and when the servants of the Dark Lords do cross the Border, they are ordered back! Is this not strange, men of the Border country?" He paused and looked around at them. Hansio alone sat cold, ummoved.

"The dead—not Seynyorean dead alone, but Kadarin and Manjipéan as well—rest now in the Tower of Vajrakota. Narmasil Hastur was watchman at that tower when we carried the dead there. He bids us make peace, saying that this is a poor time for mortal men to war on one another. Let us stop this fratricidal war, join together in defence of the land, and take our grievances before the Hasturs when the Border is quiet once more. Or let us take council now to settle our grievances, laying our weapons aside while we plan to defend and patrol the Border.

"Is it not plain that this war serves only the Dark Things? They are waiting, waiting for us to kill each other and leave the land empty—for them. When we have killed each other, our women and children shall be left to face the creatures of the Shadow. Think well, Lords of the Bordermen! Descendants of the Takkarian Kings! Already most of the ancient empire has been eaten away, while the heirs of the Old Blood fight among themselves. Shall there be nothing left of the ancient land, of the ancient blood? That is what the Lords of the Dark Things desire. Let us thwart them, and make peace."

Faint voices murmured among the Bordermen. Jagat stirred, as though to speak.

Hansio leaped to his feet. "Fool! Dog of the DiVegas!" His golden voice was a trumpet-call that drowned all other voices, all other thought. "Herald of Ojaini? Ah, how wise of the DiVegas to use you as their mouthpiece, and keep their own man silent behind you! But it is the House of DiVega you speak for, it is DiVega lies that you mouth!

"What have the DiVegas to do with the heritage of the Takkarian Kings? Do we preserve it for them? It is too late to preserve the ancient blood: Istvan DiVega has spilled it already, has slain both the heirs in direct line of the Arthavan Kings! There is no male heir to the oldest royal line in the world! The male line has died out. Your master saw to that, so there would be no other claim besides that of the upstart DiVega who sits upon the throne in Tarencia!"

Hansio's terrible presence dominated them all. Jagat buried his face in his hands. Hamir gripped his sword-hilt. Suktio's teeth were bared. A sigh like a growl passed through the throats of the Bordermen around them.

"Rinmull's herald, aye—but with a Seynyorean spy at his shoulder, a Seynyorean Seer, to see that he speaks what his Seynyorean master bids!

"Tell us, Seynyorean, of the ancient glories of the Takkarian line—now that you have ended it! Are our daughters now to marry DiVegas, to bring their heritage to your hands?

"We will not crawl either to Chondos DiVega nor to Istvan DiVega! What have the DiVegas to do with the inheritance of the Takkarian Kings?

"You tell us to beware of the Dark Things. You tell us to be frightened when they do *not* attack us, and you tell us that they will kill our children. But a DiVega has already killed our children!

"Go back to your DiVega master, licker of Seynyorean bones! Get you gone, or I will forget the ancient usage toward messengers, and rid the world of one traitor of the Old Blood. You, too, Seynyorean spy! Time for that tomorrow on the field! Go back, and tell your master that the sons of the Takkars guard the land! We have fought the Dark Things for a thousand years, and need no sword-sellers from the north to tell us how! And it is better that the land should be eaten by the Dark Ones than that the murderer of my son should rule it! I have not spent my life saving the land that a DiVega should take it from me at the end! Get you gone! Our daughters' children shall rule this land, not foreigners hired by merchant gold to kill our sons and soil our women!"

Martos flinched. Twice Jagat had moved as though to speak, and twice had paused before the barrier of Hansio's voice. Now Martos heard him draw breath again to speak; but then he hesitated, and rubbed his fingers over eyes and brow, shaking his head.

While Jagat remained silent, the Seynyorean, his face pale, said, "We offer you peace, and our aid in the defence of the land. There is no answer"—his voice was trembling—"no defence against this madness that you speak. Do not let your hatred work for the Dark Things! Will you not—"

"No!" snarled Hansio, and his voice was no longer beautiful. "Tell your master that tomorrow we crush him in the field, and that I myself, with this old hand, will give his blood to Our Lady the Earth, and avenge the murder of my son! The murder of *both* branches of the ancient line! Now get you gone, Seynyorean goblin! The land cries for your blood!"

North in Tarencia, Jodos, feeling Shachio moving among the fine-spun tendrils of mind that filled the castle and were slowly weaving out through the city beyond, made the woman who knelt at his feet let go of him and, pushing her roughly away, rearranged his clothing.

Announced by a half-mad servant, Shachio entered in haste. "Lord King," he began; then, seeing her, "My Lady!" A quick bow. "Your pardon. Commander DiVega sends important news. Prince Hansio's army is near, and he has been unable to make peace."

Jodos had already seen some of this message bubbling on the surface of the old man's mind, and it almost made him forgive the interruption, even though his breath still trembled. She remained standing in the same spot where she had fallen when he pushed her, although she had risen before Shachio entered the room. He imagined himself cutting the flesh from Shachio's bones. The old fool would probably die too quickly to be interesting.

"Lord Jagat is there also," the Seer was saying, "with all his army, so that DiVega is outnumbered by almost two to one. He is gathering his men together as quickly as he can, and it is certain there will be a battle in the morning."

And after the battle, whoever won, the Border would be nearly undefended. Jodos looked at the woman across the room, with her hollow, haunted eyes. Soon he could eat. Really eat. Not her, not yet, not until his spawn was ripe; but others like her. He would make her watch, so she would know what was coming. He would make her caress him while he ate.

"DiVega begs that you will send troops south—not to his aid, for the battle will be over long before any possible force could reach him, but to defend the Border afterward. For nearly every man on the Border will be on one side or another in this battle. Many will be killed."

Jodos fought with the triumph that threatened to bring a smile to his lips, and looked down to hide the brightness in his eyes.

"He says he is almost more afraid to win than to lose," the old Seer went on. "So many of the Bordermen are gathered in the two armies of Jagat and Hansio. He fears too that it will take such hard fighting for him to win that the greater part of both armies will be slain. He fears that whoever wins, the Border will be almost defenceless."

Jodos let his head sink down on his chest and brought his hands up to his face. Shachio thought the King deeply troubled by his tale, but Jodos was hiding the terrible triumphant laughter that forced his lips wide.

No matter who won, the Great Ones would rule; they would take back another part of the world which the Nameless One had snatched from them! It did not matter who won! DiVega would win only at the price of wiping out the Bordermen. If Hansio and Jagat won, they would bring their great army north, leaving the Border defenceless behind them.

When they had reached this city, that would be the time to send the signal, to call the Master! Before Hansio could turn his army back, the land would be eaten. The women and children left behind in the Border castles would be delicious screaming shreds of flesh. Mahapor and ancient Manjipor, Inagar and Ojaini, would all be covered by the Shadow. Demons would devour the ancient trees of the Kantara. And as the Bordermen turned, homeless and hopeless, to face the Shadow, the broken-witted soldiers from the city would fall upon their rear.

Yes, better if DiVega lost, he decided.

"Jagat and Hansio between them have close to twenty thousand men," Shachio continued. "There is also an army of three thousand or more moving in from Orissia. They have not yet declared themselves, but we know Portona's agents were stirring up trouble in Orissia months ago. So matters look very grave indeed. He hopes that Your Majesty will remember him kindly if he should fail, and begs you to remember that the Bordermen are the shield of all the kingdom."

Jodos had controlled his face by now. He looked past the Seer to where she waited for him. It would be many months before she ripened enough to eat, but he could take off a little here and there. Already, indeed, he had taken off tiny, tiny bites, where it would not show: her hair hid a mangled earlobe, and the other place was hidden under her dress.

"Lord Istvan says that he is certain now that the Dark Things are waiting, biding their time, and that they know all that happens in the kingdom. Night Walkers came to the field after his last battle, but were ordered away by a vampire. He says the Dark Lords are holding back their servants, trying to make us forget them, while they keep the Hasturs busy in the north.''

DiVega had guessed at the plan! That could have been serious— but DiVega would be dead soon.

If only this old fool would stop talking and leave! He was so excited he was almost ready to spawn. Only a few more days! He would have to think, and decide which of the women of the court to begin with. He would pick one of her special friends; that would make it more interesting. He would have to look into her mind tonight, and see whose doom would disturb her most.

Shachio regarded him intently. "You must give—*must* give—orders tomorrow, Lord King! This matter is most serious. Even though''— he smiled and shot a quick glance at the girl in the corner behind him—''I can see that you young people have other matters on your mind. But the situation is grave, and must be dealt with quickly.''

Jodos sat forward angrily, and almost lost control. How dare this thing, this creature, think such a foul idea! He was not ruled by the sickening animal instincts of the Sun People! How dare the old fool think such a thing!

But he remembered in time, and managed a weak, sheepish-looking smile. His ears felt hot, which he read as being, strangely, what Shachio expected. His brother's memories came to his rescue, and he bade the old man good night formally and cheerfully, even managing to get in a joke, the point of which he did not understand: How lovely the blood was in her face as she heard it! He licked his teeth.

At last the old fool was gone! He had her throw off her gown, revealing all the new scars on her body, and then kneel down and stroke him until he spawned in her hand. He licked her palms clean, and took the taste out of his mouth by slashing her palm with his sharp teeth and sucking as much as he dared of her sweet blood. But he must not weaken her too much: he wanted her strong for the ordeal he had planned for her tonight, and she would lose enough blood from that.

But then, thinking about it, he felt too weak and comfortable. It was very strange. He always seemed to have less energy instead of more after spawning. He supposed it was because his spawn had no time to eat before he reabsorbed them. He looked fondly through her stomach at the one developing there. That should be a different matter. It was growing nicely.

When the Great Ones spawned, they gained much power, for their spawn, the Dyoles and Demons and so on, were able to scatter to so many different sources of energy, and then, when the parent reabsorbed them, the power they had gained was all gathered—if the parent could catch them . . . or if they did not grow so mighty that they devoured the parent instead.

That was why there were Eight Dark Lords instead of One, and so many lesser Demons. Sooner or later they would all be reabsorbed by the Survivor. But that was a long time away, when this entire universe of light, and all the other universes beyond it, had been absorbed. And by then, he might himself have grown mighty, might himself be the Survivor!

But first he must transcend this fragile mortal form.

Martos, with Suktio and Ymros, escorted Jagat and Hamir back to their camp. Hamir and Suktio laughed and joked, but Jagat brooded.

"We'll have no more trouble with the Seynyoreans!" snorted Hamir, with a bark of bitter laughter. "Not even Istvan the Archer can rescue them from this! We'll crush them!"

Jagat stirred. "No doubt," he said, in a lifeless voice. "But should we?" Hamir turned, and stared at him.

"But, my Lord," Suktio began, slowly. "Prince Hansio—"

"Is mad," said Jagat, cutting him off. He shook his head. "Perhaps we are both mad." They stared at him.

"I should have spoken," Jagat murmured, as though to himself. "I *should* have spoken. But each time—twice I tried to speak, to accept DiVega's offer and end this stupid war. But each time I heard Hansio's raving drown my thoughts, and I would see my boy— dead. I'd see him dead, and hear Hansio raving that the DiVegas had . . . No!" He shuddered and straightened. "No, I do not believe it! It is madness! I do not know if Istvan DiVega killed my son or not. I do not think he did. I think—even if he did, it would have been for no gain! Certainly not just to keep Chondos on the throne! It is all nonsense! Insanity! And yet . . ." He seemed to sink down again, collapsing into himself, an old man, shrunken and tired.

"And yet I sat and said—nothing! Ever since my son died, I have been letting other men . . ." He laughed suddenly. "I am mad! I must be mad! And Hansio is mad! Two madmen leading an army to destruction! We must all be mad!"

Istvan felt sleep like glue under his eyelids, but there was still work to do, plans to make, orders to give.

Hansio's accusation haunted him. At first it had made no sense at all, until he remembered that it had been a DiVega—one of DiFlacca's men, a cousin too distant to be reckoned, one of the distant branches, from Heyleu or Solvasar—who had actually done the killing. One of DiFlacca's men . . .

But would Hansio believe it? Would it matter to him?

If you surrender, the Hastur had said, *will the war not end?*

Istvan pondered that a long time. His inner soul revolted at the thought. Generations of DiVegas rose from the family portraits in the halls of his mind to forbid. Yet, were he sure that the war would end . . .

Nearly all the men of the Border were here. All but a few thousand. Mahavara and Manjipé were both stripped of defenders, and the Kantara manned chiefly by the warriors Hansio had left there. Only children and the extremely aged would remain of the men of the Border: some of the warriors that would fight tomorrow were as young as fourteen. Only the women would be left, and a whole new generation of men would have to grow up . . .

But the Dark Ones would not give them time to grow up.

If you surrender, will the war not end? But would it? Or would Prince Hansio simply get them out of the way and march north his whole army, to carry on his lifelong struggle against the DiVegas?

Surrender! If he could only be sure that the war would end.

"Commander DiVega!" the Seer said at his elbow. "Ladeslos DiSezrotti wishes to speak with you. He says it is most urgent and begs that you permit mind-touch." Istvan blinked at him.

DiSezrotti! He was with Lord Maldeo, marching in from Manjipor!

"Very well." He felt the Seer's mind touch his, and the Seer's voice, light and high, suddenly deepened into DiSezrotti's gruff tones:

"DiVega? DiSezrotti here. I'm on my way to the Orissian camp. Our scouts caught one of their scouts blundering around, and brought him in. From what he says, it looks like we have three thousand more men on our side."

Chapter Fifteen

Dawn poured gold between fluffy white clouds. Pallid wisps of mist went spinning before the wind like fleeing ghosts. Metal flashed in sunlight. All across the plain, armoured men were bustling.

Martos, his head still stuffed with sleep, finished saddling Warflame, and brushed the big beast's crisp red hide. Bridle-rings jangled as the horse tossed his head and pawed at the piled hay.

Looking up, Martos saw long strips of blue like rivers between the clouds, and drew a joyous lungful of the scent of horse, dung, and hay. Conch-horns shrilled, and somewhere a drum boomed boldly above the noise.

"Lord Martos?" said a voice nearby. Martos turned, still grinning. "Are your men ready? I am Lord Todaro of Kirtanpor." A Borderman looked down from the back of a fine tall horse. "Prince Hansio has placed your men under my command."

The smile died on Martos' face. "Prince Jagat has not," he said sharply, and then turned away, as though that ended the matter.

"My Lord!" He heard the man's shocked voice behind him. "But my Prince said—but surely Lord Jagat must realise that now he has joined the Prince's army, his men must be subject to the Prince's commanders, and act in concert with the rest."

Martos swung around. For a moment, anger threatened to hold his tongue. He swallowed, fighting for control. "You misunderstand," he said, coldly. "Jagat, Prince of Manjipor, has accepted the aid of his ally, the Prince of Mahavara, in dealing with the Seynyorean invasion of Manjipé." He felt the stutter creeping into his mouth, and shut it. The Mahavaran's staring eyes were like coins. Martos had to fight back laughter. He drew a deep breath, and bellowed, "Stand to horse!"

All through the camp was a sudden scramble. His own men formed in a steady line beside their horses, and all about them the Bordermen were scurrying into place.

"Mount!" Martos shouted, stepping up into the sdddle. Then, secure on Warflame's back, he looked down at Todaro.

The Kalascorian horse was suddenly very small. Martos walked Warflame toward the other until he and the Mahavaran were knee to knee.

"A word to you privately," he said in a casual tone, although his heart was beating as if he had run up a hill. "Remember that you are a guest here. You *and* your Lord. You will make yourself look foolish."

Shouting to his men to form up behind him, Martos drummed his heels on Warflame's flanks and rode to Jagat's camp.

Istvan's camp was filled with the bustle and racket of arming.

"About how long, did you say?" he demanded sharply.

"If they wait for the Orissians, they won't be here until late afternoon," said D'Oleve. "Maldeo and his men could get here— oh, in four or five hours, say."

Across the dust they could hear the throb of drums and the wail of conches. Istvan pressed his teeth together, as though chewing his thoughts; his breath hissed. Coming to a decision, he turned and shouted for Ironfist.

"You say that the Orissians are all cavalry?" he said, turning back to D'Oleve.

"All, yes."

"Tell DiSezrotti to drop back and wait for the Orissians to catch up with him, and ride in with them. The rest of Maldeo's men should get here as fast as they can." He looked up as Ironfist came striding toward them, his great axe swung over his giant's shoulders, the heavy rings of his mail aglitter in the sunlight.

"Ironfist!" Istvan said. "Let me tell you before the others arrive, so that their pride does not suffer, that I depend chiefly upon you in this battle. Your men will hold a most important post: you will be the axle of our wheel. I can think of no other man I would sooner trust with such a duty. You saw the ruins, down by the edge of the Shadow?" He scarcely waited for the big man's nod. "You must march your men down quickly, settle in behind those walls, and hold them. You will have all the foot. You must be rock-steady. You will be the rock on which the rest of us stand."

"You're going to let Hansio get *that* far?" Ironfist frowned.

"Policy," said Istvan. "I'll explain it all in a moment, when the rest come—or do you really want to hear it twice?"

A few moments later they were all gathered. Istvan had ordered each captain to bring his lieutenants, that all might be aware of the plan: with almost thirty companies and several of Rinmull's Lords, there were nearly enough men to have made up a company by Kadarin reckoning.

"It is obvious," Istvan began when they had quieted down, "that if Hansio tried to bring his entire army across the dust, we could slaughter them at the neck of the road. In fact, he has already moved most of his force north, and Lord Jagat has joined him there. He will probably make a thrust across the causeway with his vanguard, but that, I think, will be a feint, to distract us while he brings him main force around the edge of the dust onto our left.

"We know that his forces outnumber ours, though we do not know by how much. He has somewhere between sixteen thousand and twenty thousand men. However, we have more men than we thought we had: three thousand Orissians are marching to join us at this moment." He watched their eyes grow as bright as their spirits, and then added, gently, "Unfortunately, we cannot expect them to reach us until after battle has been joined."

"Even if they could get here in time," a voice said from the crowd, "Orissian against Borderman is a fool's wager."

"We have Bordermen on our side, too," said Istvan in the same quiet tone. "And once upon a time the Seynyoreans considered themselves the best fighting men in the world. Or have we given up that reputation?"

That touched the fierce Seynyorean pride, and he saw them stiffen. He smiled to himself.

"So. We must leave a force to hold the road at the edge of the dust, to meet the feint there. His main body will be coming from the north, trying to turn our flank. We must make them think they succeed: lure them in. D'Olafos, your men will be stationed up at the north end of the line. I want a token resistance, followed by a feigned retreat. A feigned panic, in fact. We want them to think they're winning, when they're actually not."

"Hold them, and then run away?" said D'Olafos doubtfully. "That's a tricky business."

"My men can do it, if yours can't," snorted Palos DiFlacca. "I see what you're about, DiVega! You're planning to lure them in until they turn their flank to the northwest. Then, when the Orissians come—" He drove his fist into his palm, and made a smacking noise with his lips.

Istvan nodded. "Right! We must set up a line across the road, which looks to be our main battle-line. But the true battle-line will be well to the south, with our backs to the Shadow."

Uneasy muttering ran from man to man. Istvan had expected this. He listened, silent, letting the murmurs run their course. He knew his men. When the last murmur had died, Istvan went on, as though there had been no interruption, his voice calm.

"Our right flank must be rock-steady, an anchor that we can form on and move around. Ironfist and the foot will be holding that rockpile of a ruin down by the Border. Our first battle-line—the false one—will run up from there like a horn. It need not be more than a handful of companies—enough to look good to Hansio's scouts. Eight companies, I think, projecting up in a crescent from our second battle-line.'' He looked out over their faces, and his voice was grave.

"But we cannot afford simply to fall back to our final battle-line. Not only would it increase the risk to the advanced companies, but it might make Hansio suspect the trap. So we must have a second line, to meet and throw them back halfway. And then we must retire again, but only after they have gathered against us. Many, I fear, will fall there, defending a line that is to be abandoned.''

Istvan stood silent a moment, his eyes searching the faces that looked at him, young faces and old faces, cheerful ones and sad ones.

"Lord Rinmull, your men will hold the road where it meets the dust. I do not think it likely they will be able to drive you back. But keep your horses ready. When I give the order, your men will fly to the south and take up position next to the ruins, near Ironfist's men. DiArnac! Your men will support Rinmull's with arrows. When the word comes, you will retreat straight west on the road and take up position beside Servara, to support DiFlacca and D'Olafos when they come. Servara, you'll be stationed on the road. I'll tell you where in a minute. You, Ciavedes, and D'Ascoli, will be the new left wing on the second line.

"It will be hours yet before our full force is gathered. If they attack too quickly, we shall have to try delay, to give Lord Maldeo and the rest of our army time to arrive. But if we are lucky, it will take Hansio some time to get his army moving.

"This will be the shape of the horn jutting north: D'Olafos and Palos DiFlacca at its tip, with Ivailo and Endrios DiFlacca just south of them, with DiCalvados.'' He had planned to have the three DiFlaccas together—it simplified orders—and DiCalvados at the tip with D'Olafos. But Palos had volunteered by his outburst. "Then DiMadyar and DiBolyar, just north of the road. Be sure the road itself is kept clear! DiMadyar and DiBolyar should spread out as though there were two companies between them. The horn will be broad, but empty! Valanos Chalcondiel's company will be stationed just south of the road.

"D'Olafos, DiFlacca, you must be our false left, our feint! You will be there at the northern corner and must hold it if they come too soon! Beat them, harry them, drive them down into the narrow space between our men and the dust! DiCalvados and DiMadyar must make sure that Rinmull and DiArnac are not cut off!

"But that is only if they come before we are ready. Otherwise, your task is to fight and run away! Prick them with your arrows until they gather in strength against you; then break and run, and make them follow, run as though in panic, southwest until you reach

Servara. When Servara charges, they'll be thrown into disorder. Wheel, then—hammer them, ride them down!

"Ivailo and Endrios DiFlacca, you will join your cousin in the flight. DiCalvados, you ride on a straighter course to the south, between DiBolyar and DiMadyar. You and DiMadyar will cross the road after DiArnac has passed, join with Chalcondiel, and the three of you will ride south to take up positions next to Lord Rinmull.

"And this will be the order of our second line," Istvan continued. "First, the ruins, where Ironfist and the foot will stand. Next to them, Lord Rinmull and his men; next, Chalcondiel, DiMadyar, and DiCalvados. Next, Alon Robardin. His men will be in place, so the others can dress ranks between them and the ruins. Next, Milan Robardin, but his men will place themselves a hundred yards back, so they can charge into line if need be. Formed on him for the charge, in a crescent running up to Servara, will be DiGasclon, the two DiRonar companies, and DiBretan's company. Beyond that space will be D'Esnola's company; and beyond that, a space for DiArnac, and then Servara, on the road.

"Behind this line—" He broke off, as a Borderman came rushing in and whispered quickly to Lord Rinmull.

"Hansio's vanguard is advancing along the road!" Rinmull announced.

"To your places, gentlemen!" said Istvan. "Keep your Seers close."

Martos found the road to Jagat's camp blocked by a line of marching men, and sat fuming until they had passed. Then he spurred impatiently on. A Borderman came riding up and swore at him for blocking the road. He did not care: this was no way to run an army, and Hansio had better learn it now!

Jagat and his men had broken camp and were ready to march. Martos spurred up angrily.

"He said what?" gasped Jagat, his eyes wide. Martos repeated, as exactly as he could, Lord Todaro's words, though he stammered in his anger and had to stop often. Finally he got it all out.

Jagat shook his head. "Does the fool think he is the King already? He is mad!" Jagat frowned and bit his lip. "Now I do not know what to do! This matter—we cannot withdraw from the battle now, but if his judgment is so far gone that he cannot see the folly of—why should he do such a thing? And what will he do next? What will he do to you?"

Martos became aware that he had been much too angry to think about that. What would Hansio do? Split the army, trying to assert a wrongful authority? Attack Jagat's men? Madness!

A messenger came cantering up and reported: "Prince Hansio

begs his ally, the Prince of Manjipor, to quickly advance his army
along the edge of the dust and attack the Seynyorean left.''

The wound in Istvan's leg ached as he rode about the field,
overseeing the movements of the companies, making sure there
would be room to manoeuvre when the time came. An hour went
by, and then another.

He kept D'Oleve close beside him, to maintain contact with them
all, as well as Maldeo, marching toward the field, and DiSezrotti,
far behind with the Orissians. Where the road came out of the dust,
Lord Rinmull's men were at hard handstrokes with Hansio's van.

Word came of men moving around the corner of the dust. Istvan
cursed: Maldeo and his men would not arrive for an hour or more at
least. He sent word, by D'Oleve, for them to hasten, and to DiFlacca
and D'Olafos to delay as long as they could.

DiFlacca's company circled to wheel in for a crushing blow on the
enemy's right, catching them at open shields, hurling them into the
dust with the momentum of rushing horses, herding them helpless.

DiCalvados reported a few lone men, hunted like beasts, riding in
the corridor between his company and the dust. Men and horses
foundered in the shallow dust-bottomed water. No one pursued as
they splashed their way back.

Staring into the north while he listened to the reports, Istvan could
see only tiny unidentified figures. Some glittered with tiny sparkles;
others were mere atoms of glossy colour. The remnants of the
stricken force rallied; more came charging down to join them. Istvan
clenched his fists, impatient, impotent. D'Oleve said that Maldeo
was still far away.

Again DiFlacca's crack troop outmanoeuvred the foe. They turned
to face him, to guard—and as they did so, D'Olafos launched his
men into a wolf-wild charge that shattered their ranks as stone
shatters bone.

Still DiFlacca hovered on the flank, watching and waiting as he
moved farther north. Conch-horns screamed across the plain. A
moving forest of men and horses advanced beside the dust.

''Can't keep this up much longer, DiVega!'' DiFlacca shouted
through his Seer. ''One more trick; then they'll swamp us!''

Istvan knotted his fist and chewed his lip as D'Oleve spoke the
words: Maldeo's warriors were still many footsore miles away.

''You'll have to use your own judgment, then,'' he called back.
''Just give me a few minutes warning before you break and run.''

''One last trick!'' came the answer. ''Then be ready!''

Swift as turning swallows, DiFlacca's men whirled south and
came rushing down to join the stream of leather armour that rolled
against D'Olafos. Shouting, bright swords waving, they burst tram-

pling into the heart of the band, stampeding the horses, emptying saddles, shouldering soldiers into the slick-bottomed shallows.

In Istvan's eye, the distant dots flurried like a flock of frightened birds. Confused warriors flooded the corridor between the companies and the dust. Now both DiCalvados and DiMadyar were engaged, trying to keep the swarm from cutting off Rinmull and DiArnac.

At the same time came word of a sudden thrust along the road. Istvan realised that his whole plan could founder, and ordered Rinmull's men to fall back. Spurring his horse north toward the road, calling to D'Oleve to stay close behind, he saw the brown-armoured figures rushing to their ponies, while DiArnac's mounted troops sent a swarm of arrows against the gaudy-armoured Bordermen tearing at the barrier. Tossing steel flared above the churning riot of stamping horses. Men's voices babbled maddeningly. Riderless ponies broke from the press. In a moment the flimsy barrier Rinmull's men had thrown across the road would be down, and Hansio's van would come surging over the stones, horse and man and hungry sword, to cut off the north-pointing horn at the base.

"DiFlacca!" Istvan shouted at D'Oleve. "Is he ready yet?"

Rinmull's men, their dead and wounded slung over their saddles before them, whirled their ponies and galloped to the south.

"Ready!" shouted D'Oleve.

"Tell him to go! Tell DiArnac to get moving! Tell them all!"

Martos looked on a ferment of shoaling horsemen beneath a lacework lightning of swords. Tides of blood throbbed in his head. Warflame, warm between his spread legs, neighed and danced a step or two, the long thick muzzle plunging up and down. Martos' broad hands squeezed the reins, while his eyes hunted out death in that flickering lace of steel.

Suddenly, blocks of mail and horseflesh melted away; scattering swarms of horsemen raced glittering this way and that. All seemed confusion: some ran west, some wheeled south, while staring leather-armoured foemen stood still, amazed. Then, with a cheer, the pursuit began.

The Conch-horn of Chandra trilled shrilly. Martos heard Jagat's shouted order. His heels pounded the ribs of the horse between his knees; the saddle creaked and strained as Warflame sprang forward. Hoofbeats crashed against eardrums. In Martos' mind were snatches of old hero-songs and death disguised as a real steel blade.

Above the red stallion's head, star-sprinkled mail moved, shields turned to face him. Arrows blurred past, wind-song lost in hoof-beats, and now before him a hedge of mounted men raised steel thorns. A grating shriek of conch-horns tore at his ears; tiny horsemen swelled up, menacing.

Hoofbeat and heartbeat battered through his flesh. He saw the graceful tension of a poised sword arm coiled like a serpent to strike. The sword blurred, its edge a line of light. Martos hid it with his shield. A thunder of gonging metal boomed. His own sword arm lashed out as the shock of impact jolted through his shoulders. The sword-hilt quivered in his hand; fingers felt the familiar scrape of steel piercing steel. He ripped back the dripping blade. Over his shield, he saw mail stained bright rose: the foeman swayed, pitching over his horse's side.

The horizon was filled with the transparent silver of swords in motion: the clamour of steel stung his ears.

Istvan's sword was still sheathed. Shame gnawed at him as he saw others bleed and die. It seemed more natural to fight, to set an example for his men. But he buried that frantic thought. They needed him more here, back from the line where he could see the battle, and not just the swords that menaced him.

Before his eyes, swords mirror-bright and swords daubed with red swooped and dived above men's ring-clad backs and the lashing tails of horses. Wounded men screamed; whole men shouted.

He looked past the sparkling of swords, at the plain beyond. Around the edge of the dust, horsemen rushed, their leather armour tinted red, blue, purple, gold. Seething behind them were bright-coloured blocks of footmen. Conch-horns shrieked. Men on foot, in dark earth-coloured leather, flooded the ground.

Yes, thought Istvan, *the plan's working!* Uncountable numbers of men swarmed down into the cupped lines of waiting sun-jewelled mail.

Off to the left, sunlight rippled on the curved mirrors of Kadarin armour; beyond, still further left, he saw Ciavedes' horsemen racing in on the flanks of a mass of Bordermen, taking them at open shields and rolling the survivors to the left, where DiArnac and the three DiFlaccas had rallied and formed up again.

Jagat's dark-armoured foot came storming up in their thousands, filling the gaps between the bodies of horse that had pursued the fleeing companies. A sudden charge of horsemen swept to meet them, and drove some staggering back. But Istvan's six thousand men in that second line were far outnumbered.

"Lord Maldeo and the companies with him are in sight of the battle, Commander," D'Oleve said. "What are your orders?"

Istvan's eagle eye soared across the field; saw horsemen whirling, riding back, forming up to charge again. Near his centre was a swirling mass of circling horses, mail and plate mingled, where

Martos and his men clashed in a furious melee with DiGasclon's company.

He ordered Maldeo to move directly south, and to bring his men in along the edge of the Shadow, to join his reserve. He was tempted for a moment to send them north, to bring them in on Hansio's rear in place of the tardy Orissians—but it was too early. Hansio had not yet committed all his army, and could still absorb such a stroke.

Istvan looked again into the maddened swirl of chain and plate in the centre and, sending word to DiGasclon to retreat, ordered Turul and Attilon DiVega forward.

Death-bells of edged steel tolled in Martos' ears. Dismembered men screamed among the hooves. Sweat burned his eyes and blurred them: each breath seemed to draw the whole sky into aching lungs.

A Seynyorean bugle sang retreat. Martos' sword shaved empty air as the man he fought swerved away. Clapping heels to horse, he pursued, but the long-legged Seynyorean steed strode away with a speed Warflame could not match. Valiros shot past on a stolen bony horse; behind, Paidros shouted for men to rally and re-form.

We broke the Seynyorean line! Martos exulted at the shrinking mail-clad backs.

Then he saw blocks of horsemen ranged to the south, all along the Border. Hissing above hoofbeats, an arrow flickered in front of his face; another sank into a Borderman's leather-clad side.

Bimsio shouted a warning. From the right, a wave of horsemen rolled under upraised swords. Martos heaved his blade up to meet a glittering wheel of spinning light; startled Bordermen, caught at open shields, fell under the steel-tipped onslaught.

A horse's shoulder rammed Warflame's flank, turning the big horse around. Instinct hurled up Martos' shield: it boomed on his arm. He was blinded by tiny rings of sunglare under a twisted face with curiously passionless eyes.

Then the line was past, and he was somehow still alive, facing a second wave. He glimpsed a reeling man, white-faced before the pounding hooves, among leather-armoured bleeding forms; a riderless horse bounded up from the ground and raced away.

His spurs pricked Warflame's side, hurtling the big horse into the charging line. His long blade carried his hand like a wing of steel. He would not die alone! His shield thundered; his sword-edge shocked through crumbling metal. Agony scraped across his knee. He glimpsed Border armour, bursting through the line further down: rushing with him, the third line.

Sunlight sparked on a speed-blurred sword. Warflame breasted a wave of horseflesh that pressed Martos' knees. Swords reached out for him; and his chin cracked against his breastplate as he tried to pull his head in like a turtle. White light flared in the bell of his skull. His shield shuddered; his long blade pierced mail. Reeling in the saddle, he ripped it free and gazed about.

"Lord Martos!" Bimsio rode toward him. Flaps of leather armour had been ripped away; torn cloth dangled from a naked shoulder. "Are you hurt badly?"

"Not sure." Martos sucked in a deep breath of sky. "Is my helm—bloody?"

"No," said Suktio. "Dented in, but not pierced that I can see."

Slamming metal hammered behind them. Still stunned with wonder to find himself alive, Martos turned. Mirrored plate flashed beyond mail-covered backs and the lashing tails of horses, where Paidros fought with the rallied company.

Valiros' voice shouted from behind: he was alive! Martos' heart danced in his chest. In a few moments, Valiros and Quintis rode with Martos and Bimsio to rejoin the company, saddened to know that Erivar had vanished under the Seynyorean charge.

Pain does not hurt, Istvan reminded himself, his healing wound throbbing. *Only fear hurts.* Loudly, axes crashed in his ears; looking right he saw men riding at a wall where rose-dyed axes rose and fell, and riderless horses galloped back. Hansio's vanguard had found Ironfist's men.

His far-seeing eyes scanned the battle: in the centre, Turul DiVega's company had ridden down Bordermen in a loose array, only to reel back from a wedge of tight-packed Kadarins forming suddenly out of confusion.

Attilon DiVega charged to his kinsman's aid, but the Kadarins, displaying the horsemanship for which they were famous, whirled their mounts in place to deliver a stunning charge into Attilon's left, while their rallying Manjipéan allies swarmed into the tangle of Turul's reeling lines.

Raising his eyes, Istvan watched masses of brightly coloured leather armour deploy on the grassland to the north.

"How long before the Orissians arrive?" he asked D'Oleve, again.

D'Oleve closed his eyes. "I cannot tell," the Seer said after a moment. "They are riding through dust now, and there are no landmarks."

Istvan cursed, and watched blocks of Mahavarans gather on the plain. Then he dropped his gaze to the swords that swayed and sparked between the reeling hosts, and began to give orders.

He stopped, as conch-horns screamed like eagles. The enemy ranks shifted: some word was running through their ranks. Istvan's mind flew to mountaintop stillness, lifted above the screams and pealing of steel. He watched with gem-clear eyes.

Jagat's men were falling back. companies surged after them, but a sharp word through D'Oleve brought them back into line. The retreating host parted, and gay-hued horsemen out of Mahavara appeared. Jagat's cavalry joined them, Kadarin plate glittering in the centre.

As he watched, Istvan fed a steady stream of commands through the Seer, and his companies shifted obediently, drawing the line back, smoothing it and lengthening it, thinning the centre and leaving a small weakness there—a weakness he fervently hoped would be noticed by alert eyes.

Martos stared across the field at rows of glimmering mail, and frowned to see the line so thinly stretched. At the centre he could see a gap between two companies.

DiVega was too good a tactician for that. He remembered the blocks of horsemen he had seen during his brief time behind the enemy line, and nodded to himself. *A trap!* He glanced up at the black sky, and wondered why DiVega would put his back to the Shadow.

Jagat and Hansio came cantering by, studying the waiting ranks. Hansio's rich voice rolled out a stream of words. Martos urged Warflame out to meet them. Hansio's vibrant tones stopped as he turned cold yellow eyes on Martos.

"What is it, Martos?" asked Jagat.

"The centre—" Martos' voice dissolved in a stammer; he could only point dumbly.

"Yes, yes!" Hansio said irritably. "We have seen it, good man! We will break through there, smash them, and if you wish—"

"It's a trap," said Martos, controlling his tongue at last. "DiVega's reserve will be waiting there."

Yellow eagle eyes glared at him; and then the Prince that men had named the Fox long before Martos was born cantered off, calling for his aides.

Istvan watched the Mahavaran line. There was a sudden, faraway rise and fall of hooves; the wailing shriek of distant conch-horns grated in his ears. Eight thousand horsemen came sweeping across grass in a long line.

Six thousand Seynyoreans surged to meet them: arrows clouded the air. Istvan watched the proud horsemen of Mahavara charging, magnificent, fearless, racing over the bloody field of death to close with their famous foes. Two lines of horsemen crashed together: sparks of steel rose and fell.

Now his left wing angled their horses to the left, and Ciavedes' company curled around the end of the enemy line. The planned gap opened in Istvan's centre, and Bordermen swarmed in. Istvan smiled grimly. His reserve burst through the gaps and smashed into the Bordermen, hurling the lighter horsemen back by the momentum of their charge.

A trumpet called, and Kadarin armour moved between the charging reserve and the line, like a snake slithering through a hole. Inside his line it coiled, shifted, shaping suddenly into a wedge of steel pointing at the rear of Boros DiVega's company.

A trumpet rang, and Istvan saw his centre dissolve into a snarl of mail and plate as the Kadarin wedge ripped into his reserve from behind. His heart was rattling, but his mind was cold. The second line was broken—nothing left to do but fall back to the final line, and hope.

Where were the Orissians? How far and how long? His gaze rose above the battle, sweeping the horizon for some glint of metal. He opened his mouth to ask the Seer, but forebore: he had asked D'Oleve that same question, surely, a dozen times in the last hour. Instead he lashed out a string of commands, calling the right wing back, swinging on the pivot of the ruins where Ironfist's men were hard at work, emptying the saddles of horses that leaped the old stone walls.

But on the left, men were flying and scattering before the Kadarins. He ordered Maldeo's two thousand foot forward to plug the gap in the centre, and ordered the end of the left wing—Ciavedes, D'Ascoli, Servara—to fall back, to be a core around which the fleeing men could rally. But that was not enough. Nomenos DiGasclon's men had been breathing their horses since Istvan had ordered him back early in the battle: his men stood rallied and ready to charge.

Istvan spurred to DiGasclon's side, his sword a sudden flame.

Faces and shield-rims swam through the sweat in Martos' eyes. Warflame, twisting between his thighs, bore him joltingly through the cymbal-clash of battle, driving blurry figures, pounding them with death until the crushed crowd cringed back.

The wild eyes of horses rolled. Some, with their saddles empty and their master's blood caking their manes, ran wild, making further confusion as they hunted for a way out of the packed ranks.

"Retreat!" a voice shouted somewhere ahead. The fingers of Martos' sword hand milked the hilt as the blade flailed in soaring spirals. A horn blew sourly above the brazen drumbeat of swords—a Seynyorean trumpet, not Romulos'. The battering wingbeat of his sword went on.

Sweat-blurred eyes saw men whirl their horses, trying to get away. Swords fell on some; others went galloping off. He found Warflame galloping too, and they were rushing after the fleeing men. Sunlight flared on armour, but the sky was black ahead. To his left, he caught a glimpse of low stone walls, and red weapons sticking up behind them.

Istvan's wound throbbed as he tensed in the saddle, his sword-point a lance whose shaft was the locked bones of his arm.

Plate armour glared on the far side of a flood of mounted shapes, gorgeous and grotesque in shingled leather armour, purple, crimson, blue. Steel flared in the sunlight, waving above gay-hued leather. Istvan shouted a command. Spurs pricked hairy flanks; horses stretched long legs in a burst of speed. Colourful Bordermen raised leather shields, but chain-clad men were suddenly among them.

Istvan's rose-tipped blade whistled in the air. He stood in his stirrups, cutting to the left and thrusting to the right, disregarding the sharp twinge in his scratched thigh, opening his jaws and the trumpet of his throat to an old war-cry; and all around him, men in mail, their swords rainbows of red and silver, roared out in echo "Carcosa! Carcosa! Hastur and Carcosa!"

Even the Borderers quailed a moment then, and DiGasclon's men clove through them, swords swooping and stooping like hungry hawks. Hearing the shouting, Kadarins looked behind. Sudden startled shouts turned yet more heads. Some tried to rein their mounts around; some were caught at open shields as they wheeled, and toppled bleeding from their horses.

His saddle creaked as his steed surged like surf beneath him. His sword slammed on the closed door of a shield. The wailing of wounded men like eerie winds under the hooves filled his fingers with senseless rage. Birthran's face appeared in the back of his mind, and he wondered which of the iron-torsoed figures ahead was his old friend's pupil.

"Retreat!" someone was shouting. The heavy horses were turning away, their riders pivoting in the saddles, trying desperately to keep the steel disks of their shields between them and death.

Red-robes were running between the horses, hunting for the wounded. Istvan reined up and shouted to DiGasclon's men. The Borderers were falling back; the Kadarins, in full flight. But this was no time for pursuit. He must get these men rallied and back to the final line. The field around them swarmed with Bordermen. It wasn't over yet. If only DiSezrotti and the Orissians would arrive!

The grating screech of a conch-horn made Martos jump. Someone nearby shouted for a halt. He pulled Warflame up.

The black sky ahead filled his mind. Had he ever been this close to the Shadow before? He could see mile after mile of barren, sunless plain, stretching away to grey foothills, with the barest hint of the great mountains beyond. So close! DiVega must be in a desperate state indeed, pushed back against the Border like that.

He shook his head. That was wrong. DiVega had his reserves set here from the beginning. He had known all along that he would be driven back this far. This was some sort of trap, and the Borderers had walked right into it.

Frowning, he looked about him. His own men were clustering behind him, and all around them were Jagat's men, with a scattering of the rainbow-hued Mahavarans. A glitter of mail jerked his sword hand in reflex before he recognised Suktio, with Bimsio and Ymros. Beyond them, he saw Jagat and Hansio, side by side, conferring as they studied the field. He spurred Warflame toward them. He did not know what DiVega planned, but it was obvious that something they had not foreseen waited in his mind.

"There he is!" he heard Bimsio exclaim. "This time I'll get him!"

"Don't be a fool, Bimsio!" That was Ymros' voice. They continued to argue as Martos rode past, but he did not listen.

"Look you," Hansio was saying, "now we close, there"—he pointed—"crush their pride with a rush, then drive on their wing! See how we'll crumple them there, and then gall them, press in with the foot?" He looked up, saw Martos, and an unpleasant light filled the yellow eyes. He gestured; Jagat looked up.

Martos marshalled his tongue. "My Lord," he began, "DiVega has some plan, I am certain, something—"

"Is that how you address your Prince?" snapped Hansio, suddenly, harshly. "You called him 'Prince' before!"

"Lord Prince," said Martos, but the carefully sought words had vanished. "There is something—DiVega has something planned. I don't know what, but—he's backed up against the Border on purpose, not because we've forced him there. There must be—he's too good a leader to—to be taken this easily."

"Ha!" snorted Hansio. "I thought he'd put his back against the Shadow from fear, hoping the sight of it would keep us off! It's where he belongs. When I've slain him, I'll throw his body over the Border, leave him for our other enemies! It's what he deserves!"

Jagat stared at him, but before anyone could speak, there came a sudden loud shouting and the clamour of weapons. A quick glance over his shoulder showed Martos a tide of Bordermen, sweeping across the mass of Seynyoreans, working their way back to their lines.

The road back was blocked by Bordermen. Istvan could see the mail-clad lines of his men waiting, but the Borderers came rolling in between. Little Border ponies scuttled around them, and in a moment dripping swords leaped, and harsh tolling music sprang from shield and armour.

Steel death slashed toward Istvan's face. His shoulder clenched; the steel shell of his shield leapt up, and its gonging rang along the bones of his arm. His sword took flight, whining in the air, chopping down to crack through bone. His horse carried him past, too fast for him to know whether the bone his steel had touched would heal or lie as bloody clay with pale face and sprawled limbs.

Hooves and swords hammered like rain, pounding the field of blood. Ragged screaming knifed his ears with horror. The little ponies were everywhere; from their backs sharp steel came reaching as they darted and dodged, bewildering the eye.

A figure in shingled dark leather armour dashed in among the tall horses, spinning slick red steel over shield-rims in a deadly dance. Straight toward Istvan's horse the pony rushed. Istvan tried to rein his horse away, but the other was too quick.

Istvan heaved up his shield as blood-drenched steel lashed at him. He launched the weight of his own sword, even as the clamour of his shield ran up his arm. A bone-and-leather buckler brushed his blade aside. Was there something familiar about the man behind it? Istvan frowned.

A Borderman, bigger than most. A far better swordsman than was common, too. Where had he seen that face? He remembered the clattering rhythm of rain, the search for the road, the horsemen who'd fought him. He remembered a white-faced boy, and courtesy. But this was not that boy. *Who—?*

Steel shrieked in the air: the shield on his arm shuddered with the blow, and its bell-note rang in his bones. His bones. He was only a skeleton covered with flesh, and all around him, skeletons hidden in flesh were scything at each other with sharp steel swords.

His sword whipped out at the end of his arm. He saw past the shield-rim a flash of bare flesh where a shingle of leather had been stripped away, and the Hastur-blade hissed for that naked skin. The shield covered it, and he felt his blade lifted. As his point cleared the shield-edge, he jerked back his arm, leaning to stab, bones locking in his elbow. The shield brushed his point aside.

Pain hammered Istvan's arm. He felt his hilt slip from loosening fingers, and clenched his hand frantically, even though he was sure that the blow had severed bone and flesh and his hand was flying away, flopping empty on the earth. His fingers responded, gripping hot, slippery ivory, clutching at the weight of steel. Blood rushed in the aching arm.

The enemy sword was coming at him again, a flat red-and-silver streak. He heaved up the bell of his shield. It tolled. He glanced down to the right. The hand was still there. Mail-rings dangled loosely from his wrist. Several rings had been torn away, and where they had been was a red smear.

The red sword came around again; and as Istvan's shield rose, he shifted his grip on the sword and drew it back to cut. Death hissed in the air, clamoured on his shield. With the shock, his aching arm lashed out. He felt the edge catch, sinking into leather, and pulled it back in panic. Ruddied steel flicked across his vision, slapped his shoulder with a jingle of mail, and slid away.

The tall horse moved under him. His heart drummed air from his lungs. Death had been close. As the shield-rim dropped from his eyes, he saw the enemy curl back behind his shield, all motion, like a flame or a bird. His sword hand sailed on its steel wing, streaking the air with red. Blood flew from his arm as well as his blade.

The slope of the other shield warned him that the angle of his cut was expected even before he felt the leather rim lift his blade and send it skimming harmlessly on. The red line of the enemy's edge rose in the obvious countercut, and Istvan locked shoulder and elbow, flipping his point into the path of the flailing arm.

The arm jerked back. Swords scraped musically all along their length. The bloody point shot for his eyes. He saw it fork into two blades as he rolled frantically back in his saddle. Steel skittered and squeaked across the face of his shield: the bloody spike poked above his shield-rim, then darted away and vanished.

His sword soared on the wind again. As his eyes rose above his rim, he saw the dipped top of the climbing leather buckler and his blade swooping steeply past. Mail clashed under his arm.

A dig in his side, even as he felt his edge slice leather. Something rammed his ribs, and air gushed from his lungs. He felt his edge turn on bone; his side on fire. Looking down, he saw red steel below his shield-rim, and the point pull free from ruby-beaded silver rings.

His enemy's face was veiled in red, his helm shorn half away; but the arm was still moving, pitching up and around. Long red steel plummeted at his helm. Istvan tried to heave up his shield, but it was suddenly heavy, the side below throbbing with pain. He wrestled it up, and light flared behind his eyes as a bell banged the back of his head.

He was falling. He had just presence of mind enough to jerk his feet out of the stirrups as the ground leaped toward his face, and he caught it on his shield.

"Martos!" Jagat's voice could barely be heard above the din. Martos pulled Warflame around and rode back. Jagat sat hunched and dejected in the saddle. "You heard what that—that madman said? Throw DiVega's body—*across the Border?* What sane man could think such a horror? What have I allied myself to?''

Martos found no answer. He stared across the ringing field. Death danced in a maddened reel of men and horses. He saw silver fangs, blood-tipped, above a mass of racing horsemen, dew-shimmering mail all mixed with glossy leather.

Hansio had ridden to gather his cavalry: his footmen, in dyed leather armour, trudged toward the foe; Jagat's foot marched with them. Swords waved like grass in a high wind.

Wounded men wailed. Martos' chest ached. Blue bodies lay strewn about, rose-stained. Swords stabbed and cut. Men died screaming. Horses slipped in slick red puddles. Yet all this blood and death was not so bad as the vision of triumphant ghouls playing with the bones of Istvan the Archer.

''He—Prince Hansio—may not have meant—have really meant . . .''
But even as he spoke, Martos knew that Hansio had meant every word. ''His grief . . .'' But that was surely the wrong thing to say! He looked up quickly, guiltily, and surprised a sad smile on Jagat's face.

''His grief for his son has unseated his mind.'' said Jagat gently. ''Mine, too, no doubt about it, or we wouldn't be here! Look beyond the Seynyorean line, Martos. What do you see?''

He looked. Mail shimmered in sunlight against a black sky. Martos shivered. Through dingy, curdled air, he saw miles of dust, and the dim shapes of hills. He licked his lips, trying to imagine fighting there instead of in the sunlight. Dying there, where the Dark Things lived.

''But what are we to do, Martos?'' Jagat's voice brought him back to the sunlit world. ''It is too late to withdraw from the battle. And even if it were possible, we would deserve whatever punishment Hansio chose in reward for such contemptible sneaking treachery! And he would see that we suffered.'' He frowned, and shook his head. ''No man ever trusted the Fox without regretting it. That was why he could never overthrow the old King. All men trusted Olansos, but who would be such a fool as to trust the Fox?'' Jagat glanced away, across the field, to where Hansio was rallying his scattered horsemen, preparing another charge.

''And he was sane then,'' Jagat said. ''Now, who knows what—''

A voice shouted his name. Suktio and Ymros dashed up, urging their little ponies between the slippery puddles of blood.

''Lord Jagat!'' Ymros shouted again, and then, less loud, ''Istvan the Archer is dead!''

Martos' heart lurched.

''Dead!'' exclaimed Jagat, while Martos' tongue stumbled in his mouth. ''Are you sure?''

''I saw him fall,'' said Suktio. ''Bimsio killed him.''

"Bimsio?" Martos exclaimed.

"Where is Bimsio?" asked Jagat.

"Dead, most likely," said Suktio, "or nearly so. The Healers have him. The top of his head is—you can see the bone. But he stabbed DiVega under his shield, and even with DiVega's sword in his skull he got in one last cut—a strong one, I tell you! He took Istvan the Archer out of his saddle, as limp as wet hay!"

"When heros meet, no victory," Martos quoted softly, as though to himself.

Chapter Sixteen

Istvan's heartbeat throbbed through aching bones and drummed in his skull. *What?* he thought. *Still alive?*

Men shouted. Steel boomed. Mud caked in his beard. He felt hands tugging at his armour, lifting the skirt of his mail away from his body. *Robbing the dead already!*

His shield arm lay folded under him, but his right hand was empty. His fingers went groping in bloody mud, then found and fastened on his sword-hilt.

He rolled, his shield thrusting the earth away, mud flying from the sword's shrill edge. Red cloth flashed into sight: tightening fingers froze the sword in midair.

Wide-eyed, the Healer looked at the sharp steel so close to his paling face, drew a deep breath and blew it slowly out. "If you'll roll back and lift up a little, I can look at that hole in your side, Commander DiVega." There was the faintest hint of a tremor in his voice.

Istvan fell back on his elbows and pushed himself up to let the Healer worry the mail up around his shoulders. The thin snarl of tearing cloth was almost lost in the shouting and crashing of battle. Hooves hammered past.

Istvan's side flushed with gushing blood. Gentle fingers prodded; then the Healer's warm palm pressed down against his skin, and he felt the Healer's mind search his flesh. The ground under his elbows pulsed with hoofbeats. Death's scythe stroked chiming against a thousand swords and shields.

"Well?" he said, wanting to know the worst at once. "How bad is it?" Something cold poured over his ribs and turned to fire in the wound.

"That knock on the head may make you dizzy for a while, and you've lost more blood than is good for a man your age, but—" The Healer laughed at Istvan's start of surprise. "This?" The Healer's fingers prodded the wound. "A pinprick, a chip in the bone—it hit the rib! You must have leaned into it, for it to have pierced your mail! You just lie still while I pack some salve into it."

Lie still. Istvan shut his eyes. Hooves went pounding past. He could hear the boom of shields. He opened his eyes and lifted his head. Steel flickered like lightning. *Lie still.* He wanted to lie still.

He slid his heavy shield over the mud, and pushed himself up. He could hear men shouting and screaming and dying. He smelled mud and blood and sweet crushed grass.

"Lie still!" the Healer said again. "You've lost blood, Commander! Just lie down and—"

Istvan heaved himself up and scrambled to his feet. Pain fountained from the back of his head. The world tipped and danced behind a veil of golden light. His stomach twisted and his heartbeat pounded earth through his boot soles.

"What did I tell you!" said the Healer. "You're in no shape to play the hero at your age."

"I know, I know," said Istvan irritably. The weight of mail cut into his shoulders. His belt was lying on the ground at his feet, and the mail hung about him in a hollow tube. The Healer had undone it, of course.

He wanted to lie down. His bones cried for rest.

He slipped the point of his blade under the belt and flipped it up, while earth and sky whirled dizzyingly around. He stared as the scabbard slipped from the belt and dropped into mud.

"My men need me," he heard his own voice plead. "And there are others who need you more. More than I do! Death makes all men lazy, soon enough. Help me with my belt."

With a sigh, the Healer lifted belt and scabbard from the ground. Istvan sheathed his sword, then lifted his arms while the Healer buckled his belt around him. It caught the weight of the mail, but he still stooped; steel glare hurt his eyes.

He felt the Healer's hands on his, felt strength flowing into him. Hands and feet tingled: the world came clear, as though emerging from fog. He blinked across the steel-bright fields. Riderless horses ran past. His shield dragged at the socket of his shoulder. He opened his mouth to thank the Healer, but saw the Red-robe already dashing away. Wounded men were everywhere, and the Healers busy among them, running between them.

Horses milled in the distance with riders on their backs and a storm of tossing swords above. Nearer, riderless horses dashed by, none yet close enough to catch.

He lurched toward the hammering of steel.

Conch-horns brayed. Martos saw Hansio gesture, with need-fire blazing in his hand. Men said that Hansio's great-grandfather had won that blade: Hastur's reward for great deeds along the Border.

"Best not to tell Hansio that DiVega is dead," said Lord Jagat. "I fear he'll feel—cheated," he went on slowly, then shrugged. "I could be wrong. I hope so! But I can't tell now what he might . . ." He shook his white head, frowning at the ground.

Shields rang wildly as sharp swords battered out the fenzied beat of battle. Hansio's foot had moved up to engage the Seynyoreans while he readied the cavalry for a charge.

Jagat looked up. "We'd best get back to our men, Martos."

They rode together over blood-slick grass, with Ymros and Suktio behind them. Jagat's men cheered as they came. Hansio's eagle mask frowned in their direction. Martos left Jagat surrounded by his men and rode to where the company waited, two lines of steel-torsoed figures.

Paidros cantered to meet him. "I was wondering when you'd get back!" he grumbled. "Listen! That man"—his hand stirred toward Hansio—"has a voice like a war-horn, but have you listened to what he is saying?"

Martos listened.

". . . though we leave the sunlight behind!" Hansio's rich voice rolled over the army. "False friends, false help! They come to steal our land and till our women!"

"He's been going on and on like that," Paidros muttered, "over and over! He spews hatred!"

"We do not fear the Shadow! We have fought in that dark before! Though the sky be hid, we shall not quail! We will push them over the Border, where they belong, and there we will leave their bones! We shall kill all who try to take our land, as we have done for a thousand years!"

"You'd think he was going to lead us against night-things," said Paidros, low-voiced, "not men who come from the foot of Hastur's own mountain!"

"Men of the Border!" Hansio's voice swelled like music, and even as Martos fought its spell, it set his heart to pounding and trickled chill down his spine. "Heirs of heros! Crush the foe now! Smash them down! There they stand with their backs to the Border! See the Shadow above their shoulders! Follow my sword's flame to victory!" He wheeled his horse. The Hastur-blade flamed above his head, then dropped to point at the Seynyorean line. *"Charge!"*

Conch-horns screamed. Cheering voices drowned them. Heels spurred furred flanks. Hooves drummed thunder in the ground, and Martos found himself part of a surging line of horsemen that bore down on the Seynyorean force like an ocean wave rolling toward the ramparts of a castle of sand.

Istvan caught himself a riderless pony and rode the rough beast hard. Nightmare screams of wounded men tore at his nerves, while Red-robes rushed to drag all the living men they could find out of the way before trampling hooves came to crush them.

Behind, enemy horsemen massed like a thunder cloud. Ahead,

chiming flames of steel danced above his lines as a block of footmen pressed stolidly on against the rushes of his cavalry. If the Orissians did not come soon, there would be none left to aid.

He spurred the pony and leaned down to its mane while speed-wind lashed his face. Conch-horns shrieked behind him, and a roar of voices was followed by a rumble of hooves.

He thought of Pertap's ride, and urged the small steed on. Tiny figures shifted as the footmen fell back, and he saw his own men, clad in the sheen of their mail, brace themselves to meet the charging host that followed him, shaking the trampled earth. Naked shapes loomed before him: mountain-shouldered men slinging their great bows as they walked.

N'lantians! Istvan reined his pony sharply to the left, trying to pass behind them and around them, but one looked up and shouted. Long curved blades glittered bloodless from their scabbards. One sprang from the right, heaving up the clean, shiny steel with both hands, swirling in a watery blur at Istvan's waist.

Istvan found time to admire the precision of the stroke as he twisted in the saddle and dropped his shield into its path. His keen edge brushed across the bare throat. A second blade faltered in the air as Istvan's point sank into the flesh of a naked arm. It fell, glancing harmlessly from Seynyorean mail.

Then he was past them, and chill crawled between his shoulder blades, waiting for the shock of a shaft from one of those terrible bows, while his heels pounded the pony on. Straggling footmen scattered from his path; the waterfall of hooves drummed louder behind him, and over his shoulder he glimpsed a steel-crested breaker drowning his tracks. Someone shouted his name, and cheering deafened him as he dashed at last into his own lines, safe among his men.

"Every second man!" he shouted, hurling himself down from his pony, "dismount! Mounted men! Bows out! Seer! Where's the Seer?"

He staggered a little, his feet slipping in the mud, still unsteady. All around, men scrambled from their horses. He looked out across the narrowing space between the two armies, and saw the trampling hooves drawing nearer and nearer.

Martos rode on the crest of a wave of horses. His sword and his spirit soared above a roaring of hooves.

Seynyorean horsemen came riding to meet him. Arrows sighed in the air. He fumbled his sword back to its sheath, whipped his bow from its case. He slipped his hand from the enarmes of his shield, letting it flop loosely on the shoulder strap, banging against his thigh, while he hurled shaft after shaft at the approaching foe.

All up and down the line, arrows were flying. To left and right, horses crashed to the ground with a clamour of armour. Rage and horror filled him. The string twanged in his hand. Bordermen, too, were shooting, but their broad-headed arrows only caught in the tiny mail-rings and stuck there, while the Seynyorean spike-tipped arrows smashed through leather.

So few, he thought. This would be the end. This would roll the Seynyoreans under.

The two lines were closing. He sheathed his bow and reached for his sword, preparing for the shock. But the Seynyoreans wheeled their horses and ran, turning in the saddle to shoot behind. Wild whooping rose among the Bordermen, but Martos knew better: this was a classic manoeuvre. DiVega must have more horse in reserve.

Suddenly, shouting footmen appeared between the horses. They rushed forward, closing ranks and locking shields. Swords dipped out from the shield-wall in a row of menacing steel spines aimed at the horses' eyes. Horses checked and shied, rearing, bucking, dancing.

The light of his sword hidden by dried brown grime, Istvan spread his legs wide to grip the earth, bracing his shoulders against the shoulders of other men, and raised his shield against a stampede of moving mountains. He fought the urge to run, terribly aware of churning hooves charging to pound him into dust.

He held his point aimed steadily at the nose of the running horse in front of him. The horse checked; shied, and reared, its nose dripping blood. Through his shoulders, Istvan felt the whole line stagger. Suddenly other horses were rearing behind these, and the Border pony was looming over his shield, pushed from behind.

Horses crashed into the line of shields: Martos saw the enemy line stagger back. But the momentum of the charge was broken. Warflame pranced under him. Arrows leaped over the enemy line and fell all around.

From either side came terrible crashing and screaming as the second wave of riders ploughed into the first. The shield-wall reeled again as horses were hurled into it. A quick glance over his shoulder showed him his own second line, like living statues.

His heels urged Warflame forward. He was dimly aware of Paidros yelling commands, but most of his attention was focussed on the smoothly sailing sword that swooped and whistled over enemy shields, hunting for the flesh behind.

Istvan closed his eyes as weight smashed his shield into his chest and hurled him staggering back. The friendly shoulders fell away, and he fought for balance as his eyes snapped open. Horses bucked and reared. A bloody ribbon of steel flailed at him awkwardly: he fended it off.

He scrambled out of the path of a running horse. Behind him, hooves pounded as the mounted reserve hurled themselves on the men who had broken the line. His shield-wall had broken, but it had held long enough to dull the force of the charge. Horses were balking and bucking, the swords flailing from their backs held by men with divided minds.

Istvan ran forward, pressing in on the right of a man on a frenzied horse with a bleeding face. The Borderman's sword lashed, booming on his shield. The small figures dodging between the horses were not all his own men: Hansio's foot came running in, swords waving; the bony fingers of death, groping for him.

The diamond-hard edge of the Hastur-blade sheared through leather. Bright cherry colour poured to cover dried brown blood. The Borderman pitched from his horse. Istvan's shield rang as a running man cut at him.

The riderless horse raced away. Bordermen on foot ringed him in. His sword and shield moved in a battering rhythm. He looked behind him for the line he had been part of moments before, but saw only scattered knots of men struggling under tossing slivers of red-dyed steel. He dropped back, cannily, his shield leaping and crashing, while his subtle blade whirred about him.

Martos reined Warflame around, away from the crashing shields, and blinked sweat out of his eyes. Blurred shapes rushed toward him in the glaring sunlight. Behind him, some of the Seynyoreans had rushed out: he heard officers shouting for them to get back in line.

Bright armour flaming on either side bounded to meet him. He closed his tired eyes and let the horse's training carry them through the familiar manoeuvre.

He rode through the storm of hoofbeats that was the second line charging, his knees flinching, half expecting a collision; but he heard the crescendo pass on either side and knew he was safely through. Eyes opened then on masses of Bordermen, and his own line stretching to either side, matching his pace under a bright blue sky.

"Turn!" he shouted, and was childishly pleased that his tongue had moved without trouble.

Warflame clenched under him. Earth and sky whirled. He heard the terrible clash as his second line slammed into the Seynyoreans. The Shadow was like a black wing slapped across his eyes, and he was looking into darkness. Swords rose and fell. Shields pealed wildly. Men screamed. The Seynyorean line buckled under the impact of horses, but it held.

Martos drew his sleeve across his face. The glassy sheen of moving steel glared in his eyes. In the narrow sunlit strip in front of the Border, with the black sky and the nighted hills behind them, his men pushed the Seynyoreans back.

Off to each side the Bordermen were embroiled. Here and there, he saw they had broken through the Seynyorean shield-wall and fought with the mounted men behind it. Martos raised his sword and waved it. His men tensed on their horses. He waved to Romulos, and the trumpet ordered the charge.

The Seynyorean line crumpled before them: footmen reeled back, staggering, lost between the horses. Martos crashed through havoc, his sword sweeping the air around him. Beating steel grated on his ears. Hooves scrambled as they slipped in jellied blood. Swords skimmed through the air, and shields belled under them. Mounted Seynyoreans surged to fill the gap. Martos felt his sword-edge chisel through the fine wire of mail-rings. Red splashed up his blade. His soul pulsed with hoofbeats as he rode a triumphant wave of horses, surging over the foe.

Istvan's blade sliced leather; dying eyes stared at him in dumb reproach. Istvan ripped the sword free, hurling up his shield. Metal crashed and quivered on his arm.

His sword glided in air, and again he felt leather snag the edge. A Borderman gasped and swung again: too wildly, his buckler swaying to the side. It was child's play for Istvan to catch the cut on his shield while his sword whirled past the swaying buckler in a full circle cut that sawed through leather and metal and flesh, deep into bone. The enemy blade clattered on his shield as it dropped from nerveless fingers.

Istvan looked wildly around him. There should have been a line here, but all was confusion: men and horses crowding in a frenzied dance of battle. It was the beginning of the end, he knew. He could sense the crushing movement that would hurl them, scattered, over the Border.

Martos could feel the weight of his sword flying with his hand. The shock through steel jarred shoulder and wrist as the sharp edge scraped on bone.

"You got him!" Valiros yelled, over the tolling of metal and the slamming of shields.

But what was he doing here, Martos wondered, why was he killing men from his own part of the world, men like himself? Men against whom he had no grudge?

Sharp-edged steel squealed through the air, and he ducked back behind his shield, seeing the black sky above its rim.

What was he doing, fighting with men who had come from the foot of Hastur's Mountain, killing them and leaving their bodies at the foot of the Shadow?

Istvan rallied his sinking heart and rushed through deadly swords to where one group of his men still stood together in the press, fighting back to back. He shouted for them to gather.

A dying man in Seynyorean armour clutched at him, blood gurgling from his throat, and fell. Sword and shield rose and fell in maddening rhythm, and the slamming of swords on shield-rims was deafening. He kept shouting, swaying back and forth with lashing steel like grass in a high wind.

Men rallied to his voice. *To Istvan the Archer,* he thought bitterly. That was what gathered them, the banner of his hated fame.

Martos stood in his stirrups and looked out over the battle. There were still a few places where the Seynyoreans held their ground, but only a few. Everywhere, he saw Bordermen pressing their foes back, crushing them in upon one another, and the black sky loomed ever closer as the swirling mob staggered back.

How much easier it would be to fight against outlaws or dishonourable men he did not admire! Or against night-things!

He glimpsed Jagat nearby on a rearing Border pony, his blade blurred with whirling until it looked as though the sword-wheel was real, spinning in his hand. Hansio's Hastur-blade was flaming somewhere off to the right.

A trumpet sang: Martos puzzled at its sound. It was not Romulos', nor Seynyorean. It was not the Border conch-horns. Yet it came from behind.

Istvan's re-formed line reeled. The men they faced were suddenly crushed up against them. Istvan's elbow smarted as it rammed a lifted shield. Weight pressed his shield tight to his chest, and hurled him staggering back. He felt the whole line reel back with him, and knew it was the end.

Part of the sky was dark. They were almost at the Border. Men's hearts would fail in the Shadow; the little discipline left would break, and the Bordermen would hunt them like frightened beasts.

Shouting, louder and louder, came from the other side of the mass of crowding bodies. The enemy seemed as helpless as his own men. Wild hope leaped in his heart.

Suddenly the weight on his shield was gone, and he staggered a step forward to keep from falling on his face. He blinked across a sudden open space and saw enemy backs, turning away. And beyond them, between them, above their shoulders, gleamed bright armour and unblooded sun-silvered swords.

The Orissians had come.

"Mount!" Istvan shouted. "Mount and ride!"

Martos found himself caught in the crush of a tide, both knees squeezed in a vise of horse's bodies. Warflame was staggering, held up only by horses on either side.

He looked back, and saw fighting where there should be none. Bloodless swords, sparkling clean, waved golden with sunlight, then plunged down, rising again with a wet sunset stain. An enemy force must have hit them from the rear, coming in unnoticed in the clamour of the battle.

Seynyorean bugles rang out, mellow and sweet, and the crush eased. Martos realised that the tide had swept him far from his original position. Nearby Carrodian axes rose and fell above the ruined walls.

A Carrodian stabbed a Borderman through the throat with the sharp splintered haft of a broken axe. Ironfist Arac leaped suddenly up on the wall, his terrible axe flying around him. Seynyoreans, Carrodians, and Bordermen surged over the wall, cutting down the shaken men before them.

Seynyoreans were rallying, regrouping, while Jagat's men and Hansio's turned to face the menace on their flank. He saw the dismounted Seynyoreans running for their horses, heaving themselves up into saddles. Then he saw Jagat, bursting through the press, pushing between ponies while he shouted Martos' name. Martos spurred to meet him, Valiros at his heels. He saw Jagat stop to yell at Suktio. Suktio seemed to argue, but then Martos saw him nod, and raise his conch-shell to his lips.

"Martos!" Jagat shouted as he saw him riding up. "Where's that trumpeter of yours! We've got to gather the men and retreat!"

Martos, struck dumb, looked around for Romulos, his tongue numb. Valiros shouted the trumpeter's name, and in a moment Paidros and Romulos rode out of the swirling confusion, their armour battered and smeared with blood.

"We must rally and retreat in good order," Jagat was saying, "or this will be a massacre! We must cover Hansio's retreat—"

His voice was drowned in the crooning of the Conch-horn of Chandra. The brazen crowing of Romulos' trumpet wove above it.

Once upon horseback, Istvan could see the shining wedge of armour that flowed like a sluggish steel river through the enemy rank, swords waying like silver reeds. Men were shouting, forming into line. There were plenty of horses.

Despair had fallen from him: his heart soared. It would be over soon. And he was still alive.

"What's going on here?" Hansio's voice roared. Martos looked up, startled, and saw the Prince of Mahapor rushing toward them, his sword flaming in his hand. "Why are you falling back? Who gave the order to fall back?"

"I did!" Jagat rode up to him. From behind the eagle's mask, the Fox turned to glare at him.

"How dare you!" Hansio hissed. Jagat's men felt for their swords.

"The order of your lines is broken," said Jagat. "The right wing will be crushed, unless we fall back in order—"

"*No one* retreats in *my* army," Hansio hissed.

"You must!" snapped Jagat.

"Never!" Hansio's voice was almost a scream. "Not until I have found Istvan the Archer and made him pay for the death of my son!"

"Istvan DiVega is dead!" shouted Jagat. "One of my men killed him, and died in—"

"No!" Hansio shrieked. Strange eyes looked at them; the eagle mask crumbled. "He cannot be dead! You're lying! Fate cannot cheat me so! You lie!"

The Hastur-blade flamed high, and Martos felt his heart lurch. He launched his horse to Jagat's side, expecting Hansio to cut him down. Instead, Hansio whirled his horse away and plunged toward the Seynyorean lines. His voice was a piercing, raging scream.

"DiVega!" they heard him cry; shrill squealing ruined the golden voice. "Come out, DiVega! Stop hiding behind lesser men, letting them die for your grievous sin! Come out, DiVega! Where are you hiding? If you're a man, come out and fight!"

Istvan raised his sword for the charge, then paused as he heard a shrill voice shout his name.

"Look!" said one of the men nearby. "It's the Old Fox himself!"

Istvan saw another Hastur-blade flaming high above the space between the armies. He heard his name again.

"DiVega!" The voice was high and thin, edged with a squeal. "Come and fight, DiVega!"

The words filtered slowly into Istvan's mind. His sword snapped down before they penetrated. Trumpets sang, and a thunderclap of hooves drowned the piping voice as a dozen companies launched themselves into battle, lunging to the Orissians' aid.

But Istvan reared up his horse and wheeled toward the flaming blade and furious voice.

"DiVega!" He could still hear it, faintly, through the pounding of battle, a reedy ghost of a voice. "DiVega! If you're alive, come and fight! Don't hide behind other men! Come and fight!"

He saw the sword's fire flare above the swaying ranks of battle. He filled his lungs to shout but found himself suddenly short of breath. He remembered all the blood he had lost, the wounds he had taken that day. As he remembered them, they began to hurt. He felt old and tired, and his bones ached. *Only fear hurts,* he thought, and wiped blood from his sword onto his saddle-cloth and his horse's flanks. He stood in the stirrups, the pain of the arrow wound ripping through his leg, to raise his own bright blade high. Again he filled his lungs.

"Hansio!" he shouted. "Prince Hansio! DiVega is here!"

He spurred toward the other glowing blade.

Martos sat, sheathed in steel. His sweat-soaked clothing made him itch under the armour, where he could not scratch. Warflame, head tossing, stamped and shivered under him.

Nearby, stacked corpses stirred like drifted leaves. Wounded men groaned under the weight of the dead. Red-robed Healers scrambled among them, while Jagat's men tumbled stiff bodies about, pulling free the dead and wounded they would never leave behind. Far to the right, furious steel sparks hammered on shields.

Martos' heart hammered like the swords. Something was happening. There was movement and shouting among the Seynyoreans, but they did not charge. They were all staring over their shields.

Jagat, too, was staring. "Ymros!" he called. "Suktio!" Ymros and Suktio came rushing down from where they had been ordering the column of men. "I thought you said DiVega was dead?"

Jagat pointed: two blades flamed above the madness of rushing horses.

Istvan saw horsemen scatter out of Hansio's path. The Hastur-blade poured light on the dark, twisted face, the opened mouth in the white beard, the writhing eyes.

"DiVega!" The scream deepened to a sudden roar.

The Fox? Istvan thought. *He looks more like an eagle!*

Istvan's sword shot skyward. He pressed his shield tight to his shoulder. His horse's barrel drummed under his heels. Ground jolted up through galloping hooves. Above his shield-rim, he saw Hansio's glowing blade, streaming like a comet. A surf of hoofbeats ached in his ears. He hurled up his shield, feeling a twinge in his side, as his eyes found a path for his sword.

His shield boomed. He felt his blade brushed aside as he twisted in the saddle. He saw steel loop and fall, and his shield shuddered again on his arm. Then Hansio was past.

Istvan's horse reared as he reined around. His sword wrist ached, bruised to the bone. His ears felt an emptiness. The clamour of steel had almost stilled. Around them fighting ceased: men of both sides fell back to watch.

The horses were rushing together again, flaming swords flying above horse and man. Part of his mind was trying to find some way to tell this frenzied man he had not slain his son. Then the comet blade was hissing between his own eyes and the crazed yellow ones glaring over the rich red-brown leather shield-rim.

Istvan's sore wrist was twirling his own blade out, above the other. He pulled his shield up to cover his eyes, and felt it quake; a sharp shock shook through his bones. His shoulder strained as his own edge twisted and skipped. Hoofbeats pounded past, and his shield fell away from his eyes. Light lanced at his back.

"Die!" Hansio screamed.

He swayed under Hansio's thrust, rolling his shield up, jerking the rein. Hansio's sword arm darted above him. He saw the exposed wrist, but was in the wrong position to cut. Hansio's horse was slowing and turning. His own mount pranced around. He saw Hansio's eyes above the shield. The eyes were different. The crazed look faded. Cunning crept into them.

The Fox looked at him.

Martos galloped after Jagat. Horsemen got out of their way. Elsewhere, sky-coloured swords still chimed and clashed, but they rode into an eye of calm where both sides had drawn apart to watch.

A corridor opened between the hostile armies, and there they were: two old men on dancing horses, their swords fiery splinters lashing. Martos' eyes saw mastery in the poise of shields.

Jagat pulled up his horse, and Martos reined in beside him. All around them, men were shouting; but their swords were still.

DiVega glittered in his garment of rings. Russet-clad Hansio rushed, winged sword wheeling. Supple silver mesh rippled with stars as DiVega's shield rose and his sword pivoted, turning to a wheel of fire. Both swords struck as one: the slamming of shields crashed across the field.

Istvan stared at Hansio's eyes. It was like fighting a different man. He had always wondered about Hansio: the hero of Border song had seemed so different from the cunning politician he had known. Now he had seen the change from one to the other.

It was the Fox that circled now, and more than the eyes had changed. Istvan's trained eyes found differences in the very muscles: in the tension of fingers gripping the hilt, in the set of the wrist, in the angle of the blade. Saw signs, too, of a terrible skill. Hansio had struck two blows for each of his. Was it the frenzy that had given him added speed, or was it natural?

It was a cold-blooded, cunning killer whose horse danced about him now. Istvan watched, warily. The horse bounded suddenly into reach, Hansio's sharp sword lashing high, its edge lightning, wounds and death.

Istvan's sword arm lashed out again as his shield jerked up: he felt the gash in his ribs again. Swords crashed on shields. He turned his horse as Hansio dashed past. His shield came down. The Twin Suns flared in his eyes.

Martos saw DiVega flinch back; saw the sunlight in his face. Seeing Hansio's sword sweep around, he shouted, idiotically: his voice was drowned in the roar of a thousand men. And he knew that shout would make DiVega deaf as well as blind.

He saw Istvan roll back in his saddle, guarding his head with his sword, while Hansio's blade sprang back from the shield DiVega had clasped against his hip. The Seynyorean horse sprang away.

A thousand men cheered.

Istvan felt his shield rock as his spurs raked his horse's side. Then he was out of reach, and turning his horse to avoid the glare. Spots still burned his eyes.

Hansio had timed it neatly, a trick within a trick, forcing Istvan's eyes into the sunlight in the one crucial second needed to see the aim of his next cut. Another man would no doubt have shaded his eyes with the shield again, or frozen. But Istvan had known there were only two possible cuts—and a thrust, he had worried about the thrust—and the cut under the shield the most likely one.

"Well, DiVega!" Hansio's voice taunted from behind him. "Not like killing half-skilled boys, is it?"

Blood-guilt flooded him: the exhilaration of combat washed away. He'd not killed Hansio's son, no, but many other men's sons had died at his hand. For a second it seemed that the fathers of all the men he had ever killed were thronging through his mind, shouting for vengeance.

Hooves behind him, on his shieldless right. He heard men gasp and shout in warning, and he twisted in his saddle, jerking up his blade. The other Hastur-blade blazed in his eyes. His ears ached with the clangour of steel. The hilt was almost jarred from his hand.

He clapped heels to horse, and the next cut came on empty air. But the other horse was gaining quickly. He reined around, trying to turn, trying to get his shield side toward the enemy.

"Run, DiVega!" Hansio cackled. "Run!" He was following in a

tight circle. His horse was too fast: Istvan could not gain enough to turn.

The sword came in again, and Istvan parried with a squeal of scraping steel, thrusting the point toward the face. Hansio's shield knocked it aside, and Istvan saw dark iron, streaked with silver scratches where the leather had been torn away by his earlier cut. Other Bordermen might carry shields of leather and bone, but Hansio of Mahapor was no fool.

He could not outrun him for long. Hansio was grinning. His teeth did glitter white. *The only part of the skull that shows,* Istvan thought.

DiVega's steel darted in a blurred web of flame. But Martos' trained eye saw his arm tiring. Fine though DiVega's defence might be, it must eventually fall before that battering. And DiVega could not cut back. Hansio, safe behind his shield, would cut DiVega down the moment his sword left a defensive position.

Seynyoreans groaned; hoots from the Borderers mocked Istvan's pounding heels. Jagat was still as death.

Martos saw Istvan's horse plough to a halt, as the two blades clashed in the air. He saw Istvan jerk his horse's head around, at the same moment sending his sword hissing in the opposite direction, straight at Hansio's eyes.

Hansio's cut slashed empty air as he rode past, his eyes blinded by his rising shield. His horse checked and turned, but now DiVega faced him, shield to shield.

Still Martos bit his lip. DiVega's arm was tired, he could see, but Hansio was still unwearied, with no sign of harm. With shields the two seemed well-matched. Martos knew there was no telling how the fight would end.

Is DiVega my foe? Is Hansio my friend?

Istvan drooped. The soaring exultation that had hidden the pain of his wounds was gone. He felt his breath gasping in and out of his lungs, felt the sting of the wounds he had taken during the battle. But his joints—shoulder, knee, wrist—ached worse. Old age was closing in. Hansio was old too. But he was unwounded.

Have to do something about that, Istvan thought, and clapped heels to horse.

Hansio rushed to meet him, cunning eyes wary above the torn leather shield. "Die, DiVega!" he shouted. "But do not think you will share this land with my son! Over the Border with you! You I leave for the ghouls!"

Suddenly his horse turned sharply left, across Istvan's path. Istvan's horse checked and reared. He twisted in the saddle, hunting for the other.

Again sudden sunlight seared his eyes. He heard the hiss of Hansio's sword. "Die!" Hansio screamed.

Martos stared. Hansio's horse had suddenly danced aside, and the two men passed each other on their unshielded right sides.

"The old trick!" Jagat said. "He's killed dozens of men with that one, they say!"

Istvan cut at the hiss as he blinked his eyes free from sun-glare. Steel bounced in that second of blindness, his hilt tilting in his hand while edges shrilled. His horse surged under him.

Then his slitted, spark-filled eyes found the shade of Hansio's armour. At the edge of sight, a moving shaft of light screeched through the air, scything at his neck.

Istvan let his wrist flop, his fingers loosen, his elbow crook: only thumb and forefinger gripped as his blade tumbled into the path of the stroke; his hand clenched, milking the hilt as edges locked. Then his arm lashed out, catapulting the blade over and down at Hansio's helm. The other blade sprang to meet it: edges grated above Hansio's head. Then pivoting steel winged at Istvan's throat.

Istvan pulled his hilt down. It rocked in his hand as Hansio's blade hammered his own. He jerked the point up, under Hansio's chin, deep into the grinning skull. The Fox's eyes went blank.

A gasp ran through both armies. Martos sat staring, glory flaring through his veins, until Jagat's voice recalled him.

"Martos! Suktio! Back to your men!" Jagat's horse reared as he whirled.

A roar of exhaltation spouted from Seynyorean throats. Wails and snarls answered. The harsh tones of slamming steel hammered through the voices.

Jagat spurred his horse to a flying gallop. They rode past men who wept and screamed. At the fall of the Fox, a Border-hero had died.

Chapter Seventeen

Istvan shook his head, trying to clear it. Shouting mail-clad horsemen sent their tall steeds racing past, hunting little leather-armoured men who were running.

"Commander!" someone was saying. "Commander DiVega! Are you badly injured?"

Dull eyes hunted features on blurs of faces.

"Cousin Istvan!" the other one said. Firencio's voice. *"Healer!* Get that Red-robe over here!"

"Where are you wounded, Commander?" said the first, and now Istvan's eyes focused and he recognised the Border boy, Cousin Lucarrho's boy—what was his name? Arjun?

"I'm—" He stopped, and sucked in air. "Not hurt. Just—very—" Eyebrows clenched. What *was* the matter with him? "Tired . . ."

"The Healer will be here in a minute," said Firencio.

Istvan yawned. The horse moved under him. The heavy shield pulled on his aching shoulder. Wiping blood from his blade, he sheathed it, and Firencio held his shield while he slid his wrist out of the enarmes.

Then the red-robed Healer came, and held a flask to his lips. Something sharp and faintly sweet bit his tongue.

"Blood loss and hard work," the Healer was saying.

Istvan felt his hands and feet tingling and throbbing. The world became sharper. Men were chasing men across the plain. Wounded men were sobbing. Dead men lay in drying blood like wooden dolls. Ghostly conch-shells cried in the distance. He straightened. In the back of his mind Borderwomen wept.

"Call back the pursuit!" he ordered. They looked at him. "What—did they all break when Hansio died?"

"Hansio's men did," said Firencio. "Jagat's men moved out in a body. He seems to be rallying what's left of Hansio's troops. I'd just ordered the companies together so we could send a larger force against him. He may be able to—"

"No." Istvan shook his head. Blood was a slow drum in his ears. "This battle is over. When an enemy can run, let him run." He stared about him. The Twin Suns had hidden themselves behind the black veil in the west. The sky above was still blue.

Across the blood-smeared plain, tiny figures of men waved sunless swords of grey steel. Nearer to hand, Rinmull's men were helping the Red-robes among the heaped-up bodies, separating the wounded from the dead.

Trumpets sounded the recall above groans and shrieks of pain. Istvan suddenly remembered Hansio's words: *"You I leave for the ghouls!"* Shivering, he glanced over his shoulder at the stain across the sky, and fought the need for sleep.

His bones ached, yet he felt that he could easily fall asleep there in the saddle. But there were orders to be given: the camp must be set up, with a strong guard between the wounded men and the Border.

Chondos was wakened by the rattle of armour. His head was numb and aching, as though he had been drunk for a week. He pushed himself up from cold stone, sneezing as dust rose around him.

The nightmare hall stretched about him. Through the broken roof, he saw the sky streaked grey and black. Confused memories shuddered down his spine.

In dim areas of torchlight, starved men were dressing themselves in crude leather armour of Border-make. Some moved among them in ancient, rusty mail: men of the Chosen or the Pure-in-Blood.

Into the dim light the shrouded dark shape of the Master came like a night-wrapped toad. Chondos shrank back, and fear worse than any fear of death or pain swept over him.

Vague, impossible memories crawled in his brain: white faces, cities falling, fangs in his throat, gay-clad men and women in sunlit Rashnagar.

He saw men throw aside pieces of armour that were too greatly rent. Holes gaped in armour stained with reddish-brown grime. Old rusty swords were waved. Harsh laughter echoed from the stone. Chondos peered through the dimness and was haunted by the memory of this same hall golden with light.

He shook his head. That was not right! This was not his father's hall, nor had his father ever sat upon that throne.

But he had—

Men came in, dragging something on the floor. A smell began to filter through his dust-choked nose. The smell of death.

They stripped leather armour off the thing they had brought and tore it apart. Chondos gagged as they began to eat. He screwed his eyes shut and cowered farther into the shadows.

"Martos?" Suktio's voice came out of the darkness behind him. "Lord Jagat wishes to see you in his tent. Now. I am to relieve you." As Martos' turned, his eyes picked out the drawn, exhausted features half-hidden in the cave under the helmet. The moving moons rippled milky lines across night-darkened lacquered leather.

"My thanks, Suktio." He turned away, his mind hunting for words, and stumbled through uncertain moonlight. Thick, greasy smoke obscured new-kindled pyres. Somewhere, some voice intoned the Border Litany for the Dead.

". . . the seed of man, and man shall drink her milk . . ."

Hansio's men still straggled in, every so often: harried, exhausted men with a haunted look of shock. Hansio's death had struck deep. An aura of invincibility had grown around their leader, and now they were lost, their confidence shattered.

Jagat's tent glowed, and shadows moved on the cloth. The light inside hurt his eyes as he entered. Blinking showed Hamir of Inagar's face, Ymros, Denkrean Kru, and Lord Todaro; and others he did not know. Jagat looked around him with weary, haunted eyes.

". . . home now, without avenging either our Lord or his son?" someone was saying. "Lord Jagat, such a deed—what will our women say to us?"

"If the Dark Things reach them before you do, they will say nothing," said Jagat. He straightened. "I will hear no more of this. Set your minds to it, my Lords, swallow your pride, toughen your hearts, and live with it. We have lost, and it is better that we lose to the Seynyoreans now, then lose to the Dark Things later. You must see to your men, and rest. You have my permission to go."

"But this cannot—"

"Silence!" Jagat's voice froze them. Martos saw Jagat command as he had that long-ago day in Suknia; and once again, all eyes fell before his.

"You have my permission to go," he said again, and they shuffled from the room, Hamir, wounded, leaning on the massive shoulder of the N'lantian.

Jagat drew a deep, shuddering breath when they were gone, and Martos saw that majesty with which he had commanded them crumble. It was a tired old man who spoke.

"Martos, this wasteful war must end." His voice was sad. "It must end *now*, while enough of us are left to defend the land when the Dark Things come. And they will come!" He gestured. "They are waiting there, waiting in the Shadow, while we kill each other!" He sat back, and seemed to draw into himself. He was silent a moment, thoughtful.

"You must be my messenger, Martos, to make peace with DiVega. I shall send my herald with you, for form's sake, but I count on you to win just terms for us. You and DiVega are both outsiders, free from our feuds and foolish hatreds."

Martos stood, silent, his tongue stunned, his mind groping and blinded. Seeing the confusion on his face, Jagat smiled.

"I can trust the two of you to lay the foundation of a just peace between Chondos and myself. There will be a great deal more to it, of course. The Lords of Mahavara must be satisfied—well, you heard them! But they are leaderless now. Apparently Hansio played the Fox with his own men, too, and there are a dozen of his commanders who believe that it was Hansio's will that they take up the guardianship of the army. They'd be fighting each other, I think, if left to themselves. I control them for the moment, but we must have a truce—and quickly."

"What—what do you . . .?" Martos foundered, and licked his lips. "What kind of terms shall I offer?"

Jagat snorted a laugh through his nose, and shook his head. "Terms? We stop killing each other. That's the first thing. A pardon for the men who fought. Passage back to Mahavara for Hansio's men. And we must begin patrolling the Border. It's been too quiet. Something is about to happen." He shook his head again, sadly. "That's all I can think of now. But take whatever terms you can get. The terms can be worked out later. For now, we need a truce. I'll have to talk to DiVega before we can set up a true and lasting peace. I'll meet him whenever he wishes. We'll probably have to have a meeting with the King himself before things are finally settled. Just go, Martos—before something else happens."

It seemed to Istvan that he had barely blinked his eyes before he was wakened, and told that messengers from Lord Jagat were waiting. In darkness, the wailing of the wounded proclaimed Istvan's victory. He shivered at the screams of men in pain.

Low voices drew near. Armour creaked, and Istvan's sleep-fogged eyes found a gold-bearded figure wrapped in the ruddy glow of torchlight on curved steel.

He blinked. A smaller shape, in worn Border robes that had once been rich and fine, stepped in front of the bright-armoured Kadarin.

"I am the herald of Lord Jagat," a ringing voice proclaimed. "I bring you my Lord's chosen delegate, Martos of Kadar, who commands my Lord's cavalry."

At last! Istvan thought. "Well met, Martos! Birthran has spoken well of you, and asked me to give you greetings if I met you." The boy blushed; his beard faded to a honey brown as he moved out of the torchlight, and when he spoke, his voice was hesitant and shy.

"That is—good to hear."

"You there!" Istvan shouted. "Bring wine!" He turned courteously back. "Be welcome, for your master's sake and for your own!" They entered the tent and sat down. "I am glad that Lord

Jagat chose to send you, Martos: hearing Birthran brag about you had made me wish to meet you.'' He saw the herald frowning at such informality; Martos seemed embarrassed. ''But—to business. What does Lord Jagat propose?''

''Peace,'' said Martos. ''A truce, at least. He says—Lord Jagat says—this wasteful war—*must* end!''

Somewhere a dying man cried out above the groaning. Istvan shivered. *This wasteful war . . .*

''Yes!'' he exclaimed. ''Yes, indeed!''

''I—I'm to offer terms! Set up a—a truce, and—and a meeting between Lord Jagat and yourself!'' Martos stared at the ground. *He's not used to this,* Istvan thought.

''Well, a truce should be simple enough.'' Istvan smiled encouragingly, hoping to put the younger man more at ease. ''All we have to do is . . . Wait! What about Prince Hansio's men? Does Jagat speak for them, as well, or must I continue fighting them?''

''Lord Jagat—thinks he can control—'' Martos had been frowning; suddenly he grinned, as at some secret joke. ''In fact, I *know* he can control them—for now, at least! But—he did warn me that—if the—truce—were delayed, he might not—they might not—''

''Hansio's generals respect my Lord's royal blood,'' the herald's deep rich voice broke in. ''They know they stand upon his land. They will obey.''

''Ah!'' said Istvan, but he wondered. Leaderless Mahavaran warriors might respect Lord Jagat's will now, but would they when the shock of Hansio's death had passed? ''That worries me. You can see my position. Ojaini is still under siege, and there is still war along the Oda.''

''I do not know if—if Lord Jagat can—will be able to stop the siege of Ojaini,'' Martos said.

''Well, I'd best not make that a condition, then.'' Istvan smiled, but behind his eyes his army marched toward Ojaini, with the remnants of Hansio's forces harrying his rear.

''What conditions *do* you demand, my Lord?'' asked the herald.

''Remember,'' Istvan said slowly, ''I am not entirely my own master here. I can—and will—speak with Lord Jagat, but—'' Chondos' face rose in his mind, anger in the large dark eyes. ''I will do everything I can to bring a just peace, but I am not the King.'' Anger surged inside him. All this tangle had been made by Chondos' tongue. *If he'd been my son,* he thought, *he'd have learned to rule that tongue!*

And Istvan's dead son's face was a sudden stop; a sting in his eye's corner. Had he done so well, as a father, that he could fault Olansos? Death was all around him: dying men crying in the Healers' tents, and his son's face, Rafayel's face, the lost face . . . He brushed the thought away, forced his mind to living men, and the needs of the present.

"I assume Lord Jagat gives up the title of Prince of Manjipor, and all claim to the throne?"

Martos glanced quickly at the herald, who nodded.

"Yes."

"That's the basic condition, of course," said Istvan. "With that out of the way, there is hope. Now, in return for that, I can promise amnesty for Jagat's men—another basic, which the King can hardly deny."

"And—amnesty for Prince Hansio's men?" said Martos.

"Hansio's men? If they stop fighting, yes. And—"

"Safe passage back to Mahapor," said Martos.

Istvan laughed. "Then I will have to put ending the siege of Ojaini as a condition. I can give no one safe passage without that! Sorry. What else does Lord Jagat want?"

"He said—Lord Jagat said—we must patrol—form a regular patrol to watch the Border."

"A patrol?" Istvan looked up, surprised. "Yes, that would be good, but can we find enough Seers? Even with both armies to draw on—" He saw incomprehension in Martos' face. "There's a lot of Border to cover. I don't think anyone knows how much, anymore. You can't map the Border, because it changes with every attack, and it's been generations since anyone tried. And Jagat's conquest of Damenco must have added—oh, at least two hundred more miles! And in order to cover it all, your patrols have to be fairly small, and scattered over a wide area. Unless each group has a Seer, the Dark Things can cut them off one at a time and destroy them." Frowning, he shook his head, picturing miles of grey wasteland with the black Border looming above; little groups of men, scattered and unprotected, exposed to attack. He turned to the herald. "But *you* should know, my Lord Herald, whether there are Seers enough, or not?"

"Enough to cover the whole Border?" said the herald. "Perhaps not. Yet such a patrol is needed."

Istvan frowned.

"Well," he said at last, thinking aloud. "One of the most logical demands for me to make is that Jagat disperse his army. Now, if they disperse and ride up and down the Border, I cannot object. I can send my Seers to watch them." He laughed, then shook his head. "But Lord Jagat must understand that I cannot disperse my own army until the war is over in the north."

"But," Martos said hesitantly, "if Lord Jagat disperses—his own men—then—what check is there on—the men who came with Hansio?"

"Ah well," said Istvan, "what's the old saying? There is always a road to peace—how did that go?"

"*There is always a way to peace,*" Martos quoted, softly, "*so long as there is trust between honourable men.* That was one of Eldir's sayings." The hesitance had faded from his voice. "Atrion said, *So long as you keep faith even with your foes, men will deal with you unafraid.*"

"*But a man known to be an oath-breaker,*" said Istvan, completing the quotation as it rose in his memory, "*leaves his foes no choice but war, and may make no peace with the world.*" He smiled at Martos and met sparkling blue eyes. "When can I hope to meet with Lord Jagat?"

"He said he would meet with you wherever and whenever you wished."

"Tomorrow?" said Istvan. "Tomorrow at noon? I can bring Lord Rinmull and Lord Maldeo—they should be present—and ride to your camp."

"To the camp?" Martos said. "Would it not be better to meet on some more—neutral ground?"

Does Jagat believe I killed his son? Istvan wondered. Then, with a sharp wrench of grief, his dead son's face was ice across his heart.

"You have trusted yourself in my camp," said Istvan. "Should I do less? And if I dare not trust myself to the honour of Lord Jagat, then no one in all the world can be trusted—and you were a fool to come!"

"What?" Martos stared at him. "But—of course I trust you; we are of the same school! That makes us almost kin, like—brothers, or—or like father and son."

Father and son . . . Istvan stared.

Martos could hear Birthran's voice in his memory: *Men of the same school are brothers . . .* and Birthran had been a second father to him; what did that make DiVega? An uncle? Smiling, he looked up. DiVega's eyes were wide and intense.

His mind saw then the faces of Hansio's men.

"Even Jagat's honour might fail to protect you from men as wild with hate as some of the Mahavarans," he said. "Perhaps, instead, you could meet at the Hastur-tower—Vajrakota, I think they call it—Hansio's men would not dare break the peace in such a place."

"Lord Hansio's men must respect the truce," the herald said, "if it is sworn before Hastur.'

"Yes!" Istvan straightened. "I'd not thought of that. Thank you. And that brings another thought. Lord Rinmull tells me that we must carry our dead to the tower, until more wood comes from the Kantara. And your dead, too, must wait for wood to fuel their pyres. Let Jagat and I both, then, bring our dead to Vajrakota tomorrow, and end our strife while we lay our dead to rest.''

Chondos huddled against cold stone, feeling muscles twitch on his spine, feeling his mind fouled by the Master's touch, as fear came closer in the dark. He forced himself to raise his head: against faint torchlight, he saw black cloth writhe as the flesh crawled under it. The smell of rotting meat made him gag: the humped, swollen figure laughed.

"No appetite? That will come, little King, that will come. But in a day or so, we will have fresh meat for you. See? Your soldiers wait for you." Puffy, wormlike fingers appeared at the end of a gesturing sleeve, pointing at the men clustered in torchlight, in Border clothes and armour taken from scattered bones around them. "Soon they will follow you into the Light, and there will be food for all! Even the famished ghouls will eat, the hungry ghouls." Another laugh; then Chondos felt the wave of foulness retreat, and his stained mind was free again. He hugged himself, shuddering, and through the back of his mind he hunted for something he had lost. Something blue, and near a throne that was not the throne in this hall.

About him, Miron Hastur could feel miles of empty corridors, unpeopled caverns and chambers in the great Hastur-city of Idelbonn. And thousands of miles to the north, he could sense dragon-headed Uoght, a gliding pillar of darkness that even the rising suns could not stay, advancing against Miron's weary kinsmen on the Border.

Only three others stirred in the empty city: his kinsman Aldamir, ordered, like Miron himself, out of the fighting to the half-rest of duty here; and Elnar, whom Kandol Hastur-Lord had left in charge of the fires of Inner Earth. And the third was a cloud of swirling sparks, wise and powerful and beautiful: Tintinaré, an ancient energy-being that Narsil the Younger had wrought in ages when even Kandol Hastur-Lord was yet unborn. Agelong, Tintinaré slept under Idelbonn, until wakened by Elnar to watch undermanned towers.

West of the city, the Shadow was blank, and their trained minds were baffled by its arcane veil. As far north as Creolandis and northern Araja, the Border was still and glassy; but north of that, it seethed with deadly energies.

Aldamir laid out futures like a fan in his mind: that was his special skill. On every track, the three could see night-things swarm across an undefended Border into Tarencia: on path after path, the Shadow grew.

All three Immortals pondered the spreading tree of paths. On a few paths there was a warning; on most, there was none. But they could not see the nature of that warning. Some fundamental fact was missing: the attack could come at any time.

Rippling space-time around them seized the attention of the three Hasturs: four small figures appeared upon the glowing oval of one of the ancient gateways. Aldamir blinked his body into the chamber where they stood.

What are you children doing here? chorussed three linked minds.

We want to help! thought Alcarin, the ten-year-old brother of Elenius and Earagon. He was tallest of the four; his clear grey eyes were bold with defiance.

You let mortal wizards help, and they are in greater danger than we! That was Peridol, blond and blue-eyed, his face fine-boned as an elf's. Alcarin, Alkides, and Roderigo were all red-haired and big-boned, with brown or grey eyes.

Silence covered the surface of the adult minds; deep in their hidden depths, invisible currents pondered, seeking to explain. These few children were the hope and the future of the Hastur-kin. Others, barely twice their age, shared the dangers of the Border—and many had already died.

The four tiny figures clustered at the edge of the raised platform: the circle of translucent milky crystal lit the room with a dim glow. Air rippled above it, and a young woman appeared, copper hair swirling. The older Hasturs could sense, though the children could not, the relief and fear beneath the anger she radiated. Elnar, in his high chamber, doubled his vigilance.

Melissa Hastur reached toward the children, waves of embracing mind. *Return to Carcosa,* her liquid thought ran through them all. Defiant sparks from the children shocked her away. Mingled fear swirled in the ocean of adult mind. So few—these children surrounded, in the womb, by loving minds, by thousands of years of memory, knowledge and power; infants who spoke and studied magic before their legs could bear their weight.

Already they were so powerful that any attempt to forcibly return them to Carcosa would use up strength that none could now afford.

We could watch a tower! Alkides thought boldly. The minds of his companions chimed agreement.

The death-scream of an ancient Immortal made the four adult minds wince, but the children did not hear, and the surface of adult mind was unruffled.

In the children's minds was a vision of the tower they could man: the adults plucked the picture from their minds and mirrored it, then showed waves of darkness ravening out of the Shadow. Immature minds struggled with panic, trying to muster the concentration needed to escape.

Again the surface of the adult mind became the blank crystal of perfect calm. Yet those minds saw light burning in the battle thousands of miles to the north, where dark magic engulfed a tower. Those within winked clear—all but one—to reappear in sunlight with flames spurting from their hands. Still the children stood stubbornly. Anxiety crawled on the web of woven minds.

Miron saw inescapable truth blooming from the children's minds. They *were* needed! Already, in the south, where the Border touched desert, towers stood empty while their warders flickered north to aid their kin. Tintinaré was spread incredibly thin, to fill ten towers that their warders had left.

Now Herstes Hastur stirred in Vajrakota Tower, ready to leap into the combat half a continent away. On the grey plain below Vajrakota, armoured riders bobbed on the backs of trotting horses.

In Aldamir's mind, branching lines of future forked and spread, while his kinsmen watched. Again Miron wondered at the danger shown: Shadow growing stronger, swallowing the land, fouling the sea. He tried to see more clearly the forking-point; saw armies reel under tossing swords in a war of which he had been unaware.

Swords flickered. A man fell, royal red flooding from his veins. Were those Istvan DiVega's eyes frozen in a dead stare? Who was that standing with his long sword raised? Was that King Chondos that he faced?

The vision swayed, rippled, faded in a swirling blur.

Herstes was calling from Vajrakota Tower. Miron moved his body there, and Herstes vanished, joining his flame to the others in the north. Miron stood alone in the glowing tower, watching.

He saw the sullen blankness of the Shadow. Far across the vastness of blasted land, he could sense vague figures moving and wailing, veiled from clear sight; but other minds told him they had been there for days. At the same time, he watched the futures branching in Aldamir's mind, in the faraway room where he and Melissa faced the children.

Why do you try to keep us penned up at Carcosa? Roderigo was asking. *You let mortal wizards help, and they are weaker than we!*

They will die anyway, Elnar answered. *You need not.*

They searched Aldamir's mind, looking for a way to keep the children safe.

Two groups of horsemen rode through the rain. In Miron's mind was space to count the dead strapped to their saddles and the dead in the tower below, to study the armour and wounds of the living, and to read the symbols of the past graven in their faces and the tensions of their muscles to learn the story of the war, even as he conferred with the others about the children.

Could the children stay in the city, freeing Elnar to man a tower while they served him as living links of mind?

If only the Shadow were not so dark, Miron thought to the others, *we would have more warning. The rainy season has come at a good time for them, to weave the clouds into the spell that cloaks their movements.*

—*A strong east wind, and another from the desert south, would strip the sky of clouds, and sunlight would weaken the Shadow-spell.*

—*And it would keep needed rain from soil and crops, as well as stripping healthy vibrations from the air, leaving ill radiance that will make mortals suffer stress and despair.*

—*Gently, lest we raise a wind to lay waste the lands of men . . .*

Minds flowed together. Off to the east, winds whirling sunwise spread clear skies over the beaches of the sea. Vast minds went sweeping out, seizing pieces of air. Delicately, like the flutter of a butterfly's wings, atoms of air were diverted in their passage, and that whole massive wheel of wind rolled ponderously inland.

But will not the Dark Things take this as an attack, when we tear away their covering of Shadow? Will they not then attack?

—*Let us hope that they do! Is it not better they attack while we are watching, rather than catching us off guard?*

Hooves drew nearer to Vajrakota, squelching in the wet grass while fine rain fell.

A part of Miron's mind looked down on the riders, and studied the auric rainbow fires whirling around them. The two forces were aware of each other, and had changed their pace so that both would arrive together.

These were the two sides? Startled, he drew more of his mind away from the winds. Jagat and Hansio allied against the King of Tarencia? Manjipor divided, and Istvan DiVega fighting against Lord Jagat?

Perhaps that explained the danger Aldamir had seen. Many Bordermen had died, weakening the kingdom's defence. But surely there was more to it than that.

Far in the north, a Hastur died. The death-shock shot through his kin. Wind blew the fine rain like mist. Water gathered in a glossy coat on lacquered leather armour, and beaded like jewels on the steel rings of mail. Miron saw his own heart-pinching grief for dead kinsmen imaged in the solemn desolation that hung in the aura of the bearers of the mortal dead. But mingled with the sober colour of sorrow, he saw blaring the strangled red of hate.

Hooves squelched in the sodden grass as both parties drew rein before the tower. A door swung open at the touch of Miron's mind. Miron heard muttering: some men stroked their sword-hilts, while bloody images of hatred and revenge stained their thoughts.

Istvan DiVega slid from his horse's back. Wet grass splashed his boots. More slowly, Jagat dismounted, and the two old men walked through shimmering sadness to meet between the ranks of their men.

"Lord Istvan." Jagat bent at the waist, Border-fashion.

Istvan's knees flexed in the courtly Carcosan bow. "My Lord Jagat."

Miron watched swirling colours as each man sought for thoughts to turn into words. Their looks touched, then DiVega stepped forward, and he and Jagat clasped elbows in formal embrace.

"Let us first deal with the needs of the dead," said Jagat slowly, "and then seek justice for the living."

Shoulder to shoulder, they strode to the great arched door of Vajrakota. Other men followed, carrying stiff bodies gashed by swords, severed limbs, heads with staring eyes—men of all three of the Border provinces, and men from distant nations, far from the Shadow. Already the room was piled with dead, the leavings of the last battle. The base of the tower belled with echoing feet.

Miron's mind shook with the passion of battle as, far in the north, flame flared. Demons burst burning as his kinsmen crossed angled beams, and the fierce light pierced etheric shells and shattered evil atoms. Elation rippled through his crystal calm, but then he quieted, turning his mind back to the mortals below, the living and the dead. Istvan and Jagat stood watching while men stiff as wood were placed on the floor. Miron could see their shared sadness draw them, with small steps, toward each other, until they stood side by side. Slowly their mood was spreading to their followers: the vivid red of hate faded in the auras of Seynyorean and Borderman alike, as they moved in the depths of his mind.

"That's all of them," a voice echoed from the stone walls.

"Our dead rest together without strife," Jagat said. "Here, there is peace. Now . . ." He did not finish: the thought hung in the air, tangible to Miron's mind.

"Now let us leave the war with the dead," said Istvan.

Jagat nodded. His voice tolled eerily from stone: "I will gladly swear peace, here before the Hasturs. I speak for the men of Mahavara as well. If—" He drew a deep breath, and straightened. "*If* we can be sure that the men who joined me will not suffer for it. I shall not deliver them into the power of a cruel and capricious King. Amnesty, even for Hansio's men, must be promised: no man's land must be taken, no man banished, nor any lose his rank. Else, we fight on."

"That does you honour," said Istvan. He hesitated, and Miron saw the words waiting at his lips, and the doubt that held them back.

"For myself, I care not," added Jagat, "but I cannot betray those whose loyalty to me, or to Hansio, led them into this—rebellion."

"I myself will stand with you in this before the King," said Lord Maldeo, "but I fear that without the word of the King himself, no such promise can be made. It is for the King to decide."

Istvan's breath hissed from his lungs, and Miron could see angry sparks swirling in the calm blue of Istvan's mind.

"You see?" he said. The blue deepened, bitter. "Gladly would I agree—but I am not the King. We can make a truce, but before any final peace can be made, we must all sit at table with the King."

Miron saw wrath flare red in Jagat's mind, so brightly that he feared for the old man's heart, and reached quickly into him, lest the fury of his passion burst his heart and leave him, too, lying dead among the bodies on the cold stone floor.

Purple blood gathered in Jagat's face. Miron forced open the clenching chest, drawing air through the lungs into the blood, while he steadied the old heart, kept it beating. The attack was over almost at once: Jagat's heart was still strong. Miron let go.

"I will—I will meet my—King," Jagat said, through locked teeth. Every curve of muscle in his body screamed its protest to Miron's senses. His fist grasped the sword-hilt as though it were a throat; bones ground futilely on bone. "Lord Hamir, too, must come, and these Lords of Massadessa and Mahavara who have fought at my side—they, too, must come! And Maldeo, and you, my Lord Rinmull, for justice's sake you must be there. Yet—"

Questions thronged Miron's mind, questions kindled by the flame of Jagat's wrath. What could have turned Jagat so sharply against Olansos' son?

Then, far in the north, beyond the landlocked sea, a terrible burst of magic churned the ether.

"There is much blood between us," Jagat was saying in the vaults of Miron's mind. "You said—" His hand jerked away from his sword-hilt, as though burned. "You spoke to Martos of a plan—"

And far to the north, Uoght reared, like smoke on a still day, and glided toward the Border like a snake. Behind him something crawled into the world, forcing a tear in the plane of existence, something monstrous, ancient, shapeless. One of the great Dyoles, Miron guessed, though he could not see it clearly because a scrap of the Other World was wrapped around it, veiling all but its terrible hunger.

Fleeing Demons battered frantically against barriers of flame. Uoght swept across the Border, into the sunlight of Kadar, and before him fires faded and died, drowned in power. Frantic Demons hurled themselves against the tiny, flame-wrapped figures of the Hastur-kin.

The thing from the Dark World followed: where it passed, even the dust was gone, and its track was scratched in primal rock. Earth trembled; trees fell to dust; twisted space ate sunlight. Crackling power flared to meet it. A cocoon of rainbow need-fire seethed and wriggled onward. Waves of force sent Hasturs reeling.

And still, in the base of his mind that filled the tower, Miron could hear the tiny voices of mortal men:

"Then we will meet at Agnasta Tower, and we will leave behind all war-gear," Istvan was saying, "wearing only our court-swords, and we will lay even those aside before we enter. Not even daggers— "

"Do you not trust our word?" snarled a man from Mahapor.

"We may all trust one another's word," said Istvan gently, "but what man can trust himself to face heart-twisting grief, when hot words fly, and hate works slyly on the mind? Swords will seem to come unscabbarded by themselves. Shall we let unmeant deaths add still more blood to the flood that divides us now? We need no swords to make peace. The only weapons we shall need will be our wits and our tongues!"

"They will be sharp enough weapons for King Chondos!" Jagat said with a bitter smile. "A jest," he added, as some of the Mahavarans turned suspicious faces. "No matter. I must confess, Lord Istvan, that I would feel much better if I could take a belt or a stick to your royal master!"

"If he were younger . . ." said Istvan. He shrugged, and looked into Jagat's eyes, and Miron could see the thought that hung like a laugh between them: *If he were younger I'd do it myself!*

Miron felt power well up inside him as his strength grew. He felt Elnar searching frantically among the ancient weapons in the sealed crypts under Idelbonn. Far in the north, Hasturs were hurled back relentlessly before the Power from the Dark World. Miron poised himself to leap north to his kinsman's aid, but still he watched the Shadow behind him, and the men in the tower below.

"It were best if we wasted no time in gathering for this council," said Rinmull of Ojaini thoughtfully. "Yet it is a ride of many days from the King's city to Agnasta. I know a place that will serve as neutral ground nearer than that; it will save a day's ride at least.

Istvan and Jagat turned to him questioningly.

"There is a small fort just this side of the Yukota, north of the ford," he explained. "It was empty, so I put a garrison of my vassals there, and some others joined them after—um—the siege started. You must know the place, it's called, ummm . . ."

"Kajpor?" Jagat prompted.

"Kajpor!"

"I thought so," said Jagat, nodding. "I know the place." He turned to Istvan. "It is a good choice. It will serve as neutral ground, right enough. It is on our side of the river, but close enough to the Kantara that it could be easily—rescued, if it came to that—if any man were seriously afraid of treachery—which I, for one, am not. Kajpor would be quite safe: only a fool would attempt anything, and he would get his just price for such folly."

In the jewel of Miron's mind, mortal voices talked on while he studied the strife of flame and Shadow thousands of miles away. Veiled in whorls of power, the worm from the Dark World advanced beside Uoght. Miron poised himself to step across the miles.

"Sons of Hastur, hear us now!" The voice belled from the stones at the base of his mind. He moved his body down, to stand in the flesh before Istvan and Jagat. A man in Kadarin armour stumbled back, as though he had never seen a Hastur before.

"I, Jagat, of the Arthavan Line, Lord of Damenco, do swear, here before Hastur, that I will end the siege of Ojaini, and all other hostility, and will enforce upon my vassals and all my allies a truce, to run from this day to at least the eighth day hence, or until I can meet as arranged with King Chondos of Tarencia, at Kajpor, or whatever other place may be appointed in its stead, to conclude a final treaty of peace, or until I know for certain that there will be no such meeting."

As Jagat spoke, Miron looked deep into the mind behind the words, reading the truth of them—feeling, too, the bitter memory of Pirthio's death and the pain caused by the King's insane message.

Questions, questions—but beyond Jagat's transparent brain, Miron could see the cold eyes of dragon-headed Uoght, and feel the desperation of distant kin.

"I further swear that, providing King Chondos keeps faith with me and deals justly with my allies, I do hereby renounce all claims upon his throne and kingdom, or to any portion of his realm other than that entrusted to me by his father, King Olansos of glorious memory, my own lawful domain of Damenco; and that upon conclusion of a fair and honourable treaty, I do own him to be my lawful King and sovereign Lord, and swear to protect his land and people with all my strength and power.

"So I swear, before the Children of Hastur, and give myself to their judgment."

Istvan's voice rang from glowing stone: "And in return I, Istvan DiVega of Carcosa, Commander of all Mercenary Forces for Chondos, King of Tarencia, do swear before Hastur that I will honour this truce, and hold to it all men under my command; that I will give the fullest aid to Lord Jagat in defending this land against our common foes in the Shadow. I pledge to Lord Jagat that I will use all my influence with the King to obtain for him a just and honourable peace."

Behind the words, behind the thoughts, Miron glimpsed a blurred memory-image of Chondos the King, saying strange things, moving through the dream-castle corridors of memory.

But through the memory and through the mind, far beyond this tower where the mortals talked, he could see the monstrous, shadow-shrouded worm crushing the land where his kinsman fought. There was no time to think of Chondos: it was nearly dark, and the night-things were stirring.

He felt Elnar leap through worldless space, cradling in his arms an ancient web of jewelled fire; felt wounded kinsmen reel into Idelbonn.

"I shall join my sword with Lord Jagat's against any who threaten to break this truce," Istvan vowed. "So I swear, here before Hastur."

"Both have sworn," Miron said with his tongue, while his mind called to wounded kinsmen in Idelbonn. "And both have spoken truth." His wounded cousin, Kisil, appeared in the main chamber at the top of the tower, and turned his vigilance upon the wall of darkness.

"Trust one another," Miron said aloud, and fed all that Kisil needed to know into his kinsman's mind before his tongue had finished with the clumsy human words. As he finished speaking, he vanished from the tower.

He was crackling power, surging ether. He flickered into being beside Elnar and the others in Kadar.

Stupefied, Martos stared at the air where the red-haired man had stood. He was sure the Seynyoreans and Bordermen were all laughing at him silently: none of them had shown any sign of surprise when the blue-robed figure had appeared; they were used to the Hasturs' mysterious comings and goings.

"So," he heard Jagat saying, "the oath is sworn, and we are at peace."

"Well," DiVega's voice replied, "until we meet at Kajpor, at least—I hope. I still must notify the King."

"You—" Jagat's eyebrows were like bent bows. "Have you not consulted him?" Martos saw DiVega shake his head.

"I thought it best to present him with a peace already made."

"So that was why! I see you are learning!" He broke off with a cough and glanced quickly around, then leaned closer and spoke in a low tone Martos could not catch.

Martos felt suddenly weary. The eyes of the dead, glittering in the tower's glow, seemed to stare at him. *And even here*, he thought, *death is a smell*.

The preservative spells of the Hasturs would keep it from getting worse; but with so many hacked corpses in the room, the odour of the freshly dead was strong. He wished that there were fields of flowers outside, instead of the barren plain. If they covered the bodies with blossoms, both the eyes and the smell would be hidden.

DiVega shrugged. "I've done the best I can," he said. "It will be up to him now. But unless he orders me out of his kingdom, I will be at the peace talks as I promised, to speak for you. But I fear, that"—he smiled grimly—"my promise to my cousin was a rash one! I do not think that—that—that boy will ever be safe on his throne!"

Other men's nerves were suffering, too, Martos saw. They huddled together in little groups—Manjipéans, Kantarans, Mahavarans, and Seynyoreans, all separate from each other—and shivered in the cold fire of the walls. At least they no longer glared at each other. But waiting among the piles of hacked, pathetic dead, while their leaders talked and their dead friends stared at them . . .

"Well, patrolling the Border will give the men something else to think about," Jagat was saying. "We must—"

"Can you not talk outside?" Martos interrupted softly. Jagat looked at him in surprise. "The men can't take this much longer."

DiVega glanced around quickly at living and dead, and nodded. "He's right. Better get them moving."

A word from DiVega, a word from Lord Jagat, and former enemies filed, side by side, out of the tower. The angry glares had faded. The example of their leaders showed that war was their common enemy, and sorrow their common bond.

Martos breathed deeply as he stepped outside. The names of his dead still ran through his mind: men who had left Kadar—*part of the land*, as the Bordermen said.

Grey skies wept above Vajrakota as the mourning men passed through the wide arch. Martos looked away, into veils of rain that poured on the barren plain. Somewhere beyond, Kumari was waiting for him. Now that the war was over . . .

"There is an awful long stretch to cover," he heard DiVega saying. "Two or three hundred miles in Manjipé alone, as I recall— or is it more than that?"

"We have the men for it," Jagat replied.

Martos shivered, and glanced over his shoulder at the looming dark behind him. *Over? Hardly*.

"We have the men," said DiVega, "but not the Seers."

"Then we must do without them," said Jagat with a shrug.

Martos stared north, over the bleak, rainswept land. He sagged inside his armour, thinking of Kumari, and the child. And somewhere beyond this rain was his home, the home he would, likely, never see again, any more than the men lying in the glow of the tower behind him would ever see it. Instead, he and Kumari would have a new home, here.

Earth is the Bride of the Warrior, he thought.

"But without a Seer, a patrol will be isolated, in constant danger of being cut off, wiped out!" DiVega's voice was a rasp of exasperation. "You'll be sending men to certain death!"

"When have we ever done anything else, along the Border?" Jagat answered quietly. "Death is the Bride of the Warrior."

An hour later, Istvan watched Jagat and his men fading as they rode off in the rain and the falling light, and thought, *Now to see what the King will do.*

Cold rain lashed across his face and drummed on the thick wool of his cloak. His bones ached. His horse shivered beneath him, shrinking from the cold drip. He patted her shoulder absently. At least, if the horses could get out of the rain . . .

But why do I keep worrying about the King? What, he wondered, *could* the King say, or do, at this point? Istvan had laid down the outlines of a just peace, before the Hasturs. Even should Chondos object to its provisions, he was still subject to the authority of the Hasturs; like all Kings, one of their vassals. If Jagat or any of his followers felt themselves ill-treated, there was always the appeal to Hastur.

No matter how unreasonable the boy might be, he was still subject to Hastur's Laws.

I'm worrying too much, he decided, and started the ride back to camp, the Border looming on his right.

Once again, the King refused mind-touch. Istvan was mildly annoyed: he preferred the illusion that he was actually talking to the other person; but then, considering how offensive Chondos could be in person, perhaps it was just as well.

Jodos had been pleased when he first sensed old Shachio moving toward him through the web of the palace. He could sense news in the very tensions of the old man's body, and surely, whatever news he bore must be good.

He glanced at the girl who knelt at his feet, and ran his tongue along the edges of his teeth. Her blood was so sweet. Maybe now he could end these trivial tortures and do those things he longed to do.

If enough of the Bordermen had been destroyed in the battle, then tonight he could summon the hosts of the Shadow across the Border; by tomorrow, perhaps, they would have swept north to the city and he could rule here in truth. Then she would scream, he thought.

But then—then she would be gone. The thought sent a curious emptiness through him. No matter how careful he was, sooner or later she would die; long before he had enjoyed the last of the flesh from her bones.

Disturbed, without knowing why, he made her crawl from the room while he guided the old Seer carefully through the web of mind into his presence.

"Great news, Lord King!" cried Shachio. Jodos, gloating, listened to the Seer's cheery tones. "Istvan DiVega reports a great victory, followed by a truce!"

A truce? Jodos felt his smile freeze on his face.

"If you will permit mind-touch—"

"No!" said Jodos, then controlled himself. He felt sudden danger like a pit before him: all his work in ruins, his plans crumbled. "Go on."

"Prince Hansio is dead, and Lord Jagat has called for an end to the war. The truce has been sworn before Hastur." Jodos flinched at the naked Name. "They will help Lord Istvan to watch the Border, and all the Lords of the Border country have agreed to a meeting with you, to draw up a final treaty of peace, at Kajpor, by the Yukota."

This would mean months of torture by the Master; and at last, tiny gobbets of his flesh would be given to the ghouls and goblins in the deep tunnels.

"You must come south at once," Shachio was saying, "to set the terms for a just and lasting peace in your kingdom."

His brother's memories closed his mouth before he could give himself away, screaming at this unexpected development. Rage could destroy him now. A prudent censor in his mind turned back the flood of words.

"What is there to discuss?" he said, taking a tone of bitterness from Chondos' memory. "Those who have rebelled against me must suffer for their rebellion. Their treason! Or has my Lord Istvan delivered me into the hands of my enemies?"

"Lord Istvan says that if you feel yourself wronged in this matter," said Shachio, "you should appeal to Hastur. But the truce has been sworn at Vajrakota Tower. It is a fair peace, and will do you no dishonour, Lord Istvan says, but only great good. And this is merely a temporary truce. It is up to Your Majesty to negotiate the final treaty.''

"Then,'' said Jodos, ''if Lord Istvan has crushed the rebellion in the south, he should hurry his army to the aid of Prince Phillipos, who still fights rebels in the north.''

"Lord DiVega begs your indulgence, Lord King, but says that until you have come south and the final treaty has been signed, and adequate provision for defence against the Shadow has been made, it will be impossible for any large part of the army to leave the Border. He says, therefore, that you must come south at once, and that he will meet you at Ojaini, to guide you to the castle.''

Fear fought fury in Jodos' mind. He opened his mouth to refuse to come, to order Istvan to march his men north, and then closed it again. He was impotent under the customs of the Sun People, and the cursed laws by which the Blue-robes bound their mortal Kings.

"Kajpor is just on the Manjipéan side of the Yukota. Its position makes it effectively neutral ground—although if you prefer, we may instead meet at Agnasta Tower.''

Jodos had to hide a shudder. ''Kajpor will do as well,'' he said.

"You must ride without war-gear. That is one of the conditions of the truce. Only court-swords may be worn to Kajpor, and even they must be laid aside when we enter the Council Chamber.''

"What?'' Jodos straightened. Hope was like a drink of fresh blood. ''Would you repeat that?''

"One of the conditions is that no war-gear will be worn to Kajpor, Lord Istvan says.'' Shachio paused. ''Men will wear only court-swords, and even those will be laid aside when the council begins, left outside the Council Chamber. Even belt-knives will be laid aside. Otherwise, Lord Istvan is afraid that some hothead may lose his temper and start the war all over again.''

They would all be unarmed, he thought. All the natural leaders of the Bordermen. If there were a room near the Council Chamber, he thought, a room with a lock . . .

"Who, exactly, is attending this council?'' he asked quickly. Perhaps he could still save himself.

"Lord Jagat and Lord Istvan, of course. Lord Rinmull and Lord Maldeo. Lord Hamir of Inagar, and the Regent of Kaligaviot. I believe there is another from Manjipé, though I do not remember for sure, and there might be two; and I believe there are two Lords from Massadessa. And there are at least five from Mahavara—Hansio did not leave a single Regent to rule for his daughter. *That* is one of the things you must settle.''

"How many will there be altogether?''

"Fourteen—fifteen, I believe, counting Your Majesty. No more than that, certainly. Yes, Jagat's men and the Mahavarans will outnumber us, but I do not think you need fear treachery." Shachio was speaking now with DiVega's voice, Jodos noticed.

"I fear no rebel riffraff!" he said, his brother's mind providing stung pride. "But why must we meet with so many?"

"Jagat felt that his allies from Massadessa must be included, and the great Lords of Manjipé. Mahavara is leaderless now, until Hansio's daughter is married, or a guardian chosen. They would be fighting each other, I think, but for Jagat."

"A fine, squabbling rabble!" Jodos sneered, picking words from the ghost of his brother's mind. "Why not Jagat's whole army, and perhaps some of his horses, while we are at it? We might need their wisdom!"

He sent a shrill thought of summons to the Spider. Shachio winced: he did not catch the thought, or recognise it; it was only a sharp pain in his head.

"But you are tired, Lord Shachio," said Jodos, with a false solicitude. "Does my cousin have more to say to me, or can I allow you to rest?"

"My Lord Istvan begs you to make haste, Lord King. That is all."

"I will consider the matter," he said haughtily.

"It is several days' ride to Ojaini," the old Seer said plaintively. "And Lord Istvan says this conference is vital to the safety of the kingdom."

In Jodos' brain, his brother's ghost snarled with wounded pride: Chondos would have refused angrily and reprimanded the Seynyorean for this thinly disguised order. But there was no time for such temperament: he must seize this chance to save himself from his Master's wrath, quickly.

"Tell Lord Istvan I will start tomorrow."

All the great nobles of the Border, unarmed and in his power! He would hide Hotar and his men in some room close to the Council Chamber, and after the weapons had been laid aside, and the council begun . . .

But the men with Hotar would not be enough. Even unarmed, the Bordermen would be dangerous, and all they would only have to fight their way to the door and unlock it. There would be furniture in the room, and a table could stop a sword-cut.

He must ask the Master to send him more men.

"Good night, Your Majesty." Shachio was rising, going out. Jodos answered absently, his mind busy.

How many men did he need? He would not be able to smuggle very many men into the Council Chamber, or keep them hidden, easily. But DiVega had said there would be sixteen men at the meeting, counting himself and the King.

A man for each of the Borderers, then. And the Spider. With his flaming sword laid aside, DiVega would be unprotected. Or perhaps he should put the Spider on Jagat. There would be little that even the redoubtable Istvan the Archer could do to defend himself bare-handed against fourteen armed men.

Not even a dagger. He smiled cruelly. The girl came crawling back from the next room, but he had no time for her now. He could sense the Spider, waiting at the gate. He walked through the web of his palace. Men averted their eyes as he approached, for he had no need to be seen.

He hugged his cloak around him as he came into the night air. The Spider waited outside the smouldering ghost of the castle's broken defence. He could have tortured it by ordering it to come inside, but this was no time for petty pleasures. He went to meet it. It would need a new body soon: this one was beginning to smell.

"I must speak to the Master, in Rajinagara."

A fine thread, too shrill for any manlike mind, spun across the miles, past burning barriers and watching Blue-robes. The Master stirred, down the far, shrill corridor, all naked malice and hunger. His words spilled out of dead lips.

"Is it time at last?"

"Almost," said Jodos quickly, and sudden sweat was cold in the night. "Soon. A few more days."

"Days?" A soft, deadly voice was forced awkwardly through the dead vocal cords, and even through the Spider's mind and the miles between, Jodos could feel the rage of baffled hunger. "Days? It has *been* days!"

"Soon!" he pleaded. "Soon! The enemies make peace. But that means a chance to strike! They will meet unarmed to talk peace, and not far from the Border. I can kill their leaders, if you will send me but a handful of men; kill all the leaders and throw their armies back into war. That will be the time! Time to strike! Ten days, perhaps. No more!"

"Ten days," the cold voice said. "You will have your ten days. But on the eleventh night, we strike! And if you have failed, you will suffer far longer than ten days."

"I will not fail, Master! But you must send me the men!" Panic made his heart lurch, but he must speak. "Send but six men—men who can pass as Bordermen for a time. All the Border Lords—Jagat and Rinmull and Maldeo, and Istvan the Archer as well—all will be at Kajpor, and all will be unarmed."

He went on, explaining his plan, his voice shrill with terror. The Master listened.

"Six of the Pure-in-Blood will wait outside Ojaini," the distant whisper finally said. "This will be your last chance. Do not fail."

Before Jodos could answer, the thread was broken and there was only the Dead Man standing before him, with the Spider crawling in his hair.

Chondos woke, hearing feet scrape in darkness. Voices echoed like wordless cries from the crumbling walls. Faint red pulses disturbed his staring eyes. He blinked. Echoing feet clashed louder. Fragments of words squeaked off stone. A torch appeared. Bursts of orange sculpted tiny shapes out of the dark. Other torches followed. Stone arches and slabs leaped, gilded, from the black, and vanished again.

He sat up, shivering, and rubbed his eyes. The tiny figures seemed to float in emptiness, until perspective returned, and he realised men were crossing the dark hall toward him. They wore crude armour of Border-make; torchlight rippled wetly on lacquered leather. He stared at them stupidly, trying to think. They halted in the middle of the hall. Into the pool of light around them bobbed a bizarre shape. For a moment, he thought it only another shadow. Then he saw it was flapping black cloth.

A deep-toned sibilance rang hollow and distorted from the walls. Sdddenly, the darkness around him was no longer comforting, and cold flickers ran up his spine. He staggered to his feet and stumbled toward the light.

Echoed words became clearer. *Wait*, he heard, and *outside Ojaini, the Sun People's city* . . .

He could hear scuffing echoes of his own feet as he moved. He kicked something, clattering that sounded like stone.

Obey, the deep, inhuman voice hissed, and *kill!* As Chondos staggered nearer, more words came clear. *Hide where he tells you and strike when he tells you*, he heard; then echoes twisted the sounds again. He made out, *Immortal*, and then, *Those who fail will be food*.

Armoured men left their companions, and he saw their single torch moving away through the ancient darkness.

He stopped just outside the torchlight. The Master, like some hideous doll knotted from black cloth, faced the armoured men.

". . . preserve the remaining horses." Black cloth flapped as a long arm waved. "In ten days you must be ready to follow the other across the Border. He will open for you the castles, and their women will be yours to eat."

Kingship stirred in Chondos like a prodded lion, and rage drove his feet. Those were his people that this twisted bundle of rags was promising its followers! He lurched into the light, his fists knotting futilely, before he remembered how helpless he was.

The armoured men were marching away, except for one who stood holding a torch. Its ruddy light gleamed on lacquer, and made gold the bronze sword-hilt jutting at his waist. As Chondos halted, the lumpy black-robed shape turned to face him.

"Patience, little King! It will not be long now." Mockery filled the inhumanly harsh hiss. "Ten days only, and you may lead your men across the Border. There is a truce now, but it will not last long. It will end with the peace talks!"

And a titter like squeaking glass scraped Chondos' nerves so that his eyes clenched shut.

"Yes, small King, the truce shall end! In the fort at Kajpor, all the Border Lords will lay aside their swords, to meet with your brother, the King. They think he is you! Will you not laugh, little King, to think of it? They will lay aside their swords, yet swords will be there!" Again that shrill laugh shivered off the walls.

"Now men of the Pure-in-Blood ride to the Kantara, to join with your brother, and to ride into Kajpor as part of his train. He will hide them in the Council Chamber, and when he calls them, they will kill. What madness, then, what folly! With Jagat and Rinmull and Hansio dead, and Istvan the Archer as well, who will be left for men to obey? Only you, small King—but there will be *two* of you!"

Kingship growled in Chondos' brain: *These are my people this thing means to kill—my kingdom.*

"Soon you will be King indeed, and all those who might oppose your reign will be slaves or food."

My people! he thought. He remembered that mockery of a coronation on the throne in this hall of the ancient Kings. *King in Rashnagar!*

Then, dimly, he remembered another throne, another coronation. A blue-robed figure on the steps of the throne, and the Hastur's mind stretching all about his own. Shimmering symbols filled his mind and spilled shouting from his mouth as kingship woke with a roar.

He felt barriers rising around his mind, as he sprang at the man with the torch. The thread that had stunned him snapped: his mind was his own again. His arm stretched out; fingers gripped smooth bronze and pulled as the man staggered back. He spun, feeling the sudden weight of steel in his hand as the blade pulled free.

Something scrabbled futilely at the walls of his mind. Torchlight flamed on falling steel. Air trilled under its edge. Rotten cloth tore; and steel sank into boneless flesh. A shrill screech echoed from the walls. He turned back, pulling his sword free, and the armoured man threw down his torch and ran into the darkness.

Chondos snatched up the fallen torch, hearing something writhing and rustling horribly in the dark. He raised the light high, and in the dim illumination saw the black robe wriggling away: yellowish slime oozed from a rent in the cloth.

He leaped forward and pressed the torch against the cloth. Threads glowed, smoke rose, but the cloth did not catch. He could feel something beating against the shell around his mind. Something cold and clammy brushed his ankle, and he jumped back with a strangled shout, his sword sweeping down to gash the black cloth again. Something white and sluglike began to crawl from the cloth. Chondos' stomach cringed, and he lifted his sword again.

He heard the scurry of feet behind him, and whirled. Clusters of eyes kindled in the torchlight, and rushed toward him. Small goblin figures waved rusted steel.

He sprang to meet them, his swinging sword planing in the air. The torch's flame singed his knuckles. His blade snicked through bone, and the tiny shapes scattered, squealing. He ran through them, toward the cold air of the doorway. Behind the goblins, men stood blocking the door; but they, too, panicked and broke as he rushed them. Then a single figure stood in his path.

Red eyes glared into his own, and his mind's shield shuddered as though from a blow. Ivory needles gleamed in a gaping mouth. Already his sword was flying with his hand, and in sudden astonishment he saw the pale face tip to one side, flip upside-down, and spin away from the swaying shoulders.

The headless body fell. Dry bones crumbled under rotting cloth. Then Chondos was jumping over the sack of ancient bones, and down steps that ran into darkness, with no notion of where to go or what to do.

Frightened horses neighed and pawed the stone at the foot of the stairs. They reared and stamped, their eyes rolling in the light of his torch. Wind wailed in the streets, plucked at the torch's flame. He stood, breathing hoarsely, hearing shouts above and feet milling near the top of the stairs. He pushed the sword through his belt, wishing he'd managed somehow to grab the scabbard, and ran toward the nearest horse.

It was a gaunt, terrified, skeletal beast, scarred and starved. It stamped and danced away, stretching the reins. He heard his own voice murmur soft words; straining leather rasped his palm as he grabbed the reins. He dodged teeth and hooves, untied the reins, and scrambled onto the beast's back. It bucked, but he held on somehow, one-handed, the torch waving above him.

Feet were pounding down the stairs. Chondos gripped the saddle tightly with his knees, and freed his sword. The horse was quieting. He cut the reins that held the other horses, and they galloped off. He followed them, letting his mount go where it would.

He laughed—and suddenly, above the hoofbeats, he was roaring out the ballad of "Pertap's Ride":

> *The night-things gathered about him,*
> *And howled and screamed on his track,*
> *But he struck with his sword and burned with his*
>   *torch,*
> *And drove the Dark Things back.*

Torch in one hand, sword in the other, Chondos let the frightened horses find a way through the tangled streets of Rashnagar.

Chapter Eighteen

The comforting dark was nearly gone.

"Is everything loaded and ready to go?" Jodos asked.

"Yes, Sire." The servant he had chosen nodded. Jodos touched the other servants, the ones he did not want, with his mind, and they filed away.

"Look at me!" Jodos said.

"Sire?" The servant blinked at him, eyes wide, then stood slack-jawed and staring while the Dead Man came up behind and placed a hand on the back of his neck.

The Spider ran down the servant's arm. When it leaped from dead hand to living neck, the corpse swayed and toppled against the victim's shoulder, knocking him staggering, and jerking his eyes free. He started to turn.

The Spider bit. A scream was choked to a rattle in the throat. Jodos caught the body as it pitched into his arms. The abandoned corpse hit the stone of the courtyard.

"Get rid of that carrion!" he snarled at Hotar, angry at the Spider's clumsiness. The servant's body struggled in his arms, and he was tempted to let it fall; but there was too much danger that the rider would be crushed. It was far too useful to risk.

There was another kind of spider, he knew, that could control living men, and he wished that Emicos had given him one of those instead. Getting rid of the bodies discarded by this one was becoming a problem.

This body would have to be the last until the Border was broken. Three of Hotar's men, in their royal livery, were carrying the old body to the wall. He hoped they would throw it far enough out that it would land in the river. If it caught on the narrow, uneven ledge of rock at the wall's bottom, the townspeople might wonder. He had crushed the courtiers' curiousity, but he could not dominate an entire city. The last corpse had been no problem: Hotar and his men had been glad to get some real food. But that would not be practical on their journey south.

He wished he could take the girl with him. He would have to rush back quickly, to make sure nothing else got to her before he did. There was something disturbing in that thought. Why should it make any difference to him? There were plenty of others. They were all

335

meat. What difference did it make whether it was her, or another woman, or even a man? The ghost of his brother's mind sniggered a reason.

He shuddered at the obscene horror of it. It was not as if he were human . . .

But you are human, the ghostly memories whispered. *Your flesh is human, born of man and woman by that ritual your masters have taught you to despise. You were not spawned in the Dark Land; you did not flee from your hungry parent through the gate held open for you that you might serve in the Bright World.*

He shut the voice away, frantically. He did not wish to hear such things.

Chondos clung tightly to his mad beast's back as a flood of horseflesh poured down the mountain, free at last from the city's angled canyons, hammering the old stone road with blood-slick hooves. Tiny twisted figures had fallen under grinding hooves, gashing the horses' legs with rusty steel.

The hot torch burned Chondos' hand; its tiny circle of light showed only the churning backs of horses. He held on, shifting it from one singed hand to the other, again and again as the torch grew shorter and the cold wind that followed them down from the heights pushed the flames down to crisp the hair on the backs of his fingers. Something that looked like a bundle of sticks was strapped to the back of one of the jolting saddles, but he could not reach it.

So far, only enemies of solid flesh had attacked them, but he watched nervously, expecting at any moment to see some of the horses around him crumble into running grey skeletons. The smell would warn the horses, but Demons could move so fast . . .

At last, grey streaks barred the black sky, hinting that somewhere beyond the Shadow a fanfare of cockerels saluted the rising Twins. It came to him, then, that there was no need for the Master to store up an army of Demons here, as he had with the lesser creatures: the Demons were no doubt busy in the north. Only when the assault on the Border was imminent would they come sailing south above the mountains, moving at that speed no bird could match.

A sad echoed moaning from the rocks greeted the grey dawn, as the creatures of the night scurried to their lairs. As the day grew greyer, the horses quieted and drifted to a slow walk. Chondos was able to manoeuvre his tired mount closer to the horse with that promising bundle behind its saddle.

Horses began stopping: his own horse stood with drooping head. He slid gratefully from the saddle. Horses danced nervously, snorting wariness, and watched him with ears laid back.

He pushed the butt of the torch into soft dust, and blew on the backs of his singed hands. The horse with the torches—he was sure that was what they were—had halted a little way off, and stood eyeing him nervously, its ears flat to its mane. Its ribs poked out its hide, and he could see the marks of both whip and claw. The poor beast had been badly treated, but it had gotten used to his smell during the long ride. He talked to it softly, and froze after each slow step. He crooned to it in a low voice, watching its ears twitch, wondering if he was walking into a kick.

It quivered when at last he touched it lightly, and he had to follow slowly when it danced away, but at last he was stroking it gently, and, what seemed a long time after, the ears were lifted free of the mane and it stood quietly enough for him to get at the saddlebags. A moment's rummaging brought a sharp gasp of relief that set the horse dancing away again, as he pulled out the crude tinderbox and fire-striker he had hoped would be there.

Now, at least, he need no longer burn his hand for fear of going fireless through the haunted hills. He had been sure the Pure-in-Blood would not travel without a source of fire!

There was food in the saddlebags, too—meat which he threw away with a little shudder, knowing all too well what the Pure-in-Blood ate—and some cakes of burnt meal, which he gobbled greedily despite their taste.

The horses began to edge closer, circling warily, with little nickering cries. Nearby, some had knocked over a clump of fungus, but it was all gone now. Each of the horses had a waterskin strapped to the saddle, but that would not last long.

They were a sorry-looking lot: bony, drooping, and covered with sores and scars. If even a few of them were sound, he could make good time by switching from one back to another—perhaps even ride all day and into the night if need be. With luck he might manage fifty miles a day, or more. But he must have at least three.

What would he do, though, when night came? He glanced away from the road, where tangled upthrust rocks hid the little stream he had followed down the mountain before. He could get there, but he could not carry the horses.

The broken towers glowed brightly in his memory, but unless he could somehow get the horses there, they were of no use. Farther down the mountain, perhaps, he would be able to ride down the slope and into the valley where the old ruins offered sanctuary. But first he must pass that planed-out section where giant creatures hunted from the sky.

He found himself looking nervously into the grey blankness overhead. He must start soon. He tried to remember how long it had taken him to scrabble down the mountainside before, but the memories of that journey were all scrambled like a nightmare; and on the road, by horseback, it would not take as long.

He kept looking up at the sky. He petted the now docile horse and pulled one of the long torches from its back. He looked at it stupidly, and then looked down at the short stub that still burned where it stood upright in the dust.

I should put it out, he thought. He stepped up to it, and stood, hesitant. With a shrug, he stretched out the new torch and let the flame play around the end until it caught.

He knocked the other torch down, and kicked dust over it to smother the flame, cursing himself for an idiot. He should put this one out too, save it for the night. He had planned to sleep in the saddle, but he could not both sleep and hold the torch! Weariness dragged at him. Under the vampires' rule, he had slept during the day, as they did. Against goblins, ghouls, or men, a sword was better than a torch; and he was not likely to meet another Demon or vampire during the day.

He looked up the road, toward the dim outlines of the looming walls of Rashnagar on the heights above. *I will come back,* he thought. *Like Pertap:*

> *If I win through to Hastur's Tower,*
> *I'll tell my tale, but will not stay.*
> *I shall ride back from Hastur's Tower,*
> *Though all the Dark Host bars the way.*

"What?" Ironfist glared at Istvan. "Reasonable precautions? Against Jagat? Man, when I stop trusting Lord Jagat, you'll find me hiding under my own bed, eating nothing except what I kill and cook with my own hands! Not trust Jagat! You must be crazy as a drunken pig!"

"I trust him," said Istvan sadly. "I do trust him! But this is duty! What kind of a commander would I be if I let my private opinion endanger my men?"

"All commanders risk their men for private opinions!" Ironfist snorted. "What do you think command *is?*" He paused, and sudden deep laughter spilled out of him like a waterfall. "But you needn't look like a puppy about to be whipped! You should see your face! You look as if you'd been courting a Kadarin girl and found yourself in bed with her duenna!"

Istvan grinned. The Twin Suns broke through a patch of swirling cloud. It had rained earlier, and the air still smelled wet. But high up, a strong wind was driving the clouds in disorder back toward the Sea of Ardren.

"You may have the right of it, after all," said Ironfist, after they had grinned at each other in silence for a moment. "Jagat can be trusted, but he's only one man. I don't suppose the Fox's generals will have forgiven you yet, and from what Lord Maldeo says, not all Jagat's vassals can be trusted. Any man could set us all at each other's throats again."

Istvan nodded. "Until I have this peace signed and sealed and in my hands, I have to keep strategic control. Once it's all settled . . ." He did not finish, but stared south, where the dark wall hung like a frozen wave.

"Once it's settled," said Ironfist, "you come see me at Ojakota and we'll drink some real wine, instead of this candy-water the Bordermen have been feeding us."

"If there's any left," Istvan said with a chuckle.

"Oh, I should be able to get just about anything I want there, now," said Ironfist. "Now that Maldeo and his men have gone off to join Jagat's patrol!"

"Yes," Istvan said, frowning. "I sent all the Seers I could spare off with him. I hope they'll be enough." He stared at the Shadow.

"Something's bothering you." Ironfist looked at him sharply from under storm-cloud brows. "More than just the business about Jagat. What's wrong?"

"Jagat's patrol," Istvan hissed through his teeth. "I should do more to help. They need every Seer they can find, but it takes more than half of mine to keep up this show."

"So that's it!" The bushy eyebrows curved. "Don't they have enough Seers of their own?"

"They may." Istvan shrugged. "I don't know. Maldeo tells me Jagat must have nearly a dozen, if you count in wizards and heralds and such. But there must be two hundred miles or more around Damenco. I don't think you could patrol a distance like that with less than twenty-five Seers—fifty, if they're ever going to sleep! And Jagat wants to patrol the other two provinces, too! So they'll need around a hundred!"

"Your thirty won't make up the difference," said Ironfist.

"They might," said Istvan, "along with the Kantaran and Mahavaran Seers." He combed his beard with angry fingers. "I sent word with Maldeo that I'd provide a night patrol for the land between Agnasta and Vajrakota. That's not much, but it's the best I can manage until after the peace talks."

"Well, if you can patrol by night," Ironfist said reassuringly, "that will be the worst part. The Dark Things aren't likely to attack by daylight."

"They've been known to," said Istvan. "And if they run into one of Jagat's patrols without a Seer, I'll have killed those men as surely as any I killed in that last fight!"

Ironfist's eyes were compassionate. "You worry too much about the men you kill," he said gently. "You should have been a scholar or something, not a soldier."

"Men I myself kill in battle, deliberately, are one thing," said Istvan. "Men I kill accidentally, by my own stupidity, are another."

Chondos still held the torch as he rode on down the mountain. Twice he caught himself drowsing off just in time to keep from dropping it. *Stupid*, he thought.

He rode the horse that had carried the torches, and the three strongest beasts were tied behind him on a long lead made from the reins of the rest.

Other horses crowded behind. He had removed their saddles—they were all badly saddled-galled—and divided the loads. He had emptied each waterskin down the throat of the horse that had carried it, and thrown most of the meal cakes into a pile for the horses to eat—only making sure that those three he actually planned to ride ate first, and got enough.

The sparse fungus beside the road, and whatever water they could find, would have to serve for now. Later, perhaps, he might be able to move off the road and follow the river downstream, sheltering at night in the broken towers. But first they must pass that place where the mountain had been planed away, and where something unthinkably large lurked in the clouds.

After he had ridden for an hour or so, the horses picked up speed. Soon they were drinking at a little stream that ran under a tiny arched bridge of crumbling stone, the delicate carvings that had once made it beautiful blurred and defaced by time. When he rode on, some of the horses stayed behind—the weakest ones, the ones nearest to foundering.

The road sank now, and steep, rugged cliffs walled away the fungus that grew on the more gradual slopes. Ahead, he could see only blank greyness.

He heard nervous snorting among the horses, and switched torch and reins to his left hand, while his right fondled the cool bronze comfort of his sword hilt. After a little, he pulled it carefully out of his belt, wishing again he'd had time to get the scabbard. He cursed quietly.

Without warning, the walls of stone vanished from beside him, and he was looking out into grey, empty gulfs of air on either side, while ahead of him the straight road sloped down. Behind, to right and left, he saw a sheer and polished wall.

He allowed himself a single glance into the depths beside him, toward the unnaturally level floor of stone that lay under misty air, and then his eyes rose to search the clouds. Then he saw it, hanging fishlike and massive over a dimly seen mountain slope to the left.

Hanging masses of tentacles searched through rifts and ravines, pulling up struggling things he could barely see. They vanished into its maw, and a faint echo of distant shrieks and roars sounded underneath the pounding of Chondos' heart. His horse balked, and danced nervously. But the thing was far away, and seemed to drift sluggishly through the air.

The fishlike shape lifted, huge fins waving gently, and bunches of tendrils dangled limply—except for one, which rose slowly with a wriggling, kicking burden. His heels hit the horse's sides, urging it out onto the narrow span of stone, dragging the three led horses behind.

The road went down at a steep angle. His memory showed it to him as it looked from below: a triangle of stone. Hesitant hooves clicked behind, as the rest of the herd milled slowly out of the cutting. The road was a good broad one indeed, but the empty vastness on each side made it seem narrow. His heart lurched in his chest. The thing over the mountain was vanishing, swimming into empty air.

Air rippled overhead. The front of the creature was swimming, endless, out of the air above, as though the miles between did not exist. Coiling tentacles dropped from the sky. He heard a horse screaming overhead. A long tendril reached for him, and his sword whistled through the air—rebounded, as though from iron. The tendril dropped around him. He thrust the torch up to meet it, and a bellow shook the sky. Flame leaped: the lean tendril glowed as fire climbed. A screaming horse fell from a lashing tentacle.

His horse jolted under him; all four horses were galloping, galloping at the edge of the gulf where the horse that had fallen lay like a squashed insect, red against the planed stone. A reddish puff of light dazzled his eyes. Thunder deafened him, and a hot wind poured over his face. He fell into the horse's mane, coughing stench from his lungs. Fire was falling like snow. He blinked at the blurred line of the road's edge, and the polished stone beyond, and his heart went falling, falling . . .

But then he saw polished stone flatten; and then grey dust with patches of barren honest earth rushed past, and the road grew less steep. It was some time before he could stop the terrified horses. Not until they began to stumble with weariness was he able to rein them in at last.

He scrambled from the saddle and led them, then, legs unsteady. He heard water gurgling ahead, and suddenly hard leather pulled through his hand, and he was sprawling on his face on gritty stone. He pushed himself up and staggered after the horses. They were drinking from a small stream that shoaled and foamed over the fragments of a broken bridge. He forced himself forward to keep the sweating beasts from drinking too much. Dead horses would not help him out of the Shadow.

Down the stream, a pale light caught his eye. He shook his head, and looked again. Soft blue light in the vague dim grey. Exhaustion tugged his eyelids and settled on his shoulders. He remembered the troll crashing down the slope, and the broken tower glowing in the night. Of course! And the day could not last much longer.

It was a struggle to get the horses away from the water, and then he had to lead them, stumbling over rocks, hoping desperately that he could get the horses through.

The stream tumbled down a little waterfall, but there was a bank he could get the horses down, and then the familiar valley opened before him. The tower's broken walls glimmered upstream from him, and he led the horses toward it, racking his brain for a way to get them inside. If he could not find one, he would likely be on foot tomorrow.

The horses' heads came up, and they nickered as they smelled the green grass growing in the tower's shattered shell. He led them around the sapphire ring, looking for a place where the wall was low enough to jump them over. Blackened blocks and splinters lay scattered: where the dark power had fallen, stones had flown flaming, meteors quenched in cold magic, but the cold death had died of their burning. Steps of starry stone against the wall made a way for him to lead the horses, and soon they were grazing happily.

He tested the edge of the old rusted sword. Black stripes streaked the sky. He heard movement in the ravine they had left. Looking up, he saw loose horses burst out of the cleft, and a few moments later several were gathered around the ruined walls, grazing on the sparser yellow grass that grew here and there among the stone fragments outside. He was glad to see that some had escaped.

Grey faded from the Shadow's roof. Broken bits of stone were stars against the earth. He found a fairly smooth piece and began to use it as a whetstone. He wondered if any of the stone's magic would rub off on the blade.

Horses splashed in the water, snorting and blowing as they drank. A sudden shrill squealing and stamping. He dodged from the hooves of one of his horses as the four milled fearfully around the ring, and leaping onto the wall he peered at the river.

Something had seized one of the horses. The rest stampeded away. In the dim light of the wall on which he stood, he saw the beast struggle as it was dragged into deep water. An indistinct shape writhed like a giant snake. A great crunching and snapping sounded, and a loud splash was followed by sudden silence, while the horses inside the tower rushed madly around and around the walls.

Far out in the midst of invisible, gurgling water, something round threw back the tower's light like a huge eye. As he stared at it, he felt pressure against his mind, and Miron's spell began to chant itself. He blinked and looked away until the mystic sphere surrounded his mind; but when he looked back, the thing was gone.

Much later in the night he was again wakened from sleep by the wild neighing of frightened horses, and jumping up, he saw them rushing past in the stone's light, and heard a troll bellow in the darkness beyond. The horses in the tower went wild.

After a moment, the giant shape came shambling clumsily into the light. It paused, red eyes blinking through the glare at Chondos and the horses, then blundered on after the others.

Istvan's sharp steel whirred through the morning, shaving sound from the air as it had for forty years, a fan of flame beneath the golden moons of dawn.

The Shadow hung in the south like a wave in the night sea ready to fall, dwarfing the tiny towers that glowed like stars at its base. Between the long shreds of cloud that fled before the raging south wind, a few bright stars and tiny moons still burned through the liquid blue sky; in the ivory pallor that washed the east, moons hung gilded by the hidden Twins' light.

Istvan's feet moved rapidly in an ancient pattern, while his Hastur-blade, glowing with need-fire, wove patterns of light all about him.

Little more than half his strength was here now, bustling into armour for the ride to Kajpor and the other castles that Jagat had granted them by the terms of the truce. Ironfist and his men had marched for Ojakota the day before, along with several companies bound for Manjipor. The Orissians had started for home.

But Jagat's army, and Hansio's, would soon be dispersed all along the Border. After the peace, Istvan's men, too, could spread out to help with the patrol.

Suppose the Dark Things attack before then? he wondered. *Then, he told himself, we will act as a reserve to come to their aid.* That was fine, if the Border was attacked within a day's march, but . . .

Strange, he thought, how the horse of Time that seemed to move so fast as it bore his youth away from him, should yet walk so slowly toward the meeting at Kajpor.

As the rising Twins made trailing peacock plumes from the clouds, his blade slipped softly back into its scabbard.

In a delirium of fear, Jodos rode south with Shachio through hateful sunlight. Hotar and his men grumbled behind, while the Spider hid under the hat on its victim's head.

All things conspired against him now. Every pace of his horse brought him closer to the Blue-robes' dreaded towers, and if their vigilance fell upon him, he would be destroyed. But the Master would destroy him no less certainly.

He *must* win out! He would eat them all yet! If this truce held, and the plan failed, the Master would make him suffer forever. But the ghost of his brother's memory whispered in his mind: *You cannot suffer forever.*

Strange thoughts rose out of Chondos' stolen mind, disturbing throughts that challenged everything Jodos had ever known. The Master could not make him suffer forever, any more than Jodos could make the girl waiting for him in Tarencia suffer forever. Sooner or later, the frail flesh would die. And what would become of him then? Would he truly be part of whatever ate him? Or was that a lie?

He did not want to think about that. But he found his mind looking inside himself for some trace of all the other lives he had eaten: women, men, children, goblins, lizards, insects, part of a ghoul . . .

He tried to turn his mind away from these frightening thoughts, think instead about the woman waiting for him. He should have eaten her before he left, but there had been so little time. And he wanted to eat her slowly and carefully, savouring each shred of flesh, each scream, each moment of pain. But then she would be gone—and again he was searching his mind for the other women he had eaten, trying to find some part of them alive in him.

Vaguely, then, the dream came to him, the recurrent dream of the huge woman whose giant breast he had drunk from. Something—not blood—something sweeter. His brother's mind told him what it was, and his stomach twisted in disgust.

He had to get back to her, he thought in sudden panic. He had spawned in her flesh. If something else got to her before he did, it would be *his* flesh they were eating! They would have power over him. Or, worse still, she might escape, and the creature inside her, his own flesh, break free to grow to hunt for him.

His brother's ghost laughed weirdly in his brain. Human spawn did not hunt their parents, he remembered. And his spawn would be human. As he was human.

Eating and spawning are all mixed in your mind, said his brother's laughing ghost. Were not eating and spawning the same? He wondered. When the Great Ones had eaten, they would spawn; and then they would hunt and eat their spawn.

But you are not of the Great Ones, said Chondos' ghost.

Jodos shuddered. He would die! He was human, and that was what happened to humans. But the Great Ones would save him!

Emicos or old Isuri or some other Blood Drinker would drain his blood, and then he would rise and . . .

But would it be he that rose? Or something else wearing his body, as the Spider hiding under the hat beside him wore the bodies of its victims?

Chondos had to face the hard decision: to make his way back to the road, or try to follow the stream down the mountain.

The ravine would be far safer, he thought, remembering his earlier escape. It would be hard to get the horses down, though; it would take more time. And his people were in danger. If he came too late . . .

He got the horses back to the road, somehow, and pushed on, changing mounts often to avoid wearing them out.

He had ridden for a few hours when he saw, far, far below, a vast table of dim blue-shadowed land that rose to meet a slanting grey roof, which ended in a sunlit curtain of glowing mist.

Tears blinded his eyes even as his vision soared joyfully across the stretch of destroyed land to the bright barricade. His heel prodded the horse forward. He wanted to laugh, to shout. After a moment he found himself singing.

> *The Darkness thinned before his eyes,*
> *The mirk began to turn to grey,*
> *And he saw the fire of Hastur's Tower*
> *Burn brightly under the dawning day.*

The road curved away to the left, a broad ledge above emptiness.

> *Ah, glad indeed was bold Pertap*
> *To see the light of day . . .*

The lead rope jerked in his hand. A led horse neighed, the rope plunging as it tossed its head. The horse between Chondos' knees swayed, as it, too, raised its head and nickered. On the road behind, another neigh answered, and he heard the hard, quick rapping of horn on stone. He turned in his saddle as the galloping grew loud.

Four horses burst from the cutting. Riders on their backs waved rust-red swords. He dropped the lead rope, casting the led horses loose; slapping the nearest hard on the flank. Driving heels bounced from ribs; shouting tore his throat.

Loud behind, pounding hooves gained on him. He let his running mount pick its own way, turning his mind to the danger over his shoulder. He stood in his stirrups, and whirled his torch until it flared in air. They closed quickly, and he saw their leader prod his beast savagely with his sword. Blood dripped from its hindquarters.

Chondos hurled the torch into the man's face. The man flinched and shrieked; the horse reared, backed, and then it was twisting in the air beside the ledge. It vanished. Rider's scream and horse's mingled in a fading wail. Chondos cursed. He'd not meant the horse to die. Bronze was cold against Chondos' palm as he eased the naked curve of steel through his belt. Hoofbeats hammered at his ears.

The others had paused as their leader went over, but they were coming again, gaining swiftly. The sword's curved weight dangled oddly, not like the straight blades he knew, in the guard across his back.

A frantic horse's plunging head drew even with his elbow. A curved blade whirled. His arm jerked steel into its path, and he felt the hilt kick in his hand. A cloud of rust sprang from the echoing metal. He saw his enemy's eyes widen.

Once more the dull brown blade swung through sunless air. His muscles surged, and again steel belled—but this time a shift of his arm beat the other blade aside, his hand leaping through a shower of cool brown powder. The rust of his point was stained with ruby as it sliced the pulsing throat.

But the ledge widened, and the others closed in, their swords driving at his back like angry wings. His aching wrist lashed his blade in a wild dance, while gritty clouds of rust puffed from belling steel. Awkward, ill-timed cuts bounced from the triangle of his guard. But there were two of them, and his arm was tiring.

He leaned back against the reins, steel clashing and quivering above his ear, and wheeled his blade high to the right. The other horse blundered past as his blade sheared through the spine beneath the rider's skull.

Even as Chondos turned, the other sword was shrilling at his face, but his own flying steel clanged it back and pierced the throat, pushing the man choking over his horse's tail.

The riderless horse galloped on. Chondos drew a deep breath and looked down at the dying man. His horse danced and pawed the ground, skittish from the scent of blood. The choking stopped, the bloody throat was still. He started to ride on, then saw the scabbard in the dead man's belt. Calming his horse, he dismounted and held the beast's head until it quieted enough for him to stoop and slide the belt from the body.

The mist-curtain marking the Border was dimmer. He stared across the barren lands below. He could see the tangled foothills, and then the long flat of the plain. Dimly, he made out a winding line that must be the river he had followed down. Was it the Yukota?

It must be, if the place where he had been captured was indeed storied Kudrapor; and if he kept on, he would come out in the Kantara, beside Hastur's Tower.

He would ride to the tower, and tell them of the danger:

He rode into the Twin Suns' light,
And rode up to the tower's door,
And shouted loud at Hastur's gate:
"Men still fight on in Kudrapor!"

And that would be all that was needed: the Hasturs would deal
with his Demon brother, and all the rest—if he was in time.

Need-fire smote the hosts of night,
The Dark Things fled with wails of pain.
Ah, glad indeed was bold Pertap
To see the light of day again!

Chapter Nineteen

The fifth day after the battle, Istvan rode east under a sky scrubbed clean of clouds by a fierce south wind. Mountain-chilled air out of the Shadow made the heat almost bearable; Istvan shivered as he rode up dripping from the river into the dappled, green-gold shade of a roof of glowing leaves.

All across the wastelands of Manjipé, Arjun DiFlacca, at Istvan's side, had drowned the birdless silence by whistling "The Ballad of Pertap's Ride." He was going home, cheerfully proud of his deeds, to see to his mother and his lands, and to gather his men for the Border Patrol.

The boy's whistling stopped as birds called among the trees. He turned and smiled at Istvan, but said nothing. Istvan was glad: he'd had more than he wanted of Arjun's pompous chatter. Still, he was a good boy, and growing up to be a fine man. Lucarrho would have been proud of his son. The forest blurred. Istvan blinked wet lashes angrily. How many years now, since Rafayel died?

Tree trunks off the road shifted as Istvan rode by, red and grey, brown and black, a moving maze of pillars almost as bewildering as the twisting channels of Istvan's thoughts.

Horses' hooves thumped thick layers of leaves: the wind was a chorus of whispers in the branches overhead. A jay flashed bright feathers above him, screaming the eternal soldier's question: *Why? Why? Why?*

Dying young soldiers had often asked him that, and others trapped in their grief for the dead. He had been good at coming up with shallow but soothing answers. There was always some excuse for war.

But that was not what they were really asking, he thought: not *What are we dying for?* or even *Why do men fight?* No, it was a deeper question than that, the riddle of human life: *Why must men die?*

That was the Shadow's most terrible weapon. Sorcerers born as mortal men had menaced the world for centuries: there were vampires as old as Kandol Hastur-Lord. A man could not help wondering if death were truly preferable to the half-life of the vampire. War, death, old age, fear, evil, loss . . .

Kadarin philosophers debated the meaning of the Dark Things.

Some said that they, too, were but manifestations of the One Soul; others held that that other universe from which they came had a different soul—an evil soul.

He shook his head irritably. All this brought him no nearer to an understanding of life and death, of fear and loss.

Loss . . . How many years now? Seven? Eight? And where— *what* was Rafayel now? The body, yes, he knew about that; but was there more, and where was it? Hovering somewhere, waiting to be born, or . . . ?

Martos?

No, no, that was nonsense. Martos must have been ten or twelve when Rafayel died. He could not be Rafayel reborn. Unless that theory was right—that time did not matter . . .

It was more as though in Martos he saw his own younger self. Perhaps, if indeed the One Soul was free of time, Martos was himself in another life. Perhaps he might come back as Martos when he died, or might himself be Martos reborn—

"Commander DiVega!" Arjun DiFlacca's voice broke into Istvan's thoughts. "Do you turn off here, too, Lord? I thought you were going to—"

Istvan came to himself with a start. He'd been about to follow the young Borderman blindly down the road that led to Arjun's own lands. What was wrong with him? Daydreaming like some stupid poet!

"This way, Lord." The Seer pressed forward from where he had ridden among the men, and Istvan let him take the lead.

Arjun DiFlacca rode off down the other road, back to home and kin; his young voice called a cheery farewell as he vanished among the trees. But Istvan's party followed the Seer up a branching road that swept north of Ojaini, the road on which they could expect to meet the King.

Branches groaned as the wind rubbed them together. Leaves shook wildly as a squirrel leaped between two trees. A pheasant rose from bushes by the road with a whirring of stubby wings.

"Lord Istvan," said the Seer. "A message from the north. One of the Seers with Prince Phillipos' army says that the Prince has brought Ipazema's army to battle along the River Opontis."

"Who is most likely to win?" asked Istvan.

"No one can say yet, Lord. Ipazema's army is larger, but Prince Phillipos probably has more experienced veterans with him. But the lines are still forming." He closed his eyes for a moment, looking through the far-off eyes of another man. "And *I* would say, Lord, that the Prince has the better position, tactically."

"Good!" said Istvan. "I wish I could be there! But let me know when things start to happen. Any word from Lord Shachio? Can you tell how far away we are?''

The Seer closed his eyes, returning to trance. "Not far now, Lord," he said, opening his eyes. "Perhaps an hour's ride. I am concerned for Lord Shachio. I fear he is a very sick man. He should not have come with the King.''

"What's wrong with him?"

"Hard to say—his age, I suppose." The Seer shrugged. "It has been a long ride from Tarencia, but for some time now we have all noticed some strain, or—it is hard to explain, Lord. Looking through Shachio's mind is like looking through twisted glass. He does not seem completely aware of the things around him. He is like a man in a fever.''

Istvan frowned. "Could you not persuade him to let some younger man—''

"He is a very stubborn man, Lord, and very proud. And it is true that the other royal Seers have either gone to war with Prince Phillipos or have joined Lord Jagat's Border Patrol. We tried to get one of the guild Seers to offer to serve the King—but Lord Shachio insisted that he had served the kingdom all his life and would not leave his post now.''

"Yes." Istvan smiled. "That sounds like Shachio. They used to say he would rather use his head to knock a hole in a wall than to find the way around.''

The Seer chuckled, then held up his hand and closed his eyes. His face relaxed in trance. "The battle has begun." His voice was toneless, shrill. "Ipazema's horsemen are moving out, circling to attack the flanks. The Prince's men stand fast behind their shield-wall, defending the horsemen behind them, but some far-shot arrows must have gone clean over, for there is a horse kicking and screaming in—''

A gurgle like a death-rattle choked the words in his throat. Istvan saw glassy eyes fly open, staring wildly.

"Evil!" croaked the Seer, pulling up his horse. "Evil—something—''

"Where is it? What's wrong?" Istvan barked. His Hastur-blade flashed free. The Seer shook his head, then closed his eyes. All had halted: men waiting behind sucked breath.

After a few moments of tense silence the Seer's eyes blinked open. "It's gone now. I don't think it was anywhere near. Every Seer watching felt it—even Lord Shachio.''

"What?" asked Istvan, sharply. "What happened?"

"Just for a moment it was as though—something—something evil—'' The Seer shivered, then straightened. "One of the Dark Things was looking through me—through my mind—through all our minds, looking at the battle." He shivered again. "I think the—the pain and fear must have drawn it. I can't find it now. None of us can." He straightened. "Lord Shachio and the King are almost here now—right around that bend, ahead."

Istvan looked ahead, where the road wound out of sight among the trees. He glimpsed vague shapes moving beyond the veiling green.

"There they are now! See?" The Seer pointed. A horse trotted into sight: a man on its back gripped a staff from which the wild wind stretched out rippling night-blue cloth, where a silver hand held a golden crown.

Branches shrieked as the wind tossed the forest roof, rubbing the woven branches together so they groaned like wounded men. Istvan patted his startled mare. Gravel rolled under her hooves as she danced nervously. He calmed her, and when he looked up, the royal party was drawing rein nearby. Pale, hawkfaced men in royal livery surrounded Lord Shachio and the King; Lord Shachio did indeed look thin and pale.

"We expected you earlier, Lord Istvan," said the King, coldly. "Of course, a man of your advanced years cannot be expected to move quickly, but still . . ."

Istvan fought to hold back the angry answer that struggled on his tongue.

"The blame is mine, Lord King," the Seer cut in smoothly, while Istvan was still groping for some gentle answer. "Lord DiVega is still vigorous for a man of his years, but your Seer, Lord Shachio, is not, I fear. His weakness has made it difficult for me to locate you at all in this wilderness. He is a very sick man."

There was a whisper of protest from Shachio.

"Yes, he is," said the King, "and I should not have brought him on such a journey; but he insisted. As you can see, it has been too hard on him. He should be taken to Ojaini and put to bed under a Healer's care, rather than ride any farther. Will you take him there?"

"I?" The Seer blinked at the King.

"Will you accompany him?"

"I—it would be best, Lord King, for me to replace him, and some of your soldiers to escort him—"

"There should be a Healer to ride with him," said the King. "But I have none with me. But members of your order are also trained in these arts, are you not?"

"Well . . ." The Seer hesitated. "The preliminary training is the same for both, and the rudiments of the Healer's art are a part of our training, but—"

"Then do as I bid you!" snapped the King. "It is an order!"

Then, as the Seer still hesitated, he added, "I have been on the road for five days, and no news has reached me that could not have waited a few hours. So I do not think it likely that it will matter if Lord Istvan and I ride Seerless to Kajpor."

"But, Lord," said the Seer, still hesitant.

Then Lord Shachio ended the argument. Swaying in the saddle, he pitched forward, into his horse's mane.

"*Now* will you obey?" snarled the King, as the Seer rushed to the older man's aid. And Istvan, looking up as the King spoke, was startled by a cruel grin of triumph on the boy's face. The anger that had almost cooled flared up again, but then the King spoke.

"My Lord DiVega, will you send some of your escort to accompany these men to Ojaini?"

The names of his dead tolled in Martos' mind: Styllis, Etharthos, Darios, Rinaldo, Amando, Evarin, and more—how many more of the young men who had followed him south out of the bright dreams of their youth, to hallow the Borderers' fields with their ashes? All those bright young dreams, those bright young lives, ashes!

For days, rumbling lines of wagons had carried precious wood from the Kantara, and bales of straw and reeds. Now, drenched with oil, the pyres were ready, and in the early dawn, the wagons had creaked away to Vajrakota Tower, and returned plied high with the bodies of the dead.

Jagat set the torch to Hansio's pyre with his own hand. As the wood flamed, Jagat's deep voice boomed: "Bless us, O Fire Immortal!"

And from all the gathered army, voices echoed: *"Bless us, O Fire Immortal!"* Lines of torchbearers ran down the long avenues between the rows of pyres, setting them alight. Mingled voices rose in solemn chant:

> *Man is but a vessel*
> *In which Immortal Fire burns.*
> *Man is but a channel*
> *In which Immortal Water runs.*
> *Man is but a hollow*
> *In which Immortal Wind breathes.*
> *But his flesh is a part of the Earth.*

Flames were edged with gold; wood and fat crackled: thick black smoke rolled before the riotous wind. Martos turned his head away, sickened, and thought of marble tombs in Kadar. But you could not bury a man along the Border: bodies would not stay in the ground. If the corpse did not rise to hunt for the blood of its kin, ghouls would dig it out.

> *Earth shall eat*
> *Of the Seed of Man;*
> *And Men shall drink Her milk.*

He remembered Eldir's famous line: *Death is kind to the man who meets him serving an honourable cause.* He tried to find comfort in that. But then Armando's dead face rose in his mind, with bone splinters leering from the red gulf between his two blue eyes. There seemed scant kindness in that horror.

"Earth must be fed!" the mingled voices sang. Thick smoke rolled north. Heat burst from flaring flame. Martos felt tears and sweat drying on his crisp face.

> *For all food comes*
> *From the Breasts of the Earth.*

Ashes, he thought, ashes for the Borderers' fields. And his dreams, too, were ashes, and his burned bones would be food for the land.

> *Grain sprouts from*
> *The Breasts of the Earth*
> *To nourish the shape of man.*

Married to a woman of the land, now he would be part of the land. Istvan DiVega would ride back to the wide world, but he would be buried here, in this little Border kingdom no one had ever heard of. He would not ride home in glory, a hero from the wars, and follow Birthran as Master of the School of Three Swords. He would live out his life at the edge of the human world, tied to a plot of barren land which he must fertilise with his own flesh and blood and bones, building up soil from naked rock and leaving his ashes when he died.

> *Mother Earth rises, takes on shape*
> *To walk in the shape of man.*
> *But man is a part of the Earth.*
> *All must go back to the Earth.*
> *Now for a time,*
> *Mother Earth has walked*
> *Among us in the shapes of these men.*

But still—land! His father had been a younger son, as Martos had been, always to live on other's bounty, on other's land. Here there was land.

> *For this brief time,*
> *Mother Earth has walked,*
> *Called by the names of these men!*

But such land! Miles of grey dust, to be cleansed and reclaimed and made sacred with the ashes of your bones.

> *Mother! Earth Mother!*
> *You who walk in our shapes!*
> *We have loved you by the names*
> *Of these men!*

Land for his children? Dust and ashes!
One voice chanted: *"The warmth of life to the Fire!"*
"And the Soul returns to the Womb!" answered the others.
"The Blood of life turns to rain!" a voice called.
"And the Soul returns to the Womb!" chanted the chorus.
"The Breath of Life to the Winds!" a voice cried.
"And the Soul returns to the Womb!"
"The bones into Mother Earth!"
"And Her child returns to her womb!"

Voices soared in chorus as the black smoke rolled. All the rows of pyres were alight, and now flames filled the spaces between them, making a single tremendous bonfire in which friend and foe, Borderman and mercenary, were one.

> *Earth is our Mother!*
> *Earth is our Bride!*
> *Hollow, she awaits sweet seed!*
> *For Earth must eat the seed of man*
> *And man must drink Her milk.*
> *All life flows from Her breasts,*
> *The breasts of the Warrior's Bride.*

Twin Suns blurred in a splash of silver high in the slatey sky. Icy wind ripped at Chondos' spine. The deep river's gorge gashed the lifeless plain. He seemed to hear the wind ironically whistling the tune he had sung down the mountain, "The Ballad of Pertap's Ride."

> *The men that sleep in Kudrapor*
> *Must sleep with weapons in their hands . . .*

Kudrapor stood below him now, the stubby brown tower rearing defiant between blood-red clay banks against the prevailing grey.

Sleep with weapons in their hands, the mocking wind seemed to mutter in his soul. Yes, if the bones of their hands were still together, it was not unlikely they yet lay folded around the hilts of ancient swords. If the weapons had not been taken from them in the long centuries . . .

He thought of the rusted blades the goblins bore, and then with a sudden prickle of wonder looked down at the bronze hilt jutting from his belt. It might even be Pertap's sword!

But no. His lips remembered and shaped the song, and hurled it out across the fungi-dotted plain:

> *Ye sons of Hastur, aid us now!*
> *Take up your power and follow me!*
> *I must ride back to Kudrapor,*
> *The fate of my comrades to see.*

Hastur came in a flash of light:
He bore a bright sword in his hand.
"Now take this sword, Pertap, and ride.
No night-thing can against it stand."

No doubt *that* sword yet lay with Pertap's bones. No night-thing would dare touch blade or hilt; and most likely, Pertap's bones lay still intact, untouched, in the mouldering halls below. He straightened, and his fist clenched on the hilt at his side. Pertap's sword still lay there in the halls below!

It was madness: he knew Dark Things laired in Kudrapor—goblins at least. And yet, Pertap's own sword!

Our Power shall ride within the blade,
And its need-fire light your way . . .

He looked up quickly at the silver veil of the suns. It was as bright as a hazy day, outside the Shadow. The Dark Things were no doubt huddled in the ruins and tunnels, hiding from the sunlight that might break through the haze.

He urged his horse along the gorge's edge, leading the other reluctant beasts behind him, looking for a way down. Before long, he found a ramp of washed-down clay, still slippery from the rains. The red-walled gulch at the bottom looked familiar: perhaps it was the same one in which he had been captured by the goblins. He saw scattered bones in the mud, and wondered if they belonged to the goblins he had killed.

As he drew near the gully mouth, he slid from the back of his mount and led all three horses. The reins chafed his hands as they balked, nostrils quivering. He thought briefly of the other horses, left wandering in the mountains, and hoped their instincts would lead them out safely. In the last few days, he had caught distant glimpses of lonely horses: one pursued by a hunting ghoul.

Ahead he saw massive brown walls. Centuries had carried away many slates from the black, conical roof, but the stones of the walls were still strong. But without the veiling rain, small signs of decay stood out clearly. At the end of the long bridge, the gateless door gaped like a greedy mouth. Scraps of rust were remnants of a long-vanished portal.

He stared into the darkness beyond. Whatever safety the brightness might give him here, it would be no help inside those walls. He would be inside a lair of the Dark Things, armed with nothing but plain steel.

Plain steel and a torch, he corrected himself. But that was still madness. Fire could protect him against most of the night-things, even vampires or lesser Demons. But neither trolls nor goblins feared fire; ghouls could overcome their fear, and the greater Demons could quench flame. He did not know what he might encounter in the ruins; but then he did not know what he might encounter in the miles ahead.

Old tales said that if the holder of a Hastur-blade called upon Hastur's name, the Hastur-kin would hear him and come to his aid. It might be only a story. But if it were true, then the Hasturs, hearing their names called out of the Shadow, would have at least that much warning. Then, even if he died, the land would be saved.

If the land was saved, it would not matter if he died. What was it that the Bordermen said? *Death is the Bride of the Warrior*. Sometimes they said "Earth" instead of "Death."

Earth is the King's Bride as much as the Warrior's, he thought.

It was his land and his people: if he died to save them, he would have earned his crown. Even if that old story was not true, he would have a far better chance of reaching the towers armed with a Hastur-blade than he would with fire and plain steel.

> *The Silver Sword broke at the hilts;*
> *The Torch burned down to his hand . . .*

This sword was not even silver.

A moaning sounded that was not the wind. His arm was nearly pulled from its socket as the horses backed away, dragging the harsh leather reins against his palm.

Ye Sons of Hastur, aid us now! The moaning rose and fell eerily in the distance. He remembered the goblins talking beside the bridge. What had they feared so? Whatever it was, it was ahead of him. He would have to face it soon.

Better to face it with Pertap's sword in hand.

> *You shall bear our Light to Kudrapor:*
> *The Dark Things shall flee in dismay.*

Yet the sword had not saved Pertap at the last. The doorless mouth of Kudrapor leered like an empty skull. If he lost the horses while he hunted for the sword, he would never reach the Border in time. What had the Master said? *Ten days, no more!* Five days were gone, but anything might wait in the unknown between him and the Border.

There was no other course. The Hasturs must be warned before his brother loosed his assassins on the Border Lords. His life did not matter: a King may always die, but the land must live. The land was all.

"Wait a moment, Lord Istvan," said the King's soft voice. "One member of my party has fallen behind, and must catch up with us." Istvan blinked about him. Seven guards, Shachio had said. "My body-servant," said the King. "His horse was—limping, with a stone in its shoe. He had to clean the hoof, and rest the horse."

A body-servant? That explained it: no one ever counted servants.

The two Seers and a few of Istvan's men had ridden off to Ojaini, Lord Shachio protesting. Istvan thought of the Red Seer he remembered from his youth. *Go home, Lord Shachio, and stare into the fire!* the King had said, cruelly, Istvan thought.

The wind rolled the forest roof in great waves. Istvan had thought his horse at last used to the booming of the wind and the harsh groans it forced from the branches, but as a man on horseback came down the road behind, the mare threw up her head with an explosive snort, and bucked. All the horses were plunging, and Istvan had no time for more than a glance at the pallid man in servant's livery who joined them. The horses were still uneasy as they took the path to the ford.

Seven men in Border dress waited on the road. Istvan's hand dropped to his sword-hilt, but the King's soft voice spoke behind him.

"These are also my men, Lord Istvan." He laughed. "Did you think I had no agents in my own kingdom? I am not so young, nor so foolish, as you think! I had instructed them to meet me here: they are old in my service, and served me long before my father died. Wait you here while I meet them."

His horse surged past. From the rear, the pale servant suddenly urged his horse in a wide circle past Istvan, as though to keep as far away as possible. The horses were still nervous, frightened by the constant roaring rustle of wind in the leaves, and now once again Istvan found himself fighting to keep his mare under control, while behind him all the horses pranced and reared. The banner-bearer's horse bounded away, the wide blue cloth spreading to nearly hide the servant from Istvan's view.

After a moment, Istvan got his horse quieted, even though the branches were still creaking and screaming overhead. The King had by that time reached the Bordermen, with body-servant and banner-bearer close behind.

Istvan patted the mare's shoulder, and realised that he felt tired. *Tired and old,* he thought. Perhaps he should give it all up and go home to stare into the fire, as Chondos had advised Lord Shachio. Stare into the fire and watch his body run down.

There was something odd about these Bordermen, but he could not quite think what it was. They had gathered their horses in a circle around the King, and their voices were a faint murmur under the surf of leaves.

An odd phrase caught his ear: "Pure in blood . . ." Now what was that about? He found himself listening, but only a word here and there rose through the gruff tumult of windy leaves.

". . . escaped . . ." he heard, and after a moment of low-voiced droning, ". . . Master . . ." Scraping branches screeched and

hooted, setting his spooked horse prancing. Then the wind calmed
enough for him to make out ". . . crawled away . . ." and ". . .
wounded . . ." before the wind swelled up again. As he tried to
make these few words fit some pattern, indignation stormed inside
him. Why had the King told him to keep away? Was it not his duty
to know what went on in this war? Or had that smug, callow brat
decided he was too old to be trusted?

Suddenly he was disgusted with himself: spying on words not
meant for his ears! If it were important, surely, the King would call
him over.

Was this how it started? Spying, spreading his ears for news, until
he turned into a garrulous old good-for-nothing, always prying and
boasting about his youth? He shook his head angrily and turned
away, trying not to listen.

"Riding for the Border . . ." reached his ears, then a sharp hiss.
The voices sank.

When he looked up again, they were turning, starting to look
back. The King looked smug, and Istvan fought his anger. Let the
fool keep his little secrets! But he could not help thinking of Aimon
DiBraise and Almos DiCassio and all the other good men who had
died so that this—this ill-raised, evil-tongued child could sit on the
throne. And all because of the promise he had been foolish enough
to give a dying man!

He shook his head, wondering again if he was on the wrong side.
And yet, if this kingdom was to be preserved, if it was not to fall
apart into the little principalities that would be easy prey for the
Dark Things, what other choice was there? Either Jagat or Prince
Phillipos would make a better King—even Hansio might have. But
none of them would have been able to keep the kingdom united.
And would this fool be able to keep it united? The thought was
agony.

The King rode up, the Bordermen clumped behind his banner.

"They will ride with us," he said, jerking his thumb back over
his shoulder. Istvan nodded.

"Remember that they must lay aside their war-gear at Kajpor,"
said Istvan, casually running his eye over the oddly mismatched
armour. Suddenly he realised that that was what had struck him
about them. Each Border province had a distinct style for their
homemade leather armour, though it was hard for a foreigner to
learn to recognise them; but these men jumbled all three styles
together: the man in the lead wore a brightly lacquered scarlet
helmet of Mahavaran make, above a plain brown Manjipéan breastplate, and shoulder-pieces that could only have come from the
Kantara, with plaques of bundled wood bound and lacquered where

men of the other provinces would have used bone. And they seemed strangely pale for Bordermen.

The screeching of wind-scraped branches became too much for his already skittish mare, and she began to buck and thrash as Chondos and his pale servant rode past; Istvan had to force her head in against her knee to keep her from bolting.

The banner-bearer had drawn rein and turned his horse at the head of the column: the Bordermen lined up respectfully at the side of the road, waiting for the column to pass. Istvan heard the King's soft, mocking voice behind him.

"Well, old man, as soon as you have remembered how to ride a horse again, we will be ready to go. We have a long ride ahead."

Age again! Didn't Chondos ever talk about anything else? The stupid mockery stung him. He fought back an angry reply, and loosened up on the reins. The horse bounded forward. He fought to keep her going in the right direction, and had to pull her up sharply a few times, but she was beginning to calm, although the wind-lashed branches were still swashing wildly overhead. The Bordermen fell in behind as the column passed.

Once they left the wildly tossing, creaking trees behind, he had expected the horses would quiet down. But even after they had crossed the river and were riding across bleak plains where the ear-shattering wind could only breathe hoarsely to cover the deathly silence while stinging them with sand, the horses still gave trouble, as though some fearful thing rode behind them.

Chondos walked into the mouth of Kudrapor, the soft shuffle of his feet striking hollow echoes from the stone. Heaped debris littered the floor. His toe struck something hard, and a skull rolled clattering away from his feet. He heard the river's swift currents gnaw stone beneath him. A distant wailing rose against the wind.

Torchlight found old walls, lost them again as the darkness danced. Again they flashed forth, and the etched shape of an arch yawned and faded. He stumbled toward it.

He thought he heard a rustle overhead, and quickly looked up. Thin grey arrow-slits shone through the gloom beneath the roof: black stubs of broken beams protruded where an upper floor had been. *Echoes*, he thought. The place was like a bell. No matter how softly he put down his feet, echoes whispered along the walls; and every few steps, he kicked something he had not seen—powdery wood, or bone, or rusted metal—to set the echoes clacking.

He had tied a jagged piece of stone from one of the broken towers to his sword-guard with a thong. Its dim need-fire was like a faint star. He had loaded his sleeves with stones from the tower.

Again, that distant wailing. Or could it be, he wondered, wind firing the arrow-slits? So strong a wind must surely make some noise. He hesitated at the arch. The patch of stone ruddied by the torchlight seemed very small. He muttered Hastur's spell, and felt comforting armour close around his mind.

He pushed his torch through the door. A spiderweb flared at the touch of the flame. He glimpsed a tiny, whitish, running dot, and thrust his torch at it instinctively. It shrivelled, flared, vanished.

Drawing a deep breath of foul-smelling air, he stepped through the door. The echoes here seemed deadened. Looking up, he saw the black beams of an unfallen floor. Less of the outside air reached into this inner part of the keep, and more of the ancient wood had survived. How long had it been? Three hundred years? Four hundred?

But where was the flame of Pertap's sword? He held the torch away behind him while he peered through the darkness for some hint of need-fire. Pertap's blade should light up all around it like the sun.

> *He turned his good steed round about:*
> *Across the Border he did ride,*
> *And need-fire glistered all around*
> *And split the dark on every side . . .*

—but that had been the Hasturs, hurling their combined power into the blade.

> *The Shadow split before his sword:*
> *The Power of Hastur he bore.*

Now the sword of Pertap would be but little brighter than the stone fastened to his sword guard.

Dim light filtered through a farther door. He made his way toward it, his heart lifting. He plunged his torch through spiderwebs and bounded into the room beyond, looking about eagerly for the source of the light.

But it was not Pertap's sword he saw, but the grey of tall slitted windows, and the wide mouth of an open gate, with a glimpse of swirling, foaming water beyond.

He ground his teeth together, and his shoulders slumped. He remembered the debate between Emicos and Vidraj: *Old Pertap went first, didn't he?* The men of Kudrapor had not died fighting, most of them. They had killed themselves to keep the vampires from claiming them.

His eyes sought and found a stair that led up to a second story: no doubt where they made their final stand. He dreaded the search of that unlit floor.

He stiffened. It was not unlit. A faint radiance, more like starlight than sunlight, fell down the stairs. He rushed toward it, ignoring the things that rolled and clattered under his feet, the rising tide of echoes and sounds. A horse squealed outside the tower. He halted.

He heard wild neighing and the plashing of hooves in mud. His fingers squeezed his sword-hilt.

Jodos was furious and frightened. The Spider had almost destroyed everything, and brought death and ruin on them all, when it had looked through his mind into Shachio's. Now every Seer in the kingdom was aware that something dangerous was abroad. And what of the Blue-robes? Had one of *them* been watching? Were they now searching for the Spider? For him?

He took sardonic pleasure in ordering the Dead Man to perform tasks in keeping with its servant role that would bring it close to the blazing need-fire in DiVega's scabbard. He savoured the Spider's agony as it cringed on its victim's body.

Sprouting green blades defiled the flat land west of the river. Only here and there were patches of clean dust, but the glaring light from the sky ruined even that. There had been one good thing about the disgusting thickness of life in the forest: the Suns had been hidden most of the time.

Someday he—or that which ate him—would see those lights put out, when the Dark Lords came from Beyond the World, bursting the Barrier, to blot out the hideous blue sky, and eat both world and Suns. And then on and on, world after world, universe after universe, until all was gone, and they could settle down to eat each other, until at last only the Survivor remained, spawning and eating endlessly in a black infinity of universes.

That would be far in the future. Long before then, he would see this green destroyed, when the Great Ones' spawn came ravening from the Shadow like black wildfire, blasting grass and soil into good grey dust. Then he would return in triumph to the royal city, to eat his spawn and the woman who held it.

"There is Kajpor ahead, Lord King," DiVega said, pointing. Black stone towers rose from the green. Smaller shapes clustered about it, mere dots at this distance. "It won't be long now. An hour's ride, perhaps, or a little more."

"Good," Jodos said solicitously. "This ride must be hard on you. You will be glad to rest, I am sure." Through the clamour of the sword he could sense DiVega's irritation. When DiVega had turned away, he bared his teeth at the Seynyorean's back. The burning sword made his head ache, but DiVega would have to lay it aside in the Council Chamber. DiVega's mind would be in his power, then, and he would make him suffer. He would hold DiVega frozen with his mind, make him watch the slaughter of the Bordermen, and then let the Pure-in-Blood carve him up and eat him, slowly. But there was little of the expected pleasure in the idea. None of the thrill that he experienced in torturing the woman, for instance.

Again his brother's ghostly mind murmured obscenities, and he shuddered. It could not be true! It had nothing to do with the horrible ritual by which humans spawned, nor with the way the spawn fed.

He remembered again the dream of the giant woman, the liquid he had drunk from her breasts, and the emotion he felt when he saw her eaten. Was that why the Pure-in-Blood favoured women's breasts so highly as a delicacy? But they were only slaves, human slaves. He tried to turn his mind away then, to the woman in Tarencia and what he would to to her when he returned, while he waited for his spawn to ripen.

And then he would kill her, and she would be gone. Gone forever. The thought sent a curious emptiness through him. Even though he could already feel his flesh beginning to stir in the beginning of his feeding-frenzy.

His brother's memory provided a different reason for the stirring of his flesh. He shuddered. Whatever the outward likeness to the human breeding-frenzy, it was not the same! It was the feeding-frenzy of the Great Ones before spawning!

But the Great Ones had no flesh.

He was akin to the Great Ones! He was not just another human, with the usual human drives twisted into different channels! Yet his brother and he were the same flesh, grown in the same womb. Had Emicos not stolen him, he would have grown like his brother.

He could not bear the thought. Yet he knew, inescapably, that Emicos had taken him into the Shadow. His brother's memory forced him to look at it. He was human. He had been taken and used. He was not of the Great Ones.

Used and warped. The forms of thought, the desires and lusts natural to the Great Ones were forever beyond his reach; he could only twist his human drives into a shallow mockery of their dark delights. A fierce rage snarled at those who had used him, shaped him, lied to him. He saw himself, dimly, through his brother's mind, through human eyes.

He was trapped between the worlds, neither one thing nor the other. He was not of the Great Ones; but he could not be human, either. Rebellion seethed, but he was helpless. The Blue-robes would destroy him, for he could not change to become human now. He must serve the Master or, if he failed, be hunted by both sides.

Hopelessness hollowed him. If the Blood Drinkers did not take him, he would die. But even if they did, there was no surety they had not lied about that, as well. He knew what the newly wakened Undead were like. There seemed no way out.

Jodos dropped the barriers that he had built against his brother's mind. Perhaps, with both their minds, he might find some way out of this trap; at least part of his mind would be human.

Perhaps he should not eat the woman, after all. Perhaps he should let her escape, with his spawn. Then there would be that much of him to survive. It would not hunt him!

But could he forgo so delicious a feast?

Chondos moved quickly toward the stairs. If he rushed out now, he could not help the horses; but with Pertap's blade in his hands . . .

Something stirred in the darkness. A tall shape stood on the stairs, and red eyes glared into his. He felt a scratching at the borders of his mind, and muttered spell-words under his breath, raising his sword.

A dry rattle from the figure's throat suddenly turned to a voice, rich and vibrant against echoing stone.

There was a sudden scurry of feet behind him. Chondos heaved up his sword, and slashed at the red-eyed shape. The vampire dodged more quickly than a fly. Iron fingers closed on Chondos' wrist. He felt his numb fist unclenching from the smooth bronze; felt the sword slipping from his hand.

A wild shriek drilled through his head: his wrist was suddenly free. He gripped at slippery bronze with a hand gone dead on an aching wrist. The vampire shrieked again, shaking a hand seared as though with fire. The stone bound to the guard had brushed the undead flesh. Chondos thrust out his torch. If he could break past, reach the room with Pertap's sword . . .

The vampire cringed back from the flames. Chondos tried to raise his sword, but the steel dragged on his tortured wrist, and he could barely keep his numb hand curled around the hilt.

Feet slapped on stone: small running black figures swarmed toward him. He heaved the useless weight of the sword up onto his shoulder. Great eyes like sickly moons glowed at him out of dark faces. A rusty blade swished at his knee. He jumped away, lashing out with the torch.

Black goblins swarmed in between Chondos and the stair. High above, the doorway filled with magical light mocked him. His torch showed him a thicket of rusty, curved blades, waving at the ends of spindly arms.

"Take him alive!" The vampire's vibrant voice filled the room. "His blood is mine!" Again the brown blade cut at his knee. He staggered back, his eyes sweeping the room. There was no escape the way he had come: the door was filled with glaring eyes. It would be a fool's hope to try to fight his way up the stair to the silver light of Pertap's sword.

The vampire's bone-white face lunged at him. He hurled up the flame by reflex, and the dead thing screamed and vanished.

Small dark forms rushed at him. He swung the sword down at them. It felt as though he were swinging a heavy hammer. His arm jarred with impact and the hilt slipped in his grasp. The small black figure crumpled under the stroke. He wrenched the blade free, seeing others hesitate, their huge eyes hurling back the light of the torch. He ran for the door. They were after him at once, as he had known they would be—but where was the vampire? Lurking in some corner?

He saw mist in front of the door. The white face suddenly congealed before him, the pallid lips open, the fangs like spikes. A hand closed on the wrist that held the torch.

He threw himself backward, feeling the muscles in his arm twisting, and heaved the hammer-sword down. The vampire's laughter stopped as the sharp blade smashed through brittle bone and flesh. Chondos felt himself falling, off balance. The torch hand, suddenly free, flailed.

The vampire burst into flame. Sudden heat seared Chondos' face. Dry flesh and bone crackled. Chondos rolled away with singed hair. He had dropped the torch, but somehow his fingers still gripped the sword.

Goblin eyes stared at him. He heaved himself to his feet. For a mad moment, he thought to hurl himself among them, fight his way through to the glowing door he still saw high above their heads. But that hope faded as a dozen russet blades flailed at him. He leaped back, guarding wildly. If he could escape alive, it would be enough.

His blade rang and trembled, but he managed to keep hold of the hilt as he dodged past the towering flame. Now he had running room, and his legs were longer.

He bounded through the gate. Goblins were wading across the wreck of a submerged causeway. He rammed his awkward sword into the scabbard, and dived into the shoaling waters of the Yukota.

Jodos could sense the Spider's unease as they drew near the dark stone towers of Kajpor, and the invisible net of power that shimmered and crackled around the walls.

He would not be able to take the Spider inside until he had located the cluster of jewels at the heart of the spell, and removed one. He racked his brain for some excuse to give for keeping his body-servant outside the castle.

A camp bustled all around the fort, and he sensed there was another danger here as well. There were Seers everywhere, and Healers, too. There was no particular reason for them to take a second look at the Dead Man, but there were too many of them either to control or to avoid.

He had to grip his saddlehorn again as the horse danced under him. He glanced quickly back over his shoulder at the Dead Man riding at the rear. If it fell back too far, it would be conspicuous. But when it closed up into the party, the smell upset the horses. Inside DiVega's head, Jodos could see, dimly, through the flaming sword, DiVega's thoughts turning back toward the horses again. Time to distract him.

"Stupid beasts!" he said loudy. "Do you suppose it's the wind? It's blowing right out of the Shadow. Do you think they smell something?"

"Well . . ." DiVega considered. "We're only about twelve miles or so from the Shadow. I don't know whether they can smell so far or not."

"I thought at your age you'd know everything," said Jodos. He laughed to himself as DiVega stiffened.

Behind him, the Spider cringed. A strong Demon could break through this protection, and goblins and other crude flesh creatures could endure it for a time. But the Spider's power was too weak and its flesh too frail.

They rode into the bustle of the camp. Minds clamoured all around. Men began to curse their horses as the party rode through and drew rein before the gate of the castle. Jodos relaxed a bit. Little fear that a Seer would recognise the Spider among so many deaf and clattering minds. The maelstrom of thought was too loud and chaotic to be bearable.

This was the first time Jodos had seen an army of humans at work, and their efficiency terrified him. The Seynyoreans never seemed to get in each other's way, and for all the chaos of their thoughts, they worked smoothly and did not quarrel. He supposed it was because they did not eat each other. But then, what fear kept them working at all? They were breaking camp. He watched tents falling, vanishing into packs and wagons.

A Seer came out of the gate, and Istvan called his name. Jodos felt a touch of fear. But the Spider was already vanishing, slipping into the center of the knot of the Pure-in-Blood.

Jodos walked with DiVega to meet the Seer, drawing his brother's mind over his own like a mask.

"Tell Lord Jagat that the King is here," DiVega told the Seer. "We can meet this very afternoon."

"Lord Jagat has not kept any Seers with him, Commander. He has sent them all off with his Border Patrol."

DiVega stood blinking, and even through the flame of the sword, Jodos could see seething turmoil within him. Earlier, he had caught glimpses of this particular worry brooding in odd corners of DiVega's mind. Now it was useful.

"Why have you not sent *your* Seers to join this patrol, Cousin

Istvan? I am surprised that you take less care of my kingdom than my enemies do!'' DiVega's jaw dropped, and Jodos went on: ''This patrol is more vital to the safety of the kingdom than any mere diplomacy! We can use riders to carry messages!''

DiVega's face was torn between shock and delight: his eyes beamed, the open mouth narrowed to a twitching smile. The effect was so ludicrous that the part of his brain filled with Chondos' memories forced Jodos to laugh. And then DiVega was laughing too. The Seer stared at them with eyes goggling like a goblin's, while they shook and clutched their bellies and hurled great braying bursts of laughter back and forth.

After a time, DiVega drew a deep breath and forced himself to speak, gasping as he fought laughter back. ''Lord King, no man has ever given me a reprimand more truly deserved, nor an order it pleased me more to carry out!'' He turned to the pop-eyed Seer. ''Well, D'Oleve, no doubt you think us mad as lovesick goats, and you may be right. But you need not mention that to Lord Jagat!''

Jodos found himself laughing again. It was frightening: he held his brother's mind tight over his own, and it was all laughter-shot images and bright warm-hued ticklings. The old fear of being eaten by his food rose, but he dared not pull the masking mind from his own while the Seer was there.

''Now,'' said DiVega, sobering, ''get yourself a horse and ride to Lord Jagat. Tell him the King is here, and will meet with him . . .'' He frowned. ''How long will it take you to reach Lord Jagat's camp?''

''With a good horse,'' the Seer said, ''I can be there by dark, certainly, or a little after. I can reach him in a few hours if I kill the horse, but I'd have to walk the last few miles.''

''Take a remount,'' said Istvan. ''But it will be too late for Jagat to come today.'' He paused, thinking. ''What is it? Twenty miles or so? Four or five hours' march, walk-and-trot?''

''Somewhere between four and six,'' D'Oleve said. ''I hope! He was camped just a few miles north and east of Alpakota yesterday.''

''He couldn't arrive until—oh, noon, perhaps,'' Istvan mused. ''Very well. Tell him, then, that the King is here, and will meet with him and with the other Lords tomorrow, as agreed before. No war-gear to be worn, and so forth. Will noon''—he turned back to Jodos—''or as soon after as Jagat can arrive, be acceptable to Your Majesty?''

Noon, with bright lights burning in the sky. But it would be later by the time he had killed them all; and he would have time to set them all at each other's throats before the attack began. The Master could send men and goblins across the Border, and the dragon hidden near Rajinagara. The Blue-robes would be less wary in daytime, and the army could be across the Border before they noticed.

"Yes," he said, nodding, "I will be ready."

A young man had come out of the castle gate. He was dressed neither like a Seynyorean nor a Borderman, but wore, like Hotar, the court livery of the Royal Guards. The young man saluted and stood at attention, waiting to be noticed.

His brother's memory recognised the man: a kinsman of Lord Rinmull's, who had been among the hangers-on at Chondos' court, and had been assigned to the special Honour Guard that escorted Chondos or his father on their visits to Ojaini.

"Tell Jagat," DiVega was saying to D'Oleve, "that the King will expect him around noon. I'll keep DiVarro with me: contact him with Lord Jagat's answer. But the rest of the Seers I shall send with you to Lord Jagat, to serve in the Border Patrol."

D'Oleve saluted. DiVega saluted. The young man saluted, making DiVega salute again, and Jodos found his brother's mind trying to make him laugh again.

"Lord King, let me present the commander of our garrison here, Lord Nahos of Atavipor. I believe he has served you before."

"Yes," said Jodos, "I remember Lord Nahos well." He smiled. Chondos had not liked the man, thinking him a self-seeking toady, but Jodos had a use for him. "I am sure Lord Nahos will be pleased to show me around the castle. You need not remain, Lord Istvan. You should rest, after so long a ride! At your age, you should let the younger officers take such burdens from you. You have my permission to go!"

DiVega, eyes cold with sudden rage, bowed deeply and turned away. Jodos suppressed a wicked grin at the stiffness of the departing back, and turned to Lord Nahos.

"Shall we go inside?" he said to the somewhat startled young man, who had doubtless expected a cooler reception.

Chapter Twenty

Thunderhead snorted, and jingled his bridle savagely, his flowing mane blowing in the bitter wind. Martos clamped on the reins and patted the powerful neck. The dead lands stretched before them, grinning sores of dust, and beyond, blackness waited. Martos wondered what Thunderhead smelled in the wind that whipped their faces. It was always hard on the horses when their heads were turned to the Shadow.

Three hundred men had ridden from Jagat's camp, with the mournful black smoke of the pyres still rolling north. A third of those had already moved off to the west, to the rendezvous point from which they would patrol the land near Vajrakota. Soon those that remained would separate into the various patrols as they drew near their posts.

It would have been better, Martos thought, if they had left camp before the funeral. Yet, the deep chanting of the Bordermen sounded in his memory, and his eyelashes suddenly clouded his vision with misty jewels. No, it was best to honour the dead, say good-bye to the comrades who had ridden south with him . . .

All that Istvan the Archer might have another victory, and the Bordermen, new fields. He shook his head angrily.

This stretch of the Border had been left for the last. Seynyoreans already patrolled it by night, when the danger was greatest, and both armies were still concentrated here.

Far in the west, the men of the isolated fortress of Eikakin had maintained a sketchy patrol all through the war. Jagat had sent them several Seers, and at his suggestion, DiVega had ordered three of the Seynyorean companies there, with their Seers. Since Ekakin had remained neutral, that area could be patrolled easily.

But south from Ekakin, the Border plunged straight down to where the Tower of Ketusima flamed at the end of a long valley of sunlight between cliffs of Shadow: Jagat's realm of Damenco, where the Border had been driven back nearly a hundred miles, making close to two hundred miles of Border to be patrolled. Ymros had ridden off to Manjipor the day before, with eighteen hundred men from Kaligaviot, Manjipor, and Damenco, and with them, all the remaining Seers.

Here, where the Seynyoreans would take the night duty; here, if anywhere, was the place to patrol without Seers. Damenco, with Shadow on both sides, was a place of far greater danger, and it was there the Dark Things would be most likely to strike first.

All around was the desert of deadly grey dust, and ahead the black wall gradually grew transparent, turning slowly to a sunless stretch of land. Far away, the ghosts of mountains loomed under a dingy sky.

This barren land! Cursed land! Land for his children, and his children's children! Had his choice of their mother doomed his descendants to this? Food grown from bones would fill her breasts with milk. The land would nourish his children, and his children the land.

North in Inagar, Kumari waited, a woman flowing with milk and honey, her body swelling with his child; the child that would one day inherit dust to be cleared away, and scoured rock to be covered slowly with soil—soil that must be built up labouriously over the years out of dung and sand, kitchen scraps and the ashes of the dead—his own ashes, Kumari's ashes, the ashes of his men.

It was the land itself he had married, and now his seed would feed the Earth whose breasts he sucked. *Earth is the Bride of the Warrior*, he thought, and remembered the deep chorus chanting: *Man is a part of the Earth*.

Gone, now, the rich, exciting life in the cities of the north; lost, the joys of peace and war alike. Now there would be neither peace nor war, only the endless, ugly little struggles with creatures from the Shadow, haunting and raiding.

Nearly half his men had died here, and were food for the land. Of those that remained, most were wounded. He could barely have filled his patrol with his own men, even if Lord Jagat had not insisted that at least half the force be Bordermen. "Bordermen know the Border," Jagat had said.

The hooting of a conch-horn closed his hands on his reins. Horses slowed and stopped. It was time for one of the patrols to break off. A few shouted jokes to conceal the fear of men who might never meet again, and then a sharp command set horses trotting.

Above his right shoulder as he rode, he saw the fifty riding over dust, through sunlight, toward the sunless plain and ghostly mountains. Fifty was suddenly a pitifully small number.

Soon it would be his turn. The horses would be tired today. Over the next week, they would be ridden more slowly, sparing their strength for the effort needed if the Dark Things came, as well as taking the time to study the Border carefully. But today men must push them, simply to reach their posts.

Martos stared into the darkness across the Border. Sunless land lay floor-flat and barren. Beyond, ghostly hints of the mountain-wall showed dimly. He watched for any sign of movement.

If anything were to come out of the Shadow, would he be able to see it? Not yet, he realised. Until they had come within four miles of the Border, anything as small as a man would be a blurred dot at best.

Chondos was a strong swimmer, and had wrestled water worse than this; but both his arms ached—wrenched shoulder and crushed wrist. And he knew, remembering ropy arms that had snaked from the river to seize the horse a few nights ago, that there were more dangers here than strong currents.

He rolled to float on his back, treading water, while he looked behind. One of the goblins pushed another into the water, shrieking and screaming with rage, but the victim turned and swam back to the narrow shore, while the rest stood watching out of wide eyes. *They know too well the dangers of the river,* Chondos thought. Had he dived into life or death? He would soon know.

He rolled again, and swam with the current. In a moment, he would be past the little island where Kudrapor stood, and then he could strike across the stream to the shore. He wondered if he would ever see the horses again. The shore curved inward. Beyond the bend, he saw the shoaling above some obstacle, a fallen tree, perhaps.

His heart lurched. The curving line of waves moved upstream to meet him. He twisted in the water and made for the shore on his left. The current seized him, bearing him rapidly downstream. The bend in the river was his only hope. Water splashed across his face again and again. He saw the red shore speed past: roots of long-dead trees weaving through bright clay mocked as they passed. He felt himself lifted as the water around him swelled up, bearing him helpless as a floating leaf. Red clay, interwoven with grey, rose up before his eyes.

The wave hurled him against soft mud. His swim changed to a scrambling run, mud sucking at hands and feet. Water fell away from him. He staggered up, and a mud-caked hand closed on a jutting tree-root. It shattered into powder in his hand as something looped lithely around his ankle, and his feet were pulled from under him. His fingers clenched convulsively on his wet sword-hilt; he twisted as he fell, heaving the blade free. Mud jarred the breath from his lungs.

A taut, grey-white rope ran from his foot to the river. Something like a pallid, uprooted tree floated in the water, waving tendrils like monstrous writhing roots. His crushed wrist ached as the weight of the sword screamed down, shearing through stretched pulp. White slime spurted over his feet: the loop around his leg flexed and fell slack.

His other hand curled up into his sleeve, groping frantically. His fingers found jagged stone. He heaved himself to his feet, his hand coming free with need-fire glowing through his fingers. A thicket of lashing strands curled above him, like a hand about to close. He hurled the flaming gem into the middle where they met.

He was deafened by a bellowing screech that seemed to shake earth and sky. Water flooded his mouth and eyes, choking and blinding him; plucking him from his feet and hurling him against the mud.

Choking, coughing, he blinked water from his eyes and saw a wave fall back into the river. Glassy-grey ripples rolled and slapped. He heard dim screams. Upstream, a writhing, dirty-white tree reared out of the water by the door of Kudrapor, its lashing limbs weighted with black-furred, kicking fruit. A goblin flew through the air and smashed into the castle wall, smearing blood as it fell.

Mud churned under Chondos' feet: the sky spun; the vision vanished. He realised he was running, running in a panic down the stream, away from the screaming—but not away from all of it. Ahead of him, he heard yet more voices, screaming, howling. Through the madness of cries, he heard the squeals and snorts of frightened horses.

Kudrapor fell away from his right as he ran past the end of the island. Beyond, he saw the other bank.

Brown rough-coated ponies raced toward the water. Behind them bounded the great grey shapes of ghouls, ghostly against grey dust, long fangs glaring in their gaping jaws.

Running to cut the horses off came other shapes, smaller, paler, which wailed and moaned as they ran. Human shapes? He could not be sure, but tattered rags flapped about their limbs.

He drew a deep, shuddering breath, trying to fight the panic that raged in his legs. His heartbeat shook his body; his vision blurred.

He should swim across, now, while the river creature was busy upstream, and rescue the horses. But that would do no good. The horses were surrounded, and his single blade could not cut a path through . . .

Bright-coloured in his memory, he saw a dawn from his boyhood; saw the stone desert around Suknia, and Jagat, stern and tall, pursing his lips to whistle beneath his white mustache; remembered the Border pony grazing in the fallow field of clover, that threw up its head and neighed.

He fought for control of his heartbeat, his breath. One of the horses smashed its heels into a ghoul that had gotten too close, hurled it reeling back. Another reared, its forefeet pawing the air as one of the smaller figures dodged in front of it. A lashing hoof fell in a skull-shattering blow. The figure collapsed, and the horse's hooves crashed down again and again, trampling. Then the horse backed off, and the thing on the ground rolled over and staggered to its feet.

Chondos sucked in air and whistled. Two of the horses paid no attention, but the third, whinnying, threw up its head, and then, wheeling away from the creatures that menaced it, raced to the water's edge.

The others followed. Chondos whistled again. The horse checked at the water, pawed the mud with its forefoot, and leaped into the stream.

Behind, ghouls came bounding, and the horde of wailing, manlike shapes.

The second horse splashed into the river, and as the third hesitated, one of the smaller shapes came running, and sprang onto its back. The horse bucked, and bounded out over the water. The creature clinging to its back seemed to stiffen; it fell off and sank like a stone. One of the ghouls leaped from the bank, limbs splayed like some giant frog.

Chondos ran toward the place where the current should sweep them. So far there was no sign of danger on this shore, but that could change at any moment. He could hear faint hints of wailing beyond the clay banks.

Behind the horse-headed wedges of ripples and the splashing shape of the ghoul, he saw something bob up floating on the shiny black water, something man-shaped and still.

Only one ghoul had followed the horses into the water. The others squatted on the bank, knuckles in the mud, long muzzles snarling out across the water. One barked shrilly. There was a sudden flurry as the one in the water floundered around and began to swim back. Chondos stiffened. Was the water surging higher?

A quick look upstream showed that a vast spearhead of waves shoaled before something huge and pale that shot downstream. With a last glance at the empty land behind him, Chondos sheathed the dripping, useless sword, and began to empty the stone fragments from his sleeve.

The horses were almost ashore when the ominous rising of the water hurled waves up the bank where Chondos stood. He saw the horses' manes emerge from the water, then their shoulders. A sudden shriek from the swimming ghoul was chopped off. Ripples slapped together where it had been, and a froth of bubbles swarmed up from the depths.

Chondos whistled again, hoping the horses would hurry. He cradled a glowing stone in one hand, ready to throw it.

Water slopped over Chondos' feet. The horses, frightened now, began to scramble more quickly, but foundered in the treacherous mud. The first scrambled out, then a second. Something long and pallid licked out of the water, reaching for the third.

Chondos' cocked arm lashed out, launching the stone. Jewelled fire flew. It missed the tentacle, skipped over the water, and vanished. Already Chondos was ready with a second stone, and now he threw not at the thin target of the tendril, but at the dimly seen body behind.

A long throw, but a bigger target. A deafening shriek brought the last horse bounding from the water. Chondos leaped to catch the frightened steed, and swung himself onto its back as it pounded by. It bucked as his leg went over its back, and for a moment he clung precariously to saddle and mane, with only his foot hooked over its withers, before he managed to heave himself onto the saddle. He clung tightly as the three horses raced up the slippery bank.

He cast a quick look over his shoulder, past the frothing waters where lashing tendrils beat the river, to the brown walls of the ancient fort, where Pertap's sword still lay.

> *The Shadow split before his sword:*
> *The Power of Hastur he bore;*
> *And Hastur's power burned through him*
> *As he rode back to Kudrapor.*

Someday he, too, would ride back to Kudrapor.

Sadly he turned from legend. The three horses raced over a rise in the land, and Chondos gazed into brightness. Grey plain ran north before him, and in the distance a wall of light like crystal or opal dazzled his eyes. It chopped off the grey roof of the Shadow, and beyond he could sense a wider sky. The land there glowed, hinting of sunlit plains that stretched away forever and ever to the north.

He could see the Yukota flowing past a desolation of pillars—the branchless, leafless, barkless trunks of long-dead trees. Far away, he saw a fire beyond the wall of mist: the dimly seen glow of a Hastur-tower. Agnasta!

But he was on the wrong side of the river. The Yukota was deep and turbulent where it flowed by the tower. He must find a place to cross again.

Suddenly the horses plowed to a stop, nostrils flaring. He urged his own beast on, and managed to capture the reins of one of the others. He should change horses now, if he could: the one he rode was lathered and would collapse if pushed any harder.

Then, out of the desolate greyness ahead, a voice sobbed woefully. Another joined it, and another. A long, eerie howling jolted into the chorus of wails.

He fought down the two horses, gripping tight to the reins of the led horse while the other bucked and tried to bolt. Hooves pounded away. If his mount had been fresh, he could never have kept his seat, much less held the jerking, tensing reins with the other horse plunging to escape. But now he had only these two horses, for the third, still loose, had bolted at the first wail.

Jodos felt as though he had walked into a storm of tingling, stinging light. At the heart of that storm, the swarm of crystals glowed, as blinding as DiVega's sword. They were set in silver, and silver inlays ran between: at the centre, he saw the lines overlap in triangles and pentangles that crawled with blue sparks and flickers of liquid fire between the gems. Yet through Nahos' eyes, he saw no more than a faint glow, and felt only a heartening, faint warmth of stimulated blood.

"Here it is, Lord King," he heard Nahos say, first in his head, and then in his ears. Jodos shifted his eyes from the swirl of gems; found a flawed mark in the wall, and pointed at it with his finger.

"Look at this," he said in cheery tones. "Look closely! Can you see? Look! You see that mark? See the mark! Can you see the mark?"

"Yes."

"You can see the mark. You see only the mark. Can you see anything besides the mark?"

"Only stone, Lord King."

"See only the stone, and the mark. There is no time. You see only the stone. Time is stopped. Time is still. This is a brief moment, and you are looking at the mark. When I tell you to look elsewhere, you will look away, but you have only looked at the mark for a brief moment, and nothing happened. Soon you will forget all about it. Now you are looking at the mark. You see only the mark."

As hs spoke, he slid his dagger from its sheath, and stepped in close to the swirl of gems. There was no one in sight, and where Nahos stood, he would block the view of anyone coming by. Jodos curtly ordered Hotar to stand behind, to further block the view, and then quickly with his dagger scored across several of the silver lines. Sparks leaped, shocking his hand. He began to loosen the setting around the large glowing central stone, but when he had pried the silver away, so that the stone hung loose, he did not remove it, but instead started on one of the smaller stones at the point of one of the silver triangles.

He felt the spell's fire flicker in his nerves. It only took a moment to loosen the smaller stone's collar of silver; then his point went underneath and out it popped, as easy as gouging out an eye. He felt the crack, the sudden dimming of swirling force.

Quickly, he took a stone from each of the triangles, and with the second stone he felt the spell shatter. The swirling stopped. The dimming flame was still.

It died away to a barely felt radiance at the fourth stone. Carefully, he slid the stones into his sleeve. He would get rid of them later. He sheathed his dagger. Lord Nahos had never stirred, but stood transfixed, his eyes on the crack in the stone.

"No time has passed," said Jodos softly. "You have only glanced at the stone for a second." He changed his voice, made it loud and cheery. "And look at the top of that tower! This is *old* stonework! But come, I wish to look at the room where the council is to be held! Take me there."

"Yes, Sire," said Nahos, blinking up at the tower, and then innocently turning away, unaware that he had stood for long moments staring at a crack in the stone. "It is straight ahead."

Nahos led the way through great open doors into a broad, dimly lit hall. Back from the door, beyond the reach of the sunlight, witch-jewels glimmered faintly on each wall, and near them were sconces to hold many torches and candles. The room must once have been richly fitted: scraped places on the walls showed where ornaments had been removed. The polished stones of the floor were different from those of the wall: probably they had belonged to an older building.

Far down at the other end of the room, three steps rose to an arched door. What had once been a rich Alferridan carpet, now much worn in the middle and faded to a greyish green and blue, with only faint hints of its former bright colours, covered the three strides it took to reach the arch. The shapes of scuffing feet were worn into the carpet: in many places the stone peered through.

Doors of hammered bronze were brown as wood in the dimness. Lord Nahos seized the great handles and twisted. The doors flew back, and a sudden blaze of light picked out faded images on the ancient carpet.

When Jodos and Hotar had blinked the unexpected brilliance from their eyes, they found themselves in a room a little smaller than that they had left, under a domed and vaulted ceiling. Windows poured light from the left wall onto the polished floor, light that seemed as solid as bronze against the dark stone.

The sunbeam in the centre painted glowing golden-brown the top of a great wooden table in the middle of the room, with chairs of wood set about.

"Is it not a treasure?" Nahos said, stepping to the table to rap on the wood. "It is old, and the wooden chairs! Most of the Manjipéan castles have had to burn up such things long ago. That is the advantage of being right on the river!"

Jodos was not listening. He turned away from the windows—narrow slits set in a mirror-lined niche that gathered the sunlight to make the windows seem far larger—and looked instead at the other wall. At each end a door was set—doors with locks. A long tapestry hung between them. Old Takkarian warriors stared from the faded cloth.

"Where does this door lead?" he asked, as though casually, pointing at the nearer.

"To the kitchens, Sire," said Nahos.

"And the other?" He gestured toward the back of the room.

"There is a small anteroom, quite bare now. Do you desire to see it?" He fished in his pouch, pulled out several keys. "Here we are! These were hidden in the back of the kitchen—we found them only by chance. They were in a box covered with dust, and as like as not we were the first to open it in generations!"

As they reached the end of the room, Jodos saw with surprise that the walls did not quite join, but instead left a space that seemed to be the end of a long corridor.

"Where does this lead?" he asked.

"To the stable, Sire." Nahos was fitting the key in the lock as he spoke. The door swung open. There was no sun in this chamber: a square of floor showed in the light from the door. Jodos licked his teeth.

"Do you want this room fitted up, Sire?" Nahos asked. "We could bring in furnishings, if you like—"

"Look at me!" said Jodos. Nahos turned, and Jodos trapped the man's eyes with his own.

"Give me the key," he said after a moment, and Nahos handed the key over, his face immobile, staring. "Turn around and face the wall," Jodos said. "You will see nothing, hear nothing, until I call your name. No time is passing." He turned to Hotar. "Fetch the rest of the men. Tell them to bring their packs."

Hotar left. Jodos turned back to the little anteroom. It was bare and long unused, like some room in ancient Rajinagara. He paced its length, his eyes piercing the darkness easily. This was far better than anything he had expected! He laughed, and tossed the key idly on his palm.

He would put the Spider on DiVega, he decided. Then he would have DiVega order his troops to begin marching north, to help Prince Phillipos. Or should he do that first? That would be simpler.

Hotar came back, the men of the Pure-in-Blood behind him.

"You will be locked in this room," Jodos said. "Tomorrow, when I unlock this door and call you, you will come out and kill the men in this room. Do you understand?" Hotar nodded. "There is food and water in your packs, and you will only be here for a day."

Hotar pointed to Nahos, standing against the wall. "Leave him in with us. Then there'll be plenty of food."

Jodos considered, then decided that Nahos would be missed, and shook his head. Besides, he might scream. He did not want anything to go wrong now. Perhaps he should put the Spider on Nahos and leave the servant's body for the Pure-in-Blood to eat. But Nahos, as an officer, might be sent a message by a Seer . . .

"No," he said. "You are to be silent! No one must know you are here. If you are discovered, they will kill you. Do *not* eat each other! There will be plenty of food after tomorrow!"

He turned to Nahos.

"Nahos! You have seen nothing and heard nothing. Do not wake, but walk out through the door and turn around." Nahos stumbled through the door. Jodos followed, and handed him the key. "Lock the door. You will remember locking the door, and you will remember that we talked about—" He shuffled idly through the man's mind. "The art and history of the old kingdom." The lock clicked. "Now give me the key. You will remember putting the key in your pouch, and if you notice it is gone at all, you will decide you lost it outside. We opened the door, looking inside, and closed it again." Jodos hid the key in his robe. "Nothing else has happened. You will remember talking about the art of the old kingdom. Now wake."

Jodos looked around the room, and again at the closed door. It would be easy enough, once they were all here and unarmed, to find a pretext for opening the door. Nothing could possiby go wrong.

What if it did? What could he do? The Master would detroy him, slowly and painfully. Unless the Blue-robes caught him first, and that would be as bad. He looked about, desperate, and saw the corridor that led to the stables.

"Show me the way to the stables," he said, and Nahos led the way.

An escape route, but where could he escape to? There *was* no escape. Then he remembered the great clashing of minds he had sensed from Portona. There would be even more mental noise and confusion there than in the camp outside. Neither the Blue-robes nor the Great Ones would ever find him there!

Something urged him—something from his brother's part of his mind—to flee *now*. Just leave it all and run: run and hide in the cities of the north. But that would be foolish. Nothing could go wrong now.

Once it was over, he would lead a host of night-things to Tarencia. He smiled, and licked his teeth. *She* would be waiting. Once again his doubts rose. Perhaps he should let her escape. And his spawn too? A frightening thought.

Nothing could go wrong now. Once that door was opened, the Border would be doomed. And without his flaming sword, DiVega would be helpless.

* * *

Chondos stroked the frightened horses. The wailing noise grew louder. He held on while the nervous beasts pranced and bucked. The bright Border dazzled his eyes. He peered through thick grey air, like mist or smoke. He could not see far. Then, through the deceptive haze, he saw the things that wailed: they staggered over the dust, dirty and ragged, an army of the dead, their hair matted with grime, their skin greyish-white—men and women, and parts of children. Children that lacked an arm or leg. Legless children that dragged themselves over the ground one-handed. Some of the stumps were still raw, with splintered bones sticking through bloodless flesh. Others were nearly healed, with buds of tiny limbs forming where the scars had been.

He realised, then, from rumours, what the things must be: the newly dead, barely wakened vampires, still stupid from the shock of death, who had not yet learned to use their new powers.

He tried to hold the horses to a slow walk, to bring them quietly around and away from the pitiful horde, but the beast beneath him reared and squealed in terror. He saw heads come up, hands point, and he let the rein go loose. The horse bolted as the vampires broke into a staggering run.

He felt the tether dragging back his hand as the horse at its end stumbled. Then it was up and running again, but he saw the foam on its coat and knew it could not hold the pace for long. He wondered if the things behind would tire at all.

He tried to turn his horses toward the river; but the steed beneath him slowed and fought the bit. Then he heard shrill cries, and glimpsed dim shapes running through the haze. He gave his horse its head.

He saw the faint shimmer of Agnasta Tower fading on his right. The vague running shapes solidified. A pack of ghouls came loping from the river.

Soon the horses would tire, ghoul or vampire would catch them—and his sword was only steel. No time now to stop and kindle a torch. If only he had been able to reach Pertap's sword!

> He turned his good steed round about,
> Across the Border he did ride.
> And need-fire glistered all about,
> And split the dark to either side.

Shrieks and howls sent his horse bounding more frantically. Turning in the saddle, Chondos saw that the ghouls and vampires had met, and were fighting. He thought of the mutilated children, the crawling, limbless children who could not die. Goblins with whips appeared, lashes flailing at ghoul and vampire alike, driving the two groups apart.

Suddenly he felt the saddle rise sickeningly. The world reeled around him as his horse reared and veered. He felt the leather of the other horse's rein ripped from his hand.

A fountain of mist foamed up before them. Red coals glared from its head, and Chondos saw a white face form around them. The form was swung away on the spinning world as the scared horse whirled and ran, but Chondos looked back to see red eyes watching in a figure still as stone.

The brightness of the Border was behind him now, and both horses were bolting frantically back into the Shadow. He wrestled with the reins, wrenching the horse's jaw around, trying to turn it back toward the white-banded horizon.

"Come on, good fellow," he crooned, trying to calm the horse, keeping his tone soft and cheery. "Be a good horse, let's go the right way, easy there!" But the horse fought the bit, jerking its jaw, wrenching Chondos' hurt shoulder anew as he struggled with the strength of both arms.

Despair and fear hindered him. A horse might outrun awkward, new-made vampires stumbling in the dust, but older vampires, secure in their power, were another thing. And it was not mere death he faced, but age-long endless slavery to darkness and thirst.

A man can always die, they said along the Border.

A man, yes, he thought. But what of a King? What of a nation, a people? He could save himself with death, but not his kingdom: not the Bordermen and their women and children, nor the softer people that sheltered behind them.

The horse stopped fighting the bit, and whirled with a scream, racing back toward the pale band of the Border.

"Easy, there! Good horse!" He patted it, but it was still panicked, still running wild, though in the right direction now. "Easy there! What's the matter with you?"

Something scrabbled at the shell around his mind. He groped in his sleeve for another of the glowing stones, muttering the words of Miron's spell. The horse shuddered and bucked. Chondos felt a chill against his back.

He turned, and looked into mist. Red eyes stared into his own. A scream gagged in his throat. The mist hid the horse's tail, folding in on itself, thickening into snowy flesh and icy teeth. A shadowy arm was around him, ready to embrace him, to draw him to the white spikes forming in the ghostly mouth.

His hand closed on stone. His arm lashed out of the sleeve, and the weighted hand sank into slush.

The stone flared in his hand: flesh glowed with ruby light. Ivory spikes clacked inches from his face. The red eyes went dull. Suddenly hot, the stone burned his hand, and Chondos jerked away, feeling dried flesh flake against his fingers.

The horse bucked. Chondos seized its mane, barely keeping his seat in the saddle. A dead arm brushed his shoulder. The corpse on his horse's crupper pitched headlong to the ground. Brittle bones crackled. The stone flamed in triumph from a heap of bones and dust.

Chapter Twenty-one

"Listen!" Paidros said.

Martos stiffened, and looked toward the vast starlessness to the south. Was that a faint wailing on the wind? But then, behind him, he heard the other sound: faint jingling and tinkling and a leathery squeaking.

"There," said Suktio, pointing to the north. Across the grey vagueness of dust, the shapes of men on horseback were dim in the twilight. "Seynyoreans, I think."

The rainbow sunset had long faded from the top of the black west. Their horses gnawed new-sprung grass on the little island of unpoisoned earth they had found in the midst of the dust. The furious southern wind fanned high the flames of their tiny fire. Martos worried: it could set fire to the rest of their fuel, piled high, ready if the Border broke.

Drawing near now, he saw lean, long-legged horses and tiny glints of moonlight on mail. He mounted, and rode with Suktio to meet them.

"What?" the Seynyorean commander exclaimed. "No Seers of your own? You're brave men!" He shook his head. "A dangerous business. Well, things should change after tomorrow, eh, D'Almida?"

"Some," his Seer said with a nod. "Tomorrow Lord Jagat will ride to Kajpor around noon to meet with King Chondos. Once the peace has been made, all the available Seers will be patrolling the Border. There still won't be enough, but we hope to be able to send to Seynyor for more."

"You've seen nothing along the Border during the day?" asked the commander.

"Nothing," said Suktio. Martos shook his head.

"DiFlacca's company is patrolling near Vajrakota," said the Seer. "They reported some ghouls and trolls on the other side of the Border last night, but nothing crossed."

"What can they be eating in there?" said the commander.

"Each other, I hope!" Suktio replied.

At last Chondos' panic-stricken horse faltered and slowed, and he managed to rein it to a halt. Sliding from its back, he pulled the waterskin from the saddle and emptied it down the poor beast's throat. It was not nearly enough, but it was all there was, and he had but this single exhausted horse left, now. He had glimpsed the other, covered with bloody froth, staggering back into the Shadow.

He led the beast slowly toward the glowing band that marked the Border, swinging right toward the faint shimmer of Agnasta. He tried to estimate the distance between himself and the hazy glow, but vagueness baffled his eyes. It could not be more than another day's ride, he figured, and it might be less.

He had grown so used to the wailing of the tormented dead that he paid no more attention to it than a forest dweller does to the noise of birds and insects, until the horse came to a sudden stop, planting its hooves and jerking up its head so sharply that he felt his feet lifted from the ground. The chorus of wailing was growing louder and wilder; mingled with the moaning came the deep roars of trolls and eerie howls and squeals. And the sky above was barred with sudden bands of black.

He pulled the beast's head down and scrambled onto its back. It was cooler now, but the horse would not be able to run for long. It bounded, frantic with fear, and he struggled to hold it down to a canter, even as he fought to rein in his own galloping heart. The horse jerked its mouth against the bit, trying to turn away from the river. Dark Things must be clustered there, he realised. Most of the wailing was coming from that direction.

Something huge and dark ran toward him in the failing light. His fingers closed on his hilt. Then his mount nickered in welcome, and Chondos saw it was another horse. Night wrapped its blindfold around him. He loosened rein and gave his beast its head, only twitching the rein now and then to keep its nose pointed north, toward the narrow, night-blue band, vivid as flame in the dull black blindness of the Shadow, that marked the Border.

Soon the two beasts, seeking comfort in the haunted night, had drawn together and were cantering easily, neck by neck. A kick to his mount's barrel launched it enough ahead so that he could reach out to catch the other's bridle. The horse was both bridled and saddled, and he guessed it to be the one that had fled earlier from the wailing of the dead, but it was too dark to be sure. He talked soothingly as he slowed both horses to a walk. They were both hot and wet now, but the wailing was dying away behind them, and they began to calm. He was able to slide from the saddle and lead them both, thinking furiously. They needed water and rest, but tonight there would be no ring of glowing stone to surround them with protecting need-fire. How could they rest in the open, without the defence of a broken tower?

Chondos' own weariness dragged at him. It was not likely he would dare to sleep tonight, but he must rest the horses—find them food and water and a safe place to eat and drink.

"Great news, Lord King!" Istvan rushed into the King's rooms, and the pale, awkward servant scurried out of his way. "The Duke of Ipazema is in full flight: his troops surrender by the thousands. Prince Phillipos is master of the north!"

He saw an odd, trapped expression flit across the King's face; then the boy turned away and stared out his window into starry night. *Strange!* Istvan blinked at the King's back. The boy acted as though he'd lost a bet on the outcome, instead of having his kingdom and, most likely, his skin saved. *Has Chondos gone mad? Or . . .* Istvan's mind groped.

"Well, old man," the King said, breaking in on his thoughts, "it's over, isn't it? You and Phillipos, between you, have finished it! Ipazema running for his life; old Hansio dead, at last; and Jagat busy with this Border Patrol! You've done more than most men do in a lifetime! A dying fire burns the hottest, they say. With the kingdom at peace, perhaps you can find the time to rest."

Something about the King's praise drowned the last of Istvan's triumph. The job was done: now he would be put out to pasture like an old war-horse.

"Prince Phillipos deserves the credit, Lord . . ." He let his voice trail away. What did it matter? In the little life left to him, what would praise count for?

"You had best sleep," said the King. "Tomorrow—why, tomorrow is the crowning of all your achievements, the end of all your labour. The last resistance will be gone, and I will truly rule." He turned to Istvan a strangely crooked smile. "I have already decided how to reward you."

"No need for anything elaborate, Lord King," Istvan protested, embarrassed. "This is a family matter! I—I need no reward for helping my kin! Prince Phillipos deserves far more than I!"

"I shall be pleased to reward the Prince, too, when next we meet!" The King smiled. "But come, Cousin, it grows late: night comes on, and all grows dark! Is it not time for you to go to your rest?"

The horses jerked up their heads, wrenching at Chondos' arms, and pranced excitedly. He swore at them. Then, through the wailing of the haunted night, he heard a faint gurgle of water.

He swung himself to the back of the fresher horse, and let them go, aware of his own searing thirst. A few moments later, both horses were drinking from a small stream that flowed across their

384 PAUL EDWIN ZIMMER

path toward the Yukota: he went upstream from them and drank, too, and the first few gulps were cool and sweet. A sudden foul taste made him gag, and he stopped.

There were tough bushes and clumps of fungi growing near the stream, and after a while he dragged the horses from the water and looped their reins over a tough branch. He heard them crunching in the dark, and felt their flesh cooling under his hands.

Rest and food. But sooner or later some prowling night-thing would find their trail. Without fire, only the speed and endurance of the horses might save them. He could build a fire, but that would be seen for miles in the darkness, and bring night-things clustering like moths.

He wished he dare unsaddle the horses: their backs must be galled badly; yet he must be ready to mount and run. At least there was food: not only the branching fungus, but the leaves of the bushes. But not all the dark shapes about them were bushes, he realised as he stumbled against cold stone. Hope flared.

He hunted until he found two shield-sized slabs set near a large boulder, and in the hollow between them he gathered twigs and thin, dead branches, then rolled over a fourth stone, to hide his fire on all four sides.

The fire he kindled was small, but he piled up an immense heap of brushwood nearby, ready to light when the Dark Things came. Then, at last, he dared unsaddle the horses, and tied them to a bush close to the fire. Finally, he was able to sit down, his back warmed by the fire, his sword across his knees. Staring into the haunted night, he tried to plan the next day's journey. His eyelids were heavy, but he knew he was too nervous to sleep.

Far to the north, dragon-headed Uoght glided, a pillar of dark smoke against the Border, rolling before him a wave of cold magic that quenched shimmering curtains of need-fire. With a dozen of his kinsmen, Miron Hastur was hurled back, swept in thunder from the Dark Thing's path.

Rarely did the Children of Hastur have to face the naked power of Uoght himself. Most often, the Regent of the Dark Lords remained well to the rear, driving hordes of slaves to battle before him. Yet among all the Powers of Darkness, only the Sabuath and the Eight Dark Lords were greater. Even the great Dyoles fawned, trembling, upon Uoght: now they gathered behind him, massive powers that could barely squeeze through the rents in the fabric of space.

Miron's kinsmen left wide gaps in the line of towers as they rallied to meet the threat. Behind them, the western provinces of Kadar were scarred with trails of dust; scattered bands of night-things haunted the lonely manors and farmlands. Companies of Seynyorean mercenaries marched across the continent to stiffen the spine of the army that King Manuel the Peacemaker had reluctantly brought to the Border.

Yet, strangely, in all that tortured land beneath the blended Hastur-minds, Miron found only a few scattered bands of fleshly Night Walkers instead of the hordes that commonly gathered for the break-ing of the Border.

Martos took his turn at watch under brilliant stars, but he watched the dark half of the sky. There was nothing to see in the mile or so that was visible beyond the Border, but in the middle of the night something moved between the Shadow and the camp. His mouth opened to shout: his sword sprang from the scabbard, a fountain of starlight, but a gemmed sparkle of moonlight on mail caught the shout in his throat.

Tiny men on long-legged, spectral horses rode from right to left along the Shadow's edge, peering into the deeper darkness. Martos hoped they could see farther then he. He shivered as an icy, foul-scented wind from the Shadow chilled his face. A footstep behind him brought him around: a splendour of stars and swift moons stunned his eyes a moment before he recognised Suktio. Even the dust shimmered with moonlight. He pointed to the distant horsemen.

"Seynyoreans," he said. *Not long ago,* he thought, *they were the enemy.*

Suktio nodded. "I saw them earlier." He paused and stared at the ground. There was a long silence before he spoke. "Women say at Inagar that you will be kin to our Lord." Martos had to swallow and fight his stammer before he could answer.

"Yes."

"It is good," said Suktio very softly. "She is"—he hesitated, smiling—"very beautiful. You will be—you will take good care of her?" Martos sensed that Suktio had not meant to make that a question.

In Kadar, everything was more formal: women never took lovers before they married, and lover and husband were both bound by exacting etiquette. But it was different on the Border. Martos took his time, controlling his voice and considering his words.

"Could any man treat her otherwise? Could you?"

"I would guard her as the rarest jewel in the world!" said Suktio. "Because she is!"

Martos smiled and nodded, but did not trust himself to answer. He was deeply touched, and his tongue stricken. Border wives were widowed early: at least he knew she and the child would be well cared for.

He stared back into the black-skied wasteland to the south, and understood why the Bordermen had welcomed a human enemy. Border warfare was all grim, faceless horror, with no touch of human pity nor human glory. To such war he was doomed for the rest of his life, while Istvan the Archer rode back to his fame in triumph.

The horsemen by the Border shrank to dots and vanished. He and Suktio woke the next watch, and sought their blankets. But Martos lay a long time thinking, staring at white stars and the pearly moons that rushed among them.

Istvan DiVega woke in darkness, his eyes blinking, searching for the stars. For a moment he could not understand why there was a roof above, and the closed air of a room about him, instead of icy wind and the silver sparks of stars.

"Father!" Chondos exclaimed. The old King smiled at his son and spoke, but screaming horses drowned the sound. Chondos tried to turn, to look for the source of the sound, but his muscles were locked and could not move. His father's face vanished; cold-eyed shapes thronged the darkness.

His eyes snapped open. Stone was cold against his back. Horses neighed frantically in the dark, and he could hear the bushes where they were tied thrashing as they tried to break free. He lurched to his feet, nearly falling: sleep had stiffened him after hours in the saddle. His wrenched shoulder and bruised wrist aches as he gripped the sword-hilt. His other hand closed on a torch.

The fire had fallen to a few dim coals. Blowing on them hoarsely, he swept brushwood twigs and leaves onto the embers, his head swimming as he puffed air from his lungs again and again, willing the twigs to catch as the coals glowed more brightly. He felt eyes staring at the back of his neck, and his skin went chill with sweat.

The twigs flared. He thrust the end of the torch into the flame, hearing horses behind him kicking, stamping, squealing. He whirled, whipping the kindled torch into flame, and a dim figure dodged out of the light. The horses were rearing and backing, tugging frantically at their bridles, shaking the few leaves left on the well-picked-over bushes. He had unsaddled the poor beasts to spare their galled backs. Now he had to saddle them again, while the thing he had seen prowled outside the torchlight and the horses kicked. One good kick could leave them all at the night-thing's mercy.

He hesitated by the piled-up brushwood, and with deep misgivings, thrust in the torch. The flame would be seen for miles—but they had already been found, and the squeals of the horses would soon draw more hunters.

Green wood crackled in a golden burst of light that made the horses even wilder: branches cracked as they tugged at the bush. He saw a dark figure running out of the light, but it was gone in the gloom before he could see what it was. Lurching to the horses, Chondos murmured to them soothingly as he sheathed his sword and drove the torch into the ground. Dodging kicks and crooning, he had no time for pain, and his stiffness was drowned in fear and haste.

The touch of his hand and the tone of his voice began to work, despite the prowling fear. Slowly the horses calmed. Twice the sudden return of their panic warned him, and whirling, he saw a manlike figure lurking at the edge of the light. Each time, he snatched up the torch and strode to meet it. Each time, it faded into the darkness. But eyes threw back the torchlight.

At last he was able to get a saddle on the fresher of the horses, though tightening the cinch was an ordeal: the beast nearly kicked everything off when it felt Chondos' foot in its ribs. His aching shoulder was sorer still long before he dared to hope the cinch was tight enough, but he barely got the saddle over the other horse's back before it went flying.

The voices of the night grew louder and nearer. He began to fear the time was gone. The fire was burning dangerously low; its light echoed from paired sparks in the darkness. But he had to stop and breathe a moment, resting his back against the tall stone. The horses began to shrill and rear once more.

Claws scrabbled on the rock behind him. He leaped away, spinning. A head lifted into the firelight. Leaf-shaped eyes as big as his hand glared down a long black muzzle. A hunched body scrambled up, crouching on the rock. The muzzle gaped, and firelight glittered in golden sparks from long yellow fangs. Uncoiling legs launched it at his throat.

It was Chondos DiVega who stepped into its spring, the sword sweeping from his scabbard in a soaring cut. Foul blood splashed his robe as taloned hands closed futilely on air above his shoulder. Behind him, he heard shrill voices and a rush of feet. He turned, his body as well as his mind remembering Istvan DiVega dancing in the garden at dawn.

Ragged, emaciated, red-eyed men ran at him, their dried flesh thirsting for his blood. Bounding past them came rubbery grey ghouls, one still gnawing on a squirming little horror that kicked and bit back.

Chondos sprang to the fire. Hot wood scorched his hand as he snatched the unburnt end of a long branch and whipped it across the top of the glowing, ruddy pile. Bright coals showered in their faces, some flaring into flame as they flew. Vampires shrieked as ragged garments kindled and dry flesh blazed.

A bounding ghoul's long arms reached for him. Curved steel sighed, rippling tawny light, and sliced through meat and bone. The ghoul hooted, stumbled, and lay still.

With a sizzling crackle, a bush flashed ablaze, hurling a shower of sparks into the night. Some vampires, burning, collapsed, corpses once more; but others ran wailing, spurting flames, setting others alight. Some blundered into bushes and dry leaves exploded into searing, lurid blossoms around them.

Suddenly the darkness was lit with a sullen glow. Burning vampires ran screaming through flaming bushes, fountains of sparks swirled up, and the cold wind from the mountains seized the flames, hurling sparks from bush to bush. Chondos, sword upraised, found himself blinking into a land of fire. Forge-flavoured air dried his throat.

He turned to run back to the screaming horses. He would have to leave the saddle. Smoke and cinders stung his eyes and skin. He glimpsed the horses rearing, pulling away from the bushes before them, jerking their heads frantically, trying to dislodge their bridles.

The smoke moved aside, and he glimpsed a dark figure reeling back from a horse's hooves. He ran. The figure picked itself up, red eyes gleaming. Chondos saw with horror that the leathery flesh had been gnawed away from one arm, and the white bone protruded. As it turned to face him, he sensed a horrible familiarity about the creature, although its face, too, showed bone through flesh as tattered as the remnants of garments that still flapped about the bony frame. But it was a face he had known, somewhere.

The corpse lurched toward him, skinny arms flailing, lips drawn back from long sharp teeth, fleshless fingers clutching on the one hand it had left.

Sick with horror, Chondos sprang back, the wing of his sword wheeling on the pivot of his wrist. He was trying to place the torn face even as the line of his blade snipped beneath. It felt like cutting rotten wood. For a moment there was no blood: then a tiny ruby fountain pulsed from the neck, and the head rolled by his foot. In a frenzy of horror he stooped, seized clammy hair, and hurled it at the fires behind him.

With a popping and cracking the roots of the bush gave way. He saw the horses running through the glare, the bush between them ploughing the ground. He ran to catch them, each sharp breath burning his lungs with baked air and stinging smoke. Pounding, fur-clad muscle loomed rippling before him: sheathing his sword, he sprang to catch the flying mane. His fingers locked in horsehair that cut his hands. He scrambled to keep from being pulled off his feet as he ran alongside, building up the speed to leap onto its back.

He locked his knees on the barrel of the horse that had bucked off its saddle. It heaved him up and smashed the breath out of him, twisting and lunging between his legs. He got one arm around its neck and buried his face in its mane, clamping his legs tight again and again as its bucking loosened his grip. Somehow, he held on.

The heat of the flames singed the hair on the back of his head, and he opened his eyes to raw, twisting fire. The dragging bush beside him burst ablaze, and the horse beneath him broke into a jolting, panicked run.

Cold air slapped his face. He heaved himself up, trying to balance himself astride the bruising whip of the horse's backbone. Black sky was before them above a red-lit wasteland. A giant ball of fire raced beside them, singeing his left thigh and the horse's flank, leaving a trail of flame.

Beyond it, the other horse's side was dyed in amber light, its eyes glowing like hot iron. Behind, he saw a pulsing red cloud of fire and smoke. Sparks danced like bright insects swarming in the wind, and all around were running shapes.

A ghoul pounced on a screaming torch that ran nearby, and ripped off an arm that had not yet caught. It beat out the smouldering shoulder-stub in a patch of dead dust and began to eat, cracking the bone between massive jaws, while the flaming vampire ran on.

Chondos stared in horror, then swung his face around, desperately searching for the bright horizon, hunting the darkness for the light of the Border through flame and Shadow. Which way were the horses running? He was lost: trapped by the blindness of his horse's fear, driven by the dragging fire.

He gripped the mane tightly with one hand, while he pulled the sword free. He must cut away the mass of flame, otherwise the burnt horse would run until it died under him. Already foam from its neck soaked his chest. He pressed knees and thighs tight against heaving ribs and twisted around, the weight of the sword hanging over his head almost dragging him off into the burning branches. Fire and darkness pulsed in his eyes as he tried to find the rein and the branch to which it was tied. Senseless flares of colour dazzled him.

He leaned and slashed along the horses's side, and he almost fell. A springy branch bounced back the blade, and he almost fell. Again he cut, and again the blade sprang back. Sparks stung the horse's flank, and Chondos felt himself slip as the burnt horse jumped.

Screams sounded ahead: a mass of figures blocked his way. In the flare of the bush, he saw staring faces and rag-clad forms. Goblin shapes came running, waving spears and whips. He saw ghouls bound past him. Then they were dashing through a scattering mob of the dead. One sprang toward him, but Chondos' sword, poised above his head, lashed down, and the vampire reeled back, its head lolling on its shoulder, hanging by a thread of flesh. It lifted its hands to grip the head and forced it back on its neck; but before the wound had time to heal, a ghoul came bounding, and the two went down. Other starved shapes ran toward him, but hesitated, afraid of the fiery ball dragging between the horses. Then he was through them, and from behind came screams and the cracking of whips.

Suddenly he saw the other horse bounding ahead, and at the same moment saw the flaring branches lurch toward him. He twisted, and cut again and again at the tough branches. There was a loud *crack,* and the fire rolled to a stop. A single blazing branch dragged on the ground alongside him. On the horse raced. The wind of his speed blew lather into Chondos' face. Voices behind shrieked hunger. The burning branch left a trail of coals and sparks: bushes flared alight as they galloped past.

Ahead, he saw the saddled horse, running easily. Looking back, he could make out dim shapes chasing him, against the distant glow of fire, but they seemed far behind. Pursuit straggled and fell back: the pulsing orange glow faded in the distance. On his right a brilliant night-blue band streaked the pitch-dull sky. The horses jolted on, racing through the empty night. Only after long-clinging to the rough, churning back, did he feel the horse beneath him slow.

Water splashed suddenly over his feet. His horse stopped and stood drinking from a narrow stream. Thankfully, Chondos slid from his mount, feeling its neck wet with foam and hot as fire. On the bank, a red coal glowed at his feet: the charred stub of the branch that had dragged behind.

It took time to catch the other steed, wild with fear and pain; it took time to dry the horses—and behind him he could hear howls and screams as night-things tracked them. The horse he had ridden would not last much longer, but he could not leave it for the Dark Things: like himself, it was part of the natural world, part of the kingdom he was trying to save.

He kindled a torch from the glowing stub, and dragged both horses into the stream. Tossing the live coal into the bushes, hoping to confuse the trail further, he waded with the current as long as he dared; then he set off for the Border, leading the tired horses to spare them for the final dash. His wet shins were cold; his thighs sore from riding.

He had been driven far to the west. He could see Agnasta's clouded light, tiny on his right. Behind him, a red glow flared from the bushes by the stream. A little later he heard wild screams behind, and guessed that the fire and the stream had baffled their hunters. But as the night wore on, he heard the sounds of pursuit once more, and reluctantly scrambled onto the fresher horse's back. Alternately walking and trotting, he pressed on; behind, the savage voices grew clearer. He had to struggle to keep the horses to a lope: they wanted to run.

Far ahead, the glowing band of light brightened. Dawn was coming. He wondered if it would help him now. Over his shoulder, he saw red flecks glare in the light of his torch. With a drumming of heels, he let the horses run.

Grey light slashed the Shadow's roof. The band of light had turned creamy pale. Pallid light filtered into the Shadow. Turning, he saw ghouls loping after him on all fours, and striding merciless above them, the looming bulk of a troll. Hammering hoofbeats jolted his bones; the cold air slapped his face. He dropped the reins and drew his sword. Ahead and to the left, shrill voices shrieked, and he felt the horse swerving. Turning, he saw stumbling shapes trying to run, torn cloth flapping; but with a frantic burst of speed, the horses raced past the wailing dead.

Turning again to look over his shoulder, he saw the troll hesitate and peer up at the greying sky; then it strode purposefully forward. A ghoul screeched as gigantic hands seized it, and then the troll was striding back, carrying its struggling prey. Smiling, Chondos watched the ghouls draw near the hungry dead.

The riderless horse stumbled, pulling Chondos' mount to one side. Both horses recovered, but Chondos saw the other beast foaming and shuddering; and as he watched, it stumbled again. He cast loose its rein before it could drag his mount back. The things behind were gaining. Chondos thought of Pertap, and gripped sword and torch tightly, but his heart sank as he looked ahead: fifteen miles at least to the Border, and the horses already tiring.

The riderless horse screamed and sank to its knees. Chondos reared his steed around, sword raised, and saw ghouls' yellow fangs nearing. The dying beast heaved itself up and staggered forward.

A ghoul bounded onto its back. Others came leaping up, with the dead crowding behind. With a muttered curse of apology, Chondos lashed his sword across the horse's throat, and whirled his own mount away. The fallen beast was blotted from sight by grey bodies, and vampires fell to their knees, lapping at the spreading scarlet pool.

Hooves swirling rapidly, grinding muscles playing under skin, Chondos' horse galloped away. Some of the vampires were staggering after him, but they were soon left far behind: he saw them shrink behind him. Men said Border ponies were tough: Chondos hoped so. The curtain of light seemed far away. This would be the last lap of the race. If he did not reach the Border soon, he would never reach it, and the Dark Things would swarm into his kingdom.

When he had drawn well away, he reined the horse to a canter. He must spare the beast as much as possible. The horse would tire, but the running dead would not. Miles vanished beneath the hooves as he rode, first at a canter, then at a trot, then at the canter again. The horse was not yet badly heated.

Ahead, the band of milky light brightened. He could see hints of land beyond. Hope thrilled through him. Pertap had escaped the Shadow; so would he! Already he had ridden farther than Pertap.

He thought of Pertap's sword, still glowing in the crumbling dark halls of Kudrapor. There was one thing Pertap had done that he had not. But he would, someday. He began to sing, while the pony's rapid hooves beat out the time.

> *Need-fire flamed about his horse*
> *And drove the Dark Things wailing back.*
> *Pertap looked over his left shoulder*
> *And saw sunbeams on his track.*

But over his own shoulder, he could see only the shapes of ghouls and vampires, that grew ever larger, nearer. And smaller shapes, hunched and twisted, ran with them now: goblins, waving rusty blades.

Grim death behind, and sunlight before. The miles flew under the little horse's feet. Grey earth and sky rushed by in colourless blurs. Ahead the Shadow's roof ended, and through the thinning hazy curtain, he saw a sky that opened out to a blaze of sunlit blue.

His horse was burning, with foam forming on neck and muzzle. The smells on the cold lashed the pony on, running faster and faster. Over his shoulder, Chondos saw the vampires hesitate, staring at the brightness ahead. Some turned back, but others kept on, and with them the goblin soldiers. Chondos dropped his reins and pulled his sword out, torch ready in his other hand. He sang to the horse, defiantly urging it on.

> *Before him Demons screeched and fled,*
> *And all the night-things ran away,*
> *When Pertap rode to Kudrapor*
> *And brought with him the light of day!*

Foam from the horse's mouth and neck flew into his face, splashed his chest. He could see patches of grass beyond the Shadow, grass bright green in the Twin Suns' light. *Almost there!* Soon the sense of a Border was lost, and the sunlit land before him no longer another country, but the same soil on which he rode. The high blue sky and the endless plain spread before him, and sunlight poured down in promise beyond the Border. He could see the suns themselves, now veiled in haze.

His comrades from the castle wall
Looked down amazed, Pertap to see,
With sunbeams pouring through the murk,
To show that Kudrapor was free!

The pony staggered, lurched, broke its stride, then recovered and ran on, breath whistling through foam-filled nostrils. Each stride almost hurled Chondos from the saddle. The Dark Things were gaining. Looking back, Chondos saw a white-faced figure draw closer and closer—and others behind.

Lather flew from the pony's coat, hot as fire between Chondos' thighs. The staggering run began to falter. Foam splashed into Chondos' eyes, blurring bright blue sky and sunlit land. The staggering, off-rhythm gallop fell to a canter, to an unsteady trot, and at last to a lurching walk. Chondos slipped from the saddle as the dripping, heaving beast rocked on trembling legs and went down, tongue hanging from the slack mouth, eyes rolling wildly. It lay in convulsions at Chondos' feet, covered with bloody froth.

White faced corpses came running: starving, crimson-eyed, ragged, daring the hostile light of dawn in their hunger for living blood. Chondos looked up into red eyes glaring from a face he knew. This time he recognised it: in life, this man had been one of his guards in Rashnagar. He was not alive now: no breath sobbed from his lungs. White spikes gleamed in the open mouth as the corpse hurdled the horse's heaving body, lunging for Chondos' throat.

Chondos thrust his torch into the white face. Hair flared up; dry rags kindled; the drying flesh began to cook. The creature mewed absurdly, and staggered back.

But behind came at least a dozen more, and all around them the stunted, twisted shapes of goblins. This was no place to stand and fight. Chondos drew his sword across the dying horse's throat, and hurled his torch into a knot of running vampires. Then he turned and ran for the sunlight, now less than a mile away. Glancing over his shoulder, he saw the horse's body covered with the feasting dead. But the goblins were running after him still, waving their rusty blades.

Somewhere, he thought he heard a faint sound like a distant horn-call.

"Listen!" said Paidros; but Martos had heard it: he stiffened in the saddle. Again the sound came, the long wailing cry of the Conch-horn of Chandra.

"It's Suktio's horn!" Valiros exclaimed.

"They've seen something!" Paidros' voice was almost a whisper. "Quick!" Hooves churned silent dust: Martos' heart lurched as his fine steed swerved. It had come: dreaded, yet desired with dread during long dull watches.

Yet no need-fire marked the Border. Agnasta, in this bright sunlight, barely glowed at all. Indeed, this close, nothing marked the Border: beyond a mile or so of sunlit land, the colour was washed away, as though a storm hung over the wasteland sloping, sombre and sunless, under a high veil of dirty cloud, up into a haze that hid the feet of ghostly mountains.

Suktio's horn cried again, and Martos saw him, tiny in the distance, leading his band of little men and horses.

"There!" shouted Paidros, but he was not pointing at Suktio's men; his arm was aimed at the Shadow. Black specks milled against the grey: two-legged dots were running.

Suktio's men swept nearer, and others came galloping, gathering together, fifty men against the dark. Martos tried to count the swarming dots; failed. Sword out, shield on arm, he touched spurs to his horse's sides. The tiny flecks grew and changed as miles passed under whirling hooves. Some looked like men in ragged clothes, but others were shapes out of demented dreams: beast-headed ghouls, and hunched goblins waving blades.

"Look!" Valiros pointed. "There—ahead of the pack—looks like a man, running away from the rest." Martos saw him, mouse-small like a warrior-doll, a man running, arms and legs pumping grimly. A lightless sword swung with the arm.

Already some of the swifter night-things were closing in on the running man: Martos saw him suddenly whirl and pounce among his pursuers with a flurry of well-placed cuts, turning to run again while the bodies fell. Even at this distance, Martos could tell fine swordwork: a thrill of glory etched his nerves.

Ghouls stopped, clustered around fallen bodies. The running man dashed into sunlight, and Martos saw ragged man-shapes stop, then back away. But the goblins ran on, swarming into the sunlight with crooked blades raised.

Martos stood in his stirrups, his long sword glittering high.

"Forward!" he shouted, shaping words carefully as he fought the stammer that stalked his tongue. "Help him!" He spurred Thunderhead, and on either side, hooves churned silent dust.

The runner turned, at bay. Sunlight streaked his bloodied blade with silver. Defiance raised it high, but Martos could see the sword-arm droop with weariness.

The clatter of armour startled the goblins: they turned owl-wide eyes on the glare of Kadarin war-gear, and shrieked. Wind chilled Martos' face; Thunderhead screamed stallion rage. The dwarf-sword slashed through bone. The weary runner stumbled aside as horsemen plowed through the goblin pack. Goblins milled and ran screeching for the Border. Hooves trampled them, and sharp swords flew down from triumphant sun-glare.

Martos turned Thunderhead and trotted to meet this man—this hero!—who stood breathing hard, freed from the Shadow, ragged and weary, unsteady on his feet, cleaning the blood from his curved blade. He looked up as Martos approached and slid the curved sword into its scabbard. Martos started. Where had he seen those wide black eyes? He had met this man before, somewhere. The black curls of stubble on the cheek made the face seem round, but the flesh beneath was gaunt.

"The Lost Prince!" Suktio gasped, nearby. "Be quick!"

Suddenly a Border pony dashed at the man's back, and wheeling steel flickered in a silver film.

Before Martos could open his mouth to shout, the stranger blurred from under the spinning sword's flight, the curved blade rising smoothly from the scabbard, chiming in the air as the horse rushed by.

"Stop!" Martos shouted, finding his tongue as the stranger stepped around, sword-point lashing in a familiar move.— a *Three Swords School* move. "What does this mean?" All the Bordermen stared at him.

Suktio spoke: "It is the Lost Prince, come out of the Shadow! We must kill him quickly. Lord, before—"

"Fools!" the stranger shouted. "The Lost Prince has already left the Shadow. He sits on my throne now! I am Chondos, your King!" They all stared at him. "I have been in Rashnagar, a prisoner of the night-things! Listen to me! My brother plans to kill the Border Lords, at some gathering, while they talk peace. Then the Dark Things will come."

Martos stiffened. The meeting at Kajpor? That was today!

"It is a trick, Lord, a trap!" Suktio spurred to Martos' side. "He means to lure us into some ambush, or perhaps they wish for the peace to fail." Martos shook his head, struggling with his tongue, trying to remember what he had heard of the story of the Lost Prince. Behind his eyes he again saw the stranger—*no: King Chondos*—dance from under the descending sword, drawing his own straight up from the scabbard into the path of the falling edge; saw again the coronation, and the young King walking with a swordsman's grace.

"Was not the—the other—the Lost Prince—carried away when—as an infant? And raised—among the Dark Things?"

"Yes, Lord." Suktio frowned at him. "Or so men believe."

"Then who is Swordmaster for the Dark Things?" Martos asked.

"Who trained the Lord Prince in the Three Swords School? Did you not see him turn Nathos' cut? Could *you* have guarded so? *I* could have, but only the Masters of the Three Swords School teach that guard; it is part of the Dance of the Twelve Cuts. Who in the Shadow could have taught him that?"

"There are vampires in the Shadow who were swordsmen once," said Suktio, but Martos heard doubt in his voice. "But even—we *must* kill him, Lord! Though my own kinsman had come back from the Shadow, I would not trust him, unless he bore a Hastur-blade, or other such talisman. If he was *their* prisoner, will they not have meddled with his mind?"

"Then let the Hasturs judge!" demanded Chondos. Bordermen murmured in surprise. "Take me to the nearest tower! They will know if I lie or not! Or"—the young man straightened, and lowered his point to the ground—"if you are so sure you must kill me, at least ride to the Hasturs afterward, and let them examine the man who calls himself King of Tarencia! And stop that meeting!"

"Paidros!" Martos called, and set himself to control his tongue. The little man rode up, saluting smartly. "Take ten men—" He looked Paidros in the eye, and then, unable to think of any other signal, winked. Paidros' eyebrow rose. "Escort *King Chondos* to the nearest Hastur-tower. Defend him against *all* enemies." Again he winked.

Paidros nodded, then spoke thoughtfully. "Agnasta is the nearest tower, but there's no ford except the one at Ojaini, and they say the water's too wild to swim. Vajrakota's even farther, but if we take the Ojaini road, it will be late in the day—long after noon—by the time we get there. If what—the King—says is true, someone must ride to warn Lord Jagat."

"I will ride to my Lord's camp!" said Suktio.

"We must all ride," said Martos. Suktio began to protest, but Martos turned to the King. "You said—how does he plan to kill the Lords of the Border?"

"Is it today?" Chondos swayed, and closed his eyes wearily. "The—there are assassins—men of the Pure-in-Blood—that's a tribe in the Shadow—hidden in a place called—Kadpor, I think, Kanpor, something like that. They are to attack when the men lay their weapons aside." He shook his head. "I only know a little. They didn't tell me—everything." He drooped wearily. He must have been running and fighting for a long time, Martos thought.

"If Jagat has already left for Kajpor," Martos said, turning to Suktio, "if he is already there—we must fight our way in and rescue him. Mount one man double and give his horse to the King. We will ride together as far as the road. Perhaps we will meet Lord Jagat there. If not . . ." He shrugged. "You ride on to Jagat's camp, and hope he is there—or that you meet him on the road. Paidros will take the King on to Agnasta. The rest of us must ride to Kajpor."

Chapter Twenty-two

Jodos seethed with impatience as the hateful fireballs climbed the sky. Had he thought of everything? Could anything go wrong now? And where was Lord Jagat?

The last Seer was gone: the Seynyorean troops that had surrounded the castle had all marched away, leaving only Lord Nahos and twenty men in royal livery, unarmoured and unarmed save for court-swords.

Through the Spider he sent word to the Master, then paced impatiently in the Council Chamber, glaring every now and then at the door that hid the Pure-in-Blood. Twice, now, they had made some small noise: the first time he had unlocked the door, and, stepping inside, had snarled at their stupidity; the second time, hours later, he banged on the door with his fist, and went away, leaving the Pure-in-Blood to wonder if men would break down the door and kill them.

He prowled through the castle, trying to encourage himself with the thought of Melissa, waiting in Tarencia, and of the things he could do to her once the city was his. But even that had been spoiled for him by the corrupting humanity of his brother's stolen mind, and the doubts it had raised. Perhaps he would send her away, let her escape, bearing his spawn within her. He shuddered at the thought, sickened, all his training outraged, and yet . . .

DiVega was waiting on the Council Chamber's steps: the roar of his sword was a burning in the mind. Jodos considered how he would make the old fool suffer, once that sword was laid aside.

"Almost noon," DiVega said cheerfully. "Jagat must be on the road. He may be here in a few hours."

"Hours!" Jodos exclaimed. He wanted to scream. If there were only some way to hurt DiVega!

"No use fretting," Istvan said mildly. "There is plenty of time."

"At your age," said Jodos cruelly, "I should think you would feel time short!" DiVega's brows knitted—then, surprisingly, he laughed.

"It would be nice if I lived to see the end, true enough! But, if not, the world will go on!" Maddeningly, he smiled. "And I, at least, will be calm." He rose. "When they do arrive, I will be in the Council Chamber, meditating." He bowed, strode through the door and closed it. Jodos froze, staring after him. If the Pure-in-Blood made noise now . . .

Chondos, looking up from the saddle of his Border pony at the Kadarin war-horses bulking above, felt like a child again. Kadarin armour flared in sunlight: the northerners looked like an army of heroes out of some old legend. Border ponies churned their short legs to keep up.

They were pushing their horses, but not yet to the full. Suktio fretted, but the grim-faced Kadarin leader—Martos, his name was?—snapped at him: "Kill your horses at the end of a march, not the beginning!" He would need men like that, Chondos thought.

Chondos drowsed in the saddle, his mind floating exhausted between sleep and waking. Again and again he would dream himself back in the Shadow, with the night-things hunting him; then, waking to find himself among humans, a great joy and love would throb through him, making him wish to embrace all the men around him. He could hardly believe that this was real, and not some trick of the Master.

And there was real food at last. It was only Border hardtack, but after days of nothing but the fungus, that was royal fare indeed. Sunlight, and plain food, and the community of men . . .

Yet Pirthio, his one true and trusted friend, was dead. Everything had changed while he was gone: his kingdom split by war; and Hansio, too, gone, his most implacable foe! It was almost a different kingdom to which he had returned.

Well, they would find that their King, too, had changed.

Thousands of miles to the north, dragon-headed Uoght glided toward the Border behind waves of pain. About him Dyoles gathered: their power shook the barriers of the Hasturs.

Yet the Barrier held: blended minds weaving a fire even Uoght could not pass unscathed by daylight. Miron Hastur was a beam of light, weaving in and out of a rainbow maze: edged bars of lightning, and crystal vines of living sunlight. His body knelt gripping a sphere that pulsed with light. His mind was one with the minds of his kin. In the view of that giant, forge-welded mind, the sickening shapes of the Dyoles crawled behind the misty, dragon-headed pillar. But the Demons that had clustered around them were gone. Had they sunk underground, to wait for the night? Or were they flying hidden in the Shadow's thick roof, gathering for an attack on some distant point?

Martos and Suktio signalled the halt and drew rein together. They scanned the long stone road: there was no sign of riders east or west to tell whether Lord Jagat and those with him had not yet arrived or had already ridden on to Kajpor.

Paidros rode up with the King and the ten men chosen as escort—all Kadarins: he had understood Martos' wink.

"There's your road, Paidros." Martos turned in the saddle and pointed east. "Straight to the Ford, then follow the river down to Agnasta."

"What about you?" Paidros asked. "If you do have to rescue Lord Jagat, you'll need a strong force. Why not bring the two face to face at Kajpor?"

Martos shook his head. "No," he explained, "only the Hasturs can say which is the true King, and be believed. And if the Dark Things are coming, the Hasturs must be warned. You must get him to Agnasta, as quickly and as safely as possible."

Paidros saluted, but his eyes were troubled.

Tiny beside the towering war-horses, a pony pushed between. From its back, Chondos stretched his hand up to Martos. "Luck ride with you, Captain!"

That is a King, Martos thought, amazed, as he gripped the proffered hand, *greeting the younger son of a younger son of the House of Raquio*.

"We owe you much," Chondos went on. "All the kingdom must thank you, for you have saved not my life only, but the life of the land."

Martos' tongue stuttered silent in his closed mouth as the King rode away. Turning, he found Suktio staring at Chondos' receding back.

"If that is King Chondos," Suktio muttered under his breath, "then the world has changed."

Martos spent a moment untangling his tongue. "You'd—had better go," he managed to say. "Suktio—if—if you do meet Lord Jagat, on the road—" he tried to think of a message to send to Lord Jagat, but everything he could think of sounded foolish—"keep him away from Kajpor, until—and—and—if—if we do not meet again . . ." and Kumari, crying, was before his eyes, and his lax tongue was a lump in his mouth.

"Hush, man! Speak no words of ill-omen!" Suktio's teeth flashed and he reached up to grip Martos' arm above the elbow. "You and I shall be finger and thumb, sword-arm and shield-arm! I shall see you ere tomorrow's suns have set! May Mother Earth speed your horse's hooves, the winds ride with you, and may Hastur's flames keep you from the dark!"

"And—and you, Suktio!" Martos managed to say. Suktio's right hand swung high; his heels drummed his horse's sides. His voice rose, hawk-proud, and the three men he had chosen as companions swept from the ranks to join him as he rode. In a moment all four were shrinking with distance.

"Dis—*mount!*" Martos shouted, and slid from Thunderhead's back. "Tighten your cinches!" He set his foot in Thunderhead's ribs, and pulled till the girth was tight. All around him, men did the same. "Mount!" he shouted, swinging into the saddle. He looked quickly left and right. Suktio and his men were already tiny dots on the road to Manjipor. Paidros and his men were shrinking more slowly, pacing their horses at a brisk trot. Valiros spurred to Martos' side. Martos smiled at him, and, controlling his tongue carefully, drew a deep breath: "Trot—*out!*" he ordered.

Hooves churned, and the mass of horsemen spurred away, the few remaining Kadarins riding in perfect order while the Bordermen spread out in a cloud around them. Martos felt Thunderhead's neck: it was warmer than he liked, but not yet wet. He ordered the canter, then, as they drew farther from the old road, the gallop.

They rode north and east. The road fell away to the right. Martos raised an arm as they swept past Chondos and his escort, still trotting on the road. He glimpsed Paidros' still-worried face, and the King rising in his stirrups. Then they were behind, and he wondered, as the broad green plain spread out before him, if he could have been wrong, if it was perhaps the true King waiting at Kajpor, and if he had left Paidros and the others in the power of the Lost Prince.

Surely, he thought, no creature raised in Shadow would risk riding toward a Hastur-tower! And it was said that the Dark Things feared to speak even the name of Hastur. But that might not be true.

His saddle jouncing under him, he fought the urge to turn and race after Paidros. He pictured again the swift sword-draw of the man who called himself King—the man who was his brother in the Three Swords School. Could the Dark Things have planned so cunning a deception?

But could such an exchange have taken place at all? Had not the Hasturs examined the King's mind at his coronation? Could the Hasturs have been deceived? Legend said they had been tricked once before, long ages ago.

That meant that it had been the other brother—Jodos, if this one spoke true—whose bitter message had poisoned the loyalty of Lord Jagat. That would quickly heal the wounds of war! But for what, then, Martos wondered, had his men died? For the fields of the Bordermen? For the fame of the house of DiVega?

After this taste of civil war, Chondos would be secure upon his throne: a second rebellion would be hard to start, once men knew it had been part of the Dark Things' plan.

When men learned they had rebelled, not against their rightful

King but against a puppet of the Shadow, their view of the war would change—they would always have been loyal. With Hansio dead, the kingdom would have peace for a long time now, and Chondos, innocent in his people's eyes, could let the Shadow absorb all blame. The Dark Things, in their malice, had betrayed themselves.

"You'll kill the horses in this heat!" Valiros shouted above the clamour of hooves. The Twin Suns poured pitiless light upon the plain. Martos touched Thunderhead's neck, and his heart lurched. But the thought of Jagat, and of Kumari weeping, and the Dark Things sweeping hungry from the Shadow strengthened him.

"Then we kill the horses," he shouted back.

"At least lighten the weight on them!" Valiros pleaded. "Will we really need our armour?"

Martos hesitated, thinking. Then he pulled off his helmet and heaved it away.

"No!" he shouted, unbuckling his cuirass. Breastplate and backplate fell clanging to the ground. Hooves pounded on.

Istvan was still chuckling as the bronze doors clanged behind him. The boy's last taunt had tickled rather than stung—in part because it had been so *stupid*, and in part because of its noxious truth. However important your business might seem—however important it actually *was*—at any moment that old grinning skull could pluck you away, and the world must go on.

His age? Men younger than he died, children died: there was no age free from death.

He unbuckled his sword-belt, knelt, and laid the scabbarded blade across the floor in front of him. *You cannot fight time with a sword,* he had told Olansos, but to understand the sword would be to understand all human life. All the history of man, on this world at least, was a record of war and death.

He had to smile again at the image of himself dueling with Death's skeletal figure. *Death.* All men were dying a long and painful death from the moment they were born. And women faced death each time a child was born, though the skill of Healers made this easy to forget.

A faint sound caught his ears. He listened, but heard nothing more. He thought it had come from a nearby room. Rats? Or simply some servant about his task? He dismissed the matter from his mind and turned back to the sword.

Death: this was only one form of that sharp scythe inescapable. *Death:* the corpse, the grief of those left behind, the loathsomeness of decay. Inside his mind the bluejay darted between trees, screaming *Why? Why? Why?*

He stared at the sword, past the surface of magic and fire, stared at the innocent metal, melted out of earthen ore, heated and hammered and tempered to be Death.

There was no sword, save in the mind of man. In the natural world, this was still only metal. Its form and function was part of the mind. Yet the same shape grew in nature, in horn and fang and claw. Man's mind hammered out as a strip of steel—surely the sword grew from man's mind as naturally as horn from a deer's skull, or claws on the paws of a cat.

Alone among weapons, the sword was not used for hunting or labour: an axe could cut trees, a knife skin rabbits or whittle a stick; spear and bow were made for the hunt. But the sword had one purpose only: to kill men.

Why? The jay cried behind his eyes. With so many ways to die, why should man create another?

Women went down to Death's gates to bring back new life. What comparable prize could man bring back from battle?

He stared at the sword, alone in an empty universe: man's mind incarnate in a strip of steel. The need and the power to battle fate, to protect yourself and your loved ones from Time and Change and Death.

That was what a sword was for! And that was what men sought in war: to face Death and defeat Death—for a little while. To shape the world anew in a drama in which merely human foes could become symbols of Fate, or Evil, or Change. Sometimes—not often—those symbols became reality; but more often war merely added a new source of pain to the world's pain. But war was an illusion, a symbol, a stage where inner drama could take shape in the outer world. Death was everywhere.

The courage to face the inevitable arrival of death—that was one prize a man might seek on the battlefield. But most courage was simple common sense: knowing that your back is harder to defend than your front, and a running man is easy to kill; that unless you hold your place in line, the whole line could go, and then you and all your comrades could be killed.

He had lived *that* kind of courage for years. It was good enough for the drama of war, but in old age and peace, with Death in all his terror approaching slowly at a solemn pace, such courage was useless.

Pain does not hurt. Fear hurts. Any pain became worse if you thought it would kill you: there was an urge to bear any pain rather than face that final terror. Yet men said that suffering ceased at death.

Many men found courage in the thought that all was known about death's far side. Yet, truly, it did not matter what was beyond. Whether a man was reborn, as most now believed, or whether he entered some wondrous other realm, or even the endless torment that legends said the ancient Croytarrans had believed fated for their enemies—it was the veil that was feared, and not the mystery. It was the courage to watch the veil approaching, to feel it enfolding you, that must be found. Whatever lay beyond might be faced, even the unimaginable nothingness of not being.

No use worrying about the mystery: sooner or later you passed the veil, and then you knew, if there was a you to know. It was the loss of breath, the stopping of the heart, the end of the body that must be faced.

Pain does not hurt. Fear of pain hurts. Did death hurt, or only the fear of death? If death was quick enough, there would be no time to fear it: death in battle would be best, but it seemed he had lost his chance at that—the penalty of his long years of training with the sword. The blood on his hands doomed him to be the prey of age—the slow death that men call life.

Looking at the sword, he heard Birthran's voice: *You face Death each time you touch the sword.* Yet death meant giving up the sword and all it signified, all power to serve and defend and change. If the sword was death, it was also life, with all its striving.

Death is the Bride of the Warrior, the Bordermen said. A cold bride, one might think, but they phrased it another way too: *Earth is the Bride of the Warrior.* All life came from the Earth—and returned.

Some truth hovered: almost he grasped it, but then a faint shuffle disturbed his thoughts, like someone moving nearby. He frowned. Someone in the corridor at the rear, perhaps? His quick ears caught the sound again. A footstep?

"Who is there?" he called.

Silence.

After a moment he breathed out, and turned his mind again to the sword. In a fortress this size, there was room for many people, and no surprise if echoes made sounds seem near.

Looking at the sword which was life and death, fear and courage, he thought of the sixteen men he had killed in the streets of Tarencia to buy himself the slow death of old age. He had killed Hansio, a hero to the Bordermen, for much the same reason.

He remembered how, at the end, *She* had not been able to feel his hand . . .

The slow loss of the senses, the struggle for breath, the pain, the loss of hope—that was the worst, perhaps. The end of selfhood, of the familiar union of body and mind, identity. It was not death that was feared: it was the *idea* of death!

Identity? Despite his memories, he was no longer the young Istvan the Archer who had stood safely on a rock killing helpless men. Neither body nor mind was the same.

This body was made of the food he had eaten, the water he had drunk, the air that rushed in and out of his lungs. It was a form through which the elements flowed. This mind was a space, a blankness on which different ideas flickered.

The heart would stop, but how often did he listen to its beat? The struggle for breath? No worse than hard fighting surely. Pain? He'd faced pain before. Stripped of fear, it was only sensation. For the rest, why fear the unknown? The unknowable, surely, least of all: he could never *know* non-existence, whether it came or not. That fear was only the failure of the imagination to envision non-being. If he knew it, he would exist: a void perceived was not non-being!

For the rest, there was nothing to fear, whether meeting lost loved ones or wandering as a houseless spirit waiting rebirth. Even the torment of remembering sufferings you had caused was nothing to fear. Death once safely past, what would be left to fear? A calm joy filled him. He sat, the sword before him like a bar.

Now he himself looked out through his eyes: not the outer man that others saw; not the bundle of habits and thoughts and ways to behave that men called Istvan DiVega, but his true self. Looking through another pair of eyes, another brain, other memories, He was Martos, He was Jagat, He was Olansos, He was the glowing suns and the earth, He was the sword that crossed his gaze by his knees.

Cleansed and purified, one with his sword and with all things, he waited for Death.

One of the tough little Border ponies died on its feet, hurling its rider stunned to the ground. Martos' eyes were blurred by the foam that splashed from Thunderhead's neck.

Lathering horses stumbled and fell. Kajpor grew from the plain ahead, and one after another, horses flagged and fell behind. Nearly a third of the Bordermen would have to follow on foot.

Martos' heart ached as he felt Thunderhead hot as fire under him. Fierce pride in the powerful brute's endurance thrilled through him. Valiros, that master horseman, rode with him neck and neck, on a horse that had been dead Evarin's. Only one of the Kadarins had been forced to drop back so far: the massive war-horses had greater stamina than the Border ponies.

Behind them ponies lay stretched on the plain; others limped along at a walk, failing rapidly. Only five Border horses were still running. Now Martos glimpsed Rojero dropping back, pulling his faltering horse to a walk. They were within the last mile now. But three more Kadarins dropped out, and another Borderman, before they rode up to the gate, trotting and cantering alternately, with only fourteen men at Martos' back.

Men in royal livery came running. He pulled up Thunderhead and sprang to the ground. He found himself stammering.

"Where is Lord Jagat?" he finally sputtered, while the guards stared at him, and at the drooping, exhausted horses.

"The Lord of Damenco has not yet arrived," said the man who seemed to be in command. Martos closed his eyes. Dead horses behind them, dying in convulsions, Thunderhead covered with lather thick as wool—all for nothing! Suktio would have met Jagat on the road.

He must talk to DiVega, he thought. DiVega must be told.

Jodos waited in the cool dim hall until at last he heard the clamouring of hoofbeats in the courtyard. Lord Jagat at last! He summoned the Spider.

"Call to the Master," he said. "Tell him to begin now!"

At last the Master could unleash the hungry hordes the Spider assured him waited by the Border. Those that could stand the sun would be out before nightfall. The Demons that had flown south to gather at Rashnagar would be loosed on the towers before the Blue-robes had time to man them. Then Uoght and the great Dyoles would leave the north, and rush south to complete the task. But long before then the mortals of this land would be leaderless and confused— easy prey!

He smiled as he walked to the door: then shrank back as he saw the big men and big horses. He skimmed his mind over theirs, and saw disaster! His brother's face . . .

"Where is Istvan DiVega?" Martos asked. "I must speak to him at once!"

"General DiVega is inside." The man gestured. "Follow me."

"Walk the horses," Martos said, handing his reins to Valiros. All around him his men had dismounted and were walking their dripping mounts. As he turned away, he saw the heavy shield hanging where he had left it on his saddle. He had thought he would need it to rescue Jagat. At least he could free Thunderhead of its weight.

"No war-gear!" As the shield came down from the saddle, the commander's voice came sharp. "That was a condition of the council!"

Martos turned, the shield dangling loosely in his hand, trying to wrap his tongue around words, but a shout interrupted whatever he was going to say.

"*There he is!*" one of the Bordermen shouted. "The Lost Prince!"

The guard's sword was flying from its scabbard even as Martos saw the slim figure at the door: recognised the beardless face, the face of the man he had rescued at the Border.

*   *   *

"Treachery!" Jodos shouted. "Kill them all!" He dodged back, seeing Nahos' sword slashing at the tall man in front. Bordermen ran toward the door as he slammed it. Death was in their minds, and there were too many to control.

He ran. If the guards did not kill the intruders—and they did outnumber them—then he could release the Pure-in-Blood to fight for him. But Jagat would not come now. He must put the Spider on DiVega, if he could get him to lay aside the burning sword. With the Spider riding DiVega's body, he would start the fighting again, sending Seynyoreans to kill Jagat and the others.

A line of light lashed at Martos' eyes. He lunged back, fumbling his arm through the straps on his shield. He saw Bordermen running toward the door. Then steel whipped at him again, blocking his eyes with his rising shield while his freed hand fell to the dwarf-sword's hilt and pulled. Men in court livery came running in. He saw Gonsalo go down, and that put fury in his arm as he hurled steel through the neck and spine of the commander.

At the door where the man had stood—Jodos, his real name was, Martos remembered—the five Bordermen had hurled themselves upon a mass of guards: flashes of sunlight darted and dipped above them. Martos ran to their aid, Valiros at his side. More guards charged; their light swords battering Martos' shield.

Martos' blade whirled out, slashing soft flesh and chopping bone. Blood splashed as he and Valiros crashed through the knot of guards and rushed to the door, driving their foes before them down a long dim hall.

Belling steel and shouting reached Istvan's ears. He came smoothly to his feet, scooping up his sword from the floor and belting it around him. The bronze door burst open and the King dashed through, his pallid servant following.

"Assassins!" the King shouted over the unmuffled jangle of steel that swelled through the open door. Feet rapped on the steps beyond: the pale man lunged awkwardly aside as Istvan sprang past.

Three Bordermen rushed him with bloody swords raised. His Hastur-blade left the scabbard in a fiery sweep that sliced the lead man's throat. On his left air screamed under a falling edge. His blade reversed as he swayed away, dipping in a long slash that ripped through leather and the ribs beneath. Crouched at the cut's end, he lunged, uncoiling, brushing the last Borderer's blow aside with a squeal of steel as his point sank through the eye to the brain.

Down the hall he saw swords twirling and he heard men shout, where the King's guards battled a mere handful of Kadarins. While he watched, men on both sides died. As he sprang down the steps, over the bodies of the three Bordermen he had killed, two more Kadarins fell, and then another. Now there were only three left, fighting back-to-back.

But the King's men were dying too. Kadarin swords took a fearful toll, and the difference in numbers waned. Already there were only seven against the three: then between one step and another as he ran toward them, it became six against two.

One, he saw, was Martos, shield booming on his arm while his sunless long blade whickered in a wheel of death.

Mourning this startling treachery, he ran toward the pitching, clanging swords.

Valiros died at Martos' side, his blade wedged between a guardsman's ribs, leaving only four to menace his friend. Three were in front of Martos, and he heard running feet behind. He stamped, shook his shield, and heaved his sword high. As the three cringed back, he whirled and slashed, his sharp sword swooping to the angle where neck met shoulder. He danced away as blood spouted from the severed artery: his shield rammed a jutting sword back while his dwarf-ground edge sheared through ribs and spine as he sprang past, letting the corpse fall between himself and the other two.

Lashing light flickered over dark walls, flashing from the fiery sword hanging from a running man's hand—*DiVega!*

The remaining guards faltered as the corpse flopped in their path. Martos' hand flew on the wing of his sword. One guard fell with a cloven skull; one stumbled back, guarding, with a clatter of steel. Martos leaped with a high slash, and his shield lunged under the blade that rose to parry, holding it high while he spun away, to face Istvan the Archer.

DiVega halted in his rush, and dropped to the stance used against a shield, point slanting over his head at the domed roof. He circled in cautiously.

Stepping a pace back, Martos slid the shield from his arm, hurling it clattering to the stone, and closed both hands on the dwarf-sword's hilt. Whether pride or pity moved him he could not tell, but he would use no advantage to slay Istvan the Archer.

What am I doing? he wondered, suddenly remembering that he had come to talk to this man, not to fight him! Everything had happened so *fast*.

He opened his mouth, searching for words to tell DiVega that they were allies, not enemies, but his useless tongue would not stir.

The glowing sword whirled at his eyes. Martos's blade belled as he guarded and fell back. He saw that his edge was notched. He could not use both sword and tongue! No chance to explain to make peace now: it was kill or die.

* * *

Jodos smiled cruelly as he watched from the door. They had all played into his hands after all.

The brute fighting DiVega was one of Lord Jagat's trusted aides. If he managed to kill the old man, it would be a simple matter, now that the others were dead, to seize his mind, as he had seized Sandor's in the garden. Then the corpse would carry the Spider to Lord Jagat, and lead the Bordermen to destruction.

It would be harder if DiVega won, but this apparent treachery would be enough to start the war again. Even if he could not get the Spider on DiVega, he could order him to attack the Bordermen at once. They would be fighting and killing each other when the Dark Things poured across the Border. Then he could summon a force against them, and blot out Seynyoreans and Bordermen together as they fought.

That plan could fail. He could easily kill the Kadarin now, by seizing his mind while the sharp swords flew, but it would be better if DiVega lost. He could not reach DiVega through the flame of the sword.

He must hurry: his brother was riding to warn the Blue-robes. The slow horses would take time, but once Chondos reached the tower the Hasturs would hunt.

Istvan felt steel quiver through his palm as Martos' two-handed parry turned aside the thrust that had sprung out of Istvan's own first looping slash. He saw the dwarf-sword spinning around; a step with his left foot brought him underneath the rising blade, left hand lifted to brace his wrist above his head.

Martos pulled his hilt sharply down, foreseeing and forestalling the slash across his belly that would have answered his stroke. But Istvan barely caught the swift thrust at the throat that followed, and even as he lunged in return anticipated the ease of the Kadarin's parry.

Was it to be here, then? Death stared from Martos' point.

As well to die now, he thought. He had lived long enough, surely, It was Martos' time. But he had given his word: he alone stood between Martos and the King.

The tip of the long blade drove past his guard and left a long red rip in the cloth along his shoulder. He sank into the calm acceptance of death, his mind focussed on the lashing, hissing blades.

Martos felt a fierce joy pulse through him. He could kill this man: he knew it now. He moved in like a whirlwind, his heavier blade hurling back the other like straw, forcing the frail figure to give ground before him. He saw the counterattack he had expected, and pounced, his blade leaping up for the two-handed blow that would make him, beyond all question, the greatest living swordsman.

And saw, too late, the terrible, the inescapable, response.

The dwarf-sword's pommel struck Istvan's shoulder; the Hastur-blade's point drove almost straight up behind the ribs, through the lungs, out the shoulder. The dwarf-sword clattered to the ground. Istvan felt the ivory hilt pulled from his hand.

Freed from fear, poised uncaring between life and death, loving the foe who faced him, his mind had hung detached and calm while the well-trained sword arm, undistracted, had acted by itself, purposeless.

Istvan DiVega blinked at the man who lay bleeding at his feet. Emotion shattered perfect calm. *Like father and son,* the boy's remembered voice said in his mind. The young died, the young men always died, while he lived on. *I will have to tell Birthran,* he thought, dully.

Then he saw the twitching agony of the face, and realised the boy was still alive: still alive, and trying to speak. He knelt with a flare of hope. If he could only find a Healer, if the boy could live long enough for a Healer to come . . .

The sword in the wound kept the blood bottled still in the veins.

He saw lips moving and bent down to hear, at the same time opening his own mouth, to tell the boy to lie quietly, to let him find a Healer. Choked gasps fought to take the form of words.

"DiVe—Ch—Istvan . . ." The boy's voice was a whispered croak. Istvan saw the feverish eyes fix on his face. *"Not—King!—King not King! Not—"* Feeble muscles twitched in an attempt to move. *"Not—Chondos! Not—Chondos! Jodos! Jodos! Jodos!—not King!"* Muscles writhed in his face, the sword's flame glowed through blood. "My—chest—my—baby—take care of my baby!" Suddenly his eyes were brighter, as though the sword's light shone through them. They closed and opened and focussed on Istvan's face. His voice steadied. "Not—the King—not—Chondos!"

"He lies!" a voice screamed. Istvan turned his head. Over his shoulder he saw the King standing at the top of the steps, hands raised to claw the air, eyes glowing in a face contorted with fury and fear. "Lies!" he screamed again.

But he was too far away to have heard what Martos said! Even if the boy's voice had been stronger—

A wave of pain seared his eyes and throbbed through his brain. His strength ebbed out of him, and his mind whirled in confusion. What was happening? He was so tired, and his head—his head. . .

There was fire burning next to his head, too bright and too hot. He cringed away. A hand reached out of the fire and closed on his

own. The pain faded a little. The strong hand pulled on his, pulling
his own hand with it into the fire, until it touched a familiar smooth
hilt.

His sight cleared, and strength flowed back into his body. The
light that had hurt his eyes so was the sword in Martos' body,
glowing with need-fire—its light pulsing red through Martos' flesh.
His hand was on its hilt: Martos' hand on his.

And in the light he seemed to see pulsing lines of dark that ran like
spiderwebs across the hall, up the door where the King stood with
his pasty-faced servant, and the dark web bound them together.

"That is not the King." Martos' voice came clearly, and strong.
"King Chondos is riding to Agnasta. That is Jodos, the Lost Prince."

Istvan's legs tensed to rise, and his hand tightened on the sword-
hilt, to draw it free. If he pulled out the sword, the boy would die.
But there was no Healer close enough. No Healer could be brought
in time. Martos smiled up at him.

"Take out the sword." Pain had faded to shock and numbness.
He had needed to speak and he had spoken. In Istvan's hands now
was the future of the kingdom, of the child in Kumari's womb, and
the lives of all Kumari's people. He could feel nothing, and his sight
was going. "I am done," he said, his voice weak but level. "Take
care of my child."

Istvan pulled out the sword. Martos grimaced, and tried to say
Kumari's name, but blood flooded his mouth and drowned the word.
He smiled weakly, and died.

Istvan came to his feet, need-fire flaming in his hand, driving
back the forces from the stairs.

Jodos whirled, crying to the Spider in words of power that the
creature dared not disobey, and ran into the Council Chamber. He
ran to the door and unlocked it, calling out to the Pure-in-Blood. He
left the door ajar, and raced down the long corridor that led to the
stable.

He knew how badly he had failed. All his plans had gone awry,
and he knew well what reward he could expect. He would take a
horse and ride far, far away to the north and east, and lose himself in
the cities of men, where neither the Master nor the Blue-robes would
ever find him.

The pale servant backed away as Istvan sprang up the stairs, then
ran at him aiming an awkward cut which he easily dodged, running
his point almost by reflex into the falling wrist. No blood came from
the wound, but the sword blazed up, and a sheet of need-fire

flickered about the man's body. The figure fell to the floor, and Istvan stared. The man was dead!

He ran on, his brain whirling. The man had been dead all along, of course. He remembered now the way the "servant" had always moved to avoid him whenever they met. Whatever had ridden the corpse had feared the Hastur-blade even in its sheath.

He burst through the door into the Council Chamber, sword ready. What had Martos tried to say when he died? It could have been a woman's name—*Camilla?* Some girl in Kadar? *Take care of my child*, the boy had said. He had never known the boy had a child! How could he find it? Where was it? He did not know. He would never know.

A door was standing ajar, a door that had been locked before. He heard sounds of movement behind it. He stepped forward, and jerked it open.

The Pure-in-Blood roused from the torpor in which they had waited so long for the signal that had come at last. Hungrily they moved toward the door.

It opened, and a figure stood there—not Jodos, their Master, but a man whose burning sword marked him plainly as an enemy. A moment they cringed, then rushed in a body, blades drawn back: they were hungry, and it was only one man.

Then the greatest of living warriors was among them, and his sword was singing.